THE GODSBLOOD TRAGEDY

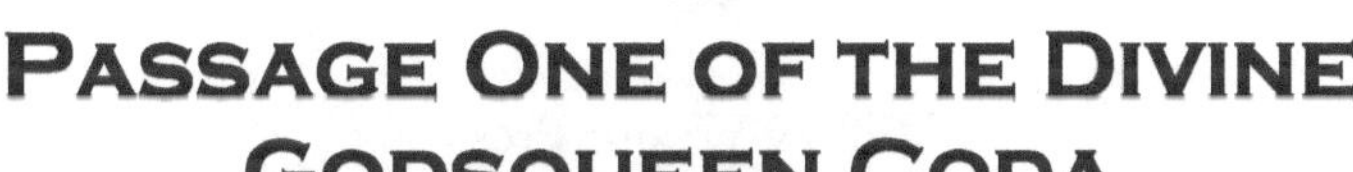

PASSAGE ONE OF THE DIVINE GODSQUEEN CODA

BILL ADAMS

Willow Wraith Press
Visit our website at willowwraithpress.com

ISBN-13: 979-8-9899405-4-7

Library of Congress Control Number: 2024911464

Cover Art by: Felix Ortiz
Cover Title Design & Interior Art by: Dewey Conway
Character Art by: Puos

Printed in St. John, IN, of the United States of America

For me, it's about godsdamned time!

Fair friends, the Passages of the Divine Godsqueen Coda are not for the faint of heart. So be warned, within these pages are scenes containing blood by the gallonful, violence & death by the plenty, profanity by the metric shit-ton, haunting past off-page sexual & emotional trauma, explicit sexy times (both wondrous & darkly themed), alcohol use, misogynistic assholes, as well as scenes of intense torture using blood magic.

TABLE OF CONTENTS

Seasandr Abyssal
The Isle of Merj
Kalderim
Golden Sea
The Forgemistress' Blades
The Forest of Calibrach
Alizarin
Shatterstorm
The Voidlands
The P
The
Dervin
Garchase
Thullyr
Wyrm Ocean
Bay of Fire
Coldpore Basin

The Mistlands
Kanja
Krylen
Wynter Expanse
Gauderll
Filfansin
Altreyia
demrae
Sis Vorum
...rulus of Eminence
Drenth
...e Imperium of the Fallen
Illigan
Drakewing deep

Aether,
The essence of Life & Death.
Pure and unfiltered Eminence, a
magical boon.
Broken and cracked Noctis, a
poisoned chalice.
Breath of fate & fire,
Of the Gods.
Their guardians, the draconem.

Imprîmîs

(Additional Appendicis in Back of Book)

Aether [*ee-ther*] – magical essence of all existence, borne of the Great Crystals, Eminence & Noctis; bequeaths the Four Tenets of Aether: *Ignis*, *Aquis*, *Terris*, and *Aere*.

Aethecite [*ee-th-e-sahyt*] – condensed & pressurized aether into an ore-like manner; its essence has been derived into a potent & valuable fuel, technology, and weaponry.

Aetheurgy [*ee-th-er-jee*] – the art of channeling aether into one of five Forms of the Pentax Gods & the God of the Void; also known as burning.

Soul Form – the purest form, borne only in those with Godsblood, the world's essence via Eminence theirs to command. Marked by pristine white pupils & irises.

Vision Form – the voice of the Pentax Gods, Bliss & Brio. Marked by one all-white eye & one all-black eye.

Burn Form – borne in the essences of the Four Enhancements of Aether. Burned via injection or ingestion of distilled aethecite called parch. Marked by a colored pupil; colors of garnet, sapphire, peridot, or emerald.

Shard Form – borne in the essences of the Four Tenets of Aether. Burned via inked runes in the flesh sparked by inhalation of the poisonous mist. Marked by a colored pupil; colors of garnet, sapphire, peridot, or emerald.

Void Form – from the darkness of the void beyond the veil of Life via Noctis, scarred runes upon breast and spine. Marked by all black pupils, irises & sclera.

The Desert City of Drenth

AN ORPHAN GIRL with no trueborn name stared past the airship's bowsprit as the Sea of Mist parted, revealing the mega-city of Drenth.

Like a crown of swords, but instead of blades, buildings rose upward from the dunes towards the skies. Home to the aethecite mines under the great desert, Drenth's outer walls were already being pummeled by an early dawnbreak sandstorm, a raging vortex imbued by the aetheric mist of the surrounding Sea.

"Look there!" yelled one of the handful of passengers aboard the aethecite-powered airship. "A vvyrm!"

The orphan followed the cry portside, a crowd gathering and pointing toward the sands surrounding Drenth. To her unnatural, all-white eyes, every person on deck bore an aura of bright yellow. Joy. Energy. Curiosity. The augurs of the Scattered Shards of the Pentax had said her gift was rare. So rare, few cases of white irises existed since the Fall of Eminence five hundred years prior.

To the girl, it was her curse.

One of the dunes undulated, like a wave rolling under the Sea of Mist. It was massive, the terrisvvyrm—or vvyrm for short. Its trail created a gully through the sand, new dunes forming in its wake, leaving mounds in the aetheric haze. A section of the vvyrm's back pierced the dune, calcified protrusions the size of an adult humir lined the entirety of its flank, allowing the draconem to tunnel. Up the pith went, then back into the sands, the Sea of Mist reforming into a cloak of unbroken grey. The poisonous haze murky in the small hours after dawnbreak.

"It's head, O Zenith, look at that!" a young woman exclaimed, her voice tinged with curious excitement, her aura blazing with peridot thrill.

Pure might exploded from the sand dune anew, shooting upward with the tenacity of Mother Marrow's Hammer, causing the gathered crowd—and the orphan—to instinctively rear back, even though they were still far away from the vvyrm.

Grit sprayed outward as if the Holy Forgemistress Herself hammered to the anvil that was the dunes, the mist clinging to the vvyrm's hundred-foot, cylindrical body like a parasite. The gaping snout roared, teeth the length of the orphan girl herself. No eyes did the monstrous beast have, for underground, it needed none. The vvyrm landed upon the sand, churning the mist that danced above it, and disappeared deeper into the earth. The sand and mist settled, leaving only the untouched hills, the Sea of Mist calming.

The orphan girl gripped the railing of the bowsprit, feeling her heart quicken as Drenth edged ever closer. Her past rising from the dunes like the vvyrm. A pool of mist clung to her ankles, swirling about her in the eager rhythm of her heartbeat.

The other aspect of her gift. Her curse.

Sixteen years, she thought.

Sixteen years of not knowing her past, her truth. Sixteen years spent in the arms of the Scattered Shards in Kalderim in the north. Sixteen years training in aetheurgy, training to become a preacher of the Pentax against her wishes.

That was why she'd fled. Drenth called to her. Her past called her.

Surrounded by the Sea of Mist, Drenth was a mega-city unlike any other. One of the few great cities to rise from the ashes of the Fall of Eminence. Protected by the searing desert that bordered the southeastern coastline of the Drakewing Deep, Drenth sprawled. Skyward as well as outward, upwards of one thousand feet. Hundreds of thousands called Drenth home.

But that's not what made Drenth stand out from the other mega-cities. No, it was something else, something far more dangerous. More ominous, foreboding. Far more connected to her past, even if not yet founded.

But as her gaze took in the city and the beast above, she knew it as truth.

A shadow at this hour, the sun still not breaking its horizonal plane, left the city bathed in umbra. Two thousand feet above, twice the height of the tallest complex, it floated. Anchored by four building-wide chains tethered at the corners of the city, the massive links straining in the early morning sandstorm. It hovered over Drenth like a god, held aloft by burning aethecite, the scree of spent fuel twinkling down upon the city like ashen rain.

Gargantua its name.

The massive floating fortress was city blocks in circumference. Rocky at the base as if Zenith had reached down from His heaven and scooped the earth. Dozens of aethecite-powered propellers fanned in a steady circuit, keeping the bulk afloat, the plumage of the fuel a storm of its own. Metal walls grew out of the stone belly, forming an outer shell. Rotating aethecite-cannons pocked the bulb like a pincushion, enough aetheric firepower to demolish cities whole.

The Fallen's greatest achievement, his most deadly of weapons. And the harbinger of the orphan's current condition. For she wasn't the only one to be torn from family and home by the Fallen and his war against the Pentax Gods.

"Think any ev'r tried to ride 'un before?"

The girl turned to find a hobgoblin standing next to her at the rail. The ugly voidspawn was all limbs and barely up to her chin. He had short, dark hair that was loosely curled around his pointed ears, and scarce any but wisps atop his gnarled, grey-green skinned skull. He was wiry, with longer arms than his legs, an angular face, and nearly black eyes.

"Have to be daft t' try, dummy," said another hobgoblin as he skittered up besides the first, whacking it upside the head. They were twins, the girl had learned. Slow on the uptick but mildly humorous to be around, unless you were the butt of their attentions. "Doubt they make hooks for et, eh, Stray Cat?"

Upon fleeing Kalderim to chase her past, the girl had stowed upon a ship called *Marrow's Lover*. She had tried to stay hidden, but one of the deckhands had chanced upon her barely two hours from the Golden Throne. The captain had demanded her name, but the girl had refused. It was unlikely the captain would've known a sprat of the Scattered Shards like her, but it helped to be careful. Luckily, the captain hadn't decided to toss her overboard. The twin hobgoblins had taken to calling her 'Stray Cat', so the name stuck, for it didn't matter to her what they called her.

The girl shrugged in response to the voidspawn, though she did wonder who'd have the seedpods to ever think of riding a vvyrm.

Like any mega-city, though, Drenth had a defined port for airships to dock, but unlike any mega-city, Drenth's was a singular, fat tower near the city's southern edge. Made of metal with bays, almost like a cylindrical piece of lace. Hundreds of feet tall, each bay a different size, larger at the base, smaller at the apex. All along the rims of each bay, lights blinked.

It didn't appear to be very full, perhaps due to the civil war raged by the man the locals called the Gutter King.

The orphan girl leaned upon the bowsprit coughing every now and again, ignoring the sibling hobgoblins as they gawked. Her body clenched from the aetheric poison ripping through her.

Drenth, the orphan girl thought. *Home.*

Her taskmaster in the Scattered Shards had once told her she was Drenth-born. A babe when the Fallen had invaded the desert city, her parentage unknown. All her taskmaster knew was that she'd been spared from the destruction, placed in his hands because she was special. Special because she was borne of aether, the magic of the Pentax Gods. A harsh taskmaster, he was, but the girl desired only one thing, and one thing only: to uncover her past.

That's why she'd fled, why she'd come to Drenth. To discover who she was. Of her blood and lineage. O, the girl had many names over her seventeen years of life, but none that were her own. She needed to know, to truly become whole. Drenth was her last chance. She didn't care that it was a war-torn place.

The captain deftly brought the airship over the outer wall, where vacuums regurgitated the mist into the raging sandstorm, toward the docking bay. *Marrow's Lover* was a sleek, seventy-footer, with its aethecite engines amidships port and starboard, and low of keel. Within the bay, people ran about in organized chaos. Some used aethecite-powered lighted sticks to guide them in, others remained ready for the crew to throw their mooring lines.

One of the hobgoblin deckhands tossed his line, a dock worker catching it and tying it off. He jumped over the railing, sliding down to the bay. His twin tried to repeat the process, but his toss was piss-poor, not even close to the worker prepared to receive it. The voidspawn let out a curse while the other cackled on the ground, taunting him.

"What kind of harebrained throw was that, Zig?" the captain demanded as she exited the pilotbox.

"I'm Zag, Cap'n," said the hobgoblin as he coiled the line, readying for another toss. "Zig's down 'ere."

"One of you needs to grow your bloody hair out or somethin'," the captain bellowed down to the one on the ground. "I can't ever tell you buggers apart. I think you do it on godsdamned purpose."

"'Course we do, Cap'n," responded Zag with a snaggled-toothed, dung-eating grin. "Where's the fun be if yous knew who yous was talkin' t'?"

"Get back to work!" Laughter roiled about the docking bay. "By Mother Marrow, you try me so." The girl chuckled softly, which drew the ire of the captain. "You think it funny, poppet?"

"Never would I dream of such a thing, Captain LeFleur," she answered, hiding her grin behind a cough that brought up some tarry phlegm.

"See to it you keep it that way, hear?" Captain Neenah LeFleur said as she rifled through her shaggy brown hair, then tugged at the ascot adorning her pristine, baggy-sleeved shirt, followed by a run of her tongue across her lips while seamlessly admiring the few golden teeth in her smile. All because the pilotbox was a flawlessly reflective surface, allowing the most dashing smuggler—her words—in the Mistlands a chance to laud herself. "Drenth isn't no place for fools, little bint."

"The hobbies on your crew tell me otherwise." Her taskmaster had always said she'd best mind her tongue lest it get herself in a world of trouble, why would she start now? "Captain," she added when an immaculate brow was raised in her direction.

The few passengers of Captain LeFleur's 'legitimate' business endeavors lined up as a plank was lowered to the docking bay. Two members of the crew—a short, broad-faced dvergir with tattoos covering the entirety of his visible flesh and a cherub-faced giantess with a wicked noose scar wrapping her neck—stood nearby, helping escort them off the airship.

Seeing the final paying guest disembark, the captain returned her attention to the stowaway orphan girl. "Neenah LeFleur suffers none herself. Remember, I could've tossed your scrawny backside overboard when Tris found you." The orphan nodded along; it wasn't the first time she'd heard such a speech. "Don't let it be said, Neenah LeFleur doesn't care for her own when she takes them in. You certain you don't want to stick with us, poppet? Drenth isn't a place for younglings your bloody age. Eat you up and swallow you whole. Seen it far too often, godsdamnit. Almost happened to me if you can bloody well believe such a thing. But no one can keep Neenah LeFleur down, not even Zenith on high."

The girl held back a comment, for once, becoming serious instead. "I have to."

Neenah appraised her. The girl knew she wasn't much to look at; skinnier than a fresh sapling with raven black hair and snowy white eyes, but she was Scattered Shards trained, so she could handle herself. Her taskmaster always said she had a warrior's heart.

"Then best be on with it. I know a place you can squat until you get your bearings. Elian's a wily bastard, not one to trust with a purse full of quadrans in a dark alley, but he's a loyal one, if I could bloody say so. Not many in Drenth's underbelly are the sort. He's one. On my word, I'll see you to his place. You godsdamned pissing mind him. I don't want my hard-earned reputation spoiled by a runaway little runt from Kalderim, hear?"

"Wouldn't think of it, Captain." This time the girl meant it. She needed a place to stay if she was going to uncover her past. And Neenah LeFleur's aura blazed a royal blue, which meant the woman had an honest heart and could be trusted.

Neenah hopped the rail, sliding down the mooring line with a graceful ease that made the girl jealous. Something about the vain smuggler made her cherish what her future might hold. It was a far cry different than her training in the Scattered Shards. More freeing, less demanding.

If anything came out of her flight to Drenth, at least she'd be making her own decisions.

The desert heat assaulted them as they entered the seventh sector in Drenth known as Marketside. It wasn't the girl's first trip to Drenth, so she knew all nine sectors, but this was the first time she had been there on her own. Liberating, it was.

In the southern reaches of the desert city's sprawl, the midday sun normally had full reign of the streets as the floating shade of Gargantua left little cover. But since it wasn't yet dawnbreak, it wouldn't be for a few more hours before the Fallen's behemoth would spill shadows into this sector. The gritty sands of the desert danced about the paved streets with the ankle-high mist a lazy swirl. The sweltering heat was growing worse by the minute.

Barely on the streets for more than ten minutes, the girl was drenched with sweat. And, O Zenith, she made sure everyone was aware of it. "It's hotter than Nocturne's coinpurse."

"Quiet," Neenah said. "Something's not gravy 'round here."

For a mega-city the size of Drenth, it was unusually subdued. Especially since Marketside was supposed to be a massive bazaar. The girl had expected more excitement, more pizzazz. Not this.

"Must be the Gutter King's work," Roland said. The big, one-eyed first mate was one-eyeing the streets, his bald head swiveling back and forth until it settled upon a smoking stack, its black plumage gracing the air in curling tufts over the ramshackle building complexes. "That's an aethecite factory. The contractor at the bay said the factory was hit two days past. The Gutter King made off with crate loads of ore."

The stench of charred aethecite hung thick in the air, along with the aroma of burnt metal. The wreckage along the street was minimal, the people of Drenth going about their days as if nothing had happened, stuffing the controlled cataclysm back into the vaults of apathy. It was said the people of Drenth were little more than slaves after the conquest, and rumor ran rampant, even as far as Kalderim, that the Gutter King aimed to take down the Fallen any way he could.

She took a gander of her surroundings, allowing herself to be swallowed by the place of her supposed birth.

Under the watchful gaze of Gargantua, rail lines weaved and twisted through the complexes, held up by steel columns that looked like upside-down fishhooks. Trams of sleek metal and glass zoomed across the rails faster than a galloping team of horses, spewing aethecite. Crammed people sullen as they were transported toward their doom in the mines, scraping by for families huddled in apartment complexes deeper in the city.

Smaller airglider transports whizzed overhead, aethecite exhaust leaving streaks of blackened smog. Most were Imperium transports filled with soldiers. Camera drones buzzed about, little motors purring from miniscule propellers as they zinged through alleys and missing windows alike. Aetheric spotlights scouring the entirety of Drenth, watching and reporting back to Gargantua the comings and goings of the city's citizens.

Lining the sky, massive aerescreens streamed everything from automaton fights to commercials or newscasts. LED and neon lights aglow, pulsing with life as powered by the aetheric spells of *Aere* housed within the magical runes etched into their outer casings.

Smoke, black as pitch, chugged from a fraction less than two dozen spouts strewn across the city. Aethecite factories, melting down the aetheric ore mined from under the sands.

"Godsdamnit, they took out my favorite chocolatier." Neenah let out a heated breath and indicated a ruin that was nothing more than timber, but a singed sign lay in the street indicated a delectable pastry establishment.

"Never knew yous liked chocolate, Cap'n," Zig said in that voidspawn trill of his. The small hobgoblin twins were arm in arm, doe eyes wide at all the sights.

"Lots you don't know about Neenah LeFleur, Zag." From the little time spent with Neenah LeFleur and her crew of smugglers, the captain could never tell the twins apart. And they certainly made a sport of it. "Legends all have foibles to uncover. That's what makes them legends, hear?"

Roland glanced the girl's way. "Ask her about the time she once tried to con a merchant out of his coffee shop in Qarthage, Stray Cat." Although he looked like he had battled an ogre over a leg of mutton and lost, she liked Roland. He was a calming presence, a stark contrast to everyone else in Neenah LeFleur's crew.

Neenah's aura became a faint shade of crimson. A dangerous color. The captain gulped back a string of curses before shushing the first mate. "We don't talk about certain things, hear?"

The one-eyed mate chuckled. "Sure thing, Cap'n."

A LED aerescreen above the street blinked neon haze borne of *Aere* as the aethecite in the two upright tubes burned into life. A heart-shaped face appeared, hair perfectly arrayed, an impeccable smile showing epically white teeth behind pink-stained lips.

"People of Drenth, my heart rejoices because I can now inform you that your loyal Imperium soldiers have cleansed the city of dissent from earlier this week. All conspirators have been apprehended. Rejoice in the Fallen's army handling the situation with ease." The smug smile nearly popped from the misty screen. ***"A gentle reminder, only three hours remain before you must take your next injection to protect you from aethecite's hateful radiation. Please ensure you refill your parch."***

"Who's that?" the girl asked.

"'Who's that?' You been locked in a bloody cage your entire life?" Neenah's aura appeared aghast at the sheer audacity of such a question. When the girl remained silent, the captain went on, "That's Solanine, poppet. Someone you don't fall in the wrong bed with. The Fallen's right hand in the Imperium."

"O."

"Don't 'O' me, little bint. You'd best watch that scrawny backside of yours now that you're in Solanine's domain." Neenah's garnet aura blazed with warning. "Besides, those eyes of yours'll get you in their sights godsdamned quick. I know aetheurgy when I see it."

The girl stiffened. "You knew?"

"White eyes ain't normal, girl. Besides, you think Neenah LeFleur hadn't bloody seen those runes marking up your left arm?"

She tried to pull her sleeve down further, even though her wrist to shoulder was already covered.

Roland's brow furrowed so deep, the caterpillars he called eyebrows might just crawl down to the bridge of his wide nose and cocoon up. "Something's wrong ahead."

It was then the remains of the aethecite factory erupted in an explosion. Shrapnel and dust, even pellets of aethecite, rained down upon the streets, soot blowing in the ongoing stormy wind. People in Marketside screamed and began a rushed flight down Drenth's many avenues, away from the blast.

Some stray ash fell upon her sweat-streaked face as she tensed, wondering if she should run as well. The hobgoblin twins were skittish, but Roland merely crossed his meaty arms while Neenah rolled her eyes.

"This is the Gutter King's work most definitely." The captain stood with her hands upon her hips, turned halfway toward the girl, noticing the grime. "Stray cat indeed, eh? Name don't suit you, poppet. You need a name that fits this city." Neenah tapped her lips. "With all that soot on your mug, Ashe is a good godsdamned name. The 'e' gives it some flavor, same as that bloody mouth of yours. Welcome to Drenth, Ashe."

Ashe was as good as a name as any. Lilia had been the name she was known by the Shards, and truth told, she'd always hated that name. Besides, Lilia had left Kalderim, Ashe would suffice until she discovered her trueborn name.

The aethecite scree lilted about the streets as further explosions erupted. As chaos devolved in the City of the Desert, the girl without a trueborn name smiled.

Home.

I

ASHE

BLOOD PAINTED EVERYTHING red.

The crimson cruor trailed down the front of Ashe's stola, staining the pale blue gown burgundy. Her hand dripped in the slick, her mind running in circles trying to comprehend all the feelings, the unsaid words just now coming to her lips, instead of before her sudden reaction with the blade. Slight guilt, part sorrow. Most of all, it got her wondering if she truly understood what she'd just done.

"O shit…" she cursed, standing over the poor dead sot she jabbed in the neck with the pointy end of her dagger. "Shit and double shit!"

It was one thing, she knew, to have accidently killed the servant, but it was another to be caught for it. That's usually how things quickly turned to slag. Killing a servant hadn't been part of the thievery job, but improvisation had been necessary when said servant had found her rummaging about the villa owner's private study. A job in which Elian said she might find clues to her past.

Sweat trickled down Ashe's temple as a low layer of iridescent mist swirled around her slippered feet, pooling beneath her stola from all nascent corners of the villa, denser as if she was pulling it toward her like a faithful familiar. The mist undulated in time with her racing heart. Ready. Eager to please. Hers to command.

The body's aura was a dark honey shade in her aetheric vision. A jaundiced yellow signifying the fear that was the servant's last emotion. Fear of her knife, fear of his death. That yellowed hue bled into his actual blood, spilling from him as the last of his life ebbed.

She shook her head, trying to forget his face, to forget his eyes when he'd found her there. The growing surprise as her blade bit into his neck.

"Snow Eyes, what've you done?"

Evander barged into the study, finding her standing over the dead servant. The soft peals of orchestral strings met her ears before he clumsily shoved the door closed.

Ashe pulled a small flask from the sheath strapped to her thigh under her newly bloodstained stola. Golden and emblazoned with filigree, she took a full draw, the harsh liquor calming her frayed nerves. "Zenith's cock, Evander, nobody was supposed to be here. I had no choice. And stop calling me that, you know I hate that name."

"By Nocturne, Snow… er… Ashe." Evander squatted by the dead body, rifling through the man's pockets. "You shouldn't have done…" The young man went silent as his eyes unfocused, glazed even, as if he went somewhere else entirely. He did that from time to time, unnerving it was. "…that," he finished.

The mist rushed up her legs, pawing like a dog returning with a hunted fowl waiting for a scratch and declaration of a job well done. It aimed to soothe her, the mist did, as the yellowed aura of the wan and pallid corpse faded.

It had to be done, she told herself. But to Evander, she said nothing.

"Elian's not going to like this." Evander's aura blazed shaded crimson with anger and warning. "You weren't supposed to kill anyone."

"I don't give a dawdle of Mother Marrow's tits what your brother wants. Would you rather I tickled his seedpods to make him forget about sounding the alarm?"

Evander pursed his lips. His face was all planes and angles, not to mention ugly to boot. He had short brown hair in tight curls. Tall and lanky. "That's not how this crew works."

"Seedpod juggling it should've been," she muttered into the lip of her flask, a tress of raven falling across her face.

A deep-rooted cough welled from within her breast. She covered her mouth as her entire body convulsed, the mist darkening around her slippers, feeling the pain with her. Entwined, they were, she and the mist. Though the thievery job brought them to the top floor of a five-story villa within Drenth's Silk Circle sector, the grey aetheric haze clung to her. And it was the poison within the mist that was destroying her from the inside out. A consumption. The nigrum pulmonem as it was called, a wasting disease borne of The Pentax Themselves. Borne from the tomb of Eminence.

The paradox of her connection to the magical aether within the grey.

"Pulmo's getting worse," Evander sighed.

Another cough, less painful. "I'm fine." She washed the coppery tang coating her lips with another shot of spirits. "Let's find that stupid safe."

"Ashe, the pulmo takes everyone eventually."

She looked over; Evander's aura shifted from angry crimson to darkened peridot fear. Fear for her. Gods, why did he care for her so? He was nothing but a partner to ride beside toward her true purpose.

Nearly a year in Drenth and she was no closer to uncovering her past. She was but a lost cause without a trueborn name, without a history. Elian's crew out of the second sector, Slag's End, remained her only meal ticket until she could find her truth.

To discover who she was. Who she'd been.

Evander, a few years her senior, had taken an instant liking to her, giving her that pet name of 'Snow Eyes' on account of her white irises and because she'd come from up north from Kalderim in Kanja, where most of the land lay covered in snow. She'd not requited his affections, didn't want to. Didn't desire to. He never touched her, though, and for that she was grateful, as she knew most others wouldn't dream of holding back.

"Enough of the heartwarming butter talk, we need to get out of here so I can have a proper drink."

Evander side-eyed her in that creepy uncle sort of manner but then relented to begin an extensive search for the hidden trigger that had eluded her before the servant had made an untimely appearance.

The soft hum of aethecite bled through the walls, pulsing like a heartbeat, sending the valuable fuel borne of Eminence's aether throughout the majestic Silk Circle villa. The desktop lamp gleamed brightly as the warmth from the aethecite engines outside the villa spewed radiant energy within, a reminder of the essence of which the ore was derived—the Great Crystal of Life.

Ashe coughed and took another drink before pocketing the flask. The mist quivered beside the dead servant, sluicing over the corpse with a probing tendril.

"Here we go," Evander said as part of the wall opposite Ashe slid open, revealing a darkened portal leading downward into the belly of the villa. He gave her a lavish grin, while his aura churned a dark forest green with greed melding with a darkened red of lust. "See?"

She shrugged.

Evander lifted an old-tech lantern from a peg just inside the hidden door, coaxing the wick to life with his firestarter. Unlike the rest of the villa, it appeared this tunnel wasn't powered by aethecite. The smell of centuries-old musk wafted up as they hurried down the winding stairway, the soft blossom of the lantern lighting the hoary passage. Ashe ran a finger across the aged stone, dust thicker than her fingernail. At the bottom, the walls were lined with catacombs. Faded sculptures lay undisturbed, covered in thick, opaque cobwebs. Doorways, arched and crumbling, led to other chambers.

She shivered as she examined a statue of some long dead bastard, as it wasn't lost on her that in the dark, dank catacombs, she was clothed in a thin-sleeved, pleated stola with slippers. Her hands roamed up and down her arms trying to coax some warmth back into her flesh. She could've burned her aether, but she decided to save her energy for what was to come.

Evander disappeared, the luminosity of the lantern fading. Ashe followed, the mist around her feet rippling. Ever present, her constant reminder that time was not on her side.

Trotting to catch up, Ashe began to brood, as she was wont to do when she was about to use her aetheurgy.

Her thoughts strayed to the dead man in the study above. How long until the Pentax judged him worthy of the Meadows in the afterlife? Or would he be sent to Nocturne's Pit with the rest of the broken and battered? Would she be deemed worthy of the Pentax when the pulmo finally ended her?

An answer she sought constantly but never learned.

None of the augurs of the Scattered Shards could answer her questions whenever she'd coyly asked the clergymen about the mist and why it was killing her even though she rarely stepped foot outside the mega-cities of the Mistlands. Priests to the Pentax the augurs may be, but as scholars, they went lacking.

"Must be 'round here somewhere." Ashe found Evander pushing stones about with the tip of his boot. "Here we go. Right where Elian said it'd be." Under the pile of stones was a circular ring, rusted with age. He handed her the lantern and pulled it with a grunt. The stone slab gave way to a cloud of dust. "Call me a firedrake's tit," he cursed, waving the earthy powder away.

"Firedrake tit."

"That's not what I meant." Evander cleared his throat annoyingly as he took the lantern and shined it upon a now-revealed safe. "You ready for this, Snow Eyes?"

As always, Ashe kept her true thoughts to herself—at least until she had a few drinks. "Stop calling me that."

Staring at the lock, Ashe painted it across the canvas of her mind, memorizing each little intricacy, any irregularity. Everything seemed to stop; all there was, shoved to the back of her consciousness. There was only her and the lock.

When the mist curling around her feet oscillated, she was ready, the memory ingrained.

Ashe drew a breath as she rolled up her sleeve to reveal intricate tattoos all along her left forearm. Aetheurgic runes inked in varying colors into her ecru-toned flesh, all of them imbued with the Four Tenets of Aether. *Aere, Aquis, Ignis,* and *Terris.* Her Shard Form of aetheurgy inked on her dominant arm by her taskmaster during her time with the Scattered Shards back in Kalderim. The tattooed runes of the Four Tenets were surrounded and connected by smaller runes in a delicate pattern linking body and aether.

The poison fog coalesced, drawn from every nook in the catacombs, forming around her body like a heaving cocoon, soaking in her emotions. She sucked it in like the addictive pipeweed drug, the poison within the aether dancing down her nostrils, flinging about her innards with deadly glee. The runes on her forearm shone in brilliance as she touched their aetheric spark, for that's all it took.

She snapped her fingers, finally burning her aetheurgy. Spark.

The world exploded outward in an invisible torrent of grey aether. Time stopped as the undulating wave crashed. Evander was frozen, like a statue. His hand still outstretched toward the safe, finger pointing. His eyes narrow in anticipation, soft brown irises under craggy eyebrows, his lips curled upward in a hopeful grin.

Aetheurgy, the magic of burning aether. Her gift. Her curse.

A gateway in the mist yawned in front of her, opening like the air itself parted, the runes along her outer forearm synapsing in the Tenet of *Aere*. A shimmer, a cut in the fabric of her reality. A clean fissure, a long, elegant slice in time and space followed by piercing screams from the void beyond. Everything hazy, a mirrored image of her world, but only a shadow of itself. A plane in the world of Death.

The Meadows, as those who believed in the Pentax called it, or the void to others, especially those who knelt before Nocturne.

Empty, the Meadows was, regardless of the wails from souls freshly wandering the realm of eternal slumber. Dark yet not. Luminance from everywhere and nowhere. Ashe reached through the misty gateway toward the mirrored safe, the mist running over her arm like a river traversing down a bank, flowing in-and-out of the runes representing the Tenets, into her palm.

It flickered brightly, the mist did. Telling her it was ready, that it was there for her to control. If her taskmaster were there, she'd long since been beaten bloody for bastardizing her Shard Form thus. But this was her choice now, her path.

After sucking in more of the poisonous haze, Ashe held her breath, then thrust her hand down, penetrating the once solid stone in her reality, gliding through the misted gateway into the safe's shell. She likened the feeling to slipping a hand into a big, steaming pile of horseshit; that's how odd it felt. Fingers found the base of the lock, twisting and turning. She exhaled the mist as if she was standing in the dead of a Kanjan winter bare-assed.

A click.

As she began to pull back on the aetheric power and sew up the gateway to the void, Ashe was drawn to something within the safe. An urge beckoning her. She dug toward the bottom, reaching. Something triggered in her mind, the mist pulsing with it. Magic.

A flash of light, of all colors and none. Ashe tried to yank her arm free, but the magic held strong, and her tattooed runes flared intensely like never before, pain shooting up her arm and into her body, deep down into her soul. Pricks along the tips of her fingers, blood pouring down, dripping freely in the void.

What the fu…

She stared into the misted gateway and found her hand wasn't empty. A thin chain of braided gold had wrapped around her wrist toward the center of her palm where a diamond in the shape of an eye lay. The golden links fanned out to auric rings on each of her fingers, each begemmed with four shards cleaved from the great crystals of the greatest crystal. Blood dribbled from underneath each ring as the shards gleamed.

What are you?

The wailing from the void grew stronger. Heartier. Angrier. The non-ground beyond the gateway trembled, a deep quake from the depths of the unseen. The mist turned opaque, dark as the void itself. Her arm disappeared into the pitch. The lantern in Evander's hand sputtered and winked out, leaving Ashe bathed in an eerie ruby-black-colored shine.

There was movement behind Evander, from the catacomb's tunnel. Someone or something ghosted toward her.

A figure, completely naked. Light brown, almost blonde hair gesticulated as if underwater. The figure was nearly translucent, like an apparition, a mixture of light reds melding with pitch blacks burned within the figure's breast, over their heart. Rune-like scars flared upon their chest, aether bleeding from them. There was a smile on the heart-shaped, familiar face, onyx irises and sclera aglow in a similar coloring to the eerie light, punctuated by blacker pupils.

Behind the apparition followed a large shadow, spreading darker than anything Ashe ever imagined possible. Kindled crimson slits formed, eyelike, in the black. Only something so sinister could be borne of Nocturne's Pit.

"GODSBLOOD!" The voice was ragged and ethereal, like the wails from the void, daemonlike.

Ashe coughed; her pulmo escaping in frazzled bursts as her arm became freed of the shimmering gate. The real world trembled as she broke the connection between the two planes, the mist fleeing into the ancient tunnel like a craven mercenary dropping blade and shield amidst flight from an overpowering enemy.

Time, otherwise, remained stopped, Evander still statuesque.

Retreating hurriedly, Ashe tried to cover her mouth to staunch the blood and tar from her pulmo. Backside hitting a stony tomb, Ashe took her fingers away, darkened blood staining. Blistering cold struck her, breaths clouding as the vaporous figure slid past Evander, a part of its arm passing right through his shoulder. By the Pentax, it went right through him! Reaching for her, slowly, mere inches away.

Ashe shook as the shadow expanded, swallowing the ghastly figure. Garnet fading, onyx slits brightening for a heartbeat. Laughter, strange and aggressive. She covered her head with her arms, tattoos burning, a scream trying to sound, dying as the void fell.

"COME, GODSBLOOD, COME TO US."

The shadow retreated and was gone in an instant. Time scurried into action, speeding back to normal. The girl sought out the apparition, but it was nowhere. The shadow was gone, leaving her alone with Evander, her heart pounding its way up her throat.

"Bloody Nocturne, Snow Eyes, you've done it!" Evander said, completely ignorant of her frightened condition. He pulled on the locking mechanism, drawing the lid away from the safe. His aura pulsing shady emerald. "Mother's milk."

Out came a woven mask, simple yet detailed. Humirish face with horse-like ears. A satyr mask. One of the relics of the old mysteries from Eminence, one of the creatures honoring the Drunk God Brio, son of Mother Marrow and Zenith. Valuable beyond reason because anything from the ancient city or of the Pentax was worth a fortune in quadrans within the Mistlands.

A fit overtook her, her stomach clenching. The use of her magic bringing forth the destruction to her body from the mist's poison, killing every little bit of humanity inside her. Her blood fire, her lungs aching with torment. Feverish and weak, she was wasting away.

This was why using aether was called burning because that's what her body felt like. Aflame like being in the center of a firedrake's pyre.

With the mask in one hand, Evander came over and pulled her upright, throwing her arm across his shoulder, the aetheric runes fading back into ink. Her legs were feeble, her insides jelly.

Evander half-dragged her through the dusty catacombs, her slippers scuffling to keep pace as he hefted her up the never-ending staircase. "For such a tiny thing, you weigh almost as much as my limp prick."

Raven hair falling into her eyes, Ashe looked over her shoulder for the wraith and the shadow but found neither. Breathing was a chore, her lungs arguing with themselves about which to do: breathe in precious air or expel the deadly poison. Neither was giving it a solid go as far as she was concerned. By the time they reached the top of the stair, Ashe was standing on her own, yet still woozy.

Ashe put a hand to the wall as Evander closed off the hidden panel, the strange bangle affixed. She gave it a solid yank, but the thin chain held strong. Breathing came easier back within the study. Out of the corner of her tear-brimmed eyes, she saw the body of the murdered servant, lamenting her undesirable fate.

The heavy oak door burst open, and a young woman hurried into the room. Wren, their lookout. "Vicars!"

Strange, unseen laughter echoed the earlier taunt.

"COME, GODSBLOOD, COME TO US."

II

Cadrianna

WIND WHIPPED AT the flags furling around the tallest spire of the citadel, oiled fabric cracking in resonating cadences.

Moonlight shone down upon the northern edges of Silk Circle; shadows of pitch bestowed by Gargantua above blanketed the fortress-like villa. A single window alight in the citadel's tower, the slight hum of aethecite engines filling the silence. There was movement beyond the tower's window, followed by the lilting laughter of a woman.

A shadow detached itself from the stone wall of the main bailey. A scourge of the Fallen's Imperium. Clothed in black-painted firedrake armor, her footfalls were silent in muffled boots. Stopping after each step, her head tilted toward the sky, listening.

Cadrianna paused as the voices of guards carried through the air.

"Oriin speared Luciatt again," a soldier said, husky and laced with scorn. "Heard she's gone and got fil't with child."

"Why you let that swine touch your sister's beyond me," a second reprimanded, tone deeper and guttural.

Goblins. Cadrianna loathed goblins.

"Can't stop her from the pricks she wants to mount," the first goblin griped. "Tried once, got a kick to the seedpods to show fer it. Ungrateful bitch, that one is. Rest my mam's soul."

"SOUNDS A FUN CONVERSATION," said the Strix in a sultry tone in Cadrianna's mind.

"Just because you have your own sheath," Cadrianna whispered back to the daemon blade gripped in her hand, "doesn't mean you'd know thing one what to do with a cock."

The Strix cackled within the void beyond. For a daemon, the Strix was all banter before the spillage of blood.

Calculating the distance to the goblin guards solely on voice pitch alone, Cadrianna hefted the black-bladed dagger. The Strix was a twelve-inch-long blade with a handle of onyx in the shape of an owl, two rubies for eyes, one on the pommel. Borne a daemon of Nocturne's Pit, the blade was sentient, full of bloodletting desire, and an eater of souls.

And, achingly annoying as men would say.

Flexing the fingers of her other hand, Cadrianna counted thirty feet to the goblins, no more. Cranking her neck side-to-side brought soft pops. A roll of her shoulders slowed her breathing.

This was her element, her fancy.

"SHALL WE?"

Cadrianna whispered a spell borne of the void as the velvet touch of the darkened mist around her coalesced. She pulled upon the aether, drawing it close, the hardened scars upon her breast smoldering as she burned her Void Form aetheurgy. Heeding. And willing. The aether came to her, spilling out of her body in a blackened mist, blood dribbling down her abdomen as the familiar sounds of wailing souls filled her ears. The mist flitted about her shoulders, making her body light as a feather as a slice within the veil between Life and Death parted.

Savior and giver, protector and shield, her Void Form aetheurgy.

Smooth as silk, she stepped into the void. Mist swirled around her in the realm of Death as she moved. In the world of Life, a torrent of black air, a tornado of translucency moved across the bailey as she traversed the void. A flurry of nothingness, anyone looking saw only what they should: an empty courtyard while she void walked.

The goblins stood a mere dozen steps away in the realm of Life, in front of carved oak doors. Cuirasses of blackened bone armor from Filfangin—the goblin homeland northeast of the Imperium of the Fallen—were adorned with the Fallen's sigil: a red moon. Greaves over leather trousers, and helms atop their ugly skulls. Their misshapen noses and pointed ears protruded inelegantly. Both had an array of piercings between nose bridges and bumpy earlobes. They carried six-foot-tall spears and had wheellock single-shot pistols and bone swords holstered and sheathed on their belts.

The churning mist drowned out their voices, only an inferno of angry souls of the void sung in her ears. Cadrianna was close now, could see their chests rising and falling, parched lips moving, knurled hands raised in gestures. She could smell their ungodsly musk through the swathe of mist, even in the void, free of doubt, free of fear, full of boorishness. The knowledge of their doom nonexistent.

"O YES. MORE SOULS FOR NOCTURNE, MY LOVE."

This was her life, the endless swarm of flesh awaiting Nocturne's Pit. She was the dagger in the night, the hand of the Fallen. Innocent or not, her sworn duty.

Close enough, the wails of the dead reaching a fever pitch, she summoned once more her Void Form, ending her void walk by stepping through the veil between the two planes. Mere feet from the unwittingly goblins, the blackened mist swarmed her, hiding her. The Strix flew from her hand by her silent command, spinning around her and separating into six blades. Hooting echoed within the mist, winging along the mist like the owl of its handle.

The goblin on her right stopped, turning as if sensing her. "Yo—"

One of the Strix's blades rammed in the gap between the goblin's helm and cuirass. Black blood spewed in a radiant arc as he crumpled to the ground, the blade shivering in his neck.

"What?" The other instinctively swung his spear, tip swishing over Cadrianna's already ducking head.

Unfortunately, the strike found her shoulder, piercing her clavicle where her armor was fastened, and set her skin aflame as the mist howled. Blood dribbled down her arm, blackened mist danced about the wound, the aether of her Void Form sewing it back up. Savior and giver, protector and shield.

Cadrianna kicked at the goblin's off-balanced leg, which sent him to his knees. She yanked the bone sword from his belt, drawing the razor-sharp ossein across his exposed neck as she willed the remaining blades of the Strix into his back. The goblin jerked as the blades dug deep, black ichor oozing as he fell.

She swung about with the bone sword, scanning the rest of the courtyard and the walls above. Nothing moved, no sounds. Only her and the corpses at her feet, the mist of the void prowling about the bodies like carrion birds over a battlefield.

"O NOCTURNE, MY LOVE," came the lusty voice of the Strix as it slurped the souls of the dead goblins. *"SO GOOD. SO BLOODY. SO FRESH."*

"You have issues," she said as she looked up at the tower of the citadel, tossing down the bone sword. "Serious issues."

"SAYS THE WOMAN WHO REVELS IN THE GAME."

"I do not *revel.* I do this only for Brynn. Now, be a dear, and clamp the void up, I'm thinking here."

"DON'T HURT YOURSELF."

Cadrianna pursed her lips, for the Strix would trade barbs all nightturn otherwise.

The citadel was a behemoth of stone; all villas in Silk Circle were. However, this keep was more akin to a fortress, augmented by dire fear of attack in the aftermath of the Fall, while still trying to remain faithful to old architectural designs. Crenellation atop fifteen-foot walls led to parapets and spires, arches of steel and stone. Battlements lined with hand-cranked aethecite cannons instead of cypress trees and gardens like most other villas. More goblin guards stalked the walls, but as shadows within the shadows.

Dropping the shroud around her, Cadrianna willed the Strix's blades from the dead bodies, reforming into one. Contentment from the blade filled her mind as she grabbed the hovering weapon. The blood it craved, and blood it had received. Souls devoured. Kneeling beside one of the dead goblins, Cadrianna pulled a key from the loop on his belt. Placing it in the lock of the oak doors, she pushed with gloved hands, a slight groan of oiled hinges.

She slipped inside.

Weaving through the empty corridors of the villa, Cadrianna made her way toward the kitchen, seeking the servant stair beyond. The succulent aroma of roasting boar wafted through the back rooms, pots clanged and voices cursed, but she crept past them, finding the stair, taking two at a time.

Not more than three steps onto the second floor, Cadrianna found herself face-to-face with another pair of goblin guards, who were startled by her sudden appearance.

Lunging with the Strix, Cadrianna sliced downward along the unprotected flank of one's thigh. He let out a stifled cry as she rammed her elbow into his crooked nose, crooking it further. His nose exploded and he fell to the ground writhing in his own black cruor.

The other goblin, fool that he was, didn't call out the alarm, instead attacked with his bone sword. She sidestepped his flimsy thrust and gave two hand jabs to his throat and one to his crotch. Before he could recover, she sank the Strix into his armpit. The bone sword fell from his useless hands as she drove twelve inches of blackened steel deeper into his innards, aiming for the heart. With one last gasp of burbling blood, the goblin died.

Pulling the blade free, Cadrianna flicked her wrist, blood splattering across the marbled floor, leaving a feculent painting.

"THE HEART IS ALWAYS MY FAVORITE. YOU LOVE ME SO, CAD," A hint of laughter and amusement—if such a thing existed for a piece of metal betwixt by a daemon. But then, a slight sadness. Strange.

A long, narrow hall with no windows greeted her. Gasless aethecite-lights hung from the ceiling, glass globes glowing dully. At the end was a set of red-painted doors, the tops fanned out in a tail-like pattern of a bird in flight. A thrush, the bird was. No guards.

It was just like Thestile to leave her rooms unguarded; she feared no one. She was the cream of the Fallen's coven, like Cadrianna. A scourge. None dared touch her.

Until the Fallen deemed her expendable.

Cadrianna stared at the bird-shaped doors for long moments. Thestile had always worn a brooch with the same symbol upon her firedrake armor or her clothing when not hunting. Cadrianna had actually never seen Thestile without it. It was odd, even to her, to be standing before these doors ready to pull the blade across flesh thinking about Thestile's brooch. But vengeance was all she had left, the only humanity flowing through her veins.

That's who she is.

All she is.

A killer made. A monster without feelings, without remorse because her heart didn't have room. Tool for the Fallen to save the last remaining shred of soul. All for her daughter.

Cadrianna eased open the door to the chamber beyond.

"They grow edgy, Richtel." Thestile's voice.

"There's nothing we can do about it," a man said. Richtel, a Guilder of Drenth, one of the city's oily politicians and leader of his House. "The Fallen will do as he will. With or without the Guild. We are but slaves to his whims. Prien agrees with me."

Cadrianna moved closer, hidden within the shadows of the bedroom. Pulling off her breather and setting it down upon the floor, her reflection in the standing mirror opposite showed the monster she'd become. Black pupils within black irises and black sclera glowered back at her like portals to her dark soul. She tightened the tie binding her shoulder-length, dark brown, nearly black, wavy hair, and flexed her fingers, waiting for the right moment to present itself.

"A thorn in our side for too long," Thestile said, face pinched, arms crossed. "He will bring ruin upon the Guild if unchecked. With the rebellion happening in Drenth, it's bound to wrap the other nations in its wake. The Gutter King will destroy us all if he wins Drenth. He'll go to Kalderim, and they'll join against the Fallen."

"THERE SHE IS. THESTILE, THE TRAITOR."

"The Fallen has Drenth by the scruff of the neck," Richtel offered, moving closer to Thestile, hand upon her bare shoulder. "He guides the Houses with his poisoned tongue. Which is why we need to stay the course. Solanine will run Drenth afoul if that creature isn't wary of the Gutter King. Lu Har's army stirs, you've seen it, Thestile. He will soon march toward Kalderim. He knows Drenth and Kalderim must not join. Prien and the other Houses are on our side."

"WHAT'S THIS NOW?" Further amusement from the Strix. *"MORE TREACHERY. I LOVE IT. AFTER MY OWN HEART, THEY ARE. I TRULY WANT TO MEET THIS GUTTER KING, THIS REBEL. HE SEEMS A SOUL WORTHY OF MY LIPS. IF I HAD LIPS, THAT IS."*

"Shhh."

"You certain of this?" Thestile continued. "How can you trust that old lout, Richtel? Even now, he throws a gala when we should be discussing our options. This can ruin all we've worked for."

The Guilder rubbed Thestile's shoulder with a large hand, mouth close to her ear. "I am." Kissing her neck, tongue moving up. "When we helped Dunleith steal the Eye, you knew this day would come. The Eye belongs to Eminence, not the Fallen." He pulled her face into his, lips crushing together as they kissed. "Together, we can oust him," he said between kisses, "and take back Drenth without the Gutter King. Once the Eye is found anew, Eminence can be reopened. Imagine what we could find."

"We will soon know."

"What of the Seal?"

"The Seal remains under Solanine's watch. Worry not, Richtel, my dear. Dunleith may have stolen the Eye but until the Godsblood is found, the Seal is useless. And the heir of Kalderim still hides."

"THE EYE? DOES HE MEAN THE EYE OF THE SOUL? FROM EMINENCE? LIES UPON LIES, CAD. STOLEN THEY SAID IT WAS. DO YOU REMEMBER?"

O Nocturne she remembered it all. Every waking moment she recalled that day seventeen years ago.

Her husband's mother and father, the former rulers of Drenth, were murdered. Her own parents and two elder brothers, murdered. Her husband, Emre Benld, throat slit. Her daughter Brynn taken as prisoner by the Fallen.

All for the Fallen's hatred of the Last Godsking and the sealing of the city of Eminence some five centuries past.

The sole reason she obeyed and was trained in aetheurgy under the ancient gaze of the Divines. Broken by the sight of brutality, bathed in the arts of Void Form, turned a gifted killer.

Cadrianna's blood warmed at the thought of killing Thestile, the magic of the Strix coursing through her. The Fallen's orders were explicit, and by her hands, she would deliver these traitors to the Divines. Traitors to Drenth. Blood meant everything. That's how she was raised. But only to save Brynn, her child bound in chains deep in the belly of Gargantua.

Obey, that's how she would finally free Brynn. To end her own nightmare.

"You're eager for action." Thestile's fingers tugged at his belt while he slid the dress from her shoulders. "You aim to take down a daemon. The Fallen is stronger than you know."

"A sullied daemon." Hands at her breasts, now exposed, skin vivid in the aethecite-powered light. Corded scars in the shape of voidspeak runes carved into the scourge's breastbone. "For far too long has Lu Har had his claws in Drenth. It's time for Drenth to break free of the Imperium. The Guild must rule, not the Fallen."

"You sound like the Gutter King." Thestile's head lolled as the Guilder's tongue moved down to her breasts, circling. His fingers found the dark between the scourge's legs. "The Fallen's time is at an end." Thestile shoved her hand down his trousers, returning the pleasure. "Immortality does not come from the proliferation of Life… O yes, O yes… but upon the wave of Death."

The Guilder lifted the scourge onto the plush bed and mounted her, a moan escaping as he entered her. The sounds of carnality sang in the room and Cadrianna smirked. Fitting that the end would come when there was nothing but the pleasure of Life to look forward to when forever surrounded by Death.

"YOU MORTALS ARE MUCH EASIER TO KILL UPON YOUR BACKSIDES. FUNNY, THESTILE ALWAYS SAID SUCH BANAL THINGS."

Through the dimly lit room Cadrianna moved, alert as the larger man pumped his hips atop the smaller woman, well-muscled legs of caramel brown wrapped around his pale torso, delicate feet clenched together. Sweat dripped down the Guilder's back as he thrust.

For Emre. His father, his mother. For Drenth. For Brynn still imprisoned.

Cadrianna grabbed the Guilder's hair, pulling his head back, the Strix slicing neatly across his throat, blood spraying the bedding and the scourge below. Thestile's eyes opened, but Cadrianna clamped a firm hand over her mouth. The blood of House Richtel streamed down the traitor's cheeks in red rivulets.

The naked scourge struggled against her hand, kicking. Her slightly slanted brows furrowed. She should know better, sex made legs weak during the throes of passion. Thestile was the one who'd taught Cadrianna that.

But the woman's connection to aetheurgy potentially presented a problem.

"DO IT," the Strix commanded, wary of Cadrianna's hesitation. Hesitation led to death, that was the core of a scourge's training.

The dying Richtel burbled on the bed, hands futilely trying to stem the flow of lifeblood, but death drew him on as he went limp, eyes rolling back into his head, convulsing. Fresh crimson rivers gushed from his neck, soaking the mussed linen sheets. The Guilder of House Richtel died without a whimper, one contract settled.

Thestile went still. Cadrianna released her mouth knowing she could still cut down the traitor with but a thought. A level of respect and trust, even amongst the Fallen's coven. A scourge to a scourge.

"It comes to this?" Thestile finally said. "The Fallen has learned the truth of my deceit? Seventeen years… ah, that was but a gift, I know it now."

Cadrianna glanced around the room. The window was open to the pale moon. Alarm not yet raised over the dead goblins. A fire burned brightly in the brazier; the room unbearably warm for summer. A portrait of a bird, a thrush within a golden frame above the fire. For a heartbeat, she thought she heard the Strix sighing in the void.

"There's none but us, Cad." Words soft and sad. Knowledge her time was over. The scourge scooted back to the headboard of the bed, not bothering to cover herself. Her Void Form scars glistened with sweat. "No words? After all this time, young Nightingale?"

Cadrianna stared at the woman, saying nothing. Nightingale, her family's surname. She couldn't muster the words. Thestile was there when it all happened. Complicit in the murders of her family, of her beloved Emre, and the chaining of Brynn.

"Then be on with it." Thestile hooked her long, fine hair over one of her pointed, elfirish ears. Thestile was well over a thousand years of age and yet, she still had a youthful glow about her. Something that had always made Cadrianna wary of trusting her. And now, with what Thestile had just confessed, maybe she wasn't wrong. "Come, I won't fight. I dare not want to see the Fallen open the way to

Eminence. What he will do once he breaks the Seals. You could only imagine the war he will bring. I was there the first time, Cad."

Thestile was from the Forest of Calibrath—one of the elfirish homelands, the other being Kanja—prior to the Fall and had been one of the finest aetheurgists the Mistlands had ever seen. But now, like Cadrianna, was nothing more than a tool. A pawn of the Fallen. A scourge and a stain upon the land.

Cadrianna was only twenty when the Fallen had conquered Drenth, barely old enough to truly understand the murder of her entire family, and her young daughter Brynn taken from her. Barely capable of making the choice of bringing death in order for the babe to live. A choice that was no choice. Then and now. When the Fallen commanded, she answered.

Thestile's face was set, determined. Bosom rising and falling in controlled, calm breaths. She hadn't moved an inch, hadn't gone for a weapon. Hadn't burned her Void Form aetheurgy. Only stared at her. "Do it, Cad. Like you've been shown."

Cadrianna put on the blank face of the Fallen's assassins, the face of a scourge. Showing nothing, feeling nothing. The vault door where her emotions sparked like a slowly dying fire was closed, leaving only the task at hand.

Thestile tapped the center of her chest, right where the runes of Void Form had been scarred centuries ago. "Do it quickly."

Cadrianna leaned forward, gripped the woman's shoulder, the tip of the Strix pressed against the woman's ribs, black on gentle brown flesh, point drawing a droplet of crimson.

Face serene, all-onyx eyes watching Cadrianna's, soft and loving as they searched, opening her soul. "Never forget the truth of who you are, Cad. You are a Nightingale. That is the real you, not the Fallen's scourge. Trust in the Pentax. Trust in Nightingale."

And that's when Cadrianna realized something: Thestile was ready for death. Had been for some time. Maybe these seventeen years had been a gift, a life already given up to help the traitor Valeria Dunleith recover the Eye of the Soul. What was seventeen in more than a millennium?

A tender hand caressed Cadrianna's cheek, and she almost pulled back, but didn't. Couldn't. A tear brimmed. The scourge smiled and lurched forward, void-wrought steel piercing the unyielding skin, passing through bone into the heart, sure and precise.

For Brynn.

"I'm sorry, Thestile, but I cannot trust the gods. Never again. Mors expectet," Cadrianna intoned the prayer of her sect. "Death awaits you in the Meadows. Fire begets, Fire taketh. Water rears, Water recedes. Earth sculpts, Earth razes. Air breathes, Air stifles. Scales ward, Scales break. Scales are All. Scales are Nothing. Immortality does not come from the proliferation of Life, but upon the wave of Death."

And finally, a single tear fell for her role in sending souls to the Meadows.

III

ASHE

PINPRICKS REVERBERATED DOWN Ashe's spine but the mist at her ankles reared in excitement, a needless anticipation because she had no desire to dance with a vicar of the Scattered Shards.

"How many?" Evander carefully wrapped the satyr mask into a cloth, then stuffed it into a pouch that was slung across his chest before buttoning his jacket up again.

"Only saw the blue cassocks," Wren answered. She was comely, not beautiful, and maybe a year or two older with a fringe of flowing blonde. Her lips turned up at the edges, and she had high cheekbones under large, perfectly round nibs of cacao. And Ashe was entirely enthralled by her. "Two or three at least."

"Godsdamnit," Evander said as he tossed his fine cloak at Ashe. "Cover up that stola." His gaze went slack momentarily, his head cocked as if listening to some unseen voice. Then, "I expect it laundered before you give it back."

"Yeah, yeah." Ashe threw the cloak around her shoulders, fastening it with a brooch over her bloodied gown. "The cloak or your dead mother's stola?"

"My what?" His aura was utterly confused.

She held out her stola's hem, stained with blood. "Your mother's stola?" Ashe glanced toward Wren for some help, but the pretty woman merely rolled her eyes. "Zenith's cock, don't you get a joke?"

Moonlight poured into the atrium from the high-ceilinged windows as Evander ignored her attempt at crude humor and opened the door, bathing the entire villa in a silvery twinkle. Long shadows interlaced the red carpet as the swell of orchestral music danced about the atrium from the ballroom on the first floor.

A set of circular stairs wound around the open-aired foyer. Each level divaricated by long hallways leading to Pentax-knew-what treasures and troves. Mosaics of visceral lands without the mist, most likely from before the Fall of Eminence, adorned the walls in an array of colored pebbles. Expertly crafted friezes above fluted columns stood near seventy-five feet in height. Ostentatious, this villa.

The three thieves of Slag's End padded across the landing, pausing beside the railing.

"Guards on the next level," Wren indicated with a whisper.

Peering over the railing, it took Ashe a few moments before she spotted a pair chatting within an alcove on the floor below, only the random glint from the flameless chandeliers glancing off their firedrake-scale armor. She noted wheellock rifles slung across their backs; single-shot pistols holstered at their hips.

"Where are the vicars?"

"Ballroom. They seem to be searching for something. Hunting almost."

Searching for what? Ashe wondered. *Or whom?*

Vicars of the Scattered Shards at a nobleborn gala in Drenth made little sense. The holy church of the Pentax typically steered clear of the affairs of the Houses across the Mistlands, let alone those living within the Imperium of the Fallen. The untainted warriors of the

Shards rarely left the mega-city of Kalderim, and only on official missions. She knew those rules all too well.

No, this was wrong. Apprehension crept up her backside.

Elian's job was marketed as a quick grab-and-flee gig. Proper quadrans paid where hands needed to be greased. But with vicars present, this reeked of a set-up.

Would Elian set us up? His own brother? Or me? He did say I might learn something about my parents with this job. But what? She wasn't about to wait and find out. "Bloody Nocturne," she breathed. "I'll go first."

Taking the steps as quickly and quietly as she could, Ashe descended to the second level, keenly slipping past the conversing guards—who didn't bother to look up, ignorant navy auras highlighting their aloofness. A small puddle of mist huddled beneath the train of her pleated stola, tickling her legs, almost as if begging for the guards to show interest in the small girl skulking in their midst. She paused; ear turned toward the hushed voices threading the music on the level below. Crouched behind the thick banister post, she scanned the nobleborn prancing through the soiree. Most wore stolae of extravagant flow or tailored suits, but she spied dark blue cassocks.

Vicar cassocks.

Ashe made to slink down the stairs but stopped when she heard a soft growl from behind. Freezing, she glanced over her shoulder to find a brindle-colored mastiff with its tail up and ears turned forward. The dog was up to her waist and powerfully built, and, worse, twitched its muzzle inquisitively, for it clearly must've smelt the blood on her gown. Its aura beat garnet.

"Easy, boy," she soothed in a measured tone and urged the aether in the mist from under her stola toward the animal. The mist enveloped the vigilant canine, and the dog's ears went flat when she plucked the Tenet of *Terris* tattooed into her wrist and sent a calming spell of earthen nature through the haze. Its tail began to wag in slow beats until it became fast. She held out her hand for the dog to sniff. "There's a good boy."

"He likes you. Virgil typically doesn't like anyone."

Ashe stiffened and summoned the aetheric mist back as she flattened her stola. Snuffing her aetheurgy, she stood straight, hoping the dried blood wasn't visible under the cloak. As she turned toward a nobleborn couple watching her, she forced a smile through the searing flames in her gut as her aetheurgy wreaked its havoc in a fight to her death with the nigrum pulmonem. "I've a kindred spirit with animals."

"Forgive me, miss." The speaker was closer to the everlasting eternity of the Meadows than that of a young buck. Rings of gold and silver cordoned fleshy fingers on hands spotted with age. Saggy bags under his dark eyes, a bowl of salt-grey hair receding ringed his pate. His aura was a ruby tint full of lust. "But I don't think I've the pleasure."

He looked like a proper bastard.

His companion was infinitely younger, still in child-bearing years. She was beautiful, with porcelain skin, bee-stung lips, and a look of unfortunate thrill toward her marriage to an old prick worn about her like a tattered robe as her aura blinked bored sapphire.

"A beauty with the eyes of a sheet of ice across the VVinter Expanse," he said graciously, lifting Ashe's hand and kissing the back of it. "I've never seen such in all my years. Prien Soabin, you may address me, host of this gala."

A small cough escaped her lips, a deeper one building. The nobleborn flinched, as did his companion. "Forgive me, Master Soabin." Ashe tried to appear contrite. "Demrae has so little mist compared to Drenth, all this travel across the Sea of Mist has made me delicate." She smiled the sincerest smile she could muster, hoping it was convincing all while trying not to retch.

"Demrae! You've come all the way from Altreyia?" the predator in noble clothing asked, raising her hand once more to kiss it while his wife frowned. "What brings you here, miss? My lovely wife is also of Demrae."

"A lovely happenstance, no doubt." Mistress Soabin sipped from the cup in her graceful hand. She truly was comely. "O Prien, I wish I'd have known some little girl from Demrae was here. I'd have pulled out Altreyian cinnamon sweets in welcome." The bored woman, with her switch of a tongue, swirled her wine as an image of her lying naked in bed flashed in Ashe's mind before she stashed it away.

"Isla cares so little of Altreyia, isn't that so, love?" The woman swallowed her wine and marched off. Prien squeezed Ashe's hand, rubbing her knuckles. "She's but a trifle, that wife of mine. I'd soon as see those exquisite eyes of yours waking next to me every day."

"Master, that's presumptuous." She extricated her hand from his, plucking a golden ring from the man's pinky, while feigning another cough. "If you'll excuse me, I best see to getting some fresh air. It helps with my cough, you see."

"Come far for this party, miss?" came a silky voice ascending the stairway.

The mist prodded her calves forcefully. It was warning her.

Prien Soabin clapped his spotted hands together. "Ah, Solanine, I wondered if you'd make my party. And so lovely as always." While the old man greeted the newcomer, Ashe looked for a way to slip away but found no such luck. She was trapped. "With all those vicars about, I was hoping they wouldn't scare away my guests."

Wait, Solanine?

The newcomer was slight and short and wore a pleated stola of soft rouge that trailed down the stair gracefully. Light brown, almost blonde hair was pinned up over a heart-shaped face that was delicately contoured. A pendant of obsidian adorned the soft curvature of her neck, a crimson rune within the crystal, unlike any rune of Shard Form.

But it was the eyes that pulled Ashe in, and not in the inviting, flirtatious way. No, Solanine's eyes were completely black, like the void. From pupil to iris to sclera. All black. Only those who used Void Form aetheurgy had eyes such as that.

O void.

Ashe's innards railed within. It was the same person from the mirrored world in the catacombs, but here in the flesh. Of all the villas in all the Mistlands. Her hands fought the urge to draw her dagger, but what would a dagger do against one of the most dangerous aetheurgists alive?

"The presence of the Scattered Shards has no bearing on me, Prien. Kalderim's foibles reach us not in the Imperium." Solanine's crow gaze bore into her, not just through her, but deep down into Ashe's very soul. There was a reassurance, one of knowledge in a serene sapphiric aura. Of mysteries and magic. "Nothing could've possibly stopped me from passing up the opportunity to view the artifacts in your collection. Life aboard Gargantua gets quite boring at times. From Eminence some of your collection, aren't they?"

The satyr mask was one such. Ashe cursed Elian. She'd thought this villa belonged to some simple nobleborn House, not one of the most powerful men in Drenth.

"You humor me, Solanine. Just admit you enjoy my company."

"I confess." A humorless tone. "Though it's odd for vicars to be here, don't you think? Almost as if sent here to watch us." They had to see Ashe's heart nearly bursting from her ribs. Solanine's lips curled upward. "Vicars wouldn't be after your newly arrived guest, would they?" A jest, but deadly serious.

Stay calm, Ashe. "Why yes, only just arrived with my brother and his wife."

"And lucky enough to be a guest of House Soabin. Fortuitous indeed. Who is your father, child?" The aetheurgist didn't blink, head slightly tilted. Prien disappeared in Ashe's vision, leaving only Solanine. "A Guilder, by chance?" A pulsing began in Ashe's chest. Tentative at first, but promising safety, of learning. "I see the rune of *Terris* upon your wrist. Not of the Scattered Shards, I hope. Old blood is he?"

Ashe hastily drew the cloak over her exposed arm. "I…"

The mist along her calf pressed against her, but there was more than just alarm. There was yearning. Urging. Growing need. Aether ready to burn.

"Old blood, hmm? With the blood of Eminence, you could be anything you wanted. They say you might be able to break the Seals protecting the city. You've heard of the Seals of Eminence, have you not?"

The very air around Solanine began to shimmer dark red, the same as the aetheurgist's ever-shifting aura. The world stood frozen, not moving, not breathing.

As if time had stopped.

Realization of aetheurgy dawned on Ashe. She cursed herself, like she'd just woken from some drunken bender only to find herself pantsless in a noblewoman's bed. Her defenses fell aside like it was nothing but air. Ashe was drawn to the aetheurgist like a moth to a flame. Though of a similar height, the girl was dwarfed by the other's presence. Her mental walls began to buckle, sliding further down into scarlet pitch. Solanine's Void Form swallowed Ashe whole.

Freed from the constraints of reality, aether owned her.

"Escape us you cannot, Godsblood."

Ashe felt herself nodding in agreement. The bloom around Solanine grew stronger, the pull harder to resist. Her eyelids grew heavy.

"Camilla, sister, there you are!"

The carmine-inky fog in her mind cleared as she became untangled from the magical shackles of aetheurgy. Time returned to motion, speeding back into action. Walls built back up, the mist climbing up her legs lovingly once more.

Evander and Wren stood upon the top step, the dog wagging its tail vigorously at his new friends. The thief made a grand showing of finding her on the landing. Hands wide, smile wider. "Dear sister, you've got to stay close to your poor brother. I worry so about you. As does my loving wife," he proffered Wren forward. "See how she worries?"

Wren and Solanine locked eyes, but the lowborn girl quickly looked away, hunching her shoulders as if trying to hide. Ashe didn't blame her, for she wanted to do the same.

"Brother," Ashe said meekly, dropping her head, more in anger at allowing herself to be unnerved than in rebuke. "Forgive…" Another pulmo cough rose and this time she couldn't hold it in. Blood speckled her lips.

Pulling free a kerchief, Evander glided beside her. "My sister does not take well to the mist in Drenth. Demrae has much less of it, you see, being closer to Kanja, I fathom. And, well, I'm sorry to say, I was the one to drag her here. Thought her seeing the Imperium while I traveled on business," he put a brotherly hand upon her shoulder, "would make her yearn for the marriage our father has set up for her."

Ashe wanted to punch him but glared at the ground instead.

"A beauty such as she deserves a good husband," the aetheurgist said, an edge like a polished blade. "Dutiful, I'd wager. Perhaps even gifted, so to speak."

Her hackles re-rose, but Evander kept his façade up. "She is dutiful." But then he paused at the most inopportune time. Gods, the man certainly had a knack for making their lives more difficult. He shook his head after a moment, continuing, "You could bet your lucky quadran on that. A dutiful and devoted sister and daughter, she is. Aren't you, Camilla?"

She nodded, trying to avoid the gaze of the petite aetheurgist.

"A lovely bangle you have there, miss," Old Prien, the bugger, commented, no longer bound by Solanine's Void Form. His grin slick. "A beauty just like you."

"One of my father's finest, wouldn't you believe?" Evander revealed, although alarm rose from the depths of his mustard-shaded aura. He hadn't seen the bangle before, and to be fair, Ashe had nearly forgotten it was there. If Prien Soabin was the owner of the mask, he must surely be the owner of the bangle.

"Eminence-wrought perhaps?" Ashe could feel the weight of Solanine's words, it meant something. But to what? "Only seen one once before."

"And only once," Evander answered, "I assure you. One of a kind, you see."

"A trader, are you? What sort?"

"O, you know, everything under the Pentax, but specifically, silks and spice. My father heard Drenth is in need of some new supply lines, and he thought perhaps I should make his case to the Guild here."

"I happen to be a Guilder," Prien said. "I'm certain with the right word from me, your offer will be listened to. Perhaps you'd like to talk it over supper this week, sir… er… I'm afraid I've not caught your name."

Wren made a tragedy of tripping over her stola, forcing Evander to catch her. "Forgive me. My wife's had too much wine this evenfall. It's best we head back to our lodgings. I'll send one of my men to treat with you about trade lines. Good evenfall to you both."

With that, Evander grabbed Ashe by the arm and dragged the two women away. She glanced over her shoulder and saw the short aetheurgist watching. Smiling.

Ashe shivered.

Two massive doors stood open at the opposite end of the foyer, a ballroom was beyond, and music roared from within. Horns and strings played, and extravagantly dressed men and women danced. Liveried lapin servants walked through the throng with trays of drink, salvers of finger food, their rabbit-like ears twitched and bobbed. Hobgoblins cleaned up any spills or messes made, their ill-shaped, small bodies squirreled amongst the tables, forgotten by the revelers. Laughter boomed loudest over the music; the party drowned out everything.

"What were you thinking, talking to Guilders like that."

"It's not like I wanted to, Evander. That was Solanine. Couldn't exactly run away. That would scream 'I'm up to something, maybe check all the blood on my dress.'"

Wren leaned in. "Evander, vicars." She pointed toward the ballroom.

Wading through the crowd were three vicars.

Ashe sucked in a deep breath, centered herself, and forced the pain in her head to knock it off. Two she could handle, but three? At least it wasn't the customary four. "This is getting better by the minute."

Evander led them away, taking a servant doorway built into the painted wall, one their contact about the satyr mask had told them of. Before long, and without seeing a single soul, they were in a back garden, exiting through a small door hidden by a row of well-kempt bushes.

Not but a step into the alley behind the villa, they stopped dead in their tracks. Three vicars stood in the soft brilliance of aethecite-powered street globes. The one in front bore a crest of blue-dyed, bristling horsehair atop the breathing helm, signifying his rank as the leader. Which, truth told, Ashe always thought looked godsdamned stupid.

Vicars weren't the Mistlands' moron class of soldiers, no, these were the special, untainted guard of the Scattered Shards, enhanced by the aetheurgy in the mist with their Shard Form. A vicar didn't wear firedrake-scale body armor, instead they donned a midnight blue cassock, which covered them from wrist to ankle and was buttoned up the sides with brass studs. Adorning the left breast of the cassock was the insignia of the Scattered Shards: a fist holding a sword with a five-pronged star within the fuller, a representation of the Pentax Gods.

The bristle-topped leader had no weapon, but upon his dominant right wrist was a golden, rune-etched gauntlet. The other two vicars carried a pair of crescent-moon-shaped, double-bladed axes of bluish-iron and nothing else. Finger-length steel cylinders with gemstone shards atop were affixed to all three vicar's belts and were linked to their tinted glass breathing mask via narrow tubes. Those cylinders were canisters of mist, which, when released, enhanced their physical capabilities as well as allowed them use of the Four Tenets of Aether. Under the pall of aetheurgy borne from the Shards of Eminence, all knew to avoid vicars at all costs, as they were near indestructible while burning.

Vicars were called the untainted warriors because their conviction to the Pentax shielded them from the harmful toxins of the mist, whereas their opposite number in the Scattered Shards, the quaestors, were called the tainted warriors. Both vicar and quaestor burned aether, but a vicar's body didn't follow into the flame as the quaestors did. Unfortunately for the quaestor, they *did* burn so their bodies resembled walking corpses.

And partly why, even in the mega-cities where the mist was nil, vicars still wore their masks. To always be one with the Pentax's punishment.

Luckily, Ashe knew all there was to know about vicars and quaestors—as well as augurs and ingeniators—and it would fall on her to stop or delay them, lest Evander and Wren be torn asunder. And that failed to tickle her fancy.

Wren drew a thin blade from the sheath at her thigh and procured a single-shot wheellock from somewhere Ashe truly wanted to know. "Always did like dancin' at a party."

Thoughts of Wren dancing sexily aside, Ashe undid the cloak and tossed it to Evander. "You two go back through the party and out the midden heap. I'll meet you at *The Colosseum*. I can launder that cloak later," she said with a grin.

Evander searched her gaze, eyebrows furrowed. He wasn't used to taking orders, especially from an eighteen-year-old girl who'd only been running with the Slag's End gang for less than a year. But she meant business. She intended to use her gift again, and there was nothing he could do about it. Even if it was three vicars.

"You owe me."

"Be safe, Ashe," Wren said with a honeyed aura. With a dismayed look, the young woman pulled Evander back into the villa.

Ashe turned to face the vicars, drawing her flask. The mist, now to mid-calf, having been drawn to her from the surrounding streets, bubbled, reading her apprehension. So, taking one more drink, liquor and pulmo-induced blood staining her lips, she smiled, specifically at the leader with the crest. "Hey Bristletop, come find me."

The runes along her arm shimmered as she burned the Four Tenets of Aether before she bolted.

IV

EMRE

NIGHTTURN WAS ASH and sand, but the coming day would carry the seeds of revenge.

Neon lights flickered *Aere* spells along the skyline of Drenth as the fearless midnight sandstorm raged through the outer sectors, those burned-out districts whistling empty songs of wind against stone. The forceful grit hammered at the remnants of the once-grand complexes, wearing away the laughing memories bound within, harkening back seventeen years before Drenth's conquest.

Homes they'd been then, now an aethecite factory.

Emre Benld waited in the foyer of one of those rundown apartment buildings straddling the boroughs of Stanktown and the Smelt in northern sectors one and four. Vengeance seared through his blood as he rolled a bead of aethecite between his thumb and forefinger. His life, and that of his city, had changed completely because of the stupid hunk of aether.

Before the week was through, he would pay it all back in full. For his child, Brynn, who was still missing. His wife, Cadrianna, who was taken from him. His parents Edric and Alandy. Cadrianna's parents from the line of House Nightingale. For all Drenth, dead or enslaved.

Plumes of ash chugged from a half dozen chimneys five hundred feet high. Grey-black smoke cascaded about the Smelt with a sulfurous stink and painted the factory with dried aethecite flakes. The precious ore dug from the desert surrounding Drenth distilled into valuable fuel within. A scant inch of mist clung to the paved streets, just as deadly as aethecite radiation from the mines.

A bell tolled twelve peals. A reminder to those still awake, or to awaken those off into the land of dreams, to inject their parch, their sole protection from the blistering radiation.

Across from the Smelt, in an open plaza of dereliction, a massive aerescreen clicked on, LED illuminating the mud-drenched street. Solanine appeared upon the screen.

"*Citizens of Drenth*," Solanine's voice clear and kindly, blaring from enlarged aethecite-powered speakers on each street corner, "*forget not your nightturn injection. Remember the death that comes should you not. Aethecite is the lifeblood of Drenth, without it, our city is nothing. Our Imperium is nothing.*"

"What a load of slag," Emre muttered to himself as the streaming message repeated Solanine's warning.

He fished out a glass vial of parch. Liquid aether within. Bringing the vial to his lips, he swallowed. It felt like fire coating his esophagus, burning his innards. His stomach clenched, but he savored the feeling, for it reminded him of what he was. What he was about to do. Emre's eyes focused on the object of his wrath. Its decadence mocking him.

Gargantua.

His fingers dug into a broken windowsill, the sleeves of his tunic riding up his tense arms. All along his forearms were crisscrossing scars. A physical memory of when the Imperium sacked the mega-city seventeen years ago. Cut flesh when his parents were murdered before his eyes. Torn soul when his daughter was taken from him. A thin scar wrapped his neck when the Fallen had his throat cut in front of his beloved Cadrianna.

But the scars had hardened him, and he would see the Fallen's imperium burn to the ground. The scars reminded him of what he was underneath. Vengeance incarnate.

"Finn," Emre said as he pushed away from the window and kicked the rotted couch upon which a man slept, "it's almost time."

Irises of the prettiest ice blue surrounding a golden pupil snapped open. "I was having probably the filthiest thoughts ever about you." A perfect smile crossed Finn's handsome face as he rose from the lumpy seat.

Though appearing of a similar age but far more handsome if you listened to him, Finnus Dunleith was not Drenth-born, but of Kalderim, which meant he was an elfir and was closer to nine hundred and twenty years old whereas Emre was nearly forty. Finn was tall and broad-shouldered, with thick, silver hair that curled around the nape of his neck. His pointed ears peeked through the waves, and he wore the same simple dung-brown mining tunic as Emre, although he had somehow found a way to make it more fashionable by slicing some unnecessary holes at the knees.

"'Bout bloody time," Kephren complained as he paced the breadth of the foyer. His hands were stuffed into his pockets but Kephren's emerald pupils glowed with delight. He was burning, for the rebel's movements were quicker than a normal man's.

"What?" Emre asked of the antsy man wasting his aetheurgy. Burn Form wasn't innate like Shard Form, and Emre didn't want any of his friends to burn out before their use was fulfilled.

"I don't trust Killian Ness."

"Killian wouldn't have crossed us." Emre leaned against the worn frame where a door had once been, toying with the pellet of aethecite. Lower, "He knows better." Lower still, "knew."

Kephren spun on his heel. "Heard some whispers Killian's been working with Bar Stock." His raven hair was in thick, corded locks, and had high cheeks of the same dusky coloring of all Drenth-born. He sported a faded shirt and narrow, cuffed trousers.

"Snuff if, Keph," Emre said, gaze going back to the shadow of Gargantua. The fortress' outline shone in the moonlight. His hands balled into fists, anger scalding hotter than the aether down his throat. He reined it in by combing his hands through his short, curled hair. "Don't waste your burn. Nothing but rumors. Killian's clean."

"You trust too easily." Kephren's face split in a smile toward Emre, but the illumination in his pupils faded as he snuffed his aetheurgic Enhancements. "The Fallen'll crush us under his boots before we can reach fifty."

"I've already seen fifty," Finn said. "And then fifty more many times over. But Keph's got a point, Bar Stock won't negotiate with us. Maybe they're working Ness under the table. Em? You listening?"

"I heard you." Emre took one last look at Gargantua, then steeled himself. *Tonight, it signals the end.* "Even if Killian is working with Bar Stock, he knows the rebellion will make him profit."

"I hate working with these gangs," Kephren said. "I don't trust the lot of them to turn us over to the Fallen the first chance they get. How many of our hits have been sussed out before we could set up? It has to be the gangs. Them Imperium rats aren't bright enough. Besides, Finn, I'd rather die young and handsome."

Finn snorted. "I'd not put you and handsome in the same closet, let alone the same city."

Emre scratched at his stubble to avoid digging at the scars on his arms. "Me too, Keph. But until the Imperium's destroyed, we're stuck working with the gangs." *That changes tonight. Kalderim will join us, they must. Finn's convinced they will.* "Without parch, the rebellion is done. And you know it."

"You think Ness will be content just working with us? None of the other gangs want anything to do with the rebellion. And you said it yourself, the factories won't trade directly. No matter how many we get inside."

Emre checked his pocketwatch instead of answering—the one his father, Edric Benld, the former regent, had given him the day before the Imperium came, the day Emre's life had shattered. The midday shift had just ended. The forges would go dark for the next hour, the furnaces would be cleaned and brushed out. The day's output catalogued and boxed up, loaded for transport before the clock hit the first hour mark of a brand-new day of enforced labor. The workers released to find food or a waiting bed.

Emre had to hope that today would be different, but hope was a fickle companion.

Cad… forgive me… "Enough chit, and that means you too, Finn. Game faces on. I want this done cleanly. Don't you goad Ness."

Finn smiled a perfect set of pearl. "Sure thing, Em. I'll play nice… for now." Which could mean any number of things where Finnus Dunleith was concerned.

Outside of the complex, in the derelict alleys of piss-yellowed lamplight and sloshing sandmud, was a burnt-out crossroads. The area used to be prosperous before the appearance of Gargantua. Four mega-roads had been built upon enlarged trusses suspended in the air of man-made mountains, but now only broken portions of pavement littered the emptiness below, the mist clawing over top. A stone portrait of decay and forgotten times.

"How did Ness get such a large shipment of first grade parch? That's stuff's been harder to get than getting Keph to bathe."

"Go bugger yourself, Finn." Kephren skipped a step to catch up. "Told you, he's been working with Bar Stock."

"Nobody gets in with Bar Stock, Keph. Tevun's been trying to get someone inside for months now. Solanine's getting smart on us."

There were eighteen aethecite factories in Drenth's nine sectors, all in the lowborn districts. All with their own standing armies. It had made getting parch for the rebellion nigh on impossible.

"That's only the tip of the iceberg," Keph continued, "hear he's got somethin' else brewin'. Ness that is."

"You ever see an iceberg, Keph?"

"I ain't never been to the VVinter Expanse, Finn, but word is they are huge underneath. Like a certain someone we all know and love." Finn choked on a cough. "But I still wouldn't trust Killian Ness as far as you could toss him full burn. He'll turn on us, mark my words."

A chorus of boots smacked wet, sandy mud in the crossroads, and moments later, five shadows emerged from under the broken mega-road, four men and one woman. Two of the men carried wooden crates upon their shoulders. The woman and the other wiry man skulked behind, heads on swivels. The glint of knives in the belts of all. At the lead was a tall, Drenth-born man, lanky and gruff. Dark hair pulled back into a tail, beard pointed and dyed green, a stark comparison to his emerald pupils. A man with Burn Form. Killian Ness and his crew stopped opposite the crossroads from them. Ness' crew was one of the larger gangs in Drenth, claiming Stanktown as their base of operations.

Emre burned his aetheurgy.

All it took was a fraction of a heartbeat and the dam holding his parch reserves exploded into his veins. Like a bubble that held the aetheric serum, the wave crushed under the weight of his Burn Form, a flare in his mind, a sear of instant inferno within.

Mind, body, and soul aflame in aetheurgy.

The air around the crossroads shimmered light silver as his sensitivity to his surroundings increased under his Burn Form. Or as the Scattered Shards called them: the Four Enhancements. They were: sense, speed, strength, and stamina.

Coated in the sterling shine, the world magnified. Shadows were pushed back into nothingness; the morbid warmth of the desert chilled his skin. Emre could feel the heartbeats of the seven others within the crossroads, pulsing in time with his own thrumming beat. Their breathing matched his, and he could taste the sands of the dunes on their tongues along with them.

Clarity now, he sensed others. Three scattered throughout the rundown buildings. Three beacons high up, spying down on the Stanktown gang and the leader of the rebellion. Lookouts who'd burned aetheurgy to find him watching back, no doubt agents of the Fallen. A leak of intel. The expectation. Spies all around him.

But he felt another presence, these ones not men but draconem. Drakken, to be more precise. A pair hiding atop an old residence. He smiled at knowing they were there. Tevun had been right.

The war begins, he thought.

Now knowing where the Fallen's eyes were, he snuffed his aetheurgy, leaving some reserves left in the tank, but having mortgaged thirty seconds of his future. Unlike the four branches of the Scattered Shards, those who burned parch traded their lifeforce for the gift of aetheurgy. Seconds at a time, that was the tithe of Burn Form. A husk he'd eventually become.

Ready he was, satisfied to begin what he'd worked so hard with Tevun to achieve. What he'd set out to do the moment his parents were murdered, Brynn orphaned, and Cadrianna turned.

To give the Fallen a well-deserved 'fuck you.'

"When I heard the Gutter King was willing to meet me in person," Killian Ness spoke like rocks tumbling down a mountainside, gravelly and booming, "I couldn't resist."

"When scourges know your face, Ness, meetings like this aren't a luxury."

"Unless you're desperate." Killian Ness surveyed Emre from head to foot. "Man's gotta do, right? You know, I thought you'd be bigger. Heard you had the seedpods to fill a wine barrel."

"Never heard that one before. Guess opinions vary," Emre said flatly. "We all have to do with what we've been given by Zenith." *We all have to do what's demanded of us, right, Tevun?* "Now, if you don't mind, I'd like to get home before breakfast."

"That's why I like doing biz with you. The Gutter King is no—"

"When my crutch is the token of the deal, I like to keep it short."

"Spoken like a true man of the streets." Killian's lips curled upward at the corners. "Does the Gutter King got what I asked for?"

Emre reached under his tunic and pulled out a pair of thin cylinders of wrapped paper, holding them for Ness to see. "Two stretches of gravy. Gold. You got my crutch?"

Ness cocked his head and the men with the crates came forward, placing them on the ground a few feet away before backing away. Emre nodded toward Kephren, who stepped up to lift one of the lids. He drew forth a tiny vial and tossed it to Emre.

It was a vial of first grade parch.

Parch. The wonder serum made from aethecite. For any regular dreg, parch stopped the torrid radiation poisoning that aethecite wreaked upon human flesh. Blisters, boils, skin melting, bones crushing inward. They may be protected from the Sea of Mist by the vacuums on the walls, but every person who went into the mines had to inject themselves every six hours. Fitting that only injecting aethecite shielded death from aethecite.

But for some, parch did more than shield the radiation, it gave them Burn Form aetheurgy. A means to fight back with aether. Something the ingeniator scientists of the Scattered Shards could never have foreseen when they created the wonder serum.

"All here," Keph said, counting the vials.

"There's more where that came from." Killian Ness had a penchant for trying to squeeze every last quadran out of a negotiation in his favor. "Hundred more, if you want."

"I wonder," Emre started as he held the vial between his fingers, "how does a gang from Stanktown get a cache so deep? Especially of this quality?"

Keph tensed. "Um…"

Ness nervously looked toward the surrounding buildings. "What's going on here?"

The gang grunts put hands to belt knives, tapping parch injectors on their wrists. Each were ready to burn should the leader give the word. Killian Ness appeared ready to give it, too.

Emre absently looked up toward Gargantua, his face grew hard. "Heard some rumors." *You will pay, Solanine, for this betrayal. And the Fallen will burn with you.* "What'd you say earlier, Keph? Something about Ness and Bar Stock?"

"I'm what?" Genuine shock burgeoned on Ness' face before it turned into a scowl of scorching hatred toward the kneeling man. "You lousy, sandbagging, piece of gutter trash."

Emre palmed the vial and stuck it into his pocket. He reached into the crate and pulled forth a handful of glass vials. Each one was semi-translucent, not opaque like the one Kephren had given him. "The deal was for two bushels of second grade, Keph. Not first. You think two stretches of gold is enough for first? Now, how would a rat like you get your grimy hands on a vial of first grade without going through me?"

Killian took a menacing step forward. His frown a deep ravine. "You sold me out."

The trap set, Emre burned his parch.

In the silver sheen of aetheurgy, the air felt denser, claustrophobic even. The silence was deafening, only the hurried breathing of those around filled the void. The many aerescreens in the sky all shifted to a vision of Solanine, but the messages had stopped as the aetheurgist merely watched with a blank cyber gaze of non-life until the screen went dark. All the small camera drones stopped buzzing; blinking lights gone dark.

A single aethecite clock across the street read the time as 00:58.

"What's that, Keph? I didn't hear your answer."

"I… I didn't… I swear."

"He's hacked the screens," the wiry grunt said. He had a compact aerescreen in his hands, his fingers typing furiously. "The entire grid's shut down. I can't… nothing."

"What's the meaning of this?" Ness demanded. "I thought this was a friendly neg—"

Emre's scrutiny flashed toward Ness, the furor stopped the gang leader in his place. In the aetheurgy-enhanced veil, Ness' blood pumped faster through his blue veins under his Drenth-born flesh. His mouth quirked, but he bit back what he'd intended to say, his breath was ragged as if he'd run a mile up a sand dune.

"You thought I'd be easy to con, Ness. Too worried about the Imperium to know what was happening right under my own nose." Emre cuffed Kephren, sending the raven-locked man sprawling under the aether-enhanced blow. "Playing both sides against each other. Smart, if not short-sighted."

The aerescreen flashed, black nothingness coming alive as aethecite bloomed in the two parallel uprights housing the *Aere* spells. Solanine reappeared. ***"Citizens of Drenth, warning. I repeat, warning. Unspecified and unverified activity in Sector 4. Early reports indicate violence. Rebel agitators assumed. Warning. Warning. All those in Sector 4, please get to safety now."***

The camera drones whizzed into a frenzy of blinking lights as the churn of tiny fans echoed in Emre's aether-enhanced hearing like a tidal wave crashing against the southern coast of the VVyrm Ocean. Lenses panned toward the crossroads in Stanktown, highlighting eight people on the aerescreen as floodlights shone down.

"Both sides." Emre shook his head. "To think, Finnus never thought you'd be useful, Ness." He heard Finn guffaw. In fact, Finn had been the one to name Ness as the Imperium spy, but Killian didn't need to know that. "You honestly think I'm going to leave *my city* in the hands of gangs?"

A guttural growl rumbled from Ness. "I'll see you de—"

"But you, Keph," Emre said to the man face down in the muddy sand, who was groaning. Or whimpering. Probably both. "I expected more from you. Brothers until the end, eh?"

Solanine's pixelated gaze shone upon the crossroads, human-like tilt of the *Aere*-spelled head. ***"The Gutter King himself, I'm surprised to see you rear your head. Tonight, of all days. Your family would be proud. She's here, you know? Of course, you do. The Gutter King knows all."***

The woman in Ness' crew pointed up, her emerald pupils glowing. "O slag, Imperium!"

Emre stuck his chin proudly toward the flickering image of Solanine and smiled wickedly.

"Nothing to say for yourself, boy?"

The clock clicked over to hour one and with it came the explosions.

A blast shook the empty street, rattling the buildings in a massive concussion, waist-thick bricks exploding thunderously. Dust and shrapnel fell all around them in a vast cloud, centuries-old architecture from before the Fall of Eminence showered down, evicted angrily from their catacombs. Curses from Ness and crew. Finn shouted at him as the elfir scooped up the crates of parch.

The images of Solanine winked out, but not before Emre saw a fraction of concern mar the heart-shaped face.

Larger detonations erupted across the city, the closest being in the Smelt. Ash and flames burst into the sky hundreds of feet as the aethecite factories went up in smoke. All eighteen. The Smelt. Bar Stock. Slag's End. All the rest. Not just one, as had been his tactic in the early days of their rebellion, but all of them at once. Chaotic screams thickened the nightturn air. Those screams were only Imperium soldiers and supervisors, as all Drenth-born workers had already left when the shift had ended.

Just like they'd planned.

And yet, when he looked up at the four-chained tethered Gargantua, the fortress barely flinched.

A rope ladder dropped beside Finn, and the elfir hooked a leg in one of the rungs as he fumbled with the heavy crates of parch. "Come on, Em!"

Alarms and squealing sirens declared Imperium soldiers headed their way. Aethecite vehicles rumbled along the sandswept streets with floodlights blooming everywhere. Airgliders puffing aethecite dropped from Gargantua's underbelly like bees. The scant mist stirred by the commotion.

Ness' crew had fled, but not Killian. The green-bearded man burned aetheurgy and leapt toward Emre with a hammer fist, his emerald pupils bled murder. Emre's aetheurgy came alive. His muscles jerked as synapses flared, speeding up his movements. He sidestepped the gang leader's initial attack, Ness' aether-protected fist crashed into the street. The man howled as he swung again, but Emre danced away.

"Em!" Finn screamed as the rope ladder rose, the airglider pulling it away.

Emre looked toward Ness, but now the man realized his folly, as he began to flee the other direction. Finn reached out his hand, and the first of many Imperium vehicles appeared, blue and orange lights blinking, siren loud. Rubber tires skidded and sprayed sand and explosion debris. Killian Ness bellowed but was trapped as the Fallen's soldiers piled out of the vehicles, wheellock rifles pointed at him.

At them.

Aetheric gunshots borne from *Ignis* spells whizzed past as Emre took Finn's hand.

Kephren was on his knees. "Em?"

They rose now, shirking aetheric bullets. "Goodbye, Keph." He nodded toward the shadow of Gargantua, his voice raised so that Kephren could hear, "Traitor or not, you had it all. But the Fallen wants everything, you stupid fool. I aim to take it all back. This is my city!"

Kephren's face fell as Imperium soldiers surrounded him. His arms went up, but not before he tried running with aether-enhanced speed down a darkened alley. Soldiers poured after him.

As their airglider sped away through the hundred-story-tall apartments, Finn cackled like a madman amid the chaos. Emre gripped the rope ladder with all he had, his bravado drained as he snuffed his aetheurgy. The warm nightturn air sent shivers down his spine.

The moonlight drenched Drenth; the only shadow was the city-sized blot that was Gargantua. It was going to be a good day for revenge.

V

LOJEN

DRENTH SUNG WITH the Hymn of War.

The first blast, blocks away from where he was crouched, rattled the unsteady apartment complex, and forcefully sent Lojen Tevunson careening off the rooftop. His clawed talons groped for something, anything, as the black funnel of aethecite smoke ruptured like a blowing geyser. Attached to the building was a ladder of entirely too much rust and sharp metal. The rungs dung into Lojen's leathery palms as he grabbed, but his claws clacked against the iron as his shoulders strained to keep him from being blown completely off the building a hundred stories to his death below.

The ladder's moorings shivered under his bulk but dislodged the uppermost twenty feet. Gathering his wits, Lojen scaled the ladder upward and jumped the growing gap between building and ladder toward the ledge. His claws found purchase in the drab concrete and slimy grime left by Gargantua's dispelled aethecite.

Aside from their holy roles as wardkeepers, drakken were renowned for their climbing abilities; their claws capable of penetrating nigh on anything. Their tails counterweight, their muscular bodies as strong as four aurochs in one. Their hides coated in impervious, lightweight but near impenetrable exoscales. Men and their aetheurgy Forms repeatedly tried, and failed, to replicate the drakken body, paling in comparison to the lower order of draconem from the Isle of Merj.

Therefore, Lojen made the roof in short order, just as another blast rocked the no-longer sleepy Drenth. His claws were coated in the ashy filth by the time he topped the once ornate but now sandblasted lip. The massive drakken deftly tightrope-walked across the apex between roof and slanting tiles, his tail swishing a blur of greyish blue.

The crossroads of the northern borough the people of Drenth called Stanktown was filled to the brim with trash, and not the vagrant humans suffering from radiation poisoning or their meager possessions. This trash was a recent endemic: the Fallen's soldiers.

Imperium soldiers filed into the crossroads like ants pouring from their disturbed hill. Armored in grey-painted firedrake scale armor head to toe and wielding wheellock rifles, the Imperium soldiers took up defensive positions all around the empty plaza, under the dilapidated mega-roads. Others shone floodlights, searching the area. Tremors rumbled under their feet, which sent some to their knees. The remaining glass in the surrounding buildings fell in the quakes from the explosions, raining down like a prism storm. Some of the soldiers ducked, but others hauled a green-bearded man toward an armored vehicle.

Through the haze, an airglider took flight, rising above the black smoke that filled the crossroads like a pitch-black avalanche. The airglider was shaped like a metal bird with wings outstretched in a forever glide, a cockpit of glass, combustion engine spewing grey smoke out its narrow tail. Small, ovular portals were cut into the riveted metal sheets both port and starboard, with a hatch and valve-like handle, though now open, a rope ladder spilled out. Two men clung to the ladder, a third on his knees below as Imperium soldiers moved in, his arms lifted in surrender.

It was the man on the ladder who drew Lojen's attention.

Like a date freshly plucked from the palm, the man's skin was flushed as the sandy wind whipped at him. Hair short and curly brown with a short-kempt beard to match. Young, perhaps forty, as far as humir went. His nose was narrow at the bridge and slightly hooked. But beyond that, even as the airglider disappeared in the fog of smoke and into the high buildings' darkness, Lojen saw the man's emerald pupils gleam with determination.

He knew that face and the man, for Lojen had been present at his birth. Emre Benld, heir to the Regency of Drenth. The true ruler of the city. Its only ray of hope. The one known as the Gutter King.

There were aetheric gunshots of *Ignis*, louder and closer than the explosions across the city, coming from the apartment buildings, including the one Lojen was hidden upon. The panging of bullets struck the fleeing airglider's hull mere inches above the ladder-climbing men, others whizzed past their unprotected heads. The bigger of the pair—a Kanjan elfir by the look of it with his silver hair whipping in the wind—shouted in defiance. A cluster of shots riddled the hull and the glider lurched dangerously. Compressed air wheezed from the engine like steam from a teakettle on the stove. The airglider dropped from the loss of cabin pressure, dipping into the smoke. Lojen unintentionally rose from behind the ledge to follow its flight as it headed out toward the deep desert.

There were other airgliders now, dropping from Gargantua at record pace, like stones in a landslide. Imperium airgliders. Some of the larger gilders circled the giant floating fortress, rotating aetheric cannons positioned in defense, while the smaller transports hurried downward, depositing soldiers into the borough to join their comrades. Others flew deeper into Drenth, heading toward the many columns of rising smoke sprinkled throughout the city. A handful of the smallest and quickest chased after the fleeing glider.

Soldiers in the plaza below shouted, forcing some to point their floodlights his way as Lojen stupidly realized his folly with a curse. Diving behind the roof's ledge, Lojen felt the rush of gunfire whiz by, chunks of brick falling across his body. Rolling to his back and grunting when a jagged piece of stone dug into his side, he found himself staring at the underbelly of the great fortress, its many engines churning that baleful fuel residue. Uncaring as the city below unfurled in chaos.

A low growl came unbidden to his lipless snout as his claw went to the smooth stump above his left eye socket, an unassailable reminder of the missing keratin horns that should curve from said stump. The horns that should have passed on to him at his father's death when the Fallen took Drenth. The ritual of being named a wardkeeper stolen from him upon his father's death, nay, Tevun's murder. The holy rite by the Pentax denied him.

But that was why he came to Drenth, to right that wrong, to seek his father's horns. To restore his honor and allow him to return to the Isle of Merj a wardkeeper.

Lojen crouched, then raced on all fours toward the other end of the building, claws digging into the tiles, smashing under his bulk. The city was din, but Lojen had seen what he'd needed to see. The rebellion had begun their attack like clockwork, attacking the aethecite factories in coordinated destruction. Loud and colorful in shades of black and grey. Random they were not.

Just like the letter that had summoned him to Drenth had said.

The drakken leapt from the edge of the apartment, his claw slamming into the weakened brick, three sausage-thick talons left deep gashes as he descended story after story. Lojen coiled his tail around his waist like a snake as he landed onto a balcony on the apartment's fiftieth floor with bent legs as he ripped his claws out of the stone, the shiver of impact running up his legs.

The many aerescreens along the skyline went black as they were shattered by rebel bombs, only a few streaming warning messages from Solanine before those burst. All the little drones in the crossroads filtered into the alleyways, searching. One passed over Lojen's head, its blinking lights taking him in but rushed onward.

A drakken was hardly cause for concern in Drenth.

Even the trams on the fishhook rails had stopped as the bombs triggered across the city brought down Imperium-wrought factories. Explosion after explosion, synchronized. Smoke painted the nightturn in varying greys. A grisly canvas rendered masterfully.

The window held no glass, so he ducked inside the old building. "Ruane."

Ruane Tevunsdotyr sat upon the ground opposite, her back against the wall, one of her legs bent, elbow resting lightly upon the fur-trousered knee. In her clawed grip, his sister held her drakken longknife, it glinted moonlight.

"Ru," he said again, louder. This time her purplish eyes slid open, black pinpoint pupils dilating. "How in the name of Zenith are you sleeping while the city sings in war?"

A frown of pointed teeth broke her snouted face, exoscales retracting in annoyance. "I was just thinking about where I'd like to stick my longknife in the Fallen. I could almost taste his misery. Savor his death."

His sister—six years shy of drakken maturity—glared at him with her predatory, slitted eyes, her long, graceful tail curled tensely around her. Though outwardly calm, Lojen sensed the anger boiling inside, she was eager, too eager by far. She wanted the Fallen dead more than he wanted his father's horns. His gaze sought the small, horny protrusions just above her eyes, rounded instead of flattened like his own stumps. A reminder that he was different, something she never failed to remind him about.

The true heir of a wardkeeper's horns.

It was the way of the Pentax for the sacred horns to pass to the firstborn hatchling upon the death of a wardkeeper when they reached the age of drakken maturity at one hundred and fifty—which was the equivalent to a humir reaching the age of twenty-five. Justice, the Arbiter of the Pentax, would bestow His grace upon the next honorbound to the horns, the holiest of rights amongst drakken.

Lojen was pushing two hundred years as drakken age and remembered his father, Tevun, fondly before he was murdered during the conquest of Drenth. But Ruane harbored a deep-seeded hatred toward the Fallen, Solanine, and any sycophant of the Imperium. A hatred so strong, Lojen feared she might be consumed by it.

Ruane slammed her serrated longknife into the rotted wood floor, her lean, light bluish, purple exoscaled arms flexed through her sleeveless, furred vest. "Today's the day the Fallen pays for Father's blood," she growled a low, sepulchral roll from deep within her throat.

"It is," he said calmly in an attempt to rein in her rising anger. Tevun had always cautioned calm, for it was the way of a wardkeeper. "This'll work, Ru. Father was revered in Drenth and by the Benld family. The scion of the Benlds will help us regain our honor. The fruits are already ripening here."

Tevun had been the Regents Benld's wardkeeper since the early days of Drenth after the Fall of Eminence. He'd been there, their father, when the Last Godsking lost control of the Crystal of Life, breaking it, and sending the heavenly city plummeting from the skies. Tevun and a handful of the Last Godsking's closest allies had survived the Fall, tasked to protect the fledgling new world.

A task Tevun took as hallowed as could be.

In the afterimage of the Fall of Eminence, the world that was became no more. Mountains had sprung from flatlands. Oceans had dried into empty basins. Once-thriving farmlands had become the Voidlands in the west. New continents had formed, new oceans had swallowed the old.

The lucky—or perhaps unlucky—survivors had struggled in the aftermath, with a new fear permeating the world: the mist. Thousands had flocked to the remnants of cities that were nothing more than ruins, a dire hope welled within the survivors' breasts, safety in numbers.

Too bad the poison had found a deadly purchase anyway.

A score of mega-cities had grown from those early ruins by plucky survivors, and Drenth, east of the tomb of Eminence, was one of the largest, and that was because the desert offered a natural barrier to the ever-poisonous Sea of Mist engulfing the continent, rendering the mist only partially deadly instead of overtly deadly.

Gouging lines into the wood with her longknife, Ruane radiated a heated violence that would rival the unbearable radiation of aethecite suffered by men. "Honor means nothing to the Fallen. Only conquest and the ore in the sand."

"The Gutter King guaranteed us the fight, Ru. It's out there in the streets singing Justice's hymns. The Arbiter will answer, reaping His holy creed."

"I don't trust anyone, Lojen." Her frown returned, teeth protruding over her bottom jaw.

Lojen shook his head knowing Ruane would never change unless their honor was restored.

Another bomb blasted frighteningly close to their building and the entire structure shook. Lojen tottered on his feet, a clawed talon went toward the windowsill to hold him upright. Ruane fell to her side, grumbling drakken curses toward the rebellion and the Gutter King.

She hefted her longknife, scorching ire. "Let's go."

Ruane nearly pulled the metal door off its hinges as she bounded into the hallway beyond. The cracked walls chipped further as another blast rocked the complex, a blunt attack that was too close for his liking. Lojen shouldered into the wall as the apartment shivered. Though she could handle herself better than any drakken he knew, Lojen instinctively reached for his sister, a brotherly need to protect her that would never dissipate. She was down on one knee, her long talons scraping the floor.

"Piss off," she snarled, "I'm fine." She tore away from his reach.

Lojen rolled his shoulders and sighed. He hoped once they found the horns, she might reclaim the innocence lost from her hatchhood. But he didn't know if hope was his ally or enemy these days.

The dilapidated hallway was bleak with fulgurating lights that dangled from the ceiling, squeaking on their mounts with each blast, chains swinging savagely. Trapezoid rays of urine-yellow left onerous shadows where the cracked grey walls met scuffed wooden floors. The rooms were filled with residents, mostly miners and their families. Or fiends drugged up on pipeweed.

A handful of frightened people were arguing in the stairways as the drakken siblings raced downward, yelling at loved ones to hurry up or at their neighbors for being in the way while they fled the drab halls in fear the bombs might strike their homes. One pipeweed-fiend roared to keep the noise down for he had a splitting headache.

Many floors later, they huddled before the fire exit, a nine-foot-tall steel door with a barred window. Lojen peered out into the streets.

"What do you see?"

"I see the patience Father tried to instill into you still hasn't manifested after all these years."

She barked a laugh.

A giant blast across the street exploded in an inferno of gunpowder and smoke. Lojen reeled from the door as the concussion hit, the after-quake from the discharge knocked them from their feet, and they clattered into a heap atop each other with grunts and hisses.

"Pissing fools," Ruane spat as she shoved him off. "The Gutter King said we wouldn't be in the blast zone here."

"This is the Hymn of War, Ru, not fun and child games."

"Yet the Fallen's bitch aims to throw a party this week's end on Gargantua to celebrate the conquest of Drenth. Sounds like fun and child games to me."

"This is our only chance to take Father's horns from her."

"You think I don't know that! It was my plan to contact the Gutter King and the rebellion. You'd still be sulking in Krylen if not for me." She looked out the window. "The Gutter King promised us help, not kill us in the process."

He ground his teeth because he knew she was correct.

They had spent the last seventeen years up in the northern reaches of Kanja, in the free city of Krylen. The snowy tundra was no place for a cold-blooded drakken, but it was the only place they could pledge themselves to after their banishment from the Isle of Merj for their father's murder and failure to protect his wards. Lojen could have forsaken his claim to the horns like his mother had wanted and taken a mate from a brood with a stronger claim, but that wasn't the life Lojen had ever desired. A mate was the furthest thing Lojen needed or wanted. No, his father's horns were all that mattered. Honor was all that mattered. The free city cared not a lick about lost honor, only saw a pair of strong arms capable of breaking the ice with claws for big game fishing in the VVinter Expanse.

Honor was everything to Lojen, and he needed those horns. He had to trust in the rebellion and the scion of the Regents Benld.

Ruane yanked open the door, "The rebels are waiting for us, once they stop bombing their city for *'fun and child games.'*" Then she was out into the streets.

Lojen threw up his talons but followed her out.

The pandemonium grew feverish. Blast after blast rocked the roadway, erupting in ten-second intervals. Huge chunks of brick littered the avenue, craters formed within the broken pavement. Aethecite-powered vehicles lay overturned, some of the larger mining trucks were torn apart. Gaping holes smiled from the abandoned buildings, shattered glass from usable rooms crunching underfoot. People covered in dust and blood.

They took off, joining the surge fleeing into the inner sectors of Drenth, away from the rebellion's bombs. Hundreds, maybe thousands, flocked the road like a gaggle of geese pouring out of Stanktown, pushing and shoving, elbowing and jostling. Babies screamed as parents held them tight with fear. Children wailed, parents hushed and swore, yelled and screamed like a tidal wave of flesh ready to crest. Sweat and fright permeated the air.

Imperium automatons—the feared Predator class, on their metal chassis and elongated gear-rotated limbs—stalked the streets as they policed the citizens. Plumes of aethecite-generated smoke spurted from the combustion furnaces in the steel bodies. Flashing orbs on head-like domes scoured the masses. Soldiers of the Imperium and their weaponry penned the fleeing group by forcing them to run faster as *Ignis* gunshots hummed in the background of the tenor of bombs.

Throw in a pair of drakken vagabonds and the tension balanced on the tip of a knife's edge as Gargantua hovered overhead like a watchful parent scrutinizing a rowdy child.

The blasts in Stanktown urged the crowd forward in sprints. Lojen grabbed Ruane's wrist to keep from getting separated, even though they stood head and shoulders above the tallest of Drenth's citizens. Surprisingly, she didn't resist. He'd seen a number of people lose their balance; their bodies flattened to a pulp by the trampling mass.

As the throng veered down a four-lane road that circled empty vehicles, Lojen angled toward the edge of the press, eventually breaking free. He leaned against a lamppost, breathing hard. Ruane bent at the waist. Before long, they were the only living souls left on the road, leaving them in eerie silence as the bombs died away.

"By the Arbiter's bloody axe," Ruane cursed in Justice's name, the patron god of wardkeepers and the drakken of Merj. "Too many humir for my liking."

Glancing up at the street name printed along the lamppost, Lojen dug a hand-drawn map from his vest pocket. "I think we've come too far east." He studied the map. "The Gutter King told us the safehouse is in Marketside."

"Then what the void are we waiting for?"

Ruane trotted west without waiting for him.

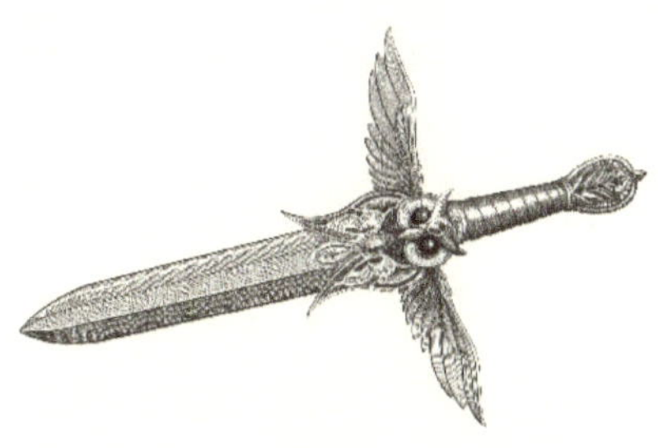

VI
CADRIANNA

CADRIANNA YAWNED AS she watched the chaos happening in the streets of Drenth below.

The underbelly of Gargantua shaded the hardened glass of the airglider's circular window, and it drowned out the moonlit clouds over the sand dunes, which left the desert city bathed in ominous neon aether and dust from their rebellion's attack below.

She fingered the quillon of the Strix. A comfort. Killing Thestile had left a hole in her soul and she didn't understand why. The elfirish woman had been a trainer, a teacher of Void Form, a hated personage in the Fallen's coven. She had been one of the many who'd made Cadrianna the killer she was, and to date, was now the only one she'd made to pay for that trauma. But the woman's last words perplexed her. *'Never forget the truth of who you are.'* What did it mean? And why bring up her Nightingale lineage? She hadn't the faintest of ideas. Should she be angry or sad, she didn't know.

All she felt was Emre's betrayal for putting her in this current state of never-ending regret. To her, but most importantly, to Brynn.

The knife was her strength, her singular obsession. It drove her, and ultimately, would sate her. Bound as they were, womanhood to daemonhood. Eager blood quickened at the thought of killing the Fallen one day and saving her daughter.

Emre, you forced me into this. Forced me into his arms.

"I'LL NEVER UNDERSTAND WHY THIS GUTTER KING ACTIVELY DESTROYS THE CITY HE CLAIMS TO WANT TO FREE," the Strix said. For a blade that spent much of its existence inside a sheath or a person's flesh, it was mighty observant of their surroundings. **"SEEMS COUNTERINTUITIVE, TO BE FAIR. FOR HOW LITTLE YOU REGARD THIS PLACE, THAT IS. SOLANINE AND THE FALLEN SEEM TO PUT GREAT IMPORTANCE ON THIS DESERT CITY."**

To the daemon blade, she merely hissed under her breath to let it know she was in no mood to discuss the past.

"Mistress Cadrianna," the soldier sitting next to her said. Her scowl stared back at her in the man's reflective breather. "We'll… be landing soon. Mistress," he added when she didn't respond affirmatively.

Annoyance rippled through her, or was that a thrill? A thrill, she decided. A thrill in the upcoming misery she intended to bring upon the Gutter King and his rebel forces. The Fallen hadn't commanded it, but she was a scourge and a scourge brought death to the Fallen's enemies without fail.

After leaving Thestile's citadel, she saw, and felt, the explosions throughout the city. Street after street beyond Silk Circle, smoke rose skyward as she had taken flight in the airglider waiting for her just outside of the traitor's keep. She knew what it meant: the Gutter King had struck. She didn't need to see the waterfall of Imperium gliders dropping from Gargantua to know that her presence on the ground was necessary. Orders came shortly after, orders that she do what she was bred for.

To do what Emre had forced her into.

The soldier harrumphed and began to check the strappings of his firedrake scale body armor—bloodred to signify his rank of captain. There were seven other soldiers seated opposite the captain and Cadrianna, all armored and armed. She was the only scourge, and thus, this team was hers to command. As if she needed any help besides the Strix. She didn't with Thestile and the Guilder and most certainly didn't now.

But orders were orders.

"Captain Arhin," one of the soldiers started, "sir, our orders?"

The captain's helmed face turned toward Cadrianna, expecting her to answer, but she only nodded before looking away. Captain Arhin muttered something low, unheard behind his breather. "Our orders are clear. Bring to task any rebel, especially the Gutter King. Rumor has it the Gutter King and some of his top rebels were spotted in Stanktown with one of the local gangs. Our soldiers have apprehended the gang leader and one of the Gutter King's own."

One of the soldiers across the small aisle shifted in his stiff harness. "What of the rebellion spies, Captain Arhin? Can we trust their word? Drenth-born can't be trusted. I don't want to walk into a massacre." The woman next to him gave him a hard elbow and flicked her helmeted head toward Cadrianna. Apparently, the dunce forgot where her husband had hailed from. "Forgive me, mistress," the first soldier said. "I didn't mean to offend."

The man withered under her hardened gaze. Cadrianna was not Drenth-born but had adopted the city as her home after her marriage to Emre. Originally, she hailed from Oldport Basin in the southern nation of Thullyr.

The Strix laughed in the void, which sounded a lot like someone choking a bird of nocturnal prey to get it to stop hooting so they could sleep.

"The Fallen swears by the words of his spies," Captain Arhin said. "Who are you to question?"

"Forgive me, mistress," the man repeated to her, chastised by the captain fully. "Hail to the Imperium!"

Fools, Cadrianna thought. *Fools all of them. They'll only slow me down.*

"WE CAN LEAVE THEM BEHIND." That ethereal tone of a daemon more humirish than she figured possible. *"WE NEVER HAD TO COME HERE. COULD HAVE..."* the Strix trailed off before she had the chance to silence the daemon. Instead, *"VERY WELL, CAD, IF IT'S FEAR YOU WANT, LET ME PLAY WITH ONE OF THEIR SOULS, THEN THEY'D ALL FEAR YOU."*

Later, Strix.

"I want all weapons locked and loaded," Captain Arhin continued. "Once on the ground, we'll be under heavy fire. I've word the rebels are rousing full assaults on our garrisons near the tethers. We are headed to Bar Stock to assist in culling this attack. Mistress Cadrianna is in charge. What she says goes. Understood?"

There was a resounding clap as fists smacked drake scale.

Cadrianna glanced out the porthole. The moon's circumference remained hidden behind Gargantua. Absently, her mind wandered to a time early in her marriage to Emre, a time when they would stand atop the Regent's Tower and watch the moon linger over the horizon in a full blaze of desert glory. Those days had been short and sweet in her memory, of a time when her life hadn't become glazed in blood.

Now, the moon's rays were but a tendril of deathly shadows as the airglider dipped in between the buildings of Drenth.

The airglider touched concrete amid the multitude of manufacturing warehouses of Bar Stock and rocked viciously as intense aetheric gunfire railed into the heavy-duty steel of its hull. Cadrianna cursed as she shoved Captain Arhin off her lap. Though she couldn't see his face nor hear his voice over the blasts of *Ignis*, by his open palms, she knew he was apologizing.

She had bitten her tongue in the landing and copper coated the inside of her mouth. An apt taste for the death she was about to bring.

The gunner atop returned fire into the lowborn sector, glass breaking as the warehouses took damage from a hand-cranked rotating cannon. Bullet casings the size of her thumb rained down on the steel hull with sharp clangs, dribbling past the portholes. Short *Ignis* bursts struck the airglider, but those were quick, almost as if the gunner's fire made the rebels hunker down. Her team unclipped from their safety harnesses and readied their wheellock rifles. The soldier closest to the exit gave a grunt as he spun the massive valve to open the hatch. In well-drilled fashion, her team jumped out and took defensive positions. A series of pang-pang-pangs riddled the outer shell of the transport, and a curdled gasp was followed by wheellock gunfire from her team. Then silence.

"All clear, mistress," one stuck his helmeted head back into the transport. "Penite's down, though."

Captain Arhin pulled the dog back on his wheellock pistol, the aethecite ore in the pan ready for firing, and sighed before he hopped out of the aircraft with a multi-barrel wheellock rifle slung across his back. Cadrianna was hot on his heels, sheathing the Strix and pulling her own multi-barrel pistol. Aetheurgy and her daemon blade were a last resort here, even though she preferred the power of the void over that of machine.

Boots striking pavement, she examined her surroundings with a meticulous eye.

The third sector known as Bar Stock was a string of roads all connected by iron and steel trusses, like gates penning in a prisoner. This sector was the lifeblood of machinery in Drenth. Gone were the sky-risen apartment complexes, replaced with squat warehouses that chugged aethecite plumage at all hours of the day, manufacturing everything from airships to gliders, from train cars to mining trucks. Those who didn't work the mines worked the assembly lines.

Smoke rose near where the giant eastern tether held one of the four chains anchoring Gargantua. The enormous links swayed by the force of the blasts, but it didn't appear as if they were greatly affected. Subtle tremors quaked underfoot. A gaping series of fourth-floor windows all down the avenue were smashed, making Cadrianna assume this was a meticulously planned attack to get the Imperium to believe all-out war was happening. She spied a handful of bloodied bodies along the bases of the warehouses, probably in flight when they realized the Imperium wouldn't surrender so easily. Dead rebels. The only kind she liked.

"I GUESS THIS IS PRETTY. A NICE PLACE IF YOU ENJOY SMOLDERING ARCHITECTURE FALLING FROM OVERHEAD."

An aerescreen across the destroyed street showed Solanine. ***"People of Drenth,"*** the camera panned away from Solaine's face and projected scenes of the explosions. ***"I'm praying for all the innocents of our fair city, for your safety. Our soldiers have been deployed in all sectors to weed out the lowbrow traitors who've caused this harm. You are in my thoughts, every one of you. Stay safe, friends of Drenth."*** Camera returning to Solanine's grim visage. ***"People…"***

One of Cadrianna's team was crouched over the corpse of another, the woman apparently named Penite. The soldier who'd questioned her earlier was pulling the identification tags from the deceased's neck and handed them to Captain Arhin. The others had their wheellock rifles pointed in the distance as they sought other potential threats. Pocketing the identification tags, Captain Arhin slapped a palm to the transport to indicate that it was safe to take off. The aethecite engine roared to life. A gust of dust mixed with the low level of mist that swarmed around their ankles as the transport rose.

Cadrianna clicked her tongue. "The Bar Stock tether is this way."

"CAD, THIS ISN'T THE WAY TO SAVE BRYNN. YOU WILL LEARN NOTHING BUT HEARTBREAK HERE."

If you've seen something in the Pit, tell me, Strix. Otherwise shut that daemon beak of yours and await the souls I'll reap for you.

"FINE, PLAY THE ANTI-HERO CARD. I'LL EAT ANY SOUL YOU GIVE ME, EVEN A BELOVED DRAKE, YOU KNOW THAT. BUT DON'T SAY I DIDN'T WARN YOU. I'LL GLADLY TELL YOU 'TOLD YOU SO.'"

With Cadrianna in the lead, the small tactical team moved deeper into the manufacturing sector, heads on swivels as gunfire near the tether cantillated through the streets. Neon aethecite clock tickers rolled across street signs. Drenth, as she remembered it, was a fragmented memory from her estranged former life as the wife to the Regents Benld's heir. Bar Stock hadn't been a sector she was overly familiar with back in her regency days, so she was extra careful of the surrounding warehouses.

The team moved quickly, craters and debris everywhere. Blood and offal filled her nostrils in the savory scent of death as they neared the tether. Imperium-controlled drones flitted about, cameras searching and scanning. Aerescreens played Solanine's sorrow on repeat. Bodies of Drenth-born workers littered the sidewalks. Not vagrants dying of aethecite radiation, but honest-to-goodness citizens of Drenth who worked the long shifts in the factories building transports. Up until now, the Gutter King had always found a way to avoid civilian casualties, but this attack on the factories reeked of desperation. Across the street was a ruined building, recently exploded by the look of it. Some injured Drenth-born workers huddled on the cobbled stones of the street, dabbing at their wounds.

"Seems like we missed the fight," Captain Arhin said. "Why would the Gutter King murder his own?"

"I don't think he did. Be alert." Something didn't feel right. A wrongness in the air. She scanned the high rises and saw nothing out of the ordinary.

Yet, something was amiss.

Cadrianna summoned her Void Form. The fire of aetheurgy blazed about her insides. The wails from the Pit surged forth as the veil between realms was breached, her scarred runes along her breastbone and spine fulgurated intensely under her drake scale and dribbled blood.

Strix, show me.

The mist around her feet turned black-red as it swirled upward in front of her. Like an aerescreen, it brought forth a picture of what might come. Aether rippled through her and the mist.

One second across the screen of mist; a shot of *Ignis* striking her, her blood spraying, a burning sensation followed by pain.

Two seconds across the screen of mist; more *Ignis*-spelled bullets, coming fierce now, clumping and rendering her body.

Three seconds across the screen of mist; bullets of *Ignis* flames tearing apart her team, blood arcing with crimson, shearing and killing, all down in a puddle of their own demise.

"Ambush!" she yelled as her Void Form rushed back into normal time. A wicked unloading of *Ignis*-infused ammunition fracturing the eerie silence in Bar Stock.

Cadrianna dove behind a mining truck. Bullets panged against the steel chassis with sparks of *Ignis*. Captain Arhin and two others had found protection behind another transport, heads covered as the rounds of aether ripped across the red exterior. Two of her soldiers lay in pools of flowing garnet in the center of the street, too slow to have taken cover.

Gunfire clanked off her refuge as she stole a glance over the transport's wheel. Four, if not five separate spouts of discharges started from a local bakery half a block down the street, one of the many small restaurants that provided much needed sustenance for the factory workers after their shifts.

Gotcha.

"AN ACTUAL FIGHT THIS TIME," the Strix commented rudely. **"NOT A MASSACRE WITHOUT REASON."**

Crouched down, Cadrianna clicked her earpiece communicator. "Captain, rebel fire from the bakery at the end of the crossroad. Cover me, I'll handle this. Over."

"Clear. Over."

The captain and the surviving soldiers popped over the hood of the car and returned fire, the shots causing the rebels to take cover. With the oncoming barrage briefly halted so both sides could reload, Cadrianna bolted down an alley across from the ambush. Aetheurgy raged through her veins as she sped up, running twice the speed of a normal person. Everything scorched. Her muscles, her mind, her blood, and her soul.

Cutting a corner, she veered west, toward the bakery. Her boots splashed sandmud as she skittered to a stop parallel to the restaurant.

The rebels had resumed firing, the clunk-clunk-clunk of a hand-cranked rotating cannon echoed. The bakery was nothing more than a two-story building crammed into a row of other shops and eateries. Cadrianna holstered her multi-barrel wheellock and drew the Strix from its sheath. She set her feet and peered into the store.

Surrounded by the silver halos of void aetheurgy were three poorly clothed rebels who knelt behind the bakery counter, the rotating cannon balanced upon a tripod. One stared down the sight while the other two cranked. It was a standard-issue Imperium model. Two other rebels were shoving aethecite bullets into wheellocks, laying the rifles out to be fired. Each wore Imperium-issue drake scale body armor, likely stolen.

"I DON'T LIKE THE LOOK OF THIS, CAD. SOMETHING SEEMS WRONG."

Taking a deep breath, Cadrianna centered her thoughts and ignored the Strix's warning. Five. Easy. "Strix, if you please."

"FINE, DON'T LISTEN." The sentient blade rose in her aetheurgic magic, separating into five blades. The outstretched wings of the owl-pommel reflected neon from the lights adorning the bakery.

In a fluid motion, Cadrianna stood, both hands leveled outward. In slow, agonizing heartbeats for the rebels, her aetheurgy shot the blades forward. Glass from the front bakery door shattered, bullets flying in the other direction toward Captain Arhin while the daemon blades struck their marks with accurate precision. Sprays of red, heads tossed back as they dug into flesh. Two dropped, rifles toppled from flaccid, dead hands. The man with the remaining rifle had a blade stuck in his shoulder but that didn't stop him from trying to turn his weapon toward her, but another Strix blade cut him down an instant later. The final blade tore through one of the surprised reloaders, her wiry body crumpling to the ground as her head painted the bakery's shelves.

The last man dropped his bounty of aetheric ammunition and took off into the back of the eatery, a half-door swung freely as he plowed through. Cadrianna swore and raced after him, urging the blades of the Strix to reform, calling the daemon blade back to her hand in a pyre of aetheurgy. Cadrianna broke into a full sprint once she hit the back alley, legs pumping in long, easy strides. She caught him within seconds, grabbing his stolen drake armor, yanking him backward. She skidded to a halt as the man fell.

Pressing her knee under the man's chin, she clicked her comm. "Situation handled. Over."

"Clear. Regrouping now," the captain responded. "Over and out."

The rebel squirmed under her, saliva and spittle spewed as he struggled. He had shaggy dark hair and a mustache. Cadrianna watched in casual amusement. His wide eyes told her everything she needed to know. He didn't want to die, not really. All she had to do was let him go, and he'd flee Drenth, never to return. Simple as that, yes, that's what she deduced from his pleading gaze.

A stab of the Strix, parting flesh. Then silence.

"Mistress Cadrianna," came the voice of Captain Arhin. "Mistress?"

"What is it?"

"I don't think these are rebels."

"NOT A REBEL, EH? THIEF, MAYHAPS?"

Cadrianna wiped the cruor of the Strix on the man's tunic. "I don't know, Strix," she answered as she reached within the tunic under the drake scale breastplate. Her fingers felt an oblong shape that hung from a chain around the rebel's neck. She drew a breath as she pulled the object free. "This isn't one of the Gutter King's."

In her fingers was an identification tag. Standard issue for all Imperium soldiers.

What is going on here?

"A pity, even Zenith couldn't protect this useless creature," said a voice from behind. "A vile thing, these rebels."

Cadrianna glanced up and found a scourge standing beside her, a man she loathed almost as much as the Fallen. A man who'd taken his pleasure in breaking her while Thestile watched on. A man who'd done things to her under the Divines' whims. A man she would one day flay alive. His name was Ratko.

"Good for bleeding," Ratko continued as he ran a finger through the blood along his short sword, leaving a streak of polished steel peeping through the river of red. A furrow of thick eyebrows over all-onyx eyes of Void Form and a beard braided down to his waist, slick with blood. "Are they not?"

The Fallen's scourges were the best within the Imperium, the fiercest of killers. But not all possessed Void Form. In fact, most were just brutes with an axe to grind. Ratko could wield aetheurgy, and he wasn't even proficient at that. She knew him to be a formidable killer, but she didn't care for him in the slightest. He had a sick predilection for killing, taking pleasure in the deaths of lowborn and noble alike, savoring each kill before the final strike of steel.

But the scourges were the prized fighters of the Fallen's coven, his inferno. She amongst them.

Cadrianna stood, ignoring the scourge as he stared at her. Gods, she hated this man. When he didn't move out of her way, she faced him. "Problem?"

The bearded scourge gave her a sickening grin. "My cock quickens when you kill, Cadrianna. Ever since you were given to me, I've watched you grow, watched you delight in the void. What say you we take a naked gander over yonder? I'm certain the master won't give a mind."

"YOU PROBABLY COULD TAKE HIS TONGUE," the Strix offered. *"DOUBT LU HAR WOULD WORRY SO ABOUT IT. HE'S GOT MORE IMPORTANT THINGS ON HIS MIND."*

"What say you, sweetling?" Ratko pressed, coming closer, his hand to his groin. "For old time's sake? You might even enjoy it this time. I promise I won't hurt you… much."

Cadrianna briefly considered slitting Ratko's throat right then and there like the Strix said, but instead marched off into the gloom of the shellshocked city. One day, she would repay Ratko for what he'd done to her.

Today was not that day, but that reckoning was coming.

VII
ASHE

ASHE SWORE AS her slippers splashed in a murky puddle and the stink-water deluged between her toes.

Unlike six of the nine sectors in Drenth where all the freedmen, dregs, and cons ready to slice a throat at the drop of a quadran crammed into sky-high apartment complexes, Silk Circle was where the upper crust Houses lived. With their wide-open spaces and their fancy abodes, their lavish parties and their little care for anyone below them.

With the vicars hounding her, Ashe wished for the cramped, scummy sectors because the myriad of twists and turns made her a less conspicuous target.

From the sound of the explosions that rocked the city, she figured the rebellion had other thoughts. It was just like the Gutter King to make his war while she was fleeing for her life. Selfish jerk.

Extravagant villas grew like wayward shoots of stone grass as Ashe raced through the paved streets of the Silk Circle. Raised mezzanines with stunning architecture, roads lined by cypress trees basking in the starlight, not bent or cracked from living within the mist. Terraces of white marble peristyles, fluted columns, three stories of balconies with stone awnings. A harmony of flowers along the rooftop trellises.

Ashe blazed ahead as she ignored the surprised looks of the many nobleborn out on the roads. Every drag of mist in Silk Circle clung to her like a fly to a pile of manure, enhancing her body through her Shard Form. She ran toward the gate between the Silk Circle and the eighth sector next, hoping to lose the vicars. The jangle of their breathing apparatuses told her she wasn't too far ahead. City guards at the gates yelled for her to stop, but on she ran into Bell End.

As she burst into Bell End—a middling sector known for the more artistic endeavors of the flesh—thousands of people stormed the streets as the bombs exploded throughout the mega-city.

It was anarchy.

The egress near Silk Circle was on the verge of being overrun by scores of miners, families, and soldiers alike. The inner set of gates groaned as a tidal wave of flesh pushed for flight. The soldiers of the Imperium tried to quell the crowd, but they were unsuccessful, and some were pulled to their deaths. The crush of people was alarming. Fires erupted along the city streets. Gunshots drowned the tenor of the frightened people.

The mist whorled within the crowd at a rate never seen in the mega-cities, somehow the Sea had breached the outer walls. Nearly black, the mist rose as high as shoulders, was as dense as the VVyrm Ocean. Its anger parallel to that of the city.

Ashe elbowed her way through the masses, throwing shoulders and fists as needed, cursing the entire way. Her anger a constant vim. She pummeled through the wave of faces. People floundered and clambered over one another as she slowed to a crawl, the mass too great even for her aetheurgy.

She punched a swarthy man as he fell upon her, his hot breath putrid, eyes crazed with fear. He grabbed her by the arms, and she nearly threw all her aetheurgy at him, but thought better of it. A woman pulled at her stola, begging her for help, but she was yanked away by the flowing tide of humanity.

A high-pitched hiss echoed behind; the vicars had released their canisters, their Shard Form aetheurgy.

Shit! Her Shard Form filled her with energy anew, so Ashe glumly plowed through the people.

Ashe raced down an alleyway between soaring apartment complexes. The press of flesh behind her now. But she was beyond tired.

A whistle in the air, and Ashe reflexively changed directions. "Shit, shit, shit!"

Chunks of rock blasted at her feet as the shrapnel tore into her thighs, leaving bloody gashes in her stola, motes of dark emerald flaring hurt about the wound. Another projectile landed on her side, exploding in hardened earth. But Ashe pressed on, despite the searing pain in her legs.

Drab, overly crowded concrete apartment complexes rose around her as she passed out of Bell End into the poorer sectors of Marketside. Most were at least sixty stories tall, if not more. One room homes with balconies, clothing draping from lines between buildings. Aethecite pipes wainscoted the walls. A handful of children, who didn't appear worried about the explosions, lounged upon the metal ladders like caged animals yelling at her while she ran below as if they were spectators and she the sport.

The bowels of Drenth were a warren of dead ends unless one knew where they were going. Blessedly, she did.

Ashe barged through the shadowed streets in no discernable pattern, and she ducked, squeezed, wiggled, or jumped over the detritus, broken carts, overturned refuse bins, and the occasional sleeping vagrant blocking her path. The vicars barreled straight through any roadblock as mercilessly as a predator. They didn't speak, didn't yell for her to stop. They only ran. Relentless.

By the Pentax, she had forgotten how frustratingly undeterred a vicar could be. What was she thinking, running from three of them? *Foolish girl. O wait a minute now, is that… yes!*

As she banked around an alley corner, Ashe sought out an anchor she'd memorized from previous flights from the city's numpty guards—a dried-up well that oozed *Terris* aether. She burned the inked rune of *Terris* on her left wrist and sent the aetheric mist toward the well. The earthen spell came alive within the horizontal zigzagged rune that resembled a volcano as the void flickered as inhumir howls moaned in her eardrums. Her body shot toward the well as if she'd been thrown like a spear.

Fortuitous because a massive truck wheel whizzed overhead.

She shifted in midair, and flung out her left arm, commanding the mist to rise in a shield-like spell of *Aere*. The fog caught the wheel, held in place by unseen threads from wind aetheurgy, mere inches from her head. Her slippers struck the street as she cut off the *Terris* anchor and she hurtled the suspended wheel back at the vicars using more *Aere*. It collided into the untainted warriors and they tumbled into a heap.

Ashe gave the vicars a very unsavory finger gesture and ran to put distance between them. Mist churned in quick vortexes, tired and drained, like she. The wails within the void grew so loud, she thought her ears would bleed. Her legs churned acid within. Her body was near the breaking point, and mist-enhancements started to fade as her tissue became weak under the flames of aether. She could already hear the vicars following. Coughing, blood dribbled down her open mouth, tongue dry as she pulled in ragged breath after ragged breath.

But she kept running, burning aetheurgy the entire way, the explosions singing her company.

Ashe ran headlong into Marketside, one of two main bazar sectors in Drenth. She barged into the meandering horde of flesh that was hunkered down within the giant rectangle of colored tents, long glass counters of goods, and shops which sold trinkets, seeking protection from the bombings. Aerescreens affixed to the surrounding buildings encroached the market like watchers. One of Gargantua's tethers was at the far end of the southern sector, its giant chain links swaying. Despite the late hour, the forum was packed to the brim with people, their auras every color imaginable. So bright, it almost blinded her, their fear the brightest.

"Citizens of Drenth, fear not," a message beamed across the aerescreens. It was Solanine, face twenty feet wide, those onyx eyes dead, but Ashe felt as if they were on her regardless. ***"We are working tirelessly to end this threat. Citizens of Drenth…"***

Reluctantly, she dove into the crowd, and tried to ignore the queer feeling of being watched by a screen-version of Solanine. She glanced behind to see that the vicars had slowed as the rush of people pressed upon them. Sensing their slightest hesitation, Ashe sucked in the mist that covered the forum's paving stones like it was the most precious thing in the world.

Breathing the fog, she burned the last vestiges within her to use it for the last thing she could think to do: to hide herself.

To all, she was simply not there. The mist wrapped around her like a cloak, a smudge in reality. A blank spot where once a girl had been. Pure aether enveloping. Just her and the wails of the dead.

She quickly moved through the crowd using her new and unpracticed spell, winding her way through the masses, squeezing between the moving people filling Marketside. Away from the vicars. The people couldn't see her, but she still danced away. Within heartbeats, she was across and behind a tent.

Ashe let go of the misted cloak as she snuffed her burn and put her back against a column. In the bazar, the vicars dovetailed through the throng, their mist-enhanced bodies glided like sapphiric water away from her as they searched but not finding her.

Her relief was brief as the onslaught of hurt from the mist seeped in. Her stomach clenched. But she pushed on anyway, gliding away from the market and the untainted warriors of the Scattered Shards.

When all was relatively silent behind her, Ashe stopped at the southern edge of the mega-city, miles from the satyr mask job, and the exact opposite side of the city from *The Colosseum* where Elian and the rest of the Slag's End gang would be. Where Wren would be.

The bombs still lingered in the background, but the only sound that hummed in her ears was the mist vacuums. Ashe violently coughed burgundy tar onto the sandy stones. The density in the air was heavier closer to the city's outer walls as the stink of the vapid mist outside filled her nostrils. It reeked of rot.

For a normal person, the scant inch of mist that layered the cobblestones of the mega-city wasn't lethal, even over the course of one's life. But outside, in the Sea of Mist, it was different. If not for the vacuums spaced along the walls, the city would be swallowed by the poisonous fog. The vacuums pulled in the haze and barfed it back outward into the Sea. Inside Drenth, the world was safe, free from the virulent disease permeating the Mistlands.

Except Ashe, for she had been cursed with the pulmo since she was but a babe.

To keep from hacking up more blood (not to mention keeping her from keeling over in what Ashe assumed a kick to the seedpods might feel like) she withdrew the golden flask. The spirits soothed her aching throat and cleared her wandering mind with a trickle of comfort as she looked skyward, cursing the Pentax for buggering her over with her consumption.

As she took another drink, she noticed the bangle on her left hand. She'd forgotten about it during her escape from the vicars.

The braided chain wrapped around her wrist was perfectly fitted and didn't appear to have a clasp of any type. The same braided gold ran in a single row of links from wrist to the diamond eye in the center of her palm, then fanned out to the four auric rings on each finger. The diamond and the gemstones on each ring were unblemished, flawless, and unmarred. The runes inked upon her arm matched those on each ring. *Ignis* on her forefinger. *Aquis* on her longest. *Aere* on the third. *Terris* on her smallest. Each stone facet and rune glimmered, while the diamond eye was warm against her palm.

The entire thing had to be worth a fortune in quadrans.

"What in Zenith's…" she said around her askew tongue as she tried digging her fingers into the diamond, pulling with all her might. The stone didn't budge. "Bah! What the void?"

She found a pointed rock and tried that, only to be rewarded with a jab into the meat of her hand for her efforts. Next, she tried to pull the rings off her fingers, but they didn't move a fraction, as if they were melded into her skin.

"Fine! Be stuck, you stupid thing." She took a drink from her flask in irritation. "Now what am I supposed to do with this?"

The mist railed against her legs, and she didn't have time to think, only react as a fist aimed for her gut. She dropped the flask as she contorted sideways, narrowly avoiding the blow, but the wall behind her was not so lucky.

"O shit!"

Ashe burned. From under her sleeve, up on her outer bicep, the semi-circle with a high tailed contrasted by a low tailed rune of *Ignis* synapsed brightly as it suffused her body with its fiery strength. The *Aere* rune—two vertical zigzag lines, one longer than the other—on her outer forearm pulsed as the three horizontal, wavy lines of the *Aquis* rune on her inner forearm bloomed, the link between thoughts and speed now connected with that of strength. The encircling connector runes glowing brightly.

One of the vicars— a short thing of a similar height and with red curls above the breather—swung at her again, but Ashe caught the punch in her mist-enhanced palm. The woman's green-grey eyes widened behind the tinted shield of her mask, her yellow pupils reflected surprise, her aura glimmered ruby.

And Red most certainly hadn't expected her to fight back.

Ashe brought up her other arm and shoved it brutally into Red's unprotected elbow, shattering the bone with her enhanced strength. Any other person would've recoiled immediately, but under the sway of aetheurgy, the vicar barely flinched.

"Godsdamn," Ashe mewled as she spied a second vicar in her peripheral vision.

The second vicar's attack struck Red in the back of the head, as Ashe ducked and pulled on the red-haired bitty's broken limb, using her as a shield. Using the other's momentum, Ashe bulled the downed vicar with her shoulder into the blue-cassocked middle, then flung the wounded bint into her curvier companion with the strength of five men. Red and Curves flew into the opposite wall.

"That wasn't very nice," she said to the vicars as the mist around her feet turned a crackling black.

Her freedom was short-lived as the third vicar joined the fray, leaping over his comrades in a single bound of aether-strengthened legs. This was the leader with the crest of dyed horsehair.

With only one heartbeat, Ashe burned a giant gust of *Aere* and caught the vicar in mid-jump. She brought both her arms around in a vicious yanking motion. Bristletop crashed into the apartment complex opposite, pummeling through brick and timber alike. Two crimson-shaded lowborn screamed in alarm as the untainted warrior got to his feet within their unfortunately destroyed home.

"HA! Take that!"

A fire burned within a brazier, so Ashe tapped its *Ignis*, drawing a gout of flame in a sudden burst of wicked heat to create a wall between her and the other two vicars, who were now untangled from each other. Twenty-foot-high flames rose and licked the walls of the buildings around her.

"Now, as I was say—" Pain blossomed and stars exploded in her sight. Her slippers were no longer touching cobblestone as Ashe found herself saying an unwanted greeting to the ground. Her hand rubbed her chin where someone had punched her with aether-enhanced strength. Head pounding, her vision fuzzy, a ring in her skull. *How'd that...?*

Three Bristletops stalked toward her as she struggled to her feet, hand against the warehouse wall for support as her head felt like kneaded dough.

A shadow stepped between her and the three versions of Bristletop. A dark cloak, hood raised over a broad head. "Leave this girl," the newcomer said commandingly. Male, voice abrasive like two skeletons fornicating. And huge. Like eight-feet-tall huge. "She's not yours to claim."

"I'm not…" Ashe started but her jaw was stiff, already bruising from the bone-crunching blow. "The fu…"

"The Scattered Shards has designs on this thief," Bristletop said, voice laboring behind tinted glass. More than slightly memorable, that voice. One she knew all too well. *O Zenith, not him…* "Crimes punishable to the Pentax. The Unfettered has called for her arrest." The shielded head cocked to the side; dark irises with red pupils glared at her. "Leave now and this thief to us."

"Her tithe is to Eminence, not your hallowed leader up in Kalderim." The newcomer was defiant and confident. The cloak rustled down by its feet and Ashe realized, with shock, that it was a tail. *Zenith's cock, only one creature's that tall and has a tail.* "Go back to your beloved Icterine the Unfettered and tell her Eminence's rise shall be fulfilled."

Ashe leaned against the building, the ringing in her ears died as the stars disappeared and her vision cleared. Tired though, really bloody tired. And thirsty. *Where's that flask?*

"You dare question the Scattered Shards?"

"You know not the mark upon this girl." The hood of the cloak drew back to reveal interlocking scales and an elongated snout. Rounded protrusions covered the crest from the nostrils to above the blue-red eyes, where it morphed into a pair of jagged stumps, as if something had been broken off. "The banalities of your church care naught for the Crystal's needs. The Crystal is all."

A drakken. One of the two lesser orders of the draconem.

What was a drakken doing here, in Drenth of all places? Apparently looking for her. She was proper buggered.

Odds she didn't care for.

"Then, by law, you're abetting a criminal," said Bristletop in that static voice of people who thought big words made them sound validated. Didn't matter a hardy drakken stood opposite. The other two vicars were now standing, Red with broken elbow cradled to her side, Curves holding an arm across her belly. "And, by law, are to be placed under arrest and brought back to Kalderim for questioning."

The drakken gave Ashe a nod. A flash of silvery aether rippled along its exoscaled talons. "Now is not the time, child. They've found you. And they'll send the darkness after you."

"Who?"

"By the Pentax's command, I ord—"

Bristletop was cut off when the massive drakken thrust out his claws; muscled, exoscaled limbs twisting as his talons moved. A groan like the gates of Drenth opening echoed within the alley, a rumbling underfoot. The vicars tensed; feet spread apart. An unearthly scream arose, like the sounds from within the void whenever Ashe burned aetheurgy. A ghastly hymn.

Then, the biggest wave of mist crashed down over the roof of the warehouse, waterfalling over the vicars, washing them backwards like they weighed nothing.

"Go!" The drakken drew upon all Four Tenets of Aether in their surroundings. *Terris* in stone. *Ignis* in candles. *Aere* in the wind. *Aquis* from shit-puddles.

"I can help."

Bristletop's Gauntlet of Justice glowed as he summoned a six-foot, double-bladed axe of pure aether and slammed it into the cobblestones. The mist redirected around him, swirling like a flowing river around a dam. Red and Curves did the same with their bluish-iron hand axes, nullifying the effect of the drakken's attack to push them backward.

"In time." The drakken threw out his claws again. A gust of *Aere* flung the wounded vicars away. The beastly head turned, there was blood dribbling from between the exoscales of its snout. Eerie it was, dark. "We will meet again soon. Your coming has been foreseen. The Eye has claimed you." His gaze settled upon the bizarre bangle on her left hand. She shoved her arm behind her back. "With it, the rebirth of Eminence. Go, Godsblood. Until we meet again."

A good thief knew when to cut and run. This was her time. So, Ashe fled into the night.

VIII
EMRE

THE AIRGLIDER FLEW over the city's tramlines until coming to a fifty-story complex nestled between much taller apartments of the southwestern seventh sector of Marketside.

Emre was ready to set foot back on stable ground as his stomach danced in knots.

Their escape had been met with gunshots from the buildings and the air. Snipers lodged on rooftops shelled the airglider with *Ignis*-infused bullets while the legion of gliders from Gargantua peppered them with their own gunnery, their casings leaving a wake of metal hail upon the denizens below.

It had taken hours, but they had finally ditched the Imperium craft over the sands of the deep desert, out near Drakewing Deep. Now, Emre had other business to attend as dawnbreak neared. A meeting of friends to be. Of family.

Atop the complex was a landing pad and under Wick's deft control, the lapin brought the airglider down. Emre patted Wick on the shoulder, and the lapin glanced sidelong at him with button-sized black eyes as he spat out the airglider's pilot box portal. "Buggerin' Imperium cocks. They can all roast."

"Ease, Wick, you'll get your chance," Emre laughed.

Sweat dribbled through the beige fur between Wick's eyes, causing his whiskered nose to twitch irritably. "Good."

Lapin had been gentler folk, once. Pious and affable, that was the lapin way until the Fallen had brought his Imperium into their peaceful lives. Ten years after the invasion of Drenth, the lapin homeland of Dervin was next in line for the Fallen's domination. Nestled between Thullyr and the Voidlands, Dervin was a simple cropping of caves and warrens.

But that was torn asunder under the Fallen. And Wick had paid the price of innocence.

Finn opened the hatch and let Emre out first. The lingering heat assailed him, regardless of the small hours before the sun rose. It was going to be a hot day, unbearable even. But Emre planned to bring more heat to the Imperium. A destructive heat.

Wick hopped from the pilot-box and his furry face bristled in irritation, most likely annoyance at himself for allowing his glider to be turned into lattice.

Emre glanced at his pocketwatch. Dawnbreak was only an hour hence. He could hear Solanine's voice over the loudspeakers at every corner, issuing warnings and spreading misinformation, as well as reminders about the dawnbreak injection of parch.

He sneered. *Soon, Solanine. Soon.*

Finn examined the inch-round apertures in the airglider's hull with a sly smile. "Godsdamned, that was a close one. What do you say, Em, plan worked like a charm? Though Wick's flying was godsdamned tight there for a moment."

"Bugger off," Wick snapped. "You know nothing about nothing, needle dick." Finnus Dunleith had a way of grinding at Wick's gears.

"I see you all made it out alive."

Emre turned to find an elfirish woman leaning against the doorway to the single staircase that led into the belly of the complex. A bikrome from Kanja with silver hair that poured from the cowl of her sleeveless tunic, her fringe shining above the aethecite mining goggles that hid her eyes. Her pale arms were crossed, and she wore dozens of bikromi seer-sight bracelets; the gold and silver reflected the dim light.

Valeria Dunleith, Finn's youngest sibling, if only by a decade as far as elfir age.

There are two types of elfir in the Mistlands: those from the Forest of Calibrath in the bowl between the Imperium, the Voidlands, Altreyia, and the mountainous range of the Forgemistress' Blades and those from the tundra of Kanja. And they were as different as boots are from slippers. One's sturdy and useful, and the other nose-sticking uppity.

Calibrathian elfir were a proud people, their hair golden or lush brown, irises the color of tree bark or newly sprouted leaves. Calm and cold, they rarely came down from their redwood villages. Canlon Carr, The Last Godsking, had been from Calibrath. Only those turning to the Divines, like Lu Har, ever left the confines of the forest without a just cause by Zenith and the rest of the Pentax.

Those of Kanja were the exact opposite, of which the Dunleiths hailed. They lived on the harsh snowlands as opposed to high in the trees. Kanjan elfir had skin so pale, it was nearly translucent, and their hair was a fine silver. Their eyes were either the darkest of black or the whitest of freshly fallen snow.

Bikromi seers had both. It was their aetheurgy, of past and future. Both Dunleiths possessed aetheurgy, but Valeria's was different than Finn's, far more chaotic. Far more potent.

"Though," Val spoke softly, her voice never rose above a whisper unless she was communing with the goddess Bliss or the god Brio, "sometimes I wonder how Finn manages it."

"Everyone's talking down on me today, eh?" The broad-shouldered elfir cracked another wry smile.

Val grimaced, "Brother-friend, does that big mouth of yours have any other use than for stating the obvious?"

"I can think of a few things," Finn responded with a wink toward Emre.

Emre cleared his throat. *'After this weekend, things will be different,'* he wanted to say, but instead, "Give off, you two."

"Yes, Dad," Finn said…

…as Val breathed a sigh of relief and added, "Thank Bliss."

Wick angrily slammed the pilot's door with his paw-like hands. "If you two'd quit bickering like the royal brats you are, we've more important things to worry about. Right, Em?"

Emre shrugged, for that was his answer to all of Finn's antics, which, again, ground Wick's gears. What could he say, Finn had a way of undoing all of Emre's problems. Most anyway, the ones that weren't buried in his past. Such as Cadrianna or Brynn.

Love made most things difficult.

"What's that, rabbit?" Finn pushed aside his silver mane to show his pointed ear in obvious mocking. Emre winced.

Though half the height of a normal humir, the lapin stepped toward the towering Dunleith, a dangerous glint in his button-sized eyes. If paws were able to go white like knuckled fists, Wick had that now. "Wanna repeat that, needle dick?"

Wick's footlong ears were shredded to ribbon-like wisps of furry flesh and tied back behind his head like hair. During the conquest of Dervin, he'd been captured by the Imperium and made an example of. He'd been one of the lucky ones, truth told. Most lapin did not survive that first incursion. Lapin did resemble rabbits, but they were far from the anxious, frightened creature at the bottom of the food chain. Resembled, yes, but lapin were highly intelligent. And though the Imperium enslaved near the entire race, those who'd escaped were some of the rebellion's fiercest and most cunning fighters.

And Wick fiercer still. A throwing knife swiftly appeared in the lapin's clenched paw.

Emre didn't have the time for Finn's mocking to become a brawl, which it often did when left unchecked. "Knock it off, all of you."

Finn muttered an apology, which for him, was barely more than a sulking glance and a tight-lipped grin.

Wick trembled with rage but tore away, the narrow blade disappearing up his sleeve. "You'd best control your man, lest he wake up without that toy between his legs you cherish so much." His angled nose twitched, but then he moved toward the bikromi seer with the two crates of parch.

"How'd it go?" Val asked as she tossed Emre a multi-barrel wheellock pistol.

He stared at the pistol. It was a simple design, the heft just right. The only ornamentation was an engraved 'B' on the wood-coated grip. It had been his father's. Tevun had given it to him after the conquest. It was the only thing Emre had left of their memory. The only physical link to the Benld name. Except the scars and the hatred.

His anger turned white-hot with the thought, but then he shoved the pistol in his waistband. *Soon, Benld. Soon.* "Exactly as planned."

"I should've seen Kephren as an Imperium traitor earlier," the bikrome said, regret tingeing her tone. "Many would still be alive today if I had."

"The Virtuous One only tells you what She wills." Bliss, also known as the Ideal Daughter, only spoke to the most devout, and Valeria Dunleith was nothing if not devout. "Don't let it get to you, Val. Keph was a jittery fool."

"Solanine released new warnings not ten minutes past. Same drivel as always, but we can assume Lu Har wants Drenth to think this random. No mention of the factories. Solanine always did have a penchant for theatrics. Even back then."

Valeria had been present at the Fall of Eminence, same as Solanine, but on opposite sides in the end. Only at the end. The bikrome had been a friend to the Last Godsking. She didn't talk much about those times; very rarely did she speak about the man called Canlon Carr or her time with Solanine. But Val had come to Drenth not long after the sack of the city, after Emre's parents' murder. She was the one who had brought him back to life after his throat had been sliced. She had saved him that day, and Emre would walk with her to the brink of Nocturne's Pit if she asked.

Only because he knew she wanted the same as he: to see Lu Har break for breaking those loved.

Emre strained his hearing as he burned. Solanine's voice rose clearly in the silvery sheen.

"Fret not, citizens of Drenth," Solanine said. **"Your protection is of the utmost importance to the Imperium. We've already begun apprehending the culprits for last night's disturbances. All shall be brought to justice. As such, expect this week's end festivities to commence as expected. I repeat…"**

Emre snuffed his burn. "That godsdamned… nevermind." *Not yet, Benld*, he thought bitterly. *Do not fall for it. Solanine will reap in the end. Lu Har will burn in the pyre. For Brynn. Cad, will you forgive me then?*

"It won't take long before word gets out that we hit all the factories." Finn sat on the ledge of the building as he chewed his fingernail with his legs crossed. Handsome as ever in the growing morning light. "Though it's probably what Lu Har wants, but Solanine's not one to mince words. You know that. The news will travel to Kalderim. I hope Mother and Father are prepared."

Finn and Val's parents were the Rēx & Rēgīna of Kalderim. For long years—and with little success—Emre had tried to get them to help the rebellion. The elfirish rulers claimed no skin in the fight with the Imperium. But Emre knew, as did the two youngest Dunleiths, eventually the Fallen would unleash his horde on Kanja. They needed to join forces now, while they still maintained the upper hand.

"Good. We need Kalderim to listen. Is everything ready?" Emre asked. *I don't think the Fallen is. Am I?* He shook his head not knowing if he was or not. The pain would rip apart his soul if he was wrong. Wrong about his friends. About Cadrianna. About Solanine and Valeria. About Brynn.

"Yes." Val's mining goggles caught the rising sun. "Everything is set. Except for your climbers. Tevun's waiting for them still."

"I sensed them before the Imperium soldiers raced in. And we should have our catalyst within the day."

"Good." The bikrome's many bracelets jingled as she made for the door. "I've drawn some outfits fit for the party tomorrow evenfall."

"What about you, sister-friend, got a dress to hug those boyish hips?" Finn quipped as they descended, leaving the bullet-riddled airglider and the smell of smoke behind.

Emre was the last to leave the rooftop, he could still hear Solanine's message below.

"…All shall be brought to justice. As such, expect this week's…"

There was a twinge in the air, the nearest speaker crinkled with static. Emre almost thought he heard the faint sound of laughter behind Solanine's streaming message.

The plan was coming together.

"Blood in the air," Wick said, his whiskers twitched as he seemed to detect answers Emre's humirish senses couldn't. The lapin set about sniffing further.

Emre exchanged a concerned glance with Finn while Val went to a knee near the main exit of the stair, a wheellock pistol ready.

Nodding to the lapin, Wick bounded down the hall on all fours. His heavily muscled back legs lifted his lithe body, while his furred paws made nary a sound on the aged floorboards. Gnarly shadows broken by flickering overhead lights, left the hall bathed in black. Wick, a darkened ghost in the low light, paused at the far end of the hall beside the door where other rebels were supposed to be waiting for them. The lapin sniffed, then pushed the portal open, and entered cautiously, a pair of dueling knives in his paws.

Long agonizing heartbeats later, a low whistle came. Emre's tension eased, the tenuous hold on his aetheurgy held in check. Even without burning, his blood pumped frenetically. *Still it, Benld. You knew this could happen.*

As he made his way down the hall, Wick stepped back outside, his whiskers florid in distress. Closer, and with the door open, Emre could smell the pungent aroma of blood. It clung to the walls like perfume, clawing an escape from the room beyond.

Inside had been a bloodied shootout.

A handful of bodies were strewn across the room. Some were his friends, three were of the Imperium. Wheellocks gripped in dead hands, others littering the floor as if thrown in the dying fight. Bullet holes pocked the drywall in clustered rents. Isolated furniture was overturned or broken to pieces by body and bullet alike. Crimson painted the walls and floor in violent streaks. A rickety ceiling fan rotated with creaky blades, a single bulb of light, the others shattered in the gunfire, broken shards on the ground a reddish prism.

"Bugger me," Finn muttered as he saw the carnage, his mouth and nose in the crook of his elbow.

Still it, Benld. Emre motioned toward the bikrome, "Val?"

Val drew down the mining goggles and holstered her pistol as she padded into the room with her eyes closed. Somehow, the bikromi seer eased around the pools of blood coalescing under the corpses, moving like a leaf on the wind, her boots barely touching the floorboards. Her arms raised as she skirted the bodies, taking in all around her. Bikromi did not use Shard Form, nor could they. This was her gift. Vision Form.

The multitude of gold and silver bracelets upon her wrists glimmered as she stopped beside one of the dead rebels. She bent close, her waist contorted in an unnatural angle, lost in the trance of the bikromi seers under Vision Form. The man's face was streaked with blood, still wet from the look of it.

Val gently wiped away a speckle of blood from the rebel's lips and leaned in to brush hers to his, mere hair-lengths apart.

"Bugger me twice." Finn winced as Emre elbowed him in the short ribs.

The bikrome's body stiffened, her sterling hair fell about her face in plaits. The air surrounding her rippled like the twang of a harp string. Body rigid, her head snapped back, a silent scream erupted from her open mouth as her breath became visible like that of a frosty morn on Kanja's tundra. Her bracelets burned like raw aethecite thrown into the forge.

She rose, then. Arms wide, inches above the floor and the body. Hoarfrost snowed from her pale, exposed flesh. Silver hair static. Slowly, her entire body rotated toward them, her head lowered, eyes level. One black eye, dark as pitch. The other entirely white, pearlescent. Onyx bound to the past of what was, alabaster attuned to the future yet to be. Both glowed in the faint light of the overhead bulb. Vision Form.

"Bugger me thrice. I hate this part."

Nothing happened for minutes, the bi-colored woman hung in the air above the corpse in a trance. Snowflakes dripped from her boots.

Then, ***"TRAP,"*** a singsong, ethereal voice broke the silence, coming from Val's mouth. Not hers, but Bliss Herself, the Virtuous One. The goddess of energy and order. Of purity. Val's lips moved not, the words continuing, ***"IMPERIUM TRAP. SPIES ON ALL SIDES. SCOURGES. TEVUN IN DANGER. MOTHER OF LIES. SHE COMES. SHE COMES. LEARN THE TRUTH. LEARN THE TRUTH. SHE COMES. BEWARE. BEWARE."***

A convulsion of body, the frost evaporated on her arms, hair drooping. Val fell, flaccid atop the corpse. It was moments before the woman breathed again, sucking in deep. Quietly, she pulled up the tinted goggles, her prophetic eyes hidden once more. "Well?"

Val never recalled what happened whenever she called upon her Vision Form. Bliss had overtaken her completely.

"A trap," Emre filled in the gap.

"No bloody void it was a trap," Finn raved as if he was on fire. "Even I could've told you that! Summoning Bliss like that. My word…" *If only you knew the truth, Finn, you'd try and stop her. But we can't. We all must do as necessary.*

"We have to get out of here, Em," Wick said, sliding between them. "You heard the Ideal Daughter. They knew we were coming here, the scourges. Nobody wants to dance with a scourge. Who knows what else Keph told them. Tevun. The others in Marketside. There are bloodied boot prints leading back down the hall, that means someone survived this onslaught. You were right, Em, there's a spy in our midst."

Emre was silent as he puzzled through Bliss' words. *'Tevun in danger'* was easy enough to understand, for this was their plan. Tevun would see it through to the end. *'She comes.' Zenith, let it be so.* "We're all in danger," Emre said quietly. *Have been since the moment the Fallen tore apart Drenth.* Steel, had to be steel today. Sacrifice. Endure the pain, that's what he needed to do. "Remember our oath, Wick."

"This is different. They've never hit us this hard before. Never known where we'd be." He pointed a paw toward the seer. "Spies. Imperium spies. That's what the Ideal Daughter said. Kephren hadn't been told this part of the plan. There's no way Solanine would've gotten it from him. The Pentax are not happy."

Emre paid for this knowledge in blood. It was going to be bloody, and it could very well end with his own.

Ashe

IX

ASHE

"YOU'VE NEVER HEARD of Neenah LeFleur?"

Ashe's mood perked up as she limped into *The Colosseum* and saw the smuggler. The exasperation in Neenah's tone was mildly amusing, for the woman was so voidbent on everyone knowing her good name. Come void or high water.

Ever since she had stowed away on *Marrow's Lover*, Ashe had retained a soft spot for the vain mist pirate. Those few days spent with Neenah and her crew were some of Ashe's best in her eighteen years. Neenah LeFleur was a regular at *The Colosseum* and always asked after Ashe whenever she was in the City of Sands. Neenah would then regale the entire bar of her daring pursuits all over the Mistlands. Most of it was probably embellishment, but for Ashe, they were a welcome remembrance of a few days of pure freedom.

"Never had the pleasure." The man sitting opposite Neenah had a head too big for his narrow shoulders, almost like a hay-stuffed doll. Wide-set eyes, black as coal, and a nose too huge for his face. Not exactly one to set hearts, let alone the privies, of whores afire.

"She's daring. And debonair, too. Her name's legendary." Neenah gave Ashe a wink and a smile of pearl and golden teeth as she shambled by before the captain's focus returned to the flabby face of the man. "I'm truly baffled you've never heard of her."

"Sounds like a working girl to me, with that name." Fat bastard that he was, the man grinned at Neenah as he spoke. Multiple chins flowered over a tight collar as if they were attempting to escape.

Wrong choice of words, Ashe thought as she moved toward the bar, slowing to hear Neenah's response.

"Neenah LeFleur isn't just some rogue, she's folklore at this point." Neenah's jaw ground some, lips pursed. "Everyone in the Mistlands is in awe of her pursuits. Really sticks her figurative prick into the cleft of the Imperium if you take my meaning. The Fallen wants her head."

"Bloody smugglers don't deserve my remembrance." Liquor dribbled down the hills of the man's fleshy neck as he slurped from a pewter mug. "They all deserve the noose. And what do I care what the Fallen wants with this scum? That man cares little for what happens here in Drenth outside of aethecite."

"Believe me when I say this, after the story I'm about to tell you, you *will* never forget Captain Neenah LeFleur…"

"Where the void you been?" asked the fat bartender, Olaf, as Ashe leaned upon the bartop, forcing her from hearing what story Neenah was about to unleash on her new mark.

Truth told, Ashe should've been there hours ago, but she took her time, for she was in no mood to get a stern talking to for her hasty act back at the villa. Olaf's aura was a cacophony of shaded hues. Greed, anger, annoyance.

The Colosseum was one of the second sector's larger taverns. It was a squat building with only two floors and was built of timber with a gloss of faded paint. An ever-present scent of sweat and drunkenness permeated through the termite-ridden arches holding up the trussed ceiling. Candles burned in dented sconces upon the walls, though the dim urine-yellow glow from aethecite-powered lamps shone down from the patchy ceiling above.

Olaf was as round as he was tall, but he was a good, honest man, especially loyal to Elian, who ran *The Colosseum* and the Slag's End gang. Though quick with a temper, Olaf kept the tavern in adequate condition. "He ain't happy you're late, girl."

"Got hung up by all the bombings." It had taken her half the nightturn and most of the morn to make her way to *The Colosseum.*

"Nasty business, that. This Gutter King's gon' bring us all to ruination."

"Still gossiping like an old hen, Olaf?" Ashe slid a quadran across the bartop and Olaf slung her a perspiring goblet of mead. Her nose wrinkled at the smell of honey. "Whiskey."

"No can do, girl," the hefty barkeep said with a grin. "Elian's word. Mead only."

"I swear to the Pentax, the bombs held me back."

"Tell him, not me. And don't you be takin' Their names in vain."

Don't tempt me, Ashe thought as she took a seat in a nearby booth. A long cloak of brocaded silver on onyx shrouded her shoulders, the hood thrown back, leaving her raven-black hair free. A simple tunic, with a simple pant. Miner's clothes. The stola stained with blood long since tossed, her current outfit stolen from a clothesline.

O Zenith she was angry. Angry at Evander. Angry at the vicars. Angry at not one, but two strangers following her, one a proper bitty in Solanine and the other a drakken. Angry that some random gold and gemstone contraption happened to fasten to her wrist and refused to come off but clearly possessing some sort of aetheric connection. Just angry.

She couldn't view her own aura, but if she could, she knew it would be blazing ruby like a thousand firedrakes shooting their flamesacs into the sky at once.

Her fingers vigorously drummed atop the tabletop as she witnessed the tragedy of a Neenah LeFleur con. The man had no clue what was happening. After a while, she grew bored. The sound of a sporting match played on the aerescreen over the bar, and a few patrons roared as one team scored. A pair of goblins were throwing knives and guzzling ale like their lives depended on it.

Vicars in Drenth should've put her over the edge, but the fact that Solanine and the shadow showed up in the Meadows was the froth on the ale. The surprise of it all, the laughter, the blinding light. Then appearing in the flesh at the exact moment of her flight. Both occurrences were not coincidence. But how? Same with that cloaked drakken. That draconem of the lesser order knew her, knew where she'd be, where to find her. A drakken, a void aetheurgist, and vicars were ingredients for a slag-tasting bread.

Yet, above it all, it was the word Solanine had called her: Godsblood. A wrinkle in her memories made her think she should know it. To whom she was.

And it angered her all the more to be left in the dark still.

"Need anything, beautiful?" a syrupy voice asked, snapping Ashe's wandering thoughts.

Ashe found a nymph-faced woman smiling shyly at her, a tray of empty mugs held in a dainty hand. Exposure between the folds of a simple pleb tunic of muted browns left little to the imagination of Mother Marrow's gifts underneath.

It was Wren.

The mist smiled with Ashe as it ran up and down her body in waves of need. "Maybe."

Wren tittered as her soft skin flushed in the flickers of the smokeless lights above them. Her ambience was a bright, lustful red. An inferno grew within Ashe now, the mist raged against her. But not in warning, O no, this was different. This was carnal.

Begging. Pleading. Wanting with a lust that had only demanded blood half a day's turn ago. Flesh touching flesh. Body heat against body heat. Fruitless passion ignited within her loins like never before. A ferocity that had never been borne within her.

Wren set the tray down upon the table, lightly gripping with porcelain fingers, leaning forward so that the folds of her tunic parted to reveal more of her flesh. "And what would that be?"

"Wouldn't you like to know, little bird?"

The thief-girl grinned, breathing heavily, hinting. Aura fulgurating. "You tease me."

Inner desire burned within Ashe; the mist curled about her legs with want. Her gaze slowly moved up the valley of collarbone to the graceful neck. Up to puckered lips of pink that were slightly open, tongue pressed against pearl, pupils dilated.

O Zenith, how Ashe wanted Wren. Wanted every inch of her body pressed against her own. Fingers roaming as they would, touching everywhere, releasing the pleasures waiting to be explored.

She leaned closer, her own heart beating furiously. Her desire was too much to hold back. "Not anymore."

Wren licked her lips.

"Yes!" One of the patrons watching the sporting match slammed the bartop, his exclamation battered down the tension-filled moment between her and Wren. "I'll drink to that. Girl! More wine."

The nymph's mouth hung open. "You lazy bastard, Olaf. Can't you see I'm busy? You fucking help them!" Wren bellowed, but not without giving Ashe a knowing smile. '*Later*,' the smile said.

"Zenith's cock," Ashe coughed into the hem of the stolen cloak. Copper on her tongue.

It had never been that strong before, the passion, the urge to toss. Or to kill. The same that had washed over her while she stood above the murdered servant in the Guilder's villa. A threshold to her childhood forever broken. The innocence of her old life gone in a blink. Ever since her first blood had the desire grown. Desire of Life and of sex. Desire of Death and of the void after. Always begging her for designs of the flesh.

Never had it been this strong, though. Never had she wanted to cross that bridge so succinctly with another person.

Life and Death.

Wren had always been a game to her. Always a flirt or a wink of intent, yet she'd not crossed that invisible bridge she couldn't uncross. No, she'd held herself in check around the young woman whose name meant 'little bird.'

Until now.

Up until the moment she'd stuck her blade into that man's flesh back in Prien Soabin's study, she'd been able to control the urge. Her willpower had always beaten back the growing dissent, cordoning off the baser part of her nature. Her taskmaster had once told her that the pull of aether sought out the vulgar needs of man, and that she must guard herself against it. Seduction by the power of aether could drown a soul.

Yet, she'd given in last night to that urge.

It was as if it offered up freedom of the body, the knowledge of all existence. The seed in need of fertilization. The silence of Death. The underlying want to hurt another. Underpinning all of her being, her thoughts and hatreds. Drawing them forth from the depths of her mind and body. From deep within her soul.

Whispers of truths from her past.

What did it all mean?

"You're finally back, Snow Eyes. Took your time."

She tamped down the fleeting visions of Wren naked atop her, beat down the longing within the mist. Stilled her flapping heart.

Evander leaned against a tabletop. He tilted his head as if looking at something that wasn't there. And then he smiled as he stared intently on the small swell of her breasts under the miner's tunic.

"What do you want?"

"Elian wants to see you. After your stunt last night at the villa, he ain't pleased. I tried to talk him down, but he wasn't having it."

His mere presence made Ashe's skin crawl as she thought back to the dead servant. Evander's red aura was a sickening tint of garnet, a far cry different than Wren's. He'd enjoyed her killing the man, she realized. Made him want her even more. Zenith's cock, she had to be even more wary of him going forward. "Why?"

Instead of answering, Evander's face glazed, jaw slack, listening to the unseen voices in his head again. He was truly a peculiar person. Blazing red around him. Back to her, "Elian wants to see you."

"You said that."

"You ever gon' accept my offer?" he asked as Ashe pushed out of the booth. She steeled her face, barren of emotion. She didn't respond. "One day, you'll be mine, Snow Eyes," he called after her.

Even the Pentax couldn't make that a reality. "Stop calling me that," she yelled back.

Toward the back of the tavern sat a man upon a gilded throne. Overweight with a balding pate of a constant flush, Elian had a scraggly yet thick beard over ruddy cheeks and a stomach as round as a column base. In the cushions that were his cheeks, sat deep brown eyes. He had no aetheurgy like some of the other gang leaders, but the man was as smart and clever as they came. Brutal too, willing to spill blood for the right amount of quadrans.

Two brutes flanked the gang leader, two of the dirtiest buggers in all of Drenth: Quick Fingers Cyrus and Red Tulio.

Quick Fingers had a rodent-like face, pinched and fuzzy. He was a shrewkin, a dubious race found in Filfangin. Shrewkin were of a similar size to lapin but much nastier in appearance and behavior. Quick Fingers had beady eyes and a wiry body. His overly elongated fingers were always in motion because he was, as were most shrewkin, a deft thief. A wheellock pistol was stuffed into his belt; a cudgel strapped to his hip. He goggled her as she approached. Quick Fingers once tried to cop a feel, but his fingers weren't so fast when she sliced a pinky off as payment for his unwelcome advance. He never bothered her again after that.

Whereas Quick Fingers was small and jittery, Red Tulio was lumbering and calm. A massive male orcir, tall and bulging with muscles under his grey-green flesh. He had a massive underbite and a misshapen nose, broken from too many fistfights, chocolate-colored eyes, and possessed a shock of red hair on both scalp and face. Most orcir were odorous and uncouth, but Red Tulio's rare orcirish coloring wasn't why he was called Red Tulio, no, it was because he liked to bathe in the blood of any poor sot unlucky to be in his path.

"Girl," Elian started, running a fat finger over the horns of the satyr mask, his aura a sickly emerald. Greed. "Sit." His gruff demeanor made her cringe but sit she did. The bastard had taken her in on Neenah's word, and she didn't want to offend him. Didn't mean she had to grovel, though. "A fine relic of Eminence. Worth every bit of coin they said it would fetch. Brio's been hot lately, what with His Festival of the Grape upcoming."

"Is it?"

"It is. But I hear you almost got nicked. Using that gift of yours in full view." Nobody outside Elian's crew and the vicars knew of her ability to use aetheurgy, so her alarm rose.

"You said this job might lead me closer to discovering my parents."

"Did it?"

"No."

He shrugged. "Guess my contact was wrong. Perhaps you should've stuck with the Scattered Shards," he continued, "being so reckless. I don't need vicars turning their steely gaze on my endeavors. Scourges are one thing, girl. Same with Solanine. Last thing we need is another gang upended."

Regardless of her trying not to, Ashe felt her cheeks flush. "I don't know what you mean."

"Killian Ness got himself seized while making a deal with the Gutter King. Tried swindling the rebel bastard. Serves him right. Resourceful, Ness may've been, but you can't outfox the Gutter King. He's entrenched deep in Drenth."

The Gutter King, the myth of Drenth. Ashe knew very little about the rebel leader. He was difficult to spy on, and no amount of aetheurgy gained her any closer inspection. The histrionics with the bombs indicated the Gutter King was making his move against Lu Har and the Imperium. Only with open warfare on the horizon would one decide to level the aethecite factories.

Say what the people of Drenth did about the Gutter King, the man had some seedpods on him.

A grin split Elian's husky face. "I know what you're thinking, your secret's safe with me, lass. You've earned me my fair share. But that means others may be wondering what you mean to my operation. Many know only Shards sprat have tattoos such as yours."

"Basing that hypothesis on a bit of ink?" Soft cough, she put the back of her hand to her mouth. "Hope Solanine's ass tastes better than that." A deeper pulmo cough followed the first. At least it kept her from saying something else stupid.

"Pulmo's an unpleasant death, I'm afraid." Elian made a sympathetic gesture, though, there wasn't much sympathy in it. But he pointed toward the *Terris* rune upon her inner wrist. "I pay to know the right information. You really think I let you join my crew without knowing all there is about you? Come on, girl, you're smarter than that."

Did Neenah tell him? She thought to look at the smuggler but refrained. "Who'd you have to slice up for that intel? Hope it wasn't the one you call mother." Much to her detriment, she couldn't keep her tongue quiet sometimes.

Elian chuckled, his flabby jowls jiggling. "Does it matter?" He handed the mask to Quick Fingers and stood, a perceptible groan of appreciation from the throne. Standing over her, he glared down his bovine gut. "If Solanine knows of a Shards-trained sprat's running amok in the second sector, then you can bet your pretty little face the other gang leaders know as well. Just remember who you can trust and who you can't. It might save your life on the next job. I don't want to go the way of Ness and I won't allow any of my crew to make it so. Drenth's no place for unwary little birds."

It wasn't empathy, O Pentax no. It was because of her aetheurgy. A man like Elian could only get so far up the gang ladder without having his grease-coated fingers in other places. But her aetheurgy had led Elian to a rung above most.

And worst, she knew he owned her.

"What's that?" he asked.

"What's what?" A lazy swirl of mist circled about her ankles.

"Don't play coy with me, girl?" Elian said, pointing at the golden braids about her wrist and fingers.

Ashe lifted her left hand, the one now garbed with the golden bangle. "It's nothing. Just a babble I bought in Marketside." The mist prodded her ankles like a toddler pestering their parents to buy them a stuffed doll. "I liked the colors," she lied.

Elian stared at the bangle for long seconds, his aura read a mash of shaded sapphire and darkened crimson. "Now, don't go cockin' up any more jobs. Wouldn't want my brother to cry over some dead girl with snowfall eyes."

With that, Elian disappeared into the back of the tavern, Quick Fingers and Red Tulio behind him.

Sliding up to the bar, she called out to the barkeep. "The strong stuff." Olaf, with a grin, plopped down a shooter glass and yanked off the cork of a darkened bottle. Ashe reached across and took the whole thing.

The liquor washed away the unease building inside. First killing a man, the vicars, Solanine and shadow, and now Elian's unsaid knowledge of her past. It all left her lost.

She spotted Wren cleaning a table across the tavern. The thief girl looked up, found Ashe watching her and smiled. The mist at her feet softly prodded her again.

Until today.

So, she tipped the bottle back and headed over.

X

EVANDER

"SHE WILL BE YOURS, EVANDER."

There it was, in Evander's mind, the ever-present voice. There was no image to accompany the voice, there never was. A shadowed man, that's how Evander envisioned the speaker. Tall and cloaked, using the figurative shadows as His mantle. Unbent but strong. The voice of a god.

A Divine.

From the second floor of _The Colosseum_, Evander nodded to the Divine's promise as he watched the girl he called Snow Eyes. That baleful Wren stood nearby, fluttering eyelashes at the object of his obsession as she toyed with her hair. Sometimes they touched each other in a dance of intimacy, teasing each other with soft kisses, coming ever closer to the levels of desire that filled him.

Ever since the girl had come with that smuggler looking like a half-starved refugee, he had been enthralled. Ensnared a more accurate description. It was her eyes that had ensnared him. Those glacial irises of the likes he'd never seen before.

And she would be his.

"When?" he asked of the voice.

"SOON." The ethereal voice of the Divine grated like bone on bone. Flickers of obsidian flashed like eyelids blinking in his mind.

"You tease, you punish me. I've done all you've asked. I've served! She's to be mine. You promised!"

"CONTINUE TO SERVE." The sound echoed in his skull, pressing down in a demanding way. Devoid of warmth, only the pressure. ***"SERVE AND YOU SHALL BE REWARDED WHEN THE TIME OF MY RETURN DRAWS NIGH."***

Evander's fists curled into a ball, fingernails digging into the flesh of his palms. "How much longer?"

There was silence, and his head cocked to the side as he sought the voice of his Divine. It had left him, always leaving him. Commanding he serve but never giving the power he craved. The power promised. The power of aetheurgy.

"You give me nothing!"

A crushing force descended upon him in a rush, driving him to his knees. Clutching the railing, his head exploded in torment, sawing at his very soul. His muscles tightened, frayed apart in a single instance, splitting.

"YOU DARE QUESTION ME, MORTAL! YOUR IMPUDENCE WILL BE YOUR UNDOING!"

A presence formed within Evander's mind, blinded by the shadows from whence it came. The shadowed form appeared, surrounded by a presence dark as the void. Crystaline. The sheer force of power bore through Evander's soul as if he were nothing but parchment. His body crumbled under the seismic compression, head touching the wooden planks of *The Colosseum's* balcony, sweat beaded his forehead and drenched his curls.

Then it was over.

He sagged; chest pulled in breath after breath. His mind cleared; the bite of acid drove upward.

"SOON. BIDE YOUR TIME. THE GIRL'S SOUL WILL BE YOURS TO FOREVER PLAY WITH IN THE COMING NIGHT WHEN I RETURN."

"Yes, master. Command me."

"PATIENCE. MY DISCIPLE WILL GIVE YOU WHAT YOU WANT. GIVE YOU THE POWER YOU DESIRE. SHE WILL SHOW YOU TRUE VOID FORM AND MAKE YOU THE RIGHT HAND OF MY FALLEN."

The voice wavered as it always did, faded and was gone. The image of the cloaked figure disappeared. Evander struggled to his feet, using the railing to steady himself. Bodily fluid poured down his face, a mixture of blood and perspiration, his jaw sore from clenching so tight.

He looked toward the girl who would be his, her head nestled upon the shoulder of the serving wench. "You will be mine, Snow Eyes. Forever."

Boots clapped on the tavern's floorboards. It was Elian.

"Brother, come," Elian commanded. Evander knew his brother was still livid over the girl's killing of the servant in the Guilder's villa. "We have a summons."

"SOLANINE CALLS. OBEY."

Yes, master. Obey I shall.

An hour later, Evander glided down a hallway aboard the fortress of Gargantua.

Elian walked by his side, as were a pair of Imperium soldiers. The guards stopped a solitary portal at the end of the hall where two additional guards stood rigid. One rapped a knuckle upon the door, which opened before the guard could knock a second time.

A solitary figure was within, clad in a robe that barely clung to narrow shoulders, almost as if it had just thrown it on. The robed one was short, with hair brownish-blonde, face heart-shaped of pale white flesh, lips full and pouty. Beautiful for truth.

He knew that face, everyone in Drenth did. Solanine.

Solanine motioned them into the room and dismissed the guards with a flicked wrist. It was a simple room within a palatial compound atop the floating fortress, a small desk alight by glowing orbs of aethecite, parchment papers stacked neatly beside the inkwell. A three-legged stand was behind the desk. A bloodied blade, a saucer, and small vials lay atop. No windows, no other seating, only the desk.

On the floor in front of the desk was a rune, of which Evander had no idea how to decipher. Bloodred as it was drawn in blood. Dark reddish-black mist seeped from the rune, as if summoned by it, for there was no mist upon Gargantua.

Elian chuckled. Glancing at him from the cowl of his cloak, Evander noted that his brother's laugh was at the expense of the dying man nailed to the far wall, arms outstretched. Wrist-thick spikes pinned him in place. Naked, crimson stained the flesh of his torso and legs from the missing strips of skin at the man's breast. Head hung, face burnt, cracked and bleeding, his thickly corded, raven locks smoldered.

"One of the Gutter King's rats," Solanine said coolly. "Captured when the man attacked my aethecite factories last nightturn. One of the others captured still rots beneath us now."

"Ness?" Elian's face was flushed behind the beard, but his eyes were hard, a man not to be crossed in the streets of Drenth. But here on Gargantua, Evander knew his brother was but a candle to Solanine's sun. "Never liked the bastard, cut into my pockets. Elian, mistress." He clapped a hand to Evander's shoulder. "My brother Evander."

"Mistress," Evander said, drawing his own cowl down. He wondered if Solanine recognized him from Prien Soabin's party. *Was that a chance meeting, master? To test me?*

As per usual, the voice of his Divine remained silent, only speaking when He sought, never the other way around.

"I am nobody's mistress, address me as such again, and I'll pluck your seedpods and shove them into your mouth raw," Solanine said with such force Evander couldn't contain the smile from breaking the planes of his face. "I've a need," Solanine continued with less vigor, "one in which your service will be valued. A girl resides in Drenth, a girl the Fallen desires."

"A girl?" The promise of quadrans gleamed in Elian's eyes. "I've lots of girls. Plenty for the Fallen to play with. Boys, too, if that's his vice."

A fool you are, brother, to try and barter with one such as Solanine. But Evander kept his tongue still, watching to see if the barb would pierce the aetheurgist's shield.

Solanine smiled, baring teeth like a predator stalking prey, venom in the accompanying hiss. "This is no ordinary girl, child."

"This girl, how will we know her?"

"O, you know this one. Clouded eyes she has. Trained in the arts of the mortal coil you call the Scattered Shards." Evander's face tightened while Elian's grimaced. "Bring her to me."

She's to be mine! he screamed into the void.

His brother's mouth quirked within the curls of his swarthy beard. "If you summoned us, you could've taken her at any moment." Elian paused, stroking his beard. "I've also on good authority she's been seen in the presence of vicar. Seems the Scattered Shards still have hold on her, too, eh mis… er… Solanine?"

Evander side-eyed his brother. *You never miss a thing, do you, brother? How do you know this information? A brutal game you play, one false step will be your end.*

"The answer matters not, child," Solanine responded. "She cannot be forced, this girl. She must come willingly, lest she serve no use. You can enter doors the Fallen's soldiers cannot. I've tried, good scourges were lost in the process. My sources still wander free, but not for long. Beware of the Gutter King. The inferno comes to him. She cannot join his cause."

Master, you promised me that she would be mine.

Elian started to speak, but Solanine silenced him with a click of tongue that sounded strangely like a Kanjan aerovern clacking their serrated draconem teeth. "Organize yourself before the inferno begins." Solanine lifted a thin, golden chain from the robe's pocket and tossed it to his brother. "A gift in the knowledge you'll do as told."

"What is this?" Elian inspected the pendant. In the center was a crimson rune within a black crystal.

"A shield against aetheurgy." Solanine handed him two additional pendants. They must contain aether. "You may go." Elian smiled and moved toward the door. Evander went to draw up his cowl, but Solanine stopped him with a curt motion. "You stay, child."

There was confusion upon Elian's flushed face, but after seeing Solanine's look, he quickly saw himself out. The Gutter King's man hanging on the wall grunted as he shifted ever so slightly. Evander's eyes darted toward the dying man.

O master, give me this power.

"How long have you served the Divine, child?" Solanine ran a hand through blonde-brown hair, regarding Evander curiously.

His gaze went slack, the voice of the Divine speaking to him.

"OBEY AND MY POWER IS YOURS. MY DISCIPLE IS AGELESS, THIS BODY YOU SEE IS NOT. SUCH IS OUR POWER OVER DEATH."

"Long as I can remember," he said. "His voice comes to me often. I serve." *I will serve, master.*

"I remember you, child, from the villa. You were with the Godsblood. Do you know this term?" He shook his head. "We shall see if you are worthy."

Solanine's all-onyx eyes closed as the robe fell. Evander drank in the aetheurgist's nudity. Stomach taut above shapely hips with a thick, curled thatch of hair in the recess of vulnerable thighs. He stared intently at the aetheurgist's ample bosom, for nestled between was a crystal shard of ebony emblazoned with a similar rune as to the one given to Elian. Below were scars that ran red with blood from the cuts procured to draw the rune on the floor. Void Form.

His manhood stiffened against his trousers. Lust filled him. There was a soft cackle in his mind, his master mocking his carnal desires.

Drawing on aetheurgy, the air around them grew cold, so cold Evander's breaths left puffs. The absence of warmth fled from his body, down his legs, into the ground itself. Evander shivered. The crystal around Solanine's neck blazed as the blackened mist draped about the aetheurgist's body, the edges became wispy like that of the red-black mist from the rune on the ground.

"WATCH AND LEARN. THIS IS TO BE YOURS. THE VOID AND THE MEADOWS WILL OPEN TO YOU. A BODY IS MERELY A BOUNDARY THAT CAN BE SURPASSED. CAN BE BROKEN AND REBORN."

Then, Solanine moved. Not the mortal body, no, but the aetheurgist's soul, he realized. A carbon copy, built from the black-red mist. Evander's gaze followed the aetheurgist's soul as it ghosted about the room. His eyes found Solanine's every phase of mist. Then Solanine was before him, touching his face, a wisp of nothingness across his cheek. He stiffened, breathing hard. Solanine went to the tips of toes, putting lips to his, the barest of touches. True life-and-death hovered between them.

His need burned like a volcano. Solanine whispered against his lips, chanting an aetheurgic spell. Without knowing what he was doing, he opened his soul, his essence spanned, shadows gathered around him, sweeping in flowing waves, black as the coldest night in the Voidlands, yet a glowing brightness within the ethereal mass.

The pleasure of touching Life and Death rampaged inside him, swelling his body's senses, tingling his manhood. Blood pulsing. Throbbing. The bliss and the sorrow. A want to expel his seed, to fertilize in the name of Life, only to see it wither and die.

Master...

"DO YOU NOW SEE, MORTAL? THIS IS WHAT I OFFER. ALL IT TAKES IS YOUR DEVOTION."

Yes, master, I see. O how I see. You have it, master. My devotion.

Solanine's ghastly soul retreated into the stiff body as the gateway to the void closed and the mist syphoned back into the rune. "You're of us, child. You could be so much more." He panted; the full brunt of their communion had drained him. "I will show you the darkness of this world."

"I'll do whatever you ask of me, master you are." He was too wild in his need to prove.

"Heed me and I'll show you the realm of aether. And its pleasures." Solanine's brow rose at his hardened crotch. "O yes, child, there is felicity in the blood. Immortality does not come from the proliferation of Life, but upon the wave of Death. Your training will start soon. But we must break your body, reform it into the mold of the Divine's warriors."

Like most children of the streets in Drenth, Evander was wiry, bereft of fat upon his bones. "Whatever it takes, I am yours."

Without answering, Solanine turned toward the man crucified to the wall. His head rose, alive, though his eyes had been sewn shut. Tears had dried long ago.

"Please, mistress. No more. I can't. O Zenith protect me."

"Ease, Nocturne will take you soon. No longer will Zenith have need of you." Solanine leaned close, inhaled the burnt flesh, the offal. Aether was strong in the air. "First you must bring me the Fallen."

Solanine's hands moved over the man's body, the aether in the mist above the blood rune on the floor flew forth, and the man screamed as the poisonous haze filmed over him, diving into his innards via his wounds. While chanting, the scarred and bleeding runes on Solanine's breast and spine burned as the aether wept from them. The man began to thrash, the spikes holding him.

From the three-legged stand, Solanine took one of the glass vials and poured it into a saucer. A handful of black powder followed the opaque liquid. It fumed with a sulfuric odor. Carefully, Solanine set the saucer below the writhing man's legs. Lifting the knife, Solanine pressed it into the man's side. He screamed loudly as the blade plunged into his kidney. The man mewled as a stream of urine fountained into the saucer.

Taking the saucer to the misty blood rune on the floor beside where Evander stood, Solanine mixed the contents with the tip of the knife. The saucer began to pulsate. Laying down the knife, Solanine lifted the foul brew and drank. Repulsiveness washed through Evander; his Divine laughed within the void of the Pit.

Over the rune of blood and mist, Solanine spat.

Instead of falling to the ground, the liquid hung suspended. Finally, Solanine took a pinch of yellowed powder from the table and tossed it. The entire liquid shimmered and then, a picture began to form, the shape of a man atop a massive red firedrake. So lifelike, so real, Evander could almost envision the wind gusting from the wings of the drake, the ripples of air threading his hair.

"Solanine," the hazy visage of the Fallen said. Full onyx eyes took in Evander. "Is this the boy He sends to us?" Evander couldn't help but shrink back from the Fallen's scrutiny. He felt so inadequate, so unworthy.

"OBEY AND YOU WILL BE WORTHY."

Yes, forever, my master.

"He is. And he knows the girl. The Gutter King will make his move soon. My forces are ready. My best scourge remains entrenched and will bring our child to us, threshold crossed. She will not betray us a second time." Evander noticed the pained look on Solanine's face, if only there for a moment.

"My favored scourge will hunt down the Gutter King and the child."

To Evander, Solanine seemed taken aback. "Are you certain that is wise? If she were to discover the truth, we could lose everything."

"Everything hinges on her," the Fallen said. "The Matron has seen the future, Solanine. Our path is now set. The war has begun, my army awakens from its slumber. Break the Gutter King and bring me the Godsblood. Kalderim cannot hold without either. But beware, the Sword of the Golden Throne will rise in this war, he must not. The bikrome must remain true. Our master's guile upon you."

Solanine waved a hand, and the air began to shimmer again. With a splash, the aetheurgic spell broke and the rune of blood sizzled.

Solanine faced the Gutter King's man, who was sobbing. "Please, mistress…"

"Mors expectet." Solanine slammed the knife into the man's heart. To Evander, "I told you, I am no one's mistress nor master. I am Solanine."

Evander waited until the man's chest fell for the last time. "What of me?" All he wanted was the power of the void.

"AND SO YOU SHALL."

"Find the girl," Solanine said. "She must cross the threshold of Life before she can become one with Death. The test of flesh must happen. See it so, our master knows what designs you have on her body. You shall reap it once her purpose to Him is done. Go."

XI
CADRIANNA

NO MATTER HOW hard Cadrianna tried to forget, every time she set foot onto Gargantua, the vivid details of her entire family's decimation tore through her.

The lines around her father's eyes burned into her memory. There was blood upon her eldest brother's face as a black-armored scourge clocked him with the butt of a wheellock rifle. The body of her middle brother lay dead, another scourge's blade protruding from his back. Terror emanated from her mother as they grabbed her and bound her hands in coarse rope. Babe Brynn cried uncontrollably in her beloved Emre's arms as the brutes covered their heads with black hoods.

A drake's roar was the only thing that drowned out the sobs.

Ever remembering.

"RELIVING THEM AGAIN, CAD? MUST IT BE EVERY TIME?"

Cadrianna brushed off the Strix as she exited the airglider into one of Gargantua's many docking bays found within the rocky underside of the floating fortress. The daemon would never understand what this place meant to her.

Aside from the steel propellers that circulated to keep Gargantua afloat, the underside was mostly stone and metal. The four tethers wormed into massive portals of the underbelly's exterior. Fifty-foot interlocking blocks pocked with slots for weaponry had steel doors for airglider access and slips for larger transports to dock. *Aere*-infused spotlights were set at six-feet intervals around the middle.

Topside was altogether a different realm, one that triggered the most hateful of memories as she emerged from the interior.

The smooth-stoned walls rose upwards into six points, complete with towers, crenellation, arches, spires, and flags. But the castle-like comparisons ended there. The interior and topside were a mash of fortified bases and extravagant living compounds. Like any mega-city, buildings rose taller than the walls. Gardens were full of color and paved avenues were large enough for trucks to fit three times over. In fact, it painted a portrait of grandeur, the antithesis of what would be expected of a flying weapon of the apocalypse.

Predator automatons stood like statues on the streets. Even though the Fallen had mastered the horde of mist daemons in the Sea, his automatons were a force to keep them cowered if they broke the walls. Spikes and weapons protruded from their chassis, standing fifteen feet tall and were difficult to destroy.

In the very center of Gargantua rose a singular tower made of ebony stone. A series of stairs led to a squat, square base, and from there, the spire shot upward. There were no balconies, save one at the highest apex where the Fallen had his chambers. Window slits lined the spire at every story. In fact, the simplicity of the tower made it feel out of place amongst the rest of the topside beauty.

Ignoring the guards standing at the bottom of the stairs leading to the tower entrance, she approached and climbed. Dull aethecite lamps lined the stairway, light layering the holy residence in obscurity despite the sun above.

A massive firedrake, easily sixty feet from snout to tail, lazily looped around the base of the Fallen's tower, its grand bulk hugging it while its folded wings draped the stairs. The drake's—one of the four greater orders of draconem; the firedrakes, seagandr, aerovern, and the terrisvvyrm—head was massive, the size of a full-grown auroch, snout-like, eyes as big as dinner plates, teeth forearm-long. Garnet orbs narrowed at the sight of her, and its finger-length spikes furrowed like eyebrows. It had a red-scaled, sloping neck with a single row of progressively larger spikes until the largest was up to Cadrianna's waist.

Cinder was the drake's name, and it was daemonized.

The scourges were the Fallen's daggers in the night, but the daemon drake was his death dealer, the symbol of Lu Har's might.

Cinder was the roaring drake the day her former life had ended.

When the hood was finally removed, Cadrianna found herself in a darkened room with arches of umbra, hands bound behind her back. Her father and mother, Efan and Jensa Nightingale, were behind her, her brother, too. Emre and the regent and regentress sat across from them. A table with glass bottles between the family members. Liquids and tiny, solid pebbles in the cruets.

The firedrake snorted, a minute flame belched along the tower's walls in a lazy dance. Cadrianna loathed the creature.

"CINDER'S NOTHING MORE THAN AN OVERGROWN LIZARD. A FAILED HATCHLING OF THE ORDER."

Cadrianna smiled at the thought. *Whatever you say, Strix.*

The guards beside the tower's door neither moved nor spoke, standing still as she pushed on the onyx portal. Armored in grey-painted firedrake scale, blades of blackened steel at their hips, wheellock rifles in hand. They wore breathers with glass shields painted like sanguine skulls even though it was unnecessary without the mist upon the fortress in the sky.

Each had a role in life. Theirs to guard the secrets within the tower. Hers to end the living. They had chosen their lot. She'd been tortured into hers.

Behind the table was a tall man. He was elfirish and one of the most handsome men she'd ever laid sight upon. Thick black beard and long fine hair, his pointed elfirish ears delicate. A smile that normally would have sent her heart aflutter. But no, not now, not in this room. It was terrifying. Terrifying because he had all-onyx eyes.

It wasn't until after that day she'd learnt what that meant.

The man walked around the table as he pushed up the sleeves to his bloodred robe. He leaned toward Jensa Nightingale, a finger running down her neck and into the folds of her torn tunic. Her father swore and the man backhanded Efan.

"WHY DO YOU STRIVE TO REMEMBER THIS MEMORY OVER AND OVER?" asked the Strix for what must have been the thousandth time.

"For Brynn." Thestile's words ran through her head, '*Never forget the truth of who you are.*' Who was she?

Her muffled boots slapped against the mosaic floor. Cinder's tail briefly flicked past the door she'd just entered, the barbed point slashing. Columns held up the grand structure as she crossed the open atrium, guards next to each, rifles held in wait.

The man stepped closer to her brother, Caridin, who's eyes were fearful. Grabbing his chin, the elfirish man turned Caridin's face side-to-side, examining it. With the slightest of nods, thick-armed Imperium torturers appeared from behind, lifting her brother, legs kicking furiously.

The torturers—shirtless orcir with bulging, green-skinned muscles, and stiff leather aprons—chained Cadrianna's brother to the table as Caridin thrashed against the metal links. He tried, O, her brother tried to fight. The beautiful man lifted a pair of bottles, uncorking them. The unforgettable tang of sulfur met her nose.

"Cadrianna," a voice came from behind. "My scourge has returned. I hope everything went according to the needs."

The Strix let out an ungodsly hiss like a cornered draconem.

In the gloom stood a man. Long black hair neatly combed around a face of creamy brown, and was still as impeccably beautiful, despite long centuries. Age did not touch this man, even though he had only been rebirthed by the Divine some fifty years ago. Beard thick and pointed, elfirish ears poking through the thick tresses of pitch. His arms were in the opposing sleeves of a dark burgundy robe that pooled the ground like a basin of blood.

Lu Har, the Fallen. Daemon master. The bloodkin and last great void aetheurgist once of the prized city of Eminence in the reign of the Last Godsking. A man most feared in the Mistlands after his hateful rebirth from Nocturne's Pit. Her master.

Instant rage filled her upon the sight of him, but it was swallowed by furious desire. Hatred ever-deep, vengeance on the tip of her tongue in contradiction to the need inside. Her lips almost curled into a snarl, but she forced her face to calm. Like a tamed dog, but if left free to do as she would, her bite would be lethal.

"The head of House Richtel is dead." She tapped her foot, the Strix was still hissing.

"Wonderful," Lu Har said without a trace of emotion. "And of my dear Thestile?"

The beautiful man glared at Emre. "Where is the Seal?" Cadrianna's beloved stared back, his face bruised and bleeding. "You won't like it if I have to ask again. Where is it hidden?"

The son of Drenth bowed his head, dark curls sagged in sweat. Looking up, his eyes smoldered. The bodies of the regent and regentress lay discarded, their corpses consumed by void aetheurgy.

"Never," her husband said defiantly.

Efan Nightingale pleaded with the torturers from behind as they took Jensa. Chained her to the table, but Cadrianna's husband held his tongue until the moment she would never forget for all of her life.

Why couldn't he just answer? She would never forgive him for this.

"The contract has been fulfilled." Inside she seethed but held the glass façade. "My team has also felled dozens of rebels down in Bar Stock."

The Fallen's beautiful face watched her, those delicately angled cheeks, slightly slanted brows. Such perfection upon a creature so evil. She loathed him, desired him equally, but Brynn's face appeared in her mind. As did what happened to her mother, and to her poor brothers. The Regents Benld. Emre…

The elfir sadly shook his head. Her father began to sob as the man poured the contents of the bottles onto Jensa's body. The scream, that's what she remembered. Flesh burning, smoke of pure white. Her mother kicked and flailed, but the chains held her tight.

O Zenith, she would never forget that scream. Never forgive Emre for doing this to her. Why?

She made to leave now that her report was complete, but the Fallen glided in front of her, his long robe undulated as blackened mist drifted from underneath. "You're late in returning. You should have been back hours ago."

Her father was next, her mother's lifeless body tossed aside, broken and burnt in a corner. Steaming. Tears streamed down her face as her father was slammed onto the table, his favorite shirt ripped open. Her father fearful. Cadrianna only wept.

"Where is it?" Those words forever there.

"Please," Efan Nightingale implored through strangled sobs. He didn't fight it, just lay there on the table staring deep into her eyes, a sad smile upon his face. Telling her, no, imploring her to remain strong.

Emre held his tongue, still. At least tears rivered down his face. He'd always been the calm one, but now he was stone and steel.

A shrill scream burst from her father. A smell of char ingrained into her memory. Forever.

"Tell him!" Cadrianna screamed to her beloved husband, begging for it to end. Emre shook his head, drooping in sorrow. She hated him then, forever.

"Two deaths do not go quickly. Nor do these rebels."

The Strix was now openly growling like an angry firedrake in her mind. Bonded they were, linked since she was twenty-one. Mind, body, and soul. One in the same.

"But of course." Lu Har's wicked lips parted in a smile, voice melodic. Face smooth as fired clay, impossibly beautiful. And hateful all at once. *By the Pentax, why did They grant such a beautiful face to such a daemon?* This was why she never trusted the word of the gods. They didn't care for such things. "I don't like delays, Cadrianna."

It took the torturers grabbing her before Emre finally gave in, by this point, her beloved husband had been tortured, his arms were gouged by aetheurgic rends. Blood covered him from head to toe. This 'Seal' as the man called the item, Emre told them where to find it. In Drenth's desert. The mines held the Temple of Mother Marrow. As was the Forgemistress of Life's sacred Hammer.

And the beautiful man thanked him, smiling like it would all end, they would be free Cadrianna had thought then.

But it was not to be.

The elfir snapped his fingers again, and the orcirish torturers cut her beloved's throat. Blood spotted her face. Tears of copper and salt went unchecked down her cheeks as she howled.

Then came a woman, a shade within the arches, holding her child, Brynn. Pale as a Kanjan blizzard, the woman's hair silver, pointed elfirish ears, dozens of bracelets affixed to her wrist.

"Master Lu Har," the woman said. Her gaze moved toward the chained Cadrianna, and she gasped despite herself. The woman had two different colored eyes; one entirely white, the other black as pitch. A bikrome, a seer of Bliss and Brio. A marked contrast to the darkness all around them. "What of the babe?"

Brynn, no, not her daughter.

She learned his name then, the beautiful man. Lu Har. The Fallen.

"Bind her." Lu Har's fingers roamed Cadrianna's face as she cried when the woman nodded and took Brynn from the room. "Take this one for my flock."

For seventeen years she had lived among the murderers of the Nightingale line, her familial heritage. They had given her a choice: live and kill or die. The hatred in her heart burned black even then. She had been a devout believer in the Pentax, but that day her devotion had shriveled. She would live only to seek a way to kill Lu Har and save Brynn. Cadrianna had slain dozens, if not hundreds in the Fallen's name. She'd murdered men, women, and children all in his name. It had been duty, her training, her art. She'd done it all without conviction, no remorse, only two things drove her.

For revenge. For love.

But her vengeance had to wait, for they had taken Brynn to make her compliant. Locked deep within the Fallen's tower, in a dungeon Cadrianna had never found on her own, only when guided blindfolded. Brynn was constantly tormented should Cadrianna refuse to obey. Her daughter was dying and alone, grown into a woman forever bathed in hurt. For seventeen summers her poor daughter had suffered, and that had only steeled Cadrianna further, added logs to the raging fire within. She would get her revenge. And she would free Brynn. The moment would come, she knew it by the Pentax, it would come. That much she believed.

But only if she could shove the disgusting love within her breast aside. She was drawn to Lu Har, bewitched by him. Yearned to please him in any which way.

Gods, she hated herself for it. For loving him and the monster he had made of her.

Cadrianna's glare cut through him as if it was made of blades. "I've been compliant since the day you brought me here."

She shouldered past. Not many dared defy the Fallen, but she'd spent the better part of her life silently fighting him, waiting, biding her time. Loving him. She would endure his demands, her heart's demands, even though she was disgusted by herself, by the pangs of desire. Bear it in the knowledge she would one day stick the Strix into his daemonized heart, the blade he had gifted her.

Many feared his magic, his mastery of aetheurgy. Of Lu Har's control of daemons borne of Nocturne's Pit. His army on the precipice of being unleashed upon the free lands.

But not her. Never her.

She wouldn't allow herself to be driven to fear by him like many others were. He would die by her hand and then, only then, would Brynn be free. She would use his magical blade upon him, feasting on his blood. She would kill that love she bore, that hateful thing that she couldn't be rid of if she tried. The Pentax had cursed her. Love and revenge.

Until then, she'd stay true. For her daughter.

She didn't look back as she marched toward her personal chamber on the lower levels of the Fallen's tower where all the scourges laid their heads. Under the main level of the tower were rooms that filtered into the innerbelly of Gargantua like an ant nest. Hundreds of rooms were stacked upon one another, an endless maze if one wasn't familiar. Torture, training, meeting, laboratories all were there.

Rooms housed poisons, weapons, money for bribery, clothing and silk. Everything the Fallen's scourges might use for a contract and stores for his army. Others for Solanine's scientists to create more deadly weapons.

Her chamber was the size of a prison cell. A bed filled with straw, a chest for her personal items, a wardrobe tailored for her to be worn while on contract, and a nightstand with an aethecite-powered reading lamp. It was all she needed, unlike the citadel of Thestile.

Cadrianna unclasped her cloak and tossed it on the bed. She unhooked her belt and cast it down as well. Pulling off the black-painted, firedrake scale cuirass, she untied her brown-black curls, letting her hair fall to her shoulders over her thin undershirt.

Drawing a thin, golden chain that held a small key from around her neck, Cadrianna unlocked the lid to her chest and pulled out a silver hand mirror and an ivory comb that had belonged to Emre's mother. It had been one of Regentress Alandy's most prized possessions, given to her upon Cadrianna's marriage to Emre.

Mirror in hand, her thoughts turned toward killing Thestile as she ran the comb through her hair. "Death comes for everyone," she taunted her reflection in the mirror.

"It does. Mors expectet," the Fallen said as he pushed through the door of her chamber. "Richtel's and the betrayer's bodies were just discovered, and word is already starting to spread. Soon the rest of the Houses will agree to free my army against Kalderim."

"Get out."

Instead, Lu Har sat upon the bed, his legs sandwiching hers as he looked up at her. He put a hand upon her thigh, rubbing it. "You've grown since I first took you into my flock." His fingers traced the contour of her hip. "Do you remember when you were brought to me?" He smiled, handsome and inviting. "Do you remember the nightturn your family was killed before your eyes?"

Blood dripped from her face, her beloved's blood. Sprayed from his throat in spectacular fonts. O Zenith, she hated Emre for what he wrought her, but by the Pentax, she still loved him. Always would.

Loved and hated. That was the lie she lived now.

"Yes. I can see it on your face. You remember every painstaking minute of it." His hand roamed higher. She didn't move, she wanted his blood, wanted to see it shower her room. To lay bare the truth. Wanted him. "You live that moment in your head every day. Every moment, every detail."

She trembled inside, truly trembled with the resounding hatred, undeniable love. Why now? Why today?

"Do you remember why you were taken?" He inched closer, knees touching, his face level now with her bosom. His hands ran up her taut stomach, grazing the bottom of her left breast, near the scars of her Void Form he himself had cut into her. Burning fire ran through her, burning desire for that's what fueled the void. Desire. "You're so beautiful, my Cadrianna." His fingers pinched her nipple through the undershirt. He licked his lips. "Do you know why I spared you?"

"CAD, DON'T."

She held still; she would not break. She would endure so she could kill him. But also to kill the love she bore for him. How could she love such a monster? Why would the Pentax curse her so?

"You look just like her. Jensa Nightingale was the most alluring woman I'd ever met. Most of Thullyr are. More titillating than Regentress Alandy Benld."

"CAD, FIGHT IT. HE TAUNTS YOU TO CONTROL YOU."

"Best lay I ever had, Jensa."

The walls around her soul crumbled in an instant.

A sigh from the Strix.

She lunged, her body a blur as her Void Form burned, the runic scars on her chest flamed as blood oozed from the cicatrice. She grabbed Lu Har by the throat, the Strix flew from the sheath on her bed and pressed its blackened steel just below his jaw, seven other blades swirling over her head in a tornado of anger. They slammed into the stone wall above the Fallen's head. Red welled at the elfir's neck from under black metal sharpness.

There was no fear in the Fallen, only mild amusement. "This is why you were chosen," he said in a calm voice. "Because of your natural gifts. But also because you are special beyond your limited understanding. It comes from your Nightingale blood."

Confusion settled around her shoulders, she tried to blink it away. "Lies!"

"LET ME ENJOY HIS SOUL. TOY WITH IT, I CAN. I'VE WAITED FOR NINE HUNDRED YEARS TO SAMPLE HIS SOUL."

All-onyx eyes grew large as the dark of the void filled her master. A pressure crushed down on her. She winced under the onslaught of his aetheurgy. Cadrianna struggled to hold him. Gods, he was so strong. Unyielding. Undaunted by her puny fight.

"I can see it, Cadrianna Nightingale." Aetheurgy pulsed, his aether fought hers. The Strix blade wavered, dropping inches. "You have a gift none else have. You have lived where others would have failed. The truth of things kept hidden for centuries. It is in your blood."

"Fuck you." Her arm tingled and her veins swelled as if they would explode.

He chuckled, the apple in his throat kissed the trembling blade. O Nocturne, his face was gorgeous, even now. The pressure loosened.

"You're mad. A liar and a killer." She recalled the blade from his neck and tossed the Strix onto her bed, the other blades still stuck in the wall. Her heart hammered at her ribs. Why did she love him so? "But so am I. Trained to be the hand of death in your name. I fulfilled the contract on Richtel and of Thestile."

"The contract isn't complete to my needs."

"Find someone else."

"It doesn't matter what you want, my Cadrianna. You were born to kill. It is in your Nightingale blood. Of the mist. Godsblood. Flesh of the void must take its ilk. Do this and Brynn is freed."

Brynn…

"I DON'T TRUST HIM, CAD."

She didn't trust Lu Har either. But she imagined the blade jabbed deep into his heart. That baleful heart spilling baleful blood, her revenge complete. Brynn freed; her own soul released from the torn loves of her life. Emre, the betrayer and beloved. Lu Har, the forbidden evil and desirer.

Both tore at her soul, at her heart. "Never trust the gods… who do I have to kill?" Her hand rose toward Lu Har's cheek, his soft beard tickled her palm. *O Zenith… Nocturne… why?*

"It's time to end the Gutter King. Bring me his head, free Drenth. Free Brynn."

For Brynn.

Then she surged forward, her lips met the elfir's in rancorous desire. Giving in, as always. Gods, she was more monster than he.

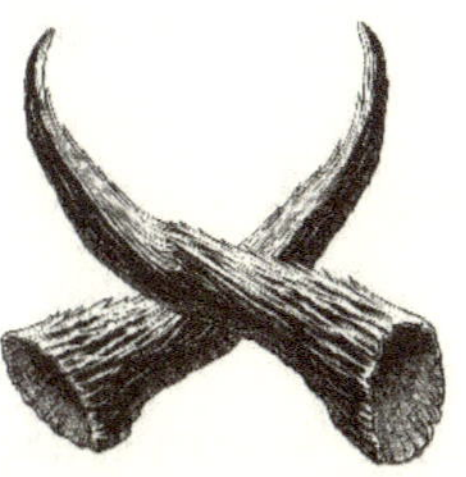

XII
LOJEN

"WAIT, RU."

Lojen grabbed his sister by the arm and dragged her back into the doorway of a red-bricked haberdashery.

"By the Arbiter," Ruane growled as he squashed her against the inlaid window.

Lojen shushed her like she was a clod fumbling about in the dark trying not to wake the hatchlings. She was like a keg of aethecite, ready to explode. "I can't tell if those are rebels or Imperium soldiers 'round the corner. They look dangerous either way."

They'd spent the better part of the day heading toward the rebel safehouse. The ruckus caused by the rebels at nightturn had long since ended, but the war for the city still waged tense as Imperium soldiers did an organized sweep. The drakken siblings had to hide for long hours in alleys and abandoned doorways or crouched with stinky vagrants. It was nearing evenfall when they'd come upon this alley in Marketside.

And it appeared they weren't alone.

By the obvious broken front window and dead bodies amongst the haberdashery, they weren't the only ones searching for the Gutter

King and his rebels. In the alley next to the haberdashery were four people. The alley was darkened, nary an aethecite lamp or neon of *Aere*. Shadows within shadows. All he could make out was the four skulking in the dark. A proper place to hide the entrance of the rebellion.

"What are we waiting for?" Ruane breathed into his earhole, hot and vapid.

"I can't tell wh—"

Just then, a camera drone zipped into the alley, dipping between the tall buildings. A bright ray of light gleamed down upon the four. It whirred above for the briefest of seconds and then zoomed away. But in that moment, in the barest of light given off by the drone, Lojen saw what he needed to see.

Imperium soldiers. And worse, a scourge.

This one's wary, Lojen thought. The scourge's head swiveled toward the mouth of the alley, almost as if hearing his inner thoughts. Lojen sucked in his breath and crushed Ruane further into the doorway.

"Who are they?"

"Humir we want nothing to do with."

"Yet, we're gonna follow them anyway?"

"They're going the same way we are. They must know about the safehouse?"

"Obviously, you dolt." She smacked him upside the head. "Look at the bodies in this shop. Efficiently killed. Don't be such a Scurred Hatch." It was a common insult among young drakken prodding one to do something they were clearly afraid to do. "What are we going to do?"

Lojen rubbed the flattened nubs where the horns should be. He was trying to think what their father would do. What a wardkeeper would do.

Ruane stuck her head around his bulk, looking at the surrounding buildings. An empty alley, no place for cover. Windows that didn't appear capable of opening without breaking the glass. That wouldn't do. A few balconies, that was about it.

"Well?"

He shrugged. "I'm thinking."

"We don't have time for you to think! The Gutter King's waiting for us. And if those soldiers are going toward the safehouse, he's in danger."

The scourge stopped, head turning back their way. *Broken shells,* he cursed inwardly. To Ruane, "Keep your voice down."

Both ducked back into the doorway, tense like fresh-made planks waiting for the scourge's gunfire to rip them to shreds like the poor sots who washed the haberdashery floor red. His leathery palms became balmy slick. Heartbeats turned to seconds turned to minutes. Silence. Easing slowly around the corner, he saw nothing. The soldiers and the scourge gone.

"Now's our chance, brother."

"I don't know, Ru."

They had to follow, even Lojen knew that. Honor bound him to this path and death meant nothing without those horns—though he preferred to keep on living if they had a choice in the matter.

He knew it, he just needed a kick in the tail to act more times than not.

Then, gunshots. The dramatic thud-thud-thud of aetheric bullets striking brick. A volley returned the first, more gunfire ricocheted, the sound was thunder.

"Guess they found the safehouse," Ruane muttered. Lojen gave her a look for stating the obvious. More shots, followed by grunts and cries of pain. "Here's what we're gonna do. I'll go fi—"

Lojen took a deep breath, cutting her off. "Stay behind me."

If drakken had eyebrows like humir, she'd be raising them as far as they could go.

Lojen crept with his scaled and spiked back against the wall of the shop, Ruane right behind as they slunk down the alley in the direction of the gunfire. It continued, the gunshots, unabated in rapid bursts, louder and fiercer the closer they stepped.

The buildings were the same as those in all Drenth's sectors where the miners resided, rundown and barely standing. Graffiti and gang symbols marred the walls. Cracked neon tubes of *Aere* lambent along the rooftops, some aerescreens still with pixels, but none shone down in the alley, which was gloomy muck in the dark of evenfall.

The shots stopped.

With a mischievous grin, Ruane raced across to the other side of the street. Lojen may have made the first move, but it wasn't an overly intelligent one, he realized. They were like sitting clay pots for target practice if anyone decided to retreat. At least on the other side of the alley were long shadows of black where the buildings blotted the minimal light in jagged strips from broken windows higher up.

Lojen sighed before overtaking her. *Too rash, Father. I seriously have tried with her.*

Around the farthest corner, Lojen noted the bodies heaped atop the pavement. Blood sprinkled the ground like someone had dropped a cask of red wine from one of the balconies above. All but one wore armored vests and mismatched miner clothing. Rebels.

A clash farther in the depths of the alley beyond. Ruane set her feet, ready for a brawl. A few gasps, a crash through broken glass. "I'm going down there."

"The Arbiter's bloody axe you are!" Lojen hissed. "You stay here."

Ruane leveled a glare at him and puffed out her chest, "I'm going with you."

Lojen rounded on her, standing to his full height, which towered over her by nearly a foot. "Stay here."

The vehemence in his voice must have startled her, for she scanned his eyes before nodding without a further complaint. Ruane gripped his claw before she hustled off into the darkness of the alley while he made his way toward the safehouse.

Heart pounding, fear rose in his stomach like Justice's wardrums. But he moved forward, finally displaying the eggs to do what he was meant to do.

His nostrils flared at the aroma of blood wafting up from the tunnel, the supposed entrance to the rebel safehouse. Bodies all about. Some were rebels, three were the corpses of the soldiers who were with the scourge, the leader nowhere to be found. Ripped asunder by metal death, bodies contorted as they lay, slumped against the walls. Blood coated everything.

It was quiet. No sounds down in the tunnel. No screams. Just emptiness.

Justice, protect me.

The tunnel swallowed Lojen as he was devoured by darkness. Luckily, drakken had excellent night vision, so even though there was a slight orange glow from quadran-sized, aethecite-powered orbs all along the copper tubes above his head, he saw near perfect as if he was standing in a field under the midday sun, nary a cloud in the sky.

Roughly hewn, the tunnel was supported by rounded concrete arches every ten paces. No doors or branches, merely a straight path to follow. Besides the aethecite tubes, Lojen noted a pair of water sewage pipes and a thin wire he figured was for communications.

Muddy bootprints pocked the ground, the freshest belonging to the scourge. Their scent mingled with the blood cloying his senses.

He drew his drakken longknife and stalked down the tunnel, only to reach a three-tined fork, each branching into further gloom. He squatted and scanned the ground. Nothing down the center, nor the righthand path indicated movement. No boot trails.

So, he went left, picking out the prints scuffed into the ground.

Minutes turned and he saw and heard nothing, just his own hurried breathing. He was on edge, worry crept in. A nervous worry. They were closer to his father's horns than ever before, so close, he could almost imagine the feel of the hard keratin under his talons.

A pair of corpses lay in the tunnel ahead. Lojen stopped well short, going to a knee, his back against the tunnel wall. Straining his eyesight to its limit, he surveyed beyond the corpses but saw nothing that would indicate a threat. Just the bodies in the stillness.

"You gon' sit here all day, Scurred Hatch?"

Lojen about near shed his exoscales as he jumped. Only after his heart retreated down his throat did he realize it was his sister and not the missing scourge. "I told you to stay back."

"Everybody's dead, brother," she said, pointing her longknife toward the corpses. "It doesn't take an augur to pronounce it."

"One of these days, you're going to listen when I say, Ru."

"Today's not that day, brother." And instead of waiting for him to take the lead, she bounded ahead.

Lojen stared at the ceiling as if toward Zenith's heavens. *Are You testing me to see if I'm worthy? If so, You have won.*

The dead bodies were rebels and they lay at the foot of the only door he'd seen in the entire tunnel. Rusted metal and ovular, a single slit with a closed hatch. A valve-like handle, rivets coated in grease.

Voices came from the other side.

Pressing his earhole to the metal portal, he tried to decipher the discussion. He jerked back when a deep, guttural string of words rose above the rest. Familiar. A laugh that sounded like a cross between a lion's growl and the hiss of a serpent.

"It can't be," he whispered in shock.

"Who?"

The conversation continued, men, these. The voice he remembered lost in the cacophony, blending into the rest. Imagination running amok.

Ruane nudged him. "Lojen?"

Standing like a statue, his mind warred with his heart. He should have shoved open the door, discover the truth, but he didn't know if he could handle it. His heart raced; his mind slowly starting to agree. The voice on the other side was who his core, no, his soul told him.

Gripping his longknife, Lojen shook the doubt away and grabbed the valve, opening the door with a squeal.

He didn't know what to expect from the safehouse, but it looked like something he could envision an army of rebels using for a brief period before moving to another secure location.

Along one wall was a map of the city, stretching from one end of the room to the other. Each street was meticulously rendered, overlaying the sewer and water lines. Districts were marked by different colors. Colored pushpins thrust into architectural drawings signified where bombs had been planted. Circles hastily drawn around the aethecite factories. A series of radio communicators were piled upon tables with operators at each. Opposite was row-upon-row of wheellock rifles and pistols. Reagents and aethecite pellets for bomb-making. Crates holding parch vials. Hand-cranked cannons with barrels that spun in rapid force. Racks held firedrake scale.

There were at least twenty rebels within the room, most of them on the radios. But none were the owner of the voice, all were humir. All were Drenth-born. They looked up as he barged into their haven.

Lojen's heart sank.

"Lojen Tevunson?" one man asked as he separated himself from the group.

It was the man from the courtyard, the one who'd escaped in the airglider as the bombs exploded all around Drenth. The Gutter King. Emre Benld.

His bearing was proud, regal even. Though he was of middle humir years, with slight grey at the temples and in his stubble, the man presented as a leader. His emerald-pupiled, brown eyes were hard yet sympathetic. His dusky face lined from the trials over the last seventeen years. A thin scar wrapped his neck, as if his throat had once been cut.

"And you must be Ruane Tevunsdotyr," the man said as his sister edged into the rebel den. "I'm Emre."

"You're supposed to be dead."

Emre Benld, heir to the throne of Drenth, grinned. "I aim to disappoint." The smaller man spread out his arms and hugged both, though it was like a child hugging a giant. Humir were curious like that. Then, the man's pocketwatch trilled. He pulled back from the hug. "Shoot up, all."

The Gutter King lifted a vial of parch to his lips and swallowed its contents. His face became strained for a moment. As one, the entirety of the rebel cabal loaded vials into their wrist injectors and shot the quicksilver of aethecite into their veins. Each shivered as the fire raced into their bodies.

"Did you enjoy the show?" Emre asked. "Solanine and Lu Har didn't know what hit them. Tevun said they'd run." The scion of

Drenth appraised him. "You look like him, you know. Color's a bit greyer, more bluish tint around your snout. But the eyes, they're certainly his. He always told me you took after him."

"But he has his mother's heart."

Four people stood in the doorway behind the Gutter King. One was lapin, half the size of the others, thickened legs and furry faced. The elfirish female, with her silver hair and eerie pale skin that glittered, was of Kanja, a bikrome most likely due to the goggles hiding her eyes. The tall one, all shoulders and legs, appeared to be a Kalderim-born elfir with similar features to the bikrome.

But it was the fourth, the one who'd spoken, who rattled Lojen's heart.

A drakken, and a mighty big male at that. He had exoscales that teetered back-and-forth between muted grey and blue in no discernable pattern. His eyes were the color of sunset pink and rows of tiny spikes poked around his sockets toward where the stumps of horns should be. His elongated tail lay flat like a lazy snake soaking in Zenith's warmth.

"Father?"

Tevun—wardkeeper to the Regents Benld, companion of the Last Godsking Canlon Carr, and thought dead for seventeen years— smiled, his pointed teeth protruding from his snout. "My hatchlings."

Ruane shouldered past in a dead sprint, dropping her longknife and leapt into their father's waiting arms. Drakken did not cry as men did, but her emotion was palpable, as was his own. She burrowed into their father's shoulder as if a young hatchling, her tail flapping in pure joy. Lojen couldn't help but smile as he went to his father. Tevun pulled him into a hug, the three of them joined tightly. A feeling he couldn't have missed more. Lojen couldn't believe it. After all these year, his father was still alive. Here in the flesh.

Thank you, Justice.

But an insignificant sound caused him to tense reflexively.

"Wait! No!" Emre shouted.

And then Tevun was shoving Lojen backward, tossing a surprised Ruane aside just as *Aere*-infused gunfire erupted within the safehouse. Lojen crashed into the racks with the weaponry, guns and armor raining down on him.

Bullets ripped through his father's exoscales, red splatter dousing the surprised rebels behind. The elfirish rebel crumpled to the ground with a wet gurgle. The bikrome and the lapin dove out of the way, same as Emre Benld. The men and women at the radios sought safety. Seconds later, the gunfire stopped, the killer out of bullets from the multi-barrel wheellocks held in both hands. Tevun sank to his knees before falling to his side, Ruane there moments later, screaming to Justice in hateful rage and sorrow.

Lojen thrust the pile of weaponry away and surged to his feet, head swinging toward the entrance, finding a single humir in the doorway, smoke climbing from the multi-barrels of their wheellock guns like cigarillos.

The scourge from earlier.

Tossing the weapons aside, the scourge tapped into Void Form aetheurgy. Lojen grunted as the scourge tackled him with inhumir speed borne from Nocturne's eternal hatred for Zenith and the rest of the Pentax Gods, hugging him close as they tumbled. Even though Lojen was bigger, the scourge's aetheurgy-enhanced momentum carried them into the gun rack.

This time, Lojen's skull cracked against the wall, and regardless of his drakken exoscales, a flash of jolting pain rocketed through his head. He tried to throw the scourge off, but found he couldn't raise his arms, they were lethargic and useless. Dizzying nausea crept up his spinal cord as his head lolled.

Then the scourge was off him, their body flying as someone bulled into them. Through the haze, he realized it was Emre Benld. The scion of Drenth bore into the scourge, his own aetheurgy blazing in his green pupils. The Gutter King pummeled the scourge with aether-hardened fists until the Imperium assassin lay still, blood pooling underneath.

Lojen crawled toward his father, trying to remain conscious. Pain in his skull threatened to turn his brain to mush. "Father…"

Emre crouched beside him, a sadness marring his face, agony in his aetheric eyes as he looked toward the bikrome crouching over her brother. Something passed between the Gutter King and the bikrome, something Lojen vowed to discover.

"Son," Tevun said, reaching for him with one talon while the other fought desperately to hold in his precious lifeblood. Red sprinkled his father's snout. Tevun gripped Ruane's claw as the blood poured from his mortal wounds. "Protect …nn."

And then the wardkeeper's eyes closed, Ruane bellowing in misery. Lojen felt empty.

XIII
ASHE

STUMBLING FROM *THE Colosseum*, Ashe tripped over the first (and only) stair and fell face-down into the hard-stone ground.

"Fucshen steppsh!" Her head was a clouded jumble, the spirits and mead tincture formed a pounding headache at the back of her skull.

"Ashe, you hurt?" Hands pulled at her tunic, turning her over.

She flopped onto her back and squinted through the darkness at Gargantua hovering above. A face poked past the floating fortress backdrop, Wren, who crouched over her.

"I'msh notta… your help." Coherent sentences seemed tricky at the moment.

"Get that little bint up," a feminine voice announced through the haze of Ashe's drunkenness as they stepped out of the tavern and hobbled past the two girls. "I thought I told you, girl, don't make a fool of me. Neenah LeFleur's reputation is all she's got. You've already ruined half my evenfall, don't deserve the other half. Make me bloody rue the godsdamned day I brought you here. Get her somewhere off to pissing sleep, you voidspawn prick-suckers."

Captain LeFleur marched off, Roland, Tris, Doll, and a young girl whose name Ashe hadn't gotten, followed after, none seemed to register Ashe's predicament. The hobgoblin twins Zig and Zag stopped to help Wren drag her limp body from the overpowering gravity of the ground. Or at least she figured they were themselves; she really only saw blurs and pops of color.

"I shhaid I wassh fine," Ashe lisped as the two lifted her by the armpits. She cocked her head, staring openly at one of the voidspawn twins. "Who… fucsh are…? And why… are… me?"

"She's bloody buggered," one said over her head to the other.

"Proper buggered," the second replied.

"You were supposed to watch 'er."

"No, I wasn't. That was suppo'ed to be yous. Cap'n even said 'Zag, you watch over her this time, this little bint made a pissing mess last time we were in town.'"

Zag pshawed so loud Ashe rubbed her ear in response, even wiping away some of the spittle. "She said notta, you firedrake's tit. I specif'cly 'member her saying 'Zig, you gots Stray Cat duty a'night cuz none else watch her drinking.'"

"Cap'n didn't say that," Zig argued. "That was supposed to be yous, and yous the firedrake's tit 'round here."

Ashe's legs wobbled as Zig let go of her arm. Zag nearly dropped her as he, too, stopped. She lazily plopped down to the ground. Slumped was more like it.

"Say it again, you… you…"

"What? Firedrake's tit?"

"Enough!" Wren shouted. Through her drunken haze, Ashe miraculously noted an air of authority around the thief-girl. "You bloody fools just shut up! You're more annoying than a fly on an ogre's ass. Gods, I hate voidspawn."

Ashe chuckled to herself over the visual of two annoying flies around a stupid ogre, and as she did, the contents of her stomach rushed up to say hail all over the ground.

"Godsdamnit," a twin grumbled. "All o'er my new boots."

"Bugger yer boots."

Wren bent down and began to rub Ashe's back as if she was a child. To the arguing hobgoblins, "Off with you now. Go get her some water." It was a commanding tone, expectant of compliance.

"She's gon' need more than that," Zag cackled. "Stray Cat," followed by a furious belch. "O Zeni—"

"'Member that time, Zag," Zig overrode his brother. "The one whe—"

"Now!" There was fire within Wren's voice. Ashe wondered when the young woman had become so demanding, usually she was quiet as a dormouse, at least around the toughs of Slag's End. Afraid, almost.

It made Ashe want her even more. The mist seemed to agree as it spun quickly about her while the hobgoblin dummies ran back inside *The Colosseum*.

Though, to be fair, she was more worried about the vomit charging up her esophagus than Wren's tone. But the mist had other thoughts. As the pounding in her head raged, her fingers dug into the hard paving stones, and Ashe's insides curdled. The mist rushed over her.

Her pulmo exploded out in tarry bursts, the mist climbing her body and filling her mouth as the fog wended down her throat. She wanted to scream but couldn't. Wanted to cough but couldn't.

"Ashe?" The mist bubbled around them, enveloping the two young women. Ashe could hear Wren's breathing, quick and frightened. "Ashe, what's happening?"

Ashe thrust out her hand, warding Wren away from her. It was only the mist, her friend. Her companion. Her eventual death.

She envisioned the dead man at the tip of her dagger back in the Guilder's study. She dreamt of Wren between her legs. Death. Life. Bound together.

Discomfort, deeply rooted in her soul, bellowed in internal strife. The roar brewed from the ground through her feet and knees, up her tense spine, and finally into her brain. Shooting urgency, aching, and destroying.

O Zenith, it hurt.

Her arms shot out into the mist; it curled lovingly around her limbs, especially the one with the odd bangle, but the torment within her body wracked her. Back arched, head thrown abaft. A silent scream erupted. Her eyes squeezed tight to keep in the hurt, tears forming at the edges. Every rune tattooed on her left arm radiated in fulguration and snapped in flashes of lurid brightness. Right arm a shadowy black.

"Ashe," more frantic came the words from far across the chasm of Life, but she knew the girl was still beside her. Yet, they seemed leagues apart. "ASHE!"

Pounding headache, a thousand hammers all battering against her skull, echoes boomed as each forging head struck bone. Ashe clawed at her hair trying to make it stop. Body shivering, not from cold, but of empty life. The mist poured over her in great fonts, as if a giant was standing over her tilting a wine glass of effluvium. The healing, soothing, poisonous-to-all-but-her fog washed over in waves, covering her entire body in aether. It wrapped around her in a cocoon, the feeling of Life and Death.

"Ashe, I can't see you."

Distant the words were. But she didn't care. All there was was the pain. O, it hurt.

Her runes synapsed, striking aglow as *Aere* cycloned. *Ignis* burned. *Aquis* stormed. *Terris* rumbled. Body alight with the aether of Eminence's Shards. The Tenets rising and falling like the tide.

It hurt.

It felt like murder.

Murder.

O Zenith, was this the tithe for the Guilder's servant?

The mist drove into her and cleared away her drunkenness. The pain brought on a clarity.

Like a tragedy upon the stage, the actors set. Fade to black.

Slowly, Zenith's cock, ever so slowly the pain in her body began to recede.

It was flushed from her as rain clears waste within the aggers on either side of the cobblestone walk. Yet, the mist spun around her unending, unyielding. She opened her eyes, lids blooming with a sudden grey light, almost as if looking into a diamond prism anew. Her mind untangled the phosphorescence to form the shapes in which were outlined by the illumination. Clearer the pictures came into focus. Silhouettes hardened by the mist. Yet, it wasn't normal, there was no sheen, no aura around the forms sending her mind pictures of emotions and wants.

No, this was different. Darker, surreal. Visionary.

A cloaked figure appeared in the mist, a woman? Something held in their arms. A child. The babe wailed, they ran, throwing out their hand, aether sparking in fonts of *Aere* and *Terris*. Flung toward something chasing them. Daemons. Garbled words, the figure hurried. The child screamed bloody void, a fierce ray from within the swaddling.

The woman led her through the darkness, almost straight through a tunnel. Then stopped.

Ashe was there, within a tower. Marble stones as tall as she. All around was a vast open chamber, fluted columns holding aloft a massive dome covered in roots. High above a massive tree, so large, so encompassing, it felt otherworldly. A spire protruded downward from the ocular opening at the top like a stalactite, piercing the roots. A humir-sized crystal of all colors and none bathed the room in rainbow. Shadowy forms moved about her. People, she realized. A throne dripped red as blood. A single figure stood before the crystal; hands outstretched upon its surface. Their body blazed in pure white fire. Giving their life, the crystal taking it.

Her mind wandered the chamber, taking in the corpses of shades. She reached for the crystal with gossamer fingers. Hand going straight through the diamond-like object, piercing wails grew, sounding like that of the void. All around her the wails, the vision turned black like obsidian, then bloodred again. Back again to clear, the crystal reformed. The wails' tenor grew, near deafening, then a shatter. Under her hand, the bangled hand with the diamond eye, the crystal exploded in a thousand pieces. Her body shivered with the explosion. Mist poured out of the remnants, driving into the eye in the center of her palm.

And then she felt it, felt the pull of her own soul toward the cracked crystal.

The woman turned toward her, holding the babe, both faces hidden. *'Godsblood,'* she called. *'Daughter of the Pentax Gods and Nightingale. Royal blood, royal. Royal. Godsblood.'*

Zenith protect…

The mist circled around her, closing in and she was within the Sea of Mist. The setting changed; the actors ready for the next scene of the play.

The woman, hair billowing silver in the Sea. The child in her arms was asleep now, a quiet thing. The woman faced her. An elfir with pale skin, nearly see-through. Her eyes were bi-colored. One black, one white. The woman held her arm out and pointed.

Ashe looked.

She could smell the bog, taste the mustiness on her tongue. Swamp as far as could see, and a shadow hung over, where she saw the face of a man within the clouds. An elfir, his face resembling the woman's. Siblings. Glaring ice blue eyes with a pupil of yellow, hidden within was pain and suffering. A polished, thin, golden sword with semi-circles of braided gold was clasped in the man's hands, radiating the color of peridot. Shadows beside him. Figures tall and short. One with large keratin horns, the other flattened, elongated ears. Drakken and lapin.

The Sea of Mist turned crimson all the way up to the moon. Bright red it was, dripping with scarlet tears down into the marshlands.

Screams of terror filled the vision, not like the wails from the void of the Meadows. These were humir mixed with creature. Daemon eyes blinked within the mist. Gunfire burst, cannons blasted within the red Sea.

The man, drakken, and lapin waited, watched as the daemons surged toward them.

The woman and child fled the Sea, aether crackled all around the swamp. The daemons hounded her every move.

Close it was, so close she could feel the screams in her bones.

Please...

She blinked. A change of scene. A flip of vision.

Opened her eyes anew and was deep within a city.

Buildings all around her reached toward the sky. Cluttered and sprawled on the edge of a desert. A temple with a rolling dune like a wave in a circle through the sands. Hovered over the city was another city. Gargantua.

She ran, frightened. The bikromi seer and the babe huddled in the frayed streets, blood seeped from the bi-colored eyes like tears, puddling at her feet.

A man with tight curls and a scar ringing his neck, clenched his fists, stared at the hovering city as anger billowed from him like the wind. He had a crown about his temple, a king, a true leader. Royalty. His eyes were pupiled in emerald surrounded by sandy brown, the emeralds breaking as the sands behind him exploded upward, a giant vvyrm punching upward toward the floating city in behemoth rage. A hammer in his hand, a green crystal shattering.

He turned toward her, his face so familiar, yet never seen. A kindness in the smile. A remembrance of her past, the past she never knew. He reached for her, lovingly, carefully.

Father.

Blink.

Dreamland shifted.

A shadow filled the sky, blotting the sun into nothing more than a disk of haze. A city that was corrupt and powerful, full of sin. A dark-haired, drake scaled woman lay in a pool of blood, a black blade in her hands, gripped as the blade dug into her gullet. Black on black on black. Scourge. Onyx handle in the shape of an owl. An actual owl sat upon her dying breast with inky eyes, opened its beak, cawing at the bloodied woman. Perched upon her shoulder and staring at the owl was a nightingale, small and full-breasted, singing a song.

The bikrome with the child hovered over the Fallen's woman. Red like a garnet flashed within the cacophony as the dream pulled back and revealed a spewing volcano, its fire hot and searing. Leaned down, the bikromi seer did, turning the babe to face the blood-soaked corpse. The owl squawked and took wing, landing upon the bikrome's shoulder, examining the babe within her arms. The nightingale continued to sing.

Laughter filled her. Sinister yet alluring in the same manner.

Ashe stretched for the body of the woman; her face glossed with red. But below, caramel skin and soft curls clinging. A face such as her own with eyes like black roses.

She recoiled.

A mirror of her own face but older. Mother. Tears flowed down her cheeks. Salty upon her lips. Ashe cried.

"ASHE!"

Words from the living echoed within her cocoon, and Ashe reached for them. *Find me…*

Blink.

But the vision shifted once again, and she only saw open warfare.

Thousands of corpses littered the ground outside a vast dead city. Kalderim it appeared to be by the snowy peaks surrounding the walls. Rivers of blood washed bodies away from the gates, over the tundra of Kanja.

A dam shuttered the river closed, two bodies bobbed up and down. One, a drakken, the same one as before. The other, a lapin, beige fur coated thick with blood. Empty sight looking up toward the sky. Kneeling beside the pair was the elfirish man from the marshlands, the peridot faded from his aura. He cried, screamed, ready to plunge the golden blade into his own flesh in unholy sorrow.

Blink.

She cringed, but a giant hand reached down for the great city, scooping into the earth, rising into the sky as a tall, beautiful man cackled voraciously. An elfir with a bloodred robe. Arms spread, aetheurgy cracked with power.

No…

The bikrome and the child were there, alive anew and hiding. The crying babe pulled close to the silver-haired elfir, soothing and shushing. *'Calm, Godsblood, calm.'* Her other hand let loose waves of aether. The mist curled around, blinking and spiking. She was surrounded by blue green, almost seafoam.

She was focused on the man.

And he turned to her, his eyes were as black as pitch, he smiled a smile that could melt the harsh snows of winter. Hair and beard black as jet. O Zenith, he was beautiful. The Fallen.

A second man appeared behind the beautiful one, a tall man with bugling muscles and scars all over his face. She felt like she recognized him, but he was not the man she had known. It couldn't be Evander. But those eyes, the lust hidden within.

Evander held a sword in his hand, a very similar sword from the elfirish man in the Sea of Mist. Though this one glowed orange, almost like flames as lightning ruptured across the sky. He slashed at the dark-haired, beautiful man with the blade, disemboweling him from shoulder to groin. The Fallen fell apart, a great red shadow spilling from his innards and settling about Evander's shoulders.

Ashe crowed as the vision of Evander thrust forth the blade and it pierced her skin. The pain erupted in her, the mist crying out with her. She went to ground, her knees slamming into the stones below. Ashe groped around her gut, searching for the wound.

But it wasn't there.

Blink.

The people shadows, wafting along the cityscape. Booming resounded. Walls crumbled as the city shook. Destruction fell all around as two figures appeared in the vision.

Raven-haired and tattooed along her left arm, a bangle vividly gold. Herself. The second figure, petite, flowing hair. The apparition from the void and Gargantua. Solanine.

The two collided as the city collapsed all around them. Solanine laughed, physical appearance shifting to that to the woman with the owl and nightingale, then to that of an orcir, then flesh sloughed off to reveal a snake-like creature underneath before reforming into the throat-slit man. Her father. Runes of the Four Tenets glowed red upon red-black exoscales under Drenth-born flesh. The mist clashed and raged with aetheurgy. Wails of unearthliness descended upon her. Her ears splintered from the sound. A fire brighter than any other exploded all around, a giant red boulder rained down on them.

The childbearing bikromi woman was crying now, huddled over the child who'd gone silent in her arms. A small, full-breasted nightingale fluttered its wings down and landed upon the babe. The bikrome reached for the small bird, petting it while it sang its song to soothe the babe.

Tears welled once more, and Ashe struggled to breathe. The mist spun faster, closing in on her. The visions faded and so did her sight. She fell forward, blackness creeping in.

The last thing she saw was a man walking through the mist, ground burning and dissolving as he went. Blackened and dying, leaving only death in his wake. But behind him shot green and fertility, replacing the Death with Life. He beckoned for her to join him, and she was tempted. He would bring her solace, to the end.

He was a god. One of the Divines. She didn't know which. Death meant one. Life meant the other.

Their hands reached for one another; fingers almost touching. And then she tumbled.

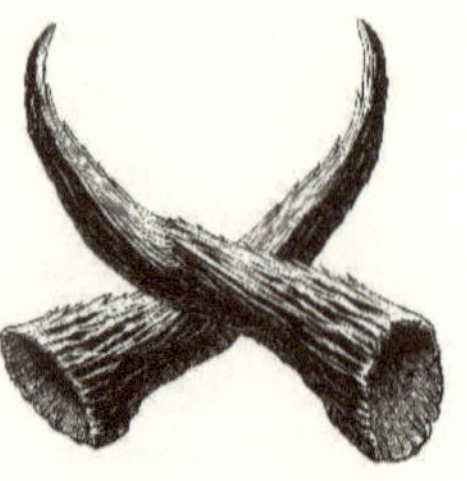

XIV
LOJEN

HIS FATHER WAS dead.

It was a thought that ran through Lojen's mind for the better part of an hour as the survivors of the scourge attack tried to bring order back into semblance. It destroyed him, seeing his father lying there upon the safehouse floor. Didn't want to admit to himself what lay before him, rent apart by the Fallen's soldiers. Didn't want to believe that things were so blatantly wrong for years were in fact now come to roost. Didn't want to comprehend that no matter how hard it had been before, nothing could have prepared him for the sight of it.

Ever since word had reached Merj of Drenth's conquest and the murder of the Regents Benld, Lojen had built a vault to house his emotions. A vault in the far corners of his mind and heart, a place where he could put his father's memory. Never forgotten, but a spot where he could hide his despair and sorrow. Life had to go on, for him, but especially for Ruane. He had to force one talon in front of the other and keep moving. The way of the wardkeeper.

But now, his soul—and his everlasting anguish—was laid completely bare.

Drakken rarely cried—it was said that the Arbiter had given His favored draconem the gift of silent mourning. An emotional armor in the face of protecting their wards. And yet, Lojen still had tears in his eyes, his mind in a fog as he helped cover the bodies of the dead.

There was no time to grieve, he knew he had to shove that grating sorrow deep down into the void and use it as the spark upon which his fire was to ignite. It's what Tevun would've expected of him. What Justice would expect of a worthy heir to the wardkeeper's horns.

When the Fallen and his cursed pets atop Gargantua crashed down to the earth, and when the Imperium was destroyed, then, and only then, would he be able to properly grieve.

"What now?" asked the lapin named Wick. The furry creature held a compress against the tall Kanjan elfir's shoulder. The elfir, named Finnus, had been hit by the scourge's gunfire, pierced through one side and out the other. Finn groaned noisily. "Cut it out, needle dick, ain't nothin' more than a scratch."

A numbness had settled over the safehouse, their apprehension taut like a stretched hide in the sun. A subdued silence had accompanied the lot of them as they picked up the pieces of the attack in their own ways.

"Em?" Wick was speaking to the scion of Drenth, who was crouched over the bodies of rebels, Tevun amongst them. Emre had pulled the bloody tarp back and was caressing the pallid face of the drakken wardkeeper smeared with blood. "Em?"

"I say bugger the Fallen and hit Gargantua with everything you've got," Ruane said. She was huddled in a corner, her drakken longknife shoved tip down into the floor. His sister simmered with barely contained rage. "You've got to have more explosives than what you did this morning at the factories. Hit them hard and fast."

"They can't do that, Ru," Lojen said as he extricated himself from his spot across the room. "It's directly over the city. They'd kill thousands."

Sadness painted across Emre's features, appearing to have aged considerably in the last few hours. The man idly scratched at his forearms, which Lojen noticed were covered in scars. "He's right. Can't risk the fallout over Drenth. Not yet at least."

"What's that supposed to mean, humir?"

"It's truly begun, eh, Em?" Finn questioned through a series of groans, really playing up his injury. It was almost comical. "I'm fine, by the way, thanks for loving me enough to ask. But Tevun?"

Both drakken stared at the scion of Drenth, who nodded solemnly. "He knew."

"Knew what?" Ruane asked…

…just as Finn exclaimed, "He knew? By the Pentax, Em. How?" Then the elfir glanced toward the bikrome sitting cross-legged beside him. "No doubt Val knew. She bloody knows everything!"

"It's not important, Finn," Emre said carefully, and Lojen realized the elfir was treading on ground Emre wasn't prepared yet to walk. "The plan was the plan. Regardless of what happened. All of this was expected. Not wanted but expected. I had hoped to avoid this bloodshed but apparently hope no longer follows by my side."

Lojen picked at a thread of his furred trousers, thinking. "My father knew this was going to happen? His own death?"

Emre sighed as he looked down upon the deceased wardkeeper. "Not exactly. There was a spy within our camp. Me and Finn nearly got nicked weeks ago. We needed to know who it was." A stray glance toward the bikrome. "And if there is more to be found."

"Imperium waiting for us at the mines," Finn added, cursing as Wick tied off the bandage at his shoulder. The elfir stifled another as he slowly rotated his arm in its socket. Instantly the bandage turned red, causing the lapin beside him to curse, untie it, and staunch it anew. "Buggers knew when we'd hit it."

"Tevun had been under the assumption for years that the Imperium would seek to infiltrate us," Emre continued. "It was slow at first, jobs and hits gone wrong. Soldiers beefing security, that type of thing. But recently, it's gotten more specific. Every job thwarted. The only thing left to us were the gangs. All our parch reserves were going stale. If we didn't start working with the gangs, we'd be ground to dust in a matter of weeks. So, Tevun, Finn, a man named Kephren, and me came up with a plan to oust the spy."

"At the cost of my father's life!" Ruane spat.

"We understood the danger, your father included. We took an oath, a blood oath. Not to give up the fight until death takes us. It was only until recently did we realize Keph was the spy, selling secrets to the Imperium. Solanine has been after the gangs for years. This was the chance to appease the Fallen." He looked toward the bikrome once more. *What did she know that only Emre did?* "But scourges? That means Kephren might have been the sacrificial lamb to get the rest of us, the gangs included."

"Then what went wrong?" Lojen asked.

"I wish I knew." A tenseness in the response. A wrongness, Lojen observed. A half-truth. *What game do you play, Emre Benld? Is this the bikrome speaking?* "We missed something."

"Broken shells, humir," Ruane cursed. "Of course, something went wrong. My father's dead for real this time and Lojen's horns by right are still missing. That bitch Solanine will pay. Then I'll gut the Fallen where he stands." Ruane pulled free the longknife and made toward the safehouse hatch.

"There's more to it than you know," Emre said softly, Ruane stopping and looking back at their father's ward. "Finn and Val are Kalderim-born. Of the Dunleith line."

"Broken shells!" Ruane cursed again. "Heirs to Kalderim's Golden Throne. Just great." She threw up her claws in angst and stalked from the room, brushing past the pale elfirish seer.

Lojen stared at Emre, but the man was still like steel. His face was hard, his eyes harder. There were secrets wrapped around him. What secrets, what truths, Lojen had no idea. There was a calm calculation, Lojen just needed to find out what it was.

"My father tried to tell me something before he died," Lojen started, looking toward the bikrome. "Protect something. I know some about bikromi seers." There was hesitation in his voice. "Can you recover it? Recover what he meant, that is?"

"I'm bikromi, not a willow wraith."

"Aren't those the flame-haired witches who shimmer in the mist and turn you to mushrooms?"

"You're an idiot, needle dick," Wick said as he pressed the bandage hard enough to elicit a squawk from the Kalderim elfir. "No wonder your parents wanted you far away from the Golden Throne."

"They didn't toss me aside, rabbit. I left that gutter-fire just for the opportunity to bug you."

"And I thank He Who Fathered the World every single day for that blessing." The lapin scrunched his nose, making his elongated teeth protrude in a frown.

"For your information, brother-friend," Val started, then paused and added *'moron'* under her breath, "Willow wraiths are the evil Lords of the Shimmer Isles and specialize in all things Void Form."

"But they also possess the ability to breach the veil of the void," Emre finished. "Just like the bikromi with their Vision Form. The voice of the Pentax."

"I'm not sure I can do anything of such nature," Val said quietly. "I've never tried. I don't know if Bliss will listen."

"You did it once, Val."

"I had Tevun's help then, Em. He sang the Hymn in aid. Alone, I don't think I can bring him back." She looked toward Lojen, who stood there in confusion. The bikrome took a breath. "I'll see what I can do."

Her smile was sympathetic but also warned that she wasn't certain she could do it.

Lojen nodded and then hustled down the tunnel, catching Ruane just before she reached the exit, grabbing her by the arm.

"Leave me be!"

"Ru, calm down," he begged, surprisingly calm even though they'd gone through the void and back this day.

She tried yanking from his grip, but he held her in a vice hold. "Let me go, Lojen."

"Not until you calm down and tell me what's wrong."

"What's wrong? Are you bloody daft? Father's dead and we're in a rebel den with blown apart bodies everywhere." That feeling he noted in her since being banished from Merj bubbled within her, that doubt creeping about. The fire for revenge still raged brightly.

Lojen released her arm. "This isn't what I wanted for you, Ru. For either of us. This is not the life you were meant to live."

"You call this a life? You're more of a fool than I thought." She took to the steps.

"Where are you going?"

"To kill anyone associated with Lu Har. Starting with Solanine."

"That's foolish. You'll be dead before you can set foot into Marketside. You don't think this place is being scoped out, even now? Think, Ru. Don't you see, Father wanted us to be here. He wanted us to be here to help Emre."

She was halfway up the crumbled stairway when she turned. Her exoscales bristled. "You would trust that humir? He's the reason Father is dead! You heard it. They planned it. I won't trust him."

"Then trust me." He needed her more than she would ever know. And as much as she didn't want to admit it, she needed him too. They were all they had left, they needed each other. "Ru?"

She bellowed as she drew her longknife and proceeded to plunge it over and over into the wall, leaving gaping holes in the crumbling stone of the sewer tunnel. Panting with rage, she left her longknife buried to the hilt in the mortar. "I want Lu Har dead, Lojen. I want them all dead."

Her anger was a detriment, an obstacle she needed to learn to control. Control it just as Lojen had done. He wanted revenge for the death of their father, they talked at length over the years about what they'd do to Solanine and the Fallen.

But now, here amongst the dead, including their father, Lojen, somehow, was cool as the dark side of a room. "I know."

He grabbed her and pulled her into a hug. Her anger wilted and she fell into his arms, the fire quelled and washed away.

"I miss him, Lojen."

"Me too, Ru," he said, holding her tight. An older brother protecting his younger sister.

Ruane pushed back. "You lead. I'll follow."

He gave her a skeptical look. "If you say so."

"Don't be such a Scurred Hatch, brother. I have sense now and then."

He laughed and they headed back toward the rebels.

"Emre, we wan—" Lojen stopped midsentence as they walked back into the room only to find the bikrome standing above the body of their father.

The bikrome's lips were pressed to his lipless snout as if kissing as man does for emotional gesture. The many bracelets around Val's wrists glowed fierce gold and silver. Ruane let out an aggressive hiss.

"Ease," Emre said, noting Ruane's astriction. "She's trying to summon Tevun's soul from the Meadows. To learn what he can impart before his soul is lost to us forever."

"By kissing him?"

"She isn't kissing him," Emre explained. "Vision Form relies upon the aether bound to one's soul. Living or dead, aether exists within each of us. Not as the mist and its poisons. But from the very life within. Bikromi seers must be able to breach the veil between their soul and another's. To breathe it in if you will."

"Gross."

Emre's shoulders moved up and down as he chuckled. Men were such odd creatures. "For those not used to it, I suppose it could be odd."

"Odd is not the word I would have chosen."

"Zip it, Ru. We have to know what Father was trying to say. This is the only way."

Val's goggles hung around her neck, nestled into the falling silver of her hair. Her eyes were closed as her back was bent near perpendicular to her feet, entire upper body stilled, breathing deeply. The bracelets glowed, alternating between silver and gold, pulsing like a heartbeat.

And that's when Lojen noticed the connection. It was subtle, but the bottommost bracelet let out a tiny vibration that left a ripple in the air. The ripple bounced off the billow created by the one just above it, creating a complex crest of wisps only visible by the shifting of the bracelets' glow. Aether, he realized. The shimmering aether moved in rhythmic pattern from each bracelet up toward Val's hands, which throbbed arctic blue down her arms, up her shoulders and into the white of her cheeks, down to her lips.

At the precipice of the bikrome's mouth pooled the aether, like a dam holding back a river. The many bracelets on her wrists twanged as she released the magical shimmer into Tevun, almost as if she was breathing the aether directly into his lungs.

"Any of you hungry?" Finn asked suddenly, breaking the tension that had built. Everyone but the bikrome looked at him with varying array of surprise. "What?"

"You wanna eat at a time like this, needle dick?" Wick glared at the big man with those beady buttons for eyes.

"What? I'm hungry, I can't help it. Em?"

"No, Finn's right," Emre said, turning toward the drakken siblings. "This may take a while. This isn't like a normal séance with the Pentax. She's trying to find Tevun in the Meadows. We could do with some rest."

"Drakken don't need to sleep like you, humir. I want to stay in case this bikrome does anything untoward."

"Truth told, Ruane, your father said the same thing many a time." The mention of their father made Ruane snap her jaws tight. A sorrow rolled through Lojen's innards. "But Val will not harm him, you have my word."

"The word of a humir means nothing."

"You have the word of your father's ward."

Ruane growled, "Fine, but if she does anything, I'll tear her limb from limb."

"I'd expect nothing less, Ruane. Come."

The Gutter King led the small group deeper into the safehouse. Though darkened by the aethecite lamps turned low, the safehouse was much bigger than Lojen originally had guessed. The room with the radios and the weapons was only a third of the entire safehouse.

A pair of barracks with bunked beds was on both sides. There were trunks for each bed bunk, most of the linens finely made, a few of the injured rebels taking up others while a handful cared for the wounded. Meeting rooms with small, rounded tables and chairs came next. Some had giant maps of the city along the walls, others had scribbled whiteboards. Things like the times of watch changes of Imperium guards, pass codes to important buildings, routes for Imperium supply chains. Intricate drawings of Gargantua and its tethers. There were some hand-drawn schematics of the aethecite mines, with notes jotted down all over.

Finally, they reached a crude mess hall. There were many long tables with benches. A couple of rebels sat eating. There were racks with dried and canned food. Boxes of fresh fruit and vegetables. Meats hung from poles, all smoked and salted for extended supply. Gallons of water and ale were stacked from ground to ceiling. An aethecite-powered stove top with metal pots and pans. Finn and Wick went straight for the racks of food, and Lojen's stomach unconsciously approved.

Emre sat at one of the long tables, Lojen across from him. Ruane took a seat beside him, her talons gouging lines into the tabletop.

"You said my father planned this entire thing?" Emre suddenly became pensive as he nodded. "The Fallen has taken everything from us. We want to help you, but we can't do anything if you don't tell us the truth. Why were we summoned here?"

XV

EMRE

"AFTER THE FALL of Eminence, when my father came to Drenth," Lojen picked at his plate while he spoke, "he said it was duty that bound him here. Said he owed it to the Last Godsking. I never knew why, and he never gave his reason."

"Here you go, Em." Wick placed a plate and mug of ale in front of him.

Ruane ravished her meal by stabbing sausages with her longknife. Finn tried to offer Ruane some boiled eggs but the drakken gave him a rueful stare.

There was hesitation in Emre about Tevun's hatchlings. Not because they couldn't be trusted to see out what he needed of them, but because the truth of what was at stake was a heavy burden to bear. Tevun had done so out of his obligation to Eminence, the Great Crystal, and to Canlon Carr.

It was unfair to place that mantle upon their shoulders. Yet, Emre had no other choice. Just as the burden had been placed on his.

Emre sighed. "Truth told, Lojen, I didn't know until after the Fallen conquered us why Tevun specifically chose Drenth to ward." The elder drakken looked up while Ruane picked at something between her teeth with the tip of her longknife. *Both borne of the same brood, yet so completely different of a hatch. O Tevun, both sides of you.* "Not many knew this after the Fall, how could they when the records were erased in the upheaval of the old world…" he tapered into silence.

The thought of Tevun caused Emre to smile fondly. All the lessons. All the teachings before and after the invasion. Love bound Tevun to him, not duty. His duty was required elsewhere. As was Emre's.

Sensing his reticence, Lojen pushed away his plate of untouched food. "My father would send communications once Drenth stabilized after the Fall. Mostly his love. And when you were born, he told us everything in his life led up to that moment. That his honor bound him to you, the child of Edric and Alandy. That you were his true ward, his calling. It was everything to him. And in his stead, now, that duty has passed to me."

"To us," Ruane said.

"To us," Lojen confirmed. He gripped Ruane's taloned claw. The younger drakken tensed slightly, some underlying animosity between them. On Ruane's part, not Lojen's.

When he was finished with his plate of greens, Wick stood. "I'm going to go sit with Val. Bring her some food."

"I guess I'll take cleaning duty," Finn offered as he stacked the plates and retreated to the sink.

"My father intended for us to do something here in Drenth. I am honor bound, as is Ruane, to do whatever it is you command of us, Emre. Til our death."

Tevun, my friend, he's more like you than you ever knew. "I hope it doesn't come to that." Honestly, he didn't know if he possessed the strength to carry it through to the end. How Val was able to, he wouldn't ever know. *Cad, forgive me. This is all for her.* "Aethecite is the lifeblood of the Mistlands," Emre started, banishing the thoughts of his beloved wife and child. Steeling himself for what was to come. "Without it, the world crumbles."

"Everyone knows that, humir." Ruane spat out the thing that had been stuck in her craw. A bone, it appeared. "Why did our father have to die? What's in Drenth that made him sacrifice his family and lead to his death?"

The young drakken was a spitfire. He hoped her resolve would remain intact. "Solanine intends to throw a party on Gargantua to honor the Fallen's annual remembrance of Drenth's conquest. When the Fallen started his war after his rebirth, he came to Drenth last. Spending decades gobbling up mega-cities all along the south before setting sights on us. Growing his Imperium until Drenth could withstand no longer."

"He wanted the mines," Ruane answered as if it was simple logic. "Take them and he controls the Mistlands."

"The truth is far more dire than that. Aether, Ruane. There is aether within the mines, the hardened ore." He drew out the vial of parch that Kephren had tried to con him with. He placed it on the table, its contents shined in the aethecite lamps. "Without the mines, not only does the Imperium control the source of fuel in all the Mistlands, but there is more." Emre tossed the vial into the air, then burned his aetheurgy. His hand whipped out faster than the eye could follow, catching the vial before it had completed its upward apex. "The mist is also borne of aether. Tell me, what do you know about Eminence prior to the Fall? The city, that is."

"The world's greatest civilization." Lojen's snouted face had a poignant look about it as he answered, the shadows of the safehouse plied over his exoscales. "High in the heavens of the Pentax it floated. A city like no other, my father once told me. Beauty unheralded. The Crystal of Life shone down from the highest spire in the center of the city. Everyone worshiped the Crystal as Zenith Himself. The All Father, He Who Fathered the World."

"Do you know what happened to a Godsking? What it meant to be chosen by Zenith to carry this honorific?" The drakken siblings shook their heads. "Mortals, that's all they were before Zenith chose them. Chosen because they have a spark within their souls. A spark of aether. The Scattered Shards have named it Godsblood. And this spark, if you will, is built upon the ideal that all Life and Death in this world is within the soul."

"The drakken are borne of aether," Ruane said. "All draconem are. Aether is our essence. There's never been mention of such Godsbloods in Merj."

"There is much in your lore that is kept from the unworthy."

"You mean only the wardkeepers know?"

"Yes, Lojen." Emre fought the urge to scratch at his scars, almost as if afraid he might tear the flesh from his bones. "Tevun broke an oath by telling me this. An oath to the Arbiter. But he had to, for it is the only way for us to defeat the Fallen."

Lojen pondered for heartbeats, staring at the table. "If aether derives within the soul, then the Godskings must have a greater purpose. Yes?"

A smile touched Emre's lips. "The Great Crystal is the source of all Life. But as you well know, life is fleeting in a harsh world. However, there is something within all of us, in our souls, that perpetuates our existence. Gives us life. Gives us purpose. Allows us to continue. This is aether, the true source of Life. And it was upon Zenith's chosen to give that life. Give that aetheric spark so the world could remain. Sacrifice their life for the rest."

"They had to give their lives?"

"It's called Soul Form, Lojen. The ultimate Form of aetheurgy. Those named Godsblood, those chosen by Zenith to bear this spark, they faced the ultimate sacrifice. By breathing their aether into the Great Crystal, the world was reborn. Each day transferring their lifeforce into the Crystal, growing weaker each time."

"Until the Fall?"

"A thousand years ago, two Calibrathian elfir were born. You know these elfir as Canlon Carr, the Last Godsking, the other as Lu Har. Bloodkin they are, but the man who became the Fallen was jealous of not being Zenith's choice. Jealous of the glory heaped upon Canlon. Jealous of being withheld Soul Form. Lu Har was one of the greatest aetheurgists during Canlon's reign. And it was Lu Har's jealousy that brought the end of Eminence."

"How?"

"Tevun only spoke of it once, for even the great drakken wardkeeper couldn't explain it. There is another crystal. One just as important to all existence as that of Eminence."

"Like the Shards?" Ruane had her taloned claw under her jaw, elbow propped on the tabletop, leaning toward him. Intently listening. Perhaps Emre had misjudged her.

"The Four Shards are but pieces shorn from Eminence. Facets of Life. But there is another. A dark crystal. The Crystal of Death. Noctis." Emre paused to let the revelation sink in. Even he hadn't been able to grasp this truth when Tevun had told him, for it betrayed everything ever believed in.

"Noctis," Lojen breathed.

"A corruption. Housed in the never-ending void of Nocturne's Pit, in the very dank, deep recesses of the Meadows. Death's Crystal. The source of Void Form aetheurgy."

"How do you know all this? My father would never have gone to the other side."

Emre glanced back toward the front of the safehouse. "Be at ease, Lojen, your father only knew of Noctis, nothing else. Valeria Dunleith is the one who knows the truth of this second crystal. Val was one of Canlon's closest confidants. But she was also the lover of Solanine when Val was barely out of her formative years." Lojen let out a small gasp while Ruane hissed. Emre heard Finn labor a disgusted sigh. "The woman you know as Solanine was one of the first to turn join with Lu Har. But Solanine is no woman. Solanine is a blooddrake." The siblings growled deep in their throats. "Yes, Solanine of Drenth is merely a blooddrake wearing the scales of some poor woman stolen along the way. It was Solanine, the blooddrake, who helped Lu Har engineer the downfall of Canlon. Their Void Form aetheurgy corrupted Canlon's Soul Form. In the end, they were too much. And when that end came, Eminence cracked, and the mist poured forth."

"And my father?" Lojen asked. "He must have known Solanine was a blooddrake. A blooddrake, by the Arbiter…We, I mean us on Merj, have always believed blooddrakes to be a myth."

"Blooddrakes are no myth, Lojen. They are very real. And very dangerous." He toyed with the vial of parch, rolling in between his fingers. "In the time before the Fall, Four Shards of the Crystal of Life were housed within towering temples upon the four corners of Eminence. At the base of each Shard was a Seal."

"You speak of the Four Tenets of Aether."

"*Aere*, *Aquis*, *Ignis*, and *Terris*," Emre said with a nod of affirmation. "The four dogmas of nature."

Lojen stiffened. "That's why he came to Drenth, isn't it? My father? The *Terris* Shard is here, in the desert?"

"Tevun always bragged about your quick skills of deduction." Although Ruane seemed to disagree under her breath, which caused Emre to chuckle. "But you are correct, the emerald *Terris* Shard was discovered in the desert, in the mines. In the Temple of Mother Marrow."

"But how is that possible?"

"When Eminence cracked, Mother Marrow reacted. Yes, the mist poured through the veil from the Meadows, aether altered forever, but She made it so Lu Har couldn't yet win his war. Eminence had to be protected at all costs. With the last of his strength, Canlon Carr summoned all the aetheurgy he could contain, gifted by Mother Marrow and others of the Pentax. The purest of aether filled him and sucked him dry, killing Lu Har in the process. As the great city fell from the heavens about to wreak its destruction on this world and creating the Mistlands, his final act came forth. The Four Shards and their Seals were thrust from their temples to the four corners of the earth. There to be hidden in the destruction and thus sealing the city within a tomb veiled by the very veil that separates the realms of Life and Death. And there they remained. Until now."

"But if Lu Har was killed, how can he be alive now?"

"The Divine, Lu Har's master, rebirthed him fifty years ag—"

A loud scream, almost unearthly, echoed from the front of the safehouse, cutting Lojen's question off. A deep wail of ghastly chorus.

"Guys!" Wick called from down the hall, "You may want to come in here."

They screeched to a halt at the sight of Val hanging in the air inches above the ground. Rime dripped from her arms, streamed from her hair. Her head lowered to gaze down on them, her black iris a deep abyss of pitch, her white a brilliant achromic. Below her feet was the corpse of the wardkeeper.

For Emre, he could only give in to the desire to scratch at his arms. Finn stood next to him, mouth agape.

Val's mouth opened but did not move as a voice drawled forth. "Lojen, Ruane. My hatchlings."

It wasn't the melodic voice of the goddess Bliss, but instead Tevun's. She'd done it. Val had found his soul in the Meadows.

"Father?"

"Forgive me… forgive me," the sepulchral growl of the former wardkeeper came from Val's open mouth. "There are no words… no words to which I could say to make this make sense. You must trust in the Arbiter. In your ability. In your soul."

Ruane went to her knees, her drakken tail flicking in distress. "Father… I… need you." Her head lowered as her body convulsed in what Emre realized were silent sobs. Lojen crouched beside her, a talon upon her back.

Val's head moved as if Tevun's soul was controlling her, a concerned parent looking upon a crying child. "You've the fire to excel in Justice's trials, my hatchling. Remember this truth. Without it, a wardkeeper is nothing."

Lojen's gaze went to the corpse before quickly averting his eyes. "Father, I don't know if I'm worthy, but I will do whatever is demanded by the Arbiter to right this wrong. This injustice."

Elfirish face blank but the pride in the voice strong. "He will deem your worth, Lojen. The way of the wardkeeper is your path. Always had been. Justice will lead you to His doorstep." Val's left arm rattled; the seer-sight bracelets glimmered as she pointed toward Emre. Emre felt Finn's fingers entwine into his. "My ward is now your ward. The Seals are your duty. Protect the Seals at all costs."

"I will, Father," Lojen said with conviction.

The bikrome's body began to shudder in the air, slowly at first but grew in ascendancy. Finn barged forward. Val's mouth began to close, her form slowly lowered to the floor. Finn caught his sister, pulling her close.

But before her aetheurgy severed with Tevun's soul in the Meadows, her face turned toward Emre. "She is… hounded." Voice fading, as if drawn back into the void. Wails of the dead began to rise in its wake. "She must… know… you. The Seal… won't… break… otherw—"

And then Val's body went limp in Finn's arms.

Emre stood there silently, contemplating. *Is this wise, Tevun? O, how I wish I had you still beside me. I don't know if I can do this.*

Lojen, now kneeling beside his father's body, ran a loving talon across the stumps where his father's horns had been.

Tevun had told Emre once, that Zenith gave the first wardkeepers their horns. The most holy of honors awarded a drakken heir, only the strong able to withstand the power associated with the horns. Over the millennia, wardkeepers were seen as beacons of truth and justice, honor bound to keeping the peace. Loyalty was given only to those deemed honest. Friendship was only given to those deserving. Should an heir not prove worthy, the horns wouldn't serve, and another wardkeeper found. Tevun's line had been the only line never to be broken, for his horns traced back to the first wardkeepers. For the first time in that ancient line, the honor was in peril of being broken. The shame that would come should Lojen fail to find the horns would be death to his family name.

Do I dare risk this shame for him? This is my folly, not his. Nor Ruane's.

Lojen went to cover his father once more, but instead sat back on his haunches, only to realize Emre watched him.

Emre knelt. "He was the most loyal soul I've ever called friend."

"He was…" Lojen couldn't finish the words, the pain too hard Emre realized. The weight on his shoulders was too heavy to carry.

They remained in silence for long minutes, neither saying anything before Emre gently pulled the linen over Tevun. *I have to use him. Forgive me.* "Lojen, I need your help."

"The party?" A nod. "Is that what Father wanted of us?"

"Finn and Wick have already secured roles within Gargantua as servants, as have others in our company. Val and I have forged invites." He scratched at his forearms while he talked, almost too vigorously, avoiding looking at Val, for if he did, he knew his voice would betray everything. "But we need stealth as well. When the Fallen's soldiers discovered the Seal of *Terris* in the mines, they took it. We need someone to climb the tethers and sneak aboard Gargantua. From there, discover the location of the Seal. We also believe that Lu Har has your father's horns and Mother Marrow's Hammer."

"Drakken make good climbers," Ruane said…

…while Lojen gasped, "The Hammer exists?"

"From what we were able to glean from our spies."

"The Forgemistress' Hammer is but a legend."

"It is no legend, Lojen Tevunson." Val leaned against her brother as she rubbed her arms as if trying to warm them. "I've seen it. Bliss has shown it to me. If a Godsblood should ever hold the Hammer, the Seals can be broken. This is what Lu Har desires most. If he should break the Seals to Eminence, Lu Har will win."

Lojen glanced down at the linen. "You are my ward, Emre Benld. I cannot falter. I will see my father's duty continued. I'll protect the Seal with my life, should it come to that."

"We'll do it," Ruane said.

Emre gave the slightest hint of a smile, just the tiniest twitch of the lip. "It'll be dangerous."

"I don't care," Ruane spat. "I want Lu Har dead. I want the Imperium to burn. Bugger your danger."

"Two thousand feet in the air with nothing between you and the ground."

"So what? We're dead if we don't get those horns. And the only way to get them is through Lu Har's corpse. Right, Lojen?"

Lojen already looked terrified, but he had no other choice. "We're in, Emre. What do we have to do?"

The Gutter King of Drenth, the heir to the Regent's throne, last vestige of the Benld name stood. *Cad, beloved, I...* "First we need a catalyst."

XVI
CADRIANNA

CADRIANNA OPENED HER eyes grudgingly as someone banged emphatically on the bedchamber door.

She stirred, a kink in her neck from falling asleep on Lu Har's chest. The Fallen's arm was still draped around her bare shoulders, his pulse rising as he came awake from the hammering outside. The scars on his breastbone, runes to the Divine Himself, tingled her palm as he shifted irritably underneath. Aether was never static, always alive. His all-onyx eyes slid open, narrowing toward the door.

"What is it?" His voice groggy, a little stiffness in his jaw.

"AFTER WHAT HE'D DONE TO YOU, I'M NOT SURPRISED IF HIS TONGUE MIGHT BE SORE FOR DAYS," the Strix joked in that unfunny way it had.

The inky blade lay on the bedside table, never far. If only she could've jammed it into Lu Har's ribs right then and there, ending him. But Cadrianna grinned, not at the joke but the thought of killing her hateful master. By Nocturne, she rued every moment she shared in the Fallen's bed, it reminded her of the murder of her parents. Of Emre. Of Brynn.

And yet, share his bed she did. Why was a question she never could answer. As much as she wanted to bathe in his blood nearly every waking minute to free her daughter, Cadrianna couldn't resist him. Something bonded her to him. A need, perhaps. Perhaps something else she couldn't decipher.

Only death would release her from him. His death or hers.

Inwardly, she seethed, appalled at what she'd done with Brynn's captor. A dishonesty to herself, to her vows to Emre. Why couldn't she just end it? What made her stop every time she had the opportunity. Gods, none of it made sense.

There was a muffled response outside as the Fallen tossed the linen sheet from his torso angrily. His bronzed flesh glowed in the soft embers of the dying fire in the far corner, black hair and beard tinted orange in the firelight. Lu Har threw a gold-worked, bloodred robe around his shoulders, tying it off before making for the door.

Cadrianna sat up, propping pillows behind her back, settling in as Lu Har drew open the metal entrance to his personal chamber in the highest spire of Gargantua. They had moved venues, his room far more comfortable than hers. She stifled a yawn, using her knuckles to knead the muscle. Her gaze fell upon the black-bladed, owl-handled knife. She snatched it up unconsciously.

A scourge stood head bowed beyond the door. A bearded scourge. Ratko. He did not raise his beady eyes to look at Lu Har, rather in her direction, ogling her nude state. A sick grin spread across his ugly face as Ratko said something low.

"SOMETHING ABOUT THE GUTTER KING. HIS HIDEOUT POTENTIALLY DISCOVERED."

"Hmm."

Before Lu Har could respond, Ratko was shoved out of the way by a short figure adorned in a green stola that flowed behind. The newcomer sneered at the scourge, took in Lu Har in his robe, and then sought out Cadrianna perched upon the bed. The womanly façade on the outside smirked but the ancient beast's true eyes bore nothing short of hate.

"One of my scourges has found them, the Gutter King and his rebels." Solanine barged into the bedchamber, slamming the door on Ratko, "but it appears your attention's been squandered on whores."

Cadrianna met the other's baleful stare, holding her chin up, betraying nothing of her thoughts. She hadn't moved to cover her nudity. One of the scourge tenets hammered into her upbringing ran through her mind. Strong as stone. Give nothing. She wouldn't rise to the insult by responding like a petulant child.

Fucking bitch.

"CAREFUL OF THIS ONE, CAD. THEIR BITE IS THAT OF A DRACONEM. BLOODDRAKE."

I know, you fool, she responded with a thought.

Solanine was a blooddrake, Nocturne's lesser order of draconem. Under the flesh of this female humir was a creature with exoscales, fierce and intelligent, cunning and clever.

And a massive pain in the privies, Solanine.

A memory flashed, one from that fateful day.

As her babe was taken from her, Emre's body not yet cold in death, a nine-foot blooddrake slithered from the shadows. Snout elongated like a firedrake's, but without the curved beak, finger-length pointed teeth. Red-black interlocking exoscales etched with aetheric runes, larger on the breast and belly, smaller like a snake's along the forelimbs. Rounded protrusions covered the crest from nostrils to above the irises, morphing into a pair of two-foot long, keratin horns sloping backward and upward to a point.

"Master Lu Har," the blooddrake had said, "what of this one?" The lesser draconem's eyes turned on Cadrianna, a chill running through her.

"She's to be trained, Solanine," the beautiful elfir had responded. "Bathe her in Void Form. I want her for the Strix. Break her."

"Can I have her scales instead? They are so pretty." The Fallen said nothing. Head back, sighing as a taloned claw combed over the keratin horns as a lady might run her hand through her hair. Deviousness in those all-onyx irises. "As you wish. I'll see her bathed in blood."

The Strix let out a noxious whine at the memory. The beginning of the end for Cadrianna, then. A hatred growing. Burning, now.

Drakken in the Mistlands openly wore their exoscales with pride, not afraid to boast the Arbiter's favor. Those blessed with the massive, magical horns of a wardkeeper, were prominent and respected by all in their devotion to the Pentax's peace.

But blooddrakes, like Solanine, used their aetheurgy to control blood and flesh. To hide and connive. Only a handful of blooddrakes had survived the Fall of Eminence, maybe less than twenty in total, for their corrupted aetheric essence had left them sterile. One or two, it was said, had turned to Canlon Carr's side during the war, what happened to them, none knew. Cadrianna knew of a few who were under Lu Har's thrall, and they were out in the world, using the flesh of others to further the Fallen's plans.

None but Lu Har and a few others, such as Cadrianna, knew the truth about Solanine. Nearly every person in the Mistlands saw a smallish woman who was a skilled aetheurgist, but little did they know of the voidspawned beast within. The scales—what the blooddrakes called the hides of man—Solanine wore was but one of many faces stolen over the centuries. With their aetheurgy borne of the void, blooddrakes were able to meld their essence and their bodies to those of man, thus taking over said person's life. A joining of souls, bonded by the runes carved into flesh and upon exoscale.

Magic was the blooddrake's aether.

"And you presume much, Solanine, to come to my chamber without invitation," Lu Har said coolly. The elfir's aura crackled like glitching aethecite engines.

"The Divine sends us as He wills, Lu Har."

"The bent knee is oft where to find the weak."

Although barely up to his chest, Solanine stood toe-to-toe with Lu Har, both staring each other down. Both were alive when Eminence fell, there at its breaking, but they bore little else in common. In manner and in presence. The Fallen radiated strength, whereas Solanine constantly sought it, which was why the drake served him.

If Solanine thought anything of the rebuke, the blooddrake didn't show it. Instead, Solanine marched across the room toward a small table with bottles of wine, lifting an ewer of red wine to the scales' nose. Satisfied by the vintage, Solanine took the entire ewer and sat down upon a plush sofa near the fireplace, tossing the greenish hem of the stola to one side with a flourish, and drank a hearty pull.

Smug, that's what Cadrianna would describe Solanine as. A smug wretch. A jealous wretch, at that.

"A COILED SNAKE IS ALWAYS A THREAT TO BITE. SAME GOES WITH A BLOODDRAKE."

Any more pearls of wisdom, dear Strix?

Lu Har was visibly annoyed even though his outward façade was blank. Cadrianna knew him too well to know he wasn't pleased with Solanine's uninvited presence. "Well?"

"It appears your little rebellion problem has finally moved their pieces across the board," Solanine said, chugging more of the dry red, gaze straying toward Cadrianna's bare legs, engorging in drink and view. "The Gutter King has set the stage as you've wanted. And per my scourge, the Godsblood has crossed the first threshold. The die has been cast."

"And the Eye?" Solanine confirmed with a nod. "Then the Gutter King will make the next move. I've buried the Oculus in Qarthage, it awaits what happens here with the Godsblood. Drenth teeters on the tip of a knife blade, we at the center. Seventeen years isn't long enough to erase the minds of the city. Fifty out of the Pit wasn't enough but it'll have to do. The people of Drenth know Gargantua's might firsthand, they wouldn't have forgotten. This Gutter King may think he knows, but he's not his parents."

Parents?

"BE WARY, CAD. SECRETS ARE KEPT, SECRETS ARE STOLEN."

What do you know about this, Strix?

If the Strix could shrug, that's what her mind relayed. *"I DON'T..."*

"They'll hit the Temple, Lu Har, at the mines. The Seal isn't safe. The Gutter King is not his parents, but smarter. You know this." Solanine's all-onyx eyes found Cadrianna's, anger and hatred within, but simmering below was something else. Knowledge kept. "Even your scourge probably knows this, else why's she here?"

Cadrianna's lips quirked, her grip tightening on the knife in her lap. Her mind raced. *Who is this Gutter King, the real man behind the hidden throne? And why now? Strix?*

"CAD..."

"I'm not pleased," Solanine continued, the wine sloshed as the blooddrake pointed with the ewer, "with how you've handled Drenth these last few years. Allowing this rebellion to sow while you've planned your war on the Dunleiths and Kalderim." There it was again, the glimmer of something else underneath. A desire once lost, Cadrianna calculated its meaning. She knew, of course, what it was. Or what it had been. "You're growing weak, old man. Spending too much time with whores."

"Watch yourself, Solanine. The Divine cares not for liars. Neither do I suffer them. Cross at your peril. I had you rebirthed first, recall. I could have left you in the Pit."

"Threats are beneath you, Lu Har," Solanine laughed. "Remember, you came to me to bring down Canlon Carr. Not the other way around. Same with Drenth and the Ben—" Lu Har cut the blooddrake-in-woman scales off with a sharp hand signal, apparently to keep the other from saying something in front of Cadrianna. "Ah, you've not included your whore. You tread a fine line, Lu Har. You know she's a Nightingale; her blood will always be that of the First Wife no matter how many times you stick your prick in her. Her child won't keep her tied to you forever. You know this." Yes, jealous, that was what it was. And palpable, too.

Brynn…

"We must move forward," Lu Har said as he poked the dying fire with a spell of *Ignis*. The flames leapt from his hand along a blackened mist and the ashes in the fireplace grew. "I want you to go to Oldport Basin, Solanine. After this deal with the Gutter King is over. Go to Oldport and find the Seal of Brio's *Ignis*. *Terris* is right where it needs to be. Right where Mother Marrow placed it."

"Rinkhal and Ialtris are in Port Sin," Solanine said around a mouthful of wine.

Port Sin was the local sobriquet of Cadrianna's home city of Oldport Basin. It was well known for, well, sin. In fact, Cadrianna's family had once owned an arena down there called *The Arbiter's Axe*. It was a place of blood and death. Before her entire family was killed, the entire Nightingale line cleansed by the Fallen.

"Finally, you send me to a place I deserve," Solanine gleefully said. "Rinkhal will be pleased we are prepared to move for *Ignis*. Long has Rinkhal waited. Same with Ialtris. What of Bliss' *Aere*? Will you now move on Kalderim? Datura waits for us, Lu Har. Or of Justice's *Aquis* in the Voidlands?"

"Cadrianna." Lu Har's normally stoic visage turned soft as he faced her. There was a deeper bond between them, something that did, indeed, border on love.

Unless she'd miscalculated the signs. Love was a funny thing, the poets said. *Why would I say that, now?* Cadrianna felt her heart flutter once in confirmation. *Godsdamnit.* No, she loathed him, wanted to kill him. Gods, she did love him, too. *Why?*

"The time has come. The Gutter King would rend Drenth further if we don't put an end to him. You know what to do."

It was almost a question, like she was some two-bit trollop sharing his bed, not the Imperium's most deadly scourge. All because of the blood in her veins. Nightingale blood. She wanted to scream. Strong as stone. Give nothing.

Because of Drenth, her entire existence was tied to this forsaken desert voidhole. Taunting her, as the former wife of the heir. Of Emre's betrayal. Of her family killed. Of Brynn.

She fingered the daemon blade as the Strix began to weep in the void, a sadness filling her as it filled the blade. *Why?*

"Go then," Lu Har said knowingly, pulling her from the sorrow defiling the black daemon blade. He had sown that hate; he knew what consumed her. He knew she would end him given the chance. "Spill blood in my name. In our Divine's name. The Gutter King shall weep when he sees your blade at his throat, my scourge. Do this, and Brynn will be given a week's reprieve."

The mere thought of Brynn's constant pain being stayed for even the slightest amount of time gave her purpose. A sickness where the only cure was a betraying lover's word. O Nocturne, how she would give anything to spare her daughter. "I want to see her first."

The liar and deceiver that was the Fallen nodded. "Done. See how merciful I can be?" She silently rose from the bed and made to leave but Lu Har held out his hand. "Come to me."

Her entire being wanted to resist, but her feet went regardless. His large hand encircled the small of her back and pulled her into a kiss. A passionate kiss. Her mind revolted, he had just threatened her daughter, but her body, nay, her soul, couldn't resist the desire. That repulsive desire that filled her. She felt his manhood stir behind his robe, her own lust rising. Solanine laughed softly and drank the wine.

"CAD, THIS ISN'T YOU." The Strix was sad, an odd feeling from a sentient daemon borne of the Pit. *"DON'T DO THIS. BRYNN WOULDN'T WANT IT. STAY CLEAR OF THE GUTTER KING, YOU DON'T WANT TO UNEARTH THINGS YOU CANNOT STOW AWAY ONCE LEARNED."*

I have to, Strix. For Brynn. Cadrianna smiled daemonly as she pulled away. One more kill, that's all it was. Then she'd be with Brynn. She'd find the way. "Allow me to see her and I will kill the Gutter King with pleasure."

"See how easy your life is when you don't resist?"

I will kill you, Lu Har. I will kill whatever this is, this vile love.

As she donned her own robe and moved toward the door, Solanine mockingly applauded. "Thanks for the show, whore." The blooddrake-in-humir scales dug into the cleavage of the gown, pushing away an obsidian pendant, and produced a silver quadran. The drake tossed it to Cadrianna, who snatched it out of the air. "Whores cost but a pittance these days."

Showing the lioness she was, Cadrianna patted the blooddrake's arm lightly. She leaned close, her robe split hauntingly low. Solanine' eyes went to the runes carved into her breastbone. Life and Death. Aetheurgy and blood. Savior and giver, protector and shield.

"Dearest Solanine, you may have broken me once." The Strix appeared, pressed against the scales' jugular. A tiny pinprick of blood welled under the sharpened tip, blackened aether accompanied the blood. Her smiled widened as Solanine scowled, "and the Fallen's dog you may be, but call me a whore one more time and I'll make certain you use your tongue again. Your true tongue, blooddrake."

Cadrianna withdrew the knife.

Solanine snorted as the drake put a hand to their scales' wounded neck. Lu Har said nothing as he watched with an arm resting on the fireplace's mantle. There was slight amusement in his eyes. Yes, it was amusement and avidity.

"You wound my pride, daughter of the beast," Solanine called after her as Cadrianna left Lu Har's chambers. "Come to Oldport with me once the Gutter King is put down and I'll show you a grand time in the City of Sin. In your old stomping grounds. I'm certain they can put you to use in the Red Moon District."

Cadrianna, scourge of the Imperium, knew she'd have to kill Solanine. One day, she'd silence Solanine in retribution for the pain she'd been through by the blooddrake's clawed talon.

Solanine. Ratko. Lu Har. Thestile already dead. Then her soul would be cleansed. But today was not that day. Another, more important death was waiting for her.

For Brynn.

"CAD, DON'T..."

XVII
ASHE

ASHE'S BRAIN FLUTTERED when her head smacked something hard, jarring her from her drunken stupor. That something hard was the canister of mist affixed to the belt of a female vicar.

She groaned, only to realize the lower half of her face was covered with a protective mask. Resembling a mastiff muzzle, it was inscribed with the connector runes of aether, and it cut her off from her aetheurgy by blocking her access to the mist. It also meant she couldn't talk either, and that angered the void out of her because she had a plethora of curses ready. She reached to pull it free, but found her hands were tied behind her back. She was stuck. And her head hurt something fierce.

The vicar carried her through the streets of Drenth like a sack of grain. Her head jounced and she squinted to see where she was, and found they were nearing Bar Stock.

When she'd first come to Drenth, Ashe had figured the factories in Bar Stock might be a good starting point to discover about her past because she knew people standing in one place all day long greasing cogs or riveting plate allowed for gossiping hens to cluck. Little did she know but come to realize within a second of stepping foot into a factory constructing airgliders, there was no talk. None at all. The workers diligently did their tasks, faces forlorn and detached from one another.

She hadn't learned a godsdamned thing about her past from the factories.

Her entire body was full of jelly as her mist-enhanced woman-carriage lugged her roughly to a heavy gate at the far end of Bar Stock, into a simple concrete building with no signage above the metal door, nor were there windows.

Drenth's prison.

Two oafish Imperium soldiers watched as she bounced against the untainted warrior's back. She smiled at them from behind her muzzle but then realized they probably couldn't see it because they frowned back, their auras a simmering bluish shade of boredom. They opened the gate to the prison. Hallway after endless stone hallway, stair after winding stair, they went into the bowels of the prison.

Ashe swore the filthiest words she could think of—muffled, of course—as the vicar dropped her unceremoniously onto the rough ground. It was the curvy vicar from the Guilder's villa.

Curves undid the magical muzzle and the binds at her wrists, and she rubbed the feeling back into them as she cursed the vicar, who ignored her. The door to her prison was pulled shut with a squeal of rusted hinges. She shouted another curse but then her pulmo burst up her lungs and she coughed for a whole two minutes before it calmed.

The prison cell left little to be desired. Solid stone on three sides, and a metal door with a small window of wrist-thick bars. A bucket to piss in, a small stool that looked like it'd break the moment she sat on it, a tray atop with a jug of water and a bowl of what smelled like porridge flavored with shit instead of spices, and a flimsy straw mattress with more lumps than an aging whore's ass.

Standing, she shuffled toward the door, getting on tiptoes to peer out.

"That you, little bint?" a voice called from the cell across the hall.

Through the crusty light, she saw a mane of shaggy brown hair, a grin of golden teeth. "Neenah, what're you doing here?" Another person moved within the murk of the cell, much larger. Roland or Doll perhaps? Said person was slurping away at that awful smelling porridge.

"Can ask the bloody same of you, poppet." Captain LeFleur slapped the big man with the back of her hand, her aetheric bearing slightly energetic honey. "Roland wanted to get his stones juggled and guess we picked the wrong pissing whore." She cackled. "Those tittering twins with you? Told them to watch over you tonight."

"Just me," she answered. "What got you in here? Was it that flabby guy? Tried to con the wrong person, eh?"

Neenah harrumphed. "I'll have you know, Neenah LeFleur doesn't get caught out by petty middlemen. Just a tad unlucky, wrong place, wrong pissing time." Roland chortled. "Shut it, you bloody one-eyed bastard, or I'll send you back to the Voidlands with only your swinging snake and nothin' else. Anyway, the pissing gangs are all in an uproar with what happened to Killian Ness, so all the prick-sucking Imperium rats are out in force. Godsdamned lucky, me."

"I heard Ness got nabbed. All over the aerescreens."

"Ness got caught on his own, little bint." Neenah leaned upon the bars of the cell. "From what we've been hearing, one of the King's own men set him up. Tried to swindle ol' King off some parch. That's when ol' King started his godsdamned bombing. Ness tried a go at ol' King. Godsdamned fool, Ness, I mean, if you ask me."

"The Gutter King showed his face?"

"Couldn't believe it myself." Neenah 's aura tuned sapphiric. "Nobody has bloody seen ol' King in many a year. But Tris, before he ran off to toss Doll, had overheard Red Tulio and Quick Fingers talking about it, said they knew of someone who was there and saw it. Makes me figure it's got to be godsdamned true."

Word on the street was that the Gutter King wasn't just a man, but a whole army of rebels. Could always kill a single man, but not an entire army, which was why the rebellion never did get squelched. To find out he was truly a single man was intriguing to say the least.

She pressed her face up to the bars. "What'd he look like? Did they say? Was he gigantic? He must be if he's lasted this long in the shadows."

Neenah LeFleur grinned, her golden teeth dull in the dim light of the prison, "Ain't no thing, little bint. He looks just like me and you. Well, ain't none who got the figure of Neenah LeFleur, hear?" She waved her hands up and down her physique to emphasize her point.

"Figures." Ashe was mildly disappointed. She'd always imagined him as some grand king, a warrior renowned. Thousands of rumors ran rampant about the famous rebel.

"What got you twisted, little bint?" Neenah asked. "I had heard Elian had something brewing in Silk Circle the other nightturn. That what got you here?"

"Nah, not that." Ashe tried to recall what had happened, but her memory was blank, aside from the visions, which Neenah nor anyone else needed to know nothing about. Everything else was just a blur. "Zenith's cock if I know. All I know is vicars running in Drenth."

"Vicars, eh? Bloody prick-buggers." Neenah straightened her tunic collar. "Rather them than scourges, truth told."

That got her thinking back to what Elian had said. He had known about Ness getting caught and intimated about the vicars. "Elian said…" She paused, wondering if she should tell Neenah LeFleur but decided against it because the woman was nothing but a smuggler, not exactly one to share secrets with. So instead, "You think the Gutter King's going after all the gangs now?"

"Nah, ol' King wouldn't let the pissing gangs be gobbled by the Imperium." But Ashe noticed the raised eyebrows, the quirking sapphire of hidden knowledge. Neenah knew she meant to say something else. "Pockets would be thinned without them, hear? Needs his parch if he's going to war with the Fallen. Ness got himself bloody nicked because he couldn't set his shit-stained ego asides."

She thought again of Elian's words. She couldn't get them out of her head. "I don't know, that bastard's slippery than an oiled up—"

"Don't even finish that sentence, little bint. Not exactly in prime locale for rumormongering."

"It had to have been Solanine, then. Maybe even the Fallen."

"What you gettin' at, poppet?"

"Solanine knows about this." She raised her bangled hand. "About my past."

Neenah LeFleur's eyes grew wide as dinner plates. "Where did you bloody well get that?"

"That Silk Circle job you heard about. Wasn't exactly trying to steal it or anything. Just sort of happened upon it."

"Must be worth a fortune if vicars are after you. If Solanine or the Fallen knows a bit about it, then you'd best keep an eye on your tiny backside, little bint. And I don't mean about your privies, hear?"

"I kn—"

As if on cue, a trio of Imperium soldiers marched into view. Two held wheellock rifles, the other held two sets of iron shackles.

"Let's go, LeFleur," the rough-looking one with the shackles said. "Time to explain to the Guild how you 'accidently' had that coffin of quadrans on your person outside the Chamber of Coin."

"Wrong place, wrong time, eh?" Ashe grinned. "Be good, Neenah."

Neenah Lefleur, the self-proclaimed dashing smuggler, flourished a graceful bow. "Neenah LeFleur's a name made for the Pentax. Innit bloody so, Roland?" She elbowed the big man as they followed the soldiers. "Be seeing you, Ashe. 'Member what I said. It's going to get real rowdy here; offer is always open. Might be better to have you aboard *Marrow's Lover* than those annoying godsdamned voidspawn."

"Be seeing you, Stray Cat," Roland said through a grin. "You know you love Zig and Zag, Cap'n."

One day, she might end up taking Neenah LeFleur on that offer, but today wasn't that day.

Ashe dozed in and out of sleep as the morn grew toward midday and then onto evenfall before a key clicked into the lock, and the door swung open.

A man in a midnight blue cassock stood in the doorway.

"You're harder to find than a maiden in a brothel," said the tall, sable-toned man. His dark eyes with crimson pupils sparkled, playful and serious locked in a never-ending battle as his aura shifted from garnet to royal. Hair cropped close to the scalp, handsome in a hard sort of way. Thankfully not wearing that stupid crested helm with the dyed horsehair.

"Been to the brothels lately, Cyan?"

Within the vicar ranks, he was Cyan the Defiant. The man was two decades older and had been her taskmaster when she had been plopped in the arms of the Scattered Shards as a wailing babe. Cyan had been the one to ink the runes upon her arm, linking her to Shard Form aetheurgy, binding her body to the Four Tenets of Aether. She didn't know much about Cyan's backstory, but he was a harsh taskmaster, which told her the man had a hard upbringing. Still, she had a soft spot for him in her heart. He had been one of the only people she saw as family when she was younger. A father almost.

Ashe sat still, never leaving her precarious spot on the rickety stool, back to the wall that was digging into her ass since she didn't have much padding there.

"Only during the Games, Lilia." Cyan's aura betrayed the jest, for the man was nothing if not devout. A virgin too. All vicars were. Untainted in all manners, they.

Lilia had been the name Ashe had been given while in Kalderim. Lilia. Camilla. Stray Cat. Ashe. Each name a different role to play. A different sense of self. She had no true name to call her own.

Ashe had always liked Cyan, alright, she loved the prickly bastard. So, she did feel slight guilt after fleeing Kalderim. "That's next month's end. You taking part in the gladiatorial games to the Virtuous One?"

"You know it, sister-friend." Cyan grew dour. "Where's the rod?"

"Ah, Bliss' rod. Sold. Hefty price for that thing. How else was I to buy my way out of Kalderim? Not many guards would allow me to waltz straight out of the Shards stronghold, let alone Kalderim without a few quadrans paid off."

Cyan regarded her with skepticism, but to Ashe's surprise, he only nodded. "It was returned a week after you stole it and fled. A benefactor looking for a reward. A shame the man didn't realize there was no blackmailing the pontifex maximus."

"Merrick crucified him, didn't he?"

"The pontifex maximus adheres closely to the sacred tablets. Stealing's a sin in Merrick's eyes. No matter who the culprit is."

It was subtext Ashe gleaned clearly: a warning to her about the spot she now found herself in. Elian's words rang free again. "How'd you find me?" Pulmo tore her lungs, a harsh cough escaped.

"Pulmo's getting worse, eh?" Ashe coughed again in confirmation. Seemingly everyone was bringing up her malady lately. "The Ideal Daughter Herself told us where to find you. Through Mindaro's sight."

Ashe should've known the Scattered Shards wouldn't let her go that easy. "The Blind still kickin'?" She ignored the comment on her disease, her death knell. "Makes sense now how you found me. Was that you earlier or are there more of you running through Drenth?"

"Cryptic as ever is Mindaro the Blind, you know bikromi, Lilia. Icterine's as surly as a goat in need of milking. The rest of the Conclave still holds." The Conclave was the high council of the Scattered Shards, it was made up of augurs, vicars, ingeniators, and quaestors. "And it was. Put me through the wall. You've grown strong. Didn't see that blow coming. The others got in my way."

Ashe grinned. "There's much you haven't seen from me yet. Sorry 'bout that, though. Wasn't exactly looking for a dance there. Also, guess you got moved up a rank? Those crests on those helms, always hated them. Makes you look like a featherless bird. But at least you have a Gauntlet now. That's neat, to be Sharded."

He toyed with the rune-inscribed Gauntlet on his right wrist. "Thanks, I suppose? Your aether has increased. Harlequin the Bloodless cried like a wailing babe after her Shard Form wore off and she felt the effects of that shattered elbow."

"I remember Harlequin back when she was Tista." The fire-haired Tista had been one of her friends under Cyan's training. A gangly girl who had grown handsome as she aged toward a teenager. Ashe always thought so, anyway. "Who else you'd bring?"

"Amaranth the Pure. You remember her?"

"Ah, yes. That would explain the voluptuous curves. Boring if I recall correct." Amaranth had trained under a different taskmaster, so Ashe didn't have much interaction with her. Although, she did remember the woman's curves all too well.

"She is quiet, that's for true. Almost wish Harlequin was as silent as the Pure."

"You never liked any conversation, Cyan, even with me."

"I've softened since you fled like a dog with its tail between its legs." Cyan's words caused an involuntarily flinch. Ashe opened her mouth to speak, but nothing came out. For once. "Anyway, time's aging. Got a long road ahead. Wanted to see if you've changed."

"Have I?"

"Not in the least. Too bad we'll have to muzzle you on the road. I won't miss your tongue lashings, to be true." There was a giddiness in his peridot shimmer.

"Where?"

"The Proving Chamber."

She sucked her teeth. "Already back to Kalderim? No time for warm returns? We've only just caught up."

"You may not've noticed," Cyan motioned to the tattoos on Ashe's arm, "but you are bound by the laws of the Scattered Shards. Icterine has deemed you rogue. And when the Unfettered speaks, we listen. That is the way of our sect. You knew that the day you were inked. Whether you adhere to the sect or not. Don't make me carry you there."

"Got anything to drink?" Cyan's lip curled as he tossed Ashe a golden flask—her flask. She unscrewed the cap and put it to her lips, but nothing came forth. "It's empty."

"You know the laws against alcohol," the untainted warrior said, smile struggling to stay concealed.

"Well bugger me, that's cold." Ashe pocketed the flask with shaking fingers. One drink wouldn't hurt, laws or not. "When do we leave?"

"On the morrow." Cyan backed out of the cell and pushed the rusted door shut. "Until then, you'll stick here, sister-friend."

"Sleep well, *brother-friend*."

Cyan's presence faded as another door closed, leaving Ashe in silence. Now she just had to figure out how to escape the prison cell beforehand.

Sometime later, in the dark of nightturn, the door to her cell opened.

She sprang from her lumpy mattress, fists balled, wishing she had the mist for company. All she had was the stool and her flask as weapons, not much to put up a decent fight with.

A lantern was lit, a small handheld one. The dim glow illumined an arm of dusky flesh covered in a crisscrossing of raised scars. As her eyes adjusted, she traced the face. A man's face. Middle aged with streaks of grey in an otherwise dark countenance that belied the emerald pupil within the man's brown iris. He had a wicked scar roping his neck.

"Who are you?" Ashe shifted her weight, ready to spring into a fight if necessary. From his colored pupils, she knew this man possessed aetheurgy.

The man crossed the cell and placed the lantern on the stool. He wasn't a tall man, she noted. But he stood back straight, facing her with his hands at his sides.

"Some call me the Gutter King," he started. Ashe couldn't stop her jaw from dropping. "Others know me as Emre Benld of the line of the Regents Benld." He couldn't be, he'd died in the conquest of Drenth. "But to you, you may call me 'Father.'"

XVIII
EVANDER

THE WOMAN GYRATED atop Evander with her back arched against his chest, his hands upon her hips, teasing at her thighs above her skirt, a throaty groan making him smile.

Her head fell into the gulch of his neck where it met his shoulder, panting breath tickling his skin while her lower half moved rhythmically against his manhood. He grabbed at her breast, caressing the tender flesh through her shift. Desire raged through him. A dark desire.

"O Evander… yes… can we?"

Lifting the small woman off his lap with ease, he tossed her atop the bed and stood over her while she giggled. Her long, stygian hair made an unruly frame around her face as she licked her tongue across her lips, pulling the hem of her skirt up, exposing the innermost holy sanctum between her legs.

O, how she looks so much like Snow Eyes.

However, the woman on the bed had unremarkable, brown irises and was a poor facsimile to the one he coveted. Not mysterious, not magical. A simple scullery maid in a Guilder's villa. Not a trained aetheurgist who could stand beside him at the feet of his Divine.

The woman's bland eyes pleaded with him as he stood there thinking of the girl who would one day be his. She held out a hand to him, urging him to come to her while she undid the laces of her shift with the other, exposing her breasts. Evander gazed down on her with a lust she would never understand. A pulsing in his body, his soul. One she could vaguely satiate. She only saw his physical arousal, knew nothing of what could cure the tempest within him.

"SOLANINE KNOWS, MY DISCIPLE," his master said, battering through Evander's desires, filling him further with the need, **"KNOWS WHAT IT TAKES TO BREAK THE BARRIER, TO THWART THE VEIL BETWEEN LIFE AND DEATH. PLAYTHINGS, THESE MORTALS. YOU CAN HAVE IT ALL."**

Solanine. No matter how hard he tried, he couldn't get the aetheurgist out of his thoughts. Ever since their meeting, he barely thought of anything else, even Snow Eyes. The power his would-be-master had wielded, the aetheurgy of the void, O, how he wanted it. He would do anything to get it. Anything.

Evander pulled his shirt over his head, the lowborn maid grinning as she admired the planes of his muscles. She sat up, running a finger—forever wrinkled from the tiresome work in the kitchens of her betters—across the valleys of his chest, down the length of his abdomen, reaching for the tongue of his belt, yanking it open. Her hand pulled him free.

"O, how I've want—" Entwining his fingers in the tresses of cimmerian, she took him into her mouth, his eyes rolling back into his head as her words died upon him.

The pleasure. O Nocturne, the pleasure. But it wasn't a lowly maid he thought of, but instead of the girl with ice in her gaze. *You are mine,*

Snow Eyes. Mine. His fingers tightened in the waves of dark black, the woman continuing her assault with practiced ease.

'She must come willingly,' the words of Solanine ran through his head. *She will be mine. Will come to me. I just need…*

An explosion of his end came forth, his thoughts only of the girl he craved more than anything in this waking life. Anything besides power. Two, both can give him all his worldly desires.

The scullery maid drew back, her hand wiping her lips, plebeian eyes glimmering in hope up at him. She smiled, but he did not let go of her hair. The black locks wrapped about his fingers. Her smile withered. "Ow. Evander, you're hurting me."

"PAIN IS BUT THE FIRST STEP TOWARD IMMORTALITY."

Evander's gaze went slack. *Pain, I can give it. What do I receive in return?*

"SEEK AND FIND OUT."

"There is felicity in the blood," he started in a coarse whisper, using the exact words Solanine had spoken after crossing the veil to the Meadows using aetheurgy. "Immortality does not come from the proliferation of Life, but upon the wave of Death."

Life and Death. His seed, her death.

"DEATH."

Death…

Just then, the door to his chamber burst inward. In strode his brother, the floorboards groaning under Elian's obese gait. Elian took in the scene, looking at the frightened woman with a slight hint of amusement. Two other shadows lurked behind, outside the room, one large, one small.

"Come, brother." Elian beckoned Evander as if he was some lost puppy in need of training. "We have things to discuss." Elian turned to leave, leaning toward Red Tulio. "Get rid of her."

The orcirish thug barreled into the room and Evander tossed the small maid at him. The putrid beast caught the flailing woman and dragged her from the room, screaming and kicking. Nocturne, how she still fought. Just as Snow Eyes would.

He shivered. "Mors expectet," he muttered, using the phrase Solanine had spoken when killing the Gutter King's rat.

"Put your prick away, brother. Come."

Evander reluctantly did as his need had not been fully sated. *Later,* he thought. Elian had denied him that end, that finish. Another tally to the list of why Evander cursed his brother.

Although *The Colosseum* was barely held together by more than sheer grit, the back halls even more so than that of the paying customer front façade. Evander's chamber was nothing spectacular, mainly four walls and some scrounged up furniture. It was all he needed, for his Divine provided all the necessities. Evander's room was on the opposite side of the building from Elian's rooms.

Aside from the brothers and Quick Fingers, the hallway was empty of souls, only their footsteps made any sound within the rowdy tavern below them.

While his own room was simple, Elian's was anything but. An office before led into a second room further back where his brother laid his head at night, but both were covered floor to ceiling with the types of furnishings one might see in Silk Circle. Draperies and velvets, carved furniture and statues. The vast majority were stolen from one job or another. Evander was drawn to a new addition: the satyr mask from House Soabin. It hung neatly upon the wall behind Elian's desk, nestled between a gemstone shard mosaic said to have been created by Canlon Carr himself prior to the Fall of Eminence and the skull of a unicorn.

"Sit." Elian might oversee the gang, but Evander knew who had the higher standing in his Divine's hierarchy. Regardless, Evander sat. "Now, what did Solanine want with you?"

"Nothing you would understand." *Nothing you could ever come close to understanding, dear brother.*

Elian glowered. He was a man used to getting what he wanted, whether that be information or elsewise. He toyed with the obsidian pendant that Solanine had given him. "Don't goad me, Evander. What did that bitch want?"

Sitting there, watching his elder brother demand information from him, Evander couldn't help but think the tides were finally going to capsize around Elian.

Growing up, both had lived a harsh life, their early days bleak. Their mother had been nothing but a street worker, their fathers some random aethecite miners with a spare bit of coin to spend on a woman of the night. They may be brothers by their mother's blood, but neither resembled each other much other than their eyes and hair, although Elian's had long since fled from his skull down to his back. Their mother had died of an easily treatable disease had she been anything more than a whore when they were but children, left to fend for themselves on the unrelenting streets of Drenth. Elian, being both older and stronger of will and flesh, had joined with the previous leader of Slag's End, working and clawing his way up the chain, all while taking care of the younger Evander.

Evander even might have loved Elian once. Loved him as a sibling, as the only family he ever truly knew. But then the Divine had come into his life and their bond, the bond between brothers, had irrevocably changed.

And now, once more, the balance teetered ever further.

"HE IS BUT A PEBBLE THAT WILL CRACK THE TILE SHOULD YOU NOT BRUSH IT ASIDE. A TAINT THAT WILL SPOIL. YET, HE MAY STILL BRING YOU WHAT YOU DESIRE MOST."

Snow Eyes. "You best not utter that word about Solanine again, brother. Master… Solanine, that is, saw me at the Guilder's villa with Sn… Ashe."

"You neglected to tell me this." Elian leaned back into his chair and turned toward the satyr mask, the wood creaking. He scratched at his scraggly beard, dry flakes snowing about his tunic front. "This complicates matters. Who else saw you at Soabin's? I'd not like to see his missing mask come back to my doorstep."

"It matters not." Evander put his feet upon Elian's desk, which drew a frown from his brother. He left them there. "None would question the word of Solanine. Soabin is but a rotten fish in a barrel of them. You have nothing to fear from Solanine. You or your operations here."

Elian squinted. "You're withholding something from me. I know when you are. It is unwise to do so."

"I'm not one of your pitiful dregs, Elian," he said angrily. "Nor your bastard son." Between the pair of them, he was the longer to anger, but once incensed, Evander had the more aggressive streak. By bringing up Elian's bastard child, he aimed to cut deep. "You may think you own Slag's End, but we are men of the Imperium now, and our standing is beside another. You best get used to it."

A chuckle with little warmth escaped Elian. "You think Solanine is going to open those legs to you like that scullery whore and just give you the breadth of Gargantua to use on your whim?" Elian put his fleshy arms upon the desk, his face darkening as he shoved Evander's boots off. "Don't you dare bring up Evzen. Where that little fucker has gone, I'll find him. You know better than most, Evander, what this city does to those who hold dreams. You know firsthand what it's like to lose those closest to us because the Fallen demands obedience."

No, brother, a god. He quivered with anger but held it in check. "Then what, pray tell, brother, are we to do with Solanine's task? Obey and hand over Ashe? One of ours?" *You would betray me if the size of the purse was large enough, but do you dare say it aloud, brother? Just like you did with your only child. Knowing that Solanine sent you off before me…*

That softened his brother's storm, if only somewhat. "The girl was never one of ours. Evzen may have had a lover's crush on her, and she's helped this imperium of ours grow, no doubt, but she's unpredictable. We cannot trust one trained of the Scattered Shards."

"And yet you're willing to trust the Fallen himself? You contradict yourself. No, brother, you would never just turn her over without assurances. And you'd truly slit your own child's throat when you find him, won't you?"

The smile returned on Elian's flabby face. "And to think I had begun to believe you too far smitten with the girl for you to see what's staring you directly in the face. O don't think I don't know what you desire with her. It's plain as day. Just as it was with Evzen." His fat fingers drummed upon the desk. "But as you say, we cannot trust the Fallen. Nor Solanine. The Gutter King has drawn in the gangs to this war, whether we like it or not. Ness was a fool. I'll not be one to follow in his footsteps. I'd rather not end up food for the worms."

"Cross the Fallen then, is it?"

"I wouldn't dream of such a thing," Elian said with a straight face before bursting into laughter.

It was a daft thing, one that would spell doom for his brother. But it mattered not. Only his oath to the Divine did.

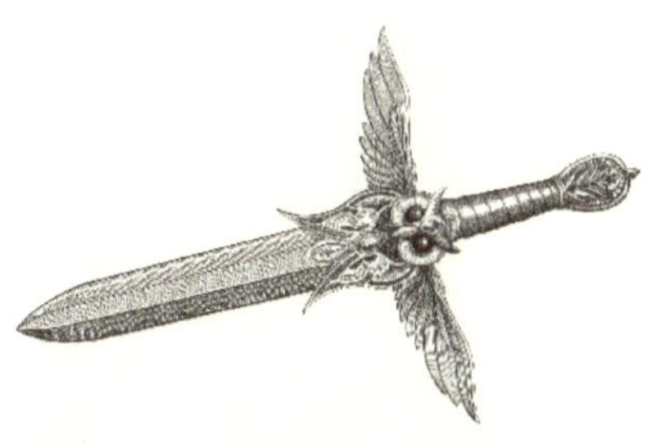

XIX

CADRIANNA

THE HUMID, PUTRID poison of the Sea of Mist had a strong scent of death. A permanence.

Southwest of Drenth near half a day, Cadrianna traveled the Sea alone. Within the thick haze, a monolithic structure emerged ahead.

As she pressed forward, her mind remained on her daughter.

Blindfolded, as she always was, Lu Har had led her down into the depths of Gargantua, into a place she could never find on her own. A winding way they went, backwards and forwards with no discernible trail she could remember. She had tried for years but couldn't. It kept her tamed. Kept her hungry.

The moment she had laid eyes on her daughter, bound in the obscurity of a darkened cell with a door that was unbreakable by aetheurgy, Cadrianna cried. Bound by aether to the wall, a crown of daggers stabbed into Brynn's head, her raven hair fallen about her dirty, young face as blood trickled in streaks. Arms raised apart, crimson at her feet. Chains with heinous bladed links crisscrossing her torso, digging into her skin.

O Nocturne she wanted to hold her child, to take her into her arms and soothe her.

Seeing Brynn had given her strength. She had needed the visual confirmation that what she was doing was worth it. To be reminded that her path was only temporary. The love that bound her to the Fallen was a dark curse, wrapped tightly in the desire for revenge. Void aetheurgy needed hatred to guide it, that was why she allowed herself to love him.

Love borne by hatred.

As she'd left the depths of Brynn's prison, Cadrianna had her resolve to seek the oracles, gain whatever advantage she could glean from them.

Sweat beaded the rim of her breather as the ground turned hard, and the ruined city of Illigan sprawled before her.

"I HATE THIS PLACE." Sheathed at her hip, the Strix radiated heat. *"REMINDS ME OF THAT TIME WHEN I WAS STILL FLESH."*

"I wish you were flesh, then I'd not have to listen to you all the time."

"FLESH FEELS MORE THAN STEEL, EVEN YOUR BARBS. YOU SHOULD'VE SEEN MY WINGSPAN. WHAT I WOULDN'T GIVE ANYTHING TO HAVE A BACKSIDE AS FINE AS YOURS."

"There you go, commenting on my backside again. Sometimes I think you just like to flirt with me."

"ME FLIRT WITH YOU? YOU'RE NOT MY TYPE."

"O, I forgot, you only have a thing for the souls of the dying."

"IF ONLY YOU KNEW THE PAIN I SUFFER FOR IT."

The ruined city rose out of the mist. Villas of mortar and wood. Multiple stories, many massive. Some were narrow and closely cobbled together. The marshland had claimed Illigan, caressing buildings as if holding them forever in place. Benches of steel and iron, rusted and bent. Windows empty of glass. Balconies collapsed. Gardens turned brown or dead, rotted away to nothing.

Illigan was nothing more than a relic of a time before the Fall.

"THERE WAS THIS ONE TIME," the Strix started and began to regale her of a time in which it'd been here when Eminence still floated above the land. But she didn't listen, she'd heard the tale countless times already.

The villas faded back into the Sea as she walked into an open expanse of uneven stones. The bones of animals and man littered the road, skulls and ivory along all the way. Daemons of small stature prowled the empty cityscape, but they were more frightened of her, than she of them. She saw tails as they fled.

"WEAKLINGS THEY ALL ARE."

"Jealous much?" A drake roared nearby, a big one. Perhaps it was Cinder, following her. Its call sent the mist careening. A blast of fire illumined in the distance, a shriek of something caught in its path. A firedrake claiming a meal. "And that one? Weak, you think?"

"O NOW YOU WANT TO TAUNT ME? I THOUGHT WE WERE FRIENDS."

The road shrunk as she reached the hub of the ruined city. Made of travertine and still somehow standing, it led to what was once a palace that reached toward the sky, so high, even broken and crumbling, it disappeared into the clouds above the Sea.

Cadrianna felt at ease in the vestiges of Illigan.

There was something calming about the empty city, the pall of death that hung over it. Almost as if the world had claimed the failings of the apex imperium and gave just punishment. It made her relish the opportunity for her own punishment against Lu Har and his coven for the death of her parents and brothers. For the capture of Brynn and repeated torture.

Even for Emre and his betrayal to allow it all to happen.

She stopped at the remains of the palace. Hands on hips.

"YOU'LL NEVER GET TO CHERISH ONE OF THESE PLACES, CAD."

"Piss off. I don't want to live here. I want to burn it further to the ground."

"I KNOW."

"Do you, though?" She clicked her tongue. "You can read my thoughts, my wants. See things only the darkest regions of my brain want to remain hidden. Yet, you've done nothing to help me achieve that."

"YOU REALLY THINK THAT? I'M HURT."

"You don't hurt. You bring hurt. That's all you want. Easy to say, you were a daemon before this."

"TOOLS WE BE, CAD. WHAT WE WERE BOTH DESIGNED FOR. I WAS FLESH AND WING ONCE. BLOOD, BLACK AS IT MAY HAVE BEEN, FLOWED THROUGH MY VEINS JUST LIKE YOURS. I WAS WITH MY OWN WANTS. MY OWN DESIRES. I HAD A LIFE ONCE. BUT THE DIVINE TOOK THAT FROM ME. TOOK EVERYTHING."

A tool. That's all she was.

"NO, NOT ANYMORE. LEAVE THIS PLACE AND NEVER RETURN. YOU CAN LEAVE ME HERE AND THEY'D NEVER FIND YOU, SHOULD YOU WISH IT."

"I can't. Brynn is still bound. I can't leave her."

A deep sigh from the Strix and the heat within the sheath cooled. *"CAD, I..."*

"Forget it. I'm Lu Har's pet, like Solanine said. Until I can find a way to free Brynn, I'm stuck with the lot I've been given. By the godsdamned Pentax. They cannot be trusted, Strix. The gods will use you until you are nothing."

"CAD..."

"The Gutter King must die. For Brynn." She couldn't stop seeing Brynn's pain. Cadrianna shook her head, trying to force it away. To steel her soul from the torment.

"YOU HEARD LU HAR, THIS GUTTER KING IS DANGEROUS. OTHERWISE, HE WOULDN'T HAVE SENT YOU. THE GUTTER KING IS THE ONE WHO GAVE YOUR FAMILY TO RUIN. SHOULD YOU BELIEVE HIM, OF COURSE."

"He didn't lie about Thestile."

"YOU CERTAIN OF THAT? THINK, CAD, YOU SAID IT YOURSELF, SHE APPEARED READY TO DIE."

"She was instrumental in the death of the Last Godsking, don't you think that's enough to be ready for the end?"

"LITTLE GIRL YOU ARE. YOUR FIRE BLINDS YOU TO THE TRUTH. BRYNN HOLDS YOU BACK FROM REALIZING THE TRUTHS IN FRONT OF YOU."

"Sometimes I wonder just how humirish you think."

"DON'T LIE, I'M THE SMARTEST DAEMON YOU KNOW."

"You're the only daemon I know."

"LIKE I SAID."

She closed off her mind from the Strix, not wanting to reopen every wound she carried with her like a boulder upon her back.

Another bridge of travertine crossed the road and Cadrianna followed it into an open courtyard of browned grass up to her breast. A woman came into view, stooped and old, hair greasy and white as bone. Her face was skeletal, cheekbones protruding through the stretched skin that was dry and chalky, almost dead looking. Empty eye sockets looked up.

"You've been expected, child," the ancient skeleton of sinew and muscle said through parched lips. She smiled, but there were no teeth, only bleeding gums. "You seek the guidance of the Matron. Come, you have much to see and learn."

The oracle turned and limped back the way she'd come, toward a basilica. Somehow the church still stood after five centuries of decay. Made of grey-white marble that interlocked without any mortar. Three arches along the façade, three additional recessed tiers of stonework above. There was a wooden door within each arch, the outer ones taller than the center portal. High above the largest arch was a metal and stone circle with four concentric circles within. A gleaming emerald in the center.

"Come, child." The emaciated oracle put a whitewash-painted skeletal hand upon the door and whispered aetheric words. The door swung inward without a sound.

Once inside the basilica, Cadrianna withdrew her breather mask and unconsciously gaped.

If one had stumbled recklessly upon the ruins of Illigan, and then toward the basilica, they might have been surprised by the entire place. Surprised that it still stood after hundreds of years. But if said person had gone into the basilica, they might have fainted at the magnificence within.

Just through the doors was a marble fountain. Carved plant-life graced the outer face of the circular reservoir, each delicate branch covered in bronzed filigree. The water bubbled out of the branches into a basin beyond in a steady stream. In contradiction to the Sea of Mist and the ruins of Illigan, the water was as clear as could be. From deep in the earth it came, cleansed by *Terris* and *Aquis*. Though the mist angrily circled the pool.

Above, the ceiling rose more than one hundred feet, supported by columns and arches, where they met at the apex of the dome. Trusses crossed a roof covered in a mosaic of people watching another ascend: the First Godsking. Behind the First Godsking was a giant crystal made of every color and none. The Aether of Life, the crystal called Eminence. The great city—christened after its namesake crystal—was in the background, floating in the heavens.

Along each wall, glass of crystal in every color was melded into scenes depicting the world while Eminence reigned. Statues atop pedestals, great, strong-looking Godskings of the past. Murals on the bases showed the homelands of the esteemed holy ruler, a shading of the color of their lands. Blue for *Aquis*. Red for *Ignis*. Green of *Terris*. And Yellow for *Aere*.

Even now, seventeen years and dozens of times stepping into the basilica later, Cadrianna was still in awe. The beauty cut through the fabric of revenge and hatred that lined her soul.

"BEAUTIFUL YOUR HUMIRISH ASS. EVERY DAEMON WORTH THEIR CLAWS KNEW NOTHING BUT SCORN FROM EMINENCE. NOCTIS IS THE GREATER OF THE PAIR."

See, jealous, she thought. *And still thinking about my backside.*

The Strix huffed, if a daemonic blade could suffer such a feat.

The oracle led her toward a small wooden door. No handle upon it, and the oracle waved her hands, chanted words of aetheurgy and the door opened. Beyond was a short stair, followed by a hall. Silent, the two walked down each. Rooms lined the hall, filled with people, the vast majority were women. Some of the women looked up as they passed, empty sockets searching her. Oracles. A few men and women were scourges, the protectors of the oracles. Each room was small, no bigger than a prison cell. Modest, some with furniture, most with none but a lumpy mattress.

The hall began a slight descent, torches in sconces, flames burning bright as the hall seemed to suck in the dark. Then the stone underfoot turned to dirt. Packed hard, it was, with cracks throughout.

"The Matron awaits you," the oracle seemed to stoop further within herself as she spoke. "Answer some of your riddles she may. Only the Divine Himself can give the answers you seek."

The oracle and the assassin came to a door made of sticks. The room beyond was dug from the earth, confined and ovular, especially crude. A few wooden struts embedded into the dirt held the soil in place. There was a table made of twisted branch, chairs of similar yield. A mattress lay on the ground, beaten and old, bugs crawling free. Ankle deep mist circulated the hovel, seeping from painted runes all along the floor and walls.

At the back, near a boiling cauldron upon a small fire pit was a kneeling woman with her back to them. A red haze rose from the pot, it formed like eyes in the smoke. "Why have you come to me now, Cadrianna Nightingale of Thullyr?" The raspy voice was harsh and unforgiving. "I saw your coming, I did."

The first oracle bowed and shuffled back up the hall, closing the door of sticks behind.

"Matron," Cadrianna said reverently, bowing her head. "I seek your counsel."

"Counsel? Do you really believe that?"

"I don't understand, Matron."

"Of course, dear child. The world you know is only a remnant of the old. There is more than what is known to you. What you think you seek is not the truth you demand. You want to know about the

Seals to Eminence. That is what your Nightingale blood demands. It oozes from you, quenched only by the Seals of the Great Crystal."

"The Seals? No, I seek to know more about the Gutter King."

The elder worked her way to standing, brittle bones creaking as she did. Turning, her ancient and wasted face found Cadrianna's. The Matron was the oldest living oracle in the Fallen's coven, older than any living creature not a god, older than the Fallen even. Her skin was emaciated and cracked, missing in some places, showing the living muscle underneath. Wispy, near nonexistent hair cascaded down the woman's blindingly pale pate as if Zenith's gentle sun had never caressed her. The creature's lower lip was gone, and where her eyes should have been, were deep, empty holes.

"Come, child of Eminence, sit with me."

Child of Eminence? She was a child of Oldport Basin in Thullyr, not Eminence. The oracle made her way to one of the twisted wood chairs, easing herself down. Cadrianna took the other one, it groaned under her weight.

The eyeless sockets drew together in what could only be described as a furrow of brow. "You are like a newborn pup in the world." Her lack of bottom lip showed the muscle underneath as she spoke, drool dribbling.

The Matron grabbed Cadrianna's hands in her own ice-cold ones. One hand was painted in whitewash, the other blackwash. Withering cold of Death waiting. Vision Form, warped and defiled from Bliss or Brio's bikromi. Only the oracles of the Divine needed no eyes to see.

"Your power has steadily been growing. Eminence awaits you. Our Divine's guile upon us. The Seals are your task. Your only goal. Yes, that is what He shows me."

"But what of the Gutter King? He's why I'm here."

"Time will come for him, child. His ruin is bound to yours. Bound to the Seals. Your path is now open before you. The balance between Life and Death is wearing thin. The four Seals will shatter and the draconem guarding them must break. They must shatter for Eminence to be reborn. For a new god to rise. Yes. Holy be thy Fallen. Your blood, your family blood is tied to the Seals. Yes, of *Ignis*. Nightingale blood. You must remember so the Seal can be broken."

Cadrianna thought a moment. The oracles only spoke in riddle, only said what they were given by the Divines, were like the bikromi seers, voices to the Pentax. "Is this why my parents were murdered?" Her family name was Nightingale, her parents had been a loyal House in Oldport Basin before they left the City of Sin and moved to the City of Sands after her marriage. Nightingale, O Nocturne, she hadn't thought of that name in so long. "Why Brynn was taken from me? Why I was trained?"

The Matron smiled the best she could with naught a lip. "The enigma of your past is strong, child. There is only the Seals for you. Temples of the old world. Yes. They await. They await your hand. Your past revealed when they are broken. Eminence demands you, calls you. It is in your blood. Eminence blood. Answer me this, why do you hate?"

"Zenith has forsaken me. Taken my family, left to rot in the ground while I suffer the living. Is vengeance not enough? Nocturne is the only god for me, now."

"Vengeance merely brings ruin." The Matron closed her empty eyes and began to hum. It went on and on, their hands conjoined. Finally, she stopped. The cauldron spat viciously in more red smoke. "Our blessed Solanine seeks the one who bears the Eye of the Soul. Seeks the way to break open the gate to Eminence in our blessed father's name. Find the Seals, they are your destiny. O," her head lulled. "Yes, this is your true path. By your hand you will help break them. By the blood in your veins, back to Eminence you are charged, Cadrianna of Nightingale blood."

"And what of the Gutter King? The Fallen wants his blood."

"And blood you shall give, child. When the last great vvyrms billow forth from the desert sands, his blood shall rain down upon you. The Forgemistress' tears sparking Her anvil, drenched in blood, by Her Hammer. Blood giveth blood. Blood begat blood. Only with the blood can the Seals be broken. Yes, O yes. You must allow yourself to see without eyes unclouded by hate, Cadrianna of Nightingale blood. Blood rules all."

The Strix sighed. *"THIS IS SOME SHIT IF I'VE EVER SHOVELED SOME."*

XX

Cyan the Defiant

CYAN'S EYES SNAPPED open as the faintest footsteps outside the temple door broke his meditation.

"What is it?" Cyan shouted.

In the throes of his aetheurgic prayers, his senses detected the plodding footsteps beyond the temple doors, a hand raised with the intention of knocking, the hesitant breathing, the reluctance to intrude.

But somehow the voice in response was lost in the aetheric haze.

Kneeling at the base of Justice's statue within the temple of the Scattered Shards in Drenth, Cyan the Defiant lowered the sleeve of his cassock over the runic tattoos upon his right arm, which faded as he let go of his Shard Form aetheurgy. Straightening his midnight blue cassock as he rose to his feet, he moved across the small temple, refitting his breather mask upon his face, the horsehair bristle swishing lightly. He left his Sharded Gauntlet upon the stone before the statue of the great god to whom he was devoted.

Cyan opened the temple's door where a young woman—barely older than a girl if he was being honest, which Cyan was in nearly all manners—stood with hands clasped behind her cassocked back, although one elbow was heavily bandaged from a recent shattering. A breather upon her face topped with red, bouncing curls.

"What is it, Harlequin the Bloodless?" he said curtly. "I'm in the middle of my prayers. Has she been prepared for our return, or has she already tried to flee? I wouldn't be surprised by the latter." A small shudder ran through him, as he hoped the latter wasn't the case. He was in no mood for another chase.

"She remains in the prison cell where you left her. Amaranth the Pure is watching her as we speak," Harlequin affirmed, her bright grey irises surrounding golden pupils betrayed a hint of elation before dimming into reticence. "But… forgive me for interrupting your prayers. I was instructed to inform y—"

"But what?" Cyan was growing impatient and cut the young woman off with a wave.

Long has the young woman overstepped when he was in his prayers, an annoyance that contradicted his teachings. Ever since the orphan girl had fled Kalderim, his other students had grown bolder, more open to disobeying his orders. Harlequin, although newly raised to the cassock, had seen what Lilia's disappearance had done to him, so she had been one to grow more brazen. He aimed to do better, to be a stronger taskmaster.

"The Unfettered has made contact."

Cyan suppressed a groan. It was just like Icterine to send word needlessly. He had found the girl and they would return to Kalderim on the morrow. The Conclave had given him the task when they Sharded him, one he was well-suited for, as well as a desire of a personal nature in the girl. If only they could just leave him to it.

"The old fools of the Conclave can wait until I am finished with my prayers."

"But… I… I was told you had to come at once." Dogmatic to the core, this girl. Most new recruits were these days, it seemed. None had the fire since the orphan girl had been placed in Cyan's hands as a babe by the mysterious bikrome. Seeing his narrowed eyes, Harlequin blustered. "I will tell…"

"No need." It wasn't her fault Icterine had sent someone so raw with him. He couldn't hold that against her. No, by the Arbiter, it was because he resented the fact the orphan had nearly escaped him once again. So much time had he put into her training, a great vicar she would've made. "I'll give into the Unfettered's trifles."

"Yes, Vicar Cyan." Harlequin straightened, though she winced when she drew her elbow close to her body. "I shall await you."

Cyan merely nodded. Harlequin was too young, but then again, Cyan was growing ever older. And ever crankier.

The poor fire-haired girl was not to blame for her over exuberance. He remembered being that young once, twenty-plus years as it was. Being that devoted to a cause after having none for most of his early life. Harlequin had a confidence about her, one that hopefully wouldn't shatter when their lives would inevitably be thrown into a den of rabid wolves, of which Cyan might consider Drenth as such. Many a faithful had lost their faith along the road set by the Pentax against Nocturne's guile.

No, he had no reason to be angry with the Bloodless for her constant badgering and questions. No, by Justice, all his bothers stemmed from one person and one person only: the girl he raised.

The Godsblood.

The orphan child had been named Godsblood by the Conclave in the early days of her training, given the name Lilia until she was to be raised to the cassock when she would be given a new name. A name worthy of the Scattered Shards. A name of a Shard color and a title of trait, for that was the way of the vicar.

In the Scattered Shards, names were everything. Given and family names were but constructs that bound a person to earthly endeavors. That wasn't what Bliss intended when She created humir. Renaming meant a cleanse from everything associated with one's past, regardless of transgressions. One became reborn with a new name.

The vicars and the augurs, both untainted by their pasts, were given names by the Shards themselves. Only a vicar was given a secondary title upon receipt of their inked runes, a title which described how each individual expressed their devotion to the Pentax. The tainted warriors, the quaestors, were tainted souls, criminals all. Many were murderers given a second chance to become a warrior of the Shards. Their renaming was a meaningful reminder of what their crime was, their punishment was their warped bodies under Shard Form. The ingeniators, they chose simple names to attach to their creations, for they were not warriors.

Cyan shook his head as he returned to the statues thinking about Lilia.

A rare and wondrous find, Lilia had been. The blood of the gods had denuded down into barely perceptible finds since the Fall of Eminence. The Scattered Shards sought out any of the blood, but found less and less each year. Until the orphan babe, they hadn't found any of the blood in almost two. Since her, they hadn't found a single child borne of the blood. Seventeen years now. It was almost like the elfir, procreation stunted after the Fall.

People like Cyan were a quadran a dozen. Broken souls in need of guidance. Once set on the road to the Pentax, retribution could be found. Warriors made.

But a Godsblood was inherently different. They were the very fabric in which the gods were made. Godsbloods became the greatest of the Shards. Icterine the Unfettered and Mindaro the Blind, Meadows, all the Conclave were Godsbloods.

Lilia could have been the best of them all. Should have been.

Her flight from the Shards was a stain upon Cyan's soul. A failure. A bane feasting upon his pride. Determined he was to find her again, bring her back into the fold. She would be the greatest warrior of the Pentax. He knew it for certain.

Cyan retreated into the temple, kneeling once more. His hand lifted the Gauntlet of Justice. Kissing the sapphire gemstone on the underside of the Gauntlet, Cyan stood, faithful gaze upon his god. Held to his breast, his heart beat furiously as he started to pray. "Take thy blood, the blood of man. Take thy heart, the heart of man. The fire in the soul, the forge it bequeaths. Show thy soul, let it burn in the pyre. Molded when white hot. In thy name, the vicars are yours. My soul is yours."

Aether of the Four Tenets sparkled from the gemstones held in the hands of the five statues of the Pentax.

Zenith in all His Glory in the center, in His hands the image of Eminence, a diamond in the middle. All the colors of the Shards filled it. Aether flashed.

Beside was His Holy Wife, Mother Marrow, and in Her hands was the image of Her Hammer. A green emerald vibrated to Cyan's words, like a quake of earth.

Justice held a set of scales in one hand and His dual-bladed axe in the other. A sapphire adorned the Arbiter's aegis and water dripped down His face like tears.

The younger children of Zenith and Mother Marrow, Brio and Bliss, were carved as young spirits. Bliss in Her virginial state and

Brio in His wanton. Bliss held a flower of peridot, its gemstone whistling like air. Brio's mantle of fiery garnet blazed like a pyre.

Nocturne, the Master of the Pit and twin to Zenith, lay amongst the shadows, no candles alighting Him, aether sucking into the void.

Feeling a wave of aether swim through him, Cyan took a deep breath. He leaned forward to kiss Justice's feet, slipped the Gauntlet onto his right wrist, the holy weapon of The Arbiter linking with his inked runes, then left the temple.

Harlequin fell in beside him as the two vicars marched through the sixth sector of Drenth known as the Revered Mark. The lone temple to the Scattered Shards was one of a handful of churches or temples within the sector, but the only one of a true religion, the rest were nothing but mummery in Cyan's eyes.

"Have you prepared the means of our return?" Cyan asked, hands held behind his back as he walked through the City of Sands.

"I have secured transport, Vicar Cyan," his acolyte said. He didn't look her way but knew she would be relieved that he was speaking to her again after his rebuke in the temple. Try as he might as a tough taskmaster, the girl known as Harlequin the Bloodless was ever full of gaiety. It was one thing Cyan wished he had more of, but his childhood hadn't been pleasant, nor allowed him to be such. "They will expect us at dawnbreak."

"Very good, vicar."

Harlequin beamed beside him. She was one of the best acolytes he'd ever trained, he had to admit, second only to Lilia. But Lilia had been like a daughter to him, and she'd reminded Cyan too much of himself.

She would have been his greatest achievement had she been raised to the cassock.

Most vicars raised to the cassock underwent strict training until their eighteenth nameday. But Cyan had been an exception to the rule. Growing up in the slums of Qarthage, he'd learned to fend for himself at an early age, fighting tooth and nail. That was the way of Qarthage—a mega-city in the eastern reaches of the Imperium—under the pall of the Fallen. His parents had been killed in a riot when he was only five, and his older brother conscripted into the Fallen's army three years later.

Scraping to get by, he learned the only way to finding your way in the world was to fight. Live and die by the blade. Only strength existed in survival. Strength of body and of mind, but most of all, strength of heart and faith. Fleeing Qarthage had been the best decision he'd made because that's when the Arbiter had come into his life, bringing a clarity to what was once a wayward soul. He had forgone any semblance of a normal life, given up a family, given up his name, all because the Pentax provided everything he needed.

And he needed to find the Godsblood's wayward soul and show her a better future.

Minutes later, the vicars climbed a ladder attached to the rear of a rundown apartment complex, making for the fourth-floor balcony of the empty room they'd confiscated and made their short-term abode while they searched for Lilia.

It was a simple room with a hearth of chipped brick. A pot for bodily refuse in one corner, their bedrolls along the far wall, their packs and supplies nearby. The door bolted shut and wood slats covered two of the three windows. Only the balcony window had bits of glass still clinging to the sill.

Cyan made toward the wall opposite their bedrolls. Sitting cross-legged, he positioned the small aerescreen they'd brought for communications with the Conclave atop a broken vegetable crate. He pressed a sequence of buttons on the device while Harlequin sat nearby. The runes on the buttons flashed as the spells of aether bound within the small device came alive. The aethecite along both foot-high uprights of the device flared with *Aere* and the aerescreen between them moved from a blank black to an image of five steel chairs that stood three feet above the ground, their legs embedded within the stone of the earth. A person sat upon each, wearing various colored cassocks. From left to right was: Zaffre, Mindaro the Blind, Icterine the Unfettered, Randol, and Tarpaulin.

The Conclave of the Scattered Shards in Kalderim.

An augur, Zaffre had light blonde hair streaked with grey, middle-aged and was a cool-headed humir. Cyan always knew him to be kind and calm for an augur. He wore a white cassock and toyed with the Beads of Bliss wrapped around his wrist.

Mindaro was ancient, blind and a bikromi seer. She was also the longest serving vicar in the history of the Scattered Shards, the elfir born centuries before the Fall. Her midnight blue cassock seemed to encase her like a thick blanket.

Icterine the Unfettered was the highest rank in all the Scattered Shards, second only to the Pentax Themselves. Strong and stone-cold, her shoulder-length grey hair coiled around her stern elfirish face, blue irised, yellow pupiled eyes wrinkled and alert.

Randol was a modest dvergir from the kingdoms under the Forgemistress' Blades. As he was an ingeniator, he wore an emerald cassock. His flat face was craggy under bushy brows, his beard and braided hair curly-grey.

Tarpaulin was a feisty, hot-tempered giantess from northern Kanja and her hair was a short wispy white and was the same pallor and desiccated flesh of a quaestor, which meant she looked like a massive, angry zombie in a red cassock.

Cyan gave a curt nod of fealty to each member of the Conclave in turn, while his gaze settled upon Icterine. "Why have my prayers been disrupted, Icterine? I already sent word ahead that we will be returning with the runaway on the morn."

As he spoke, runes of *Aere* upon the four corners of the screen oscillated as the spells of air communicated his words thousands of leagues via aether to Kalderim where similar connector runes adorned the screen in the Conclave's Proving Chamber.

"Cyan the Defiant, the name is ever apt," Icterine said, the runes on his screen glowing brighter. The woman sat with a straight back, hands in her lap. Her older face was wrinkled around the eyes, stern yet compassionate. Even for an elfir, Icterine seemed old these days, even though she was maybe fifteen centuries in age. Older appearing even since Cyan had left Kalderim to hunt Lilia. "It seems your prayers have been answered."

"How's that?"

Icterine motioned toward the ancient bikrome. "Mindaro the Blind, if you please."

"The time has come," the ancient bikrome said, her voice naught but a whisper. The runes of *Aere* amplified her voice so that Cyan could hear it clearly. "The Seals to Eminence are in danger. The Godsblood has been officially named the chosen. Come will the fires of the Fallen. Come will the rise of the Golden Sword. Eminence will be reborn. And will shatter."

Cyan was silent, nearly aghast at the prophecy revealed. "Is this true?"

The Conclave leader nodded solemnly. "The Godsblood will reap destruction upon this world and will reform it in their manner. Godsblood becometh the Godslayer. The time of Eminence's slumber is now over. The veil will be lifted and the Pentax will be waiting. The war of faith will commence, we must be prepared. The Divine's fell warriors will spare no time, neither can we."

For the first time in his life, Cyan was speechless. Since the Fall of Eminence, none dared breach its aetheric walls, none could. The Seals to Eminence were the only things keeping the horrors of the Fall at bay. The people of the Mistlands knew nothing of which resides in the ancient city, for if they did, they would all be at risk. The cold realization of what stood before them troubled his very soul. If the Seals were in danger of being broken, the end battle was nigh.

Icterine smiled in a grandmotherly way. "The Godsblood must be brought to the Proving Chamber in all haste, Cyan the Defiant. And you must guide the Golden Sword back to his rightful place upon the Golden Throne. It is the wish of the Peridot. The two must wage this war, stand upon the battlefield hand in hand. Of most import is this quest. We all know the consequences should you fail. May Justice shine His peace upon you."

Giddiness surged into him, so much so, he couldn't stop the laugh escaping his lips.

XXI
ASHE

"FATHER?"

Ashe's legs gave out as a pulmo cough burst free. She smeared the accompanying blood across the runes tattooed into her forearm. Her head began to shake near as much as her entire body, it quivered, perhaps in rage, perhaps in shock. "No… it… you can't be."

Emre Benld, the supposedly dead scion of the Regents Benld, crouched beside her, reaching for her hand. Her father. The sheer notion of it being true consumed her. It wasn't possible. Was it?

Lost at the crossroads of her past and her present.

She resisted his touch at first, glaring at him because she didn't know this man. But she relented for some reason she couldn't explain. A *rightness* because his aura was an ever-shifting tint of the four main colors borne of the Shards. From cherry to azure, from jade to daffodil. All telling her his innermost emotions without him knowing it. His hand dwarfed hers, as a father's should.

"I've wanted to seek you out," he started, his finger tracing the diamond eye in the center of her palm, "but I couldn't risk it."

"Risk it?" Ashe jerked her hand back. If there had been any mist in the prison, it would be roiling like a thundercloud. "Your own godsdamned daughter!" She hurled the flask she'd been clutching for support. He ducked the projectile, the small container clanking against the prison door.

"I know." His voice dripped regret. His aura shifted to a darkened mustard laced with shaded blue. "It's not that I did—"

"Left me an orphan," she cut him off, her anger roaring like a drake. "Not knowing who I was. Who I am."

"Brynn."

"Brynn?"

"Your name. Brynn Benld." He reached for her hand again, but she kept it balled into a fist. He smiled wistfully, sitting back on his haunches. "It was your mother's favorite. That first moment, first held you to her breast, she knew your name would be Brynn."

Brynn. The name tested across the landscape of her thoughts; the name felt real. For the first time in her life, she had an answer to the only question that ever mattered. And yet, she didn't know how to feel about it. Confused was a good way to describe it all.

"Where is she? My mother. Is she alive? With you?" O Zenith, dare she call him Father so soon? It felt right, but she also felt hesitant.

His aura darkened with blue sadness as his hand briefly touched the scar at his neck. "You were but a babe, still suckling upon your mother's breast when they took her. My Cadrianna. Your mother's name was Cadrianna Nightingale. She was a beautiful woman. They killed me, after." His aura radiated royal and crimson, the memories taking him down a dark void.

Her past laid out before her in a single, swift revelation. Eighteen years wanting to know the truth. And here she was, smacked in the face with it. "How is that possible? To be brought back to life?"

The Gutter King smirked, although there was sorrow in it. "The Pentax had other designs on my soul that day. If not for her change of heart, I'd be in the Meadows. Perhaps even the Pit of the Damned for my betrayal to your mother. But she saved me." His face hardened. The man was steel. "And she saved you."

Tundra irises flicked up to stare deeply into his, gauging and reaching for the truth of it all. Zenith, she had to know it. "She who?" But before he could answer, "A bikrome?"

Emre staggered like he took a cruel jab to the throat. She'd caught him off-guard. In a way, that made him seem more real, more humir. Less the Gutter King, more a simple man. "How do you know that?"

"I saw a bikrome with a baby. Daemons followed her. Among other things…" His aura began to steady itself, no longer waffling under his emotions. This was his true self, she realized. Hardened and stalwart. He was steel through and through. How could someone become so hard? "I saw a vision of you. And a woman in black dying while an owl pecked at her." She lifted the bangle. "Through this, I think."

"I should've known the visions would come to you sooner rather than later. I can see it now, Brynn, the aetheurgy in you has begun to change. Your pupils, they are turning white." *White? How?* Emre sighed, "Forgive me, Cad." To her, "Brynn… your mother, the Fallen took her." His aetheric aura pulsed a dangerous crimson. "She was lost…"

Although the man's face bespoke of truths, Ashe discerned there was more he wasn't saying. The Gutter King was holding something back, not her father. Something he wasn't yet prepared to speak aloud. She should press, she knew, but didn't. He was here now for a reason, why wait all these years? From all rumor and talk, the Gutter King was nothing if not tactful.

Had she not the encounters with Solanine, the drakken, the vicars, nor Elian's subtle threats all in the last two days, she probably would've been more surprised. But these were not coincidences.

"Why are you here? And why are my pupils turning white? That cannot be normal," she said through a grin, trying to make light of this quaint meeting.

"A part of me wishes I didn't have to." His hands scratched at his forearms as if trying to calm an itch, instead digging deeper as if he wanted to be free of his skin. If not for the coat he wore, she might figure he would draw blood. He almost seemed grateful for her switched topics. Almost. "It would be better had you never known me. Make no mistake, Brynn, I loved your mother. Love her to this day. She was a part of me that I could never be." Guilt threatened tears at the corners of his eyelids. "And I love you more than my own life. More than my own soul. I may be damned, but it is not a wish I have for you."

"You say that now? Like you know me? Or what I've endured without you to guide me. Father you may be, but you've not exactly crowned yourself sire of the year because of what happened to Drenth." There it was, that anger again spinning out of control. "I'm not a fucking child anymore! You saw to that when your bikrome left me with the Scattered Shards."

He took her attack with grace, which, truth told, made her more irritated. She wanted a rise out of him, to be able to hate him. It would make this easier.

"I know. No parent should ever want that life forced upon their child." His compassionate gaze turned hard. A look Ashe knew all too well. The look of a fighter. One who needed to use all at their disposal. Even family. The harsh reality of life in the Mistlands. "You ask why now? Because I need you, Brynn. More important," his gaze lowered toward her runic tattoos, "I need your aetheurgy. Without it, we cannot beat the Fallen."

"Some father you are, begging for help from a child left on her own. Think I'll just forget seventeen years without parents and come toddling about because you beckon?"

Her face must have revealed the betrayal she felt inside because he turned away from her in shame. No, in hurt his aura told. "I… The higher a person rises, the less the world sees. So, it becomes when we fall. It dogs us until the end. Plagues us." He turned back toward her. "My father used to tell me that when I was but a child. It wasn't until the Fallen took everything from me did I truly understand. I cannot erase what I've done. Had Bliss given me another choice, I would have chosen different. For you, more than anything."

"Forget it." Her tone was more acidic than she'd intended. How could it not? For years she'd imagined what she would say to her parents if ever the chance presented itself, but this was not how she'd envisioned it going. "Forget it," she repeated, more even keeled this time, "it's in the past. I'm over it."

"You shouldn't lie, Brynn. It's unbecoming."

"I am what you made me, Father."

"Fair." He knelt beside her anew and pointed at her bangle instead of reaching for it. She realized she was grateful because she didn't know if she could maintain her veneer had he touched her again. She would crack otherwise; her walls would come crumbling down. It would take time for him to earn her trust and he seemed like he knew it. "Do you know what that is?"

"This?" She turned the golden ring on her forefinger, the rune of *Ignis* etched upon the thin, auric band. "Void no. I didn't steal it, if that's what you're implying. It… this is going to sound stupid, but I was… well, okay, yes, I was going to steal something. But not this. I didn't even know it was there. All I felt was a pull. It was aether, obviously. But one second, I felt this pull, then the next, this was attached to my wrist. I tried to take it off, but it won't budge."

"You couldn't remove it shy of removing your hand from your arm. It has chosen you as its master." A pause stretched. "It's called the Eye of the Soul. A talisman of Eminence."

Eye of the Soul? "That sounds… ominous. For me, eh?" The diamond gleamed in the soft aethecite lamp that bathed the prison cell. "Do you know what a Godsblood is?"

"You've heard this before?" She nodded. "A Godsblood is one borne of the line of the chosen. Unbroken from the First Godsking down to the Last. Blessed by the Pentax."

"Cursed more like."

"As Cad once said," he lamented. "She used to say, 'Never trust the Pentax.' I now know what she meant. As you will one day. Your mother has the Blood of the Gods in her veins. The Nightingales hail directly back to Eminence. That is why the Fallen took her instead of killing her with the rest of our family. And that blood flows through you. That is why Val stole you away. Val," to her inquisitive frown, "is the bikrome you saw in your visions. She was the one to hand you to the Shards. Directly to one named Cyan, as commanded by Bliss. The Ideal Daughter chose to revive me. To bring me back."

Cyan… betrayer. Liar. How could you have kept this from me all this time? "Then I have Her to thank for this misery?"

"Misery you may think it, my daughter, but I see it as a blessing. Without Bliss' intervention, the Fallen would have had a Godsblood and the Eye. With both, he'd have a clear route into Eminence. To finish what he started five hundred years ago. On Bliss' command, Val is the one who placed the Eye in that safe. O yes, Val knew you'd one day come to Drenth. She is a bikrome, after all." The steel came back to his face, hinting at some torment underneath in need of covering. A secret hidden, perhaps? "All we needed to know is where and when you'd be."

"Lucky me." She tried to read the secret in his aura, but somehow, he was able to keep it from her. *Zenith's cock, he was a hard man to read. No wonder the Fallen hasn't been able to capture him after all these years.* "So, what's this thingamajig do?"

"Several things. Your aetheurgy is unlike any Form you might've learned by your tutelage of the Shards. But the most pressing use is the Eye is the means to break the Seals of Eminence. This might be difficult to learn."

"Godsdamn," Ashe said after her father explained about the Seals. About the final act of the Last Godsking during his war with the Fallen.

She realized now how much history the world had buried in the tomb of Eminence. Even the teaching of the Scattered Shards held nothing of this information. She was but a paint droplet in the mural of the world.

"Which is why it cannot fall into the Fallen's hands."

"Why do I sense a 'but' coming?"

Emre regarded her with raised cheeks. "You sound just like Cad when she was but your age. Your mother was one mercurial woman."

"Thanks?" Ashe then began to hack, her lungs on fire as the pulmo tore through. A glob of tar rose, and she spat it onto the prison's stone floor. "What about this? Pretty sure the pulmo'll kill me sooner rather than later."

"That is the corruption of Canlon Carr's final sacrifice. The pulmo is dangerous to all, but more so to a Godsblood, for your aetheurgy is also corrupted. Your Soul Form is tainted, and yes, it will kill you if you do not learn to control it. The mist is your tool, your weapon, your existence. Harness it, be it, and it will serve you."

"Wonderful."

He stood, maybe a head and a half taller than she. Yet there was a presence about the man. His aura blazed. She didn't know what that meant, for it had never been that strong before.

"For one who calls himself 'king' of this city, I expected you to be taller." She couldn't stop herself.

"Not the first time I've heard that." He retrieved the lantern. "Tevun once told me that height mattered not when a drowning man had the determination to reach for the surface." Another sad smile. "Tevun always had such odd parables and that one always stood out to me as one of the weirdest." A shake of his head, but it had a sort of fondness in it.

"Who's Tevun?"

"He was my wardkeeper."

"A drakken? Big boy with broken horns?"

"That's the one."

"He stopped the vicars from taking me. Well, at first. What happened to his horns? Aren't wardkeepers supposed to have some big racks atop their drake skulls?" When he didn't reply, Ashe said, "Dead?"

Her father checked a watch he dug from his pocket. "The Fallen has taken everything from Drenth, all that was good. Tevun was not only my wardkeeper, but he was my friend."

"Void, I've lots of friends. I bet being the Gutter King and all, you've got plenty."

Emre whispered something under his breath, something she couldn't make out. Apparently, her jibe had hit a nerve. "Upon

Gargantua lies the Seal of *Terris*. We cannot allow the Fallen to keep it."

"Then why not steal it yourself? I'm certain you've thought plenty about it."

For the first time since he came to her cell, the true Gutter King stood there. Anger rippled across his face, pure rage of crimson aura. "Gargantua will plummet, Brynn. By my hand, the Fallen will feel my wrath. For what he did to us. For those taken."

"O a revenge plot," she said jokingly. "I love those."

Her father grinned. "They search for you, Solanine and Lu Har."

"Yeah, me and Solanine have met."

"And they seek still now that you possess the Eye. Go to them. Find the Seal. The Blood of the Gods has no greater purpose than that." He made for the prison door, stepping through. "Solanine hounds you. They know where you've roosted. Be wary of them, they have spies everywhere. Especially in the gangs. But Lu Har will have grown tired of Solanine's dalliances, he will soon send scourges." A faraway look. "Particularly one scourge…"

"Wait, you want me to turn myself over to Solanine?" she said, noticing that there were no guards on the other side of the door. Nor Cyan or the other vicars. "How did you get in here? Void, how did you even find me?"

"Vicars and Solanine are not the only ones keeping tabs on a gangland thief with aetheurgy." He gave her a wink. "Come on, Brynn, you don't think I hadn't followed your growth since the day you were placed in the Shards' care? I'm a bastard but not an evil bastard."

Ashe sat there, hands in her lap. Finally, she stood and fixed Emre Benld with a heady stare, her bangled hand clenching into a fist. But then she smiled before another pulmo hack doubled her over, black tar staining her lips. "Zenith's cock, I need a drink first."

"I don't think you'll have the opportunity before they come for you." He pulled something from his coat pocket, holding it out to her. "They circle ever closer to us all. Soon, we will have nowhere to run except toward them with all the fire in our hearts."

It was a cloth stained with blood. Looking closer, she realized it was the same fabric as the dress Wren was wearing the nightturn prior.

Hastily, she unfolded it, finding a bloodied lock of hair within. "No… please Zenith, no." Tears stung.

"Tomorrow begins the end, my daughter. Tomorrow, my war reaches its apex. Be on Gargantua when it happens, for I aim to use the Fallen's pride to usher in his demise. Use this anger for a righteous cause." He scratched at his forearms vigorously. "You will know me by a mask of cracked marble, for that is the face of one who has suffered. A better man, or father, wouldn't dare ask this of their child. I wish I was that better man. Regret will shade me until I see the Meadows. My only hope is that one day you will have the heart to forgive me. Whether in this life or the next."

His eyes flashed as he burned, then he was gone.

The door to her cell remained open and Ashe burned her aetheurgy, bolting after, nearly tripping over the sleeping guards and Amaranth the Pure.

Emre

XXII
EMRE

AN HOUR AFTER dawnbreak, Emre sat shirtless on a stool. Val stood behind him as he angled his head backwards, a straight razor held in her steady hand as she sheared the stubble from his face.

"You ready for this, Em?" The razor slid across his chin, the soft clang of her bracelets the only sound other than a slow drip from a nearby faucet. "Once we start, it cannot be undone."

"As ready as can be. Are you?" He opened his eyes and found hers narrowed as she worked. "I know how hard this is for you, Val. Trust me, I know the pain that it will cause. Not just for you, but for him."

The blade stopped. "This isn't going to end the way you wish. She cannot be tamed. And he will get over it, he knows what's at stake."

A somber smile tinged his lips. *Steel it, Benld. You must carry the strength until the end.* "Which *she* do you speak of? Both, I suppose? If there were any other way, I'd do it."

Val nodded, sadly almost, and then resumed shaving him. Even with his outward feign at confidence, he didn't trust his own hand not to shake. When she was finished, he stood and washed his face with clean water. Toweling dry, he held the gaze of the man staring back. He didn't know how he felt about his meeting with Brynn. He was elated to finally see his daughter again, but there existed a grudging hatefulness that seeped into the edges of his mind. He hated himself for using her, just as he used everyone else. No father should do that to a child.

But he had to.

Gods, she reminded him so of Cadrianna. The face, the demeanor, void, the attitude. She was beautiful from the moment he first laid eyes on her and beautiful she'd grown. How he hated not seeing her grow to womanhood, of the probability he wouldn't see her become what she was meant for. His war against the Fallen would consume him, but it would consume her if he didn't do what was necessary.

"Why didn't you take me with you to meet her? And why would you just let her go like that?" His gaze flicked to the doorway to find Finn standing with his arms crossed, a frown marring that handsome face of his. "We could have taken her with us, Em. Hopped on a boat and sailed in luxury all the way to Kalderim. You always said you wanted to go on a cruise." There was hurt in the jest. Sorrow even.

"I want nothing more than to hold her tight and never let go." Emre clenched his fingers nervously on the sink so he wouldn't betray his thoughts. Or scratch his arms. *No, steel it!* Control came back, slightly. "Know me she must, but trust me, she cannot. I'll only bring her further ruination. What she must become must be her way and hers alone. Not mine. I can only show her the path, the trail she follows must be what she makes. She is the Godsblood. She is the chosen of the First Wife."

Though it hurt him more than anything to withhold the truth from his daughter, it needed to happen. Even after all these years, seeing her now, it brought shame. Shame in knowing that he had failed her. Failed to be the father she deserved. He had to win. And he had to use Brynn. Everything else must be cast aside.

And it cost him everything, including his soul.

"You know something you aren't telling me." Finn glanced at his sister. "Val knows. I bet Tevun did, too."

"Yes," he whispered toward the face in the mirror. The face of a betrayer. The face he crafted the day he lost both Cadrianna and Brynn.

There was hurt in Finn's eyes, like he had been slapped. "Family always comes first?"

If only you knew what role you are to play, Finn, my love. What Val won't tell you. About the coming storm to Kalderim and your family. "I'm sorry, Finn. But I can't just let her go. She's my daughter. Cad is lost to me, probably for eternity. Brynn is the only family I have left."

"You know that isn't true." The hurt in the elfir's voice only exacerbated the problem.

"You're both family. You know what I meant." *Cad… I… please don't forget why I did this to us.* For all the trials he had faced and overcome, his heart broke for what his beloved must've undertaken, what she was forced to do under the pall of the Fallen. "Finn," his voice quivered. "You know I trust you with my life." He did mean it. Some things he had to keep to himself, no matter how much it hurt him. He couldn't abide a second broken heart. "But this is bigger than both of us. You know what Brynn is. What she's capable of. We need her. I need her."

Finn reached for Emre's trembling hands. "Gods above, I know, love." The radiant smile that had captured Emre's heart returned. "I accept your apology. You owe me, though. And I can think of a few things, some that might be nas… nah, I'll not spoil the fun."

Emre grinned despite himself. Despite his heart already rending.

"You two lovebirds done grousing over hurt feelings in here?" Wick asked from the hallway.

"In fact, we were just waiting for you to show up to begin our grousing," Finn shot back.

"Pound slag, needle dick."

Emre was thankful for the lapin's intrusion, as it was getting harder for him to still the pain inside. He put on his blank face, the visage of the Gutter King. "It's time, Finn. You must get in place long before us."

"What, no joint shower as a make-up?" When Emre didn't budge, Finn huffed in mock disappointment. "Fine, be that way. Those detonators won't get to Gargantua on their own, eh?"

Finn and Wick retreated while Val moved beside him in the mirror. She had put her goggles back in place and began to comb her fingers through her hair, but there was a melancholy about her.

"What else did you see, Val?" Her goggles were nothing but black tints, although a small crease formed between her brows, her hand stopping within the silver. "When you summoned Tevun from the Meadows. Did the Virtuous One give you any glimpse of Cad? Of her soul? Did Bliss speak to you?"

Void Form left residues of one's soul in the Meadows because it harnessed Death itself, borne of Noctis in the Pit. Every rune drawn in blood created the link between the realm of the living and that of the dead. Fragments of a soul were but the recompense. And for a scourge lost in the sway of Void Form as his beloved Cadrianna, her soul was bound to the Meadows.

Cad…

"I'm not sure," the bikrome answered in her whispery tone. "I saw only fleeting glimpses of her soul and that was only because of her withering links to Tevun's. She is bound in darkness. Lies, I believe. They encase her like a tomb. But there is more, Em. Her soul isn't just bound to Nocturne, but that of something greater. It won't be easy to break that bond. It will have to come from her should she pass the bond."

"They protect her, the lies. We've seen firsthand what the Fallen is capable of." He fought down the urge to scratch his arms. "It will be the same unto her. The blade does complicate matters. Unforeseen, this is, but at least we now know the truth. The First Wife has claimed her."

"She isn't ready cede her comfort. The lies are wrapped so tightly around her; it is going to take more than what you have planned. There is but one path that will lead her astray and into redemption. The Godsblood will wake her and then will break her."

"We won't lose her this time, Val."

"Always so confident. You didn't see the fear inside of Cadrianna's soul. You didn't feel her pain. I felt it that day when she was taken by Lu Har and Solanine. I feel it every time I go into the Meadows to commune with Bliss." The bikrome shivered, rubbing her bare arms.

Emre hugged her tightly. She was cold, her skin like the ice of Kanja. "I don't have to see, I know it. She's hurting. And I won't leave her. Either of them."

"I fear more for Brynn than for Cadrianna, though both hurt equally." Val laid her head on his shoulder. They stood in silence for a while, just lost in their own thoughts before Val spoke again. "Will the strength of your conviction follow you into the Meadows? For that is the only way you can guide her."

"I… I hope so."

"Hey now, he's mine, dear sister-friend," Finn declared as he strolled into the room once more, giving Emre the latitude to not respond further, for he didn't know if the belief was strong enough. It had to be; it just did.

Finn wore a form-fitting black and red overcoat with loose sleeves, a black buttoned shirt tucked into impossibly tight dark trousers that accentuated some of his… finer qualities. Leather boots flipped at the knee completed the ensemble. The bruise on his face from the scourge's attack had been covered with a light dusting of rouge; the small cut in his eyebrow had been hidden by darkened kohl blended into the hairs, while also concealed by a strategic placement of a lock of his silver hair, the rest tied back in a tail.

The third child of the Golden Throne did a dramatic twirl, though groaned as he raised his injured shoulder. "And the best dressed servant award goes to… me!"

Emre recalled the first moment he laid eyes on the elfir moments after being brought back to life. His love would always remain with Cadrianna, but Emre fell hard for that elfir right then and there. His heart carried the love for both, and soon would break in twain.

And it hurt him in the process. He had to remember the reasons to stay the course.

"Don't get cocky, needle dick," Wick grumbled as he pushed Finn out of the way. The lapin was dressed far more simply, a similarly colored tunic and pant. The sleeves rolled at the elbow and his boots cut just above the ankle of his paws. An outfit more apt for one working in the kitchens as opposed to being in view at the party.

"You remember the plan?" Emre dug into his pocket and pulled forth a small container. Within was a new prototype in vision technology crafted by some of the rebellion's finest aetheurgists. The ingeniators would soil themselves in learning they hadn't created them first.

"Like I could forget? I planned this part, remember, love?" He opened the container and drew forth two small circular lenses. Taking stock in the mirror, the elfir put on the false lenses, leaving only blue eyes with no yellowed pupil. "Buggers, these are uncomfortable."

"Just like our escape from the mines?"

"I seem to remember that working out just fine." Finn pulled free a tiny vial from his pocket and dabbed a floral perfume on both his wrists, then pocketed a wallet of parch, somehow fitting it into the tight trousers without it being conspicuous.

They embraced, Emre clutching the bigger elfir, their foreheads pressed against another, taking in his scent, remembering. Finn leaned down and gave him a deep kiss before pulling away, the knowledge of everything going to slag palpable in the air.

"Be safe, Finn."

"And you, love." The elfir turned, but not before a fraction of indecision crossed his face. Or was it sadness?

Does he know what was to come? He can't, Val wouldn't have told him, he wouldn't be this cheerful if she did. I love you, Finnus. Forever. Don't forget me.

Finn grinned. "Come on, Wick. Time for pay back."

Emre and Val stood motionless. It was like half of Emre's soul being ripped from him. Everything was about to come to a head, all the planning, all the hours making sure everything fell into place, all the coin spent on information or the gravy paying off the guards. It all was about to start. Death and fire waiting.

And yet, it could all unravel at any moment because so much balanced upon Cadrianna and Brynn.

"I won't tell him," Val said softly. "He can't know beforehand, Em. It'll break him if he knows. Like…" The bikrome tensed as if she wanted to say more but didn't. Instead, she muttered, "I'm going to get ready."

"What's with her?" Ruane asked as she and Lojen marched into the room. The big drakken heir sullenly watched the bikrome rush by, the soft sounds of tears swallowed back.

"It's going to be a long day," Emre responded as he undid the silken bag hanging on a peg next to the mirror, revealing an immaculate three-piece black suit.

"So, what's the plan, humir?"

Despite the ache in his heart, his fingers deftly buttoned up the white shirt. "Solanine throws a party each year in commemoration of the Fallen's victory in Drenth." With the collar popped, Emre began to braid an intricate knot with his silken tie. "All the Houses under their thumb will be in attendance."

"Bugger them all," Ruane spat. "Why not just blow Gargantua from the sky, take out all those sympathetic to the Imperium in one fell swoop."

"And kill more of my people? No, that won't do, Ruane." With the knot tied, Emre pulled on the waistcoat and buttoned the three silver studs. He then slung his pocket watch into one of the vest's pockets. "As long as Gargantua is tethered above the city, I won't allow it to be blown apart. Besides, we want Solanine and the Fallen to suffer. A quick death is too good for them." He shrugged into his topcoat. "But that doesn't mean we can't still bring it to the ground."

Ruane's snout bristled in a pointy-toothed grin. "Tasty. Where do we fit into all this?"

"A few fireworks will be your task, Ruane. All the guests will be checked for any weapons upon their personages. You'll need to carry the bombs aboard and place them in carefully determined locations." Emre drew forth another container with false lenses. Staring back into the mirror, he placed them into his eyes, covering the emerald center. He blinked a few times as the aether spelled within took root onto his eyes. Finn was correct, they were uncomfortable. "Lojen, with all focused on the party, you'll have reign to find the Seal and Hammer. Your father's horns should be there as well."

"Guarded heavily, I would fathom." Lojen seemed a tad more reserved than his sister, more realistic in what was being asked of them. It wasn't a simple task, and the drakken heir knew it.

"Undoubtedly. With our showing at the aethecite factories and the rumors of the Fallen readying his war upon Kalderim, we expect the guard to be doubled. If not more."

"Why even throw this party then?"

Because they know I'm coming for them. "Solanine's ego won't allow it otherwise. I've never been, but from what I understand, Solanine goes all out. The Fallen shows his face, maybe makes a speech, but then retreats back into his spire."

"And the others?"

"Aside from the bombs you two will carry as you climb the tethers, Val and myself will need something to play with. We have other spies within Gargantua. Wick will meet up with them and then with you, Lojen, to help you find the Seal and your father's horns. Finn will be our distraction."

"And what will you be doing?"

Emre pulled at the cuffs of his sleeves, smiling. "Enjoying the party."

The look on Ruane's face did little to keep Emre from laughing. Lojen growled a deep guttural bark that Emre realized was a laugh. It felt good, the laugh.

Ruane, however, didn't seem amused. "What of the scourges? Of Solanine and the Fallen?"

Is this where my betrayal comes to demand its tithe, Cad? "Leave them to me and Val. Especially Lu Har." Ruane's anger stole across her face.

"Ease, Ruane Tevunsdotyr. You'll get your chance. You just need to focus on setting the bombs and finding the Seal."

"And where will we be planting these bombs, humir?"

"The tethers."

"But you said not to blow them." A coarse tongue licked her snout in eagerness.

"After the tethers are blown, chaos will ensue. Once we secure the Seal, the Hammer, and the horns, we'll lead Lu Har and his floating city toward the mines. If we're going to fight the Imperium, I want it far in the desert."

Lojen stared at him in a manner that reminded of Tevun. Calculating the odds of success, no doubt. Finally, he spoke, "What of your catalyst?"

Brynn... "In due course, Lojen." Emre tucked a kerchief into his breast pocket. "Let's get you prepared; we leave soon. We have a diversion to create so you can get on the tethers."

XXIII
ASHE

PLEASE, ZENITH, NOT her.

People were nothing but blurs as her Shard Form filled her as she sped from Bar Stock all the way to Slag's End. The streets were choked with warehouse workers, miners, vagrants, and Imperium soldiers. She saw nothing, only thinking about her destination. Curses met her aether-enhanced hearing as she bumped into people, but she ignored it all.

The mist had found her the moment she'd stepped outside of the prison, swirling around her like a pack of wolves. It raged inside of her, felt her hurt, fueled her pain. Swam beside her as she ran, keeping in tune with the beat of her heart.

Time was nothing until she finally slowed, her legs churned acid as *The Colosseum* came into view. It had taken her hours, far longer than it should have. The city was chaos due to the bombings and the coming party on Gargantua.

There were streaks of blood upon the ill-kempt doors. Stifling a pulmo cough, Ashe pushed them open on their old hinges. What greeted her was the sight of nightmares.

Blood—fresh and dripping—covered everything. The walls. The floorboards. The broken tables and chairs. The bartop cleaved in twain by aetheurgy, bottles broken behind. Liquor and offal cloyed her aetheric senses.

Numb and unable to grasp any sort of emotion other than raw fear as it climbed up her back like spider's legs. She should have been there with them. She could have protected them with her aetheurgy. Instead, she'd gotten drunk and captured by the vicars. Her knees felt weak, and she should've slumped to the ground, but instead forced herself to look at the bodies. To survey each. To remember them.

There were over twenty bodies. Men and women she knew, drank with, laughed with. Olaf and others of Slag's End hung limply from frayed ropes, their skin flayed from their corpses, lying in piles at their feet. Gaping, burnt holes in exposed muscles by *Ignis*. Bones blackened and protruded as if forcibly ripped free with aetheric strength. Pools of crimson cruor mixed below, bullet casings littered the floor, stuck to the gummy claret. Each face tortured. Whoever had done this had taken their time.

Her heart skipped a beat when she realized Wren wasn't amongst the dead. Neither were Elian nor Evander. Nor were any of Neenah LeFleur's crew. Thank the Pentax. Her pulmo burst from her breast so hard she retched.

"Bloodbath, innit?" someone said from behind with a raspy lisp.

Ashe spun to find Red Tulio leaning against the doorway, Quick Fingers Cyrus squatting next to him. Visions of Red Tulio bathing in the blood of his victims ran roughshod through her benumbed mind. Anger started to rise from the depths, the mist curling up her leg in blackened furor.

"Did you do this!" She sprang toward the flame-haired orcirish thug. The faithful mist surged, darkened, and demanded justice. Red Tulio sidestepped her swinging arm with surprising gracefulness.

"Bitch's got spunk, eh?" Quick Fingers snorted as Ashe swung at Red Tulio again, aiming for that broken nose of his. She snarled at the wiry shrewkin, who was fingering a black crystal pendant around his neck with those rodent-like fingers of his.

"Knock it off, girl," Red Tulio said as he caught Ashe's wrist in a fist the size of her head.

Her eyes went wide. "How?" Her aetheurgy should've rended his greenish flesh like a knife through warm lard, and yet, he countered each punch, untouched. He didn't use any Form, always drinking parch to counter the radiation of the desert every six hours like all the rest of Drenth.

And yet, somehow, he fought her aetheurgy off without breaking a sweat.

All her anger fled from her and weakness seeped in. All her gifts and she was useless as a newborn pup during a bear hunt. Her pulmo exploded as she tried to free her arm, but he held her strong in a grip of yellowed and cracked nails.

"Sorry, girl, Elian's looking for you." His breath was unbearably fetid.

"Elian? Bugger him."

With that, Ashe summoned the mist and channeled it into a quake of *Terris*. The ground rumbled under their feet, throwing all three to the muddy streets of Slag's End. She was up in an instant and ran, spelling the mist to hide her as she did with the vicars in the market, creating only an empty space of invisibility.

Quick Fingers yelled something, but she turned a corner and booked it.

Halfway across Slag's End, she finally slowed to a crawl and slid down against a brick wall. Ashe pulled her knees under her chin, arms wrapped tightly about them. Out of breath, she felt numb. She didn't care that she was in full view of those around, she didn't care that people passed by the alley mere feet away. It didn't matter that her face was streaked with tears and dried pulmo tar.

All that mattered was that she was lost.

Brynn. Father. Mother. Benld. Benld. Benld. Brynn Benld. Me.

Like a child who had wandered away from an open door and no parent around to keep her from walking out, she was prey to her inner daemons. They hounded her, circled within a storm of doubt, of self-loathing, of denial and repulse. A cacophony of tumult.

"I was a child! A baby. Damn you, Cyan!"

She screamed into her knees, clenching her fists tight, her knuckles white with animosity. The mist vortexed around her, mimicking her anger. A nearby vagrant glanced at her but then lay back down.

"You lied to me. All these years, you lied!"

The tears welled anew; the mist softly poking her in soothing touch. How could she have been so blind? A path she'd walked was one so fated. No choice had she all these years. Only to be led down one already written by the Pentax for her.

No, she'd make her own choices from now on. Godsblood be godsdamned.

Getting to her feet, Ashe wiped away the tears and composed herself, not to be some broken-hearted, weepy girl. Judging by the sun in the sky beyond Gargantua, it was nearing midday. Her mind was set. If Solanine wanted her, then she was going to step up to the wench. The vision showed them locked in battle.

Hard to argue with fate, better to meet it with a fist.

Ashe came to the base of the northern tether some twenty minutes later.

Each link of the chain was thrice the size of her height and four times as wide. The steel, itself, was greater in circumference than any of the enormous trees in Calibrath. The links were welded and riveted into fifty-foot stakes with unbroken eye-rings attached at the top. Along each chain was a gondola line. Shaped like a glass bowl with an oblong roof, the gondola rode along a pair of steel cables, motorized by a small aethecite engine. At every tether, two such gondolas rode the lines, one going up while the other came down. A chain-link fence surrounded the gondola entrance, along with six armed Imperium soldiers at all times.

However, today the guard was tripled because of Lu Har's party.

There was a line already. Scores of Drenth nobles wearing gaudy stolae and tailored suits with intricate masks or veils. She was surprised by the number of guests waiting. Scattered amongst the nobles were servants and workers. All were dressed in tight, yet loose fitting sleeved overcoats of black-and-red, while others wore simpler tunics. There was a handful of lapin within the crowd, a few hobgoblins, and a scattering of Kanja and Drenth lowborn.

A costume party? That's what the Gutter King meant when he said I'd know him by his cracked marble mask.

It was just like Solanine to have chosen a less suitable form of ostentation.

As she neared the back of the line, a tall elfir with long, silverish hair standing next to a lapin with what appeared to be ears that had been shredded like cheese winked at her. She scowled at the man, but his smile never faded.

Bugger this.

Pushing through the crowd, and accompanied by more than a few unsavory words, she made a straight line toward the gondola. An Imperium soldier muttered phrases not meant for children's ears as she approached. His face was pockmarked and tanned. Brown eyes narrowed under thin, well-manicured eyebrows, and there was a ring of kohl around his lids.

"I need to see Solanine," she said as she stopped.

He appraised her from head to toe, apparently not liking what he saw. His aura was a sickly emerald shade. "I'm sorry, young mistress, but unless you've an invitation, I can't let you board. Especially looking like you took a bath in a pile of manure."

Some of the nobles chuckled.

"Bugger your orders, you prick-sucking asshole." She stepped closer to him, the venom in her voice unmistakable. The mist echoed her by crawling up her back in dark grey fingers. "I've had a trying morning. Solanine is expecting me. Don't want to keep the Fallen's bitch waiting."

The man flinched but held his ground, uneasily glancing to the armored soldiers surrounding him, the nobles had all backed away a handful of steps. "I can send a message to the gate up top, but that'll take a few minutes."

"I don't have time to waste." Ashe brushed past the blathering idiot and boarded the gondola, taking a seat farthest away from the entrance, in the corner. "Tell her Brynn Benld is on her way up. Wouldn't want her vaunted guest to wait."

Both workers and Drenth nobles climbed aboard shortly after, taking seats away from her. There was enough room in the gondola for upwards of thirty people, but only a dozen or so decided to board with her, the rest willing to wait for the next ride. That winking elfir and his lapin buddy amongst them.

The aethecite engine hummed as it began to rev, and the gondola started to rise along the cables. Eyes behind masks made furtive glances her way, but Ashe ignored them as she put an elbow on the sill and stared out the window. The gondola rose slowly compared to the speeds in which gliders and transports were concerned, but the Fallen wanted his guests to enjoy the slow ascent to the mighty fortress in the sky, almost a full thirty-minute ride to the top. There was mild talk amongst the party guests, a few giggles behind gloved hands, shielded in obscurity behind ornate masks.

Like sheep you are. A name from the dead and all you can do is bleat.

They were just clearing the tops of the highest building in Drenth when the window shattered behind the force of steel-toed boots that connected into her sternum. Shrieks from the women on the gondola echoed as her head smacked the pane from the force of the blow.

"Zenith's co—"

Her attacker pressed as Ashe gripped the railing for support and quickly blocked a punch aimed at her head, instinctively driving her knee upward into their gut as her Shard Form came alive. Her years of training under Cyan came rushing to the fore. She parried another blow and shoved the arm away, finally able to rise to her feet.

The attacker backed away, and judging from the physique, this one was female. Curvy at the hip and bust, not packed with gobs of muscle, and standing about her own height. The woman wore full firedrake armor and a black tinted breather that hid the face behind. Scourge.

The scourge drew a knife and lunged, but the mist sprang into action, creating a dense wall before her, and she whirled away, her hand jabbing the incoming wrist with the gale force of *Aere* behind it. The bone would have shattered had the woman not been already curling her arm backward with aetheric speed.

This scourge also possessed aetheurgy, she realized with shock.

But the scourge's attack had obviously been a ploy as she kicked with her back foot and caught Ashe across her unprotected thigh with a bone-crunching jolt. Ashe countered with a series of kicks aimed at the scourge's head, but the woman used her forearms to block the assault. Ashe spun in a circle, back leg dancing away from the stab of her opponent's knife, mere inches from connecting with her artery. Her open palm struck the woman's helmet, sending a shockwave down her arm.

The unfortunate guests and workers backed against the gondola's opposite window, and the carriage swayed drastically under the intense shifts of their fight. The scourge lunged again, this time with a punch, then a feint with the dagger, jabbing quickly with both. Ashe used *Aere* to block the first two but took a fraction of a second too long on the third and a grunt escaped her lips as the woman's aether-enhanced fist pummeled her gut, her legs rising from the ground with its force. It felt like being battered by an avalanche of warhammers.

The assassin tried to strike her again, but Ashe saw the attack coming, thankfully, and countered with her own, thrusting her fingers in a stiff jab into the woman's crotch with enough force to grind seedpods into pulp had she been a man, but she wasn't, so, the scourge merely staggered with a stifled yelp and a bowlegged waddle.

Bloody void, she's strong. Ashe danced backward, wary. "Gonna have to do better than that."

The scourge mumbled something to her barb, but it was a bunch of gibberish to Ashe's ear. Then she sent a flying kick, to which Ashe blocked easily. Almost too easily.

And she was right, the woman was only trying to switch positions with her.

Now near the broken glass, the scourge grabbed one of the guests and pulled a woman in front, fighting back the woman's date with her knife. "Back."

The tall elfirish man bore a look that might kill, but the lapin stepped in front, holding him at bay. *He isn't a simple servant, is he?*

"A human shield?" Ashe set her feet, raising her fists. "Coward."

"We'll see if your conviction stands after what you've learned last nightturn." The voice was muffled but there was an air of familiarity within it, one Ashe couldn't quite place.

"What's in Zenith's buggerhole is that supposed to mean?"

Her slight hesitation cost her as the scourge lifted the quite terrified woman and tossed her toward Ashe with aetheric strength. Ashe instinctively (albeit stupidly) sidestepped the sailing woman, who crashed into the already weakened pane. There was a sharp crack, followed by a high-pitched scream. Ashe dove for the woman as her body tumbled over the railing, catching her corset in an iron grip of aetheurgy. The woman, facing downwards to a view of hundreds of feet of empty air, kicked and screamed.

"Come on, lady!" Ashe growled.

And that's when she felt the knife at her throat.

The scourge's tinted helmet leveled next to her ear as she struggled to hold the weight of the woman and maintain a grip on the gondola. "You're lucky Solanine wants you alive, otherwise I'd slit your throat right here and now."

"Fuck you," she seethed, her arms straining under the woman's mass, her aetheurgy ebbing.

"Soon enough."

The leather of the woman's corset began to tear. Ashe's head throbbed; her neck wet from sudden blood under the knife. Her fingers burned as she dug them deeper into the gondola's metal. She spared a glance down toward the woman who floundered a hair's breadth away from instant death, the woman's aura ablaze in fear. Air, clear above the buildings of Drenth, no clouds, only beautiful midday sunlight.

I've found myself. Clarity at the oddest of times. *Saving an innocent. Fitting, eh, Father?*

And then the sun was blotted out by stone girded with metal rods, as the gondola entered Gargantua's underbelly. Ashe dropped the woman, who unleashed an ungodsly screech only for it to become a pained grunt as she collapsed upon a girder, safely if not bruised.

Ashe eased herself back into the gondola, facing the scourge. "Parlay?"

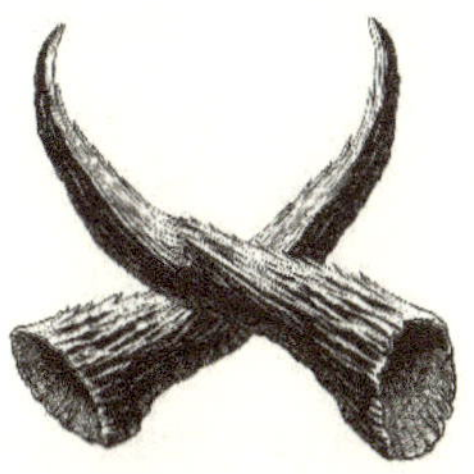

XXIV
LOJEN

"ALL THAT MATTERS is I get to poke Lu Har with my blade," Ruane said as she sharpened her drakken longknife on a whetstone. She examined the edge with the tip of her claw.

"If everything works out, you might have to wait in line."

There was something in Emre's voice that bordered on madness. Lojen wondered if the scion of Drenth was relying too much on a plan that could teeter either way. Too many cracks they could fall through, too many bridges with a chasm on either side yearning for them to lose balance.

Emre handed Lojen a satchel, then he picked up a multi-barrel wheellock pistol engraved with the letter 'B' before passing it to him. Lojen wasn't much for firearms, but he bagged the gun regardless. On the table were cylinders made of metal with capped ends that were perhaps about as wide as one of Lojen's canines. They were bound into small batches, each wrapped with thick tape. Affixed to each bundle were small mechanical *Aere*-inscribed radios that were spelled for detonation. All told, there were at least sixty bombs.

"How are we supposed to get on the tethers?"

"With these, Lojen." Emre handed him a pair of steel-shod, fingerless gloves with protruding grips on the undersides.

They were formed to fit a drakken's talon. He examined the protrusions; they were dense and was a different metal than the rest of the grips. "Magnets?"

"Those magnets will stick to any metal. Drakken can climb godsdamned near anything, but we don't want to take any chances. To unfasten them and re-grip, press downward with your palm, fingers… um, claws up to disengage from whatever surface you're on. Otherwise, you won't go anywhere."

"You tested these?"

"Your father did," Emre said. "Used it to scale the tethers."

"He did?"

"About a year ago when we started this plan. Someone had to be the test subject."

O Father…

Emre handed them both a tiny black object the size of an apple seed. "Here."

Ruane turned it over in her claw and Lojen realized it was an earpiece, designed for a drakken's earhole. His sister put the earpiece in. "It tingles."

"Soon enough you'll forget it's there. Just remember, when inside, you don't have to raise your voice any more than a whisper, these are *Aere* created and the range on these bad boys is excellent."

Whispering was not something his sister was known for. "Gon' be hard for you then, eh, Ru?"

"What you talking about?" she said quite loudly, illustrating his point. Lojen chuckled. "What?"

"You make sure they're all charged?" Valeria Dunleith asked as she flowed into the room.

Emre whistled. "Who knew you cleaned up so nice?"

The bikrome wore a dark blue stola that eerily contrasted, yet oddly highlighted her pale arms, which were bare from the shoulder down. Her bracelets didn't look out of place against the elegance of her dress. The gown hugged her hips in all the right spots, the backside poofed by layers of undertrain. A corset, almost vest-like but low cut, was tightened around her waist, revealing more of her porcelain skin. Her silver hair was coiled behind her head while thick strands hung loose at her temples in ringlets. A sheer, yet black veil covered her face from a thin golden chain at her forehead, a shining yellow gemstone just above her shielded eyes.

Valeria looked every inch the royal daughter of the Golden Throne.

Ruane grumbled under her breath about not getting to wear something nicer than the 'rags' she was wearing. Lojen elbowed her, but he smiled anyway, it was the first time in ages she had expressed anything other than anger.

Val straightened Emre's tie, then held out a mask that resembled marble for him to take. "Shall we?"

"A costume party?"

"Solanine likes grandeur, Lojen. And better for us. Makes us less obvious." Emre crooked his arm and the bikrome intertwined her hand within, laying it upon his forearm. "Although, I would assume she and the Fallen will be expecting us to make our move under such disguise. Regardless, it's now or never." Emre reached into his coat pocket and handed a folded piece of parchment to him. "Map of the inside of Gargantua and the compound. Some of it's crude. Sorry, our spies did the best they could. Your father was able to get most of the engine rooms on his initial climb."

As they left the safehouse, Lojen stopped and took one last look at his father's body. Gripping his father's talon, Lojen prayed. "Lead him to Your table, Zenith. May his actions in this life settle him at a seat near You in the Meadows. May his deeds be worthy of You. Let him be at peace, He Who Fathered the World. Until the end."

In Marketside, the people—the regular ones, not the nobles invited to the party, but the miners, the shopkeepers, the vagrants—all wandered the streets with apprehension.

All knew at the drop of a coin; the city could implode upon itself on an evenfall such as this. Rebellion had dried out these people like fruit left in the sun for too long. They had to be so accustomed to the explosions, the riots, the open warfare, that it could happen at any moment. But this time, on the day their 'benevolent' ruler opened the gate to his home, the tension was palpable in the air.

"Remember," Emre said, speaking in a normal voice through the radio in his earhole. "You'll have to jump the gondola before the final building is passed. If you aren't on the chain by then, the other ride might see you and the whole plan is ruined."

"We aren't stupid, humir."

"Em, look," Val whispered into the comm.

"What is it?" Lojen asked.

"The Arbiter's bloody axe," Emre breathed. "A scourge."

"What do we do now?" Lojen backed Ruane into an alley. "This isn't good."

"Tell me something I don't know, you Scurred Hatch." Ruane put a clawed talon to the rounded protrusions above her eyes as humir did when they were dismayed by something. Or just in frustration.

Lojen craned his neck to look over the crowd. There, ahead of them was a cluster of Imperium guards about a block away from the tether. A barricade of fence and wheellock rifles. A long line of Drenth's citizens waited to get on the gondola as the guards only allowed the people in by ones or twos. A pair of automatons hunkered across from the tether. Rounded heads with blinking orange lights.

But it was the scourge who stepped out of the recently docked gondola that drew Lojen's attention.

This scourge was a woman of medium height and covered neck to boot in drake scale. Her dark, almost black hair was cut to her shoulders. She had a mouth that seemed in a forever pout. Her all-onyx eyes scanned the crowd as she rested her hand lightly upon a blackened blade sheathed at her hip. From where he stood, it almost looked like the blade had the outstretched wings of a bird.

"Em, it's her."

"I see that, Val." There was slight panic in Emre's voice. The scion of Drenth cursed unintelligibly in the radio. They knew this scourge and it set Lojen on edge.

"Everyone keep calm," one of the Imperium guards said with a raised voice to the crowded nobles as the scourge watched on, scrutinizing the crowd. "We had to replace one of our gondolas due to a malfunction with the aethecite engine. Routine maintenance is all. Please have your tickets visible and we'll get you up to the party in no time."

"What do you think, Em?"

"A minor setback, Val. We planned for this eventuality. Maybe not necessarily a scourge right from the jump, nor her, but it'll be fine. Ruane, you still got those charges I gave you?" The urgency in Emre's tone told Lojen that they hadn't expected this.

Who is this scourge?

"Of course, you think I'd lose them?"

"You need to back away slowly, don't make a scene. If the scourge notices you, it could ruin everything. We can't let her see us. Yet."

"Why do you think we ducked into an alleyway the moment you said something?" That was the wardkeeper buried in Lojen speaking now.

"Good," Emre said. "We'll come to you."

Emre and the bikrome slipped from growing line of Drenth-born. They weaved through the throng, careful not to bump into anyone or draw attention to themselves. Most were too busy trying to get closer to the barricade, invitations held ready. After a few minutes, Emre and Valeria dipped into the alley.

"What do we do now, Emre?" Lojen asked.

"Ruane, give me one of the charges."

She reached into her vest and pulled out a small cylindrical bomb. Inside was a quarter pound of raw aethecite and some other elements mixed in the proper combination to make it go boom.

"Val?" Emre held the bomb toward the bikrome, who used her aetheurgy, summoning a small *Ignis* flame at her fingertip. With it, she drew a rune onto the *Aere*-created mechanical while Emre spoke, "We'll create a diversion for you two to get upon the chain. Make a wide berth around to the other side of the tether, and then wait for the explosion. In the confusion you can jump aboard."

"Luck, friend," Lojen said, extending his claw to Emre. "You might need this, then?" He proffered the multi-barrel pistol Emre had given him earlier.

The scion of Drenth took the pistol and then Lojen's clawed talon. "For all of us."

"Want this?" Ruane asked of Valeria Dunleith, offering the bikrome one of the other pistols.

The bikromi elfir smiled and shook her head, reached down silkily, and pulled one from somewhere under her stola.

"Where did you hide that, Val?" Emre asked.

"A lady never tells."

As the pair made their way back into the crowd, the Gutter King brushed up against a lamppost, and Lojen saw him bend down as if he was tying his bootlace. But instead, he placed the bomb upon the metal post, a magnetic field clinging tight. Then he dragged Valeria to one side.

As one, the crowd of nobles ducked instinctively from the blast that followed, shrieks and screams matching the deafening sound from the explosion. Smoke billowed into the air; the few remaining pieces of the lamppost flew in a hundred directions. The soldiers at the gondola moved with tactical precision as they herded the guests like cattle toward the far row of buildings and away from the explosion. The scourge drew that blackened blade with the bird wings and jumped the barricade with the intent of battle.

"Now!" Emre barked.

The humir and bikrome raised their weapons and fired into the air, then quickly pushed through the crowd, elbowing well-dressed men and women aside as they raced toward the opposite side of the street.

"Come on, Ru!" Lojen pulled his sister into the mass of flesh and cut a straight path to the tether base.

The barricade was right in front of them now, and the lead row of guests pressed forward trying to make the gondola in a bid for safety. The few remaining Imperium soldiers couldn't stem the tide as they crowded the carriage, rocking it under too many feet. Both Ruane and Lojen took to the fence and climbed behind the gondola. It swayed as they scrambled up to the metal roof, where they huddled upon the rounded carriage roof, Lojen huffing, Ruane grinning earhole to earhole.

"That wasn't too bad," Ruane whispered.

"That was the easy part."

"O don't be such a Scurred Hatch."

Lojen whistled relief as the gondola began to rise, the aethecite engine humming along to the Hymn of War singing in the streets of Drenth once more. The Gutter King and the bikrome disappeared down an alley as they fired their weapons. The scourge and a handful of Imperium soldiers hot on their heels.

The wind streamed over his body as Lojen clung against the smooth metal of the gondola's roof. His stomach was in his boots and there was a giant ball of fear blocking his throat. If he was humir, he'd be scrunching his eyes closed as tightly as he could, and tears would be pouring down his face with the mere thought of what he had agreed to do.

You're an idiot, Lojen. A fool who doesn't know his tail from a shadow.

He forcefully turned his head to see Ruane, and just as he assumed, his sister was loving every second of the ride on the gondola. She beamed; her mouth was open as the air whistled through her teeth. It was just like Ru to be having the time of her life while he lay here and tried to keep his lunch down.

Tentatively, he pushed himself into a plank position, forcing his body to stop shaking. When that was successful—and the overwhelming need to retch passed—he took note of their situation.

Although the gondola wasn't moving very fast, they were rising at a steady pace and had gone past most of the building tops. A few of the larger condominiums still rose like metal trees. But soon enough, they would clear them as well, breaking into open sky.

The links above his head were so large, he could barely see around them. Just below the chain were four six-inch cables in an almost square-like shape, two for each gondola. The aethecite engine had two rotating wheel-like gears between each pair of cables, and the wheels had grooves fitted to the cable.

"Lojen, we're running out of time."

The other gondola—the one coming down—was no more than two hundred feet away. If they didn't get upon the chain soon, their cover might be blown and the whole plan would fail.

Fighting the gurgle in his gullet, Lojen pulled on the climbing gloves, ready to instruct Ru to do the same, but she'd already done so.

"After you, Scurred Hatch. Or do you need your little sister to show you how it's done?"

"By Justice, Ru. Get on with it."

Rubbing her claws together, Ruane launched herself into the air and grabbed the link with the gloves, the magnetic nodules bonding to the chain. The gondola swayed under the force of her jump. She pulled herself upward by pressing her palm into the chain link, removing the magnets as Emre had shown them. Her grip faltered, though, some of the magnets jarring loose, accompanied by a screeching sound as the gloves dug into link. Steel on steel. The shrill pitch was muffled as the engine thrummed, but Ruane slipped further, her magnets not creating enough grip, not holding as they should.

Lojen's heart jumped into his throat as his sister dropped a few more inches, her feet dangling, tail flapping in the empty air. But then she found her grip again, the magnets taking hold. Slowly, she hauled herself up, climbing with primal dexterity. Soon, she was over the top of the chain.

"Justice, protect me."

Ruane was now more than twenty feet behind him, crawling deftly along the links. He spun and saw the other gondola was now a mere one hundred feet away. He couldn't waste any more time.

Gods above. I can't do this. I can't. O Gods. I can't.

"Lojen!" Ruane screamed into his earpiece. "Stop pissin' 'round!"

His throat was dry; his heart raced. *I can do this*, he told himself.

Summoning all the courage remaining, Lojen crouched, his thighs burning with tension. The wind whipped at his sleeveless vest; his tongue pressed against the roof of his mouth. *O Gods. O Gods.*

He leapt, legs pushing with all the strength he could muster. Time seemed to stop as his body flew into the air, suspended, nothing but him, the air, and the chain. His claws struck, the magnetized nodes digging in, sparks flying as the appendages ground, the magnets kissing the smooth steel chain link. His legs flailed in the emptiness, his shoulders strained, careful to only detach the magnets when he was certain he could maintain the grip. He swung sideways, kicking his leg up. Lojen grunted as he found clear purchase over the rounded lip. He threw himself over the ledge, away from the epic drop onto a rounded, yet comfortably secure section of the chain. Panting.

"Lojen. Ruane. You clear?" It was Emre's voice, and it sounded like he was running up a mountain in a thunderstorm.

Ruane crawled along the chain toward him, he could hear her spikes striking the steel.

"Remind me to kill you later, Emre."

There was soft laughter in his earpiece, followed by a grunt, a few fired gunshots, and more hurried breathing. "Take a number. Be safe. See you on Gargantua."

His sister stopped down by his boots, legs hunched under her. "That was fun, wasn't it?"

"You have problems."

XXV
CADRIANNA

A GUNSHOT RANG in the alleyway behind her, but she was only focused on the portal at the base of a stair the rebels had fled into.

Drawing the Strix, she separated it into twin blades. Weapons in hand, she descended, ready to end things. She was swallowed by darkness, the air musty and dank. Her eyes adjusted quickly. Above were dozens of thick copper tubes supplying aetheric energy. A single hall in the dark, a small set of orange lights just below where the ceiling met wall, batting in rhythmic patterns.

Cadrianna moved, calm about her. She was in her element, after all.

"BE WARY, CAD. I HAVE A BAD FEELING ABOUT THIS."

Can a daemon enclosed in steel have feelings, Strix?

"YOU KNOW WHAT I MEAN."

Do I? I'm not certain of anything anymore. Except for Brynn.

"O CAD..."

After a hundred paces, the tunnel branched into three directions. Each looked the same.

"Godsdamn. What do you think, Strix."

The Strix was silent, thinking perhaps? Then it spoke, *"BODIES TO THE LEFT. MAYBE A DAY OLD. MUST BE SOLANINE'S SCOURGE."*

"The Gutter King must be desperate. Desperation breeds rashness."

"DON'T UNDERESTIMATE HIM, CAD, HE IS A PLUCKY ONE."

"Plucky? Do you even know what that word means?"

"I'M WELL PLUGGED INTO THE YOUTH THESE DAYS, WITH THEIR SAYINGS AND SUCH."

Cadrianna shook her head. "Whatever you say, Strix."

Sliding through the darkness of the lefthand tunnel, Cadrianna ignored the corpses as she found a door closed tight, barring her from her prey. A massive lock glinted in the mild titian of the blinking light.

She could feel it in her bones, the Gutter King was here. She didn't know why she felt such conviction, but she did. He was here.

The quickened pulse of blood rushed into her heart as she summoned Void Form, Cadrianna gave a solid kick to the door as the wails of the dead blared. The hatch slammed inward with a groan, dust flying from the rusted hinges. A row of linen-covered corpses greeted her. Slipping just inside the doorway, she scanned every corner. Empty besides the dead.

A cold hand clamped over her mouth from behind. So cold her body went still, almost like the chilly winters of northern Kanja turning her into an ice sculpture. The Strix fell from her hands as hoarfrost tingled across her flesh, the metal so stinging she couldn't hold them any longer. She struggled against the hand, but despite the apparent daintiness of it, it held her contained, rooted in place.

Her entire body felt of ice.

A mouth moved near her ear, she tried to turn her head to see her assailant, but she couldn't move. The smell of the desert sands tingled her sense, breaking the feel of ice. A voice spoke. "Hello, Cad, it's been a long time, my beloved wife. Val?"

Em—

Something hard smashed into the back of her head and she fell…

…into a darkened room with arches of umbra. Looking around, she saw her father and mother, brother, too. Emre and his parents, the regent and regentress. A table with glass bottles between the family members. Liquids and tiny, solid pebbles in the cruets.

Her memory. Gods, it was so real.

The vision scintillated. Her body felt frozen, frost prickled her flesh, her hair felt slick. Cold, so deathly, enveloped her, drawing her down into the memory like a seagandr pulling a drowning man to the inky depths of the ocean.

It was the memory of the day her life ended. But this time it was different, for she wasn't seeing it with her own eyes, but those of another, she realized.

Valeria Dunleith watched from the shadows of an arch made from chiseled stone. A babe wailed in her arms; the child barely weaned. The bikrome cradled the bundle of swaddling, soothing the babe within, whispering soft words.

O, it was too much. "Is this the price I must pay for my betrayal to Canlon?" she whispered to the babe. "This can't be the path, my Divine."

A bloodcurdling scream filled the chamber, burnt flesh mixed with the moldy stink of the grey mist. In the center of the room were the captured family of the Regents Benld. Drenth burning and occupied. Gargantua hovering nihilistically overhead. All crying, whimpering, and afraid. All but one, the Regent's heir. Emre. His curled hair was drenched with sweat, his dark eyes bruised and swollen, portals into his soul that spanned chasms, a rage simmering within.

Valeria held the babe tight, they always broke, the strong ones.

Emre! Cadrianna tried to scream, but she was locked in a memory that wasn't hers. Her mouth formed the words, but only frost came forth. Nocturne, she was so cold. Her entire body shivered. Was she dead? Was this her fate for doing the work of the Fallen? For forsaking her vows to Emre and sharing a bed with Lu Har?

Lu Har, resplendent in a bloodred robe, glided around the young thrashing man. Try as she might, Valeria couldn't help but be mesmerized by him. Even now, nigh on five centuries after the Fall of Eminence and his subsequent rebirth, she still couldn't break the hold the Fallen had over her. It wasn't romantic love, no, not even platonic. It was something else. Spellbinding, he was.

Spellbinding? That can't be. The cold seeped into her very soul. Like a lake covered in a sheet of ice, cracks started to form. But the cracks were her protector and shield. The cold was trying to break in.

Valeria's hand touched the lump buried in the inner pockets of her robe. Heirloom, it was, to the greatest city ever known to man. A key. No, the key to all life. Stolen and replaced by a deft replica with the help of Thestile. It was Valeria's recompense for falling in love with Solanine and helping the Fallen defeat Canlon.

Waiting, she was, until the moment true. She just needed to stand firm until the heir faltered, hoping her resolve wouldn't waver. The babe cried softly, and Valeria shushed the cherub-faced girl with raven-black hair and pearl irises.

White… no… it can't be. This can't be…

The cracks became gullies now. The cold chipped at the stone fortress she'd constructed the day Emre betrayed her. Why now? Why this? The frost burrowed deeper into her soul, wrenching its way in the darkness within her.

The heir wept; his head bowed but still his eyes smoldered. His wife cried uncontrollably as the bodies of the Regents Benld lay discarded, their corpses consumed by void aetheurgy. The babe cried.

Lu Har glared at the heir. "Where is the Seal? You won't like it if I have to ask again. Where is it hidden?"

"Never," the heir said defiantly.

Why couldn't he just answer? Cadrianna sobbed. Why? Cadrianna cried, cried as both Valeria and as herself. Reliving it over afresh, the wound rent open, blistering ice filling the voids.

Valeria tensed as the next sufferer was Efan Nightingale. The man's clothing ripped; his ice-blue eyes fearful.

This was the pure power of Life and Death itself. The power of Soul Form. Of aether. The man bore the blood of the Gods, his ancestor was the First Wife. It was his seed that carried the Godsblood, passed on to Cadrianna, finally onto the baby girl in her arms.

The reason for all of this, the invasion, the murders. All for the Godsblood in her arms.

Cadrianna, Valeria knew, would be taken by the Fallen, initiated into his coven if she survived the trials channeled under the ancient eye of the Divines. As would the babe in her arms, the one named Brynn.

Valeria was determined to not let that happen.

The baby. Brynn…

"Where is it?" the Fallen asked calmly.

"Please," Cadrianna's father, the lineage of Nightingale, implored through strangled sobs.

Emre Benld, last of his line, held his tongue, even though tears streamed down a face of stone and steel. Valeria's heart went out to him. He would hold strong until the end, she now knew.

She mustn't let him travel the Meadows just yet. A new hope reared within her. He could help ruin the Fallen, she realized. With him, she might yet find her redemption.

It would all fall upon her old friend, the wardkeeper of Drenth. Tevun. Dare she still believe in their relationship after all she'd done?

It was possible.

"*Tell him!*" *Cadrianna screamed to her beloved husband, begging for it to end.*

Fight it, Cad. Fight it, she urged herself. This memory… no… I can't take it… stop it! Stop it!

The cracks became an abyss, thrown asunder, her soul lay bare to the cold. Like the opposite of burning aetheurgy, this feeling was utter permafrost. The same pain filled her as the aether burned, but this contained a lack of hurt, just the pain. No warmth, only floe.

The orcirish torturers lingering in the shadows grabbed Cadrianna and lifted her from the chair as if she weighed naught but the measure of her bones and dress.

That's when Emre broke.

He told Lu Har exactly what he wanted. "The Seal of Terris is in the desert," he said dejectedly. "Deep in the desert, within the mines lies the Temple of Mother Marrow. There is the Seal, as is the Forgemistress' Hammer."

The Fallen was pleased, the task complete. He snapped his fingers. Valeria turned, pulling the swaddled babe closer to her breast as one of the hulking orcir sliced Emre Benld's throat from ear to ear.

Cadrianna, the true Cadrianna, couldn't hold back the tears. Downed they flowed. O, how she sobbed. The tears steamed down her cheeks, toward a dam at her lips, something stopping the wetness. The steam crystallized at this mystifying dam. Nocturne, she wanted to wake. To end this nightmare.

Now was Valeria's moment, the time of her redemption had come. With a somber glance toward the dying Benld, she stepped forward. "Master Lu Har, what of the babe?"

"These Nightingales reek of Canlon's stink," the Fallen snarled. To Valeria, "Bind her. And take this one for my flock. If she learns, if she obeys, then the babe lives." He gripped Cadrianna's chin hard, eliciting a yelp. "If not, the babe dies."

She nodded, her heart pounding. It was time to pay her tithe.

Her boots echoed on the worn stones below the Regent's Tower in Drenth. Torches sputtered and cast shadows. A low layer of grey mist circled after, flowing in gossamer rivers of poison. Quirking and alive with aether, its fingers reaching toward the babe in her arms. Towards the Godsblood.

"Where are you going, love?"

Valeria had to breathe deep to compose herself. Turning, she noticed a man approach. Hair the color of sunset grey at the temples, a bearded face. The voice she knew, but the face was new.

"Solanine, my love, I see you've taken new scales," Val whispered. Solanine broke the plane of sputtering torchlight, a second person, a woman—much, much older and blind—leaned upon Solanine's arm. "Matron."

Solanine leaned toward the babe. "My, but she's a pretty thing. Those achromic eyes of a Godsblood. A beauty she no doubt will become."

Valeria fought the urge to pull Brynn away. "That she may."

"The Divine's guile upon us," the Matron proclaimed, her voice the sort that sounded like a rusty dagger on a whetstone. "He guides us strong. Guides us true."

"The way to Eminence will be ours once more," Solanine said, one of the scales' fingers toyed with Brynn's little hand. "And Master Lu Har will reactivate the Crystal of Life, releasing our master into the world of Life. And Eminence's glory will return."

No, no he wouldn't. Not without the true Eye of the Soul. But she had to withdraw now, lest her plan fall to ruin. "He will."

Solanine smiled sweetly to the babe, a peal of child laughter.

"The Strix has long since been dormant," the Matron said through her gritty rasp. "Will she of Nightingale's blood be enough?"

"Godsblood she be," Valeria said, uncertain if Cadrianna could master the weapon of the First Wife. She hoped the woman would never touch the blade. "If she is, your gracious tutelage awaits, Matron."

Cadrianna choked as the permafrost began to lessen. She cried out, the first sound to elicit from her frigid lips. "NO!"

The vision spurred her forward once more, the bikrome in a rush.

Minutes achingly flew by before Valeria crept out of the crypts and out one of the many secret entrances in the outer shell of Drenth. She eased open a panel of stone, exiting into the Sea of Mist. It was still nightturn, the moon the softest shade of crimson, the mist taller than she. A blood moon. Visibility was near absolute negative.

Wetness fell upon her shoulders. Rain pierced the mist. It struck her face, but it didn't taste like water. Coppery. Blood it was.

"Cyan!" Valeria called. She feared her voice would carry.

There were far more dangerous things in the heavy mist than Imperium soldiers and the Fallen's aetheurgists. Even within the mega-city. Daemons and worse prowled in the aftermath of the conquest.

She plunged into the Sea, naught but sandy dunes swallowing her. "Cyan?"

Valeria could barely see her hand stretched out in front of her, it was that dense. Her foot tangled within a low brush, one of the few types of bushes that called the desert home, a prickly thing tearing a slash in her robe. Brynn giggled. Valeria cursed.

What is she doing?

"CAD, THE TRUTH."

There, deep in her heart she felt something stir. It wasn't from the vision, it wasn't from the memory of the past, but something new, something foreign. Cold as frozen rivers but not as cold as before. Strix?

"I'M HERE, CAD. THIS IS THE TRUTH IN WHICH YOU'VE BEEN DENIED. NOT AS YOU REMEMBERED. SEE IT. SEEK IT. I'M HERE FOR YOU. ALWAYS."

But the Strix felt different. Still the same essence, but not like the daemon. No, felt more primal. More ancient. A being of aether.

"Cyan?"

"Here," a response came from the mist.

Valeria crawled over a sand dune in the direction of the voice. The gates of Drenth crashed open, aetheurgists and worse flowed out into the Sea. Hand coated in gritty sand, finding her way through the Sea until she found her man seconds later. He grabbed her wrist gently and pulled her under a withered hunk of tree.

"Never thought you'd show, bikrome." A young man in his prime, handsome in a rugged way behind the glass shield of his leather-breathing mask. He wore the cassock of a Scattered Shards vicar.

"VALERIA!" *The honeyed voice of the Divine as spoken by the Fallen.*

"This is where we go our separate ways, Cyan."

"VALERIA! I CAN SMELL YOUR BLOOD. THE FEAR WITHIN. NIGHTINGALE CRIES FOR YOU. YOU'VE FORSAKEN EVERYTHING. FOR WHAT? CANLON CARR?"

Valeria held out the child. "You must take her. Prophecy has this child marked."

Pentax, no, Cadrianna begged. But this can't be true. Brynn is locked within Gargantua. Locked in the darkness, without me.

A pressure upon Cadrianna's lips, they, too, were cold. Frozen even. The sensation ran down her neck.

"CAD, HEED THIS." The Strix had pierced the vision somehow, someway. **"THE TRUTH IS HERE BEFORE YOU. IT WAS ALWAYS HERE, LOCKED IN THE PAST. LOCKED IN THE SPELLS THE FALLEN HAS WOVEN AROUND YOU."**

Cyan nervously looked about. Shapes began to close in on them. Large shapes. "Daemons," he hissed.

"*VALERIA! THEY COME FOR YOU. THEY WANT THE BABE. THE GODSBLOOD WILL ALWAYS CALL TO THEM.*"

Valeria Dunleith drew a golden blade, the faint light of the moon shimmered upon its polished face, dripping with bloody rivulets. "They are after me, they know not about you. Take the child, Cyan. She must live at all costs. Please, Cyan. Take her and go. See her to Icterine. They will not follow you. I'll see to it."

The stinging cold coursed through her veins, freezing her blood, stopping it dead. Brynn must live. What she'd always told herself. Told herself why she did what she did. For the Fallen. For his coven.

But lies they were.

"LIES, CAD."

You knew?

"I..."

Tell me!

"CAD, PLEASE..."

Tell me!

The shapes came closer, the ground shook now with their steps. Glowing eyes burned within the muted fog. Searching, sniffing, seeking.

Cyan reached for the babe and took Brynn into his arms. "What am I supposed to do with her?"

"Run. Keep her alive. Train her in aetheurgy. No failure must she possess. You will see me again. Now I must return for the heir of Drenth." She shoved him as a lumbering creature skulked from the Sea. Valeria raised the golden blade of her family. Of Kalderim. Of the Golden Throne. Of Bliss. "Flee now. GO!"

The vicar turned tail and fled, carrying with him the child tand, if the prophecy was true, the fate of the world. The massive daemon stalked forward, thick claws scratching, jaws with serrated teeth. Arms the size of tree trunks...

…the vision ended, Cadrianna stormed awake into a swirling of an ice-cold black and white snowstorm, a woman's hands on her cheeks, her frozen lips touching Cadrianna's. Drawing away the cold, the woman released her. The Vision Form fading.

Cadrianna bellowed in the emptiness of the memory, the blistering frost in her body exploding outward. It flew from her mouth as she expunged the hoarfrost in great bouts of clear blue shards. It snowed down all around her.

Savior and shield. She thrashed against the bonds that held her wrists, the chair near to toppling over. "Please no. Please tell me that isn't so. Brynn. Please…"

A Kanjan elfir was crouched defensively a few feet away, a wheellock pistol in one hand, a knife in the other. Her argent hair swept across her face, a peridot gemstone flickered on a chain across her forehead. The black sucked in the light only to be radiated by the ivory white.

It was the bikrome from the visions. Valeria Dunleith of the Golden Throne of Kalderim.

They were in a rundown room, boards planked across the windows, the door ajar only because there was no door. It was dark, only a single aethecite-powered lantern sitting atop a warped table. Beside the lantern was the Strix, sheathed. She yearned to grab the comforting blade but couldn't.

She jerked again, trying to yank the chair's arm from its fasteners, gritting her teeth as she did. "Release me, bikrome."

A wry smile curled at the edge of the bikrome's lips. "Not until you cool the inferno inside you, Cadrianna Benld. The song of Nightingale resides in you."

"What have you done to me?"

There was a hint of curiosity within the bikrome's bi-colored gaze. "Woke you from the dreams of your past."

"Lies!"

"Forgive me for leaving you, my love," came a voice from behind. A voice she recognized, one she both loved and loathed in equal measures. The rebel she was sent to kill, she realized now that she knew the truth. The man moved into her field of vision. "I wanted, no, I tried to save you both."

It can't be.

There was no mistaking him, she'd recognize that posture, that swell of shoulder, that curl of hair, the very presence. If a thousand years spanned the time between their last words, she would know him still.

Emre Benld, her beloved husband. Her betrayer.

No, not him. Not now, not here. "Emre?" She couldn't mask the genuine fear in her. The memories had broken the lies binding her, but her mind still wasn't ready to concede the truth. "How?"

"CAD, LISTEN TO HIM. STAY. TRUST ME. THE LIES HAVE NOW BEEN BROKEN." The Strix still lay upon the table, but she could feel the daemon's sorrow. She tried to call to it, but the blade held firm, as if stuck. ***"THIS IS FOR THE BEST. I WILL REMAIN. YOU SHOULD TOO."***

"I… I… I can't." *Nocturne, O Nocturne, why?*

"Not all deaths are final, my beloved. You know this all too well." Emre's normally loose curls hung about his temples, salted grey flecked his hair. Pentax, he looked as handsome as the day she'd married him. As handsome as the day he betrayed her. "Val, release her. Until she's ready to see the truth, she cannot help us. Cannot help Brynn."

"The girl has the Eye, Cadrianna Benld," the elfir said in naught more than a whisper. "The Eye will lead her back to Eminence. You know what Lu Har desires with such an outcome. The blood of a Nightingale must claim their entitlement."

"You lured her here? Brynn?" *No!, It cannot be her. How?*

"She is the Godsblood, Cad," Emre said. "He needs Nightingale's blood." He looked toward the Strix. "Whatever he told you, isn't true. Everything that man spews is a lie. It's what drove us apart. It's what took our daughter from us."

"You took her from us! With your silence!"

"I did what I had to. Same as you would. It was the only way to save her. To save us. To save Drenth." Emre put a hand to the bikrome's shoulder. "It was the only way for us to be here for her, Cad. She needs us."

'KILL HIM!' Lu Har screamed at her in her mind.

No! Stay, Cadrianna. Stay. "You play a dangerous game, Emre," she said instead, fighting back her warring emotions with everything she had. All her training paled against it. She had to remain strong. For Brynn. But…

"No," Emre said softly, "this isn't the dangerous part." The bikrome sheared the binds on her wrists. "Brynn has the dangerous path. Ours is but a minor obstacle." He gave his forearm a scratch. "You need to see the truth, Cad. Until then, you cannot help her as I must. I wish you to be by her side when she takes that first step."

Cadrianna rubbed her wrists. She felt the urge to draw upon her aetheurgy, but also a reluctance. Cadrianna eyed the black daemon blade on the table. Emre was unarmed, all it would take was a burn of aetheurgy and she could have the blade in hand, pressed against her beloved's neck. The neck of the Gutter King. Then Brynn would be freed.

Her resolve failed her. She couldn't, not now. Not yet. There had to be truths still yet uncovered.

She turned from Emre, finding it nigh on impossible to face him. "Soon, I expect?" *Stay, Cad, stay! He is still your beloved. Don't fight him. Kill him! No… I cannot. I must!*

"Tonight, it all ends should you wish it. I cannot undo what I did. But it was what I had to do. You will understand one day, I hope."

"Never!" she screamed all while her heart ached. "Brynn suffered because of what you decided."

But she didn't, hasn't at all. *Nocturne, were the visions true? Could it be that simple? A spell to make her complicit?*

"Cad," Emre said, appearing as if he wanted to reach out to her. "My love."

'No!" She flipped over the chair and raced from the room. Tears wet her face, everything she'd ever believed flailing after her, trying to remain affixed to her.

Brynn…

XXVI

EVANDER

THE WALL PORTAL slid open into Solanine's chamber and Evander stepped through.

The aetheurgist sat upon a cushioned chair, legs folded underneath. Nude. Solanine watched him under thick lashes.

"Master," he said, taking in the nudity but not shying away. The lust within him grew with every heartbeat. He glanced at the bloody runes on the aetheurgist's belly. They were fresh, which meant Solanine had been performing spells of the void. "The girl was taken by vicars. I followed and from what I was able to gather, they are planning to leave for Kalderim."

"She's already come to me," Solanine said, surprising him with a pastoral response. Snow Eyes was onboard Gargantua? "I've got a present for you. You have served well, my child."

"WORRY NOT, MORTAL. THE GIRL MUST STILL CROSS THE THRESHOLD BEFORE WE CAN TAKE HER. SHE WILL NOT LEAVE THIS CITY WITHOUT MY FALLEN."

Yes, master. As you command.

"MY DISCIPLE, THIS IS THE BEGINNING OF YOUR SERVICE."

Solanine tilted that luscious wave of hair toward the wardrobe behind. Rising, elegant and virile. Taut body alight in the glow of the fire blazing in the brazier near the bed. Nipples hard in the slight chill. The sight titillated him, he pulsed against his breeches. Across the room the aetheurgist ghosted, delicate hand finding something along the wooden frame of the wardrobe, a false wall yawning open on silent hinges. Solanine turned toward him and waited.

Moving closer, he investigated the room beyond, and his entire body stiffened. Not in shock, but in eagerness at what he saw.

Master, you are pleased?

"I AM. TAKE THY GIFT. PATIENCE YOU MUST HAVE. TREAD THE VOID SLOWLY OR IT WILL BREAK YOU, SOUL AND ALL. THIS GIFT WON'T BE QUICKLY LEARNED. YEARS IT MAY TAKE. STEADY YOU MUST BE. THE FIRST STEP OF YOUR NEW EXISTENCE."

But Evander was an impatient man. He wanted it now. He couldn't wait years for it to become unleashed. Unbound from the constraints of his mortal life. His walking void.

Drenth was on the verge of becoming a volcano, ready to erupt. He could feel it in the people of the mega-city, on their tongues. From lowborn all the way up to the Guilders.

And Elian was planning to throw a wrench into the aethecite engine.

He'd seen nothing of his brother since their discussion of crossing the Fallen the nightturn prior. Little did Elian know, Evander had come straight to Solanine and told the aetheurgist everything. Elian had cast his die; it was Evander's turn to counter.

His Divine had approved.

'The pleasure of the mortal body awaits you. Go to it," Solanine cooed as the aetheurgist glided up, smashing warm breasts against his broad back, hand slipping into his breeches, feeling his hardness. "So eager for it to begin."

Within the room was a table, an older man bound naked upon it. Gagged and chained. He was tall, lank of form with a blond ponytail, and a dyed green beard ending in a point. A man Evander knew well.

Domed with a dry basin below, with marbled stones underfoot. Shelves lined each wall, glass containers holding every element found in the world of Life. Some even borne of the void. Varying colors, solids and liquid, all stoppered. A low layer of translucent mist danced across the basin. It was near-black, dark with envy and death. The purest of poison arisen from the Pit.

Upon the basin's floor was a rune drawn with blood, Solanine's blood. Freshly drawn. Blackened-red mist climbed from the voidspeak rune, filling the basin.

"The human body is a playground for aetheurgy," Solanine said, stroking him, sending shivers throughout his body, spasms into his soul. "A toy that is a tomb, a quagmire. A place for lust and for withering sorrow and suffering. Life and Death reigns supreme, gifting the void and the heavens alike. Two sides of a coin, the seed and the fire. Like the Pentax above, and the aetheurgies of the earth. You know him?"

"Yes," he grunted against the steady stroke. O void, he was nearing his end.

"Name him. Naming him will give claim to his soul in the void of the Meadows. And then our pleasure will begin. Name this man."

"Ness. His name… uhhh ooohh… is Killian Ness." He convulsed, the end so close. Solanine sensed this, easing back so he wouldn't yet expel his seed. His Divine laughed in his mind.

Hand removed from his swollen manhood, Solanine moved beside Killian Ness. "Disrobe, Evander."

Evander yanked off his shirt in a hurry, exposing the hard muscles of his chest where a few scars were raised, leaving small shadows along the lines of his body. He then dropped his breeches, his erect shaft quaking in anticipation.

Solanine's fingers traced the contour of a scarred rune under their right breast and began to chant in a foreign dialect. Voidspeak. Blaring red light bloomed from under hand, over stomach, over womb. The source of Life within. The pendant of obsidian burned black against pale skin.

His Divine's voice reverberated in his head. ***"REMEMBER THE PATH. REMEMBER THE CALL OF THE VOID."***

The aetheurgist placed radiant hands upon Ness' chest, ruby incandescence upon his flesh. The gang leader pleaded through his gag, but Solanine only ran a finger down his jawline. "*Ignis* burns. *Aquis* washes. *Terris* lives. *Aere* breathes. Four there are to birth the many. Aether remains." The air grew cold as the warmth fled Evander's body as he sought the calm of the void. "Fire begets, Fire taketh," Solanine continued, hands pressed into Ness.

The restrained man jerked and thrashed as fire erupted from under fingertips, charring his skin. Solanine chanted again, louder as the fire burned a bright red orange, the skin blistering as the man passed out from the pain. His head lulled to the side; spittle spilled from the corners of his mouth. Blood ran from his ears and nose.

Solanine's fists closed. "Water rears, Water recedes." The fire quelled under an influx of blue wet, it washed across the man's chest like a wave of healing. Steam rose. "*Aquis*. Create the gateway to the Meadows." The fire from the brazier in the main room winked out, plunging the entire dome into darkness, the only light glowing oceanic from Solanine's fingers. Tiny wisps of red smoke curled through the blackness from the body. "Come the void. Come Killian's soul. Seek us, take us. Fear us, love us. Own us."

Evander opened his mind, his soul, everything he was, all of him, his blood, his aether. Life and Death swirled within, teasing the passion of each. Lightning urge. Even with his eyes closed, Evander could see Ness shiver as death stalked him, watching them.

A phosphorescence, soft and pure, emanated from the center of Ness' chest. The pale brilliance grew stronger, blue essence turning from ice to the deepest of royals. Solanine hesitantly reached out, cradling the light. The mist grew surly from all corners of the basin. With the mist and the light coming together now, melting as one.

"Call the void, Evander. Call Ness' soul. Seek it, take it. Fear it, love it. Own it. Scales are All. Scales are Nothing."

Evander felt the pull of the void from beyond the bloody rune on the basin's tiles. *Come to me,* he repeated over and over. "Come to me," this time aloud. "Open the veil, let me pass. I am yours." A rune formed in the bright light over Ness' body.

His face went slack as he felt Ness' presence from the depths of the void. It was pure ecstasy, pure unbridled pleasure. A soul free from the pain of Life, awakened by the freedom of Death. It filled him with desire, filled with want. O he felt it. Life gave way unto the void, it was there, waiting for him. He reached for it, took hold of the soul. The veil between worlds parted in a laceration of light and nothingness, all and naught. Souls of the dead rushed toward him from the Void Form rune, wailing and begging for his lifeforce. Evander opened his arms to them, feeling their empty cold pass through him as the mist clawed over Ness' body.

Then, Solanine was in the Meadows, the void of the underworld. Evander followed. A quick learner, he.

A kiss of the softest contact pressed against the skin of his clavicle, trailing down the front of his body. Solanine. Intense pleasure tingled within him as the cold specter of lust rushed down his abdomen into his manhood, sending passionate flares soaring throughout. There was something tingling under Solanine's skin, something that wasn't normal. A hardness, almost like scales. Odd.

But just as quickly as it had started, the radiance faded and disappeared completely. His desire withered away into nothingness. Bitter resentment followed.

Out of the Meadows both he and Solanine went.

"*Ignis*," Solanine said, the flameless aethecite lights within the room roared into life. Fingers lifted Ness' head; his chest did not rise. "He's gone. Wasn't strong enough to hold the link."

Evander leaned over the corpse, panting. "I was there."

"The stronger the connection to the void, the stronger the link. Time it will take you. Soon, my child. Your transmutation is at hand." Solanine grabbed his hand with a delicate touch that sent more ecstasy throughout his body. It was the rapture of Life and Death. "But first we dance the dance of the void. I will show you what the curse of flesh does."

Later, while he lay upon the bed, Solanine's head rested against the cool stone rim of the basin, arms spread, fluttering back and forth as if treading the water of a bath.

Yet it wasn't water. It was blood. Ness' blood.

Warmed by *Ignis* runes drawn in the aetheurgist's blood upon the sunken stone, it lapped as Solanine moved in slow kicks, arms churning the syrupy cruor. Solanine's hair was crusted with it, pale skin claret. Sitting upright, Solanine gathered a pool within cupped hands, bringing the sanguine fluid to pink lips, swallowing the crimson. Solanine then stood, red sluiced down the womanly body, leaving trails along the porcelain skin while the aetheurgist walked to the bed. His sticky seed from their dance of the void still crusted upon their belly, white against the red. His chest rose with each peaceful breath as he watched, one arm propped behind his head.

"Now?"

"YES. THE TIME IS NIGH," his Divine said from deep within the Pit.

"Yes," Solanine confirmed. "It is time for this boy to transmute himself. The girl will soon cross the threshold. Life and Death will become hers. Now is the time. We must be ready for when she reaches her full potential."

"YOU'VE SERVED WELL THUS FAR, EVANDER. OPEN YOURSELF TO THE VOID AND MORE WILL BE GIFTED UPON YOU. YOU CAN BE MY GREATEST WARRIOR IF ONLY YOU SHOULD OBEY."

He was giddy. O yes, he was.

The aetheurgist moved toward a small jewelry box sitting closed upon the vanity, the low fire cast soft silhouettes on the floor. The room began to grow cold as the witching hour approached. Solanine pulled forth a thin-bladed dagger wrapped in worn leather. Evander scooted to the end of the bed in full attention. With the tip of the knife, Solanine pressed it between breasts, drawing a pinprick of blood from one Void Form runic scar.

Kneeling, Solanine stuck a thumb against the bubble of red and began to draw a triangle upon the smooth wooden floor, chanting. "Five Gods in the world of the living. Five worshipped as the Pentax." Next, Solanine inverted a second triangle over the first, creating a six-pointed star. "But there are six Gods. Six for the Crystals. Eminence, the Four Shards, and Noctis. Six to bring the world into balance. Six to break the scales. Never forget the sixth, Evander, for He is the most important of Them. Immortality does not come from the proliferation of Life, but upon the wave of Death."

"Yes, master."

The bloodied star began to pulse fumes as the blood began to boil. Solanine's body went rigid, holding a hand out to him. "Come." He sat across while the aetheurgist regarded him, then leaned over the bloodied star, recreating it upon his forehead. "Our master's guile upon us. Our only god."

He glanced into the domed room where Ness' slack body dangled from a series of hooks, pallid and sallow due to the blood let from his corpse. "Yes. Praise be."

A faint red-white smoke rose through the blackened mist. "The gateway has been opened. Seek it."

The cold snapped within Evander's body, his naked flesh prickling. Evander's head wavered side-to-side, curls swaying. A tingle in his groin grew, the power of the void within his loins. It ached to be released, begged for freedom. Death released from the seed of Life. The pathway to the void surged forth, the veil shattered like broken glass around them. It pulled. Death of a thousand souls and more wailing, driving, pawing. His shoulders strained, the veins in his neck protruded as he soundlessly wailed at the pain suddenly wracking his body.

Within the red-white smoke glowed a crystal of obsidian that hung in an odd non-light. Sharp fractures gleaming black glass. Noctis.

"Touch it," Solanine told him. Calm as ever. "Evander, take it. Take it within you. All this hurt, all this pain. Draw it into your soul."

He reached for the non-light of Noctis that now wafted above the blood. The mist quirked around the obsidian Crystal of Death, fuming. It snaked, black power, across the floor, diving into the boiling blood of the star between them.

"TAKE THY SOUL BEFORE YOU. TAKE THY GRIP OF THE ETERNAL DAMNED."

Tenderly, Evander sought the fiery black power of the void as he reached toward the glass jet. Thin tendrils of the power swam forth, circling around his body. Airy and weak, but then it turned darker, nearly ebony. Faster around him. Solanine smiled as the power of the void claimed him. Void Form aetheurgy challenging him.

Evander let out a scream, a piercing howl. His arms wide, fingers splayed as the mist borne of Noctis raged about his body, clawing at him. It ran up his torso, the haze funneling into his mouth, choking him, muffling the scream barking against the intrusion. His mind felt like it was being ripped in twain. His soul rent. Everything he could have possibly imagined paled in comparison to the onslaught of pain. Everything hurt. He could feel the edges of his sanity being torn asunder. Soon, he knew it would consume him.

If not for the voice of his Divine. **"DEATH IS THE TRUE PATH TO IMMORTALITY. DEATH OF YOU AS YOU WERE. DEATH OF YOU AS YOU ARE. DEATH OF YOU WHO MIGHT BE. A NEW YOU WILL BE REBORN. QUELL THE FIRE. OWN THE FIRE. THE FIRE IS FOR YOU AND YOU ALONE."**

AHHHHHHHH!

"TAKE IT, MY DISICPLE. TAKE IT AND BECOME MY WARRIOR."

YESSSSSSSSSS!

There was a loud crack, the sound of bones exploding, breaking and reforming. Popping, bulging under flesh. Tormenting and burning.

This was Noctis at work on those alive.

Evander's body convulsed as he fell onto his back, an empty wail fighting through. The muscles in his chest deflated, then doubled in size. His arms, already well-defined, shook but grew in diameter, flesh expanding. Beads of sweat dripped from his brow as he cried, the curls of his hair fell from his scalp. His eyes bled with the onyx luster. His body contorted once, and then he went limp, crumpling headfirst into the aetheurgist's lap, panting as the mist-power went absent, back into the void.

Raising the bloody dagger, Solanine carved a Void Form rune into his breastbone. The mist reappeared now, funneling into the carved rune like a pitcher of red-black wine being poured into a goblet. Evander, barely conscious, screamed as the flesh puckered and blistered before the mist burned it raw. "He is yours, master. May your guile guide him. Your blood is now His blood. And blood rules all."

Evander pushed himself to his feet, his legs wobbly. Hands to his head, once covered with a mat of silky curls was now bald and slick with sweat. Muscles rippled in valleys of taut skin across his body, new and stronger. He stood a foot taller, if not more. His eyes found hers, foreign to him, his own were. Touching them, they felt like fire, his eyes. Black, no doubt, from sclera to pupil. He no longer was the waif of a street dreg, but instead a man shaped, bent, molded into a warrior of his Divine.

"Meet me in the void," Solanine said. "Seek Ness' soul."

Evander sought the darkness, the cold. The pleasure of crossing the veil jogged through him, the gateway came with naught but a thought. A soul awaited him, of Killian Ness in the non-light of the void. One soul waiting from the depths of the great slumber.

"The soul of this man, Evander, has led you to the void on your own," Solanine announced when the newly christened Evander came near in the Meadows, the souls of the dead wailing all around him. "No longer will you need the souls of the dead to guide you. You are master of the void now. It has claimed you. Noctis is yours to master. In time, you'll be able to move about this realm with ease."

He reached out to run his hands through the gossamer form of Killian Ness, stroking it as his deathly aura beamed in his freedom of sorrow. "What now?"

"I must now see to opening the gates of Eminence for the Fallen. The stage has been set. The girl will do her part. Now we bring her to the Fallen. To her destiny."

"And me?"

Solanine put a hand that felt like a claw to his chest, the fresh scar was warm, the true sign he owned the void and its aetheurgy. "Together we will deal the final push, the final column that is keeping this city upright. As does your precious girl with pearl eyes. But first we play."

XXVII
ASHE

ALTHOUGH THE EXPANSIVE room aboard Gargantua was finely decorated and filled with ornate furniture, it felt like a prison all the same.

After being bested by that scourge (unfairly because the assassin had cheated when she'd tossed that helpless woman out of the gondola), Ashe had been taken to the room and locked inside, accompanied by only a fraction of an inch of mist clinging to her ankles. Barely enough to do more than give her gooseflesh and an aching set of lungs.

The chitter-chatter of guards outside the doors tickled her ears as she pressed against the oak. Even if she used the set of lockpicks hidden in her boot heel, she'd have to deal with Pentax-only-knows how many Imperium soldiers or scourges. Without access to the mist, her aetheurgy was as useless as a one-legged gladiator in an ass-kicking fight.

Two decanters full of wine—one a dark burgundy, the other a white—perspired upon a golden side table. Ashe hurried over and lifted the red. O Zenith, did the flow of grape taste good going down, soothing not only her throat, but also her frayed nerves. Before she took another breath, half the decanter was empty.

The oaken door of her sumptuous prison squealed open, a lapin entering. The little creature was adorable and had chestnut colored fur. Her nose was petite, her delicately long ears lowered in deference.

"Pardons, mistress, but the masters bid me help you wash for the party." In her furry paws was what looked like a stola with long flowing sleeves.

Another sip. "Pink? They had to pick godsdamned pink. I'll look like a walking cu—" the wine decanter at her lips muted the rest of her sentence.

"You don't like the color?" The lapin's aura told Ashe she hadn't understood the verbiage. "I can bring another if you wish. Pink fits you, mistress." Nervous as… well, a rabbit surrounded by predators, the lapin laid the pink stola upon the massive bed. "If you'll follow me, mistress." She grabbed Ashe's hand with her furred paw.

She followed the stuffed doll-like servant toward the far end of the room where a narrow wooden door was found hidden behind a large painting, but not until she finished the red and hoisted the white wine decanter. Beyond the painting and door was a small, domed bath with a basin-like tub in the center.

The lapin smiled. "Let me help you with those… clothes," she said as she moved to help Ashe undo the laces of her dirty outfit. "If you want, I can have these cleaned for you."

"Burn 'em. Can't wash out shit and piss." As she began to undress, her flask fell to the floor. "I'll keep the flask if you don't mind." That small liquor container and she had seen much together. No way in the void was she giving that up without a fight.

Ashe couldn't recall the last time she'd taken a proper bath, so as soon as the hot water touched her skin, she allowed relaxation to take over. If Solanine was going to afford her this moment, she sure as Nocturne's Pit was going to take it. Besides, it was better than being in that bedroom staring at the ceiling and smelling like she'd rolled about a pigsty. Drunk and clean was a far better prospect.

The lapin servant helped Ashe clean the dirt from under her fingernails and commented on how pretty her golden bangle was, then poured hot water over her head and began to wash her hair, wringing things out Ashe certainly hoped wasn't lice. Sweet rose wafted in the steamy water. For the moment, Ashe forgot all her worries. Forgot about Solanine, void, her father, even.

"What's your name?" Ashe's head rested upon the lip of the tub, a rag covering her eyes as she sipped the wine while the lapin drained the dirty water and replaced it with clean, hotter water.

"Ancantha, mistress."

"Call me Ashe. Nobody's ever confused me with being a mistress." Ancantha then scrubbed Ashe's underarm with a bar of soap with a sweet, subtle aroma. "Except this one time when I was trying to steal this one ring from… nevermind. Been here long?"

"Ashe, that's an unusual name for someone. Both me and my sister been here since we was taken from Dervin."

"What's wrong with the name Ashe?" Chilled wine melted the miniscule, affronted ire. It's not like that was her true name anyway. "You don't think Lu Har will let me free after this party of his, do you?"

"I… Master Lu Har wouldn't allow it, mis—er… Ashe."

Ashe pushed up the rag and peered at the lapin. "Couldn't hurt to try, eh?"

After Ancantha massaged oils into her scalp, the servant retreated to the bed chamber to allow her to soak. Bending her knees, Ashe slipped under the water. But a ripple across the water's placid surface broke her trance.

Above, when she opened her eyes, was Solanine, the aetheurgist's hand brushing the water between them. "*Godsblood.*"

Ashe sucked in her breath and rose from the bath, frantically pawing the wet from her vision, coughing violently, trying to spew the water filling her airways. Water cascaded over the lip of the tub. Ashe spun, searching for Solanine, but no one was there.

Ancantha rushed in. "Mistress Ashe, what is it?"

What in Zenith's cock? One hand went to her racing heart, the other reached for the wine.

"Mistress Ashe, are you a'right?"

Leaning back, Ashe nodded as she drank. "Just some water in my lungs. Fell asleep for a moment there. Just tired, Ancantha. That's all."

"Then let me help you relax, love."

Ashe peered around the lapin to see her little bird standing in the doorway. "Wren?"

Instead of answering, Wren motioned toward Ancantha. "You may go, servant."

The lapin started to protest, "I'm supposed to help he—"

Wren glanced at Ashe, then back to the lapin servant. "Come back in an hour." She leaned close to the furry creature, and through the drunken haze inhabiting Ashe's brain, she heard the words 'Solanine' and 'knows' before the rest blurred into babble.

The lapin hesitated only briefly before curtsying and left.

Alcohol whirlpooled around her skull, hazy, but coherent, understanding in the knowledge of what was happening yet not quite certain if it was real or not. The room was dark, aethecite lights left off in the bed chamber beyond the narrow door, a smoldering fire burning in the brazier across the room.

Wren sat lithely upon the edge of the tub, carefully pulling off her boots, face hidden in the gloom, smile bright and eyes even brighter. "I've waited for this." The boot dropped with a perceptible thud.

A chill ran up Ashe's spine despite the warmth of the water in the tub. So had she. "O?" Her tongue thick against the roof of her mouth.

"Yes, Mother Marrow, yes." Standing, Wren's hands went to the folds of her pleb tunic, undoing the buttons one by one.

Ashe's mind swam. The small puddle of mist that had followed her now circled around the base of the tub. Its aether sparking within as there was a craving thirst. A thirst within her own body. She should've asked Wren why the little bird was here on Gargantua when she most assuredly shouldn't be.

But she hadn't.

In fact, Ashe wanted what was to come more than anything. She knew it the moment Wren walked in. Knew it the moment they first met. That threshold she'd been unwilling to cross before killing that servant in Silk Circle. The murder had shattered something inside of her, and she knew it was her purity. She was a child no more.

This was the only door yet to be opened. And walk through it she would.

The tunic fell from Wren's shoulders, slipping so effortlessly down her curves. Soft flesh of a woman aglow in the dying embers of the fire behind. The desire in Ashe grew as she drank in the woman's body. Porcelain skin a faint umber. Breasts pert, navel flat, hips wide, dark enticement between her legs. Her aura was a blinding ruby tint.

Reaching toward the perspiring wine decanter next to the tub, Ashe sipped at it, wetting her suddenly dry mouth.

O Zenith, she was suddenly shy. Weak and shaky. What a chicken shit she'd become.

"Those eyes of yours," Wren said as she gracefully lifted her legs over the lip of the tub and eased herself in. The tub was more than big enough for both of them. "They drew me in, from the first."

Their legs touched underwater. The need grew. Nerves assaulting her again. She could stop this, should stop this. Her mind argued with her body. It wasn't much of an argument. It was her first, that was all she kept telling herself. Normal it was to be nervous. That was the best explanation she'd give herself for acting a bloody dunce in front of Wren.

She shouldn't be here.

The mist tried its best to soothe her, but it kept pushing her onward, ignoring her brain's protestations. Wren moved toward her, the water gently lapping against Ashe's chest as the little bird was inches from her face, eyes locked together. The mist churned faster below the tub, its aether growing, its pall pierced the basin directly into Ashe.

"You're shaking. Do I frighten you so?"

Ashe shook her head, which felt like a thousand pounds at the moment. "You're not suppo…" her words trailed off when Wren smiled. O it was a beautiful thing, that smile.

The woman lifted Ashe's left hand, water wove along her tattoos as Wren pulled it toward her face. O so warm her skin was. Wren gently kissed each finger around the mysterious bangle. "This fits you. Couldn't ever think of you without it even though you've only had it for a few days now."

Ashe giggled at the ticklish brush of the Wren's lips. "You know me so well? I wouldn't waste your time, Little Bird." Dark eyes glanced up at the soft rebuke, affronted, but still gleaming. "Couldn't pry it free if you tried."

"You wound me," the other jested.

Wren kissed the inside of Ashe's wrist, where one of her runes had been tattooed into her flesh. *'Many know only Scattered Shards sprat have tattoos such as yours.'* Wet kisses danced along her arm with each word spoken by Elian.

"I've heard told only those of the Shards bear these." Wren ran a trail of lips along more of Ashe's runes, leaving gooseflesh despite the warmth of the bath. "Is this true?"

Wren shifted upon Ashe's lap, a shift accompanied by a push of hips, closer as it were.

'Many know.' The words of Elian swam upstream through the sea of spirits in her mind. *She shouldn't be here.* Why would she think of him at a time like this? She forced the gang leader from her thoughts. She drank more of the wine, her mouth was still parched, but the liquid courage it brought began to seep throughout.

Her insides went to jelly, shivers shooting throughout. "Yes," she breathed as Wren drew Ashe's hand to her chest, the woman's heart beating under her touch. "No. I mean," she licked her lips, again, so dry they were. "I spent years training in Kalderim."

Blonde hair shading eyes. Heart racing under her hand. Warmth from both their loins mere inches apart now, a tempest of the coming storm between them.

"You've lived some life, Ashe."

"I… no… I mean, I have."

The tenderness within Wren was like a lit beacon ready to steer her ship back from the brink of crashing waves. The envious mist curled about the tub now, up the basin, urging her, and tripled the emotions she felt.

Want.

Desire.

Need.

Nerves be godsdamned.

Without thinking, Ashe shot forward, splashing water everywhere as she kissed Wren. Their lips met in a fury of need, the ache. The little bird pulled her close, wet arms wrapping around as Ashe ran her fingers through the blonde waves of hair. The press of Wren's tongue against her parted lips, the force of her mouth against hers drove her on, begged her to continue.

She didn't know what was happening, but she didn't care. She needed the comfort. Needed that touch, that presence. The physicality. The ardor of another. The lifeforce of someone else. A threshold to shatter.

And the mist fanned the fire of her need.

Wren's hands roamed across Ashe's skin. Enthusiasm under her touch, Wren's fingers radiated gentleness and care for her in a way she never felt before. Ashe's fingers trailed across Wren's back and clawed at her when the little bird kissed her even harder.

She was lost in the ecstasy of it all, a brilliance at the back of her closed eyelids. A diamond limning.

Wren pulled away, breathing hard. Ashe near panting as the water of the tub swelled against their skin. The little bird's gaze went to Ashe's left arm. "Ashe...your arm is glowing."

Blood pulsed through Ashe's veins, firing on all cylinders now. Her tattoos were thermal, fiery even. She needed this, wanted this more than anything. "That's kinda what they do..."

"Your eyes, your pupils have turned completely white."

Ashe suddenly felt ashamed, her hands moving to cover them. "I…"

The nymph pulled Ashe's face toward hers again, kissing her passionately. Ashe forgot all about her eyes and tattoos. Gentle hands pressed against Ashe's back. Her breasts crushed against the tender flesh of the other woman, water spilling over the lip of the tub. Their tongues caressing each other's as tingling joy, urgent and fierce, raced through her body. Utter lust raged through her blood, boiling it in white hot pleasure. An audible crackle in her ears, she would later wonder if it was the mist or just her imagination.

She decided to go with the one where it sounded like a grand choir singing their heavenly songs.

Ashe wrapped her legs around Wren, crossing her ankles, squeezing against the other's body. Wren's hands gripped her thighs, shivers ran up her spine, causing her to arch. Reason left her. All that remained was the need. Her need to be Wren's. Wren to be hers.

Wren probed the swells and valleys of Ashe's body with her hands. Down near the dark between her legs that was suddenly irriguous.

The mist fusilladed into pure fervor; pleasure demanded. Life expected. Cue choir.

Wren moved, kissing the tender curve of her neck, sending something primal throughout Ashe's body. Tongue trailed down her breasts, lingering just long enough around her nipples to heighten the passion burning within her as the little bird pushed Ashe against the tub's side. Ashe grabbed the lip with both hands and drove her hips upward, her lower body surfacing the water. Wren's arms curled around her thighs as she softly nuzzled the skin of her inner legs. Blinding flashes of bliss flared within her loins when Wren's tongue found her sex. The rhythmic nurturing of her most private areas sparked euphoric fury.

Her fingers dug into the tub's lip, her head lolled side-to-side as she moaned, water gushing overboard. "Shit, shit, O fuck!"

Seconds turned to years. Years to eons as Wren's tongue prayed to the lustful deity between Ashe's legs. Fire in her body. Water brimmed her eyes, but she ground her hips into Wren's cadence, moving in unison like a dance. Serenity flowed inside her with every flick, every measured lap. Enveloping joy wrapped her soul at each twirl. All that she had been before this singular moment in time washed away from her, leaving only rapture, only need, only pleasure.

She opened her eyes and the world seemed brighter, clearer than ever before. A diamond view, prism clear and bright.

She felt alive, felt the world alive around her. In Wren. In the fire from the bed chamber beyond. Life on Gargantua trickled into her being. Even down in Drenth. Tingles like flowing blood in every living thing. Breathing and laughter. Histories telling her stories that weren't hers. Life tracing the sounds of water, the growth of plants in the earth. The essence of the stars in the sky.

Everything alive. She could almost touch it. Could almost taste it.

Only Scattered Shards sprat… a Godsblood…

The mist swirled around the tub in fervent frenzy as the water began to steam. The anticipation of the end brought every ounce of completion she could have envisioned. When her ecstasy reached its climax, her voice was hoarse, her body shaking. The allotrope sheen of clarity faded, the lifeforce of all around her disappearing, leaving her empty.

"Fuck me," she laughed, the room spinning. "Is that what that feels like? Let's go to the bed and do it again."

And the mist was satiated.

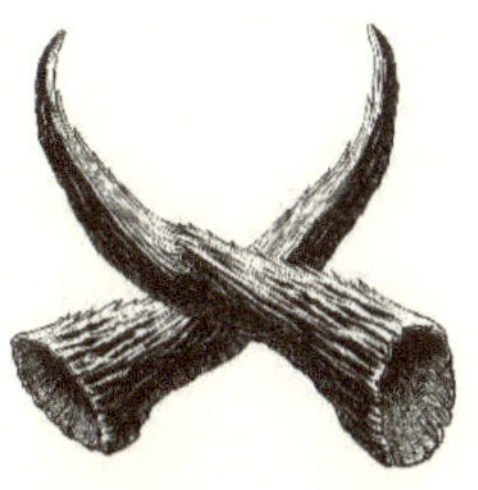

XXVIII
LOJEN

WHEN THE HISTORY books would eventually be written about the downfall of the Fallen's Imperium and his part to play in it, Lojen was dead certain that his terror at climbing the tether chain would be omitted. Scratched from existence, erased from all memory.

Despite the fact that every drakken worth their exoscales could climb almost anything, anywhere, under any circumstance, Lojen was petrified the entire climb. His stomach did back flips as he put one claw in front of the other, dragging his fossilized body inch-after-inch upward. He didn't know the dance his heart was making against his ribcage, but it wasn't a slow dance, that much was certain.

The climb felt like eons. Yard by agonizing yard. Link by link. Always upward at an unnatural angle for his rigid muscles. The tether lurched back and forth in the not-too-gentle wind, creaking upon the steel-to-steel rub.

It was quiet up thousands of feet in the air, the only sound being the chain, the wind, and the dull thrum of the engines in Gargantua's belly and propeller blades as the giant fortress in the air came closer. That and the constant ethereal song in his earholes. A steady hum that reminded him of the Hymn of War. And it was cold, frosty even for a cold-blooded drakken—which made Lojen wish he had something warmer than his sleeveless vest.

"Hurry up, Lojen." His sister was behind him, right on his tail. Ruane's voice sounded like waves crashing ferociously against a cliff during a storm. While he struggled with the height and the effort, she climbed swimmingly.

The magnets in his grips clapped against the link with each move of a claw, each push of a boot. The wind picked up and the chain began to sway violently. A high-pitched squeal of metal on metal as each link jerked against another.

He had one claw raised when a torrent gust struck the chain and his stomach lurched as his entire body shifted, his other magnet came loose. He shrieked, the Hymn growing louder within him. The grip skidded down the rounded metal as the fierce wind hammered the chain, and he frantically reached with his free claw. The magnet clamped upon the steel and his thighs clasped the link for dear life, his arms wrapped as far around the steel as he could get, urging the magnets to hold strong. The wind raged all around him and tether shook like a giant beast trying to free itself of the parasites that were crawling all over it—in this case, Lojen and Ruane.

He repeated *'Don't let me die'* over and over and over again. As he hung on, Lojen thought he heard laughter piercing the tornado-strong winds. *Zenith, Ru!*

Finally, the wind slowed, the chain straightening again. The screeching of the steel links died into silence. The calm sky returned with fluffy clouds and the soft glow of a setting sun.

He cursed the Arbiter for putting him through this sacrifice of self, this trial of worthiness. The Hymn sang in response.

"We're almost there," Ruane said with eerie delight.

He raised his head and realized they were only about fifty feet from a sewer-like opening where the chain spilled out from. His sanctuary, his safety. He only needed to climb a little bit farther and he could free himself from his nightmare.

The outer shell of Gargantua was smooth as marble, but every ten feet or so were openings in the wall for lookouts or weapon holes, but none appeared to be in use at the moment.

"Where are all the guards?" Ruane asked.

"Doesn't feel right," he answered truthfully.

"You know what doesn't feel right? Your slowtail blundering about. Get moving, you loaf of burnt pumpernickel!"

Lojen sighed and kept climbing. His arms were growing tired and being this close to the fortress, he expended that last little bit of energy and forced himself to move quicker, regardless of his fear.

Fifteen minutes later, the opening yawned over them like a giant fish swallowing a baited line. It was black within the portal, but he was thankful to be away from the sheer openness of Drenth below and surrounded by stone once more. The tether leveled out and, in the darkness, Lojen made out the anchor. Similar to the one on the ground, the link looped around an eyehole. Just below the anchor, he spotted a door, a tiny square that might be too tight for him.

His alarm rose.

Ruane, who was planting multiple bundles of bombs near the anchor, hopped off the link and made toward the door. She pulled on the circular handle, the door groaned—or the stone itself did to be more precise—as she lifted. A shaft made of steel and stone, a ladder led down, a soft glow of dull light.

"Well?" His sister looked at him.

"Guess this is our way in." The shaft might fit his shoulders, it would be tight, but he could probably squeeze through.

"You first."

"In case there are guards, you want to throw me into them?"

"Stop acting like a hatchling. Fine. I'll go first." She put her boot to one of the rungs and looked up at him again, the shadows made her look daemonic with her grinning teeth and narrowed eyes. "You know, for the heir to Father's horns, you sure are a Scurred Hatch."

He was about to retort, but she had already disappeared down the shaft, leaving him sulking in the dark.

Father, what am I to do with her?

Lojen took to the ladder and his shoulders were, indeed, too large to fit naturally, so, he sucked in his breath and curled his shoulders inward to make him as small as possible and shimmied his way down. The ladder opened into a tunnel, and it was a tight fit, not large enough for him to walk upright. He was bent, shoulders hunched, and he shuffled more than walked, trying not to drag his horn stumps along the ceiling.

"You any idea where we're going?"

Ruane was ahead in the dully lit tunnel, bent like him, though not as drastically. She glanced over her shoulder. "Didn't that humir give you the map?"

"Emre said the anchors would lead us into the innerbelly of Gargantua."

"Where do you think we are, Lojen? Krylen?" She whistled through her teeth in annoyance. "There's no tunnel but this one, it's gotta lead somewhere."

For all Ruane's bluster, they could be walking into a trap for all they knew. The emptiness and the silence didn't make Lojen comfortable. In fact, the exact opposite. "I feel like a rat in a maze."

A sound. A beep. A scrape against stone.

"Hsst." Ruane froze in place, her longknife rigid. Head cocked, listening.

Lojen's heart raced. If anyone found them in the tunnel, he'd be useless. He was like a stuffed sausage, unable to move. "Ru?" She held up a claw. Then she was moving again, slow and deliberate. "What is it, Ru?"

"Be quiet and listen, you dolt."

He snapped his jaw shut and strained his hearing. The noise was ahead, a beeping sound, and it grew louder because it was accompanied by the scraping of metal on stone. Ruane crouched, giving him a better view ahead. He drew forth the wheellock pistol and aimed it into the yellowed burrow. He hated firearms, always trusting a drakken longknife or good old-fashioned talons instead.

A flashing orange light appeared ahead. Beeping grew stronger, faster. The metal screeched louder.

And then Lojen saw it; an aethecite-powered automaton.

Eight legs like those of a spider poked out from a cylindrical body, each leg ending in a pointed metal cap. A series of tools along each leg, everything from screwdrivers to rivet punchers. Each attached via a rotating gear, able to click into place as needed upon the leg's end. A small engine attached to the automaton's back left little puffs of grey smoke. A head-like apparatus with the blinking light and a glass orb bobbed like a bird walking along the ground as it skittered through the tunnel.

The automaton was only about three feet tall, Ih made the tunnel shape logical now. But it also was coming at them fast and there wasn't anywhere to hide from the thing. They were still far enough away, and with the dim light, there was hope it hadn't seen them yet, but that didn't leave them much room for escape.

"Lojen?"

They couldn't turn back; the automaton would be on them before they could flee to the ladder back by the anchor. They couldn't press against the wall and hope the metal bot would simply pass by them without turning its little head. And if they disabled the thing, that might bring even more eyes down upon them.

They were proper buggered, as humir might say.

"Ru, we gotta climb."

"The ceiling?"

She looked at him questioningly. He pointed up, calculating the foot or two of space from the ceiling and the highest point of the automaton, then nodded. Sheathing her longknife, Ruane dug her claws into the walls near the ceiling. Her boots scuffed as little tendrils of dust trickled to the floor. Lojen braced himself, jammed his own claws into the walls with force and lifted his body off the ground and squeezed it against the rounded ceiling, wedging himself in tight.

The automaton's beep was just ahead. Lojen couldn't see it, so he sucked in his breath trying to make himself even smaller and waited.

But that's when the wheellock pistol fell from his belt and clattered below.

The metal carapace on legs skittered below them. It stopped, beeped in clicks and clacks, only mere inches from belt buckle to the automaton's glassy noggin. Metal arms prodded and examined the dropped wheellock. A series of blips not the same frequency as the automaton's beeping resounded in the tunnel. Then the automaton moved again, arms scratching the stone walls as it flitted away, the beeping proceeded down the tunnel the way they had come, disappearing. The pistol was nowhere to be seen.

Ruane dropped down. "That wasn't too bad."

"Let's get out of this place." He pushed her the opposite way from the automaton.

The purr of Gargantua's aethecite engines was steady now, and they could hear the gears turning within the man-made beasts. He hadn't seen too many large engines up close, but he did know that the amount of combustion within the internal furnace was intense. And with the sheer size of Gargantua, the engines probably could heat an entire city from the convection. His tongue hung out of his mouth as he sought to cool himself. Unlike man, drakken didn't sweat, but in that moment, he wished they did.

So, he was stuck with a lagging tongue, looking like a fool.

Up ahead, Ruane moved through the alternating shadows and overhead lights, stopping abruptly a pace from the mouth of the tunnel. Chitters and beeps sounded beyond, and as Lojen neared, he hoped that the first automaton hadn't called for backup.

In a rounded grotto were six enormous metal engines. Dozens of automatons and heat-shielded people scuttled about the furnaces, tossing in aethecite, cleaning, analyzing control panels. It was an intricate dance of chemistry and mechanics well out of Lojen's knowledge base.

"This is where we split."

"You sure about this, Ru? I don't think this is a good idea."

"It has to be this way. Otherwise, we won't hit all the targets."

"Yeah, even the ones I don't know about," Lojen muttered. Emre had pulled Ruane aside while they were leaving the safehouse and whispered something into her earhole. About a task she said nothing about to him.

Ruane frowned. "Not a big deal, brother."

"Then why not tell me?"

"You've got enough to worry about with finding Father's horns and the Seal. What Emre wants is a small thing. Not for you to worry."

"You're my sister. Of course, I'm going to worry."

"Aw, isn't that special?" Ruane punched him in the arm. Then her face softened. "Be safe, Scurred Hatch. And don't forget the Hammer."

He hugged her. "If any trouble comes your way, run. Don't fight, Ru. I'm not joking. Just run."

She patted his arm. "Talk for yourself. I don't run and you know that."

Lojen snorted. "Justice go with you."

"Justice go with you," she repeated.

And then she pushed away, hopping down from the tunnel without a sound. She raced down the grated gangplank and snaked around one of the aethecite engines just in time to avoid being seen by an automaton slinking by full of chirps and beeps.

Be safe, Ru.

XXIX
ASHE

A SOFT FLICKER, like the caress of a feather touching her cheek, woke Ashe, but she wasn't truly awake.

Yet she wasn't in the bedroom anymore, but instead in a square room. There was an odd sort of lighting to it, a non-light. And she was alone, no Wren. Mist rolled in swells along the ground that wasn't ground. She searched for an exit but found none.

It had to be a dream.

Then the walls oscillated. A soft intensity from the non-light. She knew the feeling now. Recognition bowling in.

Somehow, she was in the Meadows. Without her calling it through aetheurgy. Without being truly awake.

A door appeared where there wasn't one a moment ago. She made for it; the mist undulated before her. It opened with the barest of touches, the hall beyond was empty and alight in the non-light. A second door appeared at the end of the seesawing hall, this one made of glass, sheer, flat, and clear. A prism of light flowed through a rainbow. As she put her hand out to push the door open, her palm went right through.

"What?"

Another room yawned to her, not empty like the others. Wasn't silent, wasn't bare. An erratic wailing, soft and constant, a cacophony of words spoken in languages known and not. An eddy of spirits, souls of the dead gamboled the expanse of the void.

"Zenith's cock."

There, across from her, a man sat upon a grand-looking throne constructed of gemstone. Of sapphire, emerald, peridot, and garnet. A brilliance in battle. Behind the throne hung a massive crystal made of diamond. It was taller than the throne by at least four times. Its facets reflected the non-light.

Aged white hair cascaded down the elfirish man's broad shoulders, and covered an emaciated form that was unclothed down to his waist. Strong of jaw, covered in a flecked white beard. Flesh as pale as a moonlit night, clear and real, not like the spirits of the dead meandering around the non-room. A diamond pendant in the shape of an eye hung around his neck. The man's eyes were all white, including his pupils.

He stood, an air of confidence and wisdom about him. His aura blazed with untold knowledge, as well as unfathomable pain. "Godsblood. Long has it been since I saw you last."

"Who are you?"

"I am Canlon Carr." He purled his fingers, the wails in the Meadows briefly rose to a fever pitch, the mist a whirligig. A pair of chairs materialized. "Come, sit with me."

"You're… the Last Godsking?"

The man sat, a reassuring hand held out, beckoning her all would be well. Reluctantly and cautiously, Ashe slid into the chair. Silence held for a moment.

"You've questions, I know," the man started, "but there will be more time for us to speak of this. At present, a pressing need awaits you. A journey ahead."

"To Kalderim?"

"No, child of Nightingale. Eminence."

Eminence?

A thousand questions raced through her mind. Questions of aether. Of her connection to the mist. Of Lu Har and Solanine. Of Emre Benld. Of the pulmo killing her. Of her past.

But first: "Why would I have to go to Eminence?"

"A fire resides in you, child. A fire that will need further stoking. A day of reckoning is nearly upon us. You are the blood of Nightingale, the first of us. Of the First Wife. That is why I've come to you now. The time is no other than when you are needed."

The first of us? "I don't want it."

"Regardless, you have the blood in you. Chosen you've been." He motioned toward the bangle on her wrist. "The Eye has sought you out. The first in half a millennium to be chosen."

"I don't understand."

"The worlds of Life and Death are not meant to be understood by us mortals. Only the Divines." Canlon leaned toward her, mass of white hair flowing in the rippling dream-that-wasn't-a-dream. "You are special, child of Nightingale. Always have been. You refuse to be cowed and caged by the truth." There was pure masculinity in the Last Godsking's languid pose, it was very animalistic, pure and serene. Grace and holiness. "The mist that has spawned from my failure is growing stronger. I can see it within you. Aether fights inside of you, begging for release."

With that, Ashe coughed. Her fingers were wet with blood as she touched her mouth. Real in the mirror world of the Meadows. "But… how? Are you?"

Canlon lifted his hand and a tendril of the mist curled around his open fingers. The diamond crystal upon his neck flashed. "This poison is the price. You must beware. The Divines have marked you of Eminence, as Godsblood. And potentially so much more. A seed may yet still grow from a prophecy passed down since my fall."

"Prophecy? I don't believe in prophecy."

"And wise you are to not, for prophecy is not meant to be understood by the faint of heart. You are about to enter a world unknown to all but a few. Your blood is powerful, bound in truth, bound in secrecy."

"I don't want this." Ashe balled her hands into fists as she looked at the runes inked upon her arm. "I never did. If I could give it up, I would've long ago."

"Not all which we want can be given. It has to be, child of Nightingale. You were born to this fate. The mist is your element, don't shy from it. Duty is all we must know. It is all I knew."

"I'm not a fucking child!" The anger building inside her. The mist from the Meadows grew surly. "That part of me has been forever burned away."

"And why do you think I chose now to come to you? I tried to hide you for as long as possible. To shield you from those who'd use you elsewise. But with you crossing the threshold of both Life and Death, you've opened yourself to the Fallen. The Seals will call to you now."

A coil of anger rising. Too many unanswered questions. O Zenith, the anger was raging. She wanted to scream something primordial.

"A child you aren't any longer," Canlon continued, "this is true, but you've got a path to tread now. Taking a life and sending a soul to the void has spurred your gift into full force. But you've also given into the designs of the flesh, of creation."

"You mean Wren?"

A nod. "You've played with the aether in the mist like a child who sticks their hand in the fire knowing naught of the consequences. The mist is not to be trifled with."

Another cough. "The mist is killing me already. I won't last much longer."

"Until you learn to master the mist, to truly dominate everything within its aether, it will kill you. Master it and it will be your weapon. Harness it, be it, and it will serve you. That is true Soul Form."

The mist gurgled, almost like a feline purring when rubbed. Her father's words, as well. How?

"I've had visions. The mist showed me a throne dripping blood. A polished sword. War."

"Beware of what you think you know. Especially about the Pentax. What you've seen is the aether showing you your fate. One possible fate. Destiny has bound you to Eminence. You must go there. Be wary. A face in the crowd may not be the face you expect. Not all faces are real. Even the ones you wish to be true. Not all visions will come to pass." Canlon shifted, his body began to scintillate, becoming tiffany.

"Zenith's cock…"

"Only you can reopen Eminence. All others have been false. You have been deemed worthy by the Divines to rebirth the Crystal and use the Hymn of Soul to finish what I started with Zenith… Three trials await you. One of heart, one of body and mind, and finally, one of soul. A price to be paid for each. Four Seals to Eminence.

Godslayer you must become. Lu Har seeks to break the Seals and plunge the world of Life into Nocturne's Pit. The Mistlands that was, the Mistlands that is, the Mistlands that might be will forever fall into the depths of the void if Eminence is not revived. It is the only way to become all once more."

"I don't want to slay any gods," Ashe said. "There must be others."

"You can, child of Nightingale. You must. The Fallen, he comes. Soon." Canlon's gaze drifted. "Yes. Tonight it'll be. They will hunt you now that you've crossed the threshold. It was the only thing veiling you from them."

"Tonight? Bugger me."

Canlon gestured to the bangle on Ashe's wrist. "It seeks the Seals. It seeks its sight." He lifted the diamond eye at his neck. "Go. Seek me in Eminence. The door has now been opened for you to walk through. The journey you were born for."

"Wait, you still live?"

The Meadows shimmered, pulsed, agitated, and quailed. Ashe called out, reached for the Last Godsking, but the darkness, the shadows grew. Canlon Carr disappeared.

XXX
EMRE

THOUGHTS WANDERED THROUGH Emre's mind aimlessly like a listless summertide breeze off the VVyrm Ocean as the gondola rose toward Gargantua.

Val's head lay upon his shoulder, veil askew, her breathing shallow. Napping. Emre was equally exhausted but the adrenaline in his veins wouldn't allow him to doze. The convergence of all his plans lay ahead, and yet, he wasn't prepared.

O Cad, I should have protected you better.

The Cadrianna he'd married had been a sweet, if not slightly shy, young woman who was quick with a quip but just as quick with a lash of anger if crossed. He had loved her from their first meeting.

The Cadrianna they'd captured was not the same woman; as hurt, anger, sorrow, zealousness, pain, aloofness were specters around her. A territorial spark of aggression swallowed under a sea of suffering.

He couldn't help but bear the brunt of it all.

A woman two rows ahead of him—who was dabbing at her cheeks with fresh rouge from a compact while her partner leaned over a mini aerescreen—was talking to someone on the other side of the communicator. The man sucked in a sharp breath. Burning a smidgen of aetheurgy, the silvery sheen exploded within Emre. The thrumming heartbeats of all the guests, their idle chatter nearly overpowered him. Focusing, he picked out the pair's words.

"...said it's true," the man said, "heard it from his sister's friend, who was there."

"Can't be," the bouffant-haired woman replied. "Not been heard from since the conquest."

"That's what I said. But he swears she named herself Brynn Benld."

His scars began to itch, but he fought the urge to scratch.

Val must have sensed his state because her veil swished as she woke. "Are you okay?"

You know I'm not. He snuffed his aetheurgy. "Yes." He held her hand. *Be safe, my daughter. I wish I could have told you I love you.* "Everything is fine."

Val nestled back into his shoulder, her hair tickling his cheek. "She'll be fine. She's got your stubbornness."

Emre smiled at the thought. *Brynn and Cadrianna both. Both here, one happy family reunion.*

Although seated at what he might consider the rear of the gondola, the all-around window gave clear view of Gargantua as it grew larger. The walls overtook the gondola as it entered the interior, but not before Emre noted the massive airships docked to the lower half of the fortress. Guild airships.

Just like Tevun had predicted. The Imperium was indeed stirring for war and the Guild had thrown in their lot with the Fallen. The High Seat in Alizarin must be growing fearful the Fallen might come to Altreyia next.

Emre's plan now took on more importance than ever.

The wheels came to a stop upon the cables within the arching gateway, the carriage swaying as it locked into place. Glass doors opened and a pair of guards upon the gangplank patiently guided the guests toward a series of steps which would lead them to the party. Emre and Val were amongst the last to depart.

A second gondola carriage had been dragged to the side, shattered panes. There were maintenance crewmen repairing the damage, drilling and refitting the glass as they passed by.

"Wonder what happened there?" Val whispered as they followed the parade of party guests.

Nothing with broken windows meant good tidings. It meant a fight. "My guess is that it's our catalyst." It was a sobering thought to think of one's daughter in a fight to the death. He would have to get used to such thoughts. "Wick, Finn, where are you? Copy."

Wick was the first to answer, but it had taken them halfway up the stairs into a cavern of hanging stone lights before they received his response. "Digging the spice from the soup now," the lapin said through a bunch of static. "You up high yet? Over."

"Good to hear your voice, Wick. Topside almost. Over."

"I'm coming to you for the main course. Has Ruane delivered you the meal? Over."

"Still in the oven, Em."

"On my way, humir," came the response from the drakken. "The lapin will get his boomsticks."

"Lots of delicacies. Kitchen serving a fired roast tonight. Over and out." It was code that meant Wick was in a precarious position and couldn't talk, which was fine for Emre, he just wanted confirmation the lapin was in place. It also meant that Wick was ready to receive the bombs the drakken carried.

They walked nonchalantly through the cavern, trying to blend with the rest of the partygoers. There were hundreds milling within, looking at statues, at artwork, at the intricate stonework. But most of the crowd was overlooking the balcony, and they were 'oohing' and 'ahhing' over Gargantua's view.

Standing at a railing, Emre and Valeria joined the gaping horde.

Buildings with multiple tiers, buttresses spanning spires. Mahogany doors full of carvings, windows of stained glass. Grass-lined concrete walkways, flowers of every color, trees of long, wispy willows and others with boughs of twisting white, peeling bark. The setting of the sun left a perfect shade of pink upon it all.

Even the revenge starved Emre could stop and appreciate the beauty of Gargantua.

But then his conscious kicked in and he remembered why all this magnificence existed. Borne off the backs of his enslaved people. "Finn, you shiny?" There was silence for long minutes. "Finn? Copy?"

Nothing. Static buzzed in his ear and Emre's hackles started to rise. Did Finn get caught? Was he in trouble? His heart began racing. *Not yet, please.*

Val sensed his apprehension and squeezed his arm. "He's a rock, that one. Hardheaded to boot. He's fine."

"Finn?"

"Oh hey, love. There ya are," Finn's voice finally resounded in his earpiece. "Where you been? Over."

"Where have I been? By the Arbiter, Finn."

"I'm fine." A pause, some static. "No, I'm not talking to you, you old hag. Just admiring my handsomeness in this pot you got me slaving away at. What's that? O yeah, sure no problem. Get right to them." More static, some incoherent voices. "I'm on it. Calm down." Another pause. "Gotta go, Em. Over and out."

"See," Val said. "My brother-friend's fine."

A crier called from behind, "Everyone, please, this way. The party is about to start. If you'll follow me."

They became wedged within a crowd of stolae and suits, masks and veils, styled hair and scented oils. Amongst panache and gluttony, greed and avarice. Standing within a grand brick-formed oval entranceway, the nimiety of party guests was like livestock awaiting the bolt.

Emre felt claustrophobic. His scars itched and he struggled to fight the urge to frenzy them.

The flock of guests jostled, laughed, joked, cursed, and scowled as they waited for their gracious host. Elegantly clad servants in black-and-red overcoats stood patiently on either side of the twenty-foot oak doors. Somewhere behind the doors, music flowed sweetly.

A hush filtered within the crowd as the servants' white gloves pushed open the doors, revealing the entranceway to the party.

A spanning garden of brick led to an open veranda where a raised dais held a dance floor with balustrade stairs. Servants aplenty with trays of crystalline glasses full of wine, bubbled or chilled. Surrounding the dais were waist-high tables draped in fine silks of deep red, candelabras atop. A low wall of brick separated an open grassy area where tables for sitting were located, bearing the same linens and candle holders, but with the addition of iced buckets of wine. A hedge of green outlined the mezzanine. Suspended from yawning trees above the dance floor was a clock polished in dark stain and golden filigree. Aethecite lights along coils weaved throughout, illuminating the dance floor in a soft glow. Opposite was a grand staircase with gilded banisters, a crimson runner down the marble risers. The stairs curved upward toward a set of darkened redwood doors from the Forest of Calibrath, highlighted by a pair of aethecite globes.

But that wasn't all.

Fluted pedestals held acrobatic dancers in skin-tight clothing and ornate masks contorting their bodies in unnatural, yet beautiful ways. A pair of flying trapeze artists swung back and forth above the dance floor, where small planks nestled into the trees waited for the artists to launch themselves. A full orchestra played upbeat music from under the far arch of a tree, led by a lovely vocalist with exquisite range. Masked servants stood ready with trays of delicacies from all over the Mistlands.

One thing that stood apart from the rest was a marble fountain that spewed arcs of clear liquid. But instead of splashing water, mist rose from the bowl.

"Is that?" Val said.

"Aethecite," Emre finished, awe and anger mixed within his voice as he noted the prism of colors that threaded the arc and of the mist. Aether. "He's taunting us. Carelessly brandishing his power over Drenth. Even as dozens die daily for his quotas."

"How did they liquify it?"

"I don't know, Val. I just don't know."

The guests entered with great aplomb, happy to savor the drink and food. Willing to sacrifice their vengeful morals to curry favor with the Fallen. The servants waded through the crowd with their trays, retreating with the empties only to come back with more. Emre spied Finn amongst the partygoers. The elfir gave him a wink before spinning away with his tray.

It was another half hour before the redwood doors at the top of the curved staircase opened. The vocalist lifted a soprano note, followed by the instruments. The guests quieted at the entrance song and looked up expectantly.

Solanine appeared.

The womanly body bore a flesh-tight, crimson stola the flared out below the knees into a ten-foot train, it hugged hips as the void-born creature within swayed down the steps. Slithered more like. Hair—coiled and braided—changed from blonde to brown as the aethecite glow highlighted the outer façade's steps. No mask upon the heart-shaped face, full lips painted red as freshly spilt blood. A warpaint for a different type of combat.

"Friends of Drenth," Solanine's voice rang clear, "seventeen years ago you were liberated from the hardships placed upon your shoulders after the Fall of Eminence. Unable Drenth was in the aftermath to gain traction in this new world." The partygoers listened with bated breath. "Trials given unto your children with naught but the Pentax's curse covering the land, making it inhospitable. Until They gave us the means, a power of the earth itself. Power to warm when cold. Power to cook when weather was poor. Power to build this great mega-city from the ashes of the old world. Power of conquering the skies Zenith tried to forbid man from."

"Aethecite!" a lone woman called from somewhere within the crowd.

"Precisely, my dearest friends of Drenth. A glorious gift."

Through the death of my people, Emre thought bitterly. It wasn't a glorious gift, but one of destruction. But the guests didn't care, enthralled they were. Or uncaring only to bootlick personal favor.

"A gift to prosper." Solanine paused for effect. Murmurs of agreement wriggled through the crowd. "However, raw aethecite was the only means we know. A method so archaic, we remain shackled to it. Long hardship you've suffered within the mines. Digging for years, bent with ache. Limited vision in daylight. Death comes too soon from its radiation. All for what? A tiny shard of metal so valuable the Mistlands would collapse without it."

More whispers rose like the slow hum of an aethecite engine.

"But no longer will you have to work your fingers to the bone," the blooddrake-in-the-flesh-of-man continued as if shoveling the very ore into said engines. "No longer will your children have to work eighteen hours a day in confined tunnels that cave in without notice. No longer will your spouses or loved ones worry that today might be your last within the tunnels or from the radiation. No longer will your brethren wonder where their next meal will come from."

The crowd ate up Solanine's words like a prisoner starved for days. More and more of the nobleborn were nodding their heads in agreement, whispering affirmations, tapping glasses in hear-hears.

Arms raised, Solanine silenced the crowd. "For five centuries you've toiled. Why? Because the Pentax, no Nocturne, stole true aether from us. Giving us the cursed mist, the deathly poison. Stolen from Zenith's creations because His chosen warrior went mad. The Last Godsking did this to you, friends of Drenth. Forced you into this harsh life. His ego, his selfishness, it lies at his feet. Eminence would remain aloft in the heavens if not for him. There is a way, my friends, to bring it all back into our hands."

And that's when the firedrake roared.

The people cowered reflexively, frightened by the whooshing of wings overhead. Swooping down from the evenfall clouds, it came. Burnished crimson scales sparkled as its great bulk scythed through the sky in its descent. Eyes of blood, daemon eyes. Mouth agape as it came to a perfect landing upon the center of the raised dais, wings folding inward.

The people recovered, standing with heads raised to the magnificent beast. But Emre scratched his arms relentlessly as a dark-haired man slipped from the drake's back.

The Fallen.

"Our master," Solanine's smile was so wide it nearly broke the contours of the stolen woman's face, "plans to enter Eminence once more." The murmurs rose in question, Solanine answered, "There is but one way, my friends of Drenth. The Seals to Eminence are real. The Seals block our path into the ancient city, but we know where they are. Our great master knows the key to breaking them. Once there, he will revive the Great Crystal, return our world back to what it once was. Banish the poisonous mist forever and unveil the riches hoarded upon the city by the Last Godsking. Our master is gracious. He is kind. All will be given their share of Zenith's wealth. We will live as kings!"

The crowd devolved into a mass of cheerful hysteria, whistles and howls, claps and stamps of approval. Emre merely shook his head.

"Now, my lovely friends of Drenth," Solanine said as the applause died down. "Eat. Drink. Dance! For the Fallen plans to challenge the Pentax Themselves! But first, he will destroy the last bastion of rebellion here in Drenth, freeing you from a tyrant you didn't even realize was doing you harm. This Gutter King who spoils your lives further. Then he will march to Kalderim and end the threat of the Golden Throne. Eminence awaits!"

Solanine cued up the vocalist and the band. Music came to life and the crowd dispersed once more to passions anew. Solanine joined the Fallen as the pair mingled with nobleborn as they flocked to his side. He greeted them like old friends he hadn't seen in ages, smiles and booming laughter. A guise of friendship only discernible by the eyes of those who saw a wolf in sheep's clothing.

Emre hated everything in that minute. He tore into his scars, not caring what anyone thought.

XXXI

CADRIANNA

SHADOWS SWALLOWED THE gondola under a dome of stone and steel, coming to a final resting place upon a series of grated walkways.

Cadrianna and Captain Arhin were the last upon the glass carriage, the lagging gaggle of party guests squeezed through the slowly opening doors, insistent on not being any later to the grand to-do that had already started. Their polished boots and supple slippers sung upon the lattice walkways as they hurried about, being fashionably late as nobleborn sycophants were wont to do.

"Mistress Cadrianna," said the captain, his tinted breather reflected in the aethecite lamps lining the docking bay, "do you need assistance, or should I report the happenings of your capture?"

More than your simple mind could possibly understand, she wanted to say, but instead responded with something curter. "I'll make the report."

After fleeing Emre and the bikrome, she had wandered the streets of Drenth numb, unsure of what to think or do, in a stupor as she tried to piece together the ruins of her life. She was truly alone for the first time since being bonded with the Strix, as she had left it behind in her hasty flight. For as much as she didn't want to admit it, she missed the daemon blade. Could have used its guidance when she was so lost.

Seventeen long years sworn to do the Fallen's bidding only to keep her daughter from the everlasting pain of the void. All because of Emre's betrayal. To learn that not only could Brynn possibly be free, but that Emre was not dead was breaking to the core.

She hated him, loathed him, had wanted to berate him for everything that he'd put her and Brynn through. She had wrapped the lies around her like a protective shield. Bought into the Fallen's words, the reassurances that her daughter wouldn't suffer if she but obeyed. Gods, she even felt love toward Lu Har, even though she never stopped loving Emre.

What was she then, if not complicit?

Captain Arhin had found her staring at the remains of a small teahouse, a place that held a special spot in her heart. A memory of Emre. When the captain had rushed toward her, she brushed off his concern with a glassy-eyed dismissal, telling him they needed to return to Gargantua.

She just needed to be away from Drenth. Maybe she'd return to Oldport Basin, to her ancestral home.

"Very well," Captain Arhin said back in the present. "I shall take umbrage with the quartermaster and report my losses." The captain had been in a skirmish earlier that day with some gangland brutes in Slag's End and had suffered casualties. His focus went to the man running the controls from within a glass box at the top of the ramp. "You there, look alive. Get…" his words trailed off as there was some much ado further up the gangplank.

The distinctive clink of drake scale on metal made Cadrianna roll her eyes. And based on the gait and bearing of the form skulking toward her, it was Ratko. The last person she cared to see.

Ratko clapped his hands as he came to a stop and blocked Cadrianna from exiting the gondola. The man's beard swung free, those lustful eyes sneering as they performed a full-bodied once over. "Been slumming it in the scraps again?"

Nocturne, she didn't like the man. And especially now, of all times. "Better use of my time than whoring it up in the brothels."

"Sweetling, I'd much rather whore it up with you." Cadrianna made to pass but Ratko put a gloved hand upon her. She went to draw the Strix, only to be callously reminded she didn't have the blade. "You may have the favor of the Fallen, but that honor won't protect you forever."

She looked down at the glove on her shoulder. "Unless you want it broken, I suggest you remove your hand from me."

Ratko smiled like a viper; teeth exposed ready to bite but he removed his hand anyway. "I look forward to the day we can finally cross steel, sweetling. Then I'll play with your corpse however I wish." Ratko brushed past Cadrianna without another look.

The soldiers divided like a river going around a boulder submerged in the middle of its wake as she stalked from the gondola. Her thoughts were nothing but of Emre and Brynn, Ratko no more than a fleeting memory.

The stairs led into a man-made tunnel coated with the natural stalactites borne of the stone Gargantua was hewn from. A rail of gold-coated iron clung to the wall. Before long, the tunnel opened into a cavern where all the glory of Gargantua's conquests were housed, while also allowing any guests to view its magnificence. She noted a handful of late partygoers lingering about, taking in the statues and murals upon the walls.

Seeing these people, these leeches, she wanted nothing more than to bathe Gargantua in the blood of traitors. Starting with Lu Har.

"YOU KNOW HOW I USUALLY ENJOY A GOOD BLOODLETTING, BUT YOU SEEM LOST IN THOUGHT. SPARE A POOR DAEMON A HINT?"

"Strix?"

"I AM HERE, CAD."

"How?"

"WE ARE BONDED, NOT JUST AS A BLADE. YOU AND I ARE ONE ESSENCE. WOMB TO WOMB."

"You're a daemon, you don't have a womb."

"ONCE, CAD. THAT NEVER LEFT ONE SUCH AS ME."

"What the void does that even mean?"

"NOTHING BUT A MEMORY OF A TIME LONG AGO. WHAT BOTHERS YOU SO?"

"Really, Strix, you ask that after what that bikrome showed me?"

Cadrianna veered down a secondary tunnel for Imperium staff only. A pair of guards saluted diligently before opening a steel door for her. Beyond was the main headquarters of Gargantua, the flight deck, the barracks, the laboratories; the lifeblood of the Fallen's army above Drenth.

This section of Gargantua was comprised of dull, simplistic halls that were painted sterile white. As was the floor and ceiling. Soldiers in their scale armor doggedly patrolled the halls in small groups of threes or fours, heavily armed. Predators and other automatons stumped each corner, their blinking domes eagerly awaiting commands, especially with the party occurring.

"The Matron."

"TRUST ME WHEN I SAY THIS, CAD, THAT OLD HAG IS A FEW BOILED EGGS SHORT OF A DOZEN."

Cadrianna stopped. "What?"

"HER GEARS ARE RUSTED. THE DOGS ARE UNTRAINED AND RUNNING AMOK. A DAEMON'S BROKEN CLAW? NO? FINE, BLOODY NOCTURNE, CAD, YOU USED TO GET ALL MY EUPHEMISMS."

"Not particularly good ones, most. What are you getting at?"

"THAT HAG IS ANCIENT, LOST HER MIND WELL BEFORE THE FALL OF EMINENCE. TO BE FAIR, NOT CERTAIN SHE EVEN HAD IT BACK WHEN I POSSESSED TWO WINGS INSTEAD OF HAVING TO RELY ON YOU TO WHISK ME ABOUT."

"Yet the Fallen still relies on her counsel. Regardless, her words have left me baffled. Only more so now that the bikrome has shown me the truth of why I was kept chained."

"BAFFLED? HER WORDS HAVE THE INTELLIGENCE OF A MEWLING KITTEN MOST TIMES THAN NOT."

"The Seals, Strix. Why would the Matron even bring those up? I've never seen one, only do I know of them from my lessons from Thestile and Solanine. Calling it my true path. The true path that I must break. With you and all that. But what of Brynn?"

"RIDDLES. THAT'S ALL IT IS. THE RAMBLINGS OF A LONG-FLED MIND."

"O, just riddles. She named you. Said the Seals and Eminence are what matter to me and to you. Want to explain that to me?"

"I KNOW NOT WHAT THAT OLD, BLIND HAG MEANS. YOU CAN BELIEVE ME ON THAT, CAD. IF I KNEW, I'D TELL YOU FIRST AND FOREMOST. WE'RE FRIENDS, REMEMBER?"

"Sometimes I wonder. But why tell me that? The bikrome, void, Emre said we needed to help Brynn. How can I do such a thing? He's betrayed me, Strix!"

"YOU ASK SOUND QUESTIONS," the Strix responded carefully, almost as if hiding something.

"For sixteen years you've been my guardian, my savior and giver, my protector and shield. The aether and blood that binds us, Strix. They are the same as the Seals, as it has been said. All the aetheurgies, the Forms, in fact. She named the Seals to Eminence. My hand will help break them. I care not for any of that. I wanted only Lu Har dead, Brynn freed. But apparently Brynn has been free all this time. How? Why? It doesn't make any sense."

"AS DO I. HE MADE ME WHAT I AM. WHAT WE ARE TOGETHER. HE BOUND US, BROUGHT ME UP FROM THE PIT ITSELF. I WISH TO GO BACK INTO SLUMBER. PEACEFULLY, I MIGHT ADD."

She thought of Lu Har as he performed the ritual binding her to the Strix all those years ago.

The Fallen's breathtaking smile drank in the shadows, his onyx eyes glowed like smoldering embers. In his hand he held the blackened steel that was aflame as he pressed it to her monthly blooded womb.

Her only thought was of her daughter, taken from her. The daughter she'd carried within the womb that was now being bound by Void Form aetheurgy. A searing, a severing of the life she could and had carried, now being destroyed, replaced with the bond of another kind.

"BRYNNNNNNN!"

Hatred grew. Venom biting. "Vengeance is all I have left to me. You best not be lying to me, Strix." A laced demand.

The Strix did its best snort impression considering it had no nostrils. *"SEE, YOU DO TRY TO HURT ME. WHY WOULD I LIE?"*

"Because you come from them." The magical weapon was trying to be playful, but she was having none of it. "Brynn is all that matters. Fuck the Seals. Fuck the coven. Fuck Solanine and the rest of them. Fuck the Imperium. Fuck Emre." Now she was full of anger. "And fuck Lu Har!"

A crimson-scaled captain stopped her before she could take two steps deeper into Gargantua. "Sorry, Mistress Cadrianna, but no one is allowed to enter without clearance from Solanine."

"That's who I'm going to see," she growled.

"Orders, mistress."

She stepped up to the man, who jerked rigid. "Don't get in my way."

"I'm… I'm sorry, mistress. I have my orders." Cadrianna calculated there were at least thirty, if not more, soldiers within the hall, plus another dozen automatons. Not exactly the best of odds without the Strix handy, but doable with her Void Form. Sensing her aggression, the man cleared his throat. "Solanine is… uh… out on the main mezzanine. Ringing the party in… uh, your presence… uh… there."

Without pressing, she turned and marched away.

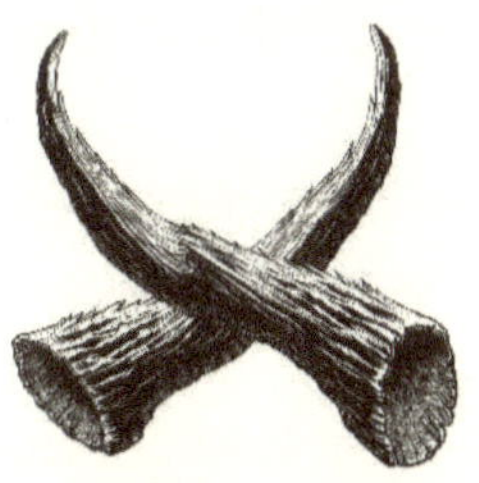

XXXII
LOJEN

IF LOJEN HAD been told how incredibly silent and empty Gargantua's inner workings would be, he would have gone straight to the nearest gambling den and placed a major wager on getting caught.

The silence was deafening.

Outside of the engines thrumming and the workers shoveling the raw material into the furnace, as well as the random beeping of an automaton, once he moved away from the main cavern, there was nothing but the sound of his boots gently kissing the walkway.

Worried that he would be discovered at any moment, Lojen probably shaved some days off his life, but at least the nervous jitters also kept him alert.

He'd left the engines by way of a series of maintenance tunnels similar—though a scant bit taller—to the one he and Ru had taken from the chain. Each was curved at the top and dimly lit. Part of him was surprised there weren't any surveillance cameras, but he encountered no one or thing in the tunnels as he placed half a dozen bombs on appropriate targets. On each bomb, he clicked a tiny lever that released a spell of *Ignis*. The rune etched onto the bombs glowed like fire, a dribble of mist from it. From there it would be on Emre to make it go boom.

Lojen soon found a winding stair that would lead him topside. He waited just inside the shadows cast by the twisting steps, listening for the sound of descent.

When he was satisfied—or at least not frightened enough to run into some unexpected worker, soldier, robot of death, or the bloody scourges themselves—Lojen raced up the staircase, taking three steps at a time. The air cooled as he climbed, the heat given off by the engines fading away. A soft buzz grew as he went upward, and before long, it developed into clear expressions of music accompanied by a voice from the heavens.

He emerged through a well-oiled metal gate—which made him feel better since it didn't squeak loudly to alert anyone to his presence—into an open terrace upon Gargantua. But more worryingly, he could see that he was opposite of the compound where, according to the map, the Seal was located. And the entire party filled the space between.

Broken shells!

He thought about going back into the tunnels and trying to find another way, but a quick check of his watch showed that was out of the question. He tried to think. Guards roamed the perimeter of the mezzanine, but they stayed in the shadows just outside of the frolicking guests, and kept a solid distance between a low hedge and the party. But that meant they were closer to him, making his task even harder.

Pressed against the building's wall, Lojen snuck as close to the party—and guards—as he was willing to get. He marked two firedrake-scale-clad soldiers patrolling in a set course, turning about face after twenty steps, then retreating the opposite way in the same pattern, only crossing paths with the other at a set point. Over and over, no stopping. Faceless helmets on swivels, watching the party, as well as those who might think it prudent to slink into the shadows for some 'fun' alone time. Even if he got past the guards, he couldn't just waltz into the crowd; a drakken would stick out like a broken tusk on a Merj mammoth. A cursory investigation of the scene didn't leave him much choice either; it was crawling on his belly near the bushes or climbing the building at his back and scale it to the hanging aethecite lights.

Neither option was a good one, but scaling the lighted string was the preferred one in his mind. Either way, it meant he had to get even closer before he could make his ascent.

Time dragged as he counted the guards' steps from the moment they crossed each other to the time they pivoted. Fifteen seconds.

Crouching with one boot forward, he cinched the satchel tighter and took a deep breath. *Twenty feet in fifteen seconds. Damnit, best be fast.*

The guards passed another shoulder-to-shoulder and Lojen hurled forward, bent as low as he could, counting in his head.

One.

Two.

Three...

He was closer now, just about ten feet from the guards.

Six.

Seven.

Eight...

His boots barely touched the ground as he broke past where the guards had crossed, aiming for the nearest cover of brush.

Eleven.

Twelve...

Diving headfirst into the low bush, Lojen whipped around, branches fluttering in his eyesight.

Fourteen.

Fifteen.

The guards turned on a heel and resumed their trek unhindered, unaware that he had just passed them without being seen or heard. The quivering branches covering his bulk resembled a gentle sway of the wind, nothing out of the ordinary. Hopefully.

Too close, Lojen. Too close.

Parting the prickly bush with his talons, he saw a low brick wall separating a grassy area from waist-high tables. Drenth's guests glided along the grass, stumbled, and spoke at length, but most were facing the dancers and the acrobats upon fluted pedestals. Slowly, Lojen darted from the bush, thorns raking across his exoscales and tearing at his vest and trousers, scraping across his snout and horn stumps. He made a direct line toward the nearest wall. Laughter and clear, concise dialogue stopped him short, so he ducked behind what could only be called a trash bin since there was an odor that made him gag.

The smell was worse than the bloody stuff drakken tanners used to clean animal hides. Lojen covered his nostrils with his claws.

A maintenance hatch was barely visible next to the trash can.

Sucking in his breath to avoid smelling the scent of another's gorge, Lojen dug his talons into the hatch, prying it open. He ducked in the tunnel and closed the door behind him.

XXXIII
ASHE

SHE AWOKE DRENCHED in a cold sweat upon her naked flesh, the dream-that-was-not-a-dream was over. Reality. Sobering truth.

She threw the blanket aside and turned onto her side to find Wren missing. Part of her wondered if the time with Wren was all part of the dream, but the slight ache in her muscles, hips and jaw, told her it hadn't been. Besides, she could remember every single second of the bliss. That was no dream, dreams always seemed to end just prior to the juicy parts.

Going to the vanity, Ashe turned on the faucet and splashed her sweaty face. Beside the sink was a perspiring decanter of wine. Her hand absently reached for it, but she stopped.

Not yet. You need answers.

The girl looking back at her was a face she recognized. The small scar just under her left eye where a training sword had clipped her at eight while under Cyan's tutelage. Cheekbones that were flushed under her sand-dusted coloring. Curling locks of luscious pitch with a cool bluish tint that coiled around her face just below her ears. Her runic tattoos forever inked into the flesh of her left arm from wrist to shoulder, inside and out.

Every little detail of the person she had become, the face of one who had been trained to pray, to survive at all costs, to not give in to anything. And yet, she didn't know this person anymore.

Her face resembled a lost little girl, one who didn't know right from wrong. Who didn't see the blinders that had been placed upon her. Who didn't defy the odds and gone to the other side when it was the tougher option. She didn't know this person, didn't want to be that person anymore.

But who was she then if not who she was raised to be?

The clock atop the wall next to her mirror chimed softly. *Emre, father.* Solanine was the key, always had been.

In her anger, she took the nearest thing on the vanity—a music box—and threw it at the mirror. The box struck the image of a Drenth-born, Scattered Shards trained thief, shattering the reflective glass in a spider's web of cracks. The series of fractures left a hundred white eyes with white pupils staring back, echoing the multitude of avenues her emotions were fleeing down.

There was movement in the doorway behind her, breaking her thoughts. "Ancantha?" She turned but saw nothing.

Ashe pushed away from the vanity and it was this movement that saved her life.

A well-placed stab of a dagger whizzed by her ear; the exact spot her neck would have been. A spine-severing attack, one stab and the victim would be dead before they'd realize it.

The attacker stumbled with the missed jab, a spray of water splashing the mirror. Ashe was already moving, her training kicking in. She grabbed a towel in both hands and wrapped it around her closed fists, pulling it taut. Only an inch-thick pool of mist filled the room, barely enough to call a puddle.

The attacker wore the firedrake cuirass of a scourge, and Ashe quickly realized, was the same one who'd assailed her on the gondola. The scourge crouched and bent her knees, feet spread. Then she lunged at Ashe with the burn of aetheurgy, most likely Void Form.

Ashe summoned her aetheurgy, already on the balls of her feet, as she had anticipated the woman's aether-enhanced attack. Without the mist backing her up, her aetheurgy was lethargic, almost as if waking from a drunken coma. She'd have to hope it was enough.

The scourge led with the dagger, so Ashe used the towel to wrap the scourge's wrist twice with the thick fabric, her aetheurgy of speed a fraction faster than the other's. The woman cursed behind her tinted breather as Ashe twisted and jarred the dagger from her hand. Ashe used her bare foot to kick it away.

"Can't be a coward here, you bitch. No one but you and me. You won't be able to toss a bitty out a window, now. Fight me fair and see who wins."

The woman responded with an attack aimed at her head and it forced Ashe to duck. Unfortunately, it caused her to loosen the grip of the towel on the woman's wrist. The scourge freed her bound arm and yanked the towel from Ashe's grip. Backing away, the scourge tossed the towel, turning her feet and raising her fists. Ashe did the same, though she bounced on her feet, staying limber like Cyan had taught her.

Both circled each other warily.

"What's with you?" Ashe pawed the strands of her hair from her eyes while never taking them from her opponent. The scourge said nothing. "I bet it's because I embarrassed your lover in front of all his friends down at the tether, eh?" The fierce killer of the Fallen swept around the room, keeping her distance, not speaking. "What's the matter, Solanine rip your tongue out for not pleasing her enough?

I bet that's it, huh?" No response. "Fine, stay quiet while I kick your ass."

Ashe attacked. She aimed a series of strikes at the woman in lightning quick succession, though not as fast as it should have been with a full complement of mist behind her aetheurgy. The scourge blocked her attacks, then reversed course and began to throw jabs of her own, forcing Ashe back, coughing while she defended the blows.

After a series of volleys and parries, they retreated from one another, pausing to catch their breath. Ashe breathed heavily, pulmo coughs making her throat raw. She was tired.

Her respite was short as the scourge lunged again, a piston of punches with aetheric speed. Ashe blocked, but her backside crunched into the vanity and the decanter of wine toppled, the glass shattering as it hit the floor. Fragments pierced the soles of her feet. Ashe roared as blood painted red smears as she tip-toed through the sharp battlefield, all the while preventing the woman's fists from connecting and making a mess of her self-proclaimed pretty face.

The woman's attacks came faster, leaving her less time to react as the nausea from blood loss swept in. Her muscles didn't want to listen to her instincts. She took a fist to the abdomen, another to the temple, then another to her sternum. All three could, no, should have been blocked had she the aether in the mist, but she couldn't. Weak she was without the mist.

She stumbled and went to her knee, blood slick underneath her. Ashe looked up at the scourge, waiting for the next blow to be her last. "You stupid bi—"

"O shut up, love," the scourge said. "You don't seem to realize you aren't that funny."

Startled, Ashe huffed. "I'll have you know, I'm hilar—"

"That's enough, love." The woman's hands rose toward the breather and removed it to reveal blonde hair, high cheeks on a cherub face, comely, upturned lips. Lips and hands that had been gentle and loving only recently. Yet now, both looked like they wanted blood. Ashe's blood.

It was Wren.

"What the fu…" her words trailed off as anger came. What little mist that remained by her side throughout her time on Gargantua darkened with the need for spilling this nymph's innards. A pressure she hadn't felt since the moments after killing that servant in the villa. "I should have known."

"Known what, love?" Wren dropped the breather. "That I was a spy for Solanine this entire time?" She smiled that little bird smile that had drawn Ashe in. Those upturned lips still beautiful. "Our little dalliance was but a side joy from my true task. To make your aetheurgy become pure and prepared. How do you think that servant found you at Soabin's? Can't lie, I did enjoy it."

"A scourge, how? No runes about your body, *love*."

Wren smirked as she reached toward her eyes and pulled something away. Her alluring brown irises revealed a crimson pupil. Wren had bloody Burn Form, not Void Form. And she was more exquisite by the revelation.

Ashe inwardly cursed the desire inside her, wanting sex at a moment like this. *Make up your godsdamned mind!* That's when she realized she was actually speaking to the mist… *O Zenith, I've lost it.*

She hefted her fists, ready to pummel the whore who had betrayed her trust and did what any self-respecting person might do to save face: she got defensive. "Not that I care or anything."

The little bird grinned while she drew forth a vial of parch, drinking it. "Don't lie, love. Your body didn't. And I'm sorry it came to this, I am. But this is business. How do you think Elian knew about your aetheurgy? Me. I set everything in motion the moment you were found here in Drenth. Lu Har always knew you'd come home. You're a good toss, just so you know before I make you kneel before the Fallen."

The mist poked the back of her calf. Now, she returned the grin. "Then come get it."

Wren rushed her with a burst of aetheurgy. Ashe lifted her left arm, the rune for *Aere* snapping along her forearm. The mist became a small gale of wind, much stronger than the mist should have created. *This is new,* she gawked at the increased power she wielded.

The spell caught Wren in dead lunge, picking her up, blowing her back toward the bed in a fury of aether. A nasty crunch against a bed post. Attacking anew, the fierce gale lifted again the woman's body.

The serving wench who'd been Ashe's object of affection was balled, tears spilling down her pretty face like a child. "Please," she begged. Arms curled against her body as if holding onto the invisible binds keeping her aloft. "The Fallen will kill me if I don't do what he commands. I didn't want to. Please?"

The keening mist tingled Ashe's legs. It wasn't angry now, it was loving. It was sympathetic. It wanted her to forgive this woman, wanted compassion shown. Odd the feeling was. Ashe suddenly felt sorry for Wren. She'd only done what Lu Har had commanded of her. Wren was just a proxy. This wasn't her. Wasn't who Ashe was.

Was she? The opposing wants fought inside of her.

And that's when the fleeting increase of power within the mist died and scattered like dried dandelion petals being blown for luck. "O… shit…"

The bonds holding Wren disintegrated and the lover-revealed-as-a-spy-turned-false-pontificator pitched a fist at her face. Ashe used the woman's momentum to grab her by the forearm and toss her ass over head. Wren landed on her backside, but was up quickly, aiming a kick that Ashe wasn't expecting. The boot cracked into her skull and sent her flying into the vanity, her head striking the rounded edge. Blood oozed down her face, stars in her eyes.

Woozy from the collision, a vice-like grip burrowed into her hair and lifted her up. She didn't have time to suck in her breath before her entire head was submerged into the sink, screaming bubbles of fury. The water sloshed over the rim as she struggled.

"You're a bigger fool than I thought, love."

Ashe clawed at the hand holding her head, but Wren put all her weight upon her, the lip of the sink digging into Ashe's breastbone. Her movements slowed; her body became sluggish as the strain in her lungs pulled every ounce of air to them.

With a last-ditch effort, Ashe released the hand and felt along the vanity for leverage. Water rushed around her as her head rose from the sink, lungs sucking in precious oxygen, but she kept thrusting with her head. It connected with Wren's pretty nose. Hellfire ran down Ashe's spine as the nose exploded, wrenching the woman's neck backward. Wren crumpled to the ground, holding her broken sniffer as blood flowed freely.

Ashe crawled toward the flopping would-be-assassin and jammed her elbow into the woman's gut. She then clamped her hands around the little bird's neck. Rage fueled her. Redemption sustained her.

"I was fool enough to fall for you, Little Bird. Won't happen again. By the way, for all your gusto, you weren't that great of a toss."

Ashe heard a gasp, the woman struggled to breathe, and then Wren went limp.

Rolling off the dead woman, Ashe nearly hacked up her lungs under the onslaught of pulmo. Blood poured from the wound on her face, her feet ached like murder. She looked up at the angled mirror on the ceiling—the one tilted just perfectly enough to view the horizontal window on the far wall. The sun was slowly setting, and it left a pinkish-orange glow within the mirror. Peaceful, serene, natural.

Probably should've asked her why, eh? Ashe thought.

The door to her chamber opened and Ancantha raced in, pure terror in her button-shaped eyes. "Mistress! Are you alright?"

Ashe stared at the lapin, sudden determination filling her. "Ancantha, give me that godsdamned pink stola."

XXXIV
EMRE

"FINN, WE READY?"

"Of course, love." Scanning the crowd, Emre found Finn surrounded by a gaggle of women. He held a tray of some cooked meat on a stick, but the women—largely older, and thus attracted to a younger buck in his prime versus their overweight husbands—fawned over the elfirish servant. "I really should be getting back," he was saying to the hens swamping him.

"Wick, making my way toward you now."

"Careful, Em, scourges everywhere. Ruane's dropped the parcel."

Under the curved stair was a set of doors. A few guests mingled, chatting about useless drivel. Men boasting about asinine victories of sexual conquest or sporting accolades that probably never even happened the way they proclaimed. Equally vapid women soaking up the boasts with giant smiles and false appreciation, more worried about their societal standing than the actual points of conversation.

But the alcohol flowed freely and the one thing all these people had in common: they had to piss.

Based on Wick's information, the privies were only a doorway away from the kitchen. Though the party was held outside, the privies were housed within the main compound itself because of the plumbing necessary to remove the filth. The double doors stood open and that's where the guests waited semi-patiently. However, at the far end of the hall, past the four individual private receptacles, was another set of doors which led to the kitchen.

He made for the kitchen when a hand clamped down on his shoulder. Emre turned to find a taller man, maybe a mix of Kanjan and Drenth blood, glaring at him from behind a golden mask. "Hey, friend, line starts back there," the man's words were a tad uneven, and the overpowering musk of alcohol like a bog.

Emre calmly pushed the man's hand away. "Ease, friend. Only going to see if they have more of those charred bits on a stick."

The drunkard's demeanor softened, and he then proceeded to slap Emre with the back of his hand like friends do when scouting a beautiful lass in the distance. "Bring me some of those, will ya? Them's good eats."

Some of the others standing in line called out other morsels for Emre to pilfer if he should find a chance. He gave a slight wave and checked his pocketwatch, moving. "Wick, nearing the door. Any scale on the other side to worry about?"

"Just one and the bugger's not paying much mind."

With a touch, the door swung on oiled hinges. The delicious smell of roasting meats, spices, and grilled vegetables overtook his nostrils. The clanging of pans, the cuts of knives against wooden boards, the clatter of spoons against pots drowned out the barks of a head cook's orders. A soldier leaned against the wall, his arms crossed, wheellock rifle hanging from his shoulder, breather helm lowered as if studying the ground, or possibly even napping.

But once Emre made his appearance, the soldier looked him up-and-down, taking in his fine-cut black suit and ornate mask. "Guests are not allowed back here."

Emre raised his hands to act innocent. "Forgive me," he said, feigning a stagger as if he'd drunk too much. "Privy line double long. Was wonderin' if there was another pot to piss in back here."

The soldier straightened and pointed back the way Emre had come. "Only privies down there."

Just then, a lapin servant wearing a red-and-black tunic rolled at the elbows came around the corner with a massive tray of food. He tripped over his own paws and barged into the guard, who in turn, shouldered into Emre, who stuttered back into the swinging doorway. The tray clattered to the ground and threw chunks of skewered meat-and-veggies-on-a-stick everywhere. The lapin gasped at his folly and dove to pick up the food. Emre regained his balance and bent down to help, while the guard muttered under his breath as the lapin servant apologized time and again.

Some of the guests were pointing and laughing at the interchange at the end of the hall. In all the kerfuffle and muttering, no one noticed the lapin hand Emre a bulky object, and they certainly didn't see him pocket said object.

Emre helped Wick to its feet and grabbed a couple of the stick delicacies. The lapin apologized loudly once more while backing into the doorway, the guard shaking his head and cursing as the door swung closed.

Sauntering toward the exit, Emre took a bite from one of the sticks before he offered one of the treats to the drunkard.

The man vigorously shook his head. "Got boot dirt all over it. Gonna make me retch more than the wine swilling in my gut."

Shrugging, Emre rounded the dance floor, where he spat out the meat in a nearby bush and tossed the others. He didn't see the bikrome anywhere. The music started again, the dance floor was full once more.

"Val, meet me by the fountain."

Emre snaked through the party. His scars itched to no end, and he fought the urge to scratch them again. With the aetheric bomb on his person and the drakken siblings no doubt nearing their targets, he was growing antsy. Years of planning had brought him to this exact moment in time, everything worked for, everything paid for, all for right now, right here.

The time to bring down the Imperium was reaching its apex, and he only had one more piece of the puzzle to click into place before the true show was to begin.

Emre came upon the magnificent fountain. Its marble was carved in the shape of four wood nymphs holding up a bowl. The shimmering liquid aethecite spouted six feet in the air, a perfect three-pronged arc landing gracefully within the bowl as the mist rose from the pool. Its aether was breathtaking.

A few guests hovered around the fountain, a couple daring to touch the aetheric liquid. A woman ran her finger through the arc and giggled as it rolled off like a gloopy syrup. Bending down as if he was tying his shoe, Emre pulled the bomb out of his pocket and tacked it under the rim of the bowl using heavy adhesive tape, then burned aetheurgy to trigger the *Ignis* spell.

"Anyone have eyes on our catalyst?"

"Nothin' by me," Finn said.

Wick mimicked with a, "Nor me."

"Keep an eye everyone. Lojen, Ruane, are we set? Over."

"The belle of the ball has arrived," said Finn suddenly. "Bless the Pentax, I think that's her?"

XXXV
ASHE

WET HAIR CLUNG to the nape of her neck, her torn feet throbbed within the haphazard bandages she'd wrapped, a welt at her temple where her head had smacked the sink, but the godsdamning thing most of all, Ashe had a fractured soul.

And yet, she kept her back straight as she marched through Gargantua as if she hadn't a care in the world.

Imperium soldiers gave her curious looks and a wide berth, taking in her long-trained stola, pinkest of pink hem flowing behind. She cared little that the wafer-thin material hugged her body, nor about the generously high slit up one leg that showed her bruised thigh. Even a thief such as herself showed little appetite for the expensive string of pearls draped across her collar.

For her, this was her armor. The gorgeous armor—she had to admit the dress was lovely despite the unfortunate color choice— she'd wear into battle with Solanine. Beautiful and angry armor. An armor of defiance.

At least the mist had returned to her, flitting under the train, caressing her legs, fueling her rage. Yet there was a minute change in the mist, as if it wanted her to march in a different direction, to go deeper into the building. Queer, that.

Some guards smiled at her, only to turn to concern when she scowled at them. Others raised eyebrows behind skull-painted breathers, more than a handful gripped their wheellock rifles tighter. Each one of them braced for trouble because they saw she meant to rain down heaps of it.

The maze of hallways ended in a double door of Calibrathian redwood, which stood open, revealing a downward curving stair. Word of her coming had already reached the exit as armed guards on either side stood with rifles at the ready, fingers on triggers.

One stepped forward, her aggressive reflection peering back at her from the man's tinted breather. "Sorry, mistress, but Solanine has requested you meet elsewhere. If you would but follow us, we will show you whe—"

"Move."

The jackass held his ground. His aura was a nervous jaundice. "Solanine has expressively declared tonight to be free of any disturbances. And you appear… well, Mistress Benld, you appear like you've seen better evenfalls. That lapin servant should never have allowed you to leave your rooms like this."

"Move," she repeated. The mist clawed up her legs.

"Mistre—" the man's words choked off as Ashe jammed stiff fingers into the gap between his breather and collar. He dropped like a sack of aethecite.

Ashe glared at the other soldiers, daring them to get in her way, the mist eager for a fight. She didn't care anymore, whatever happened from here out, would happen. But the soldiers didn't bite, they removed fingers from triggers and warily backed away.

Head held high, Ashe stepped through the threshold and found the most handsome elfirish man she'd ever laid eyes on waiting for her at the base of the stair.

The Fallen.

Anger threatened to bubble up and froth out of her in a wild rage. She wanted nothing more than to see the blood of this man erupt from his body like geysers. Every hardship in her life, every difficulty, every emotion was because of this man. She could almost savor the pride wafting from him.

"Brynn Benld," the Fallen said loudly behind a great smile, clearly a show. Murmurs and whispers arose from those close by. The Fallen held out a hand, inviting her to descend. "You could've at least washed your face, child."

"Go bugger yourself with the tip of a goblin bone sword." Many of Drenth's finest guests gasped, which brought a grin to Ashe's face. "Some party you got here, Lu Har. Paid for in blood, I suspect. Maybe even your own bloodkin, eh? Does Canlon Carr ring a bell for you?" More whispers amongst the crowd.

Although many of the guests nearest the Fallen were paying attention to her upon the stairs, not all were. Pockets of partygoers conversed and laughed, downing wine like water. The singer continued her song, the music a stirring din. There were guards everywhere, though. A handful of scourges amongst them in their black firedrake scale cuirasses. For all the merriment, it felt more like a controlled atmosphere, almost like a theater amongst prisoners.

She scanned the mezzanine and spied Solanine staring at her pensively. A tickle ran down her spine. Odd it was for the short aetheurgist to give her a chill instead of the presence of the Fallen. Perhaps it was the visions, perhaps just a sordid connection that pushed her down this path back at the Guilder's villa.

Ashe noticed a shaggy-haired woman wearing a mask layered in ribbons of varying colors. The woman reared her head back in a laugh, hand placed at her breast as if the gaggle of nobleborn surrounding her had said the funniest thing in all the Mistlands. A row of golden teeth sparkled in the woman's mouth.

Neenah LeFleur? Pulling yet another con, are you? Good luck getting off this rock.

Her gaze swept onward, stopping on a man and woman barely visible amongst the guests. Though masked and veiled respectively, the man stood out to her like a sore thumb, the woman clearly a bikrome. A mask resembling cracked marble, a fitting image of a broken piece of history. Even at this distance, she knew the man who was her father as he watched her silently, as if he was calculating her intent. Emre Benld gave her the barest of nods. Approval, it seemed.

"Back from the grave and already speaking ill of the dead," Lu Har tsked. "A child never learns."

"Then educate me," she replied, raising her bangled hand, and realizing she couldn't read the Fallen's aura. Because he didn't possess one. Something she'd never witnessed before. "Murderer," she added for effect.

His hand extended again, this time she took it, placing the diamond eye into his palm. The Fallen towered over her, his crimson robe overlapped her pink train as he led her onto the dance floor. A lively refrain ensued as dozens of other couples joined them. All moved in perfect cadence, men led, women flowed effortlessly. Laughter and joy abound, casual and free. Auras a giddy yellow.

Except for the aura-less Fallen.

Ashe allowed him to lead, his hand upon her hip, holding the bangled one aloft. She knew the steps well, the dance a Kalderim specialty. The Scattered Shards had allowance for such hobbies, and truth told, Ashe did have a passion for the artistry of dance.

"You killed my parents. Why don't we start there."

He spun her under his raised arm, letting go of her waist as she was passed to the nearest man in accordance with the dance. Ashe stymied a groan as she twirled into the waiting arms of Prien Soabin. The ancient prick smiled broadly, while his wife—the pretty Isla—frowned as she danced with Lu Har.

"My Lady of Demrae," the old bastard's spotted hands groped at her. "How wonderful to see you again. Though I must admit you look… unwell. Ahem… I've been waiting for your brother to reach out about the trade lines he spoke of."

"Sorry, Master Soabin, been a void of a week since your party," she said demurely as the dance required the changing of partners again, this time she was paired off with some lanky man with peppered grey hair. The old Guilder winked at her, and she turned away in disgust but kept the false smile.

"Lies are but the truth of the unknowing," Lu Har said as the partners exchanged again, back to the original couples. "You know nothing of which you think."

"I know the truth." He dipped her, her wet hair slapped against her bare neck. "Of what you are. Of what you did to Canlon Carr."

"Trifles, child." They did a full rotation, feet stepping in time, crossing flawlessly. A couple wearing matching masks with elongated beaks like a bird's nearly bumped into them, both appearing intoxicated. The man apologized, but the Fallen ignored him. "What matters now is what blood flows within you. Eminence awaits us. Awaits you, Godsblood."

The music shifted from the lively tune to one slower, more romantic. Some of the dancers took their leave of the floor while others pressed closer together. The vocalist's voice started from a medium alto and gradually rose into a soprano as she sang a song of love. Isla Soabin stormed from the dance floor as the old prickly bugger appeared as if he was going to ask Ashe for the dance.

Lu Har's hand moved to the small of her back and pulled her closer. The mere touch of his hand on her body disgusted her. Prien Soabin blanched before slithering away. "You're an asset, Brynn Benld. Same as your father and mother before you."

"You mean the day you destroyed my family? All for your failure to take Eminence?"

He glanced down his nose at her, the corners of his mouth tugging. "I see you've been speaking to Canlon."

How does he know? "So, it's true? All of it?"

"O Brynn, how the mind of a child manifests from a malleable pittance. A foundation built within, leading to this discovery of fate. Be pleased, child, for you have lived a life not shackled by your fate. Not all of us are given this gift."

"My past was everything!" A few of the dancing couples looked at her. "You took everything from me."

"The Pentax took that from you, not I. I am merely the tool. My Divine wants what He has been denied. The Seals await you. That is your destiny. Canlon was never strong enough to defy me."

"Then why try to kill me? Twice."

A tenseness overtook the Fallen's jaw, his eyes flickered briefly toward Solanine, who still watched them like a hawk in flight over a field of mice. *That wasn't supposed to happen, was it?*

"A tool is only as strong as the edge in which it's sharpened." His hand cupped her cheek. "Without a whetstone, you aren't of use."

The mist quirked. "You've not seen my true potential." Her hand roamed from the Fallen's arm down toward the slit in her dress, but

Lu Har grabbed her wrist. He spun her and pulled the knife sheathed at her thigh, pocketing the blade Wren had tried to skewer her with.

"You disappoint me, child."

"For that, I'm glad."

The song ended, the couples parted and cheerfully clapped. The vocalist bowed to all the applause.

"Your place is beside me, Brynn Benld, as it has always been," the Fallen said as he stepped away. "The gateway to the past has been opened to you. Your future is set. You cannot escape your fate. The Seals to Eminence will urge you toward them. It cannot be stopped. You feel it now, don't you?"

"All I feel is the thrill of seeing you dead." But before the words even left her mouth, she felt the tiniest of tugs within her, a tug toward the building she'd come from earlier. Even the mist seemed to prod her in that direction.

"That is the Seal of *Terris*," he said knowingly. "It's drawn to you. Seeks you. Try as you might, you will harness it and then break it." With that, the Fallen turned heel and ghosted across the dance floor.

"Thanks for the dance!"

Ashe stood in the center of the dance floor by herself, hands at her sides balled in white-knuckled fists as the bells tolled the time. She stood there still as stone, unmoving like the marble statues littered throughout Gargantua's walking paths. Anger roiled within.

Betrayal, the mist said.

Liar, the flames of vengeance fumed.

Killer, the enmity harkened.

By the Pentax, she was a lost soul.

Joyous couples took to the floor as the vocalist's range began anew, music striking chord once more in a style meant for the passing of partners. Women and men separated, forming a line across from one another, clapping in tune while the vocalist wailed. Prien Soabin watched her with sickening fascination.

She stumbled away, ignoring the stares accompanying her exit. Her torn feet slapped against the hardwood, leaving fresh hurtful jolts with each step. She snaked a perspiring glass of bubbly wine from an unsuspecting noble and downed it in a single gulp.

Zenith's cock, that man is maddening. We'll see what he thinks when I remove myself from this place. Shit, Father, I can't. Her anger flared. "I can't take this anymore."

"Talking to yourself are we, Godsblood?" A smirk graced Solanine's face, elbow leaning on a linen-covered tabletop nearby.

Finally, she thought. "Lu Har let you out of your cage, bitch?"

"A mastiff can still tear you apart even when not hunting, but a defanged snake is nothing more than writhing leather, Brynn Benld."

"Been working on that one long?"

The Fallen's pet's face turned hard. "Your barbs have no sting, Godsblood. I would rather you willingly join our cause. I should so hate to have to kill you right after you break the Seals."

"What do you want?"

"The rebellion dies today. Or didn't you hear?"

"And?"

"The heir of this dung heap of a city is at this party. The Gutter King, or should I say Emre Benld, is bold enough to show his face. And the rest of his inner circle. My soldiers are onto them as we speak. Your father is not prepared for the wrath of the Fallen." Solanine tittered. "But I bet you didn't know that part of the plan your father cooked up had to do with you."

"And what of Slag's End? They weren't part of it."

"I would burn this city to the ground if my Divine demands it." Solanine played with a pendant of obsidian. "Innocent or enslaved, none of it matters to me. Death is the only way to immortality. Purposes they serve, these desert ants. And when their use is over, I will gladly send their souls to the Divines as tithe. Your friends in this city have merely reached the end of their usefulness."

"You sent Wren to kill me."

"On the contrary, girl. I sent her to make you harness your aetheurgy." The small aetheurgist glided closer and Ashe couldn't help but recoil. "All to make you open the way to Eminence. The end is nigh for so many, Brynn Benld. Like I said, the rebellion dies today. You might consider it a blessing, lest you share their fate."

Ashe waved her hand in front of her face. "See this, this is my 'fuck you' face."

Solanine laughed mirthlessly. "Spoken like your mother. Ah, speak of the daemon." The aetheurgist pointed.

Ashe saw a woman dressed in the scale armor of a scourge descend the staircase. Face of flushed olive, same as her own. The mouth, the lips, the cheeks. All the same as Ashe's. Hair shorter, wavier, but the same hue of black. But with all-onyx colored eyes instead of her all-white.

The same woman from her visions.

"Mother…"

The woman, nay, her mother, marched straight across the dance floor toward where her father stood amongst the crowd.

"And it looks like she's seen a ghost. The end begins for the Benlds, Godsblood. Reap what those two have sown for you."

Lojen

XXXVI
LOJEN

ONCE INSIDE THE tunnel, Lojen dredged up the compound layout from his pocket.

Lojen crawled through the tunnel toward another hatch, this time it led into the compound itself, into a sterile hall of laboratories. Easing out, he scanned the halls for guards, but found the way clear. He could do nothing about the cameras at each juncture, so Lojen kept his back to the plastered wall as he prowled through a maze-like hallway hoping the guards on camera duty were more interested in the party than these stray halls.

Aethecite lights stuck out of both walls near the ceiling where copper tubes were riveted. The piss-yellow orbs doused the burrow in an unnatural glow. There were doorways baked into walls with signs above to indicate what was inside. Every one of them closed by an automatic locking system with a keycard access point and multiple blinking buttons. Most were machinery or service rooms, radio connections or communications supply.

But a few made Lojen's tail flick with unease.

One was named ***Munitions*** and it was painfully obvious by the darkened stone around the door that weapons and explodable things occurred beyond. There were a couple rooms called *Science Division* but Lojen didn't want to guess what went on behind those doors—though his mind could probably come up with some really frightening ideas if the colored lenses Emre showed him were any hint. The one he found himself staring at for long moments was called *Vault of the Fallen*. The room marked as his target.

"Lojen!" The drakken practically jumped free of his exoscales at the sound of his name. Heart palpitating, he saw Wick hop-running toward him, a similar hand-drawn map in his furry paw. Wick breathed a sigh of relief as he skidded to a halt. "What took you so long? The cameras are only disabled for ten minutes. We don't have time to dally."

"They are?" He glanced up at the one nearby and realized there were no blinking lights upon it. And to think he had nearly pissed his trousers in fright over being seen. He shook his massive head. *You're such a Scurred Hatch. Some wardkeeper you make, Lojen Tevunson. What would Father have to say about all this?*

"You didn't think I was only here to cut carrots and make soup, did you? I thought you trusted Emre?"

Truth told, Lojen hadn't thought about it. There was no doubt his father would've thought about it. Void, his father probably planned most of it. *Stupid, Lojen, stupid.* "I… do trust him."

"Good. Now," reaching into his tunic, Wick drew out a tiny black box with a pair of wires attached to a replica keycard, "check out this new toy I've designed specifically for the job."

The lapin lined the box just above the button mechanism, magnets on the underside clamping to the door, and then he slid the keycard into the slot. The buttons flashed red. Pressing a button upon the top of the black box with a paw, the red turned to orange and then green after a few beeps and clicks. The door swung inward.

Pocketing the keying box, Wick stepped into the darkened room with Lojen gingerly following. "Need to find the security terminal."

White beams of light from canned aethecite orbs in the ceiling turned on when their steps touched the tiled ground, though the streams were a vertical cylinder, and they didn't brighten the entire room fully. It left a path of lighted circles on the ground of shadows.

"What is this place?"

Row upon row of shelves lined the walls, most covered in glass shields. Objects of varying size sat upon them, an array of conquered goods. Pedestals stood just outside the beams of light, almost like soldiers lining a procession. Weapons, drakken ritual masks, Kanjan Pentax statues, and a multitude of other relics sat under rectangular glass shields.

"Where?"

"There." Wick pointed toward the rear of the room.

"Praise Justice," he whispered.

There, on a pedestal taller than the rest, held what Lojen could only describe as a circular disc of onyx-colored, braided steel in a full circle the size of a child's ball. Within were four concentric circles, each made of gemstone in four separate colors. Sapphire, peridot, garnet, and emerald. Within the epicenter of the disc was a six-pointed star, which must represent the Pentax Gods and Nocturne. The top and bottom point broke no planes of the concentric circles, were thicker, and touched the outer braid. The other four points pierced one of the four circles, its point ending in the epicenter.

"The Seal of *Terris*," Lojen said in awe.

Leaning against the pedestal was an object Lojen had always believed to be myth. The Hammer of the Forgemistress, of Mother Marrow, the Forger of Life. The Hammer's haft was a good three feet in length, at least twice the normal length of a common blacksmith's. Made of greenish iron, the haft was adorned with runes, which faintly glowed. The head of the hammer was a blocky rectangle of the same metal, but instead of a singular greenish color, it was a myriad of emerald shades.

Wick bounded into the room, finding a computer terminal powered by *Aere* and aethecite. His furry paws began tapping away on the keyboard of aetheric runes, his tongue askew from behind his elongated front teeth. There was a soft beep. "That'll do it." When Lojen glanced at him, he flicked his shredded ears over his shoulder. "Security shield is down. Let's grab 'em and scurry."

As they neared the Seal and Hammer, Lojen spotted another pedestal nearby, one with something far dearer to him atop. His father's wardkeeper horns. Two feet long, sloping in a delicate curve, thicker where broken, pointed in a tip. Black as the night sky, ridged, yet smooth.

"O Father…" Lojen smiled as he reached out to touch the horns when something dropped from the ceiling behind him in a grinding of metal on metal.

It attacked, throwing him viciously.

Lojen skidded across the ground, his shoulder enflamed as it sharply connected into a pedestal. He thwacked himself in the snout as his tail had a mind of its own.

In the glare of a canned light, a giant shadow rose on four metal limbs the length of a drakken's matured height. Straightening upright, it was now supported by two, smaller additional legs which held up a bulbous V-shaped torso with blinking lights and a built-in combustion furnace, a small grate covering what appeared to be a smoke releaser. An oracular-like head of crystal blinked red and orange, orbs searching. Four arms ended in claw-like blades.

"What in the Arbiter's bloody axe?"

The automaton launched itself, lightning quick, metal arms outstretched. He squealed like the Scurred Hatch Ruane claimed he was and dove aside, fleeing to the far end of the room. The automaton's torso did a full twist upon its shorter legs, facing him. It clicked its metal blades, scratching the ground as it lumbered toward him. He narrowly missed one of the automaton's blades as it whizzed toward his head but dodged in time. Lojen contorted his body to avoid another. A third almost skewered him squarely in the leg if it hadn't been for his clumsiness as Lojen tumbled to the ground and rolled away.

Things went from bad to worse when the lights blinked out one by one overhead. Beam by beam disappearing, leaving only a solitary light shining down on him. Shadows cast about the room, surrendering everything to the imagination. He drew his drakken longknife and backed down the main aisle as he mumbled a prayer to The Arbiter. Actually, it was a plea to help save his hide.

The door to the room slid open and Wick filled the void. "Lojen, where are you?"

"Wick, watch out!"

The automaton stalked on its four longer legs, the back two raised off the ground. Metal blades clipped the concrete. Snick-snick-snick-snick as it hunted, slowly as if for sport. Orbital red-orange blinked, searching, seeking. It pounced at Wick.

The lapin's muscled legs bounded out of the doorway as the automaton landed right where he'd stood. Wick bolted down the aisle toward Lojen.

"What're you doing?"

"Trying to save you, you idiot!"

A wheeze of smoke, a pressing of metal limbs, a turn of gears. The door slid shut, cutting off the much-needed extra light from the hall.

The automaton disappeared into the shadows, the blinking lights on its head going dark. It was surprisingly silent for a metal beast.

Wick sniffed the air with his whiskers. "Where'd it—" The lapin was brushed aside by a metal arm and struck the far wall with a sickening thud.

Lojen reflexively parried the first two appendages, blades glancing off his longknife. His boots slued across the concrete as the full brunt of the automaton crashed into him, the metal fingers sharp as knives slamming into the ground, the auto-beast using them as leverage. He dropped his longknife as the metal and drakken collapsed in a heap.

An anger that Lojen never knew grew within him. A rage that started as a ball of fright drew in upon itself and flamed out in an inferno of white-hot fury as a song came to life within him. A wailing song. He could hear his father's voice telling him to get up, to be worthy of his horns.

'A wardkeeper is only as strong as his conviction, Lojen,' his father had told him once. *'Lose that, and you lose everything. Conviction drives us. Binds us to our wards. To the Pentax. It is all that you can ever, and will, be.'*

His father's words galvanized him. As did the song of wails.

"I will not yield!" he growled deep within his throat, dangerous and frightening both.

His talons dug into the metallic torso, gouging into its hull, smoke escaping from the inner furnace. The blades adorning the four limbs tried to bite into his body, but his exoscales protected him, strong natural armor. Pulling with all his strength, he ripped free the back panel of the automaton's chassis in a gout of black smoke and sparks. The metal beast reared, releasing its hold on him, smaller legs kicking.

He screamed—roared really—in fury.

The automaton struggled backward, smoke pouring out of its destroyed forge, plumes of aethecite filled the room with sulfurous acridity. Lojen wrapped his massive claws about one of the metal limbs and yanked with everything he had. Gears ground, metal screeched, Lojen bellowed. The Hymn of War blaring within. Finally, the arm broke from the torso. Tossing it to the floor, Lojen sought another and pulled. The beast tried to stab at him with its remaining limbs, but a shape flew from the dark and landed upon the creature's back. Wick had two dueling knives, shining silver in the single light of the room, and he drove them into the broken circuits of the creature's metal brain, sparking and bolting electricity.

Down, the automaton went. Wick stabbing circuit boards, Lojen shattering rotating gears, both yelling at the top of their lungs. Smoke poured out of the metal furnace until it shuddered and went still.

Lojen went to his knees, his chest heaving. Wick hopped off the broken security beast, putting a furry paw to Lojen's shoulder. "Come on. Not done yet, drakken. Your father's horns. And the Mother's talisman. Hurry, before the guards come. If we're lucky, the cameras are still down."

Bending, Lojen carefully picked up the objects that had haunted him for seventeen years. Reverently, he caressed the horns. "Father."

Then they raced from the room, leaving a broken carcass of metal smoldering upon the floor just as the entirety of Gargantua trembled violently, nearly throwing them both from their feet.

"What was that?" Lojen asked as he steadied himself with a claw on a wall.

"The bombs," Wick answered, darting off.

XXXVII
CADRIANNA

SHE WAS SEETHING by the time she reached the double redwood doors leading to the party.

Standing within the doorway, Cadrianna scanned the opulence with strained anger. Before she could take another step, a low rumble made her pause. Beside the stair was the trunk of a tree, in which its branches overhung the entirety of the dance floor. At its roots, she noticed a big red blob. It rustled and she realized the blob was in fact a firedrake coiled about the base of the tree, wings folded upon its bulk. The head rose on a graceful neck, the garnet eye of a daemon glared at her.

"Well, fuck you, too," she told Cinder. "Where's your daemon master? I've got a few choice words for him."

As if on cue, the dancers upon the floor cleared when the music ended, and in that parted group of revelers, was the Fallen. His unnervingly gorgeous profile faced downward as he conversed with a young woman wearing a stola that would have made her the jealous competition of any unwed or unattached noble woman. But this woman looked as if she had been dunked in a river and beaten with a club decked out with nails then dragged through a trash heap of broken glass face first. Her hair was sopping wet, and the curls hung limp around her battered face, where blood had dried along one temple and had dripped down her cheek into her collarbone.

Unbidden, a pang of jealously germinated. *No, Cad, don't go there.* Why would she care, he was a monster, not one to love. And yet, she seemed to. Gods, her heart was a dichotomy. *Emre… beloved. Betrayer. Lu Har…*

"CAD…"

"The rage built upon lies fills you like a thousand fires upon the snow-covered hills of Kanja."

Cadrianna spun and found a silver-haired woman standing behind her. Emre's bikrome. The woman who'd saved her once already by showing her the lies that bound her. Did she already begin to believe? Nocturne, she didn't know what to believe anymore. "What are you doing here?"

"I bring you a gift, Cadrianna Benld. Should you find it useful, my help is yours. But more importantly, remember who you are, not who you're destined to be. And do not believe what the Fallen will have you believe. Believe in the First Wife."

"The First Wife?"

The bikromi woman held forth an oblong-shaped object folded within a linen wrap. Cadrianna reached for it and flipped the corner of the linen to find the outstretched wing of an owl.

"CAD, LISTEN TO HER," the Strix said. *"YOUR EYES MUST OPEN TO THE TRUTH. WITH BRYNN. WITH YOU. WITH ME."*

'*I don't need help,*' she wanted to say. '*The shadows are my protection,*' she almost said. Instead, "Why?"

"I saw your fate. And in that fate, I saw mine. We are bound by the blood of Nightingale."

Cadrianna smirked. "My husband?"

"You expect any less from a Benld? I'm Valeria Dunleith."

"That's why your lips tasted like snow."

"Your ending is yet to be written by the Pentax, Cadrianna Benld. Lu Har will be at the end of your path, waiting. The sword underfoot. The shadows fight the light and the light fights the shadows. Which do you choose?"

The shadows are your protection,' she thought of her training. "No longer. I cannot put my trust in the Pentax." She looked up but the bikrome was gone.

Holding the daemon blade to her breast, Cadrianna knew what path her life wanted her to walk: it was time for Lu Har to die. It was time to save Brynn.

Would she dare do the deed of ending Lu Har now, while he least expected it? With all the guards, the scourges, and Solanine. Not to mention Cinder and Lu Har himself, she might never make it from Gargantua alive to save Brynn.

Strix, what do you think?

"I'M WITH YOU WHATEVER YOU CHOOSE, CAD. I ALWAYS HAVE BEEN. ALWAYS WILL BE. BLOOD OF NIGHTINGALE."

Thinking violence, Cadrianna noted the locations of the guards, counting near twenty, but she knew there had to be at least a thousand more elsewhere on Gargantua. Ratko rested his arms on the low brick wall surrounding the dance floor, combing a hand through his elongated beard as he bloodlustily eyed the crowd.

Near the main guest entrance, three figures wore the midnight blue cassock of a vicar. One even sported a blue-dyed horsehair helm

"WHAT ARE VICARS DOING HERE?"

I don't know, Strix. Solanine would never invite the Scattered Shards. You don't think?

"I DO, BUT NOT SURE IF I WANT TO SAY IT ALOUD."

Not that anyone but me can hear you, dear daemon.

"POINT TO YOU, CAD. I SAY WE MOVE NOW."

Determined, she made her way toward the Fallen, but as she did, her gaze swept past the fountain spewing a crystalline liquid, and beside it a masked man of Drenth stock. Cadrianna stopped, conflicted. Lu Har was there for the taking. But Emre. The bikrome had already gifted her the blade. She had to know what was going on.

"CAD..."

Ignoring the daemon blade, Cadrianna raced down the curved steps, plunging into the crowd. Most moved once they saw a scourge amongst them, others she shoved out of her way, not caring a wit, glaring at everyone who dared voice an objection.

"Emre!"

Stiffening, the man who should be dreaming the eternal sleep in the Meadows turned toward her as she pushed aside the last remaining couple standing between them. Behind the mask that resembled a broken statue, his eyes showed nothing. No surprise, no relief. Just cold steel hardness. "Hello, Cad."

Without thinking, Cadrianna reared back and punched Emre, a clean shot to the face that sent him sprawling into the fountain. The guests gasped in shock at the savagery in their midst. But also because some seemed to recognize her. They glanced down at the man she'd socked, and realization dawned on them. Whispers broke out.

Emre sat up, rubbing his bruising jaw, his mask hung to the side, damaged. "I suppose I deserve that."

"My daughter is all that I have left of the family you ripped away from me," she hissed. "This is all yo—"

"Our daughter, Cad." Emre planted a hand on the fountain as he stood, tossing the broken mask. He faced her, hands at his sides, that hard visage plastered upon his face. No anger. Nothing. "Drenth is more than you and me. You knew this the day we wed. Drenth is everything, much more than any single person. It is a haven. A memory. A future. We cannot let the Fallen destroy it. I cannot. And I know you cannot. Break the lies wrapped around you, Cad."

She moved within inches of his face, angry, and wanting nothing more than to tear him limb from limb for all the heartache he'd caused her. To stab the Strix deep into his heart, ending him for good. This was the Gutter King of Drenth, her contract. The only way to save Brynn from Lu Har. To finally be free.

All she had to do was kill him, here and now, and it would be over.

The rebellion would falter under the Fallen's gaze, at his feet even. Clear victory in the southern Mistlands, leaving only the war on Kalderim the final path untrod.

And yet, seeing Emre once more amongst the living, she found herself hesitating. O, the anger was still threatening to boil over, but not just yet. She felt the lies which served as her savior and shield begin to unravel.

Emre slowly reached toward her, her heart and mind fought valiantly against another; heart wanting to fall into his embrace while her mind urged her to flee once more. In the end, she did neither. One of his hands wrapped her lower back, the other toward her shoulders as he tried to pull her into a hug. Her body held still.

Sensing her hesitation, Emre let his arms fall back, then he began to itch his forearms. His face became less stone if only a fraction. "I'm sorry, Cad. I had to do it."

That broke her calcification, her lapse of judgement. Her anger flared anew, this time bubbling over the kettle's edge. "Brynn has suffered for your betrayal. I've suffered." She thrust her arm out in the direction she last saw Lu Har. "Suffered for him!"

Emre took a step back as the Fallen's all-onyx eyes settled on them, and her beloved's left hand roamed toward the pocketwatch in his vest pocket. It was covered with aetheric runes in spells of *Ignis*. Emre gripped it tight, checking the time as if that were the most important thing in the world right then and there. Not her.

Smiling, her beloved's face glinted like steel. "Forgive me, my love, but I cannot stop until Drenth sees the Imperium burned to the ground. I do this for all of Drenth. But most of all, for Brynn."

His gaze was focused on the young woman who had danced with Lu Har, who was now standing next to Solanine watching the pair of them, and it forced Cadrianna to truly observe her. Then she noted the features of the young woman, the curvature of cheek, the bridge of nose. The mouth, the ears. So familiar. So like her own. So like the daughter locked within the belly of Gargantua.

Brynn? "Wha—"

Emre pressed the top button on the pocketwatch and a concussion tremored under foot. Followed by exploding marble fragments, sluicing liquid aethecite, and shattered screams rent the peaceful night air as the mist font throughout Gargantua.

Cadrianna's head smashed into the fountain, her skull aflame as the very core of Gargantua rumbled. The fountain's fuel rained down on her, drenching her while she fought to her feet, wobbly as if she'd been beaten with a cudgel.

Emre was gone.

Lu Har was down, soldiers of the Imperium surged toward him as they oozed from every orifice of the fortress and converged upon the mezzanine as if called to battle. Wheellocks and blades bristled. Cinder took to the sky, the daemonized drake's wings splintering branches and aethecite lights in the process, great ailerons flapping and sending gusts into the crowd. The drake scooped up the Fallen with its clawed back feet from the melee and careened away into the night.

Solanine—who was being supported by a tall, muscular man with a bald head and a craggy face of harsh angles and leery black eyes— yelled for the soldiers to hunt down the Gutter King. Void Form aetheurgy sent shockwaves through the crowd as Solanine then summoned blackened mist by waving their scales' hands and chanting voidspeak. Aether filled the mezzanine with the poisonous haze up to their knees.

The young woman in the pink dress was gone. *Brynn?* Couldn't be her. Could it?

The scourges cut through the crowds, hunting. The vicars in their cassocks and mist canisters waded through, holy enemies colliding in a battle of axe and blade, Shard Form and Void Form. Solanine and the bald man moved toward the vicars with deathly ease, the blooddrake's aetheurgy scything through the Drenth-born flesh, killing wantonly. The lead vicar leapt with an axe borne of pure aether toward the blooddrake and aetheurgy fractured.

More trembles unloaded upon Gargantua, deep from the innards. Wails of aethecite lines exploded as holes pierced the stony skin of the fortress like a blowing volcano. Cadrianna went down again as the fortress teetered under the strain, dipping one direction then the next as it fought to settle.

Through the thick of it, Cadrianna spied Emre as he waded the tide toward the main compound. Cadrianna, still woozy, took a step to follow after Emre, but a hand grabbed her ankle.

Ratko.

The scourge was on his stomach, a table, as well as a piece of stone fence, pinned him to the ground. Blood cascaded down the scourge's face, beard askew in dusty points. Ratko, though, had Cadrianna's leg in a vice-like grip.

"Traitor!" Ratko yelled through gritted teeth as he struggled to pull his legs free of the stone prison.

How easy would it be for Cadrianna to end his life?

"Bitch," Ratko wheezed. "Pathetic and weak."

In a moment of clarity, Cadrianna understood everything. She didn't have to be this person anymore. Ratko was goading her. That wasn't who she wanted to be any longer, the monster.

"Fuck off, Ratko." She leveled a heady kick to the scourge's jaw, knocking him unconscious. "I've always hated you."

"YESSSSSSS, CAD! FINALLY, YOU ARE FREE! BUT I DO WISH TO TASTE THE SCOURGE'S SOUL. O WELL, ANOTHER TIME."

And then she took off after Emre, barreling through the double redwood doors and into the hallway beyond, sterile and empty as a deathly scream filled the air behind her.

XXXVIII
EMRE

BLOWING THE FOUNTAIN before all the guests had left the party reeked of a desperate gamble. Perhaps it was.

Emre had expected some fallout from disentangling Cadrianna from the lies. Void, he'd even expected her to show outward violence toward him for his betrayal. But he hadn't planned for her to confront him in the center of the party.

Tevun would've had a number of unsubtle words to say about his failure to think ahead.

Like stalks of wheat being shorn by enormous aethecite harvesters, the guests of Drenth fell upon one another. Screams of pain, shouts of horror, bellows of terror pierced the once festive evenfall. The music died; the vocalist's song ended like a knife severing. Broken pieces of marble rained down, interpolated by cleanish fuel-water. Gargantua shook as the raised dance floor split.

Men and women scrambled over one another. Blood-covered faces, peppered with dust as they clawed through an undulating wave of mortality trying to escape. Tables overturned, chairs kicked, bushes trampled, glasses broken under heeled shoes and boots as hundreds scrambled through the wooden doors toward the gondolas.

Everything underfoot quailed intensely from further detonations in the interior of Gargantua. There was a thunderous snap in the air like the sound of a mountain parting from apex to base. The crowd stopped at once, afraid and terrified.

Like a giant whip being cracked, one of the tethers arched through the sky, rising like a metal seagandr, groaning in a gasp of mutilated steel. The whole of Gargantua floundered, teetering toward the lost anchor. Another blast signaled the tether opposite also blew free. The flying fortress wobbled, unbalanced as the two remaining anchors tried to keep it steady. People fell from their feet again.

Burning aetheurgy, Emre wove through the jungle of fallen people as he sought the staircase that led into the compound of Gargantua. Emre barreled through a maze of white halls and metal doors. Lapin and Imperium servants scurried hither and tither in frenzy, paying him no mind, only concerned about fleeing the shaking fortress.

A unit of soldiers hurried around a corner ahead, causing Emre to duck into a doorway. The clop-clop-clop of soldiering boots echoed in his direction, getting louder as the distance lessened. He held his breath, ready to burn his parch, and waited for the enemy to appear at any moment. But the soldiers turned, their footfalls disappearing down an adjoining corridor.

All was empty in the hall amid the aethecite lighting as another series of quakes shook the fortress, sending some glass from the light orbs crashing to the ground. Emre consulted the map hidden in his waistcoat pocket before extricating himself from the doorway.

After a series of turns, Emre found what he was looking for: a portal leading to a library. At the door's terminal, he entered the code one of his spies had given him. The door slid open silently. All was empty.

Or so he thought.

Click.

Emre dove through the doorway as he burned aetheurgy. Gunfire battered the wall where he had been moments before. Rolling into a crouch, he found cover behind a waist-high, wooden chest nestled next to a sofa. Fluffs of down exploded into the air as *Ignis*-infused gunshots riddled the cushions and embedded into the wooden chest.

The firing stopped and Emre launched himself over the couch with aetheurgy-enhanced speed. Two guards positioned behind palatial chairs with multiple throw pillows were in the middle of reloading their wheellock rifles when he landed between them.

Kicking upward, he struck one soldier upside the head. Down the man went as he drew the knife from the soldier's belt sheath. Emre lashed at the other with the blade. The soldier blocked it with his rifle, using the butt as a counter. Emre bounced away and aimed a punch into the man's opposite arm, jarring the gun loose from the soldier's grip.

The soldier backed away and Emre felt a slight tinge in the air around them. *Shit, this isn't an ordinary guard. A scourge!*

The scourge grabbed the chair and swung it at him with aetheric strength, narrowly missing his skull. The chair shattered upon the wall in a cascade of feathers and wooden bits. The scourge drew his own blade.

Emre could feel his parch reserves starting to ebb, so he withdrew, fists held up. Sensing his hesitation, the scourge attacked. His dwindling aetheurgy was no match for the other's. Emre blocked too late, and the scourge's blade left a two-inch slice upon his upper arm. Another too early, faltering judgment allowed a second gash to open along his thigh. A clenched fist connected with his side, sending misery throughout his insides as he went flying into the couch.

Reaching down instinctively, Emre brandished one of the throw pillows as the scourge stabbed with his knife, feathers pouring from the long slice within the fabric. Emre stumbled back as the pillow was yanked from his hands, making him trip over the knee-high table, and toppled to the ground. The scourge closed in, his impending doom all but certain.

A pale blur flew into his peripheral vision striking the scourge, the man's head cracked viciously to the side. Once more, twice, thrice times head flinging side-to-side by punches. Down into a battered heap the scourge went.

The pale blur turned out to be Val.

A chime of bracelets, knuckles covered in drake scale punchers reached down to help him to his feet.

"Took you long enough," he breathed.

"I had to see to things," she whispered, barely breathing hard from the assertion.

Things… steel it, Benld. You know what comes. "Let's go. Finn's waiting." With that, Emre pulled Val into the hall.

A bullet pinged off the wall nearby.

Another Imperium soldier fired from the doorway. Emre spied more rushing down the hallway. Val leapt through the air, knee raised high and brought the drake scale punchers down into the soldier's collarbone. The man dropped his wheellock rifle and yelped. In a fluid motion, Val kicked up the soldier's rifle and shot him, warm aetheric smoke rising. Lifting a hand, her bracelets glowed fiercely as her Vision Form came alive as she drew upon the gun's smoke. Throwing her hand outward, Val unleashed a torrent of *Ignis* flames into their soldiers heading their way, fire shearing through the unprotected bodies.

"So much for secrecy until the end." Val straightened the veil over her face.

"Always going to be this way. Just a tad earlier than expected."

"Lojen and Ruane sure did their part."

"Val, you didn't see Brynn after the explosions, did you?"

She shook her head, but there was something lingering behind the veil that told Emre indicated otherwise. "Too much dust." Her bottom lip quivered minutely.

"What's wrong?"

"Nothing," she said with a tight smile that showed no teeth. "She's been pushed."

"What do you mean 'pushed'?"

"Cadrianna needed to know that she was lost. Before she confronted you, I saw that she was on the fence, and if I didn't push her, she wouldn't follow through. Her will is sound, but her heart asunder. If I didn't intervene, she would fail. I had to give her the key." Even behind the veil, Emre could see the tears welling. He grabbed her hand and squeezed. "If I didn't give her the blade, she wouldn't be able to face the darkness in her soul. It has a power over her. It has given her the foundation of everything she's become. Her training, her sense of self, everything has been channeled through that weapon. She believes it the only way to save Brynn. It's bonded to one of the Gods, Emre." She looked away, ashamed. "I had to give the blade back, otherwise Cadrianna wouldn't crack. It's the last tie to her old life that must be broken." Tears trickled from the bottom of the veil. "The one that has to…" she couldn't finish.

Slow understanding came to him of the enormity of what Val had done. He pulled the bikrome in, hugging her as she sobbed. Cadrianna's aetheurgy must have frightened the seer, for Emre had never seen her break down like this before. She was always the strong one, the rock. Bliss had chosen a strong woman, but even the strong broke from time to time.

"You did what you had to do. Nothing about this day has been easy. None of what will come will make it any easier. You did the right thing."

"I… forgive me… I…" Val broke away. "Hear that?"

A scrape down the hall. A clack and a chirp. Emre burned the last of his aetheurgy, the silvery sheen of Burn Form jostled his senses. Metal shimmered in the silver glean. "Slag, automaton." A wheeze of combustion indicated the sentry drone was close, maybe a single corner down. He gave Val a wry grin. "This one's on me. Try not to get yourself killed just yet."

Val ran a finger across one of her bikromi bracelets. "You know that isn't in my future."

"The Virtuous One smiling down on you once more, eh?"

"That's not how the Pentax works. You of all should know this."

"Finn, Wick, where you at?" he asked as he pressed the comm.

Wick answered first. "With the drakken now." It sounded rushed, like he was in action. "Heading… docking bay."

It was a few more minutes before Finn responded, though his words were broken by static. "Em, I'm… waiting… are you?"

It was now or never. Emre pulled Val into another hug. "Watch her for me, will you?"

"We have more time, Em, Bliss has shown me what will come. And don't you worry about Finn, either. He'll do what is necessary. If I know that brother-friend of mine, he'll enjoy it to the fullest extent. Good luck." With that, the elfirish bikrome dashed down the opposite hallway, leaving Emre alone.

Checking his pocketwatch, Emre dug out the last of his parch, downing a quad of vials. The familiar burning sensation inside strengthened him. *Steel it, Benld. Remember why you are doing this. Be safe, Val. I'll be waiting for you. Remember I trust in you.*

Gunfire opened all around him, pelting the walls with rotating action from the aethecite-driven machine.

Emre weaved back and forth with the speed of a gale, the automaton plodding after at full velocity. He hadn't a chance to see the sentry drone before making his run, but the fact it possessed a rotating gun upon its chassis meant it was a Predator model. And now that it had detected his presence, the automaton would stop at nothing until he was dead or found a way to bring it down.

He knew he could do the latter, but the former was definitely in the realm of probability.

Up a narrow stair Emre went. The lower levels, aside from the kitchen and stock rooms, consisted mostly of areas cordoned off by mechanized doors. Based off his inside information, they were dedicated laboratories to research and development, or vaults of conquest. Rooms such as where Lojen and Wick were to meet to find the Seal and Hammer, as well as Tevun's horns. Other wings held the barracks and led to docking bays for the multitude of airgliders, others to armories.

But it was the uppermost floor where Emre needed to find: the command center of Gargantua.

As his boot hit the top step, aethecite bullets ripped through the banister and surrounding walls, resulting in a hail of plaster and wood. He dove into the adjacent hallway, catching his breath, hoping that the Predator was too unwieldy for the staircase. Unfortunately, that wasn't the case as he heard the drone's metal limbs crushing marble and carved wood. Up he got and ran onward.

The walls shivered as the Predator emerged from the stairwell, accompanied by gunfire. Emre covered his head while bent double, he zigged and zagged through the hall, avoiding the torrent of aetheric bullets around him. The onslaught forced him from the stairway that would lead him to the highest level.

His reserves started to fade, so he snuffed, saving what little he could. The Predator wasn't fast, but it was merciless. It kept up the pace as it lumbered after, showering the compound with bullets.

Emre pressed the radio in his ear. "Finn, you up top?"

Chips of grey-painted plaster exploded over his right shoulder as he slid behind an open door, wood taking the brunt of the deadly projectiles. He regained his footing and raced through a library. The Predator crashed through the door, unleashing a flurry of gunfire, books and paper rained down like the leaves at the autumn solstice, destroying Solanine's athenaeum.

"Finnus?" he panted, breaths coming ragged, tired he was without the aetheric energy feeding him. He fled the library past a row of pedestals topped with vases filled with flowers.

"Em? Em, can you hear me?" Finn's voice sounded strained, as if he was running too.

"You shiny?" Static followed by gunfire, and not from the Predator behind. This was gunfire at Finn. A grunt of pain. "Finn?" His mind rolled with the thoughts of the elfir ripped to shreds.

Heavy breathing. "Em?"

"Finn, where are you?" The Predator burst into the hall; more bullets pummeled the walls. Running. Gunfire. Repeat. "Finn?"

"Took a shot in the leg. Bugger got me good. Got him back, though." Another grunt. "Ahhh! That bloody hurts. Fucking scourges."

Thoughts of Finn bleeding and dying flashed in Emre's mind. He couldn't take the sorrow if such a thing were to occur. He'd already lost Cadrianna and Brynn to the Fallen's schemes, he couldn't lose Finn either.

But you will, Benld. He will lose you if you finish this. Steel it! But Brynn can… He forced himself to go blank, to forget both of his loves. "Has Val found you yet?"

Silence.

Gunfire circled about him as he barreled into another room, cutting through what appeared to be a study. It was empty.

Where is everyone?

"Sorry, Em." Sadness in Finn's words. Gunfire in the radio, static and metal casings melding. "Got me pinned down… dropped… when they hit… only a few…" Thudding of bullets, embedded into the walls over the radio. "…trapped… control room… ten maybe, more… outside."

A flare of voidfire pierced Emre's flesh and spun him sideways. Crashing into the wall, Emre howled in anger as blood spattered the light grey wall, streaking crimson as he bounced off the plaster, tripping over a pedestal. The Predator dogged after him, bringing down the walls along with it.

Emre forced himself onward, the stair that would lead him to the highest level of Gargantua just ahead. His feet tripped over each other. Dizzy in the head, legs pumping as if of their own accord. Blood flowed over his hand, through his fingers, arm going numb.

The wall opposite erupted, disappearing in plaster. Splinters struck his face, cutting streaks across his cheeks and forehead. Though he cried out, his bloodied hand found a railing. Determinedly, he climbed. He could hear the Predator behind, could smell the smoke of the internal furnace billowing aethecite fuel. It was at the base of the stairs; he could feel it on his heels. Instinctively he ducked, attempting to dodge the expected bullets.

But they didn't come. The Predator went silent.

Risking a glance, he saw the beast's rotating cannon still pointed at him, tiny orbs blinking within its domed head, smoke pluming soft grey. It was watching him, he knew, but for what? Why wasn't it firing at him?

Emre burned the last of his aetheurgy reserves, the silver sheen roaring to life. Beyond the stairs, he could sense life, heartbeats pulsing in sterling. Voices pierced the argent glow, not words, but enough texture to spell out multiple speakers. Then came gunfire that pounded in his aether-enhanced ears like thunderclaps. The voices became yells.

"Finn!"

Chancing getting riddled to pulp by the Predator, Emre shot up the stairs to find Finn on his knees, blood slowly pooling underneath his black trousers. His hands held behind his head. Four wheellock rifle barrels pointed at him.

"Sorry, love," the elfir gritted through clenched teeth, his face filmed with pain that turned to shock. "Wait... no... it can't be..."

"Take him," a voice whispered, one Emre knew all too well.

"Val? You?" A soldier slammed the butt of his rifle into Finn's temple, knocking the elfir to the ground. His head struck hard, and Finn's handsome eyes rolled back into his head as his sister marched into the room.

Emre turned and found Val surrounded by a gaggle of Imperium soldiers, not bound but leading them. The bikrome stared at him with a look he couldn't decipher. Was it hatred? Or was it compassion? He couldn't tell. In the end, it didn't matter, this was his tithe for his betrayal to his family.

Justice, he supposed.

XXXIX

ASHE

AS ASHE FELL to the rough brick of the mezzanine, Solanine went sprawling headlong into the crowd.

She scrambled to her feet as the guests fought one another in their attempts to flee, which, truth told, was somewhat amusing to her considering they were trapped upon an island in the sky two thousand feet above the ground.

Another quake shook Gargantua, throwing her from her feet once more. Her hands were rubbed raw as her body uncontrollably careened one direction, then abruptly rolled viciously the opposite as explosions blew through the core of the fortress in the sky. Finally, her body came to a desperate stop as she picked her gaze up in time to see a massive chain whip through the nightturn air, blotting stars and moon. It was the godsdamned anchors!

Her father had certainly gone big in his fight with the Fallen.

A firedrake extricated itself from the great tree near the compound with a roar of fury. The magnificent beast flapped its wings and took to the air, sending waves of gale down upon the already flustered crowd, not to mention raining broken branches and aethecite light fixtures. The drake dove toward Lu Har, grabbed the Fallen about the waist with a taloned claw, lifting him to safety, disappearing into the starlit nightturn, like a coward.

Solanine—surrounded now by scourges and a tall man she didn't recognize—sought calm amongst the guests, but more tremors unloaded on Gargantua from deep within the innards. Aethecite engines exploding pierced any gap or hole within the stone and metal carcass, drowning out the crowd's shrieks with tea kettle whines. Solanine fell again and was pulled up by the muscular bald man, who began to drag the smaller aetheurgist away from the destruction. The bald man punched a partygoer, dropping the poor sot in a spray of blood. His face turned in Ashe's direction and caused her to gasp as recognition seeped in.

Evander? What is he doing here? With Solanine of all people…

Her mind instantly went to Wren, the betraying scourge, before returning to all those dead at *The Colosseum*. Olaf. All the rest of Slag's End. Their bodies flayed and tortured. Remembering their faces in life, only to recall their misery in death forever etched in agony.

With the chaos all around her, she surprisingly only thought of them. Tears flowed down her cheeks. Evander had to have been the one to do it, to turn them over to Solanine and the Imperium. He had to have been working with Wren all this time.

Evander, why?

A faint touch, the mist. It hovered about her legs, it consoled, it allayed. Regardless, she was growing angrier, so she thrust it from her, and it fled, afraid.

It was then she screamed.

The bellow was deep, harsh, and full of fire. Primal and raw. The panicked crowd stopped dead in their tracks, masked and veiled faces turning towards her as one. Her runic tattoos along her left arm synapsed all at once in a brilliant gleam of iridescence. The frightened mist had come back to her, darkened and full of vigor. Her fists balled and she threw her head back, yelling upward into the nightturn sky. She could feel the anger of the mist.

But she could also feel the terror, the fear. It permeated the crowd of Drenth-born. Dismay, dread, panic all washed over her as she screamed. Fright and revulsion. Abhorrence and distress. Agony and misery. Injury and strain. Wound and affliction. From humir and creature alike. Down to the very grains of stone and ores of metal constructing Gargantua. The mist rose around her, drawing all this emotion toward her. The entirety of Gargantua was bathed in honeyed shadows, its yellowish hue damning.

O Zenith…

Her bangled left hand came up on its own accord and pointed toward the building opposite. It tugged at her, the bangle did. Begging her to follow where it would lead. The Seal, she realized. That's what Lu Har had said, wasn't it? She'd be drawn toward the Seals. The diamond burned against her palm.

The scream cut off as she coughed so hard, she retched. Blood, fresh and bright red, splashed across the broken dance floor. Her back arched, the poison in her lungs scalding every piece of her, cauterizing every vessel. She slumped forward, catching her breath as it came in ragged flushes. Her brow dripped sweat; her mouth trickled sanguine as she forced herself upright on wobbly legs.

The crowd who hadn't yet escaped the veranda, some thousands it seemed, stared at her. She smiled cruor-coated rictus. Their pervious panic resettled into even greater frenzy, their collective desire to extricate themselves from this floating prison all the more apparent.

Ashe plunged into the fleeing crowd, elbowing and jostling along with them, albeit half-heartedly as she was beyond tired. Her pulmo and aetheurgy had drained her dry, her throat raw as if she'd been eating mounds of sand for breakfast, lunch, and dinner for three straight days. She wanted to fight the urge inside her, the one her soul demanded, but she found her feet moving in the direction of the Seal regardless of her brain wishing it otherwise.

She needed to find a way into the cursed fortress that didn't involve going through Solanine. To find that blasted Seal to Eminence. To her supposed destiny she apparently couldn't avoid. She swore without abandon, her hair plastered to her skull, her anger a constant vim. Cornered, she felt. Trapped with no choice.

It felt like civil war atop the floating fortress. Skirmishes between unarmed guests and Imperium soldiers blown to epic proportions as the mezzanine holding the dance floor and the self-effacing accoutrement became a ghost town as the fighting and fleeing moved outwards from the veranda onto grass-lined walkways. Explosions attacked the buildings now, the stately architecture taking a beating. Stained glass mosaics rattled in sills before shattering and raining down crystal death. The flowers and willowy trees were trampled or pushed over. Gunshot bursts, much closer than she godsdamned wished. Pandemonium as people clawed and fought across the upper level of Gargantua, seeking any sort of refuge they could find. Be it in building or atop the low walls.

A great gout of flames sprouted from the mezzanine. A blackened mist accompanied the flames. Ashe knew aetheurgy when she saw it. It had to be Solanine.

"Girl!" A woman pulled on Ashe's dress, begging her for help. "You must protect me. With… with your aetheurgy. Please? I want to see Demrae again." It was Isla Soabin, the Guilder's attractive wife. Her sickening bastard of a husband was nowhere to be seen, probably smashed to a pulp in the melee. Isla's face was covered in grit, and blood oozed from a cut on her forehead.

Ashe felt the urge to grab her and hold her tight, but Isla was yanked away in the flowing tide of humanity before she even had the chance to respond. "Sorry," she called after.

The doors that were meant to house the party toppled and were pulled from their hinges by the frightened people as the nobleborn pressed onward toward the docking bays, toward the gondolas of the two remaining tethers. They obliterated steel, Imperium soldiers, and statues alike.

Ashe thought she spied Neenah LeFleur in the crowd, a big man in a mask next to her, who could only be Roland. But try as she might, the pair were swept away like the remains of a boat crashing upon the shoals.

Gunshots rang out from Imperium soldiers. Scourges cut through the people with little care to their safety, especially one bearing a long, braided beard and thick, unruly eyebrows over hard eyes. The fleeing tide of flesh became a killing field. Blood slicked underfoot, making the flight even more difficult. The air smelt of death.

A second conquest of Drenth, she thought grimly.

Ashe tried to cut opposite the scourges, feeling that infernal tugging in her heart toward the compound every step she made in the other direction. She made it about ten feet closer in the tight press when she spotted the vicars charging into the ocean of flesh, Cyan the Defiant at the lead.

How the fuck did Cyan get aboard?

The guest tide reeled as bodies flew into the air away from the untainted warriors of the Scattered Shards. Aetheric strength flinging thousands of pounds of body weight in a single shove. The unsuspecting guests unfortunate to be in the way were mercilessly thrown aside, tossed back into the crowd, bodies crushing others. The vicars moved so fast, even Ashe had a hard time following their movements. It was if they were wisps, or ghosts phasing from place to place. One heartbeat they were in front of the double doors, the next, closer to the dance floor, followed by thin tendrils of bottled mist. It was a dance, they did. A dance with the Pentax. Ashe ducked her head as Cyan and his two companions waded through the crowd, their midnight blue cassocks flowing, their canisters of mist releasing in spurts.

"Take thy blood, the blood of man!" Cyan bellowed the prayer to the Pentax, his companions also belting the prayer, drawing their axes. "Take thy heart, the heart of man! The fire in the soul, the forge it bequeaths! Show thy soul, let it burn in the pyre! Molded when white hot! In thy name, the vicars are yours! My soul is yours!"

Ashe always hated that prayer.

"Amaranth!" Cyan yelled, motioning with his Sharded axe of pure aether, "take the left. Harlequin, the right. Protect the Forgemistress' creations!"

Amaranth the Pure nodded, as did the fire-haired Harlequin the Bloodless. People filed around the three vicars as they confronted the scourges, bringing the Arbiter's fight to the sycophants of the Dark God. Their double-bladed axes sang the Hymn of War.

"Sister-friends!" Cyan screamed, his wispy, yet hardened aetheric axe connected with a scourge's face, leaving a bloody mess as the scourge's skull rent in twain. "Now is the time for Justice to guide us!" Cyan the Defiant grunted as he tossed the scourge away, calling upon his Shard Form. A hiss of canistered mist, aetheurgy coming to life. "For the Arbiter!"

The crowd cowered, ran from the fighting vicars and scourges, turning whichever direction they could. Ashe was carried along with them, in no dire need to meet up with Cyan again.

She made it all the way to the entrance of the gondolas when her body abruptly stopped, frozen in place. Urging her legs to move, they resisted. People tried shoving her forward, but she didn't budge an inch. Frustrated, the people moved past her statuesque form.

"What in the void?" She looked up toward the moon as if that great pale orb would give her clarity. It didn't.

Turning about, she headed back toward the mezzanine, her legs happily complying with the change in direction.

"How did I even get myself into this mess?" She shook her head as she shoved a burly man out of her way. "Move it."

To say she was growing angry again was an understatement. She was livid. The mist trailed up her legs, trying its godsdamnedest to soothe her, but it was not working. She had no other choice, it seemed. She had to find that godsdamned Seal.

To do that, she needed to find her way into the Fallen's hideout.

Before she was able to break the wall of people and reach the compound, an elbow caught her in the face, knocking her to the ground near the base of one of the spires buttressing the compound. Blood drained from her nose as she fought at the legs threatening to stomp on her. People cried out as she kicked. The mist swarmed around her, trying to protect her. She pulled on it as she pawed her wet hair from her eyes.

"Shit!" she screamed as a boot came down on her knee, bone popping in a snap.

Ashe instinctively sucked in the mist and pitched up her hands. Like the vicars using their mist canisters, she let loose. Like she had done all her life, but this time was accompanied by a scream so vicious, so angry, so full of soul.

The ground rumbled underneath her, the very fortress trembling, this time from her aetheurgy, not the bombs trying to blow it from the sky. A piercing whistle rose in pitch, becoming a wail as Ashe screamed. The mist swirling around her turned black as Nocturne's Pit, her yell and godsdamned power growing. The aether ripped through her body.

Hands pointed, eyes closed, the mist exploded from her. The people close by snapped backward violently, crashing into others. The sounds of tearing flesh and broken bones strong. Blood fell like a monsoon.

Realizing what she had just done, Ashe clamped her mouth shut, cutting off the aether-filled scream. Guilt washed over her. *Shit and double shit!*

Her knee nearly buckled when she tried to stand. She coughed bloodier tarry. But the crowd left her alone, backed away from her warily as she crawled toward the spire's gated entrance. Voices yelled for the people to move back, and the scourges stepped into the crowd, swinging their weapons and firing shots into the air, some retreated while others fell dead on the paved stones.

Ashe's strength waned as she put her hand to the gate of the spire to hold her up. Pushing it open, she dragged herself inside and closed it behind her as she slumped to her knees. She lifted her head warily when she heard footsteps approaching. A man, heavyset, thick of beard and bald of pate crouched down level with her.

"Elian?"

He smiled at her, lopsided and sinister. He motioned with his fat fingers, a strike against the side of her head. And then she drifted into darkness.

XL

Lojen

"WE WERE SUPPOSED to meet the others at the rendezvous point."

Both drakken and lapin descended down a servant stair, Wick in the lead. Lojen was haplessly lost, this route not the one Emre had planned for his escape.

"The plan has to change." Wick's shredded ears bounced as they hustled down the winding stair.

"You know where we're goin'?"

"Hsst." The lapin peered around the corner, his whiskers twitching as he sniffed. Lojen couldn't smell anything, but that's because he was breathing heavily, his tongue lolling like a mastiff after hare coursing.

The fight with the automaton had sapped him of his strength. He'd never been in a fight to the death like that and his heart argued with his ribcage in a vicious back-and-forth about staying contained.

Part of him was elated with his actions, he'd won, after all. In his first true battle, Lojen Tevunson had gone up against a formidable foe and triumphed. A wardkeeper was nothing if not a victorious fighter. But the other half of him was critical. Fear had nearly been the death of him, it had almost crippled his thinking. True, he had overcome that fear within a matter of heartbeats, but still it ate at him for being there in the first place.

But he'd almost allowed the beast within to come free. His father had once told him that every wardkeeper had two sides to themselves: the draconem chosen by the Arbiter and the beast. The draconem was the civilized half, the reasoner, the schemer, and strategist. The fearless mind, the ferocious heart. All meant to guide and guard a ward. While the beast was the baser foundation, the animal. The source of nature, unpredictable, and volatile.

He could hear his father's words, *'Beware the beast, for unleashed, it will rampage untamed. There is strength in the beast, a power only the Pentax Themselves can tap. But if you cannot chain the beast, you will be lost forever. The capability of the draconem will render unto nothingness, leaving only the beast inside.'*

Lojen had felt that power radiate within during the fight, it was addictive, and yet, he feared to even go near it again.

"Clear," Wick said.

They were in the lowest level of the compound now. Gone were the white hallways, the polished concrete. Gone were the smells of the kitchen. Gone were the sounds of soldiering boots plodding through the warren of corridors. Deep in the innerbelly of Gargantua, they were within rough-hewn stone tunnels. Ground underfoot worn, but uneven. Aethecite orbs glowed dimly, attached to heavy piping.

He briefly thought of Ruane, hoping his sister had a better run of it than he did. *Be safe, Ru...* "Where're we going?"

"Gargantua can house an entire contingent of airgliders and soldier transports. This is how they were able to attack Dervin in such deadly force without having to rely on their cannons. Like locusts, they can send troops aflight, landing with ease. But they also have airgliders ready in case of an emergency. When Emre blew the tethers, the guests would all be taken to the gondolas, and from there, to the main glider transports. All will have left by now."

Though it was subtle, Lojen could feel the slight sway of Gargantua, struggling to stay centered on the two remaining anchors. Mostly he could see it from the way the lights moved, their shadows growing and fading as the entire fortress gently rocked.

Wick slowed, putting his paw-like hand up to stop Lojen. "Wait, I think I hear something."

Absently, Lojen's taloned claw went to the pack with his father's horns, tracing the keratin curve within the sack. He felt a sudden urge to pull them free, to gaze upon the glory that was a wardkeeper's horns. A stirring in his ribs, in his heart. A yearning need.

He jerked his claw away. *No, I can't. Not yet.*

"Well?"

Wick turned, his shredded ears flopped, a stern grimace marring the lapin's face. His elongated front teeth glinted aethecite glow. "It's—"

Gunfire cut the lapin off, spurts of flashing light from wheellock barrels in the tunnel behind them. Lojen dove to the ground, Wick growling as bullets struck stone.

The lapin grabbed Lojen's claw, pulling him forward with such surprising strength that Lojen nearly tripped. "Buggers! Lojen, run!"

They took off, bent over, darting down the corridor as bullets flew overhead. Thud-thud-thud against stone, dust and shrapnel raining. Lojen blinked away the grit as the tunnel opened into a cavern, doming overhead with stalactites hanging down. The cavern was filled to the brim with technology. Airgliders by the dozens hung on steel cables like light fixtures, swaying near the domed roof. Other aethecite-generated mobiles lined the ground level with rotating guns strapped to the top. Single person drones where a driver could fit within the chassis and steer. Unused automatons hunched over in giant heaps, furnaces black and empty, lights dead in glass heads.

"Wick!"

Lojen glanced up to see a second lapin waving at them from a steel plankway up near the airgliders. A doe by the look of it.

Bullets blasting all around, they weaved through the rows of mobiles, clank-clank-clank of gunfire puncturing their path. Wick raced for a metal staircase at the far end of the cavern, Lojen overtaking the poor lapin, his legs pumping at breakneck speed.

"Ancantha, get it started!" Wick yelled as he hopped up the stairs behind Lojen.

The female lapin bounded toward the front of the queue. A quick hum of an aethecite engine roared to life, drowning out the gunfire.

"What about the others?" Lojen called back to Wick as he made the apex of the stair, stopping as he waited for the smaller lapin to reach him. Gunfire from the tunnel entrance caused Lojen to duck. He saw dozens of Imperium soldiers careening into the room, their weapons all pointed at them.

"No time. We gotta go now!" Wick didn't stop like an idiot, like Lojen had, running past. He was like a sitting duck asking to be hunted and gunned down.

An airglider swung dramatically as bullets battered into the hull. It squealed on the cable, disengaging as heavier rounds—presumably metal piercing laced with multiple *Terris*-runed spells—hit the glider. One of the wings practically took Lojen's head clean off his shoulders as the fluctuating craft nearly fell from its holding anchor.

The female lapin leaned out the window of the first airglider, waving her dainty paw frantically. "Run!"

As Lojen ducked under the bucking airglider wing, he felt the blinding sting of an aethecite-wrought bullet upon his calf, forcing him to stumble. The aetheric round shattered his exoscales like they were paper, driving through the meat of his leg. He yelled out. Another hit his thigh, the corrupted magical ore grinding into his muscle. Pain flared; his leg gave out, and he pitched forward.

The pack holding the horns, Hammer, and Seal flew from his grip and opened upon the plankway, scattering the sacred contents. Lojen watched in horror as the Seal bounced once, twice, and finally smacked the railing baluster. It clanged, the steel onyx braid wrapping the four gemstone circles striking the metal rail. He dove for the Seal, swiping nothing but air as the disc toppled off the plankway down into the aethecite-powered vehicles below.

"Lojen!" Wick screamed, button-sized eyes going wide as he noticed the dropped cargo.

Lojen crawled to his feet, blood flowing down his trouser, into his boot. "Go!" He held the horns close, ensuring he didn't lose them in the flight. He hefted the Hammer of Mother Marrow, a surge of aetheric power growing within. He glanced over the rail, but the continued gunfire gave him no choice but to flee.

The lapin reached the end of the plankway, to a control panel. Bullets ripped through the row of airgliders, at the panel, all around them. Aether sizzled as the spells struck metal, releasing *Terris*, making holey cheese out of the well-crafted airgliders, penetrating the hulls as if they were nothing. The lapin rebel slapped at buttons upon the control panel. Lojen dragged himself all the way to the glider and fell into the open hatch.

Wick must have pressed the correct button as the wall in front of them groaned. "Ancantha, go!"

The airglider shuddered on the cable. Engine raging. It moved forward, the wall opening. Lojen sat crumpled against the hull of the airglider, clasping claws to his gushing wounds. The Hammer of Mother Marrow pulsed beside his good leg, the runes upon the haft glowing. The hull rattled in a thunk-thunk-thunk as the *Terris*-infused artillery slammed into it.

Failure filled him as he bemoaned the loss of the Seal. Worthy of his father's horns, he was not. Would never be now. He had failed in the task assigned to him by his ward. That failure, that shame raged within him worse than the bullets piercing the world around him.

Lojen peeked back through the hatch. "Wick!"

The lapin held down a button on the panel as a portal along gears slid open to reveal the darkness of nightturn over Drenth. Wick ducked as a burst of bullets hit the control panel, the thing exploding in circuits and electrical fizzles. The doorway ground to a halt, not open enough for the airglider to safely pass through. The lapin slammed the few remaining buttons again, but the door didn't move.

"Wick!" the female lapin screamed from the cockpit. "No more time!"

Wick dodged through the streaks of projectiles, a graze along his shoulder knocking him aside. Lojen released the wound in his thigh and hung out of the hatch, reaching for the rebel. Wick dove for his outstretched claw, fur meeting leathery palm. With his last remaining strength, Lojen dragged the wounded lapin into the airglider as it rolled off the cable, taking flight just before the portal. The glider's wings skimmed the doors, bullets hammering the hull, the engine thrumming, the lapin pilot screaming. Grinding of metal, squealing pitch high.

And then they were free of Gargantua.

Plummeting.

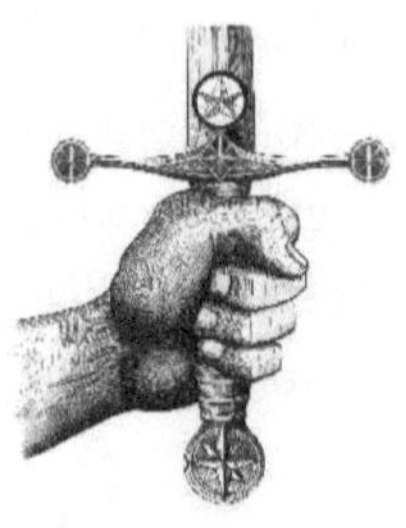

XLI

CYAN THE DEFIANT

CONSCIOUSNESS CAME TO Cyan after being kneed from behind into a chair.

His eyes fluttered open as he struggled to rub them, only to find his arms were bound behind his back. He tried to issue a complaint but found he couldn't as a leather and metal muzzle was strapped to his face, his breather long since removed. By the feel of it against his jaw and cheeks, he knew the muzzle was laced with aetheric runes. And that meant he was cut off from his Shard Form.

A figure, petite and curvy in all the right manner most men would enjoy—hip and bosom—stood off to his periphery. Face was covered in a sheen of red film, and if Cyan the Defiant was any judge, it was most likely blood. Hair was coated in the crimson ichor, falling in thick locks of drenched waves. Almost as if bathed in it.

"Watch and learn what happens to those who question the Fallen's authority in Drenth," the figure said to a massive man bulging with muscles, his bald head drenched in sweat as if he'd just run up the highest peak of the Forgemistress' Blades.

A threat and a demand borne by the mouth of Solanine.

Cyan took stock of his situation. They were in a simple room, one with sterile white walls, most likely within the main compound aboard Gargantua. There was a slight unnatural sway underneath, probably still trying to control the fortress without two of the tethers to anchor it. He was seated behind a worn and battered table, one that appeared to be perpetually stained with blood and lacerated with cuts and gouges from a blade. His arms were corded by chains linked to thick iron rings bolted to the ground, a pair of Imperium soldiers stood behind him, one with a hand gripping his manacled wrists.

Beside him, similarly bound and waking, were Amaranth and Harlequin.

Solanine pulled a chair up to the table. Cyan shot the short aetheurgist daggers, squirming in his bindings, aching to call forth his aetheurgy. "We got off to a poor start," Solanine said smoothly, sitting, the words dubious, but also macabre in the reddish-tint of the blood speckling the heart-shaped face. "Let's start anew, shall we? I want to know how you were able to get aboard Gargantua. No vicar has dared such a thing."

The soldier slammed a blade's pommel into the base of Cyan's head, forcing him to smack the table with his forehead. Stars danced across his vision. He was dragged upright by fingers digging into his scalp, the tip of steel now pressed against his neck. The other soldier released the aetheric-bound muzzle. It rattled upon the wrecked table only to be dragged aside by the soldier.

"You waste your time, heathen," he spat through clenched teeth and blurred vision. "The Pentax will cast you down for your sins."

"There will be time for that, don't worry." Solanine leaned back, legs crossing languidly. "You've a zealous tongue, vicar. I like that. Before we get to whomever helped you board Gargantua, let's get to know one another, hmm? What's your name, vicar?"

"To the Pit with you, Nocturne's whore."

Solanine glanced at the big, sweaty man, smiling. Lethal-like, with teeth. "I've heard the pontifex maximus tears out the tongues of those who use such language." Cyan trembled but said nothing. "You're the leader of these children, are you not? I know what the bristle upon your helm signifies. I know you lack your Shard Form without access to the mist in your canisters. I know what the vicars truly serve. And who. Don't make me ask you again. If you value your companions' lives, don't make me show you something you may not enjoy witnessing."

Cyan the Defiant spit in Solanine's face.

The big man—his face all angry planes—surged forward, slapping a meaty fist across Cyan's cheek. His head cracked backwards, sending more spots frolicking in his vision like fae sprites dancing between raindrops in the Forest of Calibrath. Harlequin screamed into her muzzle while Amaranth jerked in her chains.

Wiping the spittle away, the deadly smile never faltered. "I see you like to do things the hard way. Me too." Dainty fingers coated in cruor gripped the tabletop as Solanine leaned closer. "No matter, vicar, you'll beg me to stop soon enough. You'll beg me to allow you to speak. You'll beg me to let you live." Standing, the chair fell over with a dull thump that echoed around the sterile room. "Evander, be a dear and bring me my tools."

"What of his aether?" the big man called Evander asked.

Now that he had a chance to gain his wits, Cyan realized the man was the one who fought beside the aetheurgist while Lilia screamed that odd aetheurgy. Evander was the one who knocked Amaranth out cold. Through the folds of the man's shirt, he noticed a fresh scar upon his breastbone. Void Form.

The poisoned glare from Solanine was answer enough as the big man quickly grabbed a bag and placed it upon the table in front of Cyan, glass within clanking. A blackened mist rose from inside as he opened it, like a font it gushed over the lip, down the table and swirled around Solanine's feet. Cyan coughed as the mist smelt of death and offal, worse than the corrupted mist from his canisters. Evil smelling. Evander drew forth three glass vessels, placing them on the tabletop. Each contained a powder, colors ranging from bright white to clear as crystal.

Solanine lifted one of the vessels, the substance white. "Acid," the Fallen's second said as the blackened mist curled up the aetheurgist's hips, hugging like a lover. "Mix this with aether and amazing things occur. But you wouldn't know that, vicar, as the church you call master withholds the knowledge from your teachings. Teachings you rabble have neglected since the Fall of your beloved Eminence." Solanine popped the stopper and motioned toward one of the soldiers. Cyan fought but the man was stronger, brandishing his manacled hand upon the table. "Now, I'm going to ask you just once more. Be a good boy and answer, should you do so, this will go easy for you. If not..."

"Go to the void."

A smile more wicked than anything Cyan had ever seen in his life cleft Solanine's face. It was the rictus smile of a daemon for no Pentax-fearing person could revel such as this. Solanine leaned close, spitting upon Cyan's flattened hand, saliva pooling. With nary any semblance of sympathy, the aetheurgist tipped the vessel, causing crystals to fall.

The silence in the room broke with Cyan's scream.

Instant fire exploded from his flesh as the acid burned. His skin bubbled and crackled, split, and pulled away. Unreal agony. He tried to pull his hand free, but the soldier held it strong, the other pushing down on Cyan's shoulders to keep him rooted in the chair.

Gods, it hurt.

"What is your name, vicar?" Cyan's mouth opened but no words, only unrivaled pain. The burn was intense, so much pain, so much hurt. Nothing ever felt like this, not even the aether in the mist. Solanine gave a shudder, a delightful shiver. "You still fight for something as silly as your name?" The aetheurgist's head shook. "You baffle me, vicar. You'll soon realize this is only going to get worse. Much, much worse."

Solanine straightened, grabbing the other two vessels, leaving the acid tauntingly in front of him as the soldiers released their hold. He slumped, unable to bear the pain any longer. He cradled his mangled hand to his breast the best he could in his bound state, the skin blistered and raw, his tendons visible, and a knuckle bone poked through the bubbled flesh.

Cyan felt the use of aether as he glanced up under the slickness of his brow. Solanine had moved in front of Amaranth, twirling fingers. The blackened mist blew into a gale of *Aere*, yanking Amaranth from her chair, flinging her upon the table face first, and splaying her arms outward. The soldier behind stepped between the Pure's legs and pushed upon her lower back. Hard. A vicious pop, back broken. Amaranth screamed into the muzzle, her legs shaking in paralysis.

"Remove the muzzle, I want to hear her screams."

By Solanine's order, the soldier unclasped the muzzle and the broken-backed woman cried. Begging through sobs, "Please, don't… O Zenith… protect me."

"One last chance. Give us a name, vicar."

Cyan nearly bit his tongue in half. This was not the Pentax's way. *I can't… Justice… I can't…*

"You're a tough one, I'll give you that. I like it when you fight." Solanine unstoppered the pair of vessels. To Amaranth, "This is going to hurt." Back to Cyan, "You can stop this. All it takes is a name."

"Don't give in brother-friend!" Amaranth cried, panting through her teeth. "Remember our training, the Pentax will save us!"

Gods, he had to stay strong. He couldn't give away his contact. Couldn't give away the true reason they were aboard at the party. She trusted him.

"By all means, scream as loud as you want," Solanine said as the aetheurgist poured the contents onto the woman's broken back.

Cyan was a man of the Scattered Shards, trained to withstand the sight of blood and carnage in battle to the Pentax's name. He had fought many in the fight for the gods, done deeds for the Conclave of the Scattered Shards. He witnessed his best friend of ten years die before his very eyes when they were young recruits under Icterine the Unfettered's harsh and grueling training. He did not shy away then, did not mourn until well after his blue-iron axes were won. He had remained defiant.

He had done his best to remain steady when the acid burned his hand, blinding pain erupting within. To remain true to his devotion to Zenith. To Mother Marrow. To Justice, Brio, and Bliss. It hurt, to be true, but he hadn't given in. It was how he had gained his name after rising to the cassock. Defiant and true. Steadfast in everything. To the core of him, that was his truth.

But the sight before him now made his stomach churn something fierce, threatening to shit out both ends.

Amaranth's scream reverberated in his bones. The whiff of flesh tearing away from her body was unholy, the smell exploded in Cyan's nostrils. The woman's entire body convulsed, arching under the soldier holding her broken form to the table. The cauterization of the chemicals. The body heaved once more and then went still under the man's grip. The soldier stepped back and Amaranth the Pure fell off the table. Dead eyes staring up at him.

Cyan would never forget that stare for the rest of his life, sooner rather than later it seemed.

The sinner Solanine dropped the bloodstained gown. Upon the aetheurgist's breastbone from up near the collarbone down to the belly were raised scars in the form of runes. They glistened red with blood. The mist rose all around, reddish glow flickering within.

And then Solanine just disappeared.

Cyan made a sign to the Arbiter with his mangled hand, praying. He would remain strong, remain committed. He would not break his oath. He must protect the Godsblood. He spared a glance toward Harlequin the Bloodless, the poor girl sobbing behind her muzzle.

Strength, sister-friend, Cyan's eyes told the younger vicar.

Seconds ticked by and nothing happened, waiting for Solanine to reappear. The body of the Pure began to shake, torso heaving. It rose, on its own. Hanging limp, arms lifted. The vacant eyes still digging into his soul, taunting and teasing him.

Cyan gasped.

The mist coalesced as it reached toward the body suspended off the ground. That light of red flashed again in the blackened mist as it coated the body, cloaking around it. The mist became so opaque for a moment, he lost sight of the Pure, but then it quirked as black lightning flashed within, allowing him to witness the skin of Amaranth slough from her bones, but instead of splashing across the floor, the flesh just disappeared into the vaporous void. Then the muscles followed, soon again by the bones, leaving only blood vessels in the shape of a human wiring the dark mist like red circuits.

He fought the urge to retch, trying to remain stiff in his training. But it was a battle he didn't know if he would win.

A red of the deepest garnet blinked where Amaranth's eyes had been. Forming now over the blood was a hard substance, almost like marble. It knitted shapes, soon resembling a body, limbs and torso. Coarse hair grew from the form, spikes of ivory pierced the mane. Face parting in serrated teeth. Limbs ended in claws.

The distorted head reared back and unleashed a ghastly shriek that sent cold needles throughout his body. A daemon from Nocturne's Pit, molded from the soul of the dead vicar who had once been a pure disciple of the Pentax.

"Zenith, protect us," he whispered. A fear rose within him.

Harlequin sobbed harder behind her muzzle, limp against the binds holding her.

Solanine reappeared from whence the sinner had gone, covered in a sheen of sweat and fresh blood. Hair was tangled as if just woken from sleep. Dark bags surrounded the all-onyx eyes. The daemon borne of the vicar knelt before the sinner, eyes glowing crimson in fealty.

The big man with the scarred face and shorn scalp laughed and stepped behind Harlequin, yanking her head back violently. He gave the girl a kiss on the forehead and raised his eyes, expectant for another soul to be torn from this realm in the violence of Void Form.

O Justice, I have to. Had to give in to save the Bloodless. *Forgive me, O Zenith. O Mother.* "Cyan," as he broke down into tears, shedding all pretense of resistance. Finally, he would give in. "My name is Cyan."

Evander released Harlequin's hair, disappointed. Solanine stroked the daemon's head that had once been Amaranth the Pure, a true devotee, and Cyan's sister-friend.

"You just saved her life. For now." Solanine lifted the daemon's chin. "Not tell me, where is the girl?"

"The girl?"

"The one you sought to return to Kalderim. To your beloved Icterine the Unfettered. Where is she?"

"I… I don't know."

Fingers holding the daemon's jaw. "Find her, my pretty. Find her and bring her to me." The daemon's vile face split in a diabolical grin before suddenly disappearing back into the void.

Cyan the Defiant wept.

XLII
LOJEN

LOJEN GROANED, WONDERING if any of the others were having as difficult of a time as he was.

His thigh burned and his calf pulsed where the spellbound rounds broke through his exoscales. His entire body hurt and by the Arbiter, even his tail felt like it had been shattered in multiple places. He gave it a tentative wag, it protested but otherwise appeared to still be in one piece. Thankfully.

Rolling to his side, Lojen saw the crash, which explained why he felt like he got tossed off the back of a Kanjan mammoth, over an ice cliff, and slammed into each glacial boulder on the way down. The airglider lay in a smattering of pieces. Pilotbox separated from the crumpled wings. The hull was dented, gaps shorn straight through like jagged teeth. The aethecite engine vomited smoke. Both Wick and the female lapin lay amongst the wreckage.

With a claw across his somersaulting abdomen, he shuffled over and dropped like a sack of aethecite next to Wick. Lojen checked his vitals. The lapin's breathing was normal, whiskers twitching. From shoulder to chest, Wick's fur was matted with blood, almost as black as the tunic he wore. "Wick?"

The lapin jolted upright, instantly grabbing his wounded shoulder. "Buggers, that bloody hurt." Button-sized eyes found his. "You seem in one piece, drakken." Eyes like saucers. "Where's Ancantha?"

Lojen pointed some feet away to where the doe lay. Wick scrambled to her and nuzzled his nose into her neck, gently and—to Lojen's weary eye—lovingly. Ancantha moaned and Wick hugged her tightly.

"Ancantha," Wick whispered. "Don't worry me like that, hear?"

Her furry paw stroked Wick's face. "Wick."

As he leaned back into the rubble, Lojen took stock of their situation. Buildings rose into the starlight and the moon sat high in a three-quarter oval beyond Gargantua. But it was silent, the only sound was the crackling of aethecite pellets in the combustion furnace of the airglider's engine.

Where are all the people? he thought.

His watchface was cracked but an aerescreen ticker told him it was almost midnight, and yet, no one—Drenth or Imperium—had come out to investigate the crash. It was eerie, for the mega-city had been nothing short of bustling in the entire time he'd been in there. Now, it was almost like a city of shattered lights. Vagrants should at least have shown themselves, for the crash was prime pickings for looting and scavenging.

Something didn't feel normal about it, as if the world was about to fray.

He shifted because something was poking into his side, and he realized it was the tip of his father's horns. The pack with the horns and Hammer was buried under one of the airglider's seats and said seat had been forcibly ripped from the hull in the crash. Twisting with a grunt, Lojen dug the sack out. Relief washed over him now that he was holding the cherished horns.

With the utmost reverence, Lojen ran a claw down one, tracing the curve like he had when he'd been a hatchling on his father's lap. Fond memories of the horns atop his father's proud head arose from the depths. Memories of him and Ruane listening to stories of wardkeepers of old. Of heroic deeds chronicled.

A sudden urge to put the horns to his stumps swam through him, but he resisted, not yet ready to test his worthiness. Not until he found the others. But most of all because he had lost the Seal of *Terris*.

He glanced upward and found the massive belly of Gargantua. It wavered on its two remaining tethers, creaking loudly in the still night, mocking the Gutter King and his rebellion. Tiny specs floated around the giant fortress like gnats on a carcass, but when a pinprick of light turned to a beam, Lojen realized they were airgliders.

Searching the mega-city for them.

Lojen surveyed the surrounding buildings of the city. They, like the airglider, were broken and worn. This told him they were in the northern boroughs of Drenth. He tried to place the buildings against his knowledge of the city. Probably Stanktown or the Smelt if he was any judge.

Which meant they were far enough from Imperium eyes, but that didn't give them enough freedom to lounge around. They still had a job to do.

"We have to get going," he announced.

"Ready when you are, Lojen."

Shoving the horns into the sack for safekeeping, Lojen tore two long strips of leather from the broken airglider seat and began tying them around his wounds, grunting as he knotted the stiff material tight. Standing, he tested the strength in his leg. Pain shot through from foot to spine as he put his weight upon it. With a sigh, he reached down for the sack and the Hammer.

Wick helped Ancantha to her feet and the pair moved gingerly toward Lojen.

"Now what?" Lojen asked.

"We have to proceed to the mines. Just like Emre had planned."

"Shouldn't we wait for the others? Emre? Finn?"

"Look around, drakken." Wick spread his uninjured arm, the other held between his furred chest and Ancantha, who clung to him. "We may have been lucky enough that we've been knocked cold for as long as we've been and not discovered. But that won't last long."

"Protocol aboard Gargantua would stipulate search parties starting with the immediate area and spreading," Ancantha added.

"How do you know this?"

"Ancantha's been our spy aboard Gargantua for more than five years. She's been a direct servant to Solanine."

Lojen nodded, satisfied. But something still knackered his craw. "What happened to Emre? He and the Dunleiths were to meet us at the rendezvous point after blowing the tethers. Something must've gone wrong."

"You're right about that one, Lojen. Something got cocked up." Wick spoke into the communicator earpiece, "Emre, copy." No response. The lapin tried again. "Emre, copy?" More silence. "Val? Finn?"

"Where are they?" Lojen was growing not only impatient, but intensely worried.

"I don't know why they are radio silent. For all we know they could be in a dangerous spot. I vote we just go to the mines. Continue the plan."

"What about Ru? I can't leave her."

"She knows where to go."

"No!" he yelled suddenly, his shoulders tense. "I won't leave until I know she's safe. Radio her."

Wick sighed, pressed the button in his ruined ear. "Ruane? Copy." The lapin was silent for a long time before finally speaking again. "You all right? Good. Have you seen the others? Oh slag. Really? That's not good." Anger in Wick's voice. "Fine. I'll tell him. Copy, over and out." Lojen faced him with hope. "She's fine. She's in the process of performing her final task for Emre."

"She's safe?"

Wick nodded. "She's fine. Says to be safe, Scurred Hatch."

A huge weight lifted off Lojen's shoulders. Relief set in. But then the thought of Emre gone dark brought him back down again.

The Fallen had to pay.

Anger rolled through his body. The same feeling as when the automaton had attacked. It simmered within him, making him feel rage. It raced through his blood, searing him on the inside.

"Lojen?"

He wanted the Fallen dead. The man deserved it. Long had he made those Lojen cared about pawns in his game. The man deserved nothing less than death.

"Lojen?"

"What?"

"We've got more bad news."

"How could it possibly get any worse?"

"Emre's been captured." That's how it can be worse. "But that's not all." If Wick's shredded ears could wilt, they would be doing so right now. "It was… it was Valeria."

"What!"

"I know," Wick growled. Anger in his tone. "She's betrayed us all. I knew Emre was putting too much faith in Val. She played us, played Emre for a fool to trust her."

That couldn't be true, it just couldn't. Not Valeria Dunleith. She had spoken to his father in the Meadows. His father wouldn't have found her if she was turned to Nocturne. It couldn't be. Could it? "So, what do we do?"

"Continue to the mines. That was the plan."

Lojen was at a loss, he didn't know what to do. *Father?* No, he had to continue with the plan, that's what his father would have done. The loyal wardkeeper. And Emre was his ward now, whether the humir lived or not, Lojen was bound by his honor to see through Emre's goal. His ward's goal was his goal until it was completed, or death took him.

But first, "I lost the Seal," he admitted, full of shame.

"Buggers, you're right," Wick breathed. "That will complicate matters." Wick began to limp toward the pilotbox of the airglider. He rummaged about and pulled out a wheellock pistol, a length of rope, and a few other odd assortments. "We need to move. Lu Har and his scourges are not going to give us a head start."

"But without the Seal, all this was for naught."

"Probably useless now. Lu Har's probably had the remaining bombs disarmed at this point. But the plan is the plan. Emre will have to take it from here. We can only hope his daughter will prevail."

"Wait, his catalyst is his daughter? By the Arbiter, this keeps getting better and better. Then how can we even hope to fight the Fallen with nothing but sand? And do you trust in Emre enough to put our faith in a girl who only recently discovered who she is?"

"I don't know, Lojen. But Emre was insistent on going through with this. So, we'll keep going."

"I saw the aftermath of what Emre's daughter can do," Ancantha said. "She killed a scourge with nothing but her hands. A scourge who could wield aetheurgy. The girl has a stout heart, drakken."

"What about my sister? Finn? He's got to be broken knowing that his bloodkin betrayed us. If they're all in Solanine's grasp, that means the Fallen will soon have them. That's the main force of the rebellion."

"Ruane's a resourceful one and needle dick has a harder constitution than you give him credit for. They'll head to the mines."

"The Arbiter's bloody axe," the drakken cursed. They were left with very little options. He looked south. "Then I guess we better find a ride."

"Lucky for you, I know where one is."

Lojen probably would've raised an eyebrow if he had any, instead the tiny spikes along his eyehole quivered. "I suppose I shouldn't be surprised about this?"

"When will you learn that Emre has planned everything to the detail?"

"Everything but Val's betrayal," Lojen muttered.

"Come on," Wick said sullenly, perhaps even thoughtfully, limping away from the crashed airglider.

They found a truck within a garage a few streets down from where they'd crashed.

Per Wick, the place was a safehouse, though the dust that'd covered everything told Lojen it hadn't been used in some time. Wick had gotten the mining vehicle up and running within minutes, and they were racing through the empty streets of Drenth. Ancantha—

who Lojen'd learned was Wick's mate—stayed behind with the intent to send word to any rebels still alive that the time to head to Kalderim was now, where she would soon head.

The aethecite mining truck bounced along the shoddily paved road through the darkened streets, jostling Lojen within his seat.

A double-lane road broke through the high sand hills like a black river, but the winds that blasted through the desert had long made the once smooth road nothing more than a trail of potholes. There was also a train track that ran parallel, but most of the rails were covered in windswept sand.

It was cold within the desert, and to Lojen, it felt good against his scales—though Wick was constantly shivering, even with his fur. He saw nothing in the distance but the dunes, no trees, no plant life silhouettes. Sand rising high and dipping low into valleys, that was it. The Sea of Mist wasn't dense, but visibility was hardly more than twenty yards, if that. The Sea rose high above them, the fog blotting out the stars. The moonlight barely pierced through the haze, same with the headlamps on the truck.

It felt as if they were all alone in the world, a dark and dreary world aiming to swallow them whole. Thankfully, there didn't seem to be any daemons or wights roaming about out here.

Lojen had never been this far south and seeing the desert dunes up close was something he normally would've treasured. But all he could think about was the plan going to piss 'n dung. Emre and Finn captured. Valeria Dunleith betraying them. Ruane safe yet still doing something stupid no doubt.

"Not far now," Wick said. His ears flapped in the wind. Lojen hadn't been able to understand why the lapin had chosen a vehicle with no top, leaving them exposed to the elements. He tried to blink away the grit but found it nearly impossible. "Mines are just ahead."

"How far out from the city are we?" They'd been driving for a solid two hours now and they hadn't seen a single light source since leaving Drenth behind.

"Close to fifty miles," Wick answered, squinting through the Sea, then pointed. "There."

Lojen saw a solitary light in the distance just beginning to pierce the Sea. A brightness atop a lone pole, beam growing brighter the closer they got.

The dunes went from massive hills to low mounds now, and then to flat. The road grew smoother. Low-profile structures rose from the sands, tiny bulbs of light shone dimly in the hazy Sea. A gate appeared across the road, and Wick hopped out to raise it by hand. Lojen scanned the surrounding structures.

"Empty?"

"Nothin' here but aethecite and sand," Wick said as he jumped back into the driver's seat.

"I heard vvyrms like to burrow out here." Lojen'd heard that vvyrms might also be the source of aethecite, but if that was true, then the most precious fuel supply in the Mistlands was nothing more than scat, which was comical. He shook the thought away. "I'm surprised there's no guard here. With how important aethecite is."

"Ain't been a vvyrm 'round these parts in some time. Maybe a half a year. Most are saying the vvyrms are dying out. Sightings been very rare." The truck rolled past the gate. "There used to be soldiers watching the mines at all times. Workers down deep at all hours."

If the terrisvvyrms were dying out, then the world was even closer to the realm of Death than they thought. "But no more? The guards, that is."

"Happened about a year ago. Mines all closed at night. Some of the miners who would stay late swore they heard screams."

"Screams?"

"Down in the deep you hear some weird things, Lojen. Things that don't make sense. Some claimed they saw ghosts. Who knows? All I do know is that about this time last year, Lu Har closed the mines at dusk. Guards used to patrol the top level. Fully armed, too. Emre and Tevun wanted intel on the closing. But then about a month ago, everything went dark."

"A month?" Lojen leaned forward. "These are the mines you humir have been fighting over? Looks like nothing but a bunch of holes in the ground."

"That's probably the truest statement I've ever heard," Wick said dryly, making Lojen feel like a dunce for even uttering it.

The mines, he saw in the dim light, were scattered about the dunes, trussed entrances leading to darkened tunnels of aethecite. Outbuildings lined paved streets in a mishmash pattern. Trucks and carts slept dormant about the roads, some half-filled with the crystal ore. One of the roads led off further into the desert.

"Where's that road lead?"

There was a massive rumble in the ground, the entire truck shaking under them. Lojen grabbed the door and looked all around trying to find the source of the quake. When he turned back the way they had come, from Drenth, he saw the lazy moonlight within the Sea go black. Another tremble hit the sands; mounds flying. Even in the dark, Lojen could see the sprays.

"What *is* that?"

"That, Lojen, is one of your vvyrms. Guess they aren't all dead yet. Means the Forgemistress may yet still favor us this day's turn."

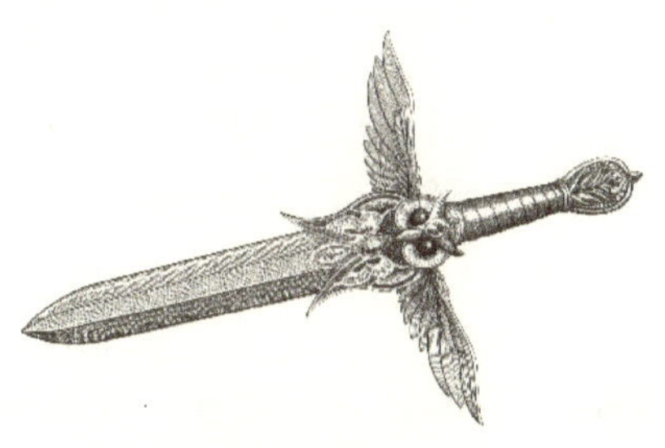

XLIII
CADRIANNA

SHAPES MOVED THROUGH the columns inside the compound, hours after the chaos of the party had died down, the last of the guests disembarking the floating fortress.

Daemons.

Moonlight pierced the blood-smeared walls, keeping a heavy mist full of umbra. It wasn't the mist from the Sea caused by the Fall of Eminence. No, this was the impenetrable void from Nocturne's Pit. Evil void. Daemon void.

The white walls ran red with bloodied runes, drawn by hand. So much blood. The ground held puddles of the cruor; more runes painstakingly crafted in the language of the Divines. The blackened mist poured from the runes. It quirked, the mist, pulsed with dark magic. Magic that sought only one thing and one thing only: death.

Figures materialized from the darkened haze. Three, to be exact. Ratko and two other scourges of the Fallen. Ratko had a sickening, lustful look, one that either wanted her body or her blood, didn't matter which order. Cadrianna ignored the scourges as they trailed on her heels as she followed the bloodied runes through the compound.

"I SMELL DEATH."

"Observant, you."

"AH, NOW THE ILLUSTRIOUS SCOURGE WITH A MAGNIFICENT BACKSIDE DECIDES TO BREAK HER SILENCE. ALL IT TAKES IS SIMPLE OBSERVATIONS."

"Enough, Strix." In truth, Cadrianna was in no mood for dealing with the daemon blade's schtick, not at the moment. She was too consumed by her overpowering emotions.

All she knew was that she needed answers.

Of the bikrome who gave her the Strix back, who then betrayed Emre. Of Brynn with Lu Har on the dance floor.

None of it made any sense.

Nocturne, why was she struggling so? She'd known only one path that would lead her to her vindication. All she had to do was obey the Fallen and Brynn would be safe. But now that road was crumbling underfoot. Every choice she'd made all came back to haunt her.

Her belief that Emre had betrayed her and made Brynn suffer.

Her hatred and her love for Lu Har. Taking to his bed in order to save her daughter, only to fall in love with him in a sick, sadistic manner.

The bonding to the Strix, giving up her womanhood so that she and daemon were one. The only creature capable of knowing her turmoil, mentally and physically.

All of it for naught. All of it lies upon lies. A series of lies wrapped around herself to make her strong. Her savior and protector. Her shield.

"I might just ask the Fallen for you when he's done with you, sweetling," Ratko said, his putrid breath upon her neck.

She hadn't heard him inch closer, so deep in her thoughts. Pulling up, she rounded on the scourge and he instinctively jerked backward, hand going to his sword. "You might want to remember your place, Ratko, before I let my blade claim your soul."

The odious scourge chuckled into his thick beard. "O, I think the times might be a changin', lass. Your little show earlier didn't sit well with the Fallen." He leaned closer, mere inches away now. His face was bruised from her kick. "But for me, it quickened my cock."

"Back off," she said with force. She kept her back stiff, her hand off her blade. She dared not let him think her flustered.

The man raised his hands. "You might wish to curb your heat, sweetling. The Fallen is the void."

"You're a fool, Ratko, if you think I don't know how to walk the void. Scourge you may be, but I am the Divines' chosen." She burned her Void Form; the edges of her body became like the mist around them. She felt the aether rage through her veins as she contained the magic within the mist, it begged for release. A letting, if it could be said.

Ratko tensed. In fact, Cadrianna was aching for a fight. Her blood boiled at the thought of spilling this man's intestines, his soul being eaten by the Strix.

"CAD, YOU KNOW I WOULD LOVE TO HAVE HIS SOUL DIPPED IN MUSTARD, BUT NOW ISN'T THE TIME."

Sensing that Ratko would hold his tongue, and his blade, Cadrianna whirled away. The scourge and his cohorts followed.

It wasn't long before the bodies came into view.

At first, it was a well-dressed man donning a conical-shaped mask, his neck sliced clean through. Then it was a woman in a warm green stola of far too many pleats, gloves above her elbows, the bare skin of her clavicle stained red from a number of deep gashes. Each step brought more and more bodies, all apparent guests of the party. All Drenth-born. All dead in pools of their own demise.

The narrow hall gave way to a large antechamber in the center of the compound. Ahead was a throne, taller than a man was high, gilded about the edges. It was haphazardly set upon the remnants of what looked to be a toppled column. Bullet holes pocked the walls all around, as if someone had unleashed a row of hand-cranked rotating cannons. The angry mist curled about the throne. It was a large thing, the throne was, but it was dwarfed by the two ominous shadows looming beyond, red eyes within the shades of shapes. Unmoving, they were, but their purpose was unmistakable: they were guarding the figure who sat on the throne.

"I THINK I SPEAK FOR ALL DAEMONKIND, SOLANINE IS A CU—"
"Shhst."
Solanine sat there. Part of Cadrianna was relieved it was the blooddrake and not the Fallen. She didn't know if she was ready to confront Lu Har just yet. Solanine's stola was covered in blood, hair matted with the ichor. Onyx gaze narrowed at Cadrianna's entrance, heart-shaped face resting upon a blood-stained hand.

There were others in the room, Cadrianna noted. Many of them soldiers of the Imperium, some daemons like the two behind. A few stragglers she knew naught. One of the daemons lithely lying before the throne wore the midnight blue cassock of a vicar, her face twisted from the void. A man stood in the adumbration of the daemons. His face scarred and hairless.

Of the bikrome, she didn't see her. *You lied to me, Valeria Dunleith. Lied to Emre.*

"Solanine," Cadrianna forced out, going to her knees rigidly. The others behind her doing the same, echoing her revered salutation but lacking the sharpness of hers. She loathed to bend before Solanine, but this was no time to silently fight back.

"Where is she?" Solanine's voice naught but the sweetness of honey and calm. It was disarming. "Where is the Godsblood?"

"She will be found," Ratko groveled. The man's face was pressed to the ground, forehead touching. "The contract remains, and we shall honor it. For you, O greatness."

What contract? What is this Godsblood?

"CAD, THIS IS EMRE'S DOING..."

Brynn?

"Silence!" It was no more than a hiss, but the vehemence in Solanine's tone was harsh.

The three scourges tensed, only Cadrianna dared look at the aetheurgist. The blooddrake smiled to reveal straight white teeth that should be pointed like a drake's but remained hidden under the scales of this woman on the throne. Chants formed on the mortal lips, whispered so Cadrianna couldn't hear. A wave of *Aere* into the center of a mini storm. Black lightning of the void raged inside the mist, Solanine snapped the scales' fingers and broke the spell.

But the blooddrake's smile did start to make Cadrianna angry. Angry that she allowed such swine to live all these years after the sack of her husband's city.

Brynn… I did it for you…

"NO, CAD, YOU DID IT FOR YOU. TO PROTECT YOURSELF."

All I did was for Brynn!

"AND YET, YOU STILL DON'T WANT TO BELIEVE THE TRUTH IN FRONT OF YOU. PLEASE, FOR THE LOVE OF YOUR DAUGHTER, OPEN YOUR EYES."

I… they…

"I had her surrounded, scourge," Solanine said, words directed toward Cadrianna. "In fact, I had her right in my sight, my fingers ready to reach out and hook her. But you, you wasteful whore, had to confront your past. Had to step in and take matters into your own biased Nightingale hands. Hands that never should have been graced with blood."

"Forgive me," a rote response came forth.

"Your little outburst destroyed our one chance at bringing the Godsblood into the fold. For Lu Har to take his rightful place upon Eminence. The willfulness of your Nightingale blood may have ground his plans to a halt, daughter of the beast."

Cadrianna held her tongue, holding firm. Try as she might, it just didn't make any sense. It couldn't be her. *Could it? What is so important about the blood of the Nightingale line? Strix, what does Solanine mean by 'daughter of the beast'? That's the second time using that phrase.*

A long pause by the daemon, one that didn't sit well with Cadrianna. Finally, *"CAD, YOUR BLOOD. THE TIES TO YOUR NIGHTINGALE BLOOD."*

I don't understand. Strix?

"SOON."

Solanine's words to Ratko and the scourges broke her concentration. "Since the girl has evaded you, it seems she's had help. Evander," the big, bald man came forward. An imposing man, but Cadrianna feared him not. He bowed reverently. "Show what you've discovered."

"As my master commands," the man named Evander said. A fire tainted by Void Form burned in him, Cadrianna could see. He held out his hand, and within was something resembling a scrunched ball of fabric. Pink and clearly from a stola.

Brynn's dress? It couldn't be her; she can't be here. She's still in her prison. I saw her before leaving!

"CAD, I TRIED TO WARN YOU. ONLY LIES WERE YOU TO MEET."
Ratko and the others took a closer look, Cadrianna was rooted like
a tree. "This was the girl's," Solanine said, "Found in front of a spire
not three blocks from this very location. Gone during the flight after
the Gutter King blew my anchors. Fled from Lu Har's grip. He is not
pleased. Nor am I."

"We searched, O greatness," Ratko said. Cadrianna looked his
way, confused. "Just as you commanded. She must have escaped via
glider."

"Not possible," Solanine said. "None have seen her, or one
resembling her."

"What of the one airglider that es—"

"Enough, scourge. Whoever helped her, will suffer my wrath."
Eerie was the proclamation, as Solanine's bloodstained face portrayed
death. Foreboding even. "This Godsblood is more than meets the
eye. She is imbued with Nightingale blood. That wretched blood of
the First… bah… she cannot have gotten far. She must be found at
all costs."

"Perhaps the girl is dead." The words trickled out before
Cadrianna could contain them. Part of her hungered for confirmation
of this girl's identity, but the other part of her feared the truth. If it
was Brynn, then everything she'd ever known was nothing but a lie.

"So much death," Solanine acknowledged. "Immortality does not
come from the proliferation of Life."

"But upon the wave of Death," the three scourges said as one,
Cadrianna silent.

"It would take more than that to kill a Godsblood. You saw her
firsthand tonight," said a voice nearby.

A coldness overcame her, a cold so deep that it drew the warmth
from her body and of the room. Her eyes snapped up in fire. The

bikrome who had betrayed her beloved husband was watching her intently behind a veil, waiting to see what she would do. Cadrianna remained still but the mist deepened and roiled. Her fingers dug into the stone.

"Temper that anger. You've still many uses, Cadrianna Nightingale," said Valeria Dunleith, traitor and betrayer. "The Seal of *Terris* has been taken."

Taken, how? Was this Emre's plan all along? Strix?

"I KNOW NOT, BUT IT ADDS UP. THE SEAL WAS ALWAYS BOUND TO DRENTH AFTER THE FALL. TO A DRAKKEN WARDKEEPER. TO THE BENLDS. YOU KNOW THIS IS WHY LU HAR CAME TO DRENTH."

I didn't…

"The girl has evaded me for long enough," Solanine said as the blooddrake slithered off the throne toward the bikrome. "Scourges and gangland thugs be godsdamned. It's time for something else."

The blooddrake drew a small dagger from the folds of the mortal's outfit, slicing across the scales' fleshy palm. Solanine squeezed crimson from the wound, not the blackish ichor of a blooddrake, but red of humir. Going to knees, Solanine's head bowed, golden-red locks fanning out. Chanting in the language of the Pit, the blooddrake drew a circle in streaks of red upon the ground. Solanine's bloodied hand began to move in a formation of symbols, ancient symbols wrought from the Pit of Nocturne. The pendant of onyx flared around the aetheurgist's neck, black eyes glowing obsidian.

"O NO," the Strix muttered, a knowing tone. *"THIS IS NOT GOING TO BE GOOD."*

What is it, Strix?

The daemon blade hissed.

The symbols hovering in the mist, started to blossom an eerie pale. A glow, as tiny as a pinprick, surged in brightness as Solanine's chants grew in intensity, expanding. Mist of the opaquest black Cadrianna had ever seen poured out of the light, a wail of deathly sorrow. The mist snaked around Solanine, gnawing at the bare skin of the scales' arms, tiny wisps fizzling. The blooddrake threw the stolen head abaft and cried out, a shriek of the void.

Cadrianna shielded her eyes as the pale intensified, radiant now like Zenith's sun. Her body was cold, devoid of anything but the fervor of the light. She forced herself to look at it.

The mist churned around Solanine aggressively. It savagely cascaded from the light, a gateway, Cadrianna now saw, from Nocturne's Pit, linking the Pit to the world of Life. A gateway that grew in size by the heartbeat of the blooddrake, the blood and soul linked to that of the void.

A shadow emerged. Long, sharp teeth. Vicious snout full of them. Hide and a cloak borne of shadows. Small horns tenting the cloak. Wailing in the mist.

The Strix inhaled, if such a feat was possible for an inanimate object. *"MELT ME DOWN INTO A TOOTHPICK. IT'S LEMURES."*

XLIV
EMRE

GLOOMY LIGHT FROM a dingy orb in the center of a rock-hewn ceiling shone down upon him as he paced. A single pipe limply affixed to the side of his prison cell sparked randomly from a splintered line.

It reminded him of his current predicament. Even a wayward path leads to power.

In a cell opposite was Finn, who lay upon a lumpy mattress that smelt of wet straw. The elfir had a bruise alongside his temple and he was sound asleep with one of his arms slung across his eyes. How he'd been able to sleep at a time like this, Emre would never know, but it was a trait he admired about Finn. One of many.

Traits he would miss when all was said and done. *Still it, Benld. Remember the why, remember the laughter along the way. Don't linger on the hurt, the unsaid words. What must be, must be. For her.*

Anger threatened to overtake him, but he fought it back as he paced, trying to contain the simmering rage as well as keep his fingers from digging into his scarred arms. He shouldn't be angry, he knew, but he couldn't help it. Betrayal was a difficult thorn to remove. Sighing, Emre stilled his emotions, harnessing them until the end.

"Psst, humir."

Ruane crouched outside his prison. The drakken hid in the shadows of the dim light, her snout pressed close to the bars.

"Ruane, you're safe."

She snorted. "You think these humir could catch me?"

"Never crossed my mind. I assume you planted the rest of the bombs?"

"Every one of them," she said. "All of it." Stressing the importance of the latter sentence.

"Good."

Ruane reached into her vest pocket and withdrew a small aetheric detonator and a leather folding wallet, handing them through the bars. Emre slipped the detonator into his waistcoat pocket next to his father's heirloom watch. He had been patted down upon his capture, but the soldiers of the Imperium hadn't taken his watch, just his engraved multi-barrel wheellock pistol. At least he had one of the two things remaining from his parents.

Within the folding wallet were four vials of parch. The liquid reflected the dingy light. How odd it was that such a small thing had been the impetus for Drenth's destruction? He brought the vials to his lips and downed them, the fires of aether burning the entire way. He felt rejuvenated and prepared for what was to come. He hoped.

The young hatchling of Tevun's brood tapped at the bars with her claws. "Your bikrome was the one to do this to you?"

"You saw?" He sighed when she nodded.

It shouldn't have surprised him, he knew the drakken siblings would learn the truth one way or another. Perhaps he shouldn't have withheld the truth from them. So many decisions he might have done differently.

"And you knew the bikrome would betray you to the Fallen?" This time it was he who nodded in affirmation. "My father, did he know?" Another nod. "And he allowed this?"

How could he possibly explain to her so she would understand that her father had sacrificed himself for the greater good? For Eminence? He didn't know if she would understand. Void, Emre wasn't certain he truly did, and it was his only goal since being brought back to life.

It was like Cad always said, *'never trust the gods.'* How right she had been.

"And yet, you still trusted her. She betrayed you. Betrayed my father. Betrayed Eminence. Not once, but twice now. How do you reconcile that?"

"That is a question I ask myself daily, Ruane. But the answer isn't what you think it means. What Val did… what she has done, it was for Brynn, my daughter. She is the Godsblood. She is the answer to reopening Eminence."

Ruane hissed. "You'd sell your soul to see your daughter break the Seals? That is not the path of the Pentax, humir. That is the path of Nocturne."

"All will become clear, Ruane. You just have to trust me. The Pentax is not what you or any of us think."

"You couldn't have done any of this without us, humir. Lojen trusts you. Me? I don't know. But if my father put his trust in you, then I have to see it to the end. For him."

Emre touched Ruane's leathery talon. She winced at being touched by a man, he knew how much she detested his race, but she didn't pull away. "Thank you, Ruane Tevunsdotyr."

"How do you reconcile your heart, Emre Benld?"

"When this is over, I will mourn. I will let it consume me. But until then, nothing."

"You're a cold one, humir. For that, I admire you."

"I'm not one to admire. But I do have a favor to ask. My daughter is here, aboard Gargantua. I expected Solanine to have her by this point, but something may have happened to her. I need you to find her and escape before we finish this. Will you do it for me?"

"How will I know this daughter of yours?" When Emre described her, Ruane's snout went wide in sharp teeth glory. "Ah, she's the wet-fish-looking one dancing?" Emre smiled at Brynn's appearance earlier. "As you've asked. I'll find her for you, Emre Benld."

"I will forever be in your debt, Ruane. There will be an airglider waiting for you here." He fingered a small piece of parchment from the seams in his waistcoat, a hidden compartment the soldiers hadn't discovered, and handed it to her. "She must go to Kalderim. Please see her there. If we cannot meet you before, take her. If she doesn't get to Kalderim, everything will be for naught."

Ruane straightened, which for a drakken female meant a six-and-a-half-foot height. She placed her clawed talon upon her breast. "I swear on my father's horns as wardkeeper to see her to Kalderim. Even if I have to shove her into a sack and carry her there."

Emre laughed. "I'd love to see that, truly, I would. O, she goes by the name Ashe, but her true name is Brynn. Brynn Benld."

Unexpectedly, Ruane grabbed Emre's hand. "Justice with you, Emre Benld. 'Til we meet again." And then she disappeared into the shadows.

"In the Meadows," he whispered into his arms as they crossed the bars, his head sinking into the crook of his elbow.

"Emre…"

He cracked open his eyes when he heard his name.

Cadrianna stood beyond the bars of his cell. She looked sad, her once-radiant beauty forever marred by their forced separation of his decisions. She still had that illustrious glow about her that had first attracted him, but it was worn with age, with heartache, and grief. His actions that day were a waking nightmare everyday of her existence, and worse, he knew there was no coming back from it.

Still it, Benld! He rose from the straw mattress and crossed the cell toward her.

She leaned upon the bars, her forehead pressed against the rusted metal, her hand gripping that daemon blade shaped like an owl in flight. Their faces were mere inches apart. He could smell her, that overpowering scent of a woman he would never forget, no matter the distance nor the void between them. Gods, he loved her still. He wanted to reach for her, just as he had when she'd confronted him upon the mezzanine by the fountain. A husband always desiring to soothe his hurting wife.

"I'm sorry for the punch," she said softly. "Couldn't help myself." A slight tug at the corners of her lips, a jest.

In the other cell, Finn's head turned from under his arm, his gaze expressing concern. Or was it jealously? Two pieces of his heart, two so near and dear to him. Emre felt torn. Felt his will breaking down.

No! Still it, Benld! What must be done, must be. Remember that. Until the end, remain on target. Finn cannot know the truth. Val promised… O Val…

Before he could speak, figures stepped from the shadows. Solanine's face was hollow, dusty, and crusted in dried blood. The normally coiffed hair was disheveled, and the once-impeccable dress was stained in crimson. Valeria stood motionless, her eyes hidden behind her veil, the peridot glimmering as she remained rigid. A third shadow hung behind, a big man, bald, someone Emre didn't know.

"The Fallen enjoyed your little show, Emre Benld," Solanine said as the blooddrake-in-humir-flesh stopped short of his cell, eyes narrowed into predatory slits, smirking. "Almost worked, wouldn't you know?"

"Val, how could you betray us like that!" Finn spat as he shot from the mattress. He grabbed the bars and if they hadn't been made of metal, might have ripped them free in his rage. "It's me, your brother. You said you'd never do that again. How…how could you?"

"O, come, brother-friend," Val said. "You always knew of a spy, you just wanted to keep the wool over your eyes."

"But Keph, he was the one…right?"

"Kephren was never a spy, Finn," Val said. "You were just too blind to see that he was a tool and the means to an end." She turned toward Emre. "You, Emre, you were growing too suspicious. Too close you came to uncovering the truth. You and that vile drakken."

"Tevun?"

"That drakken served his purpose, he helped us discover the truth about the Seal of *Terris*. But he became expendable."

"He was your friend, Val!" Finn shouted. "How could you kill him like that? You monster!"

Unlike Finn's outburst, Emre struggled to maintain the calm exterior that Tevun had instilled in him: *never show your weakness on the outside, bury the pain.* "All this time, Val? I trusted you. You brought me back, for what?"

"The Godsblood. You think we needed you all this time, Emre? Please. The Godsblood is the only one we need." The bikrome glanced toward the barely restrained Cadrianna, who gripped the daemonized blade. "O yes, Cadrianna Benld, those memories I showed you were indeed true. I did save the babe and put her in the

Shards' hands. She needed to learn aetheurgy of the Pentax. Without that training, she never could have bonded with the Eye of the Soul."

Emre retreated to the mattress, slumping down upon it, his face buried into his hands. "Val… I…"

Solanine laughed. "You're a fool for thinking your little rebellion could withstand the might of the Fallen. A fool for trusting your heart and not your head." The blooddrake's hand intertwined into Val's. "You should have chosen differently, Benld. The Dunleiths are but a sullied line that will fall into the abyss of the void. Valeria made her choice five hundred years ago. Choosing the correct side. Choosing our Divine's."

He scratched his forearms but grunted. It was time to reveal a truth. "You think I didn't know Val was the spy this entire time?" He glanced toward Finn, handsome face darkening with anger. Knuckles white on the bars of his cell, he shushed Finn with a curt wave. "You're the fool if you think I wouldn't know. You off all people, Val, you know what the Meadows can reveal. What the souls of the dead know."

Solanine turned toward the bikrome. "That's not possible, is it?"

"A bikrome's power is finite," Val said calmly, her bi-colored eyes glinting in the sparking aethecite lamplight. "I know not what the soul sees after death, only what the Pentax and Nocturne are willing to show."

"Clever move, Benld," Solanine said. "But don't think for a minute you've won. The Godsblood has slipped from your hands. The Seal of *Terris* remains aboard this ship. Eminence is for the Fallen." The blooddrake leaned closer. "I can see the hurt in your eyes. Valeria's betrayal hurt you to the core." Emre trembled. "See there, Valeria my love, he tries to hide it. You've hurt him. Bliss might have been wrong."

Still it! "You don't strike me as one who listens to the Pentax, blooddrake."

"Ah, so the Gutter King isn't one to pull the wool over so easily. It's rare that you humir can deduce a blooddrake in their scales. Valeria would not have told you, there are certain secrets that remain between each other." The blooddrake glanced derisively toward Cadrianna. "It seems you chose your husband well, whore."

Cadrianna stiffened, telling Emre he'd guessed correct, the aetheurgist had been one of Cadrianna's torturers in the life she lived under Lu Har. It saddened him to see his wife like that.

"I enjoyed your little reunion." Cadrianna death-glared the blooddrake. Solanine cackled. "O, little whore, I've waited this day to break you. Destroy what little belief you've long since clung to. I couldn't pass this opportunity, regardless of Lu Har's demands."

Cadrianna stepped closer to the blooddrake. "Recall what I said if you ever call me whore again, Solanine."

Solanine did not appear distressed, merely amused. "In time."

Emre scratched at his scarred forearms as he stood straight, willing to step in to keep his wife from doing something rash, which she was wont to do. "There's a certain stink that accompanies a frightened drake. Especially one backed into a corner. It's almost as if they know they're dead but unwilling in their ego to admit it."

"You would know, wouldn't you, Emre Benld? For I'm certain you had a full taste when our scourge laid waste to your precious wardkeeper. You rebel cairn given to us by one you implicitly trusted the most. How it must gall you to know the lives lost to you were because you trusted the wrong person."

His rage nearly boiled over, but Emre restrained it. Inside he was a keg of aethecite ready to blow. Not now, not when he was so close. The detonator felt like a wagon cart in his waistcoat pocket. Soon.

Cadrianna, however, was like a cat with their hackles raised, ready to pounce. Her hand gripped the daemon blade so tightly, Emre could almost see her knuckles popping through her padded gloves. There was an unmistakable hatred emanating between the two, and it made Emre wonder if there was something deeper in their relationship. Something traumatic.

Seeing that he wasn't going to take her baited jape, Solanine tossed him something, a small object. Emre caught it and realized it was an earpiece communicator, the one he had made specifically for a drakken. Lojen's?

Part of him wilted at the thought of Tevun's hatchling caught, or worse, dead. The wardkeeper heir's blood would be yet more staining his hands. First Kephren, then Tevun. And soon to be others…

"Where are the others?" Solanine pressed. "The lapin slave and the pair of drakken you dragged into this little game of yours." He fought to suppress a relieving sigh. They still lived, Wick and Lojen. Emre shrugged. "They can't have gotten far. Your plan was doomed from the start. Granted, it doesn't help you when everything you've planned is gifted on a platter to your enemy."

"High opinion of yourself, blooddrake," Finn said as he cleaned the dirt from under his nails, his legs crossed upon the mattress. His previous anger having been drained. The man certainly was able to turn a leaf on the drop of a hat. Another of his more admirable traits. "Who's to say you've got us all wrong." What was Finn doing, provoking her?

Finn, don't. Not because of Val. Stay your tongue, love.

The lesser order of draconem slithered toward Finn's cell. "And you, Dunleith child, you think adding your name to Drenth's rebellion would give it greater cause?"

"Don't forget raising the level of attractiveness."

"You jest, even now. Amusing. Kalderim and the Golden Throne will crumble under Lu Har's boot. And there is nothing that can stop it. Jest all you want, child, but the Dunleiths will be wiped from existence, carried away with the tide of the Divines' swell. You sister will sit the Golden Throne," Solanine held Val's hand aloft, "and will rule it in Lu Har's name when he reigns over Eminence and Noctis alike."

"Hey, Em, this one's lyrical, eh?" Solanine attacked the bars, taloned hands hidden within humir flesh rattled the cell. Finn reflexively leaned back, but then began to laugh. "Petty showmanship, love it!" But then he glared at his sister. "You chose this over us?" He shook his head.

Solanine growled. "Laugh while you can, child. I'll make certain the Fallen keeps you alive long enough to see your parents' heads upon a spike. You don't think your sister hasn't seen that future?" Finn's mischievous grin withered. Solanine turned back toward Emre. "You best say your prayers to your paltry Pentax now, dog, for the Fallen will not savor that besmirching name upon your lips."

"Is that true, Val?" Finn asked quietly. "You'd let him do that to our parents? To Titen and Jairus? They are your bloodkin, Val, just like me. You can't let him do this. Val! Please?"

A drake scaled guard shoved a key into his cell, the lock groaning as it opened. Other similarly armored solders with assault rifles pointed at him materialized in the gloom. Cadrianna appeared as if she wanted to intercede, but Emre gave her a look, letting her know it was best to back down. Her hand never left the daemon blade as she backed away.

Emre glanced at Finn, eyes locking. Knowledge that it was time to end it. Emre steeled himself, readied his heart. He could feel the parch reserves inside, swirling with the boiled rage of aether. Ready and waiting for him to break the dam holding the fire at bay.

"Be strong, Finn. Trust in me." He glanced at Val, who still remained where she was, watching in that bikromi way of hers. "Everything will be fine."

"I trust you until the end, love."

"Not you," Solanine said to Cadrianna, a hand put up as if it was a steel wall.

"What's the meaning of this?" She was crackling with rage, barely restraining herself.

Solanine seemed to be awaiting the challenge with amusement. "The Fallen is not pleased with you, regardless of the time shared in his bed." Cadrianna's gaze swept toward Emre, hurt upon her face. "You've displeased him and no amount of time on your knees will rectify your failures."

The blackened daemon dagger came whipping out, its onyx steel glimmering. "I'll kill you, Solanine."

"You best say your farewells to your husband. The Fallen will see him dead. For eternity, this time. Then you can spend all the time on your back with your legs open and beg the Fallen to take you back." Cadrianna stepped forward, the guards with their wheellocks ready to intercede. The big, bald man tensed expectantly. Emre fought the urge to reach for his wife. "Put it away before you hurt yourself. Before I embarrass you before your beloved husband."

Time, it was for him to step in and save her before Cadrianna went too far. *Still your heart, Benld. One more time.* "Cad, don't. We will meet again."

Cadrianna's face went through the gamut of emotions before finally settling on sullen acquiescence. She grabbed his hand before turning and marching away.

With one last look at Finn filled with heartbreak, Emre steadied himself. "Lead on, Solanine. Let us end this."

XLV
Ashe

GROGGILY, ASHE TRIED to rub the pain doing a sluggish jig in her skull but found she couldn't lift her arms.

"How many… going… unconscious…" she muttered unintelligibly as she came to.

The back of her head felt like a firedrake had slapped her with its tail while a vvyrm gargled on her body. From the tip of her longest toe to the apex of her hairline and everything in between hurt. Especially her busted kneecap, that hurt the most. Well, physically. Her throat was dry from all the screaming she had done, and there was so much blur in her eyesight, she godsdamned near wondered if she'd ever see straight again.

But she was plum tired of being knocked out. More so, it was embarrassing.

Blessedly, her vision started to clear the longer she remained conscious, and she found herself in a room that might be found in a villa somewhere in Silk Circle, but that didn't make sense because, try as she might, her stomach contents sloshed as the ground moved underneath.

Still aboard Gargantua, she thought as she fought the urge to cough up some pulmo tar.

It didn't last long, her willpower, as she coughed so hard it felt like her stomach might turn itself inside out. She spat the blackened phlegm that was killing her.

"Gross," she said through the gooey taste in her mouth.

Taking stock of her surroundings to avoid a second burst of pulmo, Ashe found she was tied to a bedpost, the bindings digging deeply into her sides. A window across the room was closed shut, leaving the room in shadows. An aethecite table lamp was on and an aerescreen—while not immediately visible from her captive position—sang with the sounds of an audience cheering, and from the sound of it, was some sort of sporting event. A cluster of chairs lay just out of her peripherals.

"You're awake. Finally. Was afraid we might have clobbered you too hard there for a moment."

One of the chairs gave a creaking groan as a bulk shifted. Elian's mass flopped into view, an ear-to-ear smile behind his thick, unkempt beard. A soft click and the aerescreen went blank, the cheers stopped, thankfully as the enthusiastic cheering was starting to bore into her eardrums. Two other figures moved into sight, a wiry shrewkin and lumbering orcirish tough. Quick Fingers Cyrus and Red Tulio.

Ashe grimaced, head full of murk. Nausea crept in. "Just fucking great. Exactly who I wanted to see right now."

"Wasn't easy finding you, girl." Elian's fat fingers were steepled as he glared at her. The discomfort rattling about her brain made her attempt to read his aura nigh on useless. All she saw was a spectrum of colors wafting from Elian like a stink. "Got the slip from Solanine, did you? Impressive."

"Bastards like you aren't that hard to hide from. All it takes is finding a shower stall."

"Still with the snap tongue, hmm?"

"Glad I don't disappoint."

"O girl, but you haven't. We were looking for you." He gave a slight tilt of his head toward Red Tulio. "Had to make a few stops along the way. A few ends to make dead."

The muscular orcir smiled, his lips red around his protruding lower canines. A memory of why surged forth from the depths from whence Ashe had buried it. Blood upon the redhead's shirt collar, freckled, green-skinned face flushed, smashed nose flaring. His hands, too, were stained red. There was no mistaking Red Tulio's aura, even with her jumbly head messing about. It was a dangerous crimson. Memories of hanged members of Slag's End, bodies desecrated. Blood all about *The Colosseum*.

"You bastard," she hissed. "You did kill them!" Red Tulio shrugged matter-of-factly. But how? When? He hadn't been covered in blood when she saw him the day's turn prior, when she attacked him, and he had buffeted her Shard Form like she was a gnat. Maybe after she fled? *He liked to bathe in the blood of his victims*, she recalled. Godsdamn him. "Why?"

Elian's face showed no emotion but this time he began to glow a shaded pine, a greedy green. Around his fat neck hung a black crystal pendant with a reddish rune engraved upon it. Ashe had seen that pendant before. She glanced toward Red Tulio and saw he wore the same one. As did Quick Fingers.

"They grew weak," Elian said. "Fat and useless. Even Olaf. The war that is coming is not going to be kind to the Mistlands. It will not suffer the weak. Ness is gone, so are all his grunts. Bar Stock has been wiped clean. The time of Drenth's gangs is at an end. Only those who side with the Fallen will survive. I tried to warn them but not many listened, even though they claimed allegiance to me."

"I'm going to wipe that smile from your face!" She struggled against her bonds. That tremor of rage bubbled under the surface. The inked runes along her arm started to itch. Only a fingernail's worth of mist cowered beside her, not enough to bring her aether to life. Her magic just out of reach.

"My, but you have fire," Elian said. "It's no wonder the Fallen wants you. But I've had eyes on you for a long time."

Many know only Church sprat have tattoos like yours.' Ashe wanted to scream. But she wanted blood more. His blood.

"I told you, girl, many know what your runes mean. Would hurt my investments if you were free to roam at your whim. Wasn't hard to fathom what would finally break you down. Drink was too easy, too simple for you. All it took to corner you was a bit of tits and leg. Good thing that I had the foresight to keep you cowed. Add more quadrans to my stable once the Fallen gets you."

"Wren was a scourge. Did you know that as well? Sent to spy on you for your beloved Solanine."

"Was?"

"I killed her."

Elian's lips curled upward. "My, my, girl, aren't you the perfect lover. Such a shame. Wren was useful, at least. More than my brother, that is. Wherever he might be hiding."

"Bugger a centaur's prick." Elian didn't know Evander had joined Solanine, what did that mean? Or that he was on Gargantua at the same time? Were the brothers going separate ways? Maybe she could use this information to her advantage.

"Shortsighted you are," Elian said, ignoring her comment, for people like him, centaur sex wasn't as frowned upon as it was up in

Kanja where it was considered most taboo. Which meant she needed to get more personal. "To answer your query, yes, I knew that harlot was a spy for Solanine. Wasn't hard to pick out that girl for a scourge the moment she first walked into my tavern showing off her goods to anyone willing to look. I've been at this game a long time, girl. Solanine chose the wrong gang leader to try and swindle. And the wench'll pay for it."

Time to take her chance. "Bet you didn't know Evander's in Solanine's pink pocket then, eh?"

Elian's normally flushed face went pallid, a glimmer of anger simmering below that scraggly beard of his in fiery maroon. "What my brother does is of his own devices. If he wants to sell his soul to that wench, then so be."

"Maybe he just prefers Solanine's privy over your asshole." O, now she'd done it, she realized right away her folly.

A meaty hand slapped the chair's arm audibly loud. Elian surged forward as best his bulk could. He reached for her face, grabbing her cheeks between sausage-thick fingers. "Careful, girl. You may be key to my rise, but that doesn't mean I have to play gentle with you before I take you to them." He released her face, but his nails had dug deep as her face stung.

Ashe tested the ropes as she tried to get comfortable, tied tight they were. And yet, she let her tongue continue its assault, falling back into older insults. "You got me now. What's next? A treatise on philosophy? Maybe a race around the track. Though with this busted knee, I fathom you'd win. Even with that bovine gut of yours. Wait, I know, how about a spelling contest?"

"I'd be more wary with that tongue of yours," Elian chuckled, the previous anger fully subsided. She must have struck a nerve over

Evander, which might come in handy again. "The Fallen may rip it out."

"I left all my fucks to give with Wren right up until the point she tried to stab me. In the back, I might add. What a cu—"

"Be careful what you wish for, girl," Elian said, cutting her off as he stood, the chair giving a sigh of relief. "Luckily for you, they want you alive. Otherwise, I'd have given you over to the dogs long ago."

"And here I thought you cared for me," she said with a false pout. "Shame you have to turn me over to Solanine. Here I was trying to flee from them…"

Quick Fingers put his knobby hand to his rodent-like ear, listening to something as if he had a radio. Then he leaned toward Elian, whispering something low enough that Ashe couldn't hear. Elian nodded and then waved the shrewkin off. Back to Ashe. "Solanine isn't going to lay those grimy hands on you, girl. In fact, that wench's rule here in Drenth is at an end. No, I'll take you straight to the Fallen myself. And when he's got his hands on you, you'll rue the day you were whelped."

"Don't worry, I already do."

"Suppose being the daughter of the Gutter King'll do that."

"You knew?"

"Actually, just found that out," Elian conceded. "A tad shocked with that knowledge, me. Knew you were special the moment you came into my operation, but never did know you were the daughter of Emre Benld. That was a twist I could've used had I known."

"The only twist you care about are the ones made of dough and coated in cinnamon."

Elian let out a girthy laugh, his jowls and belly jiggling. "You coulda been something in my rank. That tongue does amuse me so."

"What, leaving this reunion so soon? I thought we'd reminisce about all the good things we've done over the last year. You know, like me making you rich. Now you're kicking me to the curb. What am I, Evzen?"

Elian's aura blazed crimson. "My bastard did it to himself. You remind me of him, sometimes. Especially the fact I'd like to slap that mouth of yours clear off your face."

Evzen was Elian's bastard, birthed by a street worker. The boy was maybe fourteen summers old when Ashe had joined Slag's End but had left a few months later. Ashe had no idea why, but she knew Elian was quite angry about it still.

Elian said something to Red Tulio and waddled toward the door. "Do behave, girl, my reputation has high standing still within this city. I am to take over once the Fallen gives me my due. Perhaps even gift me Gargantua for bringing you on a platter." Ashe mumbled under her breath. "What's that?"

"I said, I heard Lu Har likes his pigs all greased up, so you might want to forgo your shower today. Not that you even know what a shower is."

Elian shook his head. "You try too hard sometimes, girl. Not all of them hit like you want. That one needed work."

"So," she said defensively, would have crossed her arms if they weren't tied. "You expect me to talk sweetly to the Fallen then?"

"No, girl, I expect you to die."

"Could you at least allow me a drink? I seem to have lost my flask and, well, you know, I'm sort of tied up."

Elian procured her small golden flask from one of his pockets. "You know, I'm going to keep this and add it to my collection. To remember you by." He shoved the container back into his waistband.

"I'm glad I'm worthy of being remembered."

With that, Ashe was left alone with Red Tulio and Quick Fingers.

"Bloodbath, innit out there?" Red Tulio said from across the room, leaning with arms crossed against the far wall, near the brazier. "Durin' the party. Not just *The Colosseum.*"

Visions of him bathing in the blood of Slag's End ran through her benumbed mind. He had said the same thing, then. "That all you know, eh, blood boy? Just up and cut people because you're told to. There's a special place in the Pit for assholes like you."

"Bitch's got spunk, eh?" The rat-faced Quick Fingers toyed with a serrated dagger, sitting upon the chair Elian had been in. Now lounging as if he was the top toady in Slag's End. Perhaps he might be, considering all the rest were dead. Or soon to be if she had her way. "She even looks like a bitch's privy with that dress of hers."

I bloody said that! Ashe glanced down upon her stola and realized it was torn in more than one place. "More than you know, ratfink."

"Always liked you, little girl. Even when you gave me this." He lifted his hand to show the maimed digit she'd sliced away when he'd gotten too frisky. He radiated dangerous vermillion. "Made me remember to watch out for little bitches like you."

"This bitch wouldn't mind taking that dagger to that little mouse between your legs you call your cock."

"A shame," the shrewkin laughed, "she'd be fun to play with."

Ashe would've put her hands to her neck and gagged if she could, but alas, she couldn't, being tied and all to a bedpost. More importantly, though, Ashe wanted to wipe that smirk from his rat bastard face. She struggled against her bindings, which were now starting to rub her wrists raw. Pentax, she was pissed. Tired and angry, that's what she was. Not the best of combinations if truth be told. Made for some rash decisions.

And she was itching to do something rash.

XLVI
EMRE

THE BUTT OF a wheellock rifle shoved him hard in the back, forcing Emre to his knees. Solanine and Val flanked him.

He was in an enormous room, nearly the breadth of the entire upper level of the large onyx-colored spire that sprouted in the center of Gargantua.

Glass, over six-inches thick, spanned the walls to his right and left, exposing the room to the starry nightturn sky, balconies on both sides. Wrist-thick metal bands cut the glass in a red-colored, six-pointed star. Sofas with tables of lacquered wood under the windows, lined in red velvet. Eiderdown of deep red. The floor was black marble, but rugs of the finest weave layered atop, each woven in intricate rune-like patterns. All red. Rows of books sat on silver-stoned racks. A giant orb of obsidian hung from the ceiling, a single aethecite power supply fired elegant light.

Under the chandelier was a throne made of ebony crystal. Sharp, jagged facets hewn in natural patterns, asymmetrical and deathly beautiful. Wrapped around the base of the throne was a serpentine tail of crimson, a larger bulk massing behind. A head the size of an auroch lazily breathed in and out from a curved, beak-like snout. Ruby red eyes watched him with a hateful gaze only a daemon could give. The firedrake yawned and a small gout of flame licked about the midnight throne.

Upon the throne was Lu Har.

The Fallen was shirtless, his broad chest corded with muscle, covered in coarse, black hair. Elbows on the rests of the cathedra, fingertips touching in front of his dark beard, all-onyx eyes dancing with the crystal's non-light.

But that's not what struck Emre, no, it was the multitude of tubes sticking out of his flesh.

Thin tubes flowed with a viscous red liquid into his body. Two at each pectoral, from his arms and back like red spider legs. Needles pierced his skin, the tubes wound over the obsidian throne, disappearing into two separate portals built into the ground.

Was this how he was rebirthed fifty years ago?

The corner of the Fallen's lip twitched. "Emre Benld. The Gutter King graces my presence at last."

Emre stood and pulled the kerchief from his pocket, wiping his lips and dry washing his hands before tucking it back in. Straightening his tie and his waistcoat. Checking the time on his pocketwatch. "Lu Har. I'd say it's a pleasure, but I'm not a hypocrite."

"The Benlds have long sought to hide what was not theirs to possess." The handsome elfir's gaze assaulted Emre like a never-ending tsunami upon the cliffs of Dervin. "You hide it so well, that hatred and vengeance of yours. You seek it, it's what drives you. You cannot hide it from me. I am the void. The Divine's guile is mine."

"You've obviously kept me alive for something, Lu Har. Why don't you just get it over with and kill me like you've done to the rest of my family?" For far too long had Emre savored this meeting, the gnawing of vengeance. He ached to scratch the scars that Lu Har had inflicted upon him, but he restrained his hands by gripping his pocketwatch, toying with the chain instead, fondly remembering his father and mother. *For them.*

"What, and delay my ascent into Eminence?" Lu Har's gaze went toward Val standing to Emre's left. "My bikrome, come to me." He held out his hand. Val glided toward the Fallen. Taking his hand, she settled upon his knee like she was his. "See, Emre Benld? We are all tools in Their battle for the heavens." To Val, "How it must hurt him so to have you betray him."

"We are not tools," Emre said softly, trying not to look at the woman he had put his trust in. "Especially those who were made into something they're not."

Laughter. "I see that fool Tevun has been filling your mind with drivel. You humir truly don't understand the gods. You play in Their name, fight for Their honor, kill in Their glory, but you don't know what it takes to truly be a god. Neither did Canlon Carr," he spat the name of the Last Godsking as if it was acid.

"And you do? The Dark God has sullied your soul with promises unfit for the heavens. He Who Fathered the World was right to cast you down. You shame His gifts. Shame His world. Shame His creations." *His creations… more lies…*

"I am the blackness, Emre Benld. The adjudicator for the Divines upon this plane. If only you knew who the true Dark God is. It is He who brought me back. But that truth is not for a mortal like you to know. His prison weakens, His reach grows daily. Shame is but a construct you mortals wrap around yourselves when you are deceived. Lies are but the foundations your temples to the gods are built upon. If you only knew the true wishes of the gods, you'd cry out in terror as the traitors we are."

"I know which Dark God you speak of, Fallen. And I know He will fail, just as he had with the Last Godsking. His prison is strong. And my city will be freed from your tyranny. Just get it over with and kill me now. You won't win, Lu Har. Others will rise up in my stead and continue what I've begun. Drenth will be free."

"You are but insects under my feet. I will make you beg, make you plead, make you cry for my mercy. And then I will finish what I started seventeen years ago. Only this time, it will be your wife who will wield the blade before I take her back into my arms."

"That's only if Cad believes your lies still." He scrubbed the thought of Cad and Lu Har together. Regardless of any truth, it mattered not. *Do not fall, Benld.* "I think we both know that will not remain. Brynn is beyond you and Cad now knows the truth. You think her cowed by the illusion you hold over her? You made her into something she's not, never was. You've created the monster, Lu Har, and now that she knows Brynn can no longer bind her, her wrath will come for you next."

"And see how that turned out in my favor, Benld. The lies gave her the strength to solidify my power while I worked to free Him from His prison. Canlon weakens, soon he will die, and the Divine will be free." He paused, as if thinking. Val hadn't moved a muscle, staring at Emre the entire time. She looked like a lost little child sitting on a predator's knee. "You'd be surprised how well your rebellion has helped my cause. Drenth was mine the moment Canlon Carr threw the Seals from Eminence. Your antics have pushed the city further under my grasp."

"Not after today. You've lost them, lost this city. Your precious Solanine killed so many, your scourges scything through my people. We've a long memory, Lu Har. We don't forget the deaths as easily as you think. It's a bastard, wanting liberty."

"And that's where you're wrong, princeling." Lu Har found a button on the obsidian throne, pushing it.

There was a grinding of gears, pistons pumping, compressed air plumed from the portals in the ground below the obsidian throne. Something moved within. Rising. The firedrake moved its massive head, resettling out of the way, eyes closing to slits.

Cylindrical in nature, it rose, top made of metal, shining like burning aethecite. The tubes connected to Lu Har snaked into the object, a prison almost. Below was glass, thick and hardened. A platinum tinted darkness. Aethecite steam rose within the contraption, shielding Emre's view of what was within. The bottoms lit up in *Aere*-spelled bulbs, each flickered in constant readings. As the steam dissipated, Emre saw two people, elderly and withered, awash in a viscous liquid, almost like the aethecite flowing from the fountain in the center of the party.

Emre crumpled to the floor. It was his parents, the Regents Benld. And they were daemonized.

One to each side of the obsidian throne, the glass prisons came to a stop. On the right, his father Edric. Suspended in the liquid, his now-white hair undulated, long and flowy. Hooked nose that Emre had inherited, chest-long beard the same color of a Kanjan tundra. His mother on the left. Alandy's gentle brown skin parched and dried with age. Both wrinkled, skin pulled taut. Both with claws and spikes sprouting where hands and bones were meant to be. Both with banded scars wrapping their necks where their severed heads had been reattached. Both with horns protruding from the center of their skulls where the pikes had pierced them when their heads had been brandished to the people of Drenth. Both with ruby eyes filled with unmistakable hate. Both with tubes piercing their scaly flesh, attached to Lu Har, the red blood passing into The Fallen and vice versa.

"By the Pentax," he whispered into his hands.

Tears fell unchecked down his face; the steely resolve having fled. Seventeen years catching up all at once. His insides felt dirty, felt empty, felt barren. All words escaped him. He, gods, how?

"I hear it told you have sound knowledge of my endeavors, Benld. Stray snippets from my bikrome that was designed to allow you to think you'd be able to best me." Val stepped away from Lu Har's knee as he descended from the throne, the tubes connecting him to Emre's parents stretching. Cinder flicked its tail, scratching at its mouth. The Fallen placed a hand upon the tank holding Alandy Benld. Those daemon eyes finding its master. "Could you ever have fathomed something such as this? I doubt you have the capacity to understand. This is how immortals die."

"I've…"

"Daemons are but simple creations of Nocturne," Lu Har said as if explaining to a child, which, truth told, Emre was in this instance. "A simple twist to what the Pentax has given with Their aether. The Four Tenets as you mortals call them. Take these husks that were once your parents. Their bodies given over to the throes of desiccation upon their deaths. To what purpose? Why must our bodies return to the earth when they can become something greater? To fill my army, it gives them a purpose, their flesh."

"Are… are they still alive?" Gods, did he really want to know?

"Portions of their souls remain tied to their bodies. What you see is but a fraction of the torment they suffer in the Pit where the battered and broken are forever ground under the will of Nocturne. Your parents suffer greatly, Benld. As will you."

"You bastard."

"And that's what makes you weak. You try to fight what you cannot withstand. Death comes for everyone. Do you truly think

Zenith cares about you as you pass the veil to the void? No, Zenith cares not." Lu Har lovingly fingered the glass over Alandy Benld. "But it's what's inside that is the crux. You call it Godsblood. Everyone borne able to burn aether contains blood of the gods, but a true Godsblood, is rare. One in every thousand or more back in the time of Eminence. Even rarer now as Nightingale's blood dwindles. Do you know the truth of who Nightingale is, Benld?"

Steel it, Benld. Try not to think of them… "I know all about your Godsblood, Lu Har. I know why you need it. Why you crave the blood in my daughter's veins. I know all about the First Wife."

"Do you now? I imagine not. Did my bikrome ever tell you the reason why a Godsblood is the only force that can destroy the Seals? Because a Godsblood must be of all the gods, not just your holy Pentax, Benld. Of Nocturne as well. Of draconem." He glanced back toward Val. "Dunleith, if you will be so generous?"

"Noctis and Eminence are but two sides of the same Crystal," the bikrome said. She was turning a wheellock in her hands, his pistol. "Life and Death. Just as we are borne of the spark of Life, we all carry the seed of Death. Immortality does not come from the proliferation of Life, but upon the wave of Death. The seeds of both lie within a Godsblood, but not just as their blood, but their connections to each. To Soul Form and Void Form. Of the heavens and the void. Of Zenith and Nocturne in the Pit. And of the First Wife, Nightingale. And Her draconem."

Emre released a choked grunt, his calm slowly returning after the initial shock of his parents being… alive. He grabbed at that steadfastness, harnessing it. "You must be confident that such a thing can be of both."

"O, it does, Benld," Lu Har said. "Your wife was but the first test." Emre stiffened. "She bonded to the Strix, a creature of the Pit.

The first in centuries who could hold the power of the Pit, the grace of Noctis. Of Nightingale Herself. Cadrianna has served me in more ways than one. And into your daughter, the nectar of all the gods resides. Eminence from your line. Noctis from Cadrianna's via Nightingale." Emre was rattled. "Let the truth wash over you, Benld. It'll be the last truth you ever learn. Except the turmoil of everlasting pain in the Pit." Lu Har smiled. "Cadrianna would have been my general, commanding my army of daemons with the Strix at her side. But, alas, she's fulfilled my needs and brought me your daughter. Both you and her will turn the Godsblood to my side. With your deaths, she will become mine."

"Zenith…"

"You'd be a fool to put your trust in Him," Lu Har cut him off. "He who cast His own Brother into the depths of the Pit over his love for the First Wife, before casting her down? If you know the truth about Zenith, is that a benevolent god? I think not." He resumed his seat upon the throne of black glass. The bikrome came forward once more, the engraved wheellock still in her hand. "Go see to my scourge. She grows unstable. We need her to witness her daughter's triumph."

"Yes, Master Lu Har," Val whispered. As the bikrome turned from the throne, her bi-colored gaze fell upon Emre. "Forgive me, Emre. You know what the cost is. What is demanded."

His head fell. "I know the tithe…"

She leaned close to him, the touch of Kanja's coldest winters as she put one hand upon his cheek, the other into his hand. He wanted to tear away but held strong. "And pay it gladly, Emre Benld. That's what you told me. Does that oath still remain?"

Emre grit his teeth. "Until the end."

Valeria Dunleith patted his cheek, her bikromi bracelets vibrated. "The heart must rend to be pieced together again." With that, she left the room, taking Emre's anger with her.

He was calm now. Ready. His hand moved toward the detonator in his waistcoat pocket, another weight reassuring in his hand. *For Brynn.*

"He knew she was the spy," Solanine said. To be true, Emre had almost forgotten the aetheurgist was there. Solanine withdrew a cylindrical metal casing from the dress. "The Dunleith boy had this on his person when the scourges took him. Another bomb meant for our control room."

No, the final nail to bring down Gargantua.

"O, did he now? Amusing game you tried to play, Benld, but very stupid. Tsk tsk tsk. How could you possibly have thought a simple supply of bombs would spell the end of me when I have a bikrome feeding you the *'the words of the Pentax'*? Shame. Blowing the tethers was a stroke of intelligence, I'll give you that. Truly brought the war to my doorstep, but you've done nothing but make my hold on this city stronger. Who have they run to in the wake of destruction you left in your city this week? Hmm? These people are fools. Fools to believe that they deserve the wealth of Eminence. They ate that up, didn't they?"

"From the Guild to the vagrants on the street, they are but stones in a pile," Solanine said. "Steps to be broken and destroyed as we march toward Eminence."

"You'd kill them all?"

"Eminence will be mine. With your daughter gifting me the greatest power known, this forsaken city will be but a ruin. I will purge this city of any not willing to bend the knee. For the Divine will demand nothing less. The rest will become my army. Like your parents. I've already started it. My soldiers firing upon Drenth's citizens, planted to look like your rebels. See, Benld? They are already being conditioned to see you as the enemy." Emre glanced at the daemons who were once his parents, hoping their souls were at peace, not bound within the contorted flesh of a daemon. "Kalderim will fall. Nobody will remain standing who does not submit. A new god will rise next to the Divine. Me."

For the first time since releasing Cadrianna, unburdening her from the lies created by the monster on the obsidian throne, void, maybe even since seeing Brynn as a woman grown, Emre truly smiled.

"You think that's a bomb?"

Emre drew the detonator from his waistcoat as well as his pocketwatch. The time read midnight, the turn of a new day. The same time as the constant reminders to be sent out to the City of Sands for its dwellers to imbibe or inject their parch to shield their radiation poisoning. The messages sent all over the mega-city.

The key to his entire plan.

"That's no bomb, Lu Har. That's a recording device, connected to every aerescreen, every radio, every communication source in the entire city. Streamed all the way to the Dunleiths in Kalderim and the Guild in Alizarin. Everyone now knows the truth. And I'm certain they aren't going to like what they've heard."

Solanine dove for him with aetheurgy forming about mortal hands. Cinder unfurled its drake wings from the throne, a rumble in its throat. Lu Har slammed a fist upon the crystal chair, shattering it into a thousand pieces as his Void Form billowed in flame.

Emre pressed the detonator, blowing a series of bombs planted all around Gargantua, but more importantly, severing the two remaining tethers. With the wheellock pistol gifted to him by Val, Emre burned his aetheurgy and began shooting.

Cadrianna

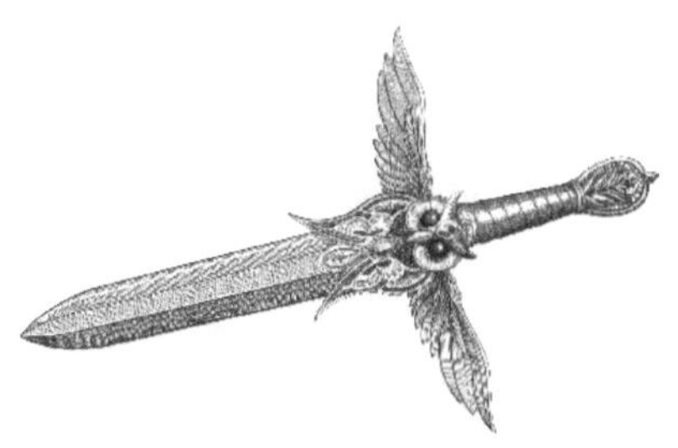

XLVII
CADRIANNA

NO MATTER HOW hard she tried, the shadow chasing Cadrianna drew nearer and nearer.

It reached for her, aiming to drag her down into the void. Perhaps even into Nocturne's Pit. She ran on, trying to stay outside of its reach, the shadow. Finger-like tendrils clamored for her, each dripping with regret.

She checked over her shoulder, saw the shape of the shadow now: a woman. Herself.

Her shadow, built by her innermost daemons, sought her. Driving home the feelings of self-doubt, of anger, of pain, of regret. Of lies. Two larger shadows towered over her own, one in the shape of a man, the other a younger woman. Emre and Brynn. Both shadow-forms absorbed her shade, then began reaching toward her.

Cadrianna stopped, crushing her hands to her head and the shadows swallowed her.

Guilt washed over her. A killer for years, taking lives as if they had meant nothing. All in the name of protecting her daughter from the villain who had taken her beloved husband from her. A deep-rooted anger toward said husband for deeds she had falsely placed upon his shoulders, not truly understanding his tribulations and reasons for doing what he did. For a daughter she sought to save, but in truth, allowed herself to become entangled, ensnared even, by the true evil. Coming to love that evil even though every fiber of her being railed against it. But she knew now that the tolls of her deeds would forever haunt her. What pain her actions had caused. What consequences her life had created.

And it tore her apart.

The shadows of Emre and Brynn wrapped around her tighter, showing her all the kills she had on her bloodstained hands. The first at twenty-two, only two years after her capture, a low-level Guilder in Drenth. Lu Har wanted him out of the way and the man had been nothing to her. So, she did as commanded, hoping the Fallen would acknowledge her potential in her bid to protect her daughter. She had cried herself to sleep that first time, that first kill taking away the innocence of her past.

The second at twenty-three. Third a month later. Four more that summer. Her hands were covered in blood by the time she had turned twenty-five. She no longer cried after that. Even when she had been bonded to the Strix—her tithe her natural-borne womanhood—she still hadn't cried. The daemon blade became her child, the one to replace the stolen.

It was all for Brynn.

By thirty, Cadrianna didn't even know the number of deaths claimed by her hands, but they all paraded through her mind as the shadows of her husband and daughter clamped tighter. She enjoyed killing by the time she turned thirty-five. Every death was a token of her ability. Every life ended became a trophy in her bid to free Brynn. She was hard, callous, and unforgiving. Her soul had been empty, only filled by death.

And she knew nothing else. Except for love. Of Brynn and her hateful desire for Lu Har.

You are a monster.

She jolted awake.

Dark blue fabric filtered out dim light. Steel vertical bars over a crisscross of grating underneath her. A blade of black steel with the outstretched wings of an owl on the ground near her face. Trembling, whole body shaking. Everything around her swayed, a distinct humming sound, as well as a blaring alarm somewhere behind her.

"Hush now," a calming voice said, as pale fingers brushed back her curls. Bracelets jingling silver and gold. Those fingers felt like fresh felled snow, cold and reassuring.

She turned her head to find Valeria Dunleith looking down on her, her head somehow in the bikromi seer's lap.

Cadrianna reached up and took hold of the bikrome's fingers, squeezing them. A bridge between the shadows of her past and the light of her present. She needed that support now more than ever. She closed her eyes again.

"NO TIME, CAD. GET UP."

Strix?

"WHO ELSE? BUT THERE IS NO TIME FOR NAPS."

I can't, she thought as Valeria continued to soothe her. In fact, she didn't want to ever move again.

"GET UP. MOURN FOR YOUR LOST YEARS LATER. BRYNN IS STILL OUT THERE. EMRE NEEDS YOU. THEY BOTH NEED YOU. WAKE UP!"

Awake now, and knowing what pain she'd caused, Cadrianna didn't know how to reconcile who she'd been to who she could be.

The guilt of every kill would follow her like an unwanted guest to the end of her days. She could never forgive herself for being the tool of the Fallen, to be manipulated by the desire to end a life.

The world only saw her as a monster, and did she even deserve to be anything else? Could she ever be the mother to Brynn again?

But maybe her true place was beside her beloved Emre. He seemed to be the only one who saw her for who she was. Even he hid in the shadows, his protection.

'The shadows are your protection.' The training she'd endured. Under Lu Har. Under Solanine. Under Thestile. *'Never forget the truth of who you are,'* Thestile had said right before Cadrianna had killed her.

Could she drop into obscurity and never face the world she'd created?

'Strong as stone.' Another of her epithets bequeathed by her harsh training.

Is that what should be expected of her?

'Trust no one.'

No, she thought. She had to learn to trust again. It was the only way she'd ever be able to make peace with everything she'd done. For Brynn. For Emre. For herself, godsdamnit. It was the only way.

And it had to start now.

"What happened?" she asked, head still rested upon the bikrome's lap, soft skin of Valeria's hand pressed to her cheek, before moving up toward her forehead. Cadrianna gasped as a sudden jolt of pain lanced. She reached up and felt her tender head, for she must have hit it on something hard. "I need to know what happened."

"Ease, Cadrianna Benld," Valeria said softly, helping Cadrianna get to her feet. "Emre blew the remaining anchors."

Cadrianna bolted upright. Emre, the bikrome. Traitor. "You!" she hissed. She reached toward the Strix, but Valeria grabbed her wrist, encasing it in her cold hand.

"I bear you no ill."

"You betrayed Emre."

"It was the only way to get close to Lu Har."

"But… wait, Emre knew this all?"

The bikrome smiled. "You must really learn to trust in your husband, Cadrianna Benld."

"How… but you… Solanine."

"A story for another day. We must go. The anchors are now free. Lu Har is wounded but won't be for long. We must make haste."

Cadrianna recalled the explosions now as she stood on wobbly legs. There was a dent in the rail, some blood upon it. She felt her forehead again and realized the rail was most likely where she'd hit her head.

Glancing around, she noticed she was not far from the prison cells where Emre had been taken.

"STRIKE YOUR SOFT MORTAL HEAD TOO HARD, DEAR CAD?"

Valeria handed Cadrianna the daemon knife—for a second time that night—and took off down the metal gangplank, her dress trailing. Gripping the Strix, Cadrianna followed.

"I LIKE THIS ELFIR," the Strix said. *"EVEN WHEN SHE BEDDED WITH SOLANINE, ALWAYS DID ENJOY THE YOUNGEST DUNLEITH'S COMPANY. NEVER DOUBTED HER FOR A SECOND."*

As they ran, Valeria held nothing back, telling Cadrianna everything. She shouldn't have been so shocked to hear Emre's plan, but somehow, she was. When they had married, Cadrianna had always known he was meant for leadership, but she had sold him short, even after all these years. Emre's plan had been nothing short of brilliant, especially the part of Valeria's double cross. No one could have seen it coming.

The guilt settled in, though. She had failed him. Had failed Brynn. She was the weak link, no other. The severe calm of the bikrome somehow soothed the frenzy building within her, eased her enough to keep the shame at a simmer.

The pair moved through the compound like ghosts. The alarms blared and they heard soldiers, but they saw no one. Valeria seemed to know exactly where to go to avoid running into armed roadblocks. She did hear gunfire every now and then, most of it higher above them, perhaps even outside the compound. Underfoot, she could feel the floating fortress moving, but wasn't certain in what direction. She recalled Lu Har's orders to prepare the troops for an assault on the mines, so perhaps Gargantua was headed southeast.

The bikrome led her into the prison and she saw why.

Finnus Dunleith, Valeria's brother, was waiting for them behind the bars of his cell.

His handsome face devolved into a semi-scowl when he saw her, his features darkening before an impish grin overtook them. "I see you are still on the side of living, sister-friend. Lu Har must have bought into your acting and therefore, the scourge hasn't seen fit to end your life."

Valeria paused before the cell. "Let us not bring to recollection of all the times your mouth nearly caused your own demise, brother-friend. Long before we came to Drenth."

"I deny all of them."

"As is your nature."

Finnus huffed, making a grand gesture of biased indifference. "Very well, I concede that my nature forces me into some, shall we call them, precarious situations. But then again," he winked toward Cadrianna, whether it was meant as jest or in jealousy, she didn't know, "some bedfellows are difficult to resist. I'm a victim of circumstance."

Maybe both, she realized with a start. This man did, indeed, love Emre. Jealousy began to rear up, but then she thought of Brynn. Far more important than sparing with a jilted lover. For whom was she to judge Emre, she had done far worse to her vows with Lu Har, and this elfirish lout knew it.

"I thought you might call it your prick."

The third son of the Golden Throne let out a laugh. "Ah, she does have some wit. I was worried we might have a broken soul on our hands. Emre has always praised your way with words."

"I DON'T KNOW IF WE ARE TALKING ABOUT THE SAME CADRIANNA BENLD," the Strix said. *"I STRUGGLE TO RECALL A SINGLE JOKE IN ALL OUR TIME TOGETHER."*

"Well, sister-friend, you just going to stand there and dally until the Fallen's ants swarm all over us or you going to let me out and we can leave this voidhole?"

"I'm tempted to leave you here. You almost jeopardized the plan with your goading of Solanine," Valeria said calmly. To Cadrianna, "Might be quieter without him."

"Wouldn't want Emre to break his concentration, now would we?" she answered, surprised at how easy it was for her to separate her jealousy of Emre and Finnus' relationship and her own need to redeem herself. "Best we take him along."

"O great and merciful scourge, I thank ye." Finnus bowed at the waist, flicking his long silvery mane as he did. "And I owed that blooddrake one. Five hundred years I've been waiting to get one up on that blasted creature."

"Never said he was bearable," Valeria added as she opened the prison cell with a key she somehow had come by.

Finnus stepped out of the cell, gave his sister a side-armed hug. "What do you mean, everyone loves me!" He gave her a once over. "We need to do something about that drake scale cuirass look, hon. It's not doing anything for you."

Valeria shook her head, muttering under her breath and took off into the underbelly. Finnus smiled at Cadrianna before following as she touched her cuirass.

"IT'S GOING TO BE A LONG DAWNBREAK..."

You're telling me.

Valeria led them deeper into Gargantua, weaving through corridors that none should have known about, especially one who hadn't made the floating fortress their home. It made Cadrianna wary, but she had no other option than to trust the bikrome. Trust was something she was going to have to learn.

Before long, they emerged into a docking bay large enough for a singular transport. An airglider filled most of the bay, a metal portal opposite.

"Get in," Finnus said.

"You know how to fly?" Cadrianna asked as she neared the airglider that hung from a cable.

"No, but she does." Finnus thumbed toward his sister. "I'll open the door; you get it ready to fly. Emre's waiting for us. He's been out there for nearly fifteen minutes now. If they haven't gotten him by now, they'll be close."

Cadrianna opened the airglider's hatch and crawled in as Gargantua shook violently as something akin to an explosion rattled the outer shell. Valeria went to the pilotbox and strapped herself in. "You really know how to fly this thing?"

"There's much more to me than just being bikrome." The daughter of the Golden Throne then clicked on the engine, it roared to life.

Through the glass shield, Cadrianna saw Finnus push a button and a doorway started to roll open along a track. The elfir leapt through the hatch and Valeria released the glider from its cabling. Cadrianna's stomach dropped as the airglider flew through the portal and banked sharply to the portside. Finnus tumbled, which caused Cadrianna to laugh. It was freeing, to be able to laugh like a normal person should. Free of the shadows. Free of the hatred within.

The bikrome flew the airship up the side of Gargantua, other gliders swooping in and out of sight. Lights bloomed from cockpits, searching for something. Buildings moved underneath them, far below in the darkness that was Drenth at this hour of nightturn. Smoke curled out of the fortress from every weapon orifice, from all the opened glider bays. The great floating behemoth listed close to the tops of the highest buildings of Drenth, nearly brushing them.

Gargantua was badly damaged, a shock. Emre's rebels had done the unthinkable, they weakened the Fallen.

"She's heading southeast," Cadrianna commented.

"To the mines," Finnus said. "Where we will head once we find our loverboy. Don't suppose we'll have to share… ah, nevermind. We can negotiate later."

The airglider rose past the flying fortress' immense walls, down through the gardens. Hundreds of soldiers trampled over the ground. The glass of the highest spire atop Gargantua was shattered. Smoke billowed out of the broken windows in fonts. The bright crystalline light spun on its moorings, bathing the room in sparkling blackish beams. Rubble lay everywhere. Cadrianna saw the gaudy throne of obsidian had cracked and was broken. She hated that thing; it reminded her of her sold soul.

Scanning the room, she didn't see Lu Har, nor Solanine. Or Cinder for that matter. No bodies whatsoever. Perhaps they were buried under the debris? "Where's the Fallen?"

"Forget the Fallen, where's Emre?" Finnus leaned out the hatch, and bullets climbed toward their airglider from below, pelting off the hull. "I see no firedrake."

"Keep an eye, Finnus," she said as she surveyed the nightturn sky, looking for any stars hidden by the bulk of the daemon firedrake. But she didn't see anything. *I don't like this, Strix. Where is the Fallen?*

"DEAD I HOPE."

That would be too easy. Besides, we have a dance still to tangle. You, me, and his flesh.

"I see him." Finnus pointed.

A person was climbing through the starburst pattern of metal. A suit, black against the night sky, dusty as if he'd been buried and had clawed his way free.

Valeria swerved the glider closer and Finnus tossed a rope out of the hatch. Emre caught it. There was still no sign of Lu Har nor Solanine. Emre took an extra-long look toward two silver-looking tanks that had shattered during the explosion, but then swung away from the building. Valeria pulled on the steering mechanism, the airglider rising fast to get away.

Cadrianna went to the hatch and helped Finnus pull Emre into the airglider. His face was bruised, nicked by cuts, and awash in grit. He was panting from the exertion of the climb.

But he was smiling as Finnus clapped him on the back.

Cadrianna fell into Emre's embrace.

XLVIII
Ashe

"WHADAYA THINK THAT gold chain will fetch?" Quick Fingers' rodent-shaped aura was a wicked crimson.

Red Tulio craned his neck. "Betcha shit all. Most likely a fraud."

"I saw it up close when she was with the boss back in the *'Sseum.*" The beady-eyed shrewkin was so close she could smell the shit-stink of his wretched breath. "'Peared real to me."

"Zenith's cock, you been eating actual shit these days?" Ashe said as her nostrils tingled.

"Take it from her."

"Sorry to disappoint, boys, the thing doesn't come off."

Red Tulio unfolded his robust arms and popped his knuckles one by one. His aura began to match the shock of red upon his scalp. And his reputation. "Cut it off then."

Quick Fingers smiled that rat-bastardly smile of his. He raised his maimed hand again, the one with the missing pinky. "That would be some circle, eh? Comes around for us all, little girl."

Ashe paled while she tried to think of a solid comeback. "I just got my fir—" The shrewkin thug grabbed Ashe by the neck with his hairy digits, constricting her air. Red Tulio laughed over his underbite.

"It won't hurt," the shrewkin said. "Much. Slice and over with."

Ashe tried to draw upon her aetheurgy, but the low level of mist didn't even budge, just lazily willowed in undefined patterns. If she had any breath to spare, she'd be cursing it something fierce.

Quick Fingers' dagger came closer. Ashe wriggled and tried to break her binds but also the restraint on her neck. Neither broke. Panic settled in instead. She wished she had the mist with her for a change, instead of it dancing about like hapless fae in drunken frolics. Her sight filled with stars. Blackening and going blurry. Again…

A grunt, then a thud like a sack of aerovern skulls being dropped upon the floor. Something happening in the haze behind Quick Fingers. A sickening sound. A muted gasp.

The rodent turned slowly, too slowly in the fading light. Shaded honey in his frightened aura. "Wh—"

Blood whipped across her face. The fuzzy hand released her neck and a figure in shadows neared.

"Brynn Benld?" came the gravelly voice of a drakken. "You hurt… well, much?"

"Who?"

"Humir, you best wake up."

The drakken shook Ashe by the shoulders until her teeth rattled. The stars in her vision rollicked like cavorting whirligigs before finally fading, bringing outlines into focus. Huge but not quite seven feet tall. Long, angled snout, rounded protrusions over a set of purplish eyes, almost horn-like but not. A light blue set of exoscales around a mouth full of sharp, pointy teeth. A woolen vest with no sleeves, muscular limbs ending in curved claws, a longknife with serrated edge dripping Quick Fingers' blood.

"Who are you?"

The drakken severed the bonds tying her to the bedpost. "Someone sent by your father to get you off this garbage heap."

"Wait," Ashe said as she rubbed at her raw wrists. "My father? Emre Benld?"

"Come on." The drakken dragged Ashe to her feet. "We gotta scurry, before Lu Har's the wiser."

"Sonuvabitch!" Ashe screeched as she put weight upon her injured leg.

The drakken's head cocked as it gazed upon Ashe's distress. "Can you walk?"

Bugger it, she'd make it work. She wasn't planning to stick around. She nodded toward the drakken. "Where to?"

"Throw this on." The lesser order of draconem tossed Ashe a cloak. "That thing stands out like an ogre amongst hobgoblins."

"Zenith's cock, I told Ancantha," she grumbled as she slung the cloak about her shoulders, covering the hideously colored stola that everyone and their brother-friends kept drawling about. "Hey, that was a good analogy, by the way. Where's my father?"

"What's an analogy? And I don't know where he is right now. He was taken by a scourge and held prisoner to be brought before Lu Har. Told me to find you and get you out of here. Been searching for you for nigh on two hours now. Whoever trundled you up here aimed to keep you out of sight. Can't stop a drakken, though."

"Care to tell me who you are?"

"Name's Ruane Tevunsdotyr. My father was your family's wardkeeper." Ruane turned away, muttering under her breath, something that sounded like *before he was killed.* "Come, humir, we must go."

"What's a wardkeeper?" Ashe asked as she tied off the cloak, pulling the hood up.

"What's a wardkeeper?" Ruane said with an air of genuine shock. "You don't know what a wardkeeper is?" Ashe shook her head. "By the Arbiter, you humir are ignorant. Gah. I knew something was fishy about this." The drakken grumbled some more, maybe let out a drakken curse, then centered herself. "Only the most important mantle bestowed by Justice Himself. The true guardian of a ward. Your late grandparents were my father's wards, then your father."

The drakken that had rescued her from Cyan and the other vicars had said something about her being a ward. She'd nearly forgotten all about it. Until now. "Your father, I think I met him."

Ruane seemed to grow agitated. "He's dead. Killed by scourges in search of your father."

"I'm sorry. Seems like my father's good for that…"

"Your father is a good humir." Ruane seemed to fight something inside of her. Drakken, unlike everyone else, didn't generate an aura for her to read. But she knew this young draconem was battling inner daemons. What they were, Ashe had no idea. "Enough soppiness, humir girl, let's move."

Stepping over the corpse of Quick Fingers Cyrus, Ashe couldn't stop herself from hocking a pulmo wad of phlegm and tar upon the wiry rodent and his neatly sliced neck. "Bastard. Fingers weren't quick enough for that longknife of yours, eh?"

"What?" The horny protrusions about Ruane's eye sockets bristled in what might be considered confusion.

Ashe pointed at his hand, the one missing the pinky. "His name was Quick Fingers Cyrus. Obviously not quick enough to stop your blade."

Ruane stared at her. "I don't get it."

"It was a joke. You know, Quick Fingers wasn't quick enough with his fingers?"

"That's not funny."

"I thought it was."

"If you say so," Ruane said dryly.

"I heard drakken are so literal, they wouldn't know funny if it slapped them in the face."

"Of course, Justice sends me to watch over a talkative runt with no sense of humor," Ruane groaned. "You humir are odd. Let's go."

Red Tulio was collapsed near the wall. He bore a slash across his thick orcirish neck, and one upon his upper arm, his shirt bathed in sanguine.

Fitting, she thought, almost like bathing in his own blood this time, but she decided Ruane wouldn't get that joke either.

"How in the Pit did you find me?" Ashe limped upon her gimpy leg, trying not to put much weight on it as they left the chamber. "And kill both without being seen. That was quick and precise. Wait, do drakken have aetheurgy? I bet it was aetheurgy. What Form do you use?"

"Drakken don't have aetheurgy, humir," Ruane grunted. They moved cautiously through the empty villa. Ashe tried to keep up, but her knee was becoming troublesome. "Draconem are borne of aether. Don't you know anything?"

"I know things," Ashe replied in self-defense. "Just haven't much interaction with drakken, that's all. Actually, the first drakken I ever met was your father." Ruane pushed through a doorway into another chamber, this one bigger than the first. "Where are we going?"

"There's an airship waiting."

"An airship? Up here?" That got her moving again.

The drakken bounded into the maze of mansion halls, Ashe trying to keep pace. Before long, they barreled into the gondola gateways. Both carriages gone. Ruane led her past the empty trough where the gondola would sit and into a small doorway half-hidden by the gear control box that generated the power to the metal carriage.

The drakken went in first, Ashe closing the door behind her. "Uhhh… where are we going?" she asked again.

Ruane grunted while she crawled. "I've spent the last quarter turn of the day sneaking about in here. All because Emre Benld asked me to. There's been so many pissing automatons and humir soldiers, this is the best way for us to reach the airglider."

Crawling on hands and knees, Ashe could hear the sounds of Gargantua's engines humming. It was dark in the tunnel, and hot. She was sweating, her breath tight in her chest as her pulmo aimed to fight for dominance of her lungs. Ashe exhaled when Ruane pushed open a small hatch and a rush of cool air filled the space. The drakken dropped into a cavern that was filled with engines and other mechanical devices.

Ruane trotted to a set of stairs and waited. "We're almost there. Come, Brynn Benld."

"My name is Ashe," she said unthinking. "How much further?"

"Need me to carry you, humir girl?"

"Bah, go fu… nevermind. Just go. I'm right behind you." Ashe wheezed and coughed the entire way as the pulmo raged inside of her. Her wounded knee throbbed with every agonizing step. She had to stop and collect herself more than once.

The mist appeared from above.

It poured down the stairs, seeking her out. A relief washed through. She'd missed the fog. It was like seeing an old friend you haven't seen in ages. A friend that took you out for the time of your life, but then stabbed you on the way home to steal your coinpurse.

Ruane reached the top of the stairs and there were gasps, grunts, and clashes of steel. Ashe took the remaining stairs and found the drakken battling with a pair of Imperium soldiers, two big brutes laden with muscle and weapons.

"Go!" Ruane sliced across one's hamstring with her longknife, the blade piercing drake scale armor. "I'll catch up." The other grabbed at the drakken and she jabbed at him with a quick thrust of steel.

She limped past the fighting. Beyond was a long walkway of stone arched above the cavern of engines. Gunfire from below exploded all around her, threatening to jostle her from the walk, the waist-high rail wouldn't support her if she went tumbling off the edge.

Ashe entered into a domed observatory; bodies crisscrossing the ground in a bloodbath. The stones were slick with gore, dozens of soulless corpses blocking her path to Ruane's supposed hangar ahead. She glimpsed a strange hulking shape moving through the hangar. It was larger than some of the buildings and wide. A fog of darkened grey swirled around it. A daemon of frightening size, its giant head was staring up at her, pinprick of red in the eyes.

Seeking her, she felt.

"Going somewhere, girl?"

Ashe turned and found Elian and Red Tulio marching up from behind, a pair of blades in Elian's fleshy fists. Somehow, someway, the green-fleshed orcir was still alive. The anger came and the mist darkened with the need for spilling this murderer's innards. A pressure she hadn't felt since the moments after killing that servant the got her into this mess in the first place.

"I see you've done a pretty job escaping, once again," the fleshy Elian said. "Red Tulio says you twisted Quick Fingers right up. A loss for me, no doubt."

"Guess I'm just going to have to kill my way off this godsdamned fortress," Ashe breathed, "and I'm taking a strong liking to gutting street rats like you."

"Foolish girl. Get her."

Ashe drew the mist around her, cloaking her body in an angry haze of black. Anger rolled off her tongue as she screamed. Aether scathed across the observatory in her fury. The bodies of the dead turned to dust from the *Ignis* burning within her aetheric call, blood pouring down her chin, fire in her throat. The walls of the observatory shook fiercely, cracked mortar fell. The mist surged and struck the hefty gangleader and his muscled orcirish brute.

She had expected them to be torn asunder limb from limb, yet there they stood. Unharmed. Unaffected.

"Impressive. But your aetheurgy won't do slag on me, girl. I've been given pardon by Solanine and the Fallen." He lifted a golden chain with a black pendant from around his pudgy scruff. His aura a putrid moss of greed. "Protected, I am. And those around me." Which explained why Red Tulio hadn't been affected either. "The Fallen can always use a man like me. I won't kill you outright, but the Fallen never said you had to be in one piece."

Elian moved toward her menacingly, albeit wasn't all that menacing since the man was a behemoth of flab. Red Tulio, though, was far more menacing. That gave her pause. But the Pentax had other designs as the drakken speared the barbarous orcir. The pair went tumbling, perhaps an even fight.

"Just you and me, girl."

"Even better."

She attacked.

Elian brought up one of his blades, blocking her flimsy dagger stolen from Quick Fingers' dead fingers. The obese man was surprisingly spry on his feet, bringing his second blade in for a quick end with a slash toward her hamstring. Luckily, she was able to squirm away mere moments before she was crippled. But her victory was exceptionally short lived as Elian's boot came down upon her balky knee and she shrieked.

Ashe backed away, holding her leg. Elian's scraggly beard was parted in a vile grin. "I thought you'd be better, girl."

A flicker of gold caught her eye from under the mountain of Elian's flesh at his waistband that was still remarkably holding strong. Filigree. It was her flask. "I'm just warming up, you smarmy bastard."

"Daddy isn't here to save you now. The Fallen is going to raze this city to the studs. The Gutter King will lose everything."

"Spare me the villainous monologue. Why don't you ask Evander what he's been up to? The Fallen chose the better brother."

The man's aura turned a fiery crimson. "I'm going to enjoy removing that tongue of yours, girl."

Sensing her chance, her runic tattoos radiated as she called upon the power of the Pentax. The world stopped as she pulled upon the veil of the Meadows, the very fabric of the world tearing as wails grew strong from beyond. A similar spell to the one back in Soabin's villa that started this mess. To where an old, crumbling well had been her memorized anchor between both worlds.

In the here and now, she had found her new anchor and pulled.

Ashe shot forward toward Elian, stolen dagger from that cursed shrewkin gripped in white knuckles. She struck him full brunt, dagger driven deep into his fleshy gullet, leaving a gaping hole a foot in diameter as she let go, flying past. The blade went straight through his innards and snapped his spine in twain as she cut the aetheric tether to the flask, flipping over him as she did, sliding, unwounded leg out, hand to the ground, the dagger left in his cold dead corpse.

"Wrong," she said to Elian's dead body.

"Now that's impressive," Ruane said, who had green blood all over her exoscales, clearly from Red Tulio. "Cut the second sector's leader in two. Wish I could've seen that."

Ashe's knee tweaked as she guffawed. "And I'm the one with bad puns? That's horseshit and you know it!"

"I don't get it."

Ashe barked a laugh/grunt as she limped toward Elian's corpse and took her flask from his belt. She thanked Zenith and His cock for making Elian take it from her. Pocketing it, "Let's get off this rock."

The hangar door was open but the outer shell was dented as if something had tried to squeeze through and got stuck. The entire place was a hotbed of activity.

A row of airgliders lined up on a cable opposite the broken door. The first appeared to be missing and the rest looked like a bunch of scrap metal used for target practice. Dozens of Imperium soldiers milled about the hangar, boarding other airgliders and giant trucks of war. Larger airship transports waited while the trucks filed into their backsides. Other transports waited while pilot-driven mechs tromped aboard. Another portal yawned open as yet another row of airgliders began to speed off their cables and into the nightturn sky.

"Hurry," Ruane said.

"To where? All those airships are laden with soldiers. All we have between the two of us is an angry drakken and my undeniable wit. Won't get far with that against a full force of Imperium soldiers."

"There's another," Ruane said confidently, dragging Ashe after, who then proceeded to wallop her knee on a railing, causing her to bleat like a sheep.

Ashe stumbled after the drakken, cursing her knee when she abruptly stopped. Her body went still, unable to go any further. It was similar to what had happened when she tried to flee the party.

"What are you stopping for, humir? There's no time." The drakken tried to yank on her arm but even the mighty strength of a draconem couldn't get Ashe's feet to budge.

"Godsdamnit. It's the godsdamned Seal, isn't it?"

"What's this voidcraft?"

Ashe began a slow turn, gaze canvassing the hangar. Her body stopped as she faced the bullet-ridden line of airgliders, and try as she might, she couldn't continue her circuit as if she was pressed against an invisible wall. Seeing as that was her destination, Ashe began to limp forward, easing behind rows of trucks. As she neared the edge of the truck line, she spied some soldiers lingering not far ahead. Burning a smidgen of aetheurgy, Ashe noticed a gleam on the ground. A glimmer of metal nestled under the overhead railing between a crate and a spare truck tire.

To Ruane, "Wait here."

Pulling the mist around her shoulders, she disappeared. Just a speck of grey as she slithered from behind the trucks toward the metal object. In moments, she was across the empty hangar bay beside the tire and the crate.

At her feet was a disc of braided black steel housing four gemstone circles. A six-pointed star filled the center of the disc, piercing the four shards.

"The Seal of *Terris.*" *What is the Seal doing in this hangar like this?*

"Talk about lucky."

"Hail! Stop there!" yelled a soldier.

"Shit!" she squealed as she realized in her stupidity, she had dropped her mist cloak and was now visible for the entire bay to see, standing like a dunce holding the valuable Seal to Eminence.

Soldiers ran toward her, some opening fire. Ashe panicked and called upon her aetheurgy. The tattoo of two vertical zigzag lines upon her left forearm burst into life and the resulting lightning created from *Aere* exploded from her fingertips. The bolts cleaved into the rushing soldiers, piercing their drake scale armor, charring bodies and the ground alike. The awe and ease in which the magical aether ripped apart what moments before had been men caused Ashe to almost drop the Seal.

Ruane called out to her. Ashe stood stunned.

It was then that a monstrosity stepped into the hangar. It was enormous, cloaked in shadows and dust, mist circling its massive hind legs. Muscles bulged and claws scraped along the ground as it barreled into what appeared to be an office, but the building merely evaporated under the daemon's swing. Two red eyes squinted through the darkness surrounding it, a wave of jet-black hair swam in the mist as the broken airgliders fell from the cable and rained down around the daemonic beast.

It roared, strangely sounding humir. "GODSBLOOD!"

Ruane yanked her off her feet. "Fucking move it, humir!"

The drakken carried Ashe toward a hatch that was no bigger than Ashe's shoulders, and it led into a smaller hangar. It was only after the hatch was closed that Ruane dropped her on the ground with a shriek. The drakken made toward the waiting airship.

It wasn't a big vessel, but it was a stout design, twenty feet from bow to stern, wings maybe half as long. Its sleek hull was curved underneath, joining two concentric circular propellers cast in metal, unlike the wooden hull.

Ruane used a taloned claw to press something, a button on the ground maybe, and a sliver of the mountain peeled away, revealing a gateway large enough for the airship to fit. Then the drakken nimbly climbed up, and the airship lurched as the engine engaged, the propellers fanning to life.

There was a heavy thud against the hatch, the wall shook with the brunt force of it.

"Time to go!" Ashe threw herself aboard as the airship lifted off the ground.

Just in time, too, as the hatch exploded into the small hangar, a deafening roar from the daemon, a claw punching through the stone, the mist raced through like a dam breaking. The beast lumbered into the hangar, hair swirling like the mist had before. It reached out with a massive claw toward the teetering airship.

"GODSBLOOD!"

Gargantua's belly rumbled by the daemon's bellow. Cracks formed along the stone walls of the floating fortress, huge chunks crashed all around them. Aetheurgy came to life. *Terris* shook. *Aere* wrapped around the stern of the airship.

"Do something!" she snarled at Ruane.

The airship zoomed forward, clear of the portal, clear of the daemon's claw, heading upward toward the sky. Bullets struck the hull, struck the propellers, causing the airship to dip. But then it steadied. Ashe pulled herself upright and saw the daemon bellowing within the belly of Gargantua.

She wiped her eyes as the city of Drenth below disappeared into the Sea of Mist surrounding the desert.

It hung in the sky like a layer of froth atop a freshly poured tankard of ale. It was dense, but not so thick the light of Nocturne's moon couldn't pierce the grey. The mist was all Ashe could see as Ruane struggled to keep the airship aloft.

"Shit!" she cursed as the vessel plummeted toward the ground. "Can't you control this thing?"

"I don't know how to fly!" the drakken yelled. The purplish exoscales of the draconem's face was ashen. Which told Ashe she was best off keeping her mouth shut because she had nothing to offer as she had never flown an airship either.

They gained unwanted speed as the airship careened downward, the Sea of Mist purling in tenuous tendrils, creating a vortex around the crashing transport. The propellers turned at different rates, one sputtered while the other thrummed diligently. The bullets had done their damage. The metal engine grated as it churned in its attempt to hold the airship steady. With a futile effort, Ruane seemed to right the airship just as the sand dunes rushed up to meet them.

Ashe braced for impact.

The gritty sand did little to cushion the impact as the bow struck first, flipping the stern completely over. Wooden planks exploded upon collision, fragments flying in every direction. The propellers snapped, whipping into the surrounding mist-covered dunes. The sound of breaking glass filled the air as the wheelhouse shattered. Ashe and Ruane flew into the sands. Black smoke rose from the wreckage and mingled with the soft grey of the mist.

And then there was silence.

XLIX
EMRE

"WELL, WHAT NOW, Emre?" Cadrianna asked.

The ragtag group—consisting of Lojen, Wick, Cadrianna, Finn, Val, and himself—huddled around a table within a squat building near one of the mine's multiple entrances. Wick had turned on the aethecite generators upon their arrival, the piss-yellow light filling the empty structure. It was a mess hall for the miners, but it hadn't seen much use lately, for there were cobwebs galore and a thick layer of dust on the floor.

"We blow the mines," Emre said calmly. He was on the verge of exhaustion, as he teetered too close to the edge, but he couldn't pull back. Not now, not when they were so close.

"Blow the mines?" Cadrianna said, aghast. His wife toyed with the steel dagger the color of ebony. "You can't be serious?"

Lojen shifted upon the bench. The aetheric rounds had gone clean through the meat of Lojen's leg. He readjusted the bandage, wincing as he tied it anew. "I'm all for taking Lu Har down, Emre, but blowing the mines seems foolish at best, erratic at worst."

He sounds just like you, Tevun. "Aethecite is the only reason the Fallen maintains his power in the Imperium. Without it, he is weakened. He touts his strength. That fountain of liquid aethecite is a mockery. All of Drenth is held ransom by it. No, all of the Mistlands. We must take the fight to him. If we do it correctly, once Lu Har is defeated, we can reopen the mines our way. Drenth can reclaim what is theirs by the Pentax." He glanced at his wife, unsaid words passing between them. *Steel it, Benld.* "How is he doing it, Cad? The liquification of aether?"

The former scourge shook her head, her grip on the black blade tightening. "I knew nothing about this."

"Pffft," Finn murmured. There was still tension brewing between Finn and Cadrianna. Their unsaid battle over one man's heart. "Even bedfellows speak of mundane things after… well, you know."

Cadrianna grew rigid and the room edged closer to the precipice of violence. Emre reached over and placed a restraining hand upon his wife's. She instantly cooled. If they survived what was to come, he best come up with a godsdamned good plan so he can navigate these treacherous rapids.

"It doesn't matter," Emre said. "Ultimately, this is a new wrinkle, nothing more." He gave Finn a silencing glare. "The plan was always to bring Gargantua down, freeing Drenth from the Fallen's vice. The tethers are no more; Gargantua is a wounded beast. You saw it listing badly. We've succeeded in getting Lu Har's gaze on us. Val's treachery will sting him, especially sting Solanine. They'll come straight for us. Now we must finish it."

"Whatever you say, love," Finn said. "Until the end." The elfir chuckled softly, his silvery mane falling over his eyes. "Reminds me of the talk you gave Keph right before the meeting with Ness, eh?"

Emre scratched at his forearms. *Don't push it, Finn.* "Well, not exactly. That is why we cannot let the Fallen leave the desert."

As if on cue, an aerescreen on one of the walls flickered on, runic static silencing the group as Lu Har's face appeared, the runes of *Aere* pulsing bloodred. Same as the Fallen's normally perfect visage, as it was now bloodstained, and here was no mistaking the threat in those all-onyx eyes and the venomous smile. Solanine stood in the periphery with shadows of red eyes. Daemons.

"Emre Benld, I should have known this would end at the Temple of Mother Marrow. You've hidden the Godsblood long enough. You've taken the only leverage over a ruthless killer." He was speaking about Cadrianna. *"No amount of aetheurgy can stop the wave of death that is coming at my feet. You'd be wise now to give in before it washes you away."*

"You hold no power over me, Lu Har," Emre said. "You are but scabs that will soon be ripped free. The Pentax has chosen Their next warrior, and there is nothing you can do to stop it."

Solanine let out a chilling laugh from behind the Fallen, the shadowed daemons shifting. *"Your pathetic Godsblood is weak. She will wilt under the Fallen's mere gaze. And you think Zenith chose her, Zenith is a lie."*

"If that is certain, then why has she evaded everything you've thrown at her?" Emre said proudly. "You fear her, fear the power she wields. Aetheurgy of the Soul. You cannot hide from it."

"There is only one path. And that is death."

"I do not fear Death, Fallen. I eagerly await the end, for when it comes, I will go to my rest knowing that you are no more. That Drenth is free. And my daughter will be the architect of Eminence's revival."

"You will not live long enough to see Eminence reopened, Emre Benld. And your wife will reap the betrayal she has wrought."

"You know where to find us, Lu Har."

The aerescreen went black.

A sullen silence fell upon the room. Cadrianna stared at the blackened blade with a scowl. Lojen toyed with Tevun's horns. Wick was chewing on an apple pilfered from the miner's storeroom. The bikrome sat quietly upon the table, legs crossed under her layered dress, hands clasped together almost as if meditating. Finn was pacing back-and-forth.

"How are we supposed to blow the mines?" Lojen asked after a while.

"You've caused enough trouble today, Emre." His wife placed the blackened blade upon the table. "We have probably only a matter of minutes before they get here. There's no way we have enough time to plant more bombs."

"No, you're right, Cad. We don't have that kind of time," Emre admitted. "It's a good thing we planned for that and have already planted the bombs." He grinned. "We just need to arm them."

"I told you to trust Emre, Lojen," Wick said around the large chunk of apple he sawed off with his elongated front teeth. The drakken merely shook his head in amazement. Wick tossed the apple core over his shoulder before reaching into his tunic to pull out a map of the mines. "Here, Em."

"Thanks." Emre eyed his wife. "Cad, you feeling up to prowlin' the dark?"

"But what about Gargantua?" The skeptical woman before him made him smile. Cad had always been a skeptic.

"Lojen's sister made sure we still had some firepower left in the tank." He gave the surprised drakken a wink for he knew Lojen was upset he had kept Ruane's task hidden. Using everyone, that's what he had to do to win. No matter what. "We just need him away from the city before we push that button."

Cadrianna stood, sheathing the black blade, his answer apparently satisfying. "You keep Lu Har busy."

"I'll go with you," Val said. "Finn and I will watch your back."

"I'll do no such thing," Finn argued, pouting. "I go where Emre goes."

"No, Finn," the bikrome said before Emre could speak, "you will come with me. Emre has his own path to tread. We must still get to the Golden Throne. Should we fail here, we cannot let Lu Har raise more daemons. Men we can kill. Daemons will be much harder." Finn appeared ready to say something else, but the bikromi seer shushed him. "This is the Pentax's way, brother-friend. Trust in the Pentax. Trust in Emre."

"Now, Lojen," Emre said, satisfied that Finn wasn't going to fight it, "I want you to come with me. We're going to the Temple of Mother Marrow."

The drakken's snouted face drooped. "Why would we need to go there? I dropped the Seal back on Gargantua."

Emre placed a hand upon his bicep, warm humir flesh upon cold draconem scales. "The Seal was never meant for you, Lojen. The Pentax has seen fit to ensure you dropped it in your flight. That means you weren't meant to bring it here. Who are we to argue Their actions? Now, it's time for you to accept the power of Tevun. And, ultimately, of Justice."

Still, the drakken didn't look too pleased, but he sighed. "Okay, Emre. I go where my ward demands."

Emre glanced at the lapin. "Wick, get the truck started. Lojen, go with him." The pair nodded and left the mess hall. To Val, "There might be something around here more comfortable than that dress."

The bikrome gave a slight smile. "Wouldn't want to ruin it any further, eh? You know how my brother-friend feels about fashion."

She lifted the many pleats and slid off the table. "Cadrianna, if you please, you seem to understand the concept of comfort."

His wife had a perplexed look upon her face, then a grin split it. "I do, don't I, Strix?" She didn't seem to realize the name she spoke. It must be the name of the daemon. It saddened Emre to think how long she'd been bonded to a creature of the void like that.

Val, ever taciturn, grabbed Cadrianna's hand, pulling her further into the building, but not before giving a slight nod to him.

Gods, I hope you're right about this, Val…

In truth, Emre needed to collect himself for what was about to unfold and Val was helping him along. For what his entire second life had brought him back for. For what his rebirth's flames were to wreak.

Emre felt a pair of lean arms wrap around him. "I forgive you, you know," Finn said softly into his ear, followed by a gentle kiss on the back of his neck.

He grabbed Finn's hands and pulled him closer, engulfed fully within the elfir's embrace. With his head resting on Finn's shoulder, he smiled. A gift for his impending sacrifice perhaps. "For what?"

"For whatever you still have planned with my scheming sister and not telling me."

Emre chuckled and intertwined his fingers into Finn's. "O really? I'm glad you've finally come around."

"And I'm sorry, too," Finn said into the curls of Emre's hair, kissing him gently, "for getting in between you two."

Spinning, Emre's hands went to Finn's face, while the elfir never let go. "Never think that. Never." A wetness threatened the corners of his eyes. *Steel it, Benld. Not yet. Not now. Stay the course.* "What we had, Cadrianna and I, that will never go away. I love her, Finn. And I love you. Both of you share my heart, both know a different Emre. Two halves to two people."

"You should be with her." There was sorrow building at the edges of Finn's voice, a misery that Emre had tried to shield, what Val had kept from him, her own brother. The path that Finnus Dunleith needed to walk. Gods, how unfair it seemed, this burden the carefree, mischievous elfirish princeps was soon to undertake. "Like one happy family. You deserve it, Em."

"No, Finn. You mean too much to me."

"You want to share?" The elfir's lips curled upward. "No, that won't do. I know I'm a catch and all, but I don't know if I can share you."

Gods above, Emre didn't know if he could miss the man more than he knew he would. "It's not in your nature," he said with a laugh, "but who knows what the Pentax will bring with Zenith's dawn."

"We could fight over you. She might be scourge and all, but I'm not helpless."

"You helpless? I would never say such a thing. Frustrating, but never helpless."

The taller Kanjan drew Emre into a kiss, a slow yet passionate kiss. Memories came of their first meeting after Val and Tevun had brought him back to life. To their first foray under his new moniker of the Gutter King. To Finn's first injury during an attack on a Bar Stock factory, the moment Emre knew losing the elfir would tear him to shreds. To their first kiss, their first nightturn wrapped in each other's arms, a new passion filling him. To the moment Emre knew he loved the big, snarky, irritatingly handsome man.

He savored every memory while he kissed Finn, for it might be the last time he would have the chance. *O Finn, I… I love you.*

Finn pulled back, his eyes finding Emre's, locked, they were, in a place of love. Of kinship. Of family. "You come back to me, hear?"

Emre opened his mouth, but the words died on his lips. He should tell Finn the truth, tell him everything right then and there, and yet, he couldn't bring himself to do so. It felt like betrayal, another on the long list he was compiling.

Instead, he nodded. "This won't be the last you see of me, Finnus Dunleith." *'In Life or Death'* he left unsaid. He would leave that up to Brynn.

"Emre, a moment?"

"Speak of the daemon," Finn said as Cadrianna stood in the doorway. The elfir leaned in and brushed his lips to Emre's, whispering, "A fight it might come down to, love." Then he let go, his familiar scent drawing away as he moved to seek out his sister. Emre locked in his memories the scent, the outline, the sardonic grin. Everything. He wanted to immortalize everything, just in case. To Cadrianna as he passed, "He's all yours… for now."

When elfir was out of sight, Cadrianna edged closer. "He's… something."

Emre smiled. "Yes, yes he is. Dare I say it, though?"

"Say what?"

"You're going to make me say it, aren't you?"

"Lu Har?"

An awkward silence settled between them, a silence that had never been in their past lives, always were they able to converse. Even if only mundane, or like now, meant in jest. But those times had long since passed.

"Cad, I'm sorry. I should never have left you with him. I should have come for you first right after I was brought back. I left you to bear such an onerous burden."

"Yes, you should have." Her hand glided toward the daemon blade sheathed at her hip. Like Val had said, the blade was a comfort to her, almost as if without it, she would wither away. "But what's done is done. We both made mistakes, I know that now. It was all an illusion. A spell to bind me to him. Brynn was, no, *is* the most important thing. Always has been. Between us…"

Gods, she's so strong. Always was. He reached toward her, she went stiff as a plank but didn't move back. Was it hesitance borne of anger, or perhaps of shameful regret? He didn't know, didn't care. They both needed this catharsis. Emre pulled her into his arms, and like he had done with Finn, he devolved into his memories.

Of their first meeting when they were ten, at a party hosted by Cadrianna's parents in Oldport Basin, an arena they owned called *The Arbiter's Axe.* Of the mischief they got into over the many years of friendship before they had expressed their love for one another. Of their marriage, their life as a couple ended so soon. Of the difficult nightturns aching to free her from Lu Har's clutches.

No matter her thoughts, he had failed her on so many levels. And that failure had torn their family apart. He would see it rectified any way he could.

Emre was tired. Everything was catching up to him. It'd worn him down like a dull knife edge. "Gods, Cad, I've missed you."

Her head nestled into his shoulder. She didn't speak, but after a few moments, he could hear her sobbing. He held her tightly, fighting the tears himself. He had to be steel. Finn would be fine, Bliss had shown Val, but Cad? He needed to keep it together for her. Until the end. He owed her at least that.

It seemed like hours but only mere minutes before Cadrianna, O, his beautiful Cadrianna, drew back, her face stained with dried tears. Again, like he did with Finn, he memorized every detail of her face—

not that he hadn't already done so the day Lu Har cut his throat. She was every bit the woman he had loved, every bit the woman she had been forced into.

"Cad…" *Where to even begin?* he thought. Would words even matter at this point after all they've been through?

Her all-onyx eyes searched his. "Tell me she's going to be fine, Emre."

"She's stronger than both of us."

"She is? Did you see her? Did you meet her?"

"I did. And she is everything we ever could have imagined and more."

Cadrianna began to cry again. She fell into his arms. "I tried to save her, Emre. They tortured her, kept her from me. I couldn't even protect her. Lu Har, he… I couldn't get to her. He made me kill to stay his hand."

"That wasn't her, Cad," he soothed, his fingers combing through her hair. "She was far from his grasp."

"And never knew us."

"It was the only way to protect her."

"She was meant to be with us. The three of us. Family. And we failed her."

"If we didn't do what we both did, then she'd be dead. There was no other way to save her. At least now, we've given her the chance to fulfil her destiny. She's going to do it; I just know it."

"I just want to hold my girl."

"You will. Bliss has spoken to Val. The Ideal Daughter says we will have ours back. Soon."

Cadrianna looked at him, searching his open soul. "What aren't you telling me?"

A smirk. "Never could get anything by you, even when we were children."

His wife instantly became the scourge, what once had been raw emotion was now blank emptiness. Her shield sliding back into place. He knew it far too well. "What's going to happen to her, Emre?"

"Nothing she cannot handle. Trust me, Cad. Bliss has seen her future, and it does not end here today."

No, not Brynn's, but other blood will be spilled. To Cadrianna, he said no more, unwilling to put it to words.

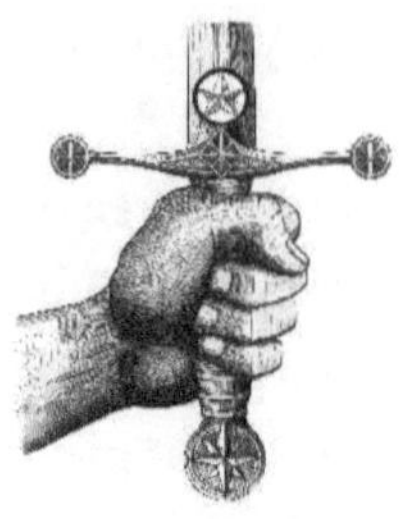

L

CYAN THE DEFIANT

"WHERE IN THE bloody void is the godsdamned latch?" a voice came from outside the darkened room.

The amount of pain lancing Cyan's neck as he lifted his head was nigh on unbearable. "Hello?" His voice was ragged and raw.

But that paled in comparison to how his soul felt. Failure would kill him sooner than the loss of blood. *Amaranth…*

"Uh… hello?" A woman's voice. "Little bint, that you?"

It was dark wherever it was Cyan was held, claustrophobic even. They were in some sort of room, but he didn't know where or how big it was. He didn't know how long he'd been there.

The pain was all he knew.

Harlequin's head lolled back and forth; the young woman was still unconscious. He could barely make out the Bloodless' form in the murk.

There was a series of curses by the unknown woman before the wall parted and an aethecite lamp pierced the obscurity. A womanly figure filled the doorway.

"What in the bloody dark of Nocturne's rearhole happened here?"

Cyan squinted against the sudden influx of light. "Who… are you?" It wasn't Solanine, and relief washed through him.

A larger shadow overtook the woman and Cyan realized it was a very large man. At first, Cyan thought it was the bald man who had been with Solanine, the man who spent a great deal of time torturing him and Harlequin after Amaranth had been turned into a daemon. But it wasn't him as this man was more fleshy, less bulging muscle.

The woman had shaggy brown hair, and she wore a tailored suit. Something flashed in the light as she smiled, and Cyan guessed it was gold. "Your pissing rescuer." She turned toward the big man, "Roland, get your one-eyed backside in here, hear?"

The big man, Roland, squeezed through the door. It wasn't large, by any means, really nothing more than a closet with a basin at the floor. It reminded Cyan of a bathroom with the basin acting as a tub. Like artwork, Cyan and Harlequin were chained to the far wall, their arms bound with inch-thick manacles, their feet hanging limply above the floor. Both were naked, their vicar cassocks tossed in the corner. Their bodies were rent and stained with dried blood. Both were bruised from head to foot.

Cyan glanced at his acolyte in the newfound light, she was hardly breathing, her red curls limp around her face. "Help… us," he forced the words out. "Solanine…"

"Solanine did this?" The woman moved beside the big man and tested the chains. Cyan knew they were inscribed with the same runes that painted the basin floor with their blood. "Roland, can you break these?"

Roland grabbed at one where it met the wall and twisted. Nothing. He then drew a knife and shoved it into a link and tried to snap it but nearly bent his blade instead. "I can't, Neenah."

"Voidspeak," Cyan breathed, his words barely audible, "the runes are voidspeak. Only the Arbiter can break such bonds. The axe…"

"Shoulda brought those godsdamned twins," Neenah said as she set the lamp down on a table, "they know voidspeak."

On the table, next to a number of vials and bottles that contained powders and liquids, lay his Gauntlet and Harlequin's axes, as well as their breathers with their mist canisters.

"Our breathers… aetheurgy… heal us."

The woman, Neenah he supposed, grabbed their breathers and placed them over their heads. Harlequin groaned. A whine of released mist fogged up their breathers as the pair inhaled. Sweet aether filled Cyan's lungs, his breathing came quicker and heartier, the magic of the gods healing him as it burned through his body.

Thank Justice.

Hefting one of the axes, Neenah said, "Alright, stand back."

"Cap'n, they're chained to a wall, where you want them to go?"

"Bugger off, Roland. Don't you talk back to Neenah bloody LeFleur, hear?"

Swinging, the chain shook under the blow of the axe, and it rattled in Neenah's hand. The bluish iron flashed as *Terris* bound within the holy weapon came alive, sparking against the voidspeak runes. Neenah swung again, her tongue askew of her painted lips, this time the aetheric runes wailed and withered, the metal shrieking as if stung. The chain shattered and both vicars slumped to the ground.

Free of his constraints, and the void runes, he started healing via his Shard Form. Cyan crawled over to Harlequin as she came into consciousness. She began to cry, so Cyan cradled the young vicar's head with his mangled hand.

"Many thanks, sister-friend," Cyan said to Neenah as he petted the younger vicar soothingly. "The Scattered Shards will repay you for your service."

"Bugger the Shards," Neenah said, helping Cyan lift Harlequin to her feet. She then handed him the axe. "Your tithe can be paid after you bash out the brains of that bloody Solanine."

Cyan's eyes narrowed at the name. The scream of Amaranth reared in his ears as he thought back to her murder. His body trembled with anger. "How did you find us?"

The shaggy-haired woman tried to calm the frayed mess with her hands. She shook out some dust. "Neenah LeFleur's not going to spoil all her secrets, hear? Just be lucky that we were doing a bloody job up on Gargantua for the Ol' Gutter King. Ol' King made a fool of the Fallen, he sure pissing well did. But, truth told, been looking for a little bint by the name of Ashe. Ol' King's been looking for that pissing sprat. The bloody bikrome sent us to find her."

"Ashe?"

"That's what she went by, Vicar Cyan," Harlequin said. The young woman had stopped her bellyaching and was pulling on her cassock, pulling the sacred robe over her battered body, wincing the entire time. "Lilia. Ashe is her name here." How did she know such a thing?

"Don't know no pissing Lilia, but she's Shards' trained, that's for certain. Been looking for her after Ol' King's bikrome found us in the chaos sprung during the godsdamned party. Got a soft spot for that bint, the girl, not the bikrome. Brought the girl to Drenth myself." The woman appraised him, only for Cyan to realize he was naked. His cheeks grew warm as she smiled a golden-toothed grin that betrayed no lie of her intention. "Looks like she might have been with you, once? Lucky bint. Though, I'd say you're more my age than hers. Savvy?"

"You were the one?" Cyan asked as Harlequin tossed him his tattered cassock. Neenah's well-manicured brow rose as he hastily covered himself. She wasn't hard on the eyes either… no, he shut that thought off. *Justice, rebuke me for my impure thoughts.* "I mean… Lilia came with you to Drenth?"

"Neenah," the big man said, his fat finger pressed into his ear, "we gotta go. Tris says the *Lover*'s been compromised."

"Bloody buggering void," the woman cursed. "Save it, vicar. We can talk about your… payment later." She gave him a throaty chuckle. "But you gotta promise you'll tell everyone in Kalderim that Captain Neenah LeFleur was the one to save you, eh? Got a legend to build."

With that, the lithe woman and the big man exited the bloodstained bath-like room. Cyan and Harlequin shared a glance before following. His winced as he slipped the Gauntlet over his mangled hand. The room beyond was a sleeping chamber, finely decorated, making Cyan wonder if it was Solanine's personal chamber. There were more bloodied runes painted upon the wooden floor. A blackened mist clawed from many of them. They appeared fresh. Cautiously, Roland checked the main entrance, he must have found the empty hall beyond to his liking and took off soundlessly. Neenah jogged after him, leaving the vicars to limp behind.

"Where are we going, Vicar Cyan?"

"I don't know. We must trust in Justice, Harlequin. For He has sent us a guide." He didn't know if he believed such a thing, but the woman mentioned a bikrome. *Couldn't be, could it? She's been the one to mastermind all this, if true…*

The captain and her mate led them into a tunnel that branched off the compound. It was hewn from the dark grey stone of Gargantua, smooth as if aether had created it. And it was eerily quiet. No soldiers, nothing.

"Madam, you mentioned a bikrome, did she have long silver hair and speak in nothing more than a whisper?" The face of the bikrome passed across the canvas of his memory, of when she'd placed the babe in his arms seventeen years ago. Little did he know, that bikrome would turn out to be the daughter of the Rēx and Rēgīna of the Golden Throne.

"Ain't no bloody madam here, vicar," Neenah said. "I'm air-born through and through. Neenah LeFleur's the name, captain of *Marrow's Lover*, and probably the greatest smuggler this side of the Voidlands, hear?"

Cyan smirked. A vain one, this smuggler. But she… "The bikrome, Captain LeFleur?" The pain in his body was lessening, more like a dull throb as the corrupted mist wove through his untainted body, cleansing his ails under the aetheric magic of his gods.

"Aye. Daughter of the bloody Golden Throne, too. Not the first time she's come to Neenah LeFleur about this little bint."

Nor for he. They were all connected, bound to the Godsblood, his surrogate daughter. But why? What roles were they to play in this game? He wouldn't… *No, you did not fail her. Only Amaranth.*

"Cap'n," came a gurgling whisper in the darkness ahead. A hobgoblin bobbled forward.

There was an audible thwack and Cyan realized Neenah must have slapped the voidspawn upside the head. "Hush, Zig, you toad-breathed hogshit. Might be Imperium bugs all around."

"I'm Zag, Cap'n," the voidspawn said while rubbing his gnarled skull.

"I don't bloody care if you're the godsdamned rēx. Shut your flaming mouth. You want to be caught in this dank buggering passage?" Cyan heard the hobgoblin mutter an apology. "You find Stray Cat at all?"

The ugly beast beamed yellowed teeth. "Nots by my eyes, Cap'n. But Zig done heard some guardies talkin' about an escaped girl with a drakken. Crashed they did into the sands."

Cyan's heart leapt into his throat. "She's in the desert?"

Beady eyes took him in. The hobgoblin shrugged. "Mayhaps it was Stray Cat."

Abruptly, the hallway ended with a metal door. The captain opened it and on the other side was a second hobgoblin who looked identical to the first. Twins, perhaps. He cackled upon seeing the captain before demonstrably beckoning them into the hangar beyond.

The hangar was a hundred feet high and half as much deep. Aethecite lights shone down, and Cyan could make out a gear-turned contraption along the far wall, most likely for opening a part of the mountain to launch an airship. Balconies and steel walkways went to and fro, some attached to the walls, others leading to different parts of the hangar or other areas of Gargantua. Boxes of wooden crate were stacked everywhere, some dozens of feet high.

At the far side of the hangar was an airship made of solid metal, and it stretched seventy feet from bow to stern and at least twenty feet wide amidships. The hull had rounded edges that curved upward toward a point at each end. At near rail level and on both port and starboard side was a cylindrical aethecite engine. A wheelhouse poked up over the metal rail toward the bow and at the stern was a high vertical fin connected to a gear for horizontal steering.

"How did you get in here, Captain LeFleur?"

The pretty captain… he scrubbed the thought away…Neenah LeFleur gave him a big grin. "That bikrome is some lady, eh? Always thought the Golden Throne stingy, but not the daughter. She bloody set this up. Ah, there's Tris."

A short dvergir and a giantess were hunched down behind a stack of crates. The voidspawn twins scuttled over toward them, whispering in voidspeak. Neenah and the others bent over and took umbrage behind the crates. The giantess gave the dvergir a sidelong glance after checking Cyan and Harlequin over. The dvergir just grinned.

"What's the word, Tris?"

The dvergir, who was covered in tattoos, popped his meaty knuckles. "Been quiet since you left for the party, but once those tethers got blasted, everything's changed. Soldiers running all over. We scrambled at first sight. Bet they've been launching everything that can fly. Ain't seen the bikrome anywhere, but Imperium rats boarded the *Lover*. Ain't been able to get her started, though. Was going to wait 'til you got back before taking the ship back."

"King's been busy, eh?" Neenah said softly. To the giantess, "Doll, give me the scope." The giantess handed the captain a single-eye scope and she propped it up on one of the crates, peering through the twin stacks. "Alright you shit-shoveling, milkmaids' tits, listen up. Looks like there's two guards standing just opposite the *Lover*. The buggers are facing away, but they are packing a wallop. Wheellocks both. With blades to spare."

Harlequin tried peeking around the crates, but Cyan pulled the willful young woman back.

"What you thinking, Neenah?" Roland asked, his face as calm as a bull ready for the sacrificial knife.

"Here's what I think," Tris said instead of the captain, twirling the long tail of his hair around one finger. "Doll and me will take these two. The twins take the other two under the hull of this here airship. And the vicar wil—"

Neenah sucked her teeth. "Nobody asked your bloody opinion! Doll, you and Tris take these two cock lumps and Zig, Zag, you buggers get 'round the ship and buckle the other two's kneecaps. And call me 'Captain', you pissing oaf!"

Zig nudged Zag with an elbow and grin. Tris rolled his eyes and Doll pinched the bridge of her wide nose. Roland just shook his head. Cyan looked toward Harlequin, but the young vicar was too busy trying to hide her smile.

"Now," Neenah continued, "there might be some Imperium buggers up near the *Lover*. Keep that eye of yours out, you prick," she said to Roland. "If you're thinking of getting dastardly on me now, at all times, bloody think again. I need you to get that portal open so we can get the void out of here."

"And what will you be doing, Cap'n?" Tris questioned. "Sittin' back while we do all the work?"

Neenah snorted. "Someone's got to fly my girl." She fixed the collar of her suit jacket. "Now, we may be skirtin' out of here to save our hides, but I want this clean." She fixed a glare on the twins. "No deaths. A clock to the skull works just as well. You muck it up, I don't need anyone bloody fingering me on this. Got it?"

Both twins looked smug. "Gots it," they said in unison.

"I swear to bloody Nocturne you better put your fingers in your ears…"

"And pull up three times," one said.

"To gets our heads out our asses," the other finished.

"Vicars, you're with me," Neenah said. Cyan stifled a chuckle but nodded.

Something about the airship captain captivated him. She wasn't hard… no, he couldn't go there. Never go there. He was a Shards man through and through. He caught Harlequin staring at him; his glare sent her gaze elsewhere.

Praise the Pentax. Ever since Lilia had gone rogue, he was having a harder and harder time remaining the steadfast taskmaster.

Cyan half-crawled, half-sprinted between stacks of crates after Neenah LeFleur, Harlequin behind. The captain stopped every few steps to listen. A few muffled cries and the soft clanking of cuirass to stone told him at least some of the captain's crew were doing what was expected of them. Holding his breath, he watched Neenah slink down the metal ramp before he and Harlequin trailed.

He looked back the way they'd come and saw two soldiers lying on the ground back near the crates, both knocked senseless—and he hoped, still alive. He spied the dvergir Tris and giantess Doll worming through the stacks, dipping over the rail of the walkway and heading toward them. The twin hobgoblins hurried over toward the ship now, both sporting big dumb grins.

"Soldier up tip top," the dvergir whispered to Neenah, flicking his thumb over his shoulder toward the ladder that was attached to the airship. "Maybe more."

"We got this," Cyan said. Harlequin only nodded; her face hard.

The two strafed around the walkway toward the ladder, climbing up hand over hand. The deck was made of oiled wood, stained a dark brown, sturdy and fitted to perfection. The wheelhouse was made of the same metal as the hull, glass encapsulating it. Inside was a plethora of buttons and levers, some tiny wheels and gauges, then obviously the big steering wheel.

Instinctively, Cyan ducked as a blade raked across his shoulders, shredding through his cassock. He twisted and summoned his aetheric axe in defense as the attacker lunged again with the sharp blade. The blade snaked off his axe's misty haft and Cyan lashed out with his aether-wrought dual crescents, struck the man in the face, a gush of blood behind shattered glass. The soldier fell back, and Cyan rammed his shoulder into the man, who hit the railing with momentum and tumbled over, followed by a sickening crunch.

"How come the vicar gets to kill, Cap'n?" one of the hobgoblins said as the voidspawn below looked up at him, the other was crouched down over the soldier, a ring of crimson beginning to grow larger.

"Do as I say, you tossing whoremonger," Neenah said, smacking the voidspawn in the head. "Get your skinny hairy asses up there on the double!"

"Notta wrong with whores," Cyan heard one say as the pair of voidspawn climbed aboard.

The airship rumbled as it came alive, the cylinders spewing fumes of black and then it began to rise. The portal ahead of the airship began opening. With all of Neenah LeFleur's crew aboard, the captain came over to Cyan, who was at the bowsprit.

"That little bint's strong, hear?"

Cyan hung his head. He had failed her once again. Failed his gods. Failed his oaths. Failed to protect Amaranth. Failure, that's all he was.

But to Neenah LeFleur, he gave her a steely glare. "We have to help her."

"Now that's what I bloody like to hear!"

Marrow's Lover pierced the clouds high above the Sea of Mist, clear evening sky above. They were out in the deep desert.

Cyan had an inkling of where the girl might be. "To the mines, Captain LeFleur, if you please."

LI

CADRIANNA

CADRIANNA ADJUSTED HER bootstraps, saying a long overdue prayer to Zenith.

Protect Emre, Great Father of the World. Not for my sake, but for Brynn's. Brynn…

"SHE IS THE GODSBLOOD, CAD," the Strix said as she tightened the other boot. The daemon blade had been quiet since they'd arrived at the mines. She wondered if it was due to all the aether built up in the area. Or if the usually quippy daemon had decided to give her some time to decompress. *"HER BLOOD RUNS THROUGH YOU. WHAT SHE IS MADE OF IS OF YOU. AND I KNOW NO OTHER STRONGER OF WILL THAN YOU. IF SHE'S HALF OF THAT, THEN WE HAVE NOTHING TO WORRY ABOUT. AND ZENITH IS NOT WHO YOU THINK HE IS."*

If only I could believe such a thing, Strix. But my worry is for Emre. He may have changed, but one thing he always was is a man with a brash streak a league wide.

"I ENJOY IT WHEN A SPADE PRETENDS THEY ARE A RAKE."

Cadrianna let out a soft chuckle, but her mood turned to focus as she finished with her bootstraps. It was time for her to atone for all the wrongs she had done under the guise of her vengeance. Emre, the lapin, and the drakken had already left for the Temple of Mother Marrow, leaving her with the Dunleith siblings to prepare for their assault on the mines. It was almost dawnbreak, almost time.

The bikrome had changed out of the graceful dark blue stola and into a simple pair of mining coveralls scrounged from somewhere in the mess hall.

"You look like shit, sister-friend," Finnus Dunleith announced. He was leaning against the doorway, arms crossed. Although he still wore the stained black servant outfit, he appeared to have found the time to wash his face and tie his silvery hair back into an intricate braid similar to the bangles wrapping Valeria's wrist. "The least you could've done is dab some rouge on or something."

Rolling the sleeves of the coveralls above her elbows, Valeria slid knuckle punchers on before adjusting the mining pouches affixed to her belt. They were filled with dynamite. "Dearest brother-friend, your droll attempts at glamour advice fall on deaf ears as we all know you received the short end of the beauty stick in our family."

Cadrianna grinned as Finnus gave a shocked gasp. "Well, if that's how you want our potentially final conversation to go, then I must regretfully tell you that your morning breath reeks of a kobold's loincloth."

"Ouch," Valeria said sarcastically. "Haven't heard that one since we were toddlers. Nothing new in that brain of yours? Probably not. Not everyone is capable of maturing and forgetting past affronts. It's hardly a wonder why Father still thinks of you as a child, Finn, because you act as if you need your ears boxed more often than not." To Cadrianna, "Shall we?"

A nod. The bikrome picked up a handheld aethecite lantern and pickaxe. Between the three of them, they had: a twelve-inch folded steel daemon blade with a knack for stating the obvious, a pair of knuckle punchers, some dynamite used by the miners to create new shafts, and a couple of pickaxes. Weren't exactly the seeds to bear the fruit of war, but at least each of them had aetheurgy to fall back on in a pinch.

Cadrianna followed the Dunleiths from the mess hall. The wind had picked up and it brushed her face with a soft spray of sand. For some reason a memory from deep within her stirred.

She was standing on a balcony, one in the Regent's Tower in Drenth. A man stood beside her at the railing, both watching the falling sun. A loving hand upon her shoulder. Emre's hand. Beloved husband. A gust of wind brought a thin layer of sand coursing through the city, and it had landed upon her young face, her newlywed face. Happy together, both. The world ripe with possibility dawning before them, they need only walk toward it. Together.

It hadn't been that way in their final interaction, Emre's and hers.

O, the love still existed between them, but they both knew they had moved on. That they weren't the same lovestruck younglings of those days upon the Tower. She could see the pain written all over his face, the same as she undoubtedly had upon hers. The world had ripped them apart, torn asunder their happily ever after, and destroyed their potential fairy tale of a life. They both understood it without having to say it.

That life was gone. Only one singular thing meant anything to either of them anymore. Both had their own reasons, but both agreed.

Brynn.

Their parting might be forever this time, and both understood the cost. And even though there would be more bloodshed and grief, Cadrianna felt joyous again. Free from the shackles that had bound her, the same ones which had buried those joyous moments of her life, those fractions of her building blocks blacked out when she threw herself into her vengeance.

She was free of it all.

It was as Thestile had said before she had killed her, *'Never forget the truth of who you are.'* This was her true self, finally free.

Free to do what she was meant to do. Give Brynn a life she deserved.

"Cadrianna?"

She shook the memory away as the bikrome had stopped, waiting for her to catch up. The night sky was finally starting to brighten, if only cautiously. It wasn't pitch, but closer to a velvety brunet. The stars were drifting out, but the crescent moon still glowed luminously over the Sea of Mist. Their path was lighted by the aethecite gleam of standing posts over the complex. Emre had ordered the entire place lit up.

"What's that?" Finnus asked, pointing toward the northwest.

Cadrianna squinted. At first, she didn't see anything, but then she burned her Void Form. Her eyesight enhanced under the aetheric spell, and Cadrianna focused on a cluster of stars, realizing they hadn't been swallowed but instead had disappeared completely. A haze seemed to drown out the pinpricks.

She knew what it was.

"They're here," Valeria said, her bi-colored eyes shimmering in her Vision Form.

"Good," Cadrianna snarled, her hand upon the Strix.

They raced from the complex to the mine shaft that would lead them deep into the sand dune where the bombs had been hidden. From there, they would set the charges and flee to the Temple. A chain-link fence squealed as the bikrome shoved open its gate. Valeria clicked on the lantern and sought out the powerbox. When she did, orbs lit up along the mine shaft's roof, brightening the tunnel.

"REMINDS ME OF WHEN WE HUNTED DOWN THAT TRIO OF CAVE TROLLS FOR THESTILE. REMEMBER THAT ONE?"

The inside of the mine shaft was enormous, about thirty-feet high. The mega-city of Drenth might be drenched in *Aere*-infused neon, but this mine was more a tomb. An elevator was attached to a set of gears that stood darkly at the far end of the cavern, heavy cable holding a platform. Mining carts filled with aethecite pellets, wooden crates topped with nailed lids stacked up on one another, a drawn map of the underground tunnels showing the open ones. A radio speakerbox was built into the wall next to the map, presumably to communicate with the foremen in the tunnels below using *Aere*.

The Dunleiths were already near the elevator, the bikrome having turned on the power with a sudden hum from the aethecite engines. Cadrianna began a careful examination of the hand-drawn map, finger tracing the carefully drawn lines, trying to decipher which would lead to their end goal. "I thi—" her words cut off as a shadow filled the entranceway behind. A flicker on black scale.

Ratko stepped into the light.

"Go!" she yelled to the siblings before squaring up to the bearded scourge. If he was here, that meant other scourges, potentially even her greatest enemy. After a brief interlude of uncomfortable silence, the turning of gears and the whine of metal on the cable told her that her companions had descended into the mines.

"Hail, sweetling. Got time for a good toss?" The Strix flew into her hand as her aetheurgy burned. Ratko stood opposite, brandishing a pair of blades. "No? Might I just take you after your dead, lass. Care to finally cross blades or were those minor threats to keep my cock quickened until I have you."

"I'm going to enjoy killing you, Ratko."

"CAREFUL, CAD."

Thanks for the vote of confidence, Strix. Daemon blade in hand, Cadrianna burned her aetheurgy and attacked.

One of Ratko's blades parried her first attack, his eyes ablaze with his own aetheurgy as he deflected the swing with ease. Another stab with her knife, but it scraped off the scourge's cuirass effortlessly. The scourge twisted and sliced her with the three-foot blade shearing through the exposed space between her left vambrace and couter, scoring her arm underneath. Cadrianna hissed as she staggered back, touching the new wound, finding blood upon her fingers.

"You thought me weak, didn't you, lass? Too blind on your knees for the Fallen to care of the others around you. You've lost your edge. Your burn is weak compared to mine. For the Divines do not tolerate weakness."

Cadrianna growled, split the daemonic blade in twain, and jumped, the dual Strix blades cut. Both blocked, Ratko's swishing the air. Steel kissing and ringing high-pitched. Both kicked with aetheric-enhanced skill, aiming for vulnerable openings, but neither hit their target as both contorted their bodies in defense. Her blades whizzed, Ratko's twins singing. Clashed forward, muscles straining as they pushed at one another with aetheric strength and speed. Faces no more than half a foot apart, eyes narrowed in the reddened haze of Void Form.

Ratko smiled through his thick beard, droplets of saliva beading the coarse hair. "Give it up, lass. You can't beat me. The Fallen owns you. Be his tool. Be his war machine." His breath nearly killed her on the spot.

"I'm nobody's tool," Cadrianna grunted through the fog of his mouth stench. Though she was strong, Ratko was larger, had a longer reach, and had more mass behind his aetheric thrusts. Cadrianna's boots skidded through the sandy ground. "The Fallen will never win."

"Then you will die, sweetling."

The scourge shoved Cadrianna back, weapons breaking contact. She stabbed with one blade, aiming towards Ratko's unprotected gut, but the scourge had anticipated it. Ratko wasted no time; his second blade rose and sliced her right wrist in the meat below her vambrace. The lancing pain arced up her limb, fingers losing grip on the Strix. It clattered to the ground.

Nursing the gash, Cadrianna swiped her other blade to keep Ratko at bay. The scourge pounced, edges whistling. Folded steel tearing another bloodied hole in Cadrianna's skin, this time up near her shoulder, inches from her neck. Her blood vessels felt flames as she dropped the second Strix blade. A kick to her calf knocked her to her knees, but Cadrianna ducked away from the surefire killing jab aimed for her temple.

But the scourge's attack left him open to a counterattack and Cadrianna took advantage of it.

She punched up, palm first into the drake scaled arm. The exoscales of the firedrake were great at stopping indirect bullets or edged attacks, but it wasn't designed for the counter-pressure of aether, so Ratko's bone snapped just below the elbow. He yowled in pain, the steel falling from his useless grip. Cadrianna burned more aetheurgy, the scars upon her breast and spine were a pyre, she could feel the blood seeping from her runes. She jammed her elbow into the man's face with a sickening crunch, head jerked backward. Blood flowed from the scourge's nose. Boot aimed at Ratko's knee. Kneecap shattered; the scourge dropped. Cradling the broken arm to his body, the scourge scooted away.

"I enjoyed that, lass," Ratko coughed blood into his beard, his back resting against a stack of crates. "Finish what you've started if you've the stomach for it."

"O you think I lack the stomach, Ratko? I've only ever spilt blood for my daughter's sake, but this one is for mine. Strix."

"WITH PLEASURE."

The blackened blades surged from the ground, forming into one as it struck the scourge in the forehead, puncturing clear through the man's skull, his brains blasting out upon the crates, the outstretched wings of the owl shivering as if in flight.

A whine of the cable and gears told Cadrianna that the Dunleiths were coming back up, which meant the bikrome had set the charges. The elevator stopped and the pale elfirish siblings jumped out.

"Done," Finnus said with gusto. "All set. It'll go boom real nice. Just like Emre wanted." He eyed the dead scourge. "Godsdamn, woman, he say something personal or is that how all you scourges work?"

She called the Strix back. The blade floated into her hand, dripping with the viscera formerly of Ratko's brain. "This isn't over, Dunleith. Save your quips for then."

Finnus glanced at his sister. "I wonder what Em ever saw in such a sad sack?"

"Careful what you say, brother-friend, your blood isn't off limits."

Cadrianna neared the entrance to the mine but had to quickly jump back as bullets ripped into the sand in front of her. Thud-thud-thud. Trapped in the mouth of the mineshaft, *Ignis* gunfire suppressed their exit, yellow light of the aethecite posts shading the surrounding area in shadows. The Sea of Mist had become darker, almost pitch, making it difficult to see anything more than a few steps ahead.

"We don't have time for this," she growled.

"There!" Finnus pointed to where a line of Predator drones stood ready within the Sea, at least five of them.

The grind of rotating guns flashed and lit up the mist as thunderous piercing rounds battered the mineshaft entrance, raining sand and support struts down around them.

"What do we do?"

For the first time, Cadrianna could almost sense a feeling of unease within. She was all out of ideas. They didn't have any firepower to counter Predators, even their aetheurgies wouldn't be able to stand up to them, they'd be torn to pieces the moment they walked into the line of fire. There was no way to sneak out and they didn't have the time to search the mines for another exit.

They were trapped.

"I've an idea." Valeria withdrew a bottle from her coveralls. It was clear, the length of her forearm, and inside was a crystalline liquid.

"Is that?"

"Yes," Valeria said as more gunfire exploded above them, causing the bikromi seer to reflexively duck. "Liquid aethecite. If we can blow the mines with it, should be useful to save my brother-friend's useless backside."

Finnus screeched as a torrent of gunfire tore into the shaft's wall behind them. Large chunks of the sandstone disintegrated. It wouldn't hold much longer. "What?" he said as both women looked at him. "That was too godsdamned close."

"Like I said."

An idea suddenly formed in Cadrianna's mind. She hastily cut a strip from her torn undershirt that was peeking out from under her drake scale and uncorked the small bottle's lid, jamming the linen inside. "Give me the lantern." As Valeria forked it over, Cadrianna pulled open the lid housing the bulb. She wrapped the remaining strand of her undershirt around the heated *Aere* bulb. "Just get ready to run. Valeria, you're on truck duty."

Falling sand, like that of an earthen blizzard, funneled down from the entrance as round-after-round of aethecite bullets thudded into the stone and metal.

She was only going to have one chance.

When there was a brief interlude in the gunfire, Cadrianna pulled the mist around her like a black-red cloak full of wailing souls, disappearing as she did a forward roll out into the open, arm flinging the glowing lantern toward the line of drones. The lantern sailed through the mist, crashing upon one of the Predators. Glass and metal shattered upon the drone's chassis, bottle breaking apart, liquid aether sluicing over the beast.

The fuel exploded in a giant ball of flames, a colossal whoosh.

Cadrianna dropped her wailing shroud of mist and darted away, the bikrome and her useless brother hot on her heels. The Predator became a metal flame husk, staggering into its companions, the liquid aethecite burning brightly, squealing of metal mixed in with the spray of bullets. The bikrome sprinted toward one of the mining trucks, throwing open the driver's door and the engine roared to life. Cadrianna and Finnus dove into the back.

"NOT BAD, CAD. RATKO'S SOUL TASTED LIKE ROTTEN MEAT IF I'M BEING HONEST."

And then the truck was fleeing the mine as the Predators fired on, metal chassis smoking and smoldering.

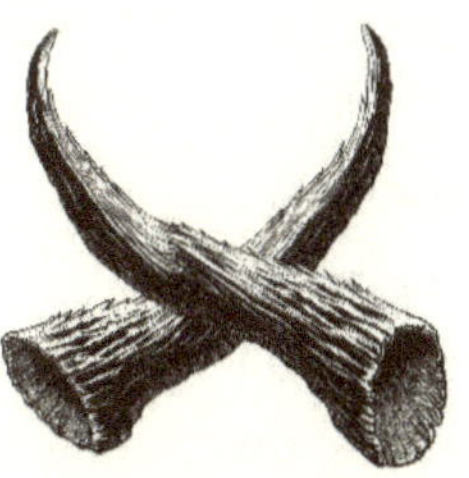

LII
LOJEN

MUTED PRE-DAWNBREAK SKY faded as the Temple of Mother Marrow materialized like a mirage.

The Temple, located about twenty minutes from the mines, was within a sandstone canyon of mountainous dunes. It seemed out of place. As they drove down the winding trail about the cliffs of the canyon, Lojen observed the Temple with a mixture of awe and reverence.

Dusky in tone, columns rose a hundred feet tall, supporting a dome laden with runic carvings. It was dark between the columns, but he noticed sandy billows moving amongst the stone, indicating an open porch, perhaps even an open cella beyond. Truncated, thicker columns lined a dusty path toward the Temple's stairs, each topped with a life-sized statue of the races birthed by the Forgemistress of Creation's sacred anvil. Humir, elfir, draconem, lapin, goblin, ogre, and all the rest.

But what caught Lojen by surprise was how immaculate the entire place was.

There was sand blowing through the canyon, but the stone corners, the fluting, the statues appeared flawless, like the day they'd been carved. Magic was clearly involved in this place of holy wonder, otherwise the stone would've long since been worn down by the constant barrage of sandstorms. Void, even the Sea of Mist stayed clear of the canyon, wending around as if the entire place was too sacred even for the aetheric poison.

Wick turned off the ignition, the mining truck going still as the lapin pulled up toward a column bearing a statue of a hobgoblin. Emre and Lojen hopped out, though he was still favoring his wounded leg.

"See if you can find a spot to wait, Wick," Emre said, his gaze never leaving the Temple.

The lapin leaned out the window, his paw resting on the frame. "You sure about this, Em? If Lu Har comes straight here, you'd be trapped. Only one way into this canyon."

He didn't want to admit it, but Lojen wished his new furry friend would stay.

"The Fallen will surely come here. But in case we should fail, I need someone to get word to Cad, Val, and that blockheaded dandy Finn."

"I don't like this," Wick said. "Splitting up, I mean."

"I don't either, my friend. But Lojen needs to commune with the Pentax. The Mother is the only means. We need to give Brynn a chance. Without Lojen gaining Justice's grace, she has none."

Brynn Benld! That's it. Emre and Cadrianna's child, a girl named Brynn. Was that where Ru was? With the Benld daughter?

"Look after him, Lojen." Lojen nodded and Wick started the engine again, heading back toward the trail leading out of the canyon.

Lojen was sullen and quiet the entirety of the short journey. And now, at the edge of the Temple of Mother Marrow, he was frightened. Frightened to fail his father, to fail the Pentax. To fail his ward. A drakken wardkeeper was the sacred right of his order and only the worthy ever received the honor.

They slowly walked the worn stone trail leading to the grand steps of the Temple, their boots stirring a thin layer of sand as if awakening it from millennia-aged slumber. A low mist roiled along the ground, but it lacked the pungent odor of death, like that of the Sea.

"I'm not sure about this," Lojen concluded as they came to the base of the stairs that would take them to the porch outside the sacred temple's cella, or innermost sanctum. Being so close, Lojen shivered.

"Your father would've pushed you for this. Live up to his name."

"I'll never live up to his name." *How could I ever live up to him? Father? Am I ready?*

"Then live up to yours."

But I can't, he almost said before hearing Ruane's voice call him a '*Scurred Hatch.*'

Envisioning her dubious grin seemed to trigger something within, his step was more assured, his body more erect, his tail low-swishing expectantly as he climbed the stairs. They passed between the massive columns, across the simple flat space before the cella, guarded by two wide columns. He could feel the radiance of aether all about the Temple. It was nearly overwhelming.

"The Arbiter's bloody axe," Lojen whispered in Justice's name.

Built upon a dais in the center of the cella was a statue, all marble. A woman stood near twenty feet tall, clothed only in a flowing linen wrapped about her waist, her bust was not humir, instead corded with muscle and coated by interlocking exoscales like those of a draconem but mottled with flower petals. Biceps bulged with strength, one hand humir, the other claw-like. Carved fur lined one side of the neck, graceful sloping like a feline, the other gnarled like an old oak. But the head—Mother Marrow's head, Lojen amended—bore the markings of more races than he could imagine one able to sculpt without it turning to muck. Eyes rounded like lapin, angled snout of draconem, humir mouth, elfirish and goblin ears, a dvergirish brow, orcirish underbite. And so much more. Whiskers and scales. Spikes and long hair. Curved horns atop Her head.

It was both eerie and magnificent at the same time. *How?*

"Now is the time for you to become who you were meant to be. For your father. For your sister. For Zenith and Mother Marrow. The Children: Justice, Brio, and Bliss."

I'm not ready, he wanted to say, but as he gazed upon the face of the Forgemistress of Creation, Lojen felt his legs inching closer toward the statue, compelled. Emre stayed behind, for this was Lojen's path and his alone. He went to his knees, mere inches from the dais, never taking his eyes from the carved marble. Lojen pulled his father's horns—identical to the ones on Mother Marrow's head he realized—from his vest pocket. Like two curved spikes, he held them aloft, arms outstretched.

Warmth washed over him, like the heat of a fire nearby. It settled across his shoulders, his body, his soul like a blanket cocooning him. He closed his eyes, taking it all in. Calm, collected, unafraid.

Aether.

A siren song, soft and gentle at first, swirled around him as if coming from everywhere and nowhere, coming to a point at the horns in his claws. It flitted through the air and channeled into the sacred horns as if it pierced the abyss between time and space. Soothing, powerful, fulfilling. Lyrical resonance grew within the song, words forming, spinning around his soul, into his heart.

It was the Hymn of Justice.

"LOJEN, SON OF TEVUN. BLOOD OF SIRELAR, DESCENDANT OF DELIOS. WARDKEEPER HEIR." The heavenly voice of Mother Marrow spoke to him.

My Goddess. Lojen was scared; worried he would say the wrong thing. Terrified he wouldn't be deemed worthy to succeed his father's place. Fearful he wasn't as strong, as loyal.

"YOU KNEEL BEFORE ME, HONORED AND GLORIFIED AS A CHILD DOES BEFORE THEIR MOTHER. YOU BESEECH MY GRACE AND THAT OF MY CHILDREN?"

He summoned every morsel of courage within his breast. *I only wish to honor You, my Goddess. My loyalty shall only be to You, He Who Fathered the World, and my ward. To Your children. To Justice.*

"YOUR HEART IS KNOWN TO US, LOJEN TEVUNSON. THERE IS NOTHING BUT GOODNESS AND HONOR WITHIN YOU. YOUR FATHER TRAINED YOU WELL. WORRY NOT ABOUT YOUR OWN FAILINGS, EVERY SOUL FALTERS, EVEN A GOD LIKE HE WHO FATHERED THE WORLD. IT IS ABOUT HOW YOU COME TO STAND AFTERWARD. SOME COWER, OTHERS REMAIN CAGED. BUT THOSE WHO STAND FREE, THEY ARE THE TRUEST WARRIORS."

He'd done his best to listen to every word, every oath, every task his father had ever given to him. Lojen'd spent his entire hatchhood trying to be worthy for this honor in hopes to impress his father. It's the only thing he'd ever wanted with his life, to be a wardkeeper.

The magical presence of aether filled him with hope.

*"YOUR FATHER SERVED EMINENCE WITH ALL HIS HEART. AS DID HIS FATHER BEFORE HIM, AND SO BACK TO THE FIRST OF OUR WARDKEEPERS AFTER THE SCHISM BETWEEN ZENITH AND NOCTURNE AND THAT OF THE BIRTH OF THE PENTAX. YOU WILL

DIGNIFY OUR PRESENCE IN LIFE BY ACCEPTING OUR OFFER TO BECOME A WARDKEEPER IN OUR STEAD."

Lojen shuddered, not in fear, but in sheer joy. *My Goddess, it would be the greatest thing I could ever ask for. I will not fail You. Any of You.*

"WE KNOW YOU SHALL NOT FAIL, OUR WARDKEEPER. TAKE OUR GIFT UNTO YOU. SERVE US WITH RESPECT. LAUD YOUR STRENGTH AND NEVER WAVER IN YOUR DUTY. EMINENCE AWAITS YOU."

His heart filled with furor, pulsing with fire. Claws raised the horns, slowly, lingering doubt still. But then Lojen drew a deep breath and brought the horns to the stumps over his eyes, touching the hardened spikes to the waiting emptiness, locking home.

A brilliant light of crystal clapped like lightning, sending rivulets of pure energy crackling around the entire statue in a diamond sheen. Healing energy birthed from aether rose from beneath his body, filling him with ease. The gunshot wounds in his leg disappeared as spells formed of the Four Tenets of Aether tended him, weariness of the previous days washed away. His scales hardened, even more than normal. They interlocked seamlessly, strengthening.

Whole, he felt.

Fulfilled, he was.

Able, he knew.

He pulled his claws away from the horns and stood. The weight upon his head was the same, but he could feel them, the curves, the length, the power to do right swimming through him. The power of the Pentax and the Crystal of Life.

"NO OTHER WARDKEEPER BEARS RESPONSIBILTY TO EMINENCE AS DOES YOU. EMINENCE IS WEAKENING, WITH IT, THE WORLD WE HAVE SO VALIANTLY FOUGHT OVER REMAINS

BROKEN IN ZENITH'S JEALOUSY. WITHOUT A GODSBLOOD ASCENDING TO EMINENCE, WE WILL ONLY FEAR THE END. A GREAT TASK IS NOW AT YOUR FEET."

Zenith's jealousy? What jealousy? *What task, my Goddess? If it is in my bones and soul, it shall be done.*

"THE SEALS TO EMINENCE MUST BE SHATTERED."

No! They mustn't. We cannot allow the Fallen into the city.

"THIS IS THE ONLY WAY, LOJEN TEVUNSON. THE GODSBLOOD HAS THE POWER TO BECOME GODSLAYER. IT MUST HAPPEN. SHE MUST BEAR MY HAMMER BEFORE SHE CAN WIELD THE AXE, MANTLE, AND CROWN."

I can't. That goes against everything a wardkeeper stands for.

"HEED US. THIS IS THE ONLY WAY. THE SEALS MUST BREAK. AND THE DRACONEM GUARDING MUST ALSO PERISH FOR THEY ARE THE TRUE SEALS."

The draconem? Those are Your favored children, my Goddess. How can I do this?

"YOU MUST CALL THEM FORTH. THE GODSBLOOD MUST SING THE SONG OF WAR. ONLY THEN WILL THEY KNOW THE GODSLAYER HAS COME FORTH. IT IS WHAT THEY GUARD FOR, LOJEN TEVUNSON. THEY AWAIT THE GODSLAYER. SEE IT SO."

But I lost the Seal of Terris, I failed You.

"THE SEALS WERE NEVER MEANT FOR YOU, WARDKEEPER. THE SEALS ARE MEANT FOR ONE AND ONE ONLY. MY HAMMER IS MEANT TO SING THE SONG AND BRING OUR GUARDIANS HOME."

"Your Hammer?" It was then Lojen noticed that the humir hand of the statue was in a fist-like grip, a hole between, as if something was missing from it. "The Hammer!"

"Lojen." Emre stood a few steps behind, in his hands he held the Hammer of Mother Marrow. The greenish steel glowed from the runes etched into the haft.

"TAKE MINE HAMMER TO THE GODSBLOOD. SEE TO IT THAT THE GODSBLOOD BECOMES THE GODSLAYER. PROTECT EMINENCE."

"I will."

Pride swelled within him. Pride at becoming a wardkeeper, being deemed worthy. Pride at proving to his father he could follow in his clawsteps. Pride that he was chosen to become what he'd always dreamt of. Pride in knowing that he could avenge his father's death. Pride in knowing his family name was redeemed.

"Impressive." Lojen spun to find Lu Har standing at the top of the stair. Dozens of scourges, all armed to the teeth with wheellock rifles and swords. "Too bad it's too late."

Time stood still as the Fallen raised his arm, aetheurgy leaching from his flesh. A spark, a flash ripping as it struck Emre in the stomach. Aether tore through the scion of Drenth and sent him sprawling amongst the columns.

An overwhelming need to protect his ward pricked every nerve ending. A hymn orchestrating the song of war. He knew Justice had brought him to this exact moment, His Hymn of War coming to this crescendo alongside his own canto.

Everything filtered from his vision except for Lu Har. The Temple, the scourges, the statue of Mother Marrow, even Emre who was now dragging himself toward cover amongst the tall columns. Only the Fallen.

Lojen crouched and then flung himself at the source of his ire.

Bullets ricocheted off his exoscales from all directions. None pierced his scales because they were now stronger than diamond, the bullets a mild irritant. His legs pumped, tail parallel to the ground, eyes slitted, roar rumbling in his throat. One man, tall and dark of hair, that's all he focused on. The cause of his rage. The fire that hurt his ward.

Lojen smashed into the Fallen, the elfir's body crunching against his, shoulders driving into the other's gut, legs lifted off the ground, aether crackling. His momentum carried them out of the Temple completely. Tumbling into the sands of the canyon, bodies jostling, flipping, and bouncing. A drake screeched somewhere nearby.

He rolled to his feet, but armed scourges were already firing upon him, the ground a plumage of sand. Barricading the entire Temple grounds were scourges and automatons. Rotating guns and aethecite-powered tanks. All closing in and shooting. Gargantua reigned overhead, blotting out any sunlight that wasn't held back by the black mist surrounding the canyon.

Lu Har staggered to his feet and was encircled by his scourges, barking orders, gesturing with his hands. Lojen heard only sounds, the words drowned out by his inner inferno. The gunfire ceased as it did no damage to his body, somehow, someway he was unhurt. He knew it was the horns of a wardkeeper, of the aether in his essence. Robotic arms creaked as weapons were drawn back. Down came a red streak, plucking the Fallen from the scene in a whoosh of wings.

Lojen wanted blood.

He roared at the top of his lungs, raising the Hammer of Mother Marrow. The runes all along the haft were near blinding. Aether filled his vision, engulfed his soul. Berserk he went.

Scourges with aethecite-electrified batons raced in to subdue him with aetheurgy-enhanced strength and speed, but Lojen was far past the threshold of an enhanced humir. His muscles strained as he jumped into the pack, grabbing men and women by their arms, shoulders, anything he could get his claws on and flung them about. He swung the Hammer, its radiant emerald head colliding with flesh and metal alike. Electric barbs prodded him, sending jolts throughout his body, but his mind barely registered the pain.

Lost in the dance of wardkeeping he was.

He grabbed a scourge by the arm and lifted the hapless man, then swung the flailing body in a full arc, using him as a weapon, knocking others back. Releasing the man, he plummeted into his companions, bowling them over, Lojen leaping after, Hammer raised high. Green iron head crushed limbs, snapping, and breaking as he tore through the soldiers with swing after swing.

The scourges retreated from his deadly attacks, giving Lojen a chance to scan the battlefield. Dozens lay dead or wounded. Emre was nowhere to be seen, neither was the Fallen nor the firedrake. He looked skyward but saw nothing but jet-black mist, and it took him a few moments to spot the reddish shape weaving in and out. The great drake discharged a commanding roar and breathed fire.

Lojen's blood quickened as he gripped the Hammer tighter.

Three humir-driven drones stomped toward him from beyond the ring of scourges. Ten feet tall, broadly built metal chassis draping over the drivers like a harness. Feet and arms clicked into place, controlling heavy metal limbs. Hardened glass protected the driver's face and upper torso. Robotic arms tipped with gun and sword, aethecite furnaces upon their backs, smoke melding upward into the mist.

Lojen bellowed and crashed into the nearest one, driving one of his claws into the glass shield, cracks formed but it held strong as he brought down the Hammer. The drone's arm stabbed into his side, sword breaking upon his exoscaled hide. With both fists clutching the Hammer, Lojen beat at the glass, shattering it after the fourth try. He ripped the driver from the harness and tossed him aside, the drone toppling.

The other two attacked him simultaneously, but Lojen was much quicker than the metal beasts. He ducked under one swinging arm and grabbed it, flipping his body into the other, knocking it on its back. The aethecite furnace smashed under his weight, spewing molten pellets everywhere.

Lojen vaulted onto the final metal beast's back, digging into the space between the shield and the furnace. His claws tore through the gaps and piece by piece he flung metal. The driver tried to throw him off, but Lojen hung on, digging deeper, tearing further until the driver squeaked in fright, opened the harness, and fled. The drone went slack.

The ground all around them shook in the biggest explosion and tremor yet. Lojen spun and saw a humongous pillar of fire and smoke smear the last remaining darkness over the mines where Cadrianna Benld and the Dunleith children were. They had done it, blown the mines.

Everything balanced upon the edge of a sword.

Bloodied but still swimming with aether wrought from Mother Marrow's grace, Lojen finally spotted Emre. Hammer held before him Lojen fought toward his ward.

LIII
ASHE

ASHE GROANED AS she rolled onto her back, staring at the dawnbreak sun streaking the Sea of Mist on the desert dunes.

The air was blessedly cool, not the normal stifling acrid of the barren sands. She blinked a few times to verify she was still alive (she was) and then sat up gingerly. Her entire body felt as if she had fallen from Gargantua and hit every sky-risen apartment complex of Drenth on the way down. Every bone ached, her muscles were like sun-dried fruit, taut and twisted. She rubbed a hand against her forehead in a futile attempt to quell the splitting pain in her skull.

"Zenith's cock."

Two dozen feet away, the airglider was little more than a pile of kindling. The wings, or what was left of them, stuck out of the dunes, oil spurting from one of the hull's multiple interior pipes like a cut artery. All told, it was more a smoking pile of slag instead of an airglider.

A rustling in the sands to her left drew her attention as Ruane dragged herself into view, bent over on claws and talons. Purplish blood dribbled between a plethora of the drakken's exoscales and her tail swished experimentally as she dug through the wreckage to scavenge her longknife, coming up with a pointed grin when she procured the serrated blade.

Suddenly, Ashe burst into laughter.

"What's so funny?"

Ashe shook her head, still laughing. "Zenith's cock, Ruane, we survived a crash which surely should've killed us!" She stuck both hands out like she was gripping the steering device of the airship. "Arghh," she mimicked flying the ship, "we're crashing! Arghhh!"

Ruane grunted. "Remind me never to get in another of those godsdamned things again."

"We made it," Ashe said with a triumphant smile. It was a while before Ashe's laughter subsided, but the stabbing in her side kept pricking her. She surmised it might be a cracked rib or two. "Not bad if I do say so myself."

"There is seriously something wrong with you, humir."

"That's what I always hear," she countered, trying to stand. But her knee buckled and down she went. "You hurt, Ruane?"

"Fine enough to kill the Fallen when I see him." The drakken thrust her longknife out in demonstration.

"My knee is proper buggered," Ashe said. "And I think I broke some ribs. See if you can find anything to help me wrap it up." She pressed her hand to her tender side and choked upon a gasp. Ashe dug into the folds of her gaudy pink stola and found her flask, but it was empty. "Sonuvabitch."

She heard Ruane rummaging through the wreckage. Loud the drakken was, almost too loud for the Sea. She was about to tell the draconem to knock it off, but something came flying through the mist. Ashe recoiled as it bounced on the ground, which sent further shouts of pain through her body. It was a glass-breathing mask.

"Put it on," the drakken said. "Hear the Sea is bad for you humir."

Ashe lifted the breather and thought better of it. A cough ached to come up, but she tried her best to keep it inside with her ribs and all being shattered like a clay pot. "Fuck it. I'm already dying of the godsdamned pulmo." She tossed the breather back into the dunes where it was claimed with a slurp.

Ruane must have found something as she moved over toward her. "Let me see the damage."

Her entire left side was slick with blood. There were no protrusions, so that was good, but there was a considerably deep cut from her pelvis to her underarm and it bled freely after she peeled away the hideously colored stola. Her knee was a swollen mass of red and purple, and looked like the backside of a hag's thigh.

The drakken began tearing strips away from what appeared to be a linen bag, slowly tightening it around the wound in her side. Ashe glanced away and took deep drags of the mist the best she could with her battered ribs. The poisonous grey swarmed her insides, her pulmo flared quickly in her lungs, but she could feel the mist flouncing through her veins, heading straight for her injury, the aether within healing along her bruised and cut flesh, warm and tingly. Aether at its finest.

The haze above shifted, and a massive blur filled the void. The sound of engines whirred through the desert calm. "Is that?"

Gargantua.

An itch pulled her toward the direction of the floating fortress, the mist around her swirled like an arrow the same way. A warmth below her and she dug the Seal of *Terris* from the sand, holding it in her hands. The Seal and the diamond in the bangle both gleamed aether. A pulmo cough. "Fuck."

"What?"

Godsdamn you, Father. "That is where the Pentax is forcing me."

She rose to her unsteady feet and began to walk toward where Gargantua hovered.

The Sea of Mist sizzled with the unmistakable sensation of aetheurgy as Ashe crested a dune that swooped downward into a canyon that housed a monumental temple. The impressive lump of stone and metal that was Gargantua hovered directly over the domed shrine, the undercarriage of the hulking fortress a stone's throw above, smoke pouring out of it. Her father had seriously done a number on the floating fortress.

The mist turned from opaque grey to the inky jet of a seagandr's blood. Aether surged with such a force, Ashe knew it wasn't borne from anything other than Nocturne's Pit. There was a feeling of hatred bound within the mist, a desire for necrosis. The icky feeling prickled at her flesh. The mist surrounded the canyon, almost as if unwilling to move any closer.

"Did you see that?" Ruane was squatting with her clawed talons resting upon her knees as she scanned the canyon below. Her claw holding the longknife thrust forward toward the temple. "See there it is again."

The tattoos along Ashe's left arm flared as she burned her aetheurgy. A clarity came, expanding the scene below as the Sea disappeared as if nonexistent, but the aura of necrosis remained, stronger than ever. The temple rushed to the forefront in her sightline as if she was standing on the grounds themselves. A man in a red robe stood with hands stretched outward toward a shorter man and a large drakken with some epic horn action. Aether burst from the robed man's hands, striking the smaller man, sending him flying backwards into the temple's cella while the drakken roared.

Ashe took off down the dune at a mad sprint with a shout, her janky knee giving her discomfort, but she ignored it as the frayed train of her rose stola trailed behind because Lu Har had just pummeled her father with aether borne of the Pit.

"Stupid humir." Ruane came flying down the mound on all fours, sending granules of earth flying. It took half a yard before the drakken overtook her and forced Ashe to nearly trip into a stop. "What are you doing, you foolish child?"

That primal urge bloomed inside of her, the same as when she was aboard Gargantua during the party. It was the darkness within the mist. What had her father called it? Noctis. *Father…* "That's my father down there."

"And so is my brother. But this place is crawling with Imperium soldiers. I'm all for finding a way to stick my knife into Lu Har's black heart but running around screaming like a chicken on fire is not going to solve our problems. There's only two of us."

She tamped down a pulmo cough and looked between the drakken's arm and torso toward the temple. Her father was nowhere to be seen and Lu Har was ascending the stair to the raised porch. Circling the domed top was the daemon firedrake. "Then what do you suggest? Pray to Zenith and ask Him to magically whisk us down there? Or would you rather we take the long route in, punching each and every soldier in the seedpods or privies on the way down?"

Ruane rolled her eyes. "The fate of the world rests on you? By the Arbiter's bloody axe, this world is buggered if that's true."

"Hey now."

"Come on, humir. Let a drakken show you how this is done." With that, the drakken darted into the compressed curtain of black mist, swallowed with nary a blip.

Ashe cursed under her breath but followed anyway because it's not like she had any choice. Her path led straight to that temple.

What was in there, she didn't know, but the Seal in her makeshift belt was a beacon being pulled in that direction.

There was no direct route into the canyon, but Ruane seemed to have found a way down regardless. A series of step-like outcroppings of sandstone no bigger than half of Ashe's foot. It wouldn't be an easy route, especially with her injured knee, but they had no other choice as there were gobs of soldiers ringing the entirety of the canyon opposite. All of Gargantua it seemed. Her father had really gotten into the Fallen's head.

Ashe leaned over the lip and whistled. "This isn't going to be fun."

"Don't be such a Scurred Hatch."

"A what?"

"Just be careful, you little whelping. I don't want your father angry that you've been bruised more than an apple kicked miles down the road."

"After you." Ashe waved her hand over the nearly vertical route to the bottom.

Step after careful, agonizing step, they descended. Well, careful and agonizing for Ashe because the drakken made the descent look awfully easy. The drakken probably could have gone down, up, and down again at least five times before Ashe would make the bottom once. Her knee gave out the last few feet and she slid down, rocks crumbling underneath.

Ruane hissed at her while crouched behind a boulder. "Quiet, humir."

"Sorry?"

"Let's move."

"Yes, boss."

"If Emre Benld survives this, I'm going to kill him just for making me promise to watch you all the way to Kalderim. I'm of a mind to let the Fallen have you."

Ashe crossed her arms. "I'll do just fine without you." The drakken mumbled something in draconem-speak as she slithered from the protection of the boulder, heading toward the temple. "Crybaby."

The odd pairing of humir and drakken skulked about the rear of the temple grounds. Thick columns ran in rows from end to end, all supporting statues. Ashe wondered if this temple was in honor of Mother Marrow. Either way, the temple became the 'Temple' in her mind. A little honor toward the Pentax might do her some good at a time like this.

As they neared the Temple, soldiers of the Imperium appeared amongst the artwork. All faced inward, and there were far too many for it to be anything but an enclosing circle meant to capture or contain, clearly for her father. The mist quirked with the crackle of aether, a voice almost lingering about the fog. Could it be the Fallen?

They were nearing the Temple's twenty-foot-tall porch when two figures emerged from within. A short woman and a burly man began to descend the stair. She recognized the aetheurgist Solanine on sight, she'd never forget those all-onyx eyes and heart-shaped face. But the bigger man took her a second longer to realize who he was. *Zenith's cock, he didn't...*

The aethuergist's voice carried over the spanning distance, "Bring me the girl alive. The Fallen awaits her while he deals with her father. And don't forget the Seal of *Terris*."

A gaggle of Imperium soldiers nearby turned toward the aetheurgist's words, then saw Ashe and Ruane. Weapons came upright, swords and rifles. Forward they came.

"Brynn?"

Ashe's lips convexed into a frown as she bolted toward the row of soldiers and summoned the mist around her, a slit opening in the world of Life as she hacked something globby. It felt of Death. Of murder and revulsion. A stink of the Pit itself.

The gateway came, mist glowing like a billion fireflies coming to life all at once. The non-stone walls of the canyon in the Meadows shimmered, translucent. The wails of the dead along with, their ghastly shrieks deafening. How she summoned the Meadows without memorizing the path or having an anchor, she didn't know. It just came alive with her need.

But in the Meadows, the mortals of the real world were frozen in place as time stopped. Blades in midair. Stirred sand hung pendulous.

A tug on the mist, the world of the dead strumming. She coughed hard. Blood coated her mouth. Pulmo tore apart her innards. Then she was dumped back into the world of Life as if she was no longer welcome on the other side of the living, time speeding back up.

A dozen Imperium soldiers rushed toward her with swords raised, prepared for close combat. Ruane leapt into the swathe of soldiers, stabbing with longknife, cracking her powerful tail like a club, snapping at humir flesh with her jaws.

"No!" Ashe screaked, throwing her voice toward the oncoming soldiers with a laced blast of aether. Her scream sent most toppling, tossing the drakken from her feet unintentionally. Ashe sought to control the aether within her veins, begging for it to stop. Her left arm coruscated with burning runes, the bangle and the diamond alight.

The drakken scrambled back to her feet, glaring at her from across the grounds before returning to the fight. Scores of others resumed their hunt in her direction. Solanine and Evander still stood motionless upon the Temple's stair. What were they waiting for? And where was Lu Har? And her father?

Ashe was drained from her aetheurgy. Tired from the crash. Zenith's cock, she was tired. And, truth told, she needed a drink.

Despite it all, Ashe drew the dagger she confiscated from Quick Fingers Cyrus' dead fingers, and the mist around her feet darkened within anticipation. The front-most soldier brought his blade down in an arc toward her with the intent to maim and she slid to one knee, expecting where his momentum would take him, and brought her own steel upward into the man's stomach, cutting as she passed. She met the next man with a downward slice. Both fell to the ground in agony.

She wobbled back to her feet, having had forgotten about her wounded knee. It still held, but she'd wrenched it in her stupid attempt to appear dangerous.

Two more soldiers—clearly not the most advanced lot of murderers—came at her from the side and she glided between them, cutting with her dagger at their legs. The men's swords clattered to the ground as they clutched at their wounds. Meat for the carrion birds.

Facing the others, Ashe slowly backed away, stepping over the fallen men. She bent down with a grimace and grabbed the nearest wounded bastard by the drake scaled gorget. Smiling, Ashe cut the man's throat as the mist awakened in glee around her. She felt the man's essence cross the veil. Pleasure and yearning soared. Building her body in strength she wouldn't have otherwise possessed. Her own soul swelling with the quietus.

The other soldiers fell back.

A warning in the back of her mind sprung to life. *This isn't right*, it repeated over and over. Killing to kill was not her.

The ground trembled as a massive explosion blew through the black mist, but that's not what drew her attention, no, it was the after tremors. So many of them, as if something tunneled underfoot.

Could it be?

Her gaze sought out Solanine. On the Temple's stair stood the aetheurgist and Ashe's former thievery companion. *Them*, the urging was for. Solanine's face turned upward toward Evander, words spoken, then the aetheurgist was gone, the big man as well. Disappeared into the void.

She screamed as she ran to where they had stood, a deathly wail. Taking to the stair of the Temple, Ashe scanned the porch, searching for them. Ashe skidded to a stop between the soaring columns, her dagger dripping blood as she lowered it. In the single beat of her heart, the mist parted, and a hand reached for her throat, grabbing it with aetheurgy-enhanced strength borne of the Pit.

"Hail, Snow Eyes."

LIV

EMRE

"LOJEN, NO! STAY back!" Emre cried as he backed his way into the statues, leaning against one that depicted a drakken. Fitting.

The drakken wardkeeper must have heard him, because Lojen disappeared into the protection of the Temple as a barrage of aethecite-powered wheellocks and aether ping-ping-pinged the stone all around.

Lu Har's daemonic firedrake deposited him upon the Temple's porch, where the Fallen stood with hands coated in onyx aetheurgy. The drake reared its fiery head and roared a defiant outburst borne of the Pit.

As aether barreled toward him, Emre tumbled twenty feet from the porch, landing forcefully upon a scourge who had ringed the stairs below, his engraved wheellock pistol bouncing from his grip, his wind knocked from his lungs. Luckily for him, the scourge took the brunt of his fall, and nothing seemed broken except the scourge's neck. But despite his shock, Emre pressed the aether-induced wound closed with a hand, could feel his back slick with his lifeblood, drenching his suit coat.

He picked up the scourge's fallen wheellock rifle and held the barrel to his forehead, eyes squinted, he breathed deeply, hoping that his final moments would see it done to the end. *Steel it, Benld. You knew this was the path. For Brynn.*

Burning all aetheurgy reserves at once, golden fire in his veins. Silver glow showed and felt everything in the surrounding canyon. White-hot inferno filled his body with strength of the Pentax. The wound in his gut was the harshest of fires. No amount of burning could stem a wound already made such as that. It was unlike any fire he had ever felt. This was something else. Something sinister. Something forbidden.

Of the void.

"You cannot hide from me, Emre Benld." A crackle of aetheurgy pinpointed Lu Har's location from within the Temple above. "You've made yourself worthy of my attention, but now is the time to end you. To end what you have sown in Drenth. Your stunt with the communication to the people will be handled effectively. I will raze your city to the sands. All that blood will be on your hands."

"Go to the Pit," Emre yelled through clenched teeth.

Laughter from the Fallen. "I have already seen it and know of its majesty. Untapped its power remains. What you've seen, what this world has seen, has been but a pinprick of what Noctis can do." Lu Har began chanting in a language Emre could only describe as grim. A coldness settled over the Temple grounds. "I'll give you a taste, Emre Benld."

He could feel the raging flames of the parch coursing through his body, but as it neared the wound, the world, his world, felt like he was standing upon the sun. Pain, nothing but pain. The hurt flared into his bloodstream, into his muscles, gnawing away at the parch, stopping and quenching. Snuffing the enhancements on its own.

"Shit."

What had Lu Har done to him? It felt like a siphon. He could feel the siphon destroying the reserves in his body, eradicating the parch serum he'd swallowed, aiming for his soul. It was rendering his aetheurgy null. And worse still, the pain felt like fire. Liquid fire.

All his aetheurgy snuffed out, leaving him a mere man.

How is this possible?

"Do you now see what Noctis is capable of?" Lu Har sounded closer to where Emre hid. "A scratch at the surface of what is possible. Let it consume you. Let it consume all those you hold dear. This is what awaits your daughter."

Black-red lightning bolts cratered into the sandstone, sending shards of rock flying in all directions, sand and dust misting as the ground became churned by the corruption of *Aere*. The mist of the Sea came rolling down the canyon walls, but it was black as the abyss, denser than he had ever seen. The sable fog circled the Temple grounds like a shroud, almost as if the Forgemistress was struggling to keep it at bay. Was this the true horror of Noctis?

Mustering all he had left, Emre barged around the column and fired the wheellock in the direction of Lu Har. The Fallen had his hands out to the sides, palms up. Emre's bullet stopped in a wall built of black mist, the projectile dropping to the sandstone at the Fallen's robed hem.

From behind, shots rang out. Emre ducked and he dove between a set of columns, grunting as he hit, hard. The sky was lighter now as dawnbreak fully broke over the desert, its wonderous rays fighting through the veiling haze of Noctis, which made his eyesight lag in adjusting under the blinding sunlight and the vastness of the emptiness. It was as if Life and Death were meeting in a grand battle with Gargantua and the Temple of Mother Marrow at the center.

Lu Har's laughter echoed. "Escape, you cannot. This is where you meet your end, Emre Benld. I might even leave you alive long enough to see your daughter break the Seal."

More gunfire and black-red lightning bolts all around him. Emre half-shuffled, half-dragged himself away from his precarious resting spot into the surrounding statues. Nestled between were benches and altars of sandstone, of pedestals and rock-hewn vases. He tripped, falling, his wheellock rifle bouncing away. Emre reached for it, but there were bullets thudding-thudding-thudding into the earthen creations, the ground, and canyon dunes. He curled into a ball, his gut wound on fire, hands covering his head in protection.

"Emre!"

Partially visible through the hazy mist borne of Noctis, Lojen crouched behind a stone bench that was pocked with bullet holes, the horns upon his head magnificent.

"I told you to stay away," he croaked.

"Bugger that." Lojen crawled on his belly the distance to where Emre was huddled, keeping head low as bullets whizzed all around. "Lu Har has this place surrounded. That mist is evil, it's very touch stings. The Hymn of War is weakening."

Emre forced himself into a kneeling position, trying to keep the wound tight, but it was a losing battle. He coughed and blood trickled out the corners of his mouth.

"You don't look so good."

"I've felt better." It hurt to crack a smile.

"You prolong your death, Emre Benld." The Fallen stood calmly at the top of the stair, his all-onyx eyes glimmering like ebony in an inky statue as the black mist swirled around him.

Stone erupted, flinging shrapnel as the Fallen unleashed a blast of black-red lightning. Emre took umbrage, but all around him were the sounds and seeds of destruction. Predators and human-driven drones stomped into the Temple grounds as Lojen and Emre squirmed through the debris, avoiding gunfire and aetheric sparks alike. Blood left a telling sign of his passage. Lojen was practically carrying him now, his arm slung across the drakken's shoulder, the seven-foot-tall draconem bent nearly in half. He was weakened, body ready to go into arrest at any moment. Lojen carried the unloaded gun, his fingers without strength.

The drakken dragged him deeper into the labyrinth of columns, but Emre had no idea to where, he just focused on putting one foot in front of the other—troublesome as it was. A crash nearby, a column exploding and ground shaking as stone masonry broke and lurched like a tree felled in the Forest of Calibrath.

Emre slid off Lojen's bracing arm, falling to his face. He rolled over, eyes blurry. "Too far, Lojen. My time has come." A coughing fit full of blood balled him up, knees up to his chest. "Save yourself." Final thoughts flit through his foggy mind: *I don't regret my choices. For Brynn, it was worth it. For Tevun, Val. For Wick, O my friend, I'll miss you. And for Finn, I'll always love you. For you, Cad.*

Lojen's claws pulled Emre's underarms. "Like void I'm leaving you. You're my ward. The Dark God of Death will take me first. Hold on, Em." Lifting him as if he were an infant, Lojen carried him on through the forest of columns and brush of stone.

Emre's head lulled. In one of the rare times his eyes were open, Gargantua was all he saw above the blackened mist. The quarter mile-wide flying fortress suspended a mere hundred feet in the air, a giant blotch in the sky as if bobbing atop the Sea. A thousand or more aethecite lights shining about the fortress.

Gods, it's beautiful...

He thought about the day the fortress of the Fallen had come to Drenth, but the memory was fleeting, the pain in his wound drowning out his questions. He knew why he loathed everything about Gargantua, of what he had planned. Planned it all, even his...wait, what did he plan?

A chill ran through him. No, he realized, not a chill, but Death. It was the icy fingers of Nocturne coming to claim him.

"Almost there, Em. Hang on."

Emre mumbled incoherently.

A massive concussion struck nearby, and both were thrown from their feet, Emre's body striking a column base. He crumpled, too dazed to care or protect himself. In a bit of clarity—or a fitting moment of it—he realized the scars along his forearms did not itch. Those physical memories he used to fuel his anger, his desire for revenge, they no longer fed him.

And here is the end.

His mind was nearly empty now, the moment coming for him like the dawnbreak sun coming for the day. A chasm spanning the breadth of Emre's connection to the world of Life. He struggled to open his eyes, head groggy, breathing shallow. Shadows poured over him, draping him in their peaceful darkness. Rough claws grabbed him by his arms, his legs and body.

"Perhaps it best I let my daemons show you the way to the Pit, Emre Benld."

The ground underneath began to tremble. Statues toppled from their columns. Aged vases plummeted and shattered. The billowing shroud of onyx fog rippled.

From the mist emerged two figures. Wrinkled figures with claws and spikes. Figures with thick banded scars around their daemonic necks and a singular horn warping upward. Figures with bright crimson eyes.

Edric and Alandy Benld. His parents.

"By the Arbiter's bloody axe," Lojen swore. Emre could barely register them as the pair of daemons who had once been his parents circled closer. The drakken looked his way. "What do we do, Em?"

He couldn't imagine taking any other route to this point. To get closure from Cadrianna. To get Brynn back. It had been all for them. For his family. It'd been worth it.

"Sur…vive."

Edric Benld bent over, the former regent's front claws digging into the sandstone as the daemon's back legs pushed with a sudden burst of speed. The daemon in the body of Alandy Benld threw back her horned head and bellowed an ungodsly sound, then charged. Their claws scrapped the earth, their crimson eyes illumining hatred.

Stepping in front of him, Lojen crouched, his talons extended on one hand, the Hammer of Mother Marrow in the other. Emre tried to tell him to stand down, but his words came out as a babble. The drakken braced himself as Edric tackled him, Alandy a mere heartbeat behind. The three tumbled backward, missing Emre completely as they fell into the copse of columns.

Emre's head lolled to the side as he saw Lojen kick his powerful legs and thrust the daemonic version of his father away. His sweet, loving, caring mother tore at the new wardkeeper's snout with her claws, his exoscales taking a beating, some ripped away, leaving exposed meat and purplish blood. Lojen screamed in a berserker rage as he grabbed the lithe daemon by the waist and tossed her. She slammed into a column, sending the cyclopic statue crashing down.

Lojen, they are…

The drakken's freedom was short-lived as Emre's doting, honorable father bore down on him anew, the former regent's claws rasping across his back, ripping through his sleeveless furred vest, tufts of mammoth hair flying everywhere as the vest was ripped clean off. Lojen brought the Hammer to bear, swinging with all his strength, the muscles of his back and arms stretched to their limits. The greenish-ironed head whirred as the runes glowed ferociously. The Hammer shattered the scaly flesh of Edric's chest, the skin parting like ripped linen threads. The beast howled but Lojen brought the Hammer down upon the creature's horned skull, crushing its daemonic life.

Father… Tevun… like you…

Alandy leapt at Lojen like a harpy smelling offal. She scrabbled up the drakken's back, ripping and gouging with claws like steel. Lojen's exoscales gave way under the daemon's blows, daemonic fire from beyond the veil of Life scoured his muscles. The drakken dropped the Hammer. Lojen grabbed the daemon's head with both his claws as Emre's mother tried crawling towards his prone body, and yanked her away with the last of his will. The beast vaulted over Lojen's head, shoulders grazing his wardkeeper horns, which elicited that ungodly howl, and the berserk drakken slammed the former regentress into the sandstone. She tried to flip, but Lojen brought his boot down into her withered face, smashing through leather and bone alike. The regentress' legs flailed as life fled from her.

Emre's arm reached for his mother's clawed fingers. *Mother…*

"I grow tired of this game." Lu Har stepped into view.

The drakken wardkeeper stood over Emre as the Fallen's hands became encased in blackened aether. The Fallen's palm came up and lightning sparked above, dancing from his fingers. The electric blast struck Lojen clear in the breast and the wardkeeper went sprawling, his exoscales smoking. Emre's torso bled freely, his eyes rolled back into his skull.

This is it. Papa, Mama, I'm coming. Brynn…

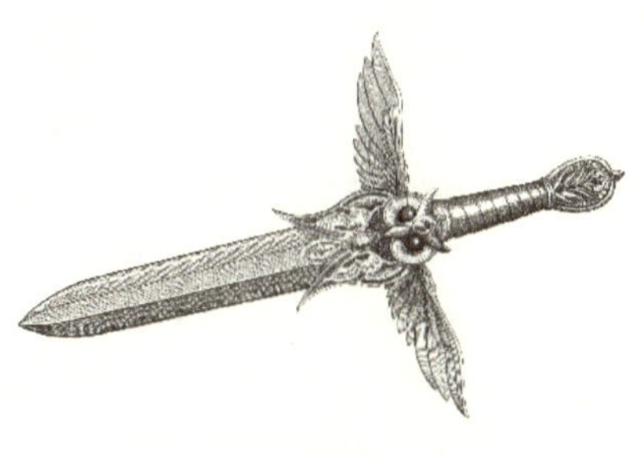

LV

CADRIANNA

VALERIA WHEELED AROUND a large dune as the sands tremored below.

Soldiers dawdled about the edge of a canyon underneath Gargantua and when the truck came bearing down on them, they opened fire with bullets and *Ignis* alike. Cadrianna and the Dunleiths ducked as the bikrome floored the vehicle. Bullets clanged off the metal grill, shattering the windshield, thin smoke rising from the engine. Valeria spun the wheel, jerking the truck off-road, sand spraying as *Ignis* flames flashed overhead. Panging of more gunshots as they wove into the heavy fog that was so black it was as if the void had come into the world of Life. Cadrianna half-expected the sound of wailing souls to be heard.

The ground undulated even more, as if something was coming closer.

"We'll worry about these bastards," Finnus said, his peridot pupils glowing as he burned his aetheurgy. Yellowed air of *Aere* whirlwinded around his hands. "You find Emre. Protect him for us."

The bikrome slammed on the brakes, tires skidding through the sand, truck nearly flipping sideways. Cadrianna jumped out as bullets ripped into the side of the vehicle. Finnus unleashed his twin yellow tornadoes in the direction of the gunfire. Valeria hit the pedal and flung arcs of sand everywhere as the Dunleiths raced off.

Cadrianna sprinted to the edge of the canyon. A figure stood in the center of the Temple grounds, looking up. Lu Har. And he was waiting for her.

"CAD, I DON'T LIKE THIS. THESE QUAKES, THEY ARE DRAKES."

Gripping the Strix tight, she made her way to the trail leading into the canyon, steadying herself against the quaking dunes. Predators lined the trail, soldiers with their wheellock rifles. All watched her, not gunning her to shreds. Seems she was expected.

Lu Har looked a bit worse for wear, his long locks disheveled and sandy. There were tears in his bloodred robe. The black mist blew about his feet. Cinder circled above, the drake's great wings flapping.

Emre lay at the Fallen's feet.

"DON'T BE HASTY. HIS SOUL HASN'T YET CROSSED THE VEIL. THESE DRAKES, THEY COME FOR THE SEAL."

Seething, Cadrianna stopped a dozen paces from the Fallen. She gripped the daemon blade so tight her hand started to throb. Emre was lying face up, breathing, but barely. His suit jacket and shirt were soaked with blood, his vest ripped apart in his abdomen. Face ashen.

"Remember your place, Cadrianna, my love," the Fallen said in his silky tone, the one that she up until recently thought devilishly handsome. Gods, how could she ever? "You were bonded for just this purpose. To be here and finish what was mine own plan. To kill in mine own name."

"I was never yours in the first place."

"You are mine. Always have been. I've put too much into your molding. Spent too much time making sure your heart and soul were beleaguered enough to become my weapon. You were made to be my scourge. See how it fits you. The blood of Nightingale flows through your veins. Diluted, but still it flows. Nocturne wouldn't have bonded you if you weren't meant to rule His blade."

Strix?

"DON'T LISTEN, CAD. HIS WORDS ARE FLAWED. I... I MEAN NOCTURNE DOES NOT CHOOSE LIGHTLY, GOD THOUGH HE BE. THERE ARE ALWAYS REASONS..."

"Cad…" Emre raised his hand, outstretched, eyes opening, hair drenched in sweat and blood. "Cad?"

"Emre," she whispered. Tears flowed down her cheeks unabated, flooded with all the anguish from the last twenty-four hours. All the revelations. The reconciliations. The shredding of her lies.

"You must…" Cough filled with blood. "…not give…" Another hack. "…in. For Brynn…"

It was wrong, utterly and totally wrong. Here, in this holiest of places with the twin loves in her life. Her beloved dying, her hateful love still standing mere feet away. But something in the back of her mind made her calm. Emre had been in control, manipulating everything up until this point. Could he be planning something, even now? In his dying breaths?

"USE IT. USE THIS PAIN. END HIM."

She leveled her gaze upon the Fallen. Red colored everything in her sight. She pointed the blade at Lu Har. "This ends now."

Lu Har spread his arms and his eyes a black void as he tapped into his aetheurgy, the surrounding mist turning an uglier shade of ebony. His hands burned white-hot. "Then your service is ended."

But then a giant blur crashed into the Fallen and sent him flying. Lojen, in all his drakken glory, landed upon the Fallen with pure hatred. Rage carried him, propelled him just as it flowed through

Cadrianna. Lojen rained punch after punch, slamming down the Hammer of Mother Marrow. Arms flailing, the Fallen fought back with aether-enhanced abilities, even though Lojen outweighed him by more than half. He walloped the elfir's body, claws tearing at the robe, at his flesh but neither seemed to penetrate Lu Har's aetheric defenses. Strength on strength. Guile versus tact. Instinct versus honed logic.

Cinder roared from above and folded her wings and dove, intending to skewer the drakken with her barbed tail. But before the firedrake could reach the lesser order of draconem, another drakken burst onto the scene, a simple longknife forged on the Isle of Merj thrust forward. The second light blue drakken collided with the firedrake's neck, tearing scales asunder, which threw the diving drake off track. The higher order draconem plowed into the sandstone with a sickening crunch. The smaller drakken scampered up its graceful neck and stabbed over and over, sending crimson ichor flying.

Lu Har had regained his feet as a cloud of black mist encircled Lojen and pulled him off. Time it was for her to uphold the bargain she made with herself all those years ago. With Brynn free, nothing would stop her from killing Lu Har. All the pain he'd caused her demanded it, her prison of lies commanded it. Lu Har would pay with his life.

She leapt.

The Strix slashed at his back, but the Fallen turned, parrying it with his aether-coated hands, almost like a shield. Lu Har then went on the attack with his other hand, forming the black mist into a translucent blade aimed at her heart. She parried with the Strix, but his aetheric blade found her arm anyway, searing her flesh in molten fire, making her scream in fury rather than pain. Blood flowed down her arm regardless.

With inhuman strength, Lu Har shoved Lojen away while parrying one of Cadrianna's ripostes, the Strix striking the shielded hand. The drakken dropped the Hammer, and the Fallen brought an elbow down, jacking him in the back, sending him straight to the ground as black-red lightning sizzled upon the drakken's exoscales.

Cadrianna, in the throes of aetheurgy, separated the Strix into half a dozen blades, aimed at Lu Har. A wall of the mist borne of Noctis rose up in protection, the Fallen's savior and shield. The six owl-handled blades stopped, hanging helplessly. Lu Har surged forward, bringing his white-hot fist into Cadrianna's sternum. Her body jerked in what felt like a direct strike of lightning to the chest. She flew backward and rolled around in hurt, feeling broken inside.

Lojen stood once more, his berserker rage firing on all cylinders, claws ready to rip the Fallen apart. The second drakken, with crimson firedrake blood dripping from her longknife, circled around Lu Har. The three appraised each other.

"Ru, get back," Lojen said to the other drakken. A sibling?

"For Father, Lojen."

A shadow darker than anything Cadrianna had ever seen pooled under the Fallen, it sucked in the light. A void of never-ending darkness. The shadow continued to grow, not expanding but instead rising, dimensional and erect. Hand-like shapes rose from the shadow, fingers reaching for Lu Har. They grabbed at the man's clothes, his limbs.

The Fallen smiled. "The Godsblood is ready." His all-onyx gaze fell on Cadrianna, disappointment within the void. "Your daughter will be the greatest warrior our Divine has ever produced. Too bad you won't be by my side to see it."

The ground opened under the Fallen, the shadowed hands pulling him down into the void. A concussion, the shadow convulsed then contracted. A snap, an instant of intense, unbearable heat. The shadowed hands retreated into the ground again, leaving only the black mist. The Strix blades clattered to the stone.

"Where'd he go?" the smaller drakken asked in bewilderment.

"CAD, YOU MUST GET UP," the Strix said in her benumbed mind. Breathing was a chore, her entire breastbone felt broken into a thousand pieces. She rolled to her side and spat blood. Her Void Form wilted. *"THIS IS WHERE YOU MUST FIND THE STRENGTH TO CARRY IT TO THE END. FOR YOUR DAUGHTER. I CAN HELP HER."*

What?

"YES, PUT ME INTO HER HANDS. IT IS THE ONLY WAY."

I can't do that to my daughter, bond you to her as I was."

"TRUST ME."

A pale figure appeared from the mist, the bikrome, followed by her brother. They moved closer and crouched near Emre's body, the Kanjan seer lifted Cadrianna's beloved's head, cradling it in her lap, his lifeblood lathered down her silver-and-gold bracelets. Emre's lover ran his hand through his hair, tears staining his handsome face.

Emre…

"THIS IS WHERE YOU MUST DECIDE, CAD. A SOUL FOR A SOUL."

She crawled toward Emre and gripped his hand, "Emre." She pressed a kiss to the back of it.

His weakened fingers clutched at hers. "Brynn…"

Summoning what little strength she could, Cadrianna got to her feet, called the Strix to her, and moved toward the Temple.

LVI
ASHE

ASHE DIDN'T FIGHT, there was no point.

She limped along beside Evander through the Temple of Mother Marrow, his hand gripped her neck, constricting her air just enough to keep her alive and moving. Evander dragged her past the impressive statue of the Forgemistress and down a stair behind the statue's base into a dreary tunnel full of cobwebs and smelling of the grave.

"What happened to you, Evander?" A sliver of pain ran up her leg, replaced by warm healing. There was mist flowing along after her while she walked, light tendrils of haze.

At first, seeing Evander had been alarming. His body must have been altered using Void Form. The once luscious curls no longer remained, leaving only a smattering of new scars on his barren pate. His face was stronger, craggier, and scarred. His eyes, though, were his, even though they were ink.

But seeing him there in the flesh, she didn't know what to feel.

Ashe supposed she should have hated him, but she really didn't. Dregs did whatever they had to on the streets. Death was the only constant. In a perverted way, she was amused he had survived over his bastard brother Elian.

The tunnel opened into a chamber. A colonnade held up an arched ceiling with inlets that reached upward to where the statue of Mother Marrow resided above ground. It was musty and dark. There was another passage on the opposite side of the colonnade, one that held sputtering torches.

Evander smirked. "You wouldn't understand, Snow Eyes." The voice was still his, at least. "This world wasn't meant for people like us. We are but shit the rest of the world wipes from their asses." His fist clenched. "Such power. Aetheurgy. Death and destruction. You don't und—" Evander's words were cut off as his body jerked forward, blood gushing down the back of his skull as he slumped to the ground.

"For Amaranth," Cyan said, hefting his aetheric axe, the one that had cleaved Evander's head. Harlequin limped into view, carrying her axes, red curls matted with sweat. "Sister-friend, you alright?"

"Snow Eyes," her one-time companion sputtered through bloodied lips. "What… sorry… forgive…" His voice left him, and his eyes glazed.

"I always hated that stupid name." She was too tired to come up with something punchier. To Cyan, "Where the void did you come from?" The mist at Ashe's feet warned her. Danger, it said. Solanine was still somewhere ahead. "Stay here," she said to the vicars.

Ashe summoned the Meadows. That elegant cut in the fabric of the real world and that of the dead. The rend shimmed, almost liquidly, non-light of shades faithfully recreating the Temple's innerbelly. Ashe stepped in. The wails of the dead grew, then faded when they recognized her.

A scene similar, the colonnade, the portico, the dome of inlets. Real but not. No Evander, nor of Cyan or Harlequin. The place was still and unmoving, even as the walls rippled like a slight breeze upon a lake. She sniffed the non-air, focusing on the trepidation within the mist.

There, across the colonnade in the mouth of the dark passage, something waited for her. It was then the daemon lunged at her.

Ashe fell backward, tripping over her feet, landing in a ball outside of the Meadows, thrown from the land of the eternal slumber. The daemon bounded into the world of Life without a sound, standing tall as Ashe scrambled to her feet.

The daemon was twice her size, black in color, as if wearing naught but a cloak. The head was hooded, the outlines of horns left little tents of shadowy fabric. A flat nose within, almost pig-like. Red eyes, beady and lucid, piercing. It was the same daemon who had chased her in Gargantua, of that she was certain.

She heard the vicars gasp behind her, the red-haired sprat praying to Justice while Cyan groveled to the entire Pentax.

"YOU'VE GROWN STRONG, MORTAL," the daemon rasped, like gravel grating against a boot. *"YOUR SOUL FORM IS CLOSE TO COMPLETE."*

Ashe tilted her head, trying to peer into the red eyes. "My life's been thrown upside down since that ratfink who summoned you flew into my life. So, let's just say I don't have time for this shit, asshole."

Daemon claws shot out of the cloak of shadows, Ashe raised her hands to block as her aetheurgy came alive, but she wasn't quick enough. The back of her head slammed into a column. The mist rose all around her like a geyser, separating her from the daemon.

Vision blurry, she spied the vicars swinging their holy axes at the daemon. Cyan unleashing his canistered mist. Harlequin leapt with both axes raised, bringing downward, her mist canisters popping in the tune of a steaming sinfonietta. The daemon bellowed as the blue iron struck. Cyan shouldered into the creature of the Pit, knocking the hulking thing over.

Ashe's mind told her to act now or she'd not get another chance.

She summoned aetheurgy, her innate aether wrapping around the daemon as she screamed, binding it in dense bands as strong as steel. The creature writhed, claws tearing in an attempt to free itself. In her mind, Ashe dragged the daemon toward the veil of Life and Death, rending at the edges of the Meadows as she sought to contain it. The daemon fought her pull, shoving Ashe back with fingers of Void Form, her feet almost giving way. But the mist—and the aether borne of the Crystal of Life within—urged onward, struggling against the frenzy. The behemoth flailed, ripped from the ground in a font of black mist, lightning sparking, leaving the beast hanging, still.

"YOU CANNOT BREAK US. YOUR HYMN OF THE SOUL IS NOT YET COMPLETE. I AM LEMURES AND WE ARE LEGION."

Ashe sought the calm within, drawing forth the connection between the daemon and that within the Meadows. No, not the Meadows, Nocturne's Pit. She screamed, head thrown back, arms out, mist vortexing. Her pulmo grew like hellfire, blood and globules of gods-knew-what swarmed up and out in her call, sprinkling throughout the mist. That only added more fuel.

Finally, the bond holding the daemon's link gave way, the body beginning to fade. A sallow red glow in the center of its mangled form pulsed and waned. Its beady eyes were the last thing Ashe saw before it was gone, sent down into the farthest reaches of Nocturne's Pit.

The Meadows oscillated around her, as the mist sewed up the gateway.

The tunnel beyond the chamber where Ashe had defeated the daemon was empty, down further into the desert it went, to the very core of the world it felt.

With a hand to the rough-hewn walls, Ashe made her way down the slight decline, the two vicars close behind. Dark as a moonless night, tepid with shadows. Mist rolling in waves at their waists. A singular irradiance in a chamber at the far bottom.

"Lilia, you certain about this?"

"I need to end this, Cyan. And Lilia is not my name."

"Then what is it?"

Ashe snorted. "That's what I need to fucking find out. Let me do all the talking."

Cyan nudged the red-haired runt. "Then we're buggered."

Harlequin mocked the elder vicar. "Language, Vicar Cyan."

Solanine stood in the center of a small room, cloaked in a white robe laced with red runes, reminding Ashe of streaks of blood. The aetheurgist's hair was wild, all-onyx eyes narrowed as the three entered, standing behind an altar made of emerald crystal shards.

The altar of crystal glowed a verdant emerald, leaving the chamber a pulsating green. The altar seemed alive, the pulse like that of a heart. There was life within, Ashe realized. And not just a small lifeforce, no, this was something enormous. The entire place buzzed with *Terris*, the essence of Life and Creation.

"Come, child of Nightingale," Solanine said, beckoning her forward with a bloodstained hand. "The Seal awaits you."

"By order of the Scattered Shards, I hereb—"

The aetheurgist's fingers moved and Cyan's mouth froze. Same with Harlequin. Neither moved, neither blinked. Ashe rolled her eyes; she *did* tell them...

"That's better." Solanine's hands motioned over the altar and Ashe saw that a circular dent was atop the faceted crystal, as if something was missing. The Seal? "It is time, Godsblood." Solanine drew a wickedly curved blade as the linen robe fell. An onyx gemstone with ruby runes hanging over the bloodied runes between breasts. "Let's see how strong you've grown."

With the curved blade, Solanine carved a rune into pale flesh, aetheurgy creating a slice in reality that was coated in blackened mist. The aetheurgist stepped through.

Ashe called forth her aetheurgy and entered the Meadows.

Time seemed to slow to a crawl. There were wails from all over the Meadows. That sound was becoming second nature with every entrance. Shades, the spirits of those long dead who were doomed to wander the realm of eternal slumber, roared out of the distance of non-light. Bright shapes of men and women and everything in between and beyond flew in great force, they came at Ashe, hands outstretched. Mouths open with deathly echoes.

This was new, these were the souls of daemons. Of the Pit in the deepest, darkest, dankest abyss of the void.

"You think you're a master of a world you know nothing of." Ashe looked around for Solanine, following the voice, but saw nothing. Only the non-light of the void. "Time flows to my whims in this realm. Not yours, child."

Ashe cowered, throwing her hands up to protect herself as the daemonic shades beat at her in a whirlwind of moans and screams. The terror grew as the torrent of spirits assailed her. Circling in a tourbillon of howls, the shades brought torture with them. They promised her eternal suffering in the fields of punishment within the Pit. Glimpses of never-ending death.

"It can all end if you give yourself to the Fallen," Solanine's voice said from outside the circle of swirling shades, ethereal. "Become the Godslayer, child of Nightingale. Break free from the Crystal of Life and take your place upon Eminence. Bow before the Crystal of Death and the Divines."

Visions of being crushed slowly by heavy stones. Skin flayed from her body in agonizing ways. Body ripped apart piece by piece. Mist daemons eating her insides—one conspicuously appearing like Amaranth the Pure.

"Give yourself to Him. End the suffering."

A weight pressed upon her, pushing Ashe into the non-floor of the Meadows. Ashe pulled her legs to her chest as she sobbed.

The visions of death and suffering continued unabated. Body was strapped to a giant, slow-turning wheel that was aflame. Tossed from a thousand-foot mountain onto a bed of daggers. Hooks piercing her skin attached to ropes and pulled limb from limb.

"You will only be the beginning. Everyone you have ever cared for will feel your suffering. They will witness your pain tenfold. Their souls will wither and die into nothingness. Your mother, your father. This is the power of Noctis if you don't allow the balance to become one with Eminence. Balance is needed."

Images in the swirling mass of spirits showed her Emre Benld. Of Cyan the Defiant. Neenah LeFleur. Roland, Tris and Doll, the twins Zig and Zag. Two pale Kanjan elfir, a bikrome and her brother. Of the drakken Ruane Tevunsdotyr and her sibling. The soul of sinless Ancantha. A face that looked just like hers, older with all-onyx eyes. Her mother named by Emre as Cadrianna Nightingale. A mother she had never known. All were splayed upon a cross, torsos bleeding profusely as daemons danced around the bases. Their pleading eyes found her, searing into her soul.

Ashe screamed, her voice cracking as she did, aetheurgy weak this time. Pulmo coursing her lungs instead. The corruption of the Pentax's aether. Her curse, her death.

The aetheurgist laughed. "Serve and they are free. Serve the balance, and they can be at ease in the eternal slumber."

"But what of the living?"

"The living will suffer as they suffer every day, with every breath. Life is suffering, child. Mortality is suffering. Immortality does not come from the proliferation of Life, but upon the wave of Death. Life and Death are balance for all existence. Flesh dies, the soul lives forever and can be reborn. Do you not see? Everything is cyclical. Which is the more important; flesh or the soul?"

"And what of my soul?"

"Serve and live eternal. Death is but the first step. It doesn't have to be agony. But the Divines can make it so for everyone you've ever loved. The body you know is but a construct bound to the laws of the Pentax. With Noctis, your soul can transcend those laws. You can be anyone you wish." The shades of the dead laughed as the aetheurgist did. "The balance must always remain. Zenith and Nocturne. Two sides of the same coin. Nothing can change that. Just who serves where."

Servitude.

The screaming cyclone of shades instantly fell silent, the weight pressing her down disappearing, leaving only the altar of emerald. The altar to Mother Marrow. She could sense the sound of someone, or something, sobbing. *Who?*

The non-light of the Meadows blazed as a figure approached. The non-walls of the temple vacillated. The mist fled. Solanine held out a hand, delicate, yet strong, beckoning for Ashe to take it.

Freedom, it said.

Empathy, it offered.

Redemption, it suggested.

Ever so slowly, her hand began to rise toward the acceptance. It was her only opportunity to save her mother's soul. Her father's. Everyone's. Zenith's cock, everyone's soul at the tips of her fingers.

Ashe went to her knees, her hands pressed against her skull as the pressure returned tenfold. "AHHH!" Death, torture, pain, terror. It all blended into one. Her vision darkened as she lost the connection to the mist. "No!"

"IT CAN ALL END." The words echoed in her mind. A voice she didn't know. The Fallen's? No, Zenith's cock, she knew it was one of the Divine's. But which? ***"ALLOW ME TO BECOME ONE WITH YOU. TOGETHER WE WILL RULE. FREE NOCTIS."*** The words pounded in her head. Over and over. ***"TAKE THY PLACE AT THE AETHER OF LIFE. BE THE BALANCE."*** Agony. Torment. Her fingers dug into her skin, tearing at her hair. Misery. ***"ALL OF LIFE WILL BE YOURS. GIVE ME MY NIGHTINGALE."***

She began to nod. She understood now. She had to do what was right. This was what Canlon Carr meant. This is what he had done as the chosen of the gods. Her soul was the token to save all of theirs.

Safety. Preservation. The tension in her body relaxed. Happiness. Ecstasy. Joy.

"Yes," she decided, voice hoarse.

Solanine's hand remained posed before her, mouth within the heart-shaped face agape, the voice definitely spoken via the aetheurgist for the Divine. Ashe reached up to take it, their fingers touching, the barest flicker of Life passing between them. ***"YOUR SACRIFICE WILL OPEN THE WORLD. OUR BLOOD IS SHARED. EMINENCE IS OURS, CHILD OF MY NIGHTINGALE."***

The hand of the aetheurgist morphed from tender, pink skin into hardened crystal, proliferating in verdant tones, like the color of a freshly plucked apple underneath the skin. A multi-prism of color outlined in onyx. Solanine's hand grabbed onto hers, holding it tight. The Eye of the Soul clamped to the aetheurgist's palm, Ashe's tattoos glowing like fire.

The affliction that had been assaulting her mind subsided, replaced with effervescent energy. She smiled as the crop settled into her. Her hand, in Solanine's right, began to harden into crystal, joined as one. The crystallization sprung to life like a vine. It burrowed deep into flesh, Ashe's blood, her muscles, her soul.

And then Ashe felt the world.

Far to the west beyond the Voidlands in lands so arid, nothing lived there except a wellspring of sapphire blue. Down south near the VVyrm Ocean, a singular volcano of ruby. North where the world was layered under snow, past the rocky teeth-like mountains of the Forgemistress' Blades lay a yellowed flower. The sands of Drenth. The earth called to her.

Terris one and all.

The people. Every culture under the sun. Lowborn, noble, those with no class, freedmen, slaves. Animals and plants alike. Voidspawn, draconem. Tiny sparks of life moving along the facets of the earth.

"THE GREAT CRYSTALS CAN BE YOURS, CHILD OF MY NIGHTINGALE. EMINENCE AND NOCTIS. ALL YOU MUST DO IS BREAK THE SEALS. DESTROY THE DRACONEM, NAY, THE GODS YOU CALL THE PENTAX."

*What? That cannot be…*Canlon mentioned the guardian draconem. Could they be the Pentax?

"YES, CHILD OF THE GODS. THE PENTAX AND THE GUARDIAN DRACONEM ARE ONE. THOSE ARE WHO YOU WORSHIP. THOSE ARE WHO YOU MORTALS DIE FOR. FOR WHAT?"

The mist, it came alive, weak, and dying. It pulled away from her, cleansed and free.

'The mist is your tool, your weapon, your existence. Harness it, be it, and it will serve you.'

Ashe gasped at that unbidden thought. Words spoken by her father. By Canlon Carr. A memory from the past telling her this was wrong. The corners of her mouth turned down and the expanding emerald crystal froze, the whole left side of her body from hand to foot was lucent.

No! This is wrong! Her mind screamed in anger.

She tried to free her hand from Solanine's grip, but it was molded solid, mist dancing along their faceted touch. In the aetheurgist's other hand was the curved knife, and it was coming down, aimed for Ashe's head.

"DESPAIR NOT, CHILD OF THE GODS. THIS IS TRUE LIFE."

Never! I am my own soul.

"THE AETHER CAN CLEANSE YOU."

'The mist is your tool.' Her father's words. Canlon's words.

Desperately Ashe sought the mist and it flickered to life, weakened, yet there. Concentrating on the corrupt grey, she breathed the essence into her arm, that primal notion, the carnal fire. The fog jumped to her bidding and rode the vessels of her lifeforce.

As the mist's existence touched the crystalline atoms encasing her, there were audible snaps as the lattice began to splinter and crack in explosions of black. It dissolved back into the Meadows, her flesh becoming alive again. The Meadows clapped like thunder directly overhead. Solanine was thrown backward, arm shattered, right hand completely gone, under the flesh was purple blood and exoscales like a draconem. The aetheurgist snarled in pain as the non-walls of the Meadows began to ripple like rain pelting a clay-tiled roof, strong and fierce.

Ashe wasted no time and leapt toward the altar, colliding with Solanine, arms wrapped around the suddenly-non-humir aetheurgist, their bodies jolting from the Meadows as Ashe connected. Both tumbled. Scrambling to her knees, her head ringing, Ashe raised her arm as Solanine jumped at her, the wicked blade coming at Ashe's face. She winced as it cut into her, through flesh and bone alike. Solanine fell upon her, knocking out her air. Ashe began to swoon as her lungs burned. The pulmo burst, firestorm. Lights danced in her mind.

And then, somehow, Solanine was off her. Ashe sucked in a breath, and sweet air filled her lungs.

Ashe found Solanine held between Cyan and Harlequin. A muzzle slapped upon the heart-shaped face, the runic covering keeping the aetheurgist from using aetheurgy. Solanine struggled against their grips, but was no match for them without aetheurgy, or without an exoscaled arm that bled orchid.

Finding the curved blade on the ground next to her, Ashe got to her feet.

Solanine's all-onyx eyes narrowed as Ashe neared. *This isn't over,'* the threat said from behind the muzzle.

"For you it is," Ashe rammed the dagger into Solanine's heart. The aetheurgist jerked, and the light faded in those all-onyx eyes. "See your soul in the Pit, you cu—"

"A pity."

LVII
ASHE

ASHE TURNED TO find a man standing in the shadows, a pooling robe worn. Bathed in green light from the altar, the Fallen was.

"The Seal of *Terris* awaits your hand, child of Nightingale." The sound of his voice was pure elegance and brought gooseflesh to her arms.

The vicars dropped the corpse of Solanine, ready for the fight that was expected, a fight they've trained for their entire lives. A fight in the Arbiter's name. Then they were both tossed by a gust of *Aere* laced with black lightning across the ritual chamber, clattering to the ground, axes and canisters of mist clanking on stone.

Ashe pointed at the corpse. "You made me do this. You allowed her to die."

"Loyal Solanine was. Until the end."

"You bastard." Ashe coughed, her pulmo bringing up blood.

"It is in your blood. Godsblood. That is what you are. Blood of my blood. Blood of Eminence and the Pentax. You are bound. Until you realize that, the nigrum pulmonem will rage through you."

"Fuck you."

He smiled. "Fire in you for certain." Then he turned, a smudge of shadows flew past.

The Fallen brought up both hands, great crimson robe fluttering. Aetheurgy crepitated, the smudge flung across the chamber. Crashed against the ritual chamber's wall, the blur fading as the shadows of mist evaporated, revealing a figure. A woman, arms splayed, an owl-shaped dagger in one hand.

"BRYNN!"

Ashe gaped at the woman.

A woman grown, face of southern olive, same as her own. The mouth, the lips, the cheeks. All her own. Hair shorter, curlier, but the same hue of black. O Zenith…

"BRYNN!"

The owl-shaped blade was yanked forcefully from her grip, and to Ashe's surprise, the blade divided into six equal blades, all twelve inches of blackened steel. There was a cawing, almost a tearing sound accompanying. Then the blades, one by one slammed into the woman, pinning her to the wall. Limbs pierced, torso. Crucified. She screamed, cried in pain. A single blade hovering at her throat.

The Fallen laughed as he toyed with the wearer of an Ashe mask. *It's… it's… Mother…*

"Enough, Lu Har."

Standing in the entrance of the chamber was her father. Well, not precisely standing as Emre was held in the arms of a massive drakken, his body practically limp, blood everywhere. Behind came Ruane, the bikrome from the visions, and another Kanjan elfir who also resembled the man in her visions. The bikrome held a hammer in her pale hands.

"You lied to me!" the crucified woman hissed. "You never had her. You lied." She cried harder, tears streaming. *Mother… I…* "You showed me nothing but false guises."

"A tool, that's all you are, Cadrianna Nightingale," the Fallen said. "All you've ever been. Honed to a fine point. To bring us to this exact moment. You all seem to think this chronicle hasn't been written yet by the scribes. Even with Bliss guiding you, this was all preordained. Fight it not. Fight it you cannot."

"Brynn." Cadrianna's head lulled toward Ashe. "My Brynn…" more crying. "Please. O Strix, stop the pain… never trust the… Bliss… the Pentax… O, the pain…"

Ashe staggered like she was hit with a thousand-pound hammer. She looked at her hand, the one with the Eye of the Soul. It radiated heat, diamond flickering prism, each gemstoned ring near bursting with light. The ground shook. The entire Temple pulsed. The altar of emerald quaked. A verdant ray shot from the altar, shooting upward through the chamber ceiling, up through the very Temple of Mother Marrow itself. Blinding and strong. The Seal at her waist yearned for the holy luminescence.

"Choice you have, Godsblood," Lu Har was saying through the blaze of green. "Break the Seals or be consumed by the fire. That is no lie. Balance there must be, Solanine held no lie there. Break the Seals. Give balance. Or there will be suffering for more than just these whom you love." He motioned toward her mother, toward her father dying in the drakken's arms. To the others she didn't know.

"She will do no such thing," her father said softly.

"And yet you, her loving father, held the knowledge from her. This makes you better than I?"

Ashe looked between the two. "Father?"

The bikrome stepped forward. "A necessity. Knowledge she wasn't yet ready to possess, Fallen. You'd weigh her down with the entirety of it without her able."

"Who you calling able?" Ashe demanded in heated agitation, it's not like she wasn't standing right there.

"Child, you were, you needed to grow," the handsome bikrome continued, remembering how she had cradled her as a babe through the potential fates of the future. The bikrome of the present raised the hammer in her hands, the silver and gold bracelets flickering in the green light shooting through the Temple. "Needed to learn on your own, without the restriction of knowledge. Think, Brynn Benld. Don't let his words sway you. Trust in yourself." She smiled.

Then the bikrome sprang into action, aetheurgy coming to life in her hands.

A blink of lashes, agonizingly slow, and the bikrome whipped out her arm, swirling waves of the mist rode the dozens of bikromi seer sight bracelets, her fingers summoning aether. An audible pop as the essence of the fire's lifeforce came alive with *Ignis*. Flames licking, growing, and melting down the walls like a waterfall of liquid fire.

The earth under them trembled greatly.

A giant wave of mist crashed behind Ashe, like a tidal of grey aether spurred by *Aere*. It struck, chipping stone and flutes alike. Debris rained down on her as the Fallen thrust aetheurgy of his own at the bikrome, using the black fog as his weapon, squelching the fiery aether. Coming to life, the haze turned opaque, hardened like marble yet malleable and deadly.

Ashe recoiled. Cadrianna whined upon the wall, crying out the name 'Strix' over and over. The elfirish man and the drakken siblings moved for cover.

Arm raised to ward off the dust and marble chips, the bikrome flung the coiled mist using *Aquis* from the sweat now drenching her face. Like the greatest storm upon the ancient seas, the mist wetly rose, a wall stopping the attacking wave, two living barriers colliding and dissipating upon touching.

The bikrome yanked the dust, twirling her fingers and sharpening the particles, sending it flying down the hall like a thousand tiny arrows. But the Fallen's aetheurgy broke the barrage with *Aere*. Then the most powerful aetheurgist in the land cradled *Ignis* and *Aere* together, flung it out toward the bikrome. Prepared, the bikrome was not, the full brunt of the two Tenets of Aether hit her and sent her sprawling. Unconscious. Breathing still.

The Hammer clattered upon the stone at Ashe's feet, the Seal urging her toward it.

The ground was shaking so hard, Ashe wondered if the Temple would cave in above them.

Lu Har appeared contrite, annoyed even, his ruby red robe covered in dust from the Temple's walls. He turned to Ashe. "Time it is, Godsblood. Your choice before you. Maintain the balance or bring the world into everlasting suffering."

"Zenith's cock, I thought I was done with this shit." Ashe knew there was only one choice. She looked toward her mother pinned to the wall by that strange owl blade. To her father now lying on the ground, his eyes half lidded. To the pair of growling drakken. Toward the unconscious bikrome and vicars. To the Kanjan. Words meant for the Fallen. "If I break the Seals, will you let them go?"

"That is up to them."

"Brynn, no. Kill him!" cried her mother.

"What is your choice, child of Nightingale? Kin of mine."

"Fuck, I'll do it. I'll break the fucking Seals to Eminence."

As the Fallen waved his hands, his aether rushed to do his bidding as the blades of the owl-shaped dagger pulled from her mother's body. She dropped to the ground and curled up, clutching at her bleeding wounds.

The mist prodded her legs, pushing her toward the altar. *The mist is your tool, your weapon, your existence. Harness it, be it, and it will serve you.'* She looked toward her father; his words rang true. Trust in the mist, she must. Served her to this point, it will continue to serve. Trust in herself. Choice now made, Canlon Carr would be proud.

The quaking was closer now, shivers sent up Ashe's legs as she reached for the hammer, hefting it. The tool possessed no weight, simply greenish metal in the shape of a forger. Instantly the runes in its haft began to radiate as the diamond in the Eye of the Soul began to blaze. Her runic tattoos glowing in tune. With her right hand, Ashe lifted the Seal of *Terris*.

The path now lay before her. A path only for her. The Pentax had chosen her to be their warrior. Chosen her for Eminence. Warrior she must become.

"Brynn!" The green light of Mother Marrow filled Ashe's vision, shielding her crying mother under the hunter mist. "Please don't leave me again!"

But she must, "Trust me, Mother."

"Brynn, no. He is the… father of lies…. never trust…the gods… and Their…" Coughing, dying slowly. "Strix, help…"

The six blades reformed into one, the owl embedded in the cross guard faced her, and the oddest of things happened, Ashe thought she heard the blade speak within the din of her mind and that of the quaking earth. *"TRUST."*

With the Seal now in hand, Ashe moved toward the altar, each step a chore as the trembling ground underfoot made it nigh on impossible to walk. Pausing before the vertical green brilliance, she took a deep breath, then stepped into the light, standing before the crystalized table. With the black braided steel Seal held above in both her hands, the hammer in the crook of her elbow, she watched as the circle of emerald in the Seal glimmered in conjunction to the surrounding light, the three othe circles of gems fading into shadows.

As had in the Meadows with Solanine, the fruitful lifeforce of Mother Marrow engulfed her. She felt the void of the Pit within the Fallen beside her. Felt the breath of the Forgemistress fleeing both her mother and father. The strong aether flowing in the drakken siblings. Of the others, hearts all beating fiercely, defiantly against the black of the oncoming void.

Deep in the earth underfoot she could feel the true spirit of the world. Of Mother Marrow, the Forgemistress of Creation. That was the quake. Mother Marrow and Her children. The guardian draconem. She knew.

Lu Har leaned close, his face bespeaking what his aura didn't: pride, eagerness, victory. "Do it, Godsblood."

She glanced once more at her father, who was barely awake. His lips moved, but no sound emanated. His aura was a wildfire of sapphire, as if he knew what she had in mind. A barely perceptible nod of agreement.

"What do I do?"

"Place the Seal upon the chantry." Ashe did as told and placed the circular braided steel into the indent upon the altar. The glow of mid-summer forest leaves grew so bright she had to look away. The ground underfoot stopped rumbling. "Place the Eye upon it, channel all your anger, all your rage into the Eye. Your aether will pass through Noctis, claiming it as your own."

Ashe held out her hand bathed in the greenish glow, the Eye in the bangle around her wrist reflected a thousand mirrors of her own face. She recalled her meeting with Canlon Carr, the Last Godsking. With her father. With Solanine.

All of them told her she was the key. Her Godsblood. She was the balance.

Gazing upward through the emerald light, she saw the statue of Mother Marrow. Even down deep in the ground, she saw it. The majesty. The elegance of nature. The iridescent beauty of creation.

Balance.

A pulmo cough escaped her lips but the fiery tattoos upon her flesh brushed aside the burn inside of her. Aether swam in her veins as the mist swirled like a cyclone about her bare feet. Everything was balanced about her. Life and Death.

Now she understood, truly understood. With that knowledge came a grin.

"Life and Death," she whispered, as her aetheurgy billowed out of her like a bonfire. She hefted the greenish hammer in her left fist, the runes upon the haft and the diamond eye in her palm turned white-hot. With her other hand, she reached outward toward the owl-shaped black dagger lying beside her mother. The daemonic blade whooshed from the pooling blood and connected with her palm.

A ghastly voice from beyond the veil to the Meadows spoke, *"HELLO, GODSBLOOD. A PLEASURE IT'LL BE TO SERVE YOU."*

Lu Har blinked once before trying to bring his aetheurgy alive, but she was faster. The daemonic blade sunk into the Fallen's innards as Ashe screamed. Aether, pure and uncorrupt, poured from her mouth as the black Void Form of the Pit-wrought blade seared the Fallen's flesh in a blast of black-red. Both aetheurgies of Life and Death, of Eminence and Noctis funneled into the elfir, lifting him off the ground as if he was weightless. With a heave, Ashe threw him across the chamber, away from her family and their friends, away from the downed vicars who were hers.

The Fallen tried to stand, but Ashe was already bringing the white-hot hammer down upon the Seal of *Terris*. A flash of blinding green, the Seal, followed by the emerald altar, shattered into a million shards, a rainbow of colors exploding forth, every spectrum known in nature.

"NOOOO!" the Fallen wailed.

The ground swelled under them with such conviction. The beam of light expanded, sending her backwards as the ground exploded as a great mass emerged, so large it swallowed half of the chamber as it rose, including the Fallen, the altar, and the broken Seal. The greatness burst through the ceiling, upward straight through the Temple, clear into canyon. Straight upward into Gargantua.

It wasn't until Ashe cursed before she realized what the bulk was. It was a terrisvvyrm.

The vvyrm, all grey and earthen brown flesh, with its keratin protrusions and gaping mouth, was easily three hundred feet as it heaved upward from underground, colliding with the floating fortress of doom, piercing the stony underbelly. Other vvyrms rose from the dunes, crashing into the Fallen's soldiers and war machines. The behemoth roared as its mouth unfurled upon the metal innards of Gargantua. Shooting through like an arrow, swallowing tower and spire alike, rising past the blackened mist of the void, splitting the fortress in twain as Mother Marrow's aether ripped through like firebolts. Emerald aether sparking and discharging through the Fallen's fortress.

For the briefest of instances, from below the Temple, Ashe saw Zenith's sunlight high overhead. A calmness.

Then, the great draconem reached its apex, its roar a finality, and began to fall. Like a tree felled in the forest, the vvyrm crashed into the canyon—thankfully away from Ashe and everyone in the ritual chamber. The bulk crushed the outer rim, sending sand and stone launching into the Sea of Mist. The other vvyrms all fell, dead in a circle around the canyon. The blackened fog retreated.

Both halves of Gargantua toppled down amongst the Temple's grounds, sending further aftershocks rippling through as the emerald aether of the Forgemistress of Creation continued its havoc. Walls of perfect interlocking marble shattered in a spider's web of cracks and divots. The husk of the flying fortress burned as buildings collapsed upon themselves, spires and outer walls breaking under the stress of the holy aetheric heat. Fires high into the sky, aethecite fuel creating the source. Smoke as dense as mushy dung billowed, filling everything with near-black haze. Dust and tremors across the dunes, wiping away entire mounds, flattening the landscape in a busted semi-circle all around Her Temple.

Ashe's mouth was still agape when an airship appeared over the gigantic hole left by the vvyrm. A shaggy-haired woman was at the rail, waving down. "You bloody buggers need any godsdamned help? Stray Cat?"

She began to laugh at the absurdity of it all.

Her mother lay coughing, her face ashen, blood spilled everywhere. Sadness filled Ashe, her laughter subsided, knowing that she would never know the woman behind the drake scale armor. Never know her mother the way a child would desire.

The drakken with the horns brought her father near, setting him beside her mother. He was barely breathing. Cadrianna's hand reached out toward Emre, gently pushing back his curls, speaking softly before she balled up with another cough.

Ruane lingered behind while the Kanjan elfir tended to his bikromi sister. Cyan and Harlequin stirred.

"Brynn," her mother said as Ashe crawled over to her. Ashe lifted the woman's head, hugging to her breast. Cadrianna gripped her arms and held on with all the fleeting strength remaining. "My… Brynn."

"Mother…"

"Forgive… me." She coughed, blood spilling down her lips, reminding Ashe of her own affliction. Her mother's eyes found hers, all-onyx focused on all-white. "Please…Strix… over her."

Her mother nodded in her arms after a moment as the daemon blade's voice sounded in Ashe's mind. *"YOU KNOW I WILL, CAD. I ALREADY KNOW SHE WILL BE JUST AS FUN AS YOU WERE."*

Emre Benld's hand found Cadrianna's upon Ashe's arm. And for a moment, they were a family again. Fleeting as it might be.

A wry smile came to Ashe's face as she looked around at those within the chamber, at her parents, etching their faces into her memory. "Guess they better call him the Flyin' instead of the Fallen now." There were groans from the others, her parents' shoulders both lifted in soft amusement. Even close to death, they found the humor. Gallows though it may be. "Wait, what about the Swallowed?"

Her father laughed the best he could, wincing as his life ebbed away, his stare wandering toward the Meadows. "Just as…funny…as…mother."

"Funnier… right… Strix…" her mother struggled. "Forgive… you… Emre…"

Both Ashe's mother and father smiled, the three forever bound together. Tears crept down her cheeks as she held both while the last breaths left them. The family she had always wanted.

Finally found.

THE DESERT CITY OF DRENTH

AT THE STERN of the airship, an orphan girl with the trueborn name of Brynn Benld watched as the Sea of Mist closed about the mega-city of Drenth like a curtain dropping after a fine performance.

Like a crown of swords, the famed city jutted from the dunes, but instead of blades, were sky risen buildings that no longer had a giant shadow overhead. Once home to the aethecite mines, but those were now caved in and buried deep under the great desert with the last remnants of the magnificent terrisvvyrms as headstones. At least a dozen of the vvyrms were now entombed, the last of the largest draconem. Drenth's outer walls were already being pummeled by an early dawnbreak sandstorm, a raging vortex imbued by the aetheric mist of the surrounding Sea.

The girl gripped the railing with a bangled left hand, fingering the handle of a black steel blade with her right. "Home," she whispered to the mega-city as it disappeared into the grey.

Home.

For so long, the girl had sought that elusive place that she could call her home. Now she could, no, now she would. Home was where a family placed their roots, it didn't matter where, just where the family was, that was home.

And Drenth was home for her. Now and forever.

"YOUR MOTHER USED TO HATE THIS CITY, KNOWING WHAT HAD HAPPENED TO YOU AND YOUR FATHER."

"It's not the best, but it served well, I suppose."

"YOU ARE JUST AS DEEP AS CAD WAS, NEVER MET A MORE SOMBER PHILOSPOHER IN ALL MY YEARS."

"Didn't realize philosophy and daemonkind went hand in claw. Or wing. Or whatever you had."

It was an odd thing, but the daemon blade laughed in her mind. Odd because she now had a daemon talking to her through a dagger or if said daemon possessed a personality that bordered on facetious, she couldn't decide. *"BY THE PIT, YOU ARE JUST LIKE HER. DRY AND DROLL. MUST BE BECAUSE OF THE DESERT SAND ALL AROUND. DRIES OUT THE SKIN AND THE WIT."*

"Thanks?"

"I'D SAY IT'S A COMPLIMENT. BE WARY, THOUGH, I DON'T TEND TO GIVE OUT MANY, RUINS MY REPUTATION HERE IN THE VOID."

"I'll keep that in mind."

"I'LL MISS HER, YOU KNOW. WELL, BEING WITH HER IN THE WORLD OF LIFE. HERE IN THE VOID, I'M CERTAIN SHE WILL BOTHER ME FOR ALL ETERNITY."

She smiled at the thought. Her mother and father, together at last, buried side-by-side at the base of what had once been the Regent's Tower. Buried upon the place of her birth, of their home when the world had not been destroyed by the Fallen. Buried in the heart of the city that was everything to the three of them.

There was a sense of loss about her leaving behind the graves of Emre and Cadrianna Benld, a loss she couldn't explain. She knew them both only mere hours, not even days. And yet, she felt she knew each her entire life. She understood the magnitude of their decisions, their trials. Fault them, she could not. Not them, never them.

It was in their blood. In her blood. A part of her heart would forever remain in Drenth. A part of her felt she failed them, failed to live up to their name. Perhaps this was the trial of heart Canlon Carr had told her of.

"You certain about this, Stray Cat?" Captain Neenah LeFleur asked as she sauntered up to the rear of *Marrow's Lover*, "back to bloody Kalderim? A place I stowed you away from. Looks bad on me when Neenah LeFleur bloody brings back what was godsdamned stolen in the first place."

"I'll keep your name out of my mouth," she said with a grin. "Don't want your ego dropped a notch or two because of me."

Neenah put her hands on her hips. "Godsdamned right, hear?" Then she softened, ruffling a hand through her shaggy hair nervously with an aura of sorrowful honey. "Sorry 'bout your folks, poppet. I know you never knew them and all, but I had passing relations with that bikrome and if that buggering wench ran with Emre Benld until the end, then I'd wager that's high praise indeed. Ain't nobody worthy of Bliss like Her bikromes. Especially the daughter of the Golden bloody Throne."

The bikrome in question sat upon the pilotbox, legs crossed, bi-colored gaze staring north. Toward Kanja. In Valeria Dunleith's lap was a fragment of the Seal of *Terris*. Ashe still felt drawn to the piece, perhaps she always would.

"I know the woman behind Bliss' gifts," Cyan the Defiant said as the vicar placed his elbows on the ship's rail.

The daemon blade called the Strix hissed. ***"VICARS, PFFT. OVERZEALOUS LOUTS."***

"She's the one who placed you in my arms, Lil… Brynn," Cyan continued, clearly not lucky enough to hear the Strix's scorn. "One does not bring a wailing babe like you from the clutches of Lu Har without having a few screws lose upstairs or guided by the grace of the Pentax."

"Lucky you, Cyan." It seemed like everyone aboard was connected to her somehow. The Scattered Shards taught that the warriors of the Pentax would always find another. She had never put stock in such banal ideations, but it appeared she better brush up on her teachings from the Book of the Scattered Shards.

"How long to Kalderim, Captain LeFleur?" Cyan asked. He had not pushed for Ashe to return, but his aura had told her how relieved he was when she told him of her plans to return to Kalderim.

"Depends on the bloody Pentax… O, sorry, forgot you bug… er, you vicars don't care for foul language."

Cyan puffed a light chuckle, giving the orphan girl a nudge with his shoulder. His aura beat a soft crimson tint. *Zenith's cock, really, Cyan?* "After spending time with this one here, I've learned to care less about things of that nature. Besides, when they're as dashing as one Neenah LeFleur, even less so."

Neenah's face broke into a smile of gold and pearl. The captain's aura turned from a curious yellow to a dark ruby. "Neenah LeFleur is a dashing one, isn't she? Best smuggler in all the Mistlands, aye." She gave Cyan a full once over. To her, "Not bad on the eyes, this one, hear?"

Ashe rolled her eyes. "If you say so."

Inwardly, she was surprised at Cyan's new outlook on life. Vicars were celibate in their devotion. But Ashe had learned of their escape from Gargantua. Needless to say, she hoped her old taskmaster might change. Perhaps the Defiant had learned a thing or two while chasing her. Maybe some good would come from it all. But then again, Cyan was basically as bland as a fallen log.

"You certain about this path, Brynn?" Cyan asked. She nodded. "It'll be two years before you're raised to the cassock because you ran. I don't think Icterine the Unfettered will care for such things. I can talk to her, but my word might be for naught."

"It is what it is." It's what she needed to do, for herself. She needed this, it was almost a cathartic reason, maybe selfish. But she felt it in her bones, this was the path to take.

"Brynn?" The girl turned to find the massive drakken, Lojen, standing almost nervously behind her. Ruane sat perched upon a crate, picking at something in her teeth with that longknife of hers. Beside her was the lapin, Wick. "I know my ward… your father, well, he did say you were to go to Kalderim, but I'm not certain he intended for you to… you know… go back to the Scattered Shards. I think he meant to go to Finn and Val's parents."

Finnus Dunleith hadn't been topside since they had left Drenth. In fact, the entire trip back to the City of Sands, the Kanjan elfir had been quiet, which the girl had learned was a rarity for him. She had also learned he had been her father's lover, and his death must have hit him especially hard.

But she had made up her mind, she would go back to the Scattered Shards and finish her training. With Lu Har and Solanine dead, the Imperium of the Fallen was no more. Drenth was free now, there was nothing left for her there. No reason to remain. It was time for her father's victory to be celebrated.

"What of Eminence and the other Seals?"

"What about them?"

"You heard your father. Heard Lu Har even," the drakken added. "The Pentax chose you. The Seals call to you now. Eminence awaits."

"Bugger that," she said. "Everything I ever wanted died in that Temple, Lojen."

She glanced to where the Temple might have been situated in the Sea of Mist. The entire eastern sky was an emerald shade, only the eastern horizon. It was as if Zenith had taken a paintbrush to His heavens and decided to shade the east green. It was a peculiar sight, but she knew it was Mother Marrow's aether, the Forgemistress had released her essence through the guardian vvyrm. Day or nightturn, it didn't matter, a greenish glow illumined the east.

But Mother Marrow was now dead, Her favored terrisvvyrm guardians along with Her, one point of the Pentax slayed and ended. Who knew what that would do to the world. Would the world even know the truth of Her sacrifice or only see the death of the greater order of draconem? Not to mention the downfall of the aethecite mines. Even the bikrome hadn't an answer.

The Hammer of Mother Marrow tugged at her belt. She felt the goddess' aether within.

"You can't just step off the path the Pentax puts in front of you," Lojen continued. For as large as the drakken was, not to mention with his epic horns, he truly was a fastidious one. And if she wasn't careful, one who might begin to grate on her. Which was why she needed to release him of his self-proclaimed duty to protect her in her father's stead.

"Watch me."

The drakken wardkeeper sighed. "Then to the Scattered Shards we will go. You are my ward now. I will follow you into the void."

She shook her head. "No, Lojen. My father was your ward. No buts, he was. Not me. I'm done with the Pentax forcing me into something I'm not." She paused as a pulmo cough wove up her throat. "I… nevermind. Just heed me, Lojen Tevunson, I'll be fine."

"That goes against everything a wardkeeper stands for."

"Listen to the humir, Scurred Hatch," Ruane said around the tip of her longknife, still digging for whatever was stuck in her craw. "She can handle herself."

"But the Forgemistress said…" the drakken wardkeeper trailed off as Finnus Dunleith appeared from belowdecks.

The elfir wore Kanjan funerary braids in his silver hair over his pointed ears, kohl circling his yellow-pupiled eyes. Pale face even paler than normal, almost like the very ice of Kanja. His shirt, trousers, and overcoat were black, pressed and immaculate. In mourning he was.

Everyone on Neenah LeFleur's airship paused what they were doing—even the hobgoblin twins, who were wrestling over the last bone of the evenfall prior's dinner—and watched as the Kanjan elfir of the Golden Throne walked up to her. His bikromi sister turned her veiled gaze upon him, and if the girl was any good at reading auras, she could tell that the bikrome had seen all this coming and had withheld it from him. Stoic bitch.

Finnus Dunleith drew up before her. With tears streaking the rings of kohl, he reached into his overcoat, and pulled forth a hunk of metal. She realized it was a multi-barreled wheellock pistol. The elfir kissed the grip of the revolver and held it out to her. "He would have wanted you to have this."

Taking the pistol, she noticed the 'B' engraved in the grip. B for Benld. A sob threatened her throat, so she swallowed it back. "Thank you."

"Wherever you go, Brynn," he said softly, "know that he goes with you. Just as he does me and my sister-friend up there." He turned toward Valeria, a sad smile breaking that somber façade of his. "You know, it's just like Emre Benld to leave us hanging when the going was gettin' good. There was this time with the mines…"

She turned back toward the desert city of Drenth hidden within the Sea of Mist while the elfir went on. She fingered the engraving upon the pistol's grip. The Hammer of Mother Marrow was slung at her hip, opposite the Strix. Each pulsed with aether. Life on one side, Death on the other. All bound within her.

One day, perhaps tomorrow, maybe years from now, she'd have to go to the ruins of Eminence. But until that day, the girl with the trueborn name of Brynn Benld would make her own path.

REBIRTH

WAILING.

O Nocturne, they heard the wails. It was the sweetest sound. Which meant their wayward soul had a mortal body waiting.

Excruciating.

Demanding.

Irate.

There was pressure upon the veil protecting the Meadows from that of Nocturne's Pit, a thin, yet strong barrier of elemental material comprising the threads of the entire world. It, the Aether of Life, warded the souls of the damned within the black cauldron of the ethereal void. Their ancient, centuries long lifeforce pressed against the gulf, spanning eternity, yet still nothing at all. Flares burned within them with each second passing.

Time meant nothing in the Meadows, especially to those under the thrall of the Pit. Time was all they had, all they were, all they would ever be until released. Seconds felt like eons, eons passed like seconds.

The veil pulsed, rippling like flowing water. Undulating in waves great and small. Their being, nay their essence, their soul, pressed harder, thrust elemental tendrils at the resistance. It convexed outward toward the Meadows, groaning within the non-walls hemming wandering shades into non-rooms of Death. Snapping and popping along the tethers that bound the essence of their soul to Nocturne's Pit.

Behind their essence was a crystal of obsidian so large it dwarfed anything else within the Pit. Multi-faceted of crystalline black, the Crystal of Death held a link to their soul. It was the final binding between souls locked in the Pit with those allowed to the Meadows and the peaceful slumber. A prison, a chain keeping a soul bound within the abyss.

Some of the souls were warped, twisted into daemons, others were those of man turned to Nocturne. All were howling in forever torment, all begging for release. But that rarely happened here in the Pit where the heinous reaped their failures in agony.

They felt the god, but it felt wrong, felt incorrect. Nocturne was pure Death, this felt of Life. What did it mean?

And then the heave of the void, felt it within their being. It tensed, the void did. It fought back. The wails of the hateful souls locked in the Pit raged like a volcano ready to burst, spewing forth molten aura. The Crystal of Death pulsed with anger, with hatred, with every negative emotion and desire, and yet, there was that underpinning of Life. Odd. The links between the bound souls faltering under the evil bound within the deathly aether.

But they heard the voice. Soft, delicate, ancient. Muffled sounds, broken words. Their soul latched onto it through the tiniest of cracks within the veil. The wails roared from deep within the Pit. Dank, black, and down near the center of the world. Down near Nocturne Himself, a corrupted prison for their Divine near Noctis. That's where the source of Life felt the most wrong, yet, there it was.

Fleeting, the sparks of their soul sent shivers throughout the void as memory returned, the dark pushed back at the transparent nothingness as their soul sought purchase within the realm of the slumbering dead. It clawed, their soul did, yearned and stretched from the empty chasm of the Pit, searching for the voice, demanding release.

Like a claw reaching out, they grasped onto the voice. It pulled, yanked them from the depths of their prison. Through the veil, past the withering souls of the dead, upward toward a light-that-wasn't-a-light. Glorious, it was. Bright and burning with the force of a thousand suns. Fire and glistening dew.

And they knew, finally, they did. Life, succulent and enveloping.

Their eyes opened, bloodred film sluiced down their snouted face as the blooddrake barged into the world of the living like a newborn birthed from a mother's womb. Crimson cruor poured down the blooddrake's forelimbs as they sat upright, dribbling down their throat, rivering over their crimson and black exoscales. The blooddrake swallowed the sanguine antidote and felt alive once more.

Vision cleared, red haze giving way to sputtering torches in damp, musty air. Only one clawed hand, the other missing below the elbow on their right, lined with the thick liquid—which the blooddrake now remembered its name: blood—gripped the edge of a hollow tub of stone and mud. Feeling, the sense of touch under hard keratin, sending memories shooting through their snake-like body that floundered in broken remembrance of what it was meant to live.

Restored and rebirthed. Again.

A low, distinct murmur met the blooddrake's earholes. One voice louder than the others. Chanting, all, the language that of Noctis and Void Form aetheurgy. A voidspeak the living knew naught. A cabal of withered and desiccated, hunched forms locked hands on skeletal forearms, swaying back and forth in the ancient rituals of aether.

Slithering into an S position, the blood coursing down their exoscales as one of the decrepit forms righted itself—herself—as the others continued to chant. The woman was old, older than any living creature not a god. Her skin was emaciated, missing in some places showing the living muscle underneath. Wispy, near nonexistent hair cascaded down the woman's blindingly pale pate. The creature's lower lip was missing, and where her eyes should have been were empty holes.

The Matron was the name recalled.

"Solanine." Raspy, the voice sounded like a dagger on a whetstone. The Matron bowed her head.

Solanine, yes, that was the name the blooddrake was born with. Memories surged into Solanine's mind. Years, decades, centuries of thoughts, schemes, dreams, and death raced into them. But one regret loomed larger than everything else.

Lu Har and the Godsblood.

"You've done well, my faithful servants," came a melodious voice in the shadows behind the coven of oracles who watched without eyes.

Solanine squinted into the shadows. A man, once handsome, now wilted and scarred, sat with linen stained by blood draped over his shoulder. His body, that which was visible, was burned, as if the acidic blood of a vvyrm had showered him. Yet, his all-onyx eyes bore the hunger of revenge. "Lu Har?"

Two other forms slithered out of the shadows. Blooddrakes. Both large, both in their own scales, not the scales of man. They bowed their snouted heads. Rinkhal and Ialtris were their names.

"Wounded we've been, Solanine," Lu Har said, straightening with a grunt, his face contorting in pain. "Life stolen from us. Betrayed us, she did. That shall not go unpunished. Mother Marrow and Her draconem guardians are dead. The first to fall. Three remain. The daughter of Eminence is still at hand. Find her, we must, the child of

Nightingale. Take what is ours. Take what was mine. To Kalderim and the Seal of *Aere*. Of *Aquis* lost in the Voidlands."

The memories of failure raced inside Solanine's mind. With the remaining claw, the blooddrake stroked the horn over one of their eyes. "How long has the Pit claimed me?"

"Half a year's turn."

Could it be so long? It felt like nothing.

"My Imperium has fallen, Solanine, in its place something else grows. This Guild. It is but the worms who worshiped us who have claimed my throne."

"Am I allowed to finally paint this world in blood as should have been from the beginning?"

Lu Har leaned forward, a quiet contemplation before answering. "I have a gift for you, a set of scales you've long since coveted. Bring me the child's head and you can leave this land swimming in blood. In our master's name."

The Fallen motioned toward the cabal of corpse-like oracles. Two shuffled through the rest, carrying something in their deathly grasp, something that resembled a cloak made of leather. But it wasn't a leather cloak, instead it was the stretched skin of an olive-toned woman with raven hair, a face where the hood might be.

Solanine felt a smile cross their snout. "This is how you repay me in full, Lu Har. Now you give her to me. After making me suffer her training. Bonding her to the Strix. Taking her to your bed." The blooddrake slithered out of the blood bath toward the scales held in the oracles' arms, the cruor staining the rough ground in their wake like a slug. Solanine ran their remaining claw over the stretched face. "Mine…"

"We must bide our time, Solanine. The child of Nightingale must come to us." Lu Har coughed, his withered body convulsing. Weak, yes, that's what Solanine would call him. They had never seen Lu Har be weak, but the Godsblood had wounded him so. "Work, we have. Our army has been scattered; men are worthless. I must raise the daemon horde. Time it will take me. In the meantime, this Guild must crumble, but more importantly, the Seals remain to us. With these scales, you must bring the Godsblood back to us. I command you to destroy the Guild from within. Rinkhal and Ialtris will join you. Datura is already amongst them in Alizarin. Destroy what hope this world has built. With it will come the child of Nightingale."

The blooddrake glanced up. "The Seal of *Ignis* in Oldport Basin?"

"Kalderim is mine. *Ignis* is yours. You know what power the blood of Nightingale had there. Use it."

Solanine caressed the set of scales with a claw. "Yes." But their words were to their Divine, not Lu Har. The elfir had long since overstayed his use, Solanine knew it now. For in the Pit, during their torture, Solanine had heard the truth. Now was their chance.

"BRING ME THE GODSBLOOD," the voice of the Divine spoke from beyond the veil. **"MY LOVE, MY NIGHTINGALE WILL RISE AGAIN."**

Yes, my master.

With a chant of aetheurgy borne of the void, Solanine felt the power of aether. So sweet, so freeing. The claw of Solanine's left arm disappeared into the set of scales held by the oracles, melding together like a bladesmith forging steel. The oracles pulled the scales' flesh taut as Solanine dove snout first, worming inside. Aether bloomed as the two worlds collided, a blooddrake stealing the memories and the life of the scales. Everything that was the scales' former life filled Solanine. Dreams, wishes, loves, memories, failures, achievements. All. Two at the forefront. A husband and a daughter.

Solanine became the scales.

When the chanting was done, Solanine stood taller than their previous scales with the heart-shaped face, wider of hip and smaller of bosom. Black-red blood of a drake dribbled down the olive flesh, over hardened muscles trained by rigid use in the arts of killing, down into the thatch between athletic legs. Though Solanine couldn't command the humir's right hand, the blooddrake ran the left through the shoulder-length waves of raven-black, memories of a daughter with white eyes filled the chasm that was Solanine's now to command.

Cadrianna Nightingale, scourge of the Fallen, daughter of the line of Nightingale, now stood in the flesh reborn. But not the failure that was Cadrianna married to Emre Benld, no, this was Solanine, the blooddrake that would see the world burn.

The blooddrake that would bring the world of Life to the Pit.

Here Ends Passage One of the Divine Godsqueen Coda

The Coda Continues in:

Lady Drakeslayer

APPENDICIS

THE DIVINES

The Divines [dih-**vahyns**] – The ultimate deities of Life & Death.

Zenith [**zee**-nith] – The divine of Eminence & the realm of Life. Also known as He Who Fathered the World and the All Father.

Nocturne [**nok**-turn} – The divine of Noctis & the realm of Death (the Meadows). Also known as the Master of the Pit or the Dark God.

The Pentax Gods [**pen**-taks gods]**, also known as the Hatch** borne via **Nightingale** [**nahyt**-n-geyl] & Zenith:

Mother Marrow [**muh**_th_-er **mar**-oh] – Goddess of the east, guardian terrisvvyrm of the Emerald Shard. Patron goddess of creation, healing, & life, as well to the ingeniators of the Scattered Shards. Associated with _Terris_. Holy artifact is the Hammer of Mother Marrow. Also known as the Forgemistress of Creation, the Forger of Life.

Justice [**juhs**-tis] – God of the west, guardian seagandr of the Sapphire Shard. Patron god of peace, law, & war, as well to the vicars of the Scattered Shards. Associated with _Aquis_. Holy artifact is the Aegis of Justice. Also known as the Arbiter.

Brio [bree-oh] – God of the south, guardian firedrake of the Garnet Shard. Patron god of desire, stimulation, & lust, as well to the quaestors of the Scattered Shards. Associated with *Ignis*. Holy artifact is the Mantle of Brio. Also known as the Wayward Son, the Drunk God.

Bliss [blis] – Goddess of the north, guardian aerovern of the Peridot Shard. Patron goddess of purity, order, & time, as well to the augurs of the Scattered Shards. Associated with *Aere*. Holy artifact is the Crown of Bliss. Also known as the Ideal Daughter, the Virtuous One.

THE ORDERS OF DRACONEM

Draconem [drey-**koh**-nem] – Greater & lesser orders of drakes.

Firedrake [fahy*uhr*-**dreyk**] – Greater order. The smartest, as well as the cruelest, grand of size, & notoriously violent. As such, these savage beasts tend to lair on fiery peaks far from the races of man. Their scales are near impossible to breach, thus are used in body armor manufacturing.

Seagandr [see-***guhn***-dyr] – Greater order. The bane of every sailor, for they possess multiple heads & rise from their gloomy depths only when cargo ships are bulging with drake essence or aethecite. Their oil offers an alternative fuel source to aethecite, as well as a suitable machine grease.

Aerovern [**air**-oh-vern] – Greater order. The smallest in size, with a wingspan half the size of their firedrake cousins but possesses a healthy dose of claw & lightning breath. Their scales drip poison & frost, but once past their exteriors, they make for excellent food seasoning.

Terrisvvyrm [ter-**uhs**-vurm] – Greater order. All have perished during the destruction of the aethecite mines & Temple of Mother Marrow. The largest drake, but simplest of intelligence. These subterranean behemoths had slimy scales & no eyes. Instantly after death, vvyrm corpses become fetid & rotten, making a perfect source of fertilizer.

Drakken [drey-**kuhn**] – Lesser order. Anthropomorphic, these drakes live amongst men. Renowned for their warrior-heart, some become wardkeepers, or counselors & generals to rēgis & rēginae.

Blooddrake [bluhd-**dreyk**] – Lesser order. Cunning & secretive, most owing allegiance to the Divines. These loathsome drakes utilize aether to wear the flesh of men, stealing their identities to further the Divine's endeavors. Wily & hateful.

Aetheurgy Forms

Soul Form [sohl fawrm] – the purest form, borne only in those with Godsblood, the world's essence via Eminence theirs to command. Marked by pristine, white pupils & irises. Manipulation of all Forms.

Vision Form [**vizh**-*uh*n fawrm] – the voice of the Pentax Gods, Bliss & Brio. Marked by one all-white eye & one all-black eye. Manifests in prophetic visions of past, present, & future, as well as manipulation of the veil between Life & Death.

Burn Form [burn fawrm] – borne in the essences of the Four Enhancements of Aether. Burned via injection or ingestion of distilled aethecite, called parch. Marked by a colored pupil; colors of garnet, sapphire, peridot, or emerald. Enhances senses, speed, strength, & stamina.

Shard Form [shahrd fawrm] – borne in the essences of the Four Tenets of Aether. Burned via inked runes in the flesh sparked by inhalation of the poisonous mist. Marked by a colored pupil; colors of garnet, sapphire, peridot, or emerald. Enhances strength, speed, & senses, as well as allows manipulation of the four elements.

Void Form [void fawrm] – from the darkness of the void beyond the veil of Life via Noctis, scarred runes upon breast & spine. Marked by all black pupils, irises & sclera. Manipulates the body by use of blood, as well as manipulation of the mist.

THE RUNES OF AETHEURGY

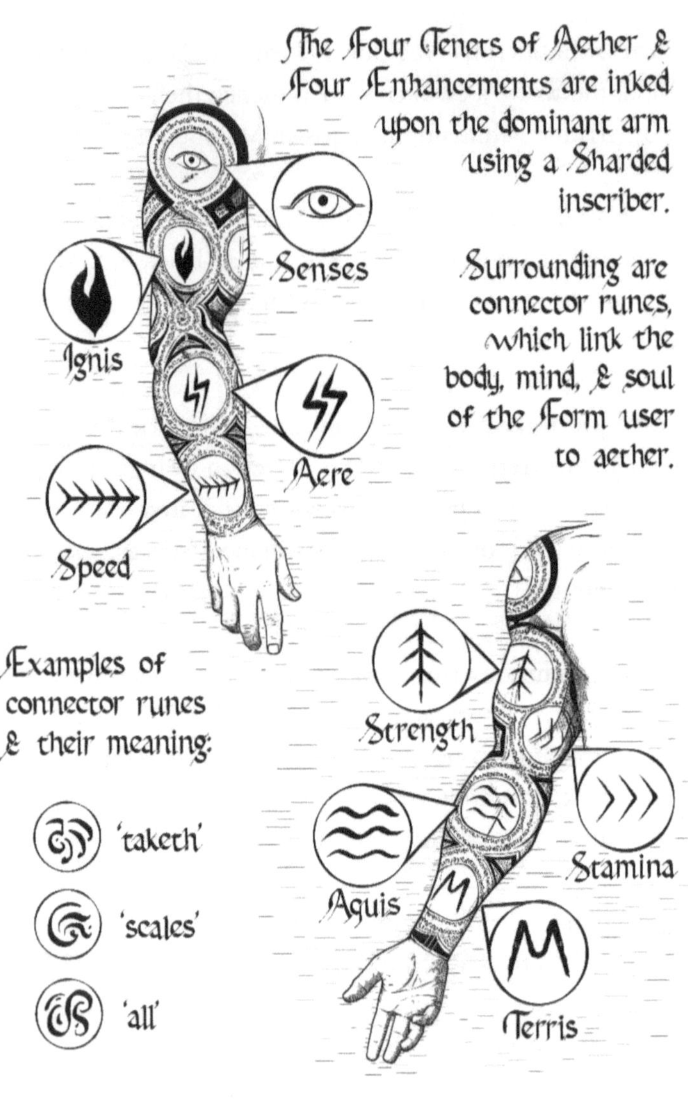

THE AURAS OF SOUL FORM

Aura [**awr**-uh] – the art of reading a person's emotions and/or intent by a color. Used solely by a wielder of Soul Form aetheurgy.

Blue – the ideal of Trust.

> **Tints** – Serenity, Wisdom, Stability, Contentment, Intimate, Nurturing
> **Shades** – Distancing, Aloofness, Inferior, Apathetic, Bored, Guilty

Green – the ideal of Awareness.

> **Tints** – Health, Fertility, Faithful, Confident, Eager, Powerful
> **Shades** – Greedy, Sickness, Jealousy, Wanting

Red – the ideal of Stimulation.

> **Tints** – Loving, Passionate, Lusting, Strengthened
> **Shades** – Anger, Danger, Warning, Critical, Hateful, Hostile

Yellow – the ideal of Energy.

> **Tints** – Joyous, Optimism, Playful, Daring, Amusement, Excitement
> **Shades** – Cowardice, Fear, Anxious, Rejected, Submissive, Bewildered

FACTIONS OF THE MISTLANDS

The Scattered Shards [thuh **skat**-erd sharhds] – the religious order formed after the Fall of Eminence. Broken into four sects, each branch devoted to one of the Pentax Gods. Headed by the Conclave & pontifex maximus in Kalderim.

Augur [**aw**-ger] – the preachers of Bliss' words & healers of the ill. Denoted by a pristine white cassock. Upon attaining the cassock, an augur receives a new name, determined by their Shard preference. An augur's Shard Form is held within the Beads of Aether wrapped around their wrist, each sharded Bead contains one of the Four Tenets & will crack upon use. Untainted by the corruption in the mist.

Ingeniator [in-**ge**-ni-ator] – the followers of Mother Marrow, creators & scientists using aether. Denoted by an emerald cassock. An ingeniator carries a smaller version of the Forgemistress' green-iron hammer but are not warriors. An ingeniator's Shard Form is tattooed upon their arms, which allows them to combine aether with science. Untainted by the corruption in the mist.

Quaestor [**kwes**-ter] – the tainted warriors of Brio. Denoted by a crimson cassock. Former criminals allowed to repent. Upon attaining the cassock, a quaestor receives a new name, determined by their crime. A quaestor's Shard Form is tattooed upon their arms & is only accessed by inhalation of the corruption in the mist, thus their tainted bodies wither & die. A quaestor carries a red-iron mace. All Shards strongholds are headed be a grand quaestor.

Vicar [**vik**-er] – the untainted warriors of Justice. Denoted by a midnight blue cassock. Upon attaining the cassock, a vicar receives a new name, determined by their Shard preference, plus given an honorific denoting a physical or emotional attribute. A vicar's Shard Form is tattooed upon their arms & is only accessed by inhalation of the corruption in the mist. They are, however, untainted by the corruption.

The Imperium of the Fallen [thuh im-**peer**-ee-*uh*m ovh thuh **faw**-l*uh*n] – the physical embodiment of the Fallen's coven, in both lands conquered & soldiering force.

Scourge [skurj] – the assassins of the Imperium. Broken by torture, they are the blade of the Fallen. Some scourges are trained in Void Form.

Oracle [**awr**-uh-k*uh*l] – aged aetheurgists living in a basilica in the ruins of Illigan. Blind, these seers paint one hand in whitewash, one in blackwash in a corrupted Vision Form. Led by the Matron.

The Guild [thuh gild] – the growing affiliation of Houses within each mega-city, each pledging fealty to the High Seat in Alizarin.

The Golden Throne of Kalderim [thuh **gohl**-d*uh*n throhn ovh kald-**er**-im] – the imperium & formal seat of power in Kanja. Led by the rēx & rēgīna.

The Legion [thuh **lee**-j*uh*n] – the soldiering force of Kanja. Legionnaires are trained in hand-to-hand combat as well as artillery. Each stronghold is led by a primus pilus (captain) & serve under the guidance of the praetor (general).

The Golden Sword [thuh **gohl**-d*uh*n sward] – a title & a weapon held by the eldest heir.

The Holy Order of the Vird [thuh **hoh**-lee **awr**-der ovh thuh vurd] – a sect of devout believers in the Shards of Eminence & Noctis. Found upon the highest peak of the Forgemistress' Blades, they are the creators of the rune inscribers for the Scattered Shards.

The Matriarchy of Krylen [thuh **mey**-tree-ahr-kee ovh krahy-len] – the leadership of the free city of Krylen.

The Wardkeepers [thuh wawrd-**kee**-pers]– drakken chosen. They bear the horns of the Pentax & sing the Hymn of Justice. They are the generals, counselors, & protectors of a ward's bloodline until their death, then the honor is passed on, along with the horns.

The Isle of Merj [thuh ahyl ovh murhj]– the homeland of the drakken. Each wardkeeper bloodline can be traced back to Merj & the first wardkeeper.

The Broken Quarry [thuh **broh**-k*uh*n **kwawr**-ee] – a forgotten bloodline found in the Voidlands near Shatterstorm. Led by the Goldkeeper, these wardkeepers are the guardians of the Sapphire.

ACKNOWLEDGEMENTS

Where to start? Family first, probably. I suppose I should start with my parents because they showed me that nothing is better than burying myself in a good book. To my sister, who reads far more than I do, this is probably too big and dark a book for you. To my extended family, you rock! To my BIL, I'll get you to read some indie fantasies soon enough. To my lil goblin, you tire me out, but I wouldn't change it for the world and to the biscuit still baking, I already am filled with love for you. To my wife and biggest cheerleader, you probably won't read this book, but I still love you.

A huge shoutout to all the writing friends I've met along the way. Amanda, my first writing friend. Claire, my voice of narrative reason, guardian of stakes, and pusher of bettering my craft. Sam, my ever-present ear, always listening to my crazy ideas and reading everything I send your way. Dewey, my grumpy brother, my great friend, my fellow quester, I couldn't have gotten to this point without you. To AJ and Mario who beta read this chonker, your feedback was ever helpful. To Mike, Tim, Andrew, the Silverstones Books gents, the Secret Scribes, and the rest of the indie community rockstars who've adopted me into their tribe, you are simply the best!

Finally, to those who read this coda, I hope you've enjoyed following my stabby, sarcastic little bint. Without you, none of this is worth it. And I'm not sorry if I killed off your favorite character…

Love you all!

About the Author

When not writing, Bill is a product manager for a company that tests food using analytical chemistry and microbiology.

During his collegiate days at the turn of the century, he began to develop his passion for writing, especially within the epic fantasy genre about unlikely heroes. It was there, Bill began to formulate the story that would eventually become Ashe's unwanted journey and *The Divine Godsqueen Coda*.

Aside from writing, Bill loves movies and reading, especially SFF B-movies. He likes to know all the useless trivia, like who played who, and what the stories were behind the curtain. He is a master at Scene It. Bill's few other hobbies include soccer, good whiskey, a slice of pizza, and growing a beard. It is the little things he enjoys most.

Bill currently lives in the greater Chicago, IL area with his wife, young son, and soon-to-arrive daughter.

Gentle Reader, my eternal gratitude goes to you for taking the time to read Passage One of the Divine Godsqueen Coda. I sincerely hope you enjoyed this tale. Self-publishing relies on word of mouth and reviews/ratings on sites such as Goodreads and Amazon.

If you can find the time, please leave your thoughts on The Godsblood Tragedy wherever you can, good or bad, every little bit helps. My thanks.

Scan the QR Code above to be taken to The Godsblood Tragedy's Goodreads page.

Willow Wraith Press is a collective of nerds who write the types of books we want to read. If you have enjoyed this book, please check out the other Willow Wraiths.

<u>Dewey Conway & Bill Adams:</u>

The Tenacious Tale of Tanna the Tendersword

<u>Andrew D. Meredith:</u>

Deathless Beast
Bone Shroud
Gloves of Eons

Thrice
Four Scored

Quaint Creatures: Magical & Mundane

<u>Michael Roberti:</u>

The Traitors We Are
A Grave for Us All
The Revenge of Thousands

<u>Timothy Wolff:</u>

Platinum Tinted Darkness
Tears of the Maelstrom
Age of Arrogance

The Whisper that Replaced God

To visit the Willow Wraith Press
website, scan this code

The Secret Scribes are an affiliation of independent fantasy authors. If you have enjoyed this book, please check out the other books from some great authors & show them some support!

Tom Bookbeard:

The Corsair (Winter '24)

E.H. Bradley:

The Ranger (Summer '24)

L.M. Douglas:

Gharantia's Guardian

Bella Dunn:

The Dreams Thief

Damien Francis:

The Tome of Haren

Dave Lawson:

The Envoys of War (Fall '24)

Seán O'Boyle:

The Ballad of Sprikit the Bard (and Company)

R.E. Sanders:

A Path of Blades
Tann's Last Stand
Demon's Tear

R.A. Sandpiper:

A Pocket of Lies

Alex Scheuermann:

The Odyllic Stone

G.J. Terral:

Bloodwoven

www.ingramcontent.com/pod-product-compliance
Lightning Source LLC
Chambersburg PA
CBHW061848310726

48972CB00004B/931